INTO THE NARROWDARK

The finest in imaginative fiction by Tad Williams

MEMORY, SORROW AND THORN
The Dragonbone Chair
Stone of Farewell
To Green Angel Tower

THE LAST KING OF OSTEN ARD
The Witchwood Crown
Empire of Grass
Into the Narrowdark
The Navigator's Children

The Heart of What Was Lost
Brothers of the Wind

THE BOBBY DOLLAR NOVELS
The Dirty Streets of Heaven
Happy Hour in Hell
Sleeping Late on Judgement Day

SHADOWMARCH
Shadowmarch
Shadowplay
Shadowrise
Shadowheart

OTHERLAND
City of Golden Shadow
River of Blue Fire
Mountain of Black Glass
Sea of Silver Light

Tailchaser's Song

The War of the Flowers

TAD WILLIAMS

INTO THE NARROWDARK

Book Three of The Last King of Osten Ard

HODDER &
STOUGHTON

First published in Great Britain in 2022 by Hodder & Stoughton
An Hachette UK company

1

Maps by Isaac Stewart

A CIP catalogue record for this title is available from the British Library

Hardback ISBN 978 1 399 70659 9
Trade Paperback ISBN 978 1 399 70660 5
eBook ISBN 978 1 399 70661 2

Typeset in Bembo Std by Jim Tierney

Printed and bound in Great Britain by Clays Ltd, Elcograf S.p.A.

Hodder & Stoughton policy is to use papers that are natural, renewable and recyclable products and made from wood grown in sustainable forests. The logging and manufacturing processes are expected to conform to the environmental regulations of the country of origin.

& Stoughton Ltd
melite House
ria Embankment
on EC4Y 0DZ

.hodder.co.uk

Dedication

It's still the same story, just divided into volume-sized pieces, so the dedication still remains the same as for Volumes One and Two, to wit:

These books are dedicated to my editors/publishers, Betsy Wollheim and Sheila Gilbert, and to my wife and partner, Deborah Beale. I can't imagine what my life would be like without them, and I certainly can't imagine these books happening without them, either.

Acknowledgments

My books, by the time they get to readers, are always the product of far more than just one person. I'd like to thank some very important contributors.

Top of the list: Ron Hyde, Ylva von Löhneysen, Jeremy Erman, and Angela Welchel have been the reader-curators of these new Osten Ard books in so very many ways, from vetting my manuscripts to overseeing map geography and working on the indexes (they did all of those for this volume) and even writing an occasional synopsis. I would have been completely overwhelmed returning to my own fictional world without their help.

We lost our dear friend Cindy Yan in 2020, who was also a big help and inspiration in the early stages of these books, and we miss her terribly. This will be the first volume she wasn't here to read, and I can't tell you how sad that makes me.

Lisa Tveit has bravely and skillfully kept the *tadwilliams.com* website running for many years, giving my community of readers a place to find Tad-news and make (well-deserved) fun of me and my four-book trilogies.

Olaf Keith continues to do kind things for my books online and in Europe, and he's also a super good guy. Thanks, Olaf!

Isaac Stewart has created beautiful maps for this whole series, and is so nice and easy to work with that it's a little frightening. What is he hiding?

Marylou Capes-Platt has brought her considerable copyediting skills to this volume, as she did with the previous books. Not only does she save me from some of my worst mistakes, she also cheers me up when she writes supportive notes in the margins. (She has high standards.)

Joshua Starr of DAW Books has, as always, worked efficiently and cheerfully with me and most of the folks cited above to get this book into published form. He's very chill, and I'm grateful for that.

Matt Bialer is my agent and friend. Along with others listed here, he is a central reason why I still like the publishing industry. Too bad he's kind of a Yankees fan, but even the saints had flaws.

And of course I must bow to the single most guilty group of usual suspects in getting my books to you, the editorial team led by Betsy Wollheim and Sheila Gilbert, my excellent publishers at DAW Books, with whom I have been working harmoniously since somewhere back in the last century, something I never take for granted.

I also am very lucky to have fine publishers at Klett-Cotta in Germany and Hodder and Stoughton in the UK.

And last but certainly not least—as if!—I want to thank Deborah Beale, my wife and partner, but also a damn fine publisher and businesswoman herself.

Author's Note

The original (and much scoffed-at) plan was for me to finally capture, subdue, and present to the readers that most elusive beast (at least for me)—an actual three-volume trilogy. I have tried and failed several times before, but I was plucky and optimistic again this time, certain I could constrain my tale to three convenient volumes.

Short version: I failed. Again.

Thus, anything unusual about this volume—a bit less long than either of the first two, for instance—can be ascribed to it originally being the first half of what would have been a very, very, *very* long third volume. But the publishing industry has changed since the days of the first Osten Ard series and *To Green Angel Tower,* and it quickly became clear we couldn't manage that long a third volume this time even in hardcover, á la TGAT.

Fortunately, the monstrous last book split pretty evenly, and the first half still works as a single volume, I think, because it was already paced to have a watershed at the original mid-point. And the final volume is coming soon, I promise.

Thank you for your patience. My books and I are still a work in progress.

Synopsis of
The Witchwood Crown

More than thirty years have passed in Osten Ard since the end of the Storm King's deadly, magical war—a war that nearly doomed mankind. *King Simon* and *Queen Miriamele*, scarcely more than children when the Storm King was defeated, now rule over the human nations from the High Throne, but they have lost touch with their onetime allies, the immortal *Sithi* folk. Then *Tanahaya*, the first Sithi envoy since the end of the war, is ambushed on her way to the Hayholt, the ancient castle that is the seat of the High Throne.

While *Tiamak*, scholar and close friend of the king and queen, works with his wife *Thelía* to save Tanahaya's life, Queen Miriamele and King Simon are away from the castle on a royal progress. Currently they are visiting the neighboring country of Hernystir and its *King Hugh* as part of a royal progress to the north, where Simon and Miriamele are troubled by the behavior of Hugh and his new love, the mysterious *Lady Tylleth*. Dowager queen *Inahwen* warns the royal couple's advisor *Count Eolair* that King Hugh and Tylleth have revived worship of the *Morriga*, an ancient, dark, and bloodstained Hernystiri goddess.

Even while accompanying the royal family on their progress, *Prince Morgan*, the seventeen-year-old grandson of Simon and Miriamele, spends his days drinking and womanizing with his knightly companions *Astrian*, *Olveris* and old *Porto*. Morgan's father, *Prince John Josua*—the only child of Simon and Miriamele—died of a strange illness some years earlier, leaving his wife *Idela* a widow, Morgan and his younger sister *Lillia* fatherless, and the king and queen, John Josua's royal parents, still grieving.

When not nursing the poisoned Sithi envoy, royal counselor Tiamak is collecting books for a library to commemorate the late John Josua, but when his helper *Brother Etan* investigates some of the dead prince's possessions, he discovers a banned and dangerous volume, *A Treatise on the Aetheric Whispers*. Tiamak is filled with foreboding, because the *Treatise* once belonged to the wizard *Pryrates*, now dead, who collaborated with the *Storm King Ineluki* to destroy humanity, though they ultimately failed.

The threats to Simon's and Miriamele's peaceful reign are increasing. In the icy north, in the cavern city of Nakkiga beneath the mountain Stormspike, the ageless ruler of the Norns, *Queen Utuk'ku*, has awakened from a years-long magical slumber. Her chief servant, the magician *Akhenabi*, summons the High Magister of Builders *Viyeki* to an audience with the queen, who declares her intention to attack the mortal lands again. The queen leads a strange ceremony that resurrects *Ommu*, one of the chief servants of the Storm King, though Ommu was thought to have perished forever during the Norns' failed attempt to destroy the Hayholt and the mortal kingdoms.

In Elvritshalla, the capital of Rimmersgard, King Simon and Queen Miriamele are reunited with their old ally *Sludig* and his wife *Alva*, as well as their dear Qanuc friends *Binabik* and his wife *Sisqi*. They also meet the trolls' daughter *Qina* and her betrothed, *Little Snenneq*.

The royal progress reaches Elvritshalla just in time to say farewell to *Duke Isgrimnur*, who dies shortly after their arrival. His last request to Simon and Miriamele is that they renew their search for *Prince Josua* (Miriamele's uncle, Simon's mentor, and John Josua's namesake) and his twin children, *Derra* and *Deornoth*, who mysteriously vanished twenty years earlier. Later Little Snenneq, who is Binabik's apprentice, meets Prince Morgan and predicts that he will become as important to Morgan as Binabik became to Morgan's grandfather, King Simon.

In a castle in southern Rimmersgard where the royal party is guesting on their way home, Simon realizes he has not dreamed in many days. He consults Binabik, who creates a talisman to help him. That very night, Simon dreams of his dead son and the voice of the child *Leleth*, who had once whispered to him in dreams three decades earlier. Leleth tells him "the children are coming back". After Simon frightens the whole household while sleepwalking, Miriamele destroys the talisman, and Simon again loses the ability to dream.

In the still more distant north, the half-blood Sacrifice *Nezeru*, daughter of Norn noble Viyeki and human woman *Tzoja*, is sent as part of a "Talon" of Norn warriors to retrieve the bones of *Hakatri*, brother of Ineluki, the defeated Storm King. Nezeru and her fellows, commanded by their chieftain *Makho*, find the bones being venerated by mortals, but Makho and the Norns take them and escape from the angry islanders. During the escape, Nezeru fails to kill one of their enemies (a child) and is severely punished for it by Makho.

However, before the Talon can return to Nakkiga with Hakatri's remains, they are met by the Norn Queen's arch-magician Akhenabi, who takes the bones and sends the Talon on a new quest to Mount Urmsheim to collect the blood of a living dragon. To aid in this dangerous feat, he sends with them an enslaved giant named *Goh Gam Gar.*

While traveling eastward towards Mount Urmsheim, the Norn Talon encounters a mortal man named *Jarnulf*, a former slave in Nakkiga who has vowed to destroy the Norns and their undying queen, Utuk'ku. Because the Talon has lost its Echo—their trained communicator—Jarnulf, hoping to further his own private aims, convinces the Norns to take him on as a guide. They all travel eastward towards the mountain, last known home of dragons, and on the way Jarnulf overhears the Norns discussing their queen's great plan to defeat the mortals by recovering something called "The Witchwood Crown".

In central Rimmersgard, the Talon encounters the royal party, and Jarnulf is able to get a secret message to Queen Miriamele and King Simon that the

Norn Queen is looking for something called the Witchwood Crown. Simon, Miriamele, and their advisors are alarmed, and they have seen enough signs of renewed hostility from the Norns that they take Jarnulf's message seriously, though this is the first they have heard of him.

In the City of Nabban, a Wrannawoman named *Jesa* cares for *Serasina*, the infant daughter of *Duke Saluceris* and *Duchess Canthia*, Simon's and Miriamele's allies. Tensions in Nabban are rising: *Count Dallo Ingadaris* has allied with Saluceris's brother *Earl Drusis* to fan fears of the nomadic Thrithings-men whose lands border on Nabban. Drusis accuses Saluceris of being too cowardly to properly punish the barbarians and drive them back into the grasslands.

Meanwhile, on the plains of the Thrithings, gray-eyed *Unver*, an adopted member of the Crane Clan, and his companion *Fremur*, participate in a raid on a Nabbanai settlement. As they escape, Unver saves Fremur's life, perhaps in part because Unver hopes to marry Fremur's sister, *Kulva*.

Sir Aelin catches up with the royal party, bringing messages for his great-uncle, Count Eolair. *Lord Pasevalles*, Eolair's temporary replacement at the Hayholt, sends his worries about Nabban, and Queen Inahwen of Hernystir sends news that King Hugh and Lady Tylleth are growing ever more open in their worship of terrible old gods. Eolair sends Aelin with this bad news to a trustworthy ally, *Earl Murdo*. But while seeking shelter from a passing storm, Aelin and his men spend the night in a border castle with *Baron Curudan*, leader of King Hugh's private, elite troops. During a storm that night, Aelin sees the dim shapes of a vast Norn army outside the fort, and then watches Curudan meet with humankind's deadliest enemies. But before Aelin and his men can escape with the news of this treachery, they are captured and imprisoned by Curudan's Silver Stags.

In the Norn city of Nakkiga, Viyeki is sent by Lord Akhenabi on a secret mission to the mortal lands with his Builders, but he is accompanied by a small army of Norn soldiers as well. Tzoja discovers that with Viyeki gone, her life is threatened by her lover's wife, *Lady Khimabu*, who hates Tzoja for giving Viyeki a child, Nezeru, when Khimabu could not. Tzoja knows she must escape if she wishes to live.

As Tzoja thinks of her past with the Astaline sisters in Rimmersgard and her childhood in Kwanitupul, it becomes clear Tzoja is actually Derra, one of the lost twins of Prince Josua and his Thrithings wife *Vorzheva*. Tzoja flees to Viyeki's empty lake-house in a cavern deep beneath the city.

Their royal progress finally returned to the Hayholt, Simon and Miriamele ask Tiamak to honor Isgrimnur's dying request with a new search for Prince Josua. Tiamak sends his assistant Brother Etan south to try to discover what happened to Josua when he disappeared twenty years earlier.

Meanwhile, challenged by Little Snenneq, Morgan climbs Hjeldin's Tower, the Hayholt's most infamous spot, and is almost killed. He believes he saw long-dead Pryrates while he was atop the tower, and swears Little Snenneq to secrecy.

With evidence of the Norn resurgence everywhere, Simon and Miriamele realize these ancient and magical foes are too powerful to face alone. They decide to try to contact the Sithi, especially their old allies *Jiriki* and *Aditu*. At Simon's urging, Miriamele reluctantly agrees to send their grandson Prince Morgan with Eolair and a host of soldiers to Aldheorte Forest to find the Sithi and return their poisoned messenger Tanahaya for more healing.

Viyeki travels south from Nakkiga toward mortal lands, accompanied by an army of Norns who plan to attack the mortal fortress of Naglimund. Viyeki is told that he and his Builders are going to excavate the tomb beneath the fortress of the legendary Tinukeda'ya *Ruyan Vé*, called "the Navigator", and salvage his magical armor, though Viyeki does not understand how this can happen without causing a war with the mortals. Tinukeda'ya, also called "Changelings", came to Osten Ard with the Sithi and Norn, though they are not the same as these other immortals. In Osten Ard, the Tinukeda'ya have taken on many shapes and roles.

Prince Morgan and Count Eolair finally contact the Sithi at the edge of Aldheorte Forest. The immortals have abandoned their settlement of Jao é-Tinukai'i and their matriarch Likimeya was attacked by humans and has fallen into a deep, magical sleep. *Khendraja'aro*, of the ruling Sithi Year-Dancing House, has declared himself Protector of their people and refuses to help the mortals in any way, causing friction with Likimeya's children, Jiriki and Aditu. Aditu is pregnant, a rarity among the Sithi. The father is Yeja'aro, nephew and militant supporter of Khendraja'aro.

In the Thrithings, Unver challenges and kills his rival for Fremur's sister Kulva. But Kulva's brother, *Thane Odrig*, does not want to give his sister to an outsider and slits her throat instead. Unver kills Odrig and flees the Crane Clane to return to the Stallion Clan of his mother Vorzheva. Unver, we learn, is actually Deornoth, the other of Josua and Vorzheva's twins. When Unver demands his mother tell him why he was sent away and where his sister has gone, Vorzheva says he was sent away by order of her father, *Thane Fikolmij*, and that Derra ran away shortly after.

Thane Gurdig, husband to Vorzheva's sister *Hyara* and Fikolmij's successor, comes to attack Unver, and in the confusion Vorzheva kills her now old and infirm father, Fikolmij. A giant flock of crows appears out of nowhere to attack Gurdig and his allies, causing many Thrithings-folk to declare that Unver may be the new Shan, the universal monarch of the Thrithings. Unver kills Gurdig, and is then declared the new thane of the Stallion Clan.

Far to the northeast, the Talon and Jarnulf manage to capture a small, young dragon, but then the mother dragon appears. During the struggle Chieftain Makho is badly burned by dragon blood and one of the other Talon members is killed, but the rest manage to escape and begin dragging the captive young dragon down the mountain.

Eolair and Morgan are returning from their embassy to the Sithi to their camp beside Aldheorte Forest, but discover that their party has been attacked and all the soldiers wiped out by Thrithings-men, some of whom are still there, looking for victims and pillage. Eolair and Morgan become separated and the prince ends up lost back in ancient Aldheorte.

Back in the Hayholt, Queen Miriamele and King Simon are invited to attend an important wedding in populous and troubled Nabban. Hoping the presence of the High Throne will help solve the problems between Duke Saluceris and his brother Earl Drusis, Simon and Miriamele accept the invitation. With the increased threat of the Norns and disturbing news from Hernystir they cannot both go to Nabban, so they decide Miriamele will attend the wedding while Simon stays in the Hayholt.

Royal counselor Lord Pasevalles meets his secret lover Princess Idela, John Josua's widow. When she gives him a letter from Nabban he had dropped, Pasevalles sees the seal is broken and fears she has read the letter. He pushes Idela down a flight of stairs and when the fall does not kill her, he breaks her neck with his boot.

In Aldheorte Forest the onetime Sithi envoy Tanahaya at last awakes from her terrible illness and is reunited with Jiriki and Aditu. Despite her recovery, the future seems dark. It is clear that the Norn Queen Utuk'ku intends war on both the Sithi and the human world.

Synopsis of Empire of Grass

Osten Ard has fallen into confusion and struggle after years of peace. And at a time when *King Simon* and *Queen Miriamele* most need each other, they are far apart.

While Simon remains in their castle home, the Hayholt in *Erkynland*, Miriamele is at sea, headed for *Nabban* to attend the wedding that will unite two powerful families. *Drusis*, feuding brother of *Duke Saluceris*, is marrying young *Turia Ingadaris*, whose family are the duke's greatest rivals. But before Miriamele can even begin to worry about Nabbanai politics, she gets the terrible news of a death back home, her daughter-in-law, *Princess Idela*, who (although everyone thinks it an accident) was murdered by the Lord Chancellor, *Pasevalles*.

At the Hayholt, Simon has to deal with not only the death of his daughter-in-law, but the disappearance of grandson *Prince Morgan*, the heir to the throne. Morgan and *Count Eolair*, after a mission to meet with *Jiriki* and *Khendraja'aro* of the *Sithi* people, have been attacked by *Thrithings-Men* on the broad grasslands west of Erkynland. Eolair has been captured and Morgan has disappeared into the vast Aldheorte Forest. While the old knight *Sir Porto*, and the four trolls—*Binabik*, *Sisqi*, their daughter *Qina*, and her betrothed *Little Snenneq*—hunt for Morgan, the lost prince is in real danger of starving in the forest until he saves a squirrel-like animal he calls *ReeRee* and nurses her back to health. Living in the trees with ReeRee and her troop of creatures that he names *Chikri*, he learns to survive in the unfamiliar environment.

Count Eolair is taken by his bandit captors to the Thanemoot, where all the Thrithing-folks gather at mid-summer every year. This year the most powerful thane, *Rudur Redbeard*, has heard reports about *Unver* (born "Deornoth," one of *Josua*'s and *Vorzheva*'s twin children) who many of the grasslanders think might be the *Shan*, a great leader foretold in legend. Jealous Rudur captures Unver and sentences him to torture and then exposure, but after being brutally flogged, Unver survives being chained to a pole overnight, and there are signs that wild wolves have come to bow before him—or that is the story that his friend *Fremur* and Unver's mother Vorzheva make sure the other Thrithings-folk hear. Now in a difficult position, Rudur tries to poison Unver, but somehow the shaman *Volfrag* gives Rudur the wrong cup and Redbeard himself drinks the poison. With Rudur dead, Unver is freed and is acclaimed the Shan of the Thrithings people.

While all this is happening, *Queen Utuk'ku* of the *Norns*—the Sithi's equally immortal kin—seems to have designs on mortal territory, even planning to renew outright conflict with the mortals despite their disastrous loss in the Storm King's War. The Norns make a bargain with *King Hugh*, the mortal king of Hernystir, who allows them to cross his lands in secret, but this betrayal of humankind is discovered by *Sir Aelin*, Count Eolair's young relation. Hugh's soldiers try to imprison Aelin and his men, but they escape, meaning to warn others of Hugh's treachery and the approaching Norn army.

Meanwhile, High Magister *Viyeki*, an important Norn leader, is beginning to have real concerns about what Queen Utuk'ku plans—he does not think another war with the mortals is a good idea after the terrible defeat the Norns suffered in the last one. But he is one of the few with doubts, and it soon becomes clear that the Norns are going to attack the mortals' important fort, *Naglimund*.

Sir Aelin and his men race to Naglimund to warn the defenders, but on the same evening they arrive, the Norn armies also show up. The battle is brutal but swift, with the Norns throwing down Naglimund's walls and killing most of its defenders. The only mortal survivors are those Viyeki claims he must have as laborers to fulfill his given task of opening the grave of *Ruyan the Navigator*, hero of the Tinukeda'ya people (or "Vao"), a changeling folk who came to Osten Ard with the Sithi and Norns thousands of years earlier on the *Eight Ships* when their shared homeland, the *Garden*, was destroyed by a deadly, unstoppable force called *Unbeing*.

Viyeki's mortal concubine *Tzoja* was born "Derra," and is Josua's and Vorzheva's other lost twin. After Viyeki has left Nakkiga on his mission for the queen, Tzoja faces retribution from Viyeki's murderous wife, *Khimabu*, but escapes and goes into hiding in the depths of Nakkiga, where she meets a strange, deformed group called *The Hidden*. Tzoja is eventually captured, but to her surprise, instead of being given to a vengeful Khimabu, she is instead assigned as a healer to Queen Utuk'ku because of Tzoja's previous experiences with the Astaline sect. Utuk'ku, the only living being who saw the Garden, is suffering both from sheer age and the loss of the *Witchwood Trees*, whose fruits have extended her life for thousands of years. And when Queen Utuk'ku leaves Nakkiga for the first time in memory, headed for captured Naglimund, she takes not just Tzoja but hundreds of Norn nobles with her into mortal lands.

Back in the Hayholt in Erkynland, King Simon and others have learned of the destruction of their embassy to the Sithi by Thrithings raiders, as well as the disappearance of Count Eolair and the royal heir, Prince Morgan. Since he thinks the new Shan of the grasslands, Unver, may be holding Morgan hostage, Simon sends out an army under Morgan's other grandfather, *Duke Osric*, to negotiate with Unver for Morgan's return. Meanwhile, Unver Shan has purchased Count Eolair from the bandits who captured him, intending to use the Hernystirman as an envoy to negotiate between himself and the High Throne of Erkynland. But instead Eolair is rescued by *Sir Astrian* and *Sir Oliveris*. As they escape Unver's camp, Eolair tries to convince Vorzheva to come with them, since Simon and Miriamele have been hunting for her and her missing husband, Prince Josua, for years. But Vorzheva refuses and attacks Eolair with a knife. She accidentally stabs her own sister *Hyara*, then blames Eolair, who escapes. Unver and the rest of the Thrithings leaders consider this an act of treachery by King Simon, and when a battle is provoked between Duke Osric and the grasslanders, Unver decides he must invade Erkynland to avenge what he sees as King Simon's double-dealing.

In Nabban, far to the south, Queen Miriamele meets with the elders of the *Niskies* and is told that they (and other descendants of the Tinukeda'ya or Changeling race, who came from the lost Garden with the Sithi and Norns) are having powerful dreams in which they are called to go north. But Miriamele has greater worries, and soon finds herself in the middle of a deadly rivalry between Duke Saluceris and powerful House Ingadaris (into which the duke's brother, Drusis, has just married) that threatens to turn into a civil war. While mobs of the two houses' supporters clash in the streets of the ancient city, and as Miriamele discovers lies and treachery even within the duke's own household, Drusis is murdered and Saluceris is naturally blamed for it. The dead man's widow, child-bride Turia Ingadaris, tells Miriamele that she should leave Nabban, because violence is coming. It is more of a threat than a friendly warning.

In Aldheorte forest, where Prince Morgan has been living with little ReeRee and her tree-dwelling troop of Chikri creatures, he is separated from his small allies when they climb the steep hills into a mysterious valley full of fog and odd creatures. Before Morgan can follow them along the valley floor, a gigantic, monstrous ogre chases him through the mist and he only survives because he is saved by *Tanahaya*, the Sithi envoy sent to the Hayholt in *The Witchwood Crown*, who was attacked on her way to the castle and almost died. Morgan's own mission with Count Eolair returned her to her people, who have cured her, and on her way back to Erkynland she has stumbled onto Morgan's trail and decided to investigate. But she is not the only one. A group of Norn soldiers are tracking Morgan as well, but he and Tanahaya escape and flee the valley. She leads him to what should be a place of safety, the hillside home of her mentor, *Master Himano*, but they discover that the Norns have been there first and have murdered her old teacher. Tanahaya finds a parchment on Himano's body that suggests the Norns are seeking witchwood seeds that were buried under the Hayholt long ago, back when it was the Sithi stronghold called *Asu'a*. Tanahaya is desperate to get this information to Jiriki and *Aditu*, her two close Sithi allies, but she has no Witness—a magical device for communication—and so leads Morgan toward the ancient Sithi city of *Da'ai Chikiza*, hoping to find a Witness there. But they are captured by the current inhabitants, a breakaway Sithi sect called *The Pure*, and because Morgan is a mortal, he is threatened with execution. But when Tanahaya tells the Pure of Himano's death and the parchment, they reluctantly allow her to use a Witness to inform Jiriki about the witchwood seeds that may be hidden beneath the Hayholt. She has time only to tell him that it seems likely Utuk'ku will try to conquer the Hayholt, then they are interrupted by a force of Norn soldiers attacking Da'ai Chikiza. In the ensuing fight, Tanahaya manages to bring down the ceiling of the chamber, killing many Norns, but she and Morgan and all the others are buried under collapsing stone.

Not far away, Aelin and his few remaining men escape Naglimund only to be captured in Aldheorte. But they are fortunate: their captors are Sithi, not Norns.

Back in the Hayholt, Simon and *Tiamak* and Tiamak's wife *Thelía* are struggling with many problems. Tiamak's helper *Brother Etan* is away in the south searching for news of Prince Josua, missing for many years, but *Bishop Boez* informs them that he has discovered many thousands of gold pieces are missing from the royal treasury. All the news seems bad—Simon has just heard of the civil war flaring in Nabban, and is frightened for Miriamele, who is still there.

And in fact, things have gone from bad to worse in Nabban. Angry citizens, enflamed by several mysterious murders and the propaganda of House Ingadaris, now storm the ducal palace. Duke Saluceris is killed by the mob, but Queen Miriamele helps the duke's wife, *Duchess Canthia*, to escape with her two children and *Jesa*, the children's Wrannawoman nurse. Miriamele gives Canthia her wedding ring so that Simon will know the message the duchess carries is truly from her, but then Miriamele herself barely escapes the mob and the destruction of the palace. Miriamele must ride north alone, through wild country, in a desperate attempt to get back to Erkynland and safety. But she is attacked by bandits, and though she escapes, her horse is killed and Miriamele falls down the hillside and is struck senseless. Canthia and Jesa are even less lucky. Their carriage is chased by Thrithings mercenaries and set on fire. The duchess and her little son are killed, with Canthia burning to death in the wagon after it is hit with flaming arrows. Canthia's friend Jesa manages to escape the carriage with infant *Serasina*, but the two of them are now stranded in an unfamiliar land and still being mercilessly hunted.

In Aldheorte forest, Binabik and the other trolls are searching for Prince Morgan, but the Norn invasion of Da'ai Chikiza prevents them from finding him. They have also discovered that many people and creatures—humans, ghants, even kilpa—are moving north as if drawn by some invisible force. They decide to split up, Binabik and Sisqi to take news of what is happening south to the Hayholt, their daughter Qina and her betrothed Little Snenneq to continue searching the forest for Morgan.

Inside the conquered fortress of Naglimund, Queen Utuk'ku herself has arrived—the first time she has left her mountain city of Nakkiga in living memory. Viyeki, his Builders Order, and his conscripted mortal slaves open the ancient tomb of Ruyan the Navigator and find the Tinukeda'ya lord's fabled armor. In a strange ceremony, Utuk'ku's Order of Song sorcerers put the bones of the Storm King's brother *Hakatri*, burned by dragon's blood and in terrible pain until his death, into Ruyan's armor. (The bones had been found and retrieved earlier by Nezeru and her Norn companions.) Then the dragon that Nezeru and the rest captured on Urmsheim is sacrificed and the blood is poured into armor as Queen Utuk'ku invokes a terrible spell. *Jarnulf*, a mortal who insinuated himself into the Urmsheim expedition but then left afterward, is hoping to have a chance to kill the Norn queen with an arrow from a high spot overlooking the ceremony, but the forces Utuk'ku unleashes are so terrible that Jarnulf is overcome with terror and flees. Even Viyeki, who had already seen the resurrection ceremony that brought *Ommu the Whisperer* back to the world, is sickened when Ruyan's armor comes to life, inhabited now by Hakatri's tormented spirit. The resurrected Sitha lets out a cry of horror so dreadful that it kills birds flying overhead.

In the Hayholt, and already overwhelmed by terrible news—the Norn attack on Naglimund in the north, Unver's grasslanders invading over the western border—Simon and his closest advisors learn that a corpse has been found in the ashes of a carriage on the border between Nabban and Erkynland. The body inside was burned beyond recognition, but it wears Miriamele's wedding ring. Simon is devastated, and all Erkynland is plunged into mourning for their beloved queen.

Nakkiga
Urmsheim
To Tumet'ai
Hikehikayo
THE NORNFELLS
Tungoldyr
Mintahoq
Sikkihoq
DIMMERSKOG
Elvritshalla
Skoggey
YIQANUC
Kaldskryke
RIMMERSGARD
Naarved
Vestvennby
Saegard
THE FROSTMARCH
THE CIRCOILLE
Naglimund
THE WEALDHELM
Da'ai Chikiza
ALDHEORTE
Mezutu'a
Hernysadharc
HERNYSTIR
Nad Mullach
Enki-e-Shao'saye
Sesuad'ra
The Westfold
ERKYNLAND
Erchester
Hayholt
(Asu'a)
Falshire
Gadrinsett
Crannhyr
Abaingeat
Grenefod
HIGH THRITHING
Meremund
Wentmouth
THE SILVER SEA
Kementari
MEADOW THRITHING
WARINSTEN
LAKE THRITHING
PERDRUIN
Ansis Pelippe
BAY OF EMETTIN
NABBAN
Nabban
N
Kwanitupul
BAY OF FIRANNOS
THE WRAN
NARAXI
HARCHA
NASCADU
OSTEN ARD
2017

Foreword

Tanahaya stood at the edge of an orchard valley and knew she must be dreaming. This lush vale, with blossoming groves that embraced both banks of the river, could only be Shisae'ron. She knew it achingly well—she had spent her childhood here. But even as the limbs of the fruit trees quivered in the gentle breeze, a part of her knew the scene was impossible, because though the river might still flow, the orchards and the home of her youth were long gone.

Full of confusion, she made her way down the slope through tumbling petals that danced like snowflakes. A single thought drew her on, though she knew she walked through her own past: *Where is my mother? If the orchards are in bloom, she is still here. And Willow Hall must still stand!!*

Just as some part of her knew that she was dreaming, she also knew that the orchards her father had planted so carefully had not long outlived her mother. During Siriaya's long decline, as her mourning for Tanahaya's father slowly became something darker and closer to madness, most of the members of her Heart-Seed Clan had deserted her and the beautiful settlement had begun to die—as if, like Siriaya herself, it had lost the desire to continue. But here it stood once more, alive and burgeoning, and if the orchards lived, then so did her mother. Their house must still stand above the valley, watching over the river and the trees. Everything could be reclaimed. Time's previous, terrible path could be changed and both Siriaya and the House of Heart-Seed could be saved.

The branches of the orchard trees, at first only a lacy fretwork, grew thicker and closer together as Tanahaya passed deeper into the valley, until she could barely see the sky. The limbs reached toward her like hungry ghosts, hemming her in, and soon she was completely enwrapped. She struggled, but soon the sky was gone, the darkness complete, and she could not move.

Protect it! A voice filled her head, the voice of someone she knew almost as well as she knew herself but for some reason could not name. *Do not let it be harmed!*

The egg, Tanahaya remembered, swiftly and unquestioningly melding one dream with another. *The witchwood egg I found—it is in danger!*

And even as she thought of it, she could feel the ovoid shape clutched against her body, curved and smooth and warm.

The trees now closed so tightly around her that she almost felt she was becoming a tree herself. *But these are not our ancient willows,* she thought in dismay. *These are the trees of the new land, not our beloved Garden. They will strangle me, they will destroy the egg, they will grow over us and leave no trace of what went before!*

She was being held more tightly, sinking ever deeper beneath a thickening rind of bark that sealed her away from the air, from the sky, from everything that mattered. And the witchwood egg she clutched against herself was dying—she could feel that.

Protect it! the voice said. *It must grow!*

Who are you? Tanahaya cried, though she did not speak with lips, lungs, or air. Her mouth was sealed with bark, her limbs pinioned by heartwood. *Help me! I cannot get free!*

And then, suddenly, someone was with her. Tanahaya could not see through the strangling darkness of limbs and roots, but she felt a presence like a cool breeze on fevered skin.

You are walking the Road of Dreams, daughter of my heart, if not of my flesh. The faint voice seemed to come from some echoing place far, far away. *You can only hear and be heard by those who also walk that road or stand near it. But you must leave your dreams of the past and awaken now—that is all that matters. You must save what has been gifted to you—and you must beware the queen's device!*

In the first moments, Tanahaya had thought it might truly be her mother's voice, but now she knew such fierceness could not come from Siriaya's broken, hopeless spirit.

Who are you?

My name does not matter here, the voice told her, *nor can I recall it. For the moment, I am only memory—the memory of all our people, something that cannot be destroyed except by Unbeing. You must save yourself and help save our folk, or even the memory of us will die. Only you!* The voice grew fainter, as if it tumbled way down a deep hole. *But remember—watch for the queen's device!*

And then the presence was utterly gone. The darkness was still solid around her, but the moment had given something back.

My mother's heart broke and she surrendered—but I will not. I cannot.

And in that not-place, whether a dream or her life's ending, she fought as hard as she had ever fought against a foe that made no sound, uttered no words.

It's death, she realized as she struggled against the smothering darkness. *My enemy is death. It comes for everyone at last—everyone, even the deathless silver queen. We can only keep it at bay as long as we fight.*

But I will not stop fighting when those I love are in danger. I cannot—I dare not!

★ ★ ★

At first the only difference between the dream and waking life (which returned to her now in a shudder of immediacy) was pain. Everything hurt. Tanahaya realized with growing alarm that she was just as trapped as she had been in her dream, but instead of crowding trees, she was prisoned beneath an incomprehensible weight of fallen stone.

She could not move her leg and at first could not even feel it. She reached down and discovered it was caught in a crevice in a chunk of stone column that had once, long ago, supported the crystalline roof of Da'ai Chikiza's Place of Sky-Watching. As she touched her leg, she felt something wet. When she drew her hand back she saw a flash of bright red and realized that she had reached through a beam of daylight, but also that her hand was covered in blood. Still, the fear caused by the sight of blood was less than her relief at knowing the sun was in its rightful place in the sky, that she was not stuck in the endless twilight of the dreamlands. She was not even certain that the blood was her own.

Tanahaya had to twist her entire body, slowly and with great care, but as she wriggled her foot loose, she decided that although she ached all over, her ankle and foot hurt particularly fiercely. She did her best to ignore it; her dream was still with her, at least in memory, and the desperation it had fired in her had not lessened with her return to the world.

The witchwood. The dream-egg. The warning voice. Far more than just her own life hinged on her escape. There were secrets to be uncovered and understood—in fact, she carried secrets within herself.

"Beware the queen's device," the voice had told her. But what could that mean? Had someone truly spoken to her on the dream-road, or had it only been Tanahaya's own memory prodding her to save herself?

At last, with a scraping of her flesh that made her gasp, she managed to twist her foot and slide it free, but she was still caught beneath a tumble of broken columns and perhaps badly injured. She began to clamber slowly through the jumbled pile, trying to stay silent even through the worst of the pain. She remembered now that she had not been alone in Da'ai Chikiza's crumbling ruins. She and Vinyedu and the rest of the Pure had been under attack by Queen Utuk'ku's Sacrifice soldiers; the fight had been going poorly before Tanahaya brought the ceiling down. Her allies and the poor mortal Prince Morgan might all be dead. And the invading Hikeda'ya might be only a short distance away, listening for any sounds of survival.

Squirming like an earthworm, almost blind but for the single chink of light she could see, Tanahaya slowly crawled through spaces so small and so painful that they made her want to cry out in agony. At last she felt rain on her face; then, a few moments later, her head emerged from the pile of fallen stone. She could see roiling gray clouds above the shattered roof. Nothing else moved in the ruins of the Place of Sky-Watching.

Tanahaya dragged the lower half of her body out and onto the top of the rubble, still listening for any sign of either her enemies or surviving allies, but she heard only the soft plash of rain on stone: if a battle was still being fought in the tunnels beneath Da'ai Chikiza, it was too far away to hear. What surrounded her instead was the silence of death. Her heart felt cold and sickly. She could not hope to shift the stones, to look for Morgan or any of the Pure, but she also could not believe anything else had survived that terrible collapse. A pang of fury and regret gnawed at her. She had lost the mortal youth she had tried so hard to protect—in truth, might have led him to straight to his death—and now she could not even find his body.

Grieving, Tanahaya tallied her wounds. It was hard to tell where the worst injuries were, since she had been scratched and scraped in many places, but her ankle and foot hurt the most. She was relieved to find she could still bend them, though every movement made her gasp for breath. She tore a piece from her shredded tunic and bound the ankle as tightly as she could. When that was done, she pulled her bloody boot back on and began to climb down the piled rubble, taking care to protect her most vulnerable parts. She could not forget the words she had heard in the dream.

"You must save yourself, save our people, or even the memory of us will die."

What could that mean? Had it been only a call from her dreaming self to the part of her that had already awakened? Or had someone else spoken to her—some spirit or lost traveler on the Dream Road?

She slid off the last shattered column and winced as her wounded foot struck the floor, then realized she had not been protecting her injured ankle or foot as she climbed down. Instead, she had curled one arm protectively over her belly.

By my clan and the Garden, she thought. *Those dreams, even when I was in the grips of fever. The precious egg. "Protect it,"* the dream-voice—perhaps her own voice—had told her. *"It must grow! It is the seed of our salvation."*

My dreams knew before I did, she realized. For long moments she could only sit beside the rubble, amazed and terrified. *The egg I had to protect. My dreams knew!*

I carry a child inside me.

PART ONE

Time of Gathering

The substance of an arrow is wood,
But the arrow's spirit is air.
Is that why, when the wind makes the
forest trees shake and murmur,
I am struck to the heart?

—BENAYHA OF KEMENTARI

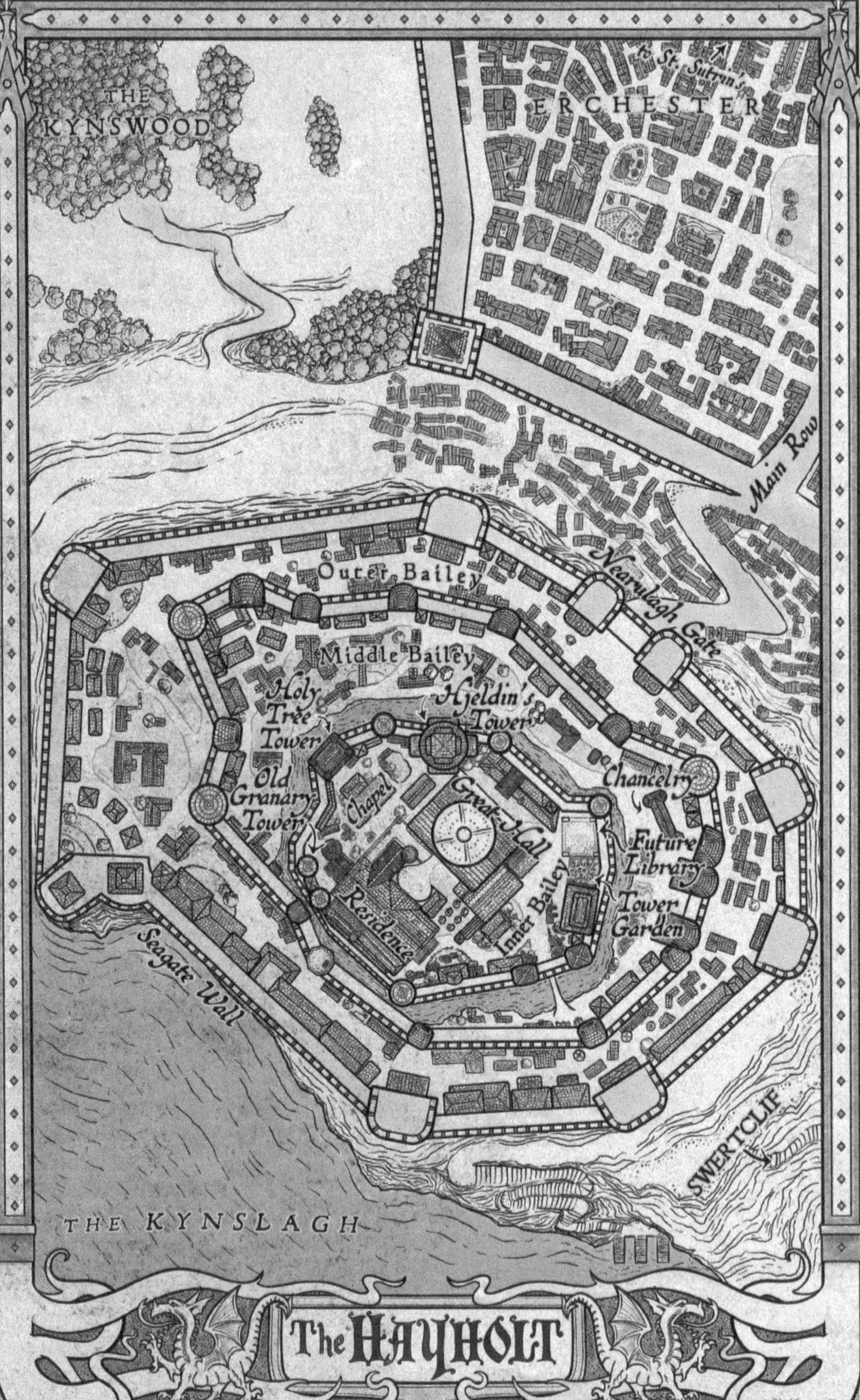

THE KYNSWOOD
ERCHESTER
to St. Sutrin's
Main Row
Nearulagh Gate
Outer Bailey
Middle Bailey
Holy Tree Tower
Hjeldin's Tower
Old Granary Tower
Chapel
Great Hall
Chancelry
Future Library
Tower Garden
Inner Bailey
Residence
Seagate Wall
SWERTCLIF
THE KYNSLAGH
The HAYHOLT
2017

1

The Keen Edge

They crouched together in deep darkness, his captor's chill, firm hand pressing the knife against Morgan's throat. Each time quiet footsteps passed their hiding place, his heart raced. Whether they were found by Sithi or Norn, Morgan did not think the discoverers would care that he belonged to neither army.

The sounds of pursuit faded at last. After a long silence, he whispered, "There's no one else coming. You can let me go now. I promise I won't tell anyone."

His only reply was a quiet hiss. It might have been laughter but could have been something less pleasant. The keen edge of the knife was cold against his skin. It seemed like such a small thing, that edge, thinner than a broom straw, barely more perceptible than a smear of water or a waft of cool air, yet he did not doubt it could end his life.

The one who holds me is a Norn—one of the White Foxes. They have no souls. They hate us and they want our kind dead. But for some unknown reason he was still alive.

The Norn put her feet into the small of his back and shoved him hard enough to send him sprawling forward onto his hands and knees. "Get up," she said quietly. "Slow. We go now."

He considered trying to crawl away and then make a run for it but remembered that both the Norns and Sithi could see much better in the dark than he could. He started to get to his feet and knocked his head painfully against the stone above him.

"Go," she said. "Move. I am just behind."

"Go where?" he asked, rubbing his aching head. "Deeper into the tunnels?"

Again the hiss. "Fool. I never have been in this place but still I know more than you. Below this city much farther—below the river—the water comes in everywhere. Can you live without breath?" He felt the point of a heavier blade than the knife push against his spine. "We move now," she said. "But quiet. Do only what I say."

Do all immortals speak Westerling? he wondered. *Is it some magic?*

She made him lie face down on the stone as she climbed over him to get out of the crevice. She felt surprisingly light but moved with such swift purpose that he did not even consider trying to fight for his freedom. He followed her out into the passage and nearly walked into the point of a long, sharp sword.

"Do I need to say *no tricks*?" she asked.

Morgan shook his head. Now that they had left the crevice, the light from the glowing stones shone on them again, dim but steady. He could see that the woman—no, the immortal creature, he reminded himself, perhaps many centuries old—was a little shorter than he was and much more slender. Still, the sword in her death-pale hand did not waver, as though it were lighter than a birch wand. But it was the narrow oval of her face that caught his attention: her eyes were large and tilted upward, like the those of the Sithi-folk he had met, but this creature's eyes were not molten gold like theirs but dark as a starless sky, a difference made even more prominent by her almost invisible, cobweb eyebrows. He had never seen a Norn, and he was startled by how much she looked like a very pale-skinned mortal: her face was narrow, but her features would not have been outlandish on one of his own kind.

"You stare," she said, sounding almost amused, though Morgan would not have wanted to risk his life on that. "You find me horrifying? Or you think me comely?"

He *did* find her comely, even with her sword only inches from his throat, but he quickly looked down. "No. I just didn't know who it was that . . . that caught me in the dark." He lifted his eyes until he met hers—bottomless wells, inky depths. "Now I see."

She made a noise of derision. "Move, then. I do not stay here—no, *cannot* stay here. Soon the Sacrifices will have all the city, then they make a careful search of even these deep places."

Morgan was exhausted, every muscle trembling, and yet there was that unarguable sword pointed directly at him, the gray blade so slim it was almost invisible. "What do you want me to do?"

"Walk before me. Do nothing foolish."

He lifted his hands in a gesture of resignation. "And my own sword?"

To his surprise, she laughed. "Wear it if you like. But draw it against me and you learn fast what a Sacrifice knows."

"Sacrifice? Is that what you call yourself?"

The laugh again, swift and harsh. "Hah. Once I did, with much pride. Now I do not. Walk, mortal boy."

"Not a boy," he muttered, but his captor gave no sign of having heard him.

The Norn moved so silently that Morgan kept looking back to see if she was following. Each time, he found her only an arm's length or so behind him, and each time she gestured fiercely for him to keep moving.

Despite her earlier words, she forced him down into Da'ai Chikiza's ancient depths. Tunnels that had been shaped to a smooth finish in the upper levels and freely carved with figures and symbols barely touched by time now grew more crude. The few carvings they encountered were simple constructions of straight lines, and Morgan suspected they were nothing more ambitious than direction markers. It would certainly have been easy to lose oneself in the maze of tunnels, which seemed just as shapeless and haphazard to him as the arrangement of the city above ground. Here, though, there were no distractions except the occasional net of roots splayed across the tunnel ceiling or clusters of mushrooms clinging to the damp walls. In some places the palely radiant stones still shone in the walls and roof, but as they descended, these pools of light became less frequent, and the tunnel floors were often clogged by debris fallen from the ceiling. Several times they had to get down on all fours and crawl through a particularly narrow spot, the Norn's sword poking at the soles of his boots.

They had been walking for what seemed at least an hour, and Morgan was finding it hard going. Overwhelmed by weariness and the ache in his bruised chest each time he took a deep breath, he finally broke the silence. "Where are we going? Do you know?"

Something jabbed him in the back of his neck, nasty and shocking as the sting of a bee. Morgan reached up to feel it; when he brought his hand down it was smeared with blood. He turned to say something angry, but the look in his captor's night-dark eyes silenced him immediately. She lifted a finger to her mouth but the poke in the neck and her hard stare had already made the message clear: he was not to talk.

He still couldn't understand his captor's plan. He had seen with his own eyes that the ruined city of Da'ai Chikiza stood beside a wide, often swift river, and after such a long time walking downward, Morgan thought the two of them must now be below it. In some places water seeped out of cracks in the wall and ran beside their path for a short while before disappearing down into other crevices, but otherwise the river seemed no closer than it had been when they started.

At last his captor began to guide him upward once more through a series of sloping passages. The change from carefully excavated and finished corridors to crudely hacked tunnels now reversed itself: intricate carvings began to appear on the walls again. They passed several caverns enlarged into storehouses, and he could even see the remains of earthenware jars in some. Most of the vessels had long since broken into pieces.

Just as the fear in his belly and the painful throb of sore muscles had driven him to a serious contemplation of throwing himself down on the ground and letting the Norn end his suffering, she poked him again, but more gently this time. They had reached a place where three tunnels came together. She slipped past him to examine the faint scratches in the wall, then pointed down one of the passages. Morgan groaned quietly but began to walk again.

At first he sensed the difference more than saw it, because the great space into which they entered was much darker than the corridor. He stopped, befuddled by the different feeling of the air and the dying echoes. A dim light kindled above him, then another, and another, until half a dozen slabs of crystal glowed faintly in the ceiling of the wide chamber.

And it *was* a wide chamber, though as in other parts of the tunnels, the floor was cluttered with fallen stone and broken pottery and even what looked like the rotting remains of wooden furniture. The ceiling stretched upward three times his own height and the nearest walls on the far side looked to be a long stone's throw away.

"One of the city's great vaults." She spoke in a whisper. "Here you may rest for a while."

Morgan's weariness overwhelmed any curiosity he might have felt. He staggered forward until he found a place where the stone floor was empty of jagged potsherds, then stretched out in the ancient dust. Within moments he had tumbled into sleep.

"First you said you did not want to travel so close to the river, Snenneq." Qina was trying to keep frustration out of her voice but not entirely succeeding. "Now you say that we are too far from the river. You are like a mountain wind, first blowing this way, then that." She pointed. "Should I ignore these tracks, all these signs of Prince Morgan's passage? I thought we were sworn to look for him."

"You said yourself that they did not all seem like his tracks."

She thought Snenneq was dangerously close to pouting. "We do not know how he is traveling, nor with whom," she said. "The Norns leave almost no sign of their passage. The same is true for their kin, the Sithi. But here are tracks that speak of several travelers. Perhaps they have captured Morgan and carry him. Should I ignore the tracks because they no longer follow the river?"

"The river is what will lead us to the old Sithi city," Little Snenneq replied. "I did not wish to travel too close to its bank only because we saw those kilpa things, those water monsters. Perhaps you are following the trail of those horrible creatures and will bring us right to them."

"Now you are just making up objections," she said in exasperation. "What I am following is neither kilpa nor . . . what was that tree-beast we killed, with a shell like a beetle? A ghant? These tracks are not from either of those—unless they wear shoes. Look." She pointed at the soft ground. "Those are the marks of stitching. *Stitching.*"

"Daughter of the Mountains, you are stubborn!" Snenneq straightened up, shaking his head. "But you are right. No, I do not think that kilpa, even so far from their home in southern waters, have taken to wearing shoes. But I fear we are following these tracks so far that I will not be able to find the river again."

"Listen. I can hear its noise clearly." Would their marriage be like this too—

every disagreement a stalemate, neither with the power to overrule the other? Qina was not certain she could bear a lifetime of argument, though she feared Snenneq would see nothing wrong with the prospect. "What can we agree? I suggest we keep following the tracks until the river is barely in our ears, then we will head back, as you wish, to follow the water toward the old city."

Snenneq thought this over. "This is a good idea, my beloved. I am glad you have a *nukapik* like me, so reasonable, so willing to let you have your way. Not all men of the Qanuc are so accommodating."

She clenched her teeth. "If you say so."

The long afternoon wound down. The sun still shed light, but it had dropped behind the veil of forest. Little Snenneq kept talking about finding something to eat, and Qina could not much blame him. Their progress had been slow. In many places the strange tracks had all but disappeared, and each time it had taken all her skill to find them again, sometimes by a sign as faint as a single bent blade of grass.

"The sad thing," Snenneq said, "is we are so far from the river now that we will probably eat only dried fish as old as our journey, when fresh fish swim just a short distance away to catch."

"For me to catch, you mean," Qina said. "You do not like to come so close to the water, remember." She rose, weary and unhappy. "Snenneq, my heart," she began, "I know it is difficult sometimes—" She fell silent. Her husband-to-be was not even looking at her but staring instead at a strange figure in a hooded cloak that had risen from the bracken before them. Qina gasped and fell back a step, fumbling at her belt for her knife. "Be careful, Snenneq!"

The stranger was almost twice their height, as tall as a flatland mortal but somehow different. For a moment she thought he might be one of the Norns or even a Sitha. The tilt and size of the stranger's eyes seemed like theirs, although the color of his eyes and skin did not look quite like either one.

"Kikkasut's Nest," Snenneq said quietly. He stood very still. "What sort of person are you?"

The stranger raised one arm and his wide sleeve fell back, revealing a hand with such long, slender fingers that it became even clearer this person was neither Hikeda'ya nor Zida'ya. "Peace," he said in recognizable if strangely inflected Qanuc speech. "Come with me." He beckoned with long fingers. "No harm will come to you. That is a promise." Then he turned and walked back into the trees.

For long moments Qina and Little Snenneq could only look at each other, stunned and uncertain.

"Is that what we have been following?" Snenneq whispered.

"I think so. Should we trust him?"

"No. But we should follow, though carefully. He spoke our tongue. He said, 'no harm.'" Snenneq quickly pulled apart his walking stick and slid a wool-wrapped dart into the hollow tube made by half of it. "Only a middling poison," he explained as she watched. "Enough to put something that size to sleep. Or so I hope."

"I am frightened, dear one," she said. "First those horrible beasts, now this strange person—neither a mortal nor an immortal as far as I can tell. What madness is happening here? Creatures that should not be, creatures I have never heard about."

"It makes me fearful too," he said. "But meetings are rare in such a place, and he might have seen something of Morgan. Let us follow but keep ourselves ready to fight or run."

"I have been ready for both since I came into this queer, dark forest," said Qina.

They had not followed the stranger far before they noticed the tang of woodsmoke in the air. Their guide threw back his head and let out a strange, mournful call that sounded more like the cry of a loon than mortal speech. From somewhere in the trees ahead an answering call came back.

"Now we must be ready," Snenneq whispered.

"Again, dearest, you seem to think I am not already as tight as a bowstring."

The smell of smoke grew stronger as they stepped into a clearing at the center of a ring of ancient linden trees and saw the campfire, its flames shielded behind a circular wall of flat stones. Several creatures like the one who led them sat huddled around it, but these others were big-headed and slow of movement, and looked even less like either immortals or men than did their guide.

One of the figures turned slowly toward the trolls, watching calmly as they approached. His face was like the first stranger's but sagging with age and all but hairless, skin dry and wrinkled as ancient parchment. Qina thought he might be the single oldest-looking person she had ever seen.

"Welcome to our fire." The ancient one's Qanuc speech was effortless and perfect. "Peace be upon you. I am sorry if Tih-Rumi's sudden appearance was alarming."

"Who are you?" said Snenneq.

"I will tell you all you wish to know soon enough," said the wrinkled one, smiling. "But first I wish to greet you properly, and for that I will need your names. I promise we mean you no harm."

The trolls exchanged a look. "Little Snenneq, son of Snenneq, am I," he said at last, "of Mintahoq mountain. This is Qina, daughter of Mintahoq's Singing Man, and also granddaughter of our Herder and Huntress. How do you come to speak our tongue so well?"

"I give you greetings, Qina and Little Snenneq. May the beloved Sea be your haven. May you dream extravagantly." The ancient stranger folded his hands as if in prayer—hands smaller than those of most of his companions but still large and long-fingered. "To answer your question, I speak many tongues—those of all the first tribes of humankind, the Qanuc, the Qo'sei, the high hill-folk, the water-seekers of the desert and the dwellers in the marshy and distant Wran. I also speak the tongues of the Keida'ya, our onetime masters, and of all my sundered, time-lost kin, whom the immortals call Tinukeda'ya."

"You are Tinukeda'ya?" Snenneq nodded slowly. "Yes, of course you are. But you and your companions do not look like Niskies. Are you the *Agaki*, as are told of in our old mountain stories? The diggers in the earth?"

Qina took a breath. If that was true, it was more unexpected to her than even southern swamp creatures roaming the woods. The deep-dwelling Agaki were almost as legendary among her people as Sedda or Kikkasut or any of the other gods, goddesses, or world-spirits.

"Our companions are delvers, yes," the old one said, "—or *dwarrows*, as men name them in the Westerling speech. But I am of an older sort of Tinukeda'ya, and so is my apprentice, Tih-Rumi." The faintest hint of a smile curled the thin, cracked lips. "My name is Kuyu-kun Sa'Vao. I am the Voice of the Dreaming Sea. I wish you both good health, though I fear it cannot last long now that we have come to the end of the world."

It took a moment before the stranger's words sank in, then Qina felt the blood go cold in her veins like a winter stream freezing into ice.

Morgan awoke to find the Norn's narrow, ghostlike face directly above his own and her hand clamped firmly over his mouth. He struggled, but she set the tip of her knife against his cheek just beneath his eye.

"Silent," she hissed. *"Hounds coming."*

"I don't hear . . ." he began, but a prick from her knife convinced him to close his mouth. She pointed to her nose, then toward the far side of the cavernous space she had called a great vault: she was saying that she could smell them.

He climbed onto his feet as silently as he could. *Hounds?* he wondered. What did that mean?

Another of his grandfather's stories came drifting up from his memory, a tale about young Simon being chased through the forest by huge white dogs. But Morgan couldn't remember how that story had ended, except that, obviously, his grandfather had escaped. A quick look at his captor told him that though escape might be possible, it would not be easy: her pale features seemed an empty mask, but her posture and her drawn weapons—long knife and silvery-gray sword—told him she was prepared for a deadly fight.

Morgan slid Snakesplitter out of its scabbard and moved to her side just as half a dozen or more pale, silent animal shapes burst into the high chamber from an opening at the vault's far end. As the beasts sprang toward them, toothy mouths gaping, the Norn leaped to one side. For a panicky instant Morgan thought she had deserted him, but the pack immediately split into two groups, two of the huge hounds heading toward Morgan while the rest continued toward his Norn companion.

The beasts were huge, nearly the size of ponies, their white fur so short that even in dim light he could see their muscles and tendons almost as clearly as if they had been skinned. They made no sound except for their panting breath—no barking, no howling, not even the click of claws on stone. The two bounding toward him each looked to weigh at least as much as he did, so Morgan did the only thing he could do, backing up until he could clamber onto one of the fallen roof stones and gain the advantage of high ground. He had barely turned back when the first hound sprang at him from almost a dozen paces away, an astonishing leap he would never have guessed possible.

Time seemed to slow to a snail's crawl. The great pink mouth opened wide like a blooming flower, yellow fangs visible to the gums; it was all Morgan could manage to get the point of his sword in front of him. His jab caught flesh, but it was only a glancing cut. The massive beast missed him by a handsbreadth; the blood from its wounded muzzle, warm as a summer rain, sprayed his face as it flew past. Then the second hound attacked.

This animal was more cautious than the first: instead of jumping, it put its front paws up on the stone and, like a striking snake, darted its head at Morgan's legs. He knew he had only wounded the first hound, so he jabbed hurriedly at the second and by a lucky chance managed to plunge his blade into the creature's mouth, piercing its jaw. The white hound let out a strangled yelp and whipped its head back and forth like an eel as it tried to get free of the sword. Morgan managed to hold onto Snakesplitter, but the dog slipped over backward and its weight tugged Morgan off his stone perch.

His fall to the cavern floor knocked out his breath. The hound managed to yank the sword from his grip but seemed more intent on getting free of the painful piece of metal in its jaw than coming after him. Still, Morgan was terrified that the other hound would attack while he was unarmed, so he grabbed the first object he could find, a jagged piece of pottery, and when the struggling second dog turned toward him, he swung the shard into the creature's eye. The pottery broke into pieces, but the dog stumbled and fell. Before it could get up again, he yanked his sword free from its jaw and thrust it as far as he could into the thing's belly.

Something struck him from behind, knocking him over the hound's corpse so hard that he rolled several times. Before he had even stopped tumbling a great weight landed on top of him—the first hound, snapping at Morgan's head and neck. He rolled onto his back and punched at it, then pulled up his knees until they were against the dog's heaving midsection. He tried to push it off him, but the beast kept lunging, still eerily silent, spittle and blood flying from its muzzle. Morgan managed to get Snakesplitter up and flat against the dog's neck, his other hand wrapped around the blade to hold back the creature's snapping jaws. Blood from his palm ran down his wrist but Morgan did not even feel it, not with the hound's carrion breath fouling his nostrils.

The creature's weight bent the sword and kept Morgan from turning the edge of the blade toward its throat. Then, as it strained toward him, bending

Snakesplitter even farther, the dog abruptly twitched violently, shivered, and thrust its snout high in the air before collapsing on top of him.

For several heartbeats Morgan could only gasp for breath. When he tried to move the hound's body, he felt the hilt of a knife sticking out of its broad ribcage.

"Not safe yet." The Norn appeared beside him and freed him from the pale, canine corpse.

Morgan struggled to sit up. With the hound's weight gone he felt light as a feather and not much more substantial. His limbs were trembling. "What?"

She yanked the knife out of the dog's bloody side. "Not safe yet."

Morgan stared at the scatter of animal bodies on the other side of the room. One, two, three, four . . . and the one on top of him made five. She had killed four of the white monsters in the time it took him to kill one, and then managed to kill the sixth as it tried to bite off his face—and she was not even breathing swiftly. "How did you . . . did you *throw* that knife . . . ?"

"Get up!"

He scrambled to his feet just as three more shapes ran into the storeroom—two-legged newcomers, all of them carrying long knives and short spears. The parchment-white faces told him instantly that they must be Norns.

"*Kaddara*!" one of the figures cried, and all three sprinted toward Morgan and the Norn. Their speed shocked him, but the swiftness of his companion was even more astounding: in the blink of an eye she leaped forward to meet them at the center of the great vault, her sword cocked at an angle above her head that made no sense to Morgan. She blocked one almost invisibly fast spear thrust. Then, so swiftly that Morgan could not quite make sense of it, she blocked the stab of a second attacker, then flipped his spear out of his hand and sent it clattering into the shadows along the cavern's edge.

To Morgan's shame and relief, all three of the attackers now surrounded her, ignoring him completely. He considered trying to escape while they distracted each other: after all, he was the Norn's prisoner, not her ally. But he could not make himself run—not least because he could not tear his attention from the spectacle unfolding before him.

Morgan had watched the Sitha Tanahaya fighting alongside the Pure only a few short hours earlier and had been amazed by her grace and facility with a blade. But the Norn who had captured him was something else entirely. She moved with what seemed like impossible speed, dancing through a storm of ringing blades and stabbing spearheads, leaping, ducking, kicking. Several times she used the thrust of one enemy to block an attack from another. It would have been exceptional even if they had been clumsy fighters in heavy armor, but the Norn warriors were her own kind, capable of swift and startling feats of their own. Yet every time they seemed to have pinned her down and were trying to finish her, she slipped away like windblown smoke, and they were forced to defend themselves from a new angle of her attack.

Morgan had not given up entirely on the idea of fleeing this struggle between two different enemies, but something beyond mere admiration for the Norn's skills was holding him. He had survived being lost in the forest, but it had not been all his own doing: only joining the troop of Chikri forest-creatures had kept him from starving. He still wanted desperately to get back to his home and family, but he had lost Tanahaya in the collapse of the roof and now was deep beneath the earth in an unfamiliar place, surrounded by creatures who would cheerfully slaughter him. His Norn captor seemed to be his best hope now—his *only* hope.

He raced across the room and snatched up the spear that she had knocked away from one of her attackers. When he turned, he saw that, though one of the Norn soldiers had been downed, he was not badly injured and was about to rejoin the fight. Morgan dashed forward and shoved the spear into the Norn soldier's back even as he rose, all ideas of fairness and chivalry gone in the terror of real combat. The Norn arched in agony as Morgan yanked the spear back out, his blood gushing black in the dark vault before he tumbled forward and lay motionless.

One of the other attackers was distracted by his fellow warrior's death-gasp, and in that instant Morgan's Norn captor put the tip of her slender gray blade into his eye, then snatched the spear from his suddenly strengthless hand and blocked a desperate blow at her neck from the third Sacrifice soldier. A moment later her blade passed through his stomach and tented his cloak behind him. She yanked out the gray sword with a flourish like a courtier presenting an expensive gift; the Norn soldier slumped to the stone floor and did not move again.

As she cleaned her blade on her dead enemy's cloak, she looked over at Morgan, her face still preternaturally calm, as if she had not just destroyed two skilled fairy-warriors and several monstrous hounds in a matter of moments. "What did you say your name was, mortal?"

It took a moment—he was still short of breath. "I don't think I did. You had a knife to my throat, remember?"

Her expression did not change. "Your name?"

"Morgan." He considered listing his titles, letting her know how important he was, but decided against it. "Morgan of Erchester. And I've forgotten your name."

"Nezeru." She slid her blade back into its scabbard, still fixing him with that stony look. "So, Morgan of Erchester, I will say only this—you may have thought to win my trust, but do not involve yourself in my battles again. I do not need your help. I do not want your aid. In fact, I want nothing at all from any mortal."

2

Wolves at the Doør

Each morning when Simon awoke, everything felt ordinary. He surfaced from his always-dreamless sleep and lay with his face pressed deep into the pillow as the world reassembled itself around him. And then he remembered.

The pain was so big, so overwhelming, that he rolled over onto his back and cried out. "Oh, God! Oh, God, why?"

"Your Majesty?" Avel, his young chamber servant, had crawled from his pallet on the floor to stand swaying at the foot of Simon's bed. He rubbed his eyes with his knuckles and stifled a yawn. "It is morning."

"I know. I know it's morning." It was almost too difficult to speak, as if some huge beast were sitting on his chest. The king sank back into his bed and closed his eyes. "It doesn't matter whether you want it or not. It always comes."

"Majesty?"

"Morning. Damnable, damnable morning." The first innocent moment was gone as if it had never existed, a bare heartbeat or two in which Miri was not dead, in which the world still had meaning. Now everything had climbed back on top of him again. Simon rolled over and buried his face in the bedding. He did not have the strength to bear such a terrible burden. He couldn't believe he would ever have that strength again.

"Majesty, there is a note by the door," Avel announced.

Simon said nothing. A note, an armed rebellion, a raging dragon—he could not imagine anything outside this chamber that was worth the struggle against the awful weight of being alive.

"It is from Lord Tiamak, sire. I recognize his seal." There was a long silence. "Do you want me to open it?" the boy finally asked.

"Do as you wish." Simon tasted sweaty linen and pushed the covers away from his mouth. "Read it or do not read it. Take it to Market Square and announce it to the crowds there. Set it on fire. I leave it to you."

He heard Avel fumbling with the folded parchment. When he spoke, he sounded anxious. "Should I read it out loud to you? I am not good with spelling and words, Majesty, but I will try."

Simon pulled the pillow off his head. He was not angry, he was not worried, he was not *anything*. He sat up. The young servant looked thin, and he had a touch of blue beneath his eyes. "No. Give it to me, lad. Then go and get yourself something to eat."

"But you, Majesty? Will you break your fast?"

"Just go."

When Avel had gone out of the bedchamber, walking on tiptoe as though the king had only pretended to be awake, Simon sat up, the message from Tiamak open and unread on his lap.

Someday I will see her again in Heaven, he told himself, but it brought him scant solace. *I would go and join her now—they could bury us side by side on Swertclif—but the church says it is a sin to end your own life. I would be denied her not just for now but for eternity.*

There was no way out he could see, and nothing to do but wait through the weary years. He fell back again, the unread letter already forgotten. *Oh my God, why would You take her and not take me? Do You hate me so much? There is no crueler thing You could do to me.*

But someday, unless the church is a liar, we will be together again. That was all he could hold onto, all that kept him moving in a semblance of life. *We will be together in Your infinite grace.* A colder thought intruded. *But the sermons say we will be with all the others that have gone before us, together forever in the unwavering light of God.* He did not want Miriamele back only to share her with everyone. The best moments of his life had been their times alone, private talks where they made each other laugh until tears flowed, quiet, irreverent asides to each other at the most important of moments—and of course, the glorious secrets of their marital bed. If Heaven denied him those private moments, how could it be all the priests promised?

It did not matter. Even if she would be given back to him in Heaven, the empty years still stretched before him—days, months, seasons that would trudge past like exhausted prisoners being marched to an unknown fate.

Simon made a sound of despair and struck at the bed with his fists, but he did not weep. He had used up his tears for good on the day they had lowered Miri's casket into the earth on Swertclif, and since then his eyes had been dry as dust.

Eolair, Count of Nad Mullach, had been gone from the Hayholt a long time, and was surprised by how different Tiamak looked. The Wrannaman had always been small, but now seemed shrunken, as though something vital was slowly leaking out of him. Obviously, it had not been a good time to be the king's counselor.

But how must I *look, this battered old man I have become?* the count wondered. *I feel my age as never before. Or is it the world that has aged around me? Where have all the colors gone?*

"Welcome back, my lord," said Tiamak, bowing. "This place has missed you more than you can guess."

"And I have missed it, though I would have much preferred to return in happier times and bearing better news from the world outside."

"It would not much matter, at least at this moment. The world outside seems to be of little interest to the king right now. I wrote to tell him you were here, but it is almost noon and I have not had any word regarding when he will see you."

Eolair shrugged. "He sleeps a great deal, does he?"

"Well, he is in bed a great deal. How much he sleeps, I cannot say." Tiamak frowned. "He suffers, our old friend. He mourns. In truth, he shuffles around the castle like a ghost—as though he was the one who died but has not realized it yet."

"He truly loved her," said Eolair. "They were no arranged joining of dynasties like many royal couples—there *was* no dynasty when they came together, only two young people who needed one another. Simon has lost a part of himself." He certainly knew how that felt: it was an unusual day when he did not think of lost Maegwin, despite all the intervening years.

"You spoke of dynasties," Tiamak said slowly. "I hate to turn so quickly to practical thoughts, but Prince Morgan is still missing. We must begin to consider what we should do if something were to happen to the king."

"Something?" Eolair felt his skin prickle. "What are you saying, man? Is he ill?"

"No, at least not in body. But he is . . . the queen's death has affected him badly."

"Surely that is no surprise. He loved her. We all loved her."

Tiamak shook his head, then looked around as though he feared to be overheard, but the retiring room was empty but for the two of them. "No surprise that he is mourning her. But it feels like something worse."

"Tell me your thoughts straightly, my friend."

"The king seems to have given up on everything, Eolair. He barely leaves his chambers, and when he does, he scuttles back to them as quickly as he can, like a crab to its pool. At the queen's funeral, Lord Chancellor Pasevalles and I were so afraid he might collapse altogether that Pasevalles stood close and held his elbow while Captain Zakiel stood on his other side. Even so, we feared Simon might throw himself into the grave after her." Tiamak shook his head. "I am afraid he might do himself harm, Eolair. I have never seen him like this."

"Then we shall talk about the succession, if we must." But Eolair felt now as if his own weight was pulling him down into a hole from which there would be no emerging. He had visited the queen's grave early in the morning—it had felt like a bad dream. Eolair had never considered that he might outlive the queen. "It is hard not to feel that Heaven is against us," he said heavily. "So many terrible things all at once."

Tiamak gave him a quick, startled look. After studying Eolair's face for a moment, he said, "We will talk more of that later, too. But for now, I want your news and I will give you mine. Perhaps the king will meet with us later."

"I know we must talk of Hernystir," said Eolair, "but King Hugh's treachery fills me with shame so deep it presses out my breath. I was already in horror that Hugh let the cursed Norns pass through Hernystir, which we would not have even known about but for my grand-nephew Aelin, but I thought Hugh would at least wish to keep his crimes secret. Now I hear he outright refused Simon's request for aid."

"That is for the best, I think," Tiamak said. "If Hernystir's king is now our enemy in truth, better not to have him beside us where he could do even more harm."

"But making compact with the Norns! I am told those monstrous things have attacked the fortress of Naglimund."

"Attacked it and took it in a single terrible night, if the reports of survivors are to be believed." Tiamak sighed. "This is heavy work, my lord. I think despite the earliness of the hour, I need a cup of strong wine. Will you join me?"

If the usually abstemious Wrannaman was indulging before noon, thought Eolair, what was the point of staying sober? "Yes, I think I will," he said.

"Tell me again about what happened on the River Laestfinger," Tiamak said when the servant had gone. "The king took your letter away with him and I have not had a chance to read it again more carefully."

"It was shocking—and strange," Eolair said. "Unver, this so-called Shan, this grassland king of kings, gathered his fighters on the river across from Osric's camp, although it was only a fraction of what numbers he might have mustered, at least from what I saw at the Thrithings-men's great gathering. We thought Unver would wait for more warriors and try to overrun us by sheer numbers. But he is a very different creature than the other Thrithings leaders we have faced—more complicated, and certainly a better general.

"While Duke Osric's men were reinforcing their defenses, Unver sent a troop of riders across the river farther south so that they could come silently around behind our camp in the night. No word came to warn us, and they struck just before the first light, catching our soldiers by surprise. Then Unver himself led his other troop across the river. Osric and the rest of the Erkynlanders fought bravely but it was no use—we were outnumbered and turned two ways, fighting at the front and the rear. We were nearly caught between them and destroyed." He paused as the memories of that terrible dawn washed over him—shouting grasslanders riding down the Erkynguard, the hail of arrows ending lives all around him. "Then Duke Osric fell. His herald and the rest of his household dragged him off the field. Others saw them retreat and it became a full-fledged rout, which is probably all that saved us—Osric would have fought until every Erkynlandish soldier was dead, so much does he hate the grassland barbarians." Once the memories had been summoned, it was hard to dismiss them. A little wine spilled over the rim of his cup and Eolair realized his hands were shaking badly.

"I am told Osric lives, at least," Tiamak said quietly. "How many men did we lose?"

"Still no true idea. Hundreds. But in a strange turn, Unver did not try to stop us when he might have finished us off. We retreated across the fields in a shambles until we reached Fellmere Castle. Unver followed, but slowly and with surprising caution. I even hear that he has kept his army from plundering anything that was not in his direct path. Perhaps Unver means to protect what he plans to rule someday." Eolair was silent for a long moment. "I fear that man, I will not lie to you. And I fear that my own actions may have been what began this."

"I have heard the story," said Tiamak. "I do not blame you. You saw Vorzheva, who we have been seeking for years, and you tried to get her to come back to Erkynland. Any of us would have done the same."

"She tried to stab me!" Eolair was still astonished. "As if she would rather be a servant in Unver's household than the widow—I beg pardon—than the wife of a missing and beloved prince."

"She was always a difficult person to know or understand. But what you say about this Unver Shan worries me." Tiamak took a sip of his wine, then another, as if he sought courage before his next words. "Could Unver have ordered the murder of Queen Miriamele? Thrithings arrows were found at the scene of her death."

The count shook his head. "It seems unlikely to me, but I can offer you no proof. There are many men of the grasslands who have become sell-swords, so Thrithings arrows do not prove who ordered the attack. And it may be that I have lost my ability to judge people, or perhaps the Thrithings-folk are too strange and different for me to understand, but Unver seemed truthful when he talked to me of wanting peace with Erkynland and the High Throne."

"Lost your ability? Do not rate yourself so lowly, old friend. When I consider that the Sitha woman we saved was felled with poisoned Thrithings arrows within sight of the Hayholt's walls, I can only agree with you. Else we must believe that this Unver began a campaign against us a year ago and risked the anger of the Sithi as well. No, there is some other player at work in this game, I suspect, though I cannot say yet who it might be. Too many things have gone wrong for it to be pure chance."

"You do not think it King Hugh, do you? By all the gods, is my shame to be made even greater? Could he really be so foul? Striking at the heart of the High Throne even while the king and queen were dining at his table last spring?"

"I put nothing past Hugh," said Tiamak sourly. "But I rather suspect that we are seeing another hand—perhaps a pale, immortal one—behind our many troubles."

"The Queen of the Norns, you mean."

"She is unquestionably at the back of all this. But she may have a cat's-paw closer to us who is responsible for our current calamities." He put his cup down and sat straight. "But this is too much speculation for so early in the day. You and I will speak more of all these things later, good Eolair, but now I think we should see the king. Perhaps you can breathe some resolve into him where Lord Pasevalles and I cannot. You are, after all, the Hand of the High Throne, and you have been badly missed."

"I hear Pasevalles has been more than capable."

"Oh, he has done all that he could," said Tiamak. "But the throne needs you now more than ever."

Eolair started to say something, then decided against it. "Lead me to King Simon, then. His heart is heavy, I know. Perhaps it will help him to have another old friend to share the burden."

"King Simon," said Tiamak and knocked again. "Majesty, it is Tiamak. I've brought Count Eolair, just returned from the east. He has news for you."

A young servant opened the door. "Very sorry, my lords," he said, unable to meet their eyes. "But the king is feeling unwell and asks you to come back another time."

"Ha!" Tiamak assumed a bluff tone that Eolair could tell was as false as a lead fithing-piece. "Then it is good I am here because I am the king's physician. I will see him now." And he slipped past the servant and limped through the anteroom toward the royal bedchamber.

"Bring some food and wine," Eolair told the serving boy. "Do not stint. If I know Tiamak, he will make the king eat something, so be sure to give His Majesty a rich choice."

The king was sitting up in his great wooden bed. His haggard face and long, unkempt beard startled Eolair: Simon looked like a man who had been lost and adrift at sea for many days.

"Straighten up, fellow," he said as Eolair bowed before him. "Who is that? I can scarcely see you."

"Perhaps if you opened the drapes, Simon, you would see your visitor better." Tiamak spoke as if to a sullen child instead of a monarch.

"But I don't want the light in here." Simon squinted. "Eolair? Is that you?"

"It is, Majesty." He rose. "Here to give you my deepest condolences, and to offer any assistance I can."

"Huh. Can you raise the dead? Can you bring back my wife?" Simon pulled his coverlet up almost to his chin as if he was contemplating disappearing beneath it altogether. "If not, there is little you or anyone else can do for me, Count."

"If I could, I would, Majesty," said Eolair. "As would every one of your subjects. We all loved Queen Miriamele."

"Love." Simon leaned back against the headboard, his stare flat and empty. "Love is a trap that God sets for us, Eolair. And it is also the bait."

"Majesty," said Tiamak quickly, "the Hand of the High Throne has journeyed all the way from Fellmere to see you. Eolair witnessed the battle with the Thrithings-men firsthand, and before that he was a prisoner among the grasslanders for some time. Is there nothing you wish to ask him?"

Simon lowered the coverlet again, staring with eyes so full of pain that it almost took Eolair's breath away. "Then tell me the truth—is my grandson really lost? Or do the barbarians hold him prisoner?"

For a moment, Eolair was startled into confusion. He had written the entire story of his trip with Prince Morgan and their meeting with the Sithi, of returning in time to see the attack on the Erkynguard camp, and of his own subsequent capture. Had the king not even read it, he wondered, or had grief driven it from his mind?

"Ah . . . as I said in my letter to you, Majesty, Prince Morgan fled the field and back into the forest at my direction. He was no coward and would have stayed to fight, but I knew his duty to your subjects outweighed it. I have no certainty of what happened to him afterward, I am very sorry to say, but I am sure that he is not being held by the Thrithings-men. Unver was preparing to ransom me. Why would he have done that if he had the prince to use as a bargaining piece instead?"

Simon, whose body had tensed as if he feared a blow—or hoped desperately for some relief—slumped once more. "I recollect your letter now. I had forgotten, that is all. The days have been dark, you see. Since Miri. Since we heard." His expression remained bleak and empty. "They murdered her. She was terribly burned, you know. Tiamak did not want me to see what they had done to her, but I could not—I could not believe until I saw."

Eolair wanted desperately to change the subject. "I bring at least a little good news, Majesty."

Simon looked at the count and his eyebrow rose; for a moment he looked a little more like his old, familiar self. "Truly? I had forgotten that such a thing even existed."

"The Thrithings leader Unver is angry, Majesty, but he does not seem to intend a true invasion of Erkynlandish territory. He besieges Fellmere but has not done anything like the damage to the surrounding countryside that he might have. There are other, softer strongholds not far away, ripe for plunder, but he has left them alone."

Simon made a noise of disgust. "Ah, good. So, we may be grateful that the barbarians are behaving themselves and only killing the Erkynlanders directly in their path. Obviously 'good news' has changed its meaning in these evil days, Count."

Eolair was silent for a long moment, considering. "Such sarcasm ill becomes you, Simon," he said at last, and saw the king's eyes widen a little at the reproof and the calculated use of his name. "Yes, we are fighting against invaders, but every Erkynlandish subject of yours they do not kill when they might is indeed a good thing. And although you may no longer wish to get out of bed and face it, the rest of us have enough to worry about that we are glad—yes, glad—that Unver seems intent on nothing worse than punishing us for my escape. An escape," he said with slow emphasis, "that I did not wish, and tried to resist."

"Did you really?" Simon looked at least mildly interested. "I had not heard."

"The men you sent, they forced me. I told them I was negotiating with the one called Unver Shan, but they would hear none of it."

Simon nodded. "Yes, I recall you put that in the letter as well. Still, it is all water over the dam and cannot be undone now." The eyebrow rose again. "Unless you are volunteering to return to this Unver's custody?"

Eolair was not happy with this current version of the king. Even when Simon acted as if he cared about the state of the High Ward, there was a hollowness behind his words that Eolair had never heard before. "I do not think that would help now Majesty, or, indeed, I would readily return."

"Then what should we do, High King's Hand?"

Eolair looked at Tiamak, but the little man showed no hint of what he was thinking. "Resume the search for your grandson, Majesty." Eolair took a breath. "And let me return to Hernystir."

"What?" Simon was actually startled. "What folly is this? Have you given up on us entirely?"

"Count Eolair," Tiamak began, "do you really—?"

"Hear me out, please, both of you," Eolair began, "and let me have a little more of that wine, because I have been dreading this for days."

When the servant boy had refilled his cup and stepped away to a discreet distance, Eolair took a long swallow. "My king—Simon—you know that I have pledged my life and honor to the protection of the High Ward and your throne. I beg you to hear me out. Everything I say begins with that pledge—and ends with it, for that matter."

"Go on," said Simon, but he seemed to be holding back anger.

"What I hear from Tiamak and others suggests that Pasevalles has ably replaced me in my long absence. It seems to me there is little I could do here at the Hayholt that would change our situation."

"Except to stay at your king's side when he most needs you."

"Please, Simon. Hear me out, I beg you. Of course I will do as you wish, and if my presence will bring you comfort, you have only to tell me and I will stay. But listen to my thoughts and see if I am so far off the mark." He took another sip. "The attack on Naglimund is a terrible, terrible thing and should be uppermost in our thoughts. We know that the Norns did not lightly enter our lands, and that they would not have done so unless they intended something more than merely taking that one castle. I fear—we all fear—that they mean to bring war all the way to the Hayholt, as they did so many years ago. We also know we face a grave situation in the east of Erkynland. So far, Unver seems interested only in making his displeasure clear, but we must defend against his invasion anyway. Many Erkynlandish troops are besieged in Fellmere, and others are being readied here to relieve them. Nothing can change that need.

"The news from Nabban was bad even before . . . well, enough to say that Nabban is in chaos, with the nobles of House Ingadaris apparently seizing power after the death of Duke Saluceris. We can change nothing there without using armed force, and you and I and Lord Tiamak know that would be a foolish, pointless thing even to contemplate. We need every soldier we have, and it still may not be enough to save the High Ward in this hard time. So for now Nabban must boil and bubble like a pot left too long on the fire, and we will wait to see what is left afterward.

"The people of Rimmersgard and Isgrimnur's son, the new duke, are still true to the High Throne, but Grimbrand will not be able to send us much help. He is fighting against the Norns too, as well as against treacherous Hugh on the Frostmarch borderlands. But that is to our good."

"To our good?" Simon scowled. "We have no allies anywhere, the Norns may march down on us any moment, and you say it is to our good? And what does this all have to do with you deserting me to return to Hernystir?"

"You misunderstand me, Majesty. I mean it is good that Hugh is pushing against his borders with Rimmersgard. Though it means he holds Grimbrand back from helping us, it also means that his attention is divided and many of his soldiers are committed there."

"I see a flicker of sense in all this now," said Tiamak. "I am sure His Majesty does too."

"No, I do not," Simon said, but anger had brought a little life to his face and voice. "I see disaster on all sides."

"Only a fool would tell you we are not in danger," said Eolair, nodding. "We are—all the lands of men are in danger. But we must still make careful decisions. Now listen, please, both of you. My young kinsman Aelin was the first to see the Norn army. We know that because he told Lord Murdo, Earl of Inbarh, who passed it along to our mutual friend, Count Nial, who brought the news here. Murdo is a good man, one of the High Throne's staunchest supporters, and there are many more like him in my country, nobles who do not love what King Hugh has done and will love it even less when they learn he has made compact with the Norns. Hugh is ambitious, that is clear, and he has apparently made some bargain with the Norn Queen and her White Foxes. What if she demands that he attack Erkynland from the west while she attacks from the north?"

"This is not making me feel better," said the king.

"I think Eolair may have a solution," Tiamak told him. "Or at least an idea."

"My idea is simple. We must rally the Hernystiri nobles against Hugh. If we force him to defend the capital, Hernysadharc, he will have little freedom to make mischief against us here. Murdo and Nial will be with us, but their dislike of Hugh has been known for a long time, and the other nobles might think an uprising only their own ambition. With all humility, Majesty, I can say that I am one of the few men trusted by the Hernystiri lords we need to unseat Hugh—or at least keep him greatly occupied. In Hernystir I can raise a rebellion. Here in the Hayholt I can only wait to see what trouble comes upon us next."

Simon thought about this, frowning and tapping his fingers on his knee, but he looked even more weary than he had when they came in, and Eolair feared they might not have his attention for long.

"What the count says has good reason behind it," Tiamak offered.

"You said we must search for Morgan as well," said Simon. "You are right. What good to save the kingdom if I lose him?"

"We must do our best to save both, Simon," said Eolair. "You sent men to find me—not an army but a pair of useful fellows, though I could have wished they would have listened to me better. Perhaps the same men could be put to work, tracking him down. But I beg you to consider, Majesty, what I said about Hernystir. I do not see all of Hugh's plans yet, but I fear them, whatever they may be. I will be of more use to the High Throne there, I feel that strongly."

"Yes, I understand." Simon waved his hand. "But I cannot give you an answer now—it's too much to think about and my head hurts. Leave me now and we'll speak again later."

Eolair was afraid of losing the moment. "But, Majesty, I think . . ."

"Enough!" Simon balled his hands into fists and shoved them against his temples. "Enough. My head is splitting. I am doing my best, curse it all—would you bleed me like a pig? Go. I said we will speak again and we will, Count Eolair. But for now, I am tired and angry. And whether we find my grandson or save the kingdom, the truth is that my queen—my wife—will still be dead."

I am . . . alive. Yes, I think I am alive.

But Miriamele was not entirely certain. Her head throbbed like a hive full of angry bees, and she could see blood pooled on the ground where she had lain. She reached up and felt her scalp, gasped when she found the stinging gash, and then stared down at her own bloody fingers, working to make sense of it all.

She clambered back up through the tangled vegetation of the hillside, following the path of broken pine trees. Halfway up she found her horse's remains. Wolves had found brave Orn, who had died carrying her, and she could not bear to look at the ruin of his flesh crawling with flies. She closed her eyes as she rummaged in the saddlebag. For her trouble she found only a bit of bread and a bit of dried fish, but it filled her aching stomach.

Noble Orn, you and your master Sir Jurgen saved me, she thought, *and even in death you have helped spare my life. If the wolves had not found an easier meal, they might have dined on me instead.*

When she reached the top of the slope she stepped onto the road and looked around. The marks of her mount's last staggering steps still scarred the hard earth, but otherwise the road was empty. Miriamele lingered for a moment, listening for the sound of pursuit, but heard nothing, so she began walking. She was still unsteady and her head throbbed fiercely, but she was alive, alive.

She did not follow the road for long, though she slept in a tussock of grass beside it the first night, cold in her tattered court dress. The next day a few farm wagons and oxcarts came rumbling along the wide track, forcing her to scurry off the side and into the trees: she could not afford to trust anyone in this part of the world, since she was not even certain she had crossed out of Nabban and into Erkynland. Whatever else she did, she knew she must continue northward to be sure of reaching her own country.

As the day went on, she could see far enough ahead at times to know that the road was descending from the heights and the tree cover was growing thinner as the dirt track wound its way down into bare meadows. Soon there would be nowhere to hide when people passed by, so when the last, long slope of the hill had begun, leading her downward into a broad valley, she stepped off the road for good and made her way downhill toward a line of alders, trees which often grew beside streams.

She found something more than a mere stream flowing at the bottom of the valley. The river was not wide, but its calm though fast-moving waters seemed deep, and she suddenly thought of fish—fresh fish, freshly caught. She had finished the little bit of food she had salvaged the previous night: her stomach felt as sadly empty as an abandoned cottage. Still, she followed the course of the river until she was far from the road and the sky was darkening before she stopped to try to catch something.

She had no hook or net, so she picked out a backwater, took off her shoes and hose, then rolled up her skirts. The weather was cool, not cold, but she did not want to spend the night shivering in a heavy, wet dress.

Fishing by hand was harder than it seemed: every time she sighted a small, shining shape, it slipped easily through her fingers before she could lift it out of the water. At last, after what seemed at least an hour, she managed to hold onto a silver bitterling no longer than her palm. For a moment she contemplated making a fire, then decided she did not want to make smoke and give herself away to anyone who might be out wandering in the vicinity, so she opened and cleaned it with her fingers, then ate her catch raw.

Her swift and only slightly satisfying meal finished, she tossed the well-picked bones into the water and found a place to curl up for the night, high enough on the riverbank that the ground was dry but the spot was still sheltered from the wind. The sun had set some time earlier, a fat new moon had risen, and the stars were now fully visible. She prayed silently for the lives and health of her husband and grandchildren, then for the safety of the troubled lands of the High Ward. Afterward she lay for a long time watching the white fires wheel slowly through the sky, the Hare, the Shepherd's Crook, and the wide Spinning Wheel, until sleep overtook her in her hollow above the murmuring waters.

Days slipped past as Miri followed the winding course of the river north, each one bringing her a little closer to home, though how far she would have to travel to reach it was still a mystery. She thought she must be on a tributary of the Coldwater River, which rolled down from Nabban's Nearulagh Hills and poured into the sea at last in Erkynlandish territory south of Wentmouth. But even if that was true, she did not know what point along the river she had first struck, and whether she was still on the Nabbanai side of the border. It was strange to realize that she could not tell the difference between her mother's land and her own, between the nation that had once ruled the earth and the one that ruled it now, where her husband and friends and family waited for her.

We make marks on maps to separate one country from the next, then write treaties to make law of those separations, she thought. *But in truth, unless people contest the borders, the differences mean little. Most folk who live on the edges speak the language of both sides, and there is little else to separate one nation's people from another's.*

So is there something wrong in the way men rule each other? she wondered. *Animals walk and birds fly freely from one land to the next and no one thinks to stop them doing it. And God makes no lines across His Heavens—the sky is blue from one horizon to the other with scarcely a difference to be seen, let alone a boundary. And yet His children fight each other to the death over lines they can only imagine.*

The thought stuck in her head and would not be dislodged, not even by the distractions of her slow, difficult, and very muddy journey beside the river.

I hope I'm right about what river this is. Then I only need to follow it to reach Erkynland. For drinking, a river's name does not matter. But for finding my way home, the name matters much.

Perhaps this truly is the Coldwater, she thought one morning as she made her way along the river's upper bank, following its leisurely twists through the valley. Its northward flow certainly suggested that it must come down from the Nearulagh Hills, and when she drank from it, it was certainly cold enough to have had its birth in the heights. It was variable, too: in places the river widened until she could not have shot an arrow across it; at other spots it narrowed to a frothy, hurrying thing scarcely more than a dozen ells across. As she followed its course from the bank, the river turned and sped through a narrow gorge, and though she did not like to walk where she could be seen, to follow it Miri had to climb up the rocky slope then and walk along the crest, the water hissing and booming far below her, filling the air with spray.

On the other side of the gorge the river swirled through a boneyard of pale stones that turned the water to white spume. A little farther on it finally fell back and began to behave itself once more, widening into its previous slow progress, and Miri finally felt safe to clamber down the slope and make her way along the river's brushy bank once more. It was hard going in places, choked with shrubs, small trees, and stands of reeds, but the slope above her looked even more tangled. Then she reached a place where a large, rounded stone jutted into the river, blocking her path along the bank. After a moment's consideration, she decided that she could make her way around it through the water more easily than climbing past it through the thick brush on the slope above.

She rolled up her skirts, then stepped into the bitingly cold shallows, moving slowly to make sure the footing was firm, leaning on the stone for balance as she crept around it. The water reached as high as her hips, but the tug of the current was not too bad, and when she was halfway around the obstacle she saw that the river spread into a wide, calm backwater just ahead. This reassured her, and she even dared to take her hands off the stone as she negotiated the last few cautious steps. When she had reached the far side she stopped, contemplating with relieved satisfaction the placid spread of the river and the bank covered with gently swaying reeds. Then something caught her leg and yanked her off her feet and into the green water.

It happened so suddenly that in the first thrashing startled moments as the river closed over her head, Miriamele thought that she must have stepped into a deep hole. But when she managed to get her face above water for a moment, whatever held her immediately yanked her back down, pulling on her leg and twisting so that she spun as she descended, and all her struggling could not bring her back toward the surface. In terror, she opened her eyes, and through the green water she saw a shape that she at first thought was a man beneath her, wide across the shoulders, with grasping fingers that flailed as it turned to look up. Its mouth was so big that she could not see her attacker's eyes, could see nothing but the wide jaws that held her foot and ankle in an unbreakable grip and a squirming, wormlike tangle on either side of the huge mouth. *Kilpa!* she thought, but even as her lungs began to burn, she realized the thing was too bulky and squat to be any kilpa she had ever seen. She kicked hard at the broad, smooth head, but the thing did not loosen its hold and her foot slid off it.

The creature dragged her farther away from the bank, and as she spun, her hand closed on a piece of wood. She jabbed it at the creature's face—or at least where a face should be. For a moment the rasping mouth gaped, and Miriamele yanked her foot away. She swam hard for the surface and managed to get her head above water and suck in a life-giving breath. In that fleeting instant she saw that the bank was now much farther away, then the clammy mouth closed on her leg once more and dragged her back down.

She had only managed to take in a small amount of air. Already darkness seemed to be flowing over her thoughts like spilled ink.

Simon, she thought. *Simon. Home.*

The thing had now engulfed her leg almost to the knee. She shoved at her attacker's tough, smooth skin, and kicked as hard as she could with her failing strength, but she might as well have tried to kick loose an anvil. She looked up to a circle of light shining in the murky green above her.

Is it Heaven?

Then the thing that held her spun again and she lost sight of the shining spot, the light fading in a whirl of green and black and green and black.

Hakatri

First Interlude

For an unmeasurable time he knew nothing except that he had died. The intrusive chaos of being alive had become so distant as to be utterly without importance. He had died, and now he slept, though his sleep was not entirely dreamless: he had thoughts, though they were slow and cold as fish in a frozen winter stream. Still, the ending of his life had finally brought him a kind of peace. Instead of squeezing him in its cruel grip, time now flowed around him without touching him, slow and heavy as a river of mercury. Somehow, he had escaped its awful tyranny and the pain that living had inflicted on him—or so he believed as the world, which he could hardly recall, spun on without him.

But if he had almost forgotten the world, that did not mean the world had forgotten him.

After a seeming eternity of this glorious nothingness, something began to prod at his sluggish thoughts, drawing him up from his vegetal slumbers toward a greater awareness—and, unavoidably, toward the living world he had so willingly left behind. Something in that world was calling him. He did not want to be called, but try as he might, he could not ignore it. With that return to awareness came something else: a memory of life and its unending, unendurable pain. And with that memory came horror.

Like some underground creature dragged from the dark safety of its burrow into harsh daylight, he tried desperately to wriggle away from the increasing pull, to escape back down to shadowed, dreaming unconcern. Life was *agony*, he remembered now with horrifying certainty, and he would do anything not to experience it again.

But whatever sought to awaken him would not let him escape so easily, did not care that all he wanted was to be left alone. And as the cruel, nameless thing drew him closer to life and light, torment returned—a growing and horrific pain, not just of the body but of the spirit too, a terrible gash in his being that he knew would split him open and expose every part of him once more to life's merciless attentions. But struggle though he might, he was drawn ever upward, and as he rose the old agony burst out in full force, blooming like some scorching fire-flower, growing with each passing instant until it overwhelmed everything else.

He could think again. He could feel. But after so long at peace, he could imagine nothing worse.

Pain and madness came rushing in together like a burning wind, and his thoughts became a firestorm. Wordless words thundered through him, drawing him up ever faster toward the terrible, terrible light.

Then life caught him in its jaws and shook him. The glare of the living world came blazing in from everywhere at once—a dreadful, scalding radiance. He screamed and heard his own voice, no longer just curls of dream but something that shrieked real words made of real breath. He screamed until it felt as though the sky itself must crack open and the firmament shatter and fall. Pain was everywhere. Pain was everything. Treacherous, hateful life had stolen his peace and dragged him screaming back into endless suffering. He could not bear it. All he wanted . . . all he wanted . . .

"We summon you!" The words cascaded over him, burned through him like sparks landing on fine muslin. *"We summon you!"* The words were in a tongue he did not know, but they forced their way into him as the dragon's black blood had done so long ago. Was it one voice or many that dragged him upward? Whatever it was sang a harmony that gripped him like the claws of some great hunting bird as the terrible words thundered on. "*We speak the Word of Command! You are summoned back. Return! The hour has come and your blood calls you!"*

He could not form words or even the shapes of words, but his whole spirit seemed to shudder in horror.

"Come back to us! You cannot turn away from the Word of Command. RETURN!"

And then he was pulled out into the blinding, burning light, into the monstrous grip of time, and he howled and howled like something skinned alive.

3

Mummers' Parade

It was never less than terrifying to attend the Queen of the Norns, but this was even worse. Today Tzoja, High Magister Viyeki's mortal mistress, needed to ask Queen Utuk'ku a question—a question whose answer she feared. Just thinking about it made her tongue grow large and useless in her mouth and her heart race until it seemed to rattle against her ribs.

Shrouded in layers of darkness—her blindfold, the heavy mask, and the inky shadows inside the queen's wagon—all of Tzoja's attention was fixed on her fingertips as they slid over the queen's slender body, pushing here, palpating there. But what she was really trying to do was to summon her courage. *Do I dare speak to the Mother of All unbidden?* This lean frame, which felt so ordinary, belonged to a creature who could destroy her as easily as Tzoja herself might flick a bit of catkin fluff from her sleeve. And the more she thought about the uncountable years the queen had lived and the power that was in her, the more Tzoja wanted to say nothing, to simply finish what she was doing and scuttle away, back to her dark wagon.

She knew she dared not wait any longer. "Your Majesty."

The pause was long. Tzoja wondered if the immortal queen had fallen asleep. Then Utuk'ku's voice was inside her head, intimate as a kiss but cold as the lips of a corpse. *What do you want, mortal?*

Tzoja took a breath. "Your Majesty, is . . . is anything I've done . . . the tinctures, the ointments . . . is any of it helping?"

Another long silence passed. *No. Or perhaps there is a fraction less suffering than there would be without your mortal remedies.*

Tzoja could only wait, trembling now that the truth of her failure had been acknowledged, wait for her service to the queen to be ended and perhaps her life as well. But the queen stayed silent; for a moment Tzoja had the shuddersome feeling of sharing the room with something dead.

Was there more you wished to ask? Utuk'ku's question was without weight: she was apparently thinking about something else.

The serpent is sleeping today, Tzoja decided, unutterably grateful for whatever was distracting the queen. *I still live. But I must poke it again.* "Forgive me, Great Majesty," she said out loud. "I have done what I can, but I could do more. With respect, if you wish me to help you then I must know what works and what does not. I need truth." Tzoja's skin was prickling badly now. She was an eyelash away from disputing with the sacred Mother of All, or so any Hikeda'ya courtier would see it. As Tzoja waited for an answer, the darkness and silence seemed to swell. She had become little more than a small, frightened animal and had to struggle not to turn and run. The whole world seemed to tilt inward, as though the queen's supine body were a deep pit whose vertiginous depths could cause Tzoja to lose her wits and fall simply from being too near. But when the queen's words finally sounded in her head, they felt shallow, almost sullen.

Foolish little mortal creature. You cannot understand.

Tzoja swallowed, took a breath. "Please, then, Majesty—help me to understand. Tell me what else I can do for you."

You can do nothing, slave. My own healers have long since exhausted their lore and their experience without curing my pain or even much diminishing it. The queen's words were as bitter as rotting grain. *I have eaten the last of the witchwood fruits. The sacred trees we brought from the Garden are all dead now—every last one. Help me? Little mortal, little buzzing fly, I was old already when your ancestors lived in caves, when they heard giants shouting in anger every time thunder cracked. After so long, nothing but the* kei-t'si *itself could prevent death from dragging me down into darkness—but the witchwood fruits are all gone. And on my way down the long descent, I will suffer for all those fleeting centuries I kept death at bay.* The queen's thoughts were as heavy and cold as the lid of a stone sarcophagus.

Tzoja had never heard the Mother of All say so much at one time. Despite knowing the terror and destruction that the silver-masked queen had brought to so many, at this moment, with her hands on Utuk'ku's spare and chilly flesh, Tzoja could not think of her as entirely inhuman. A little pity, even, bloomed deep inside her, a single early wildflower emerging from a snowbank.

But do not misunderstand me, child. Harder thoughts now, sharp as icicles. *I must stay alive—I must stay strong. I have one last, important task I must perform for my people, and only I can do it. So, you will continue to search for your herbs and simples. Continue to make your potions. They do not seem to harm me, and it could be they will help me to last that little bit longer . . . for the sake of my people.*

"I will do as you ask, Your Majesty."

But do it swiftly. We will not stay in this place long, so take this chance to gather whatever you can.

Tzoja had been so concerned with merely staying alive that she hadn't considered that things might change now that Naglimund had fallen. "Where are we going, Your Majesty?"

This time the silence went on very long, until the blackness seemed to spin around her. Tzoja could almost feel the queen's disapproval through her fingertips. With an involuntary gasp, Tzoja pulled the shroud back up over Utuk'ku's body.

"I h-have b-been . . . been foolish, Majesty." She could barely hear herself above the thundering of her own pulse. "I had no right to ask such a question of the Mother of All. Because of your generosity, I forgot myself. Please forgive me, Your Majesty. Forgive an ignorant mortal."

Go. The word fell into her thoughts and lay there like a discarded dagger. Tzoja gathered up her flasks and her bag of herbs and hurried out.

"Follow me, Viyeki-tza." The voice was a familiar one—his old master, Yaarike. But High Magister Yaarike had been dead for a long time.

Viyeki accompanied the dim shape deeper into the tunnel. Even though he knew he must be dreaming, he still looked for landmarks. "Where do we go, Master?"

"You are the master now, Viyeki-tza." The figure before him was little more than a shadow, except for the ni'yo *gleaming in its hand like a tiny star. "That is why you must see the crossings before you reach them and discern the seams that will reward excavation from those which might collapse. If you choose wrongly, you will not be the only one to pay the price."*

"Do you mean my family, Master?"

"Not just them." The dim shape abruptly stopped. They were in a place where many corridors met, some rough and hand-hewn, others smoothed and polished by expert hands—so many corridors that Viyeki could not count them all. Some led upward, others down into the depths or away toward every quadrant of the compass, like a single, invisible knot that tied together dozens of cords. "You must choose," the shadowy figure said.

"How could I choose from so many ways, Master? I do not know any of them. I have never been in this place before."

"Precisely," said Yaarike's shade. "That is precisely the problem you must solve, Viyeki-tza. Choose carefully. All of the passages are dangerous, and most lead directly to disaster and death. You will need all your wisdom and luck to pick the one passage that might lead you back to the air and the sky."

Confusion and fear now overcame him. "Air and sky? Our people would never choose that! How could we be safe in such a place?"

"We could not. But that is the choice you must make, nevertheless."

The walls of the tunnels began to slump inward. Stones and dirt began to patter down on his head. Viyeki tried to cry out, but earth filled his mouth and he could not spit it out. It surrounded him, weighing down his arms and legs, smothering him. He would be lost and forgotten for all the ages to come . . .

"High Magister! High Magister, wake up!"

As he struggled to claw free, he felt the heavy, prisoning earth changing beneath his fingers, until he realized he was gripping cloth instead of sliding soil.

"High Magister, please be careful—you are hurting me!"

As he recognized his secretary Nonao's voice, Viyeki discovered that he was sitting on his bed, tangled almost painfully in his blanket, and that he was twisting Nonao's arm. A moment later he realized where he was—in his chambers in the conquered mortal fortress.

"You are to be summoned, High Magister." Nonao just managed to hide his angry, hurt expression, though he could not make his bow look properly servile. "I have heard that the queen will call for you within the hour."

"It would be dangerous to anticipate it, but I will go the moment the Mother of the People summons me." Viyeki felt his throat tighten and his stomach writhe at the thought of facing her. He would almost rather have been back in his dream, smothering. "But how did this early news come to you?"

His secretary's face was now carefully expressionless. "By chance, Magister. High Marshal Muyare has just come from the queen's wagon. One of his body-servants told me."

So Nonao had an informant in Muyare's household. Viyeki set that bit of intelligence aside to be considered later. "And did this body-servant tell you anything else of interest?"

Nonao nodded. "Yes, Magister. It seems the high marshal and the army are being sent south to attack the mortal castle that once was Asu'a."

More unhappy news, Viyeki thought. If a siege was coming, his Builders would certainly be expected to join the Order of Sacrifice in the flames and chaos of battle. And where was his only child now—Nezeru, his warrior daughter? Would she be one of those caught up and maybe killed as war blazed across the mortal lands? A chill settled in the pit of his stomach, but all he said was, "We live to serve the queen, Nonao. Make order of my things and prepare yourself and the others to leave as soon as possible."

Viyeki crossed the blackened wreckage of the mortal fortress, doing his best to ignore the lingering stench of death wafting from the burial pits. The queen's huge, linked wagons stood just inside the castle's ruined front gates. Two silent Queen's Teeth guarded the entrance at the nearest end, but a more welcoming figure was waiting for him there as well. Viyeki stopped and bowed deeply. "High Celebrant Zuniyabe. It is good to see you."

The ivory mask inclined to show acknowledgment. "And you as well, High Magister." The ancient celebrant was the final source other than the queen herself on all protocol and precedent. He was also one of the few ranking nobles that Viyeki did not actively distrust.

"I did not know you were here, my lord."

"When the queen leaves Nakkiga, where else should I be?" Zuniyabe beckoned him up the stairs and into a sort of antechamber, a small room at the front of the wagon with a cushioned bench, the walls clad in beautifully carved wood that might have come straight out of the palace back home in Nakkiga. "These are strange days, are they not?" Zuniyabe said as Viyeki seated himself. "Who would ever have thought the Mother of All would not only leave our sacred mountain, but come so far?"

Viyeki nodded. "Strange days, indeed. But how are you, High Celebrant? Are you well?"

"As well as can be expected." Zuniyabe sat on a nearby stool and folded his gloved hands in his lap. "Like most of us, I have not tasted the life-giving elixir of the *kei-t'si* for almost half a Great Year and I feel my strength ebbing. It is one thing for those of you who are still young, but we of the first generation here, the Landborn, are stretched already beyond what is natural. It is . . . uncomfortable."

Such honesty from a high official almost felt like an invitation. Viyeki made a gesture of dignified concern. "Perhaps when all has been arranged to the queen's satisfaction, you and I might find time to share a celebratory cup. I have saved a jar of very fine *analita-zé* for just such a happy occasion."

"Perhaps. I would certainly enjoy that." But the High Celebrant now sounded as if he might be regretting his unguarded remarks. His ivory mask showed only his eyes, making it hard for Viyeki to guess what he was thinking. "Please excuse me now, High Magister. I have duties for the Mother of All still awaiting me."

When the High Celebrant had gone out again, Viyeki arranged himself to wait. After a span that might have been an hour but seemed like longer, more guards appeared and at last ushered him into the queen's presence. At first, Utuk'ku's white garments and silver mask were the only thing in the dim chamber he could see, but after a moment he made out the magician Akhenabi standing silent and motionless behind her high-backed chair, like a templar bug waiting to snatch a victim out of the air. A heartbeat later he realized that the queen had one more companion on the raised platform, an unmoving, seated figure at her left hand whose grotesque silhouette provoked Viyeki to a sudden, surprised intake of breath.

It's the thing she summoned back from death—Hakatri, the Storm King's brother.

Had he not already encountered the queen's first summoning, Ommu the Whisperer, Viyeki might have wondered if this truly was the dead Zida'ya princeling, since almost anything or anybody could have been inside that crystal armor. But even from several paces away, Viyeki could feel the same otherworldly emptiness that he had felt during his unwanted audience with the Whisperer, the unmistakable chill that settled not in his skin or bones, but in his heart.

The revenant sat with a gauntleted hand on each arm of the chair, head lowered as if in thought or slumber. In contrast to the glittering armor of crystal tiles laced together by almost impossibly slender gold wires, Hakatri's helmet seemed crude, the three circles that made up its eyes and mouth completing the simplest possible sketch of a face. As Viyeki stared, the helmeted head slowly lifted, then turned toward him with the heavy inevitability of a millwheel, until the twin flames burning in the eye holes seemed to stare right at him.

His heart speeding so swiftly that he could not distinguish between beats, Viyeki dropped to his hands and knees, fortuitously facing the queen.

High Magister Viyeki. Utuk'ku's words rang in his head like hammerblows on stone. *You have done us useful service here in the mortal fortress. Prince-Templar Pratiki has told me of how you overcame several obstacles to open the traitor Ruyan Vé's tomb.*

It was unutterably strange that he should find the queen's attention the lesser of two terrifying things, but even though he could swear he felt Hakatri's fiery but empty stare, he also knew he could not afford any slackening of attention while in the queen's presence. Such mild compliments as she had just given him were often the last thing a noble heard before being condemned and dragged off to execution. He kept his eyes resolutely on the flagstones as he summoned the courage to answer, although it was very hard to keep his voice steady. "The Mother of the People is too kind to her servant. It was your Majesty's wish—I could do nothing other than fulfill it."

Of course. And now I have another task for you. You are to take your Builders north, under Pratiki's leadership.

Even the chill of death's farthest regions emanating from Hakatri could not prevent Viyeki's surprise. He had been certain that he and his workers would be traveling south with Muyare as part of the queen's attack on the mortal kingdoms. "But, Majesty—!" he began before he could swallow the startled words, then set his forehead against the stone floor and waited through a daunting silence. When she did not speak again, he took his life in his hands to explain his outburst. "My regrets for my foolish outcry, Majesty. Prince-Templar Pratiki told me we are at war with the mortal kingdoms. Will you not need my Builders for the sieges and other battles of that conflict?"

The prince-templar should practice discretion. Her words came with a swift stab of pain in Viyeki's temples—a mere twitch of irritation from the queen—and though the discomfort was minor, it reminded him how easily the Mother of All could obliterate him, and how quickly afterward even his name would be effaced from history. His family would vanish too, including his beloved daughter and his mortal mistress. "I apologize, Majesty, if my question sounds of anything but surprise," he added quickly. "I want only to do your bidding."

Then go and prepare yourself and the minions of your order, Magister. Utuk'ku's thoughts now felt flat and heavy and faintly disapproving; it was all Viyeki could do not to knock his head against the floor in shame and terror. *The prince-templar will give you what information you need. General Kikiti and two legions of Sacrifices will lead the company.*

Pratiki will be furious with me for offering him as an excuse, Viyeki thought. *He is my only ally—I must be more careful.* But any unconsidered thought was dangerous in front of the Mother of All, so he spoke up quickly. "Of course, Majesty! Thank you, Majesty! You honor me with your trust." He did his best to force down all confusion and doubt—the Garden forbid that the queen should sense them! "If I have your leave, I will begin preparing at once."

Go, she told him.

As he backed toward the door, Viyeki kept his mind as empty as he could manage. Hakatri's helmet swiveled to follow him, slow as some great war engine being swung into position. The pulsing sparks in the dark depths of the eye holes were the last thing he saw as the door closed.

As he made his way back across the mud and tumbled stones, heart racing, Viyeki could at last begin to think clearly again. *What possible task can there be for me in the north? Where am I to go now? Wait—could she be sending us back to Nakkiga?* A momentary hope flared in his breast. He longed to see his home again, to hold Tzoja in his arms. His wife Khimabu would also be grateful to have him back, especially if she knew that the queen had complimented his work on Ruyan Vé's tomb.

But of course, wondering would avail nothing, and many lives depended on him. He would be told where the queen wanted him, and he would go there. The Mother of All could hear thoughts. She could summon abominations like Hakatri from beyond the veil of death. Viyeki would wait to be told what to do, then he would do it. Anything else was unthinkable.

The lands around the conquered fortress of Naglimund were empty of life now, nothing but trampled grass, mud, and the scorched and shattered remains of buildings. Still, when the queen's guardsman carried Tzoja on his horse down to the river, she discovered that life had not been entirely erased.

Even with the Season of Withering almost upon them, the stony riverbanks were alive with storksbills and blue gentians. To her delight, she even found a cluster of agate mushrooms, delicate fans of concentric stripes that peeped from the grass grown over a fallen log. She gathered them up greedily, then went looking for others, eventually finding several more clusters along the banks of the river. The mushrooms provided one of the most sovereign remedies for many of the pains of old age—the Astaline healers who taught her had prized it especially. They were far too tough to be chewed and swallowed but could be dried and then ground into powder for tinctures. It was one of the remedies she had not tried on the queen, and she was anxious to see if it lessened Utuk'ku's suffering.

But how can anything lessen the suffering of someone like her? Viyeki called her the oldest creature in the world. She would have died long ago if not for the witchwood fruit. A sudden realization struck her: that must have been the fruit that Lord Jijibo had brought to the queen when he had forced his way in some days before.

Tzoja returned to her search, wading through the grass as the sky grew ever darker and frogs began to murmur in the reeds. She found other useful plants, too, and for a while forgot everything else in the simple pleasure of the hunt. Then the helmeted guard, who had been watching her from horseback the whole time, motionless as a statue, raised his gauntleted hand to signal it was time to go.

As they neared the top of the hill, Tzoja was surprised to see a large troop of

Sacrifices and others marching away northward along the road that ran beneath Naglimund's great outer wall, though the wall itself was now little more than a cemetery of broken stones and rubble. She could dimly make out the forms of the officers who led the procession, and the Hamakha serpent banner that flew above them, and she wondered where they were going. There was nothing significant to the north, that she knew of, though she had traveled across much of Erkynland in the days before her capture and slavery.

Perhaps they are taking a roundabout way back home, she thought. *Perhaps now that this stronghold has been conquered, they are returning to Nakkiga.* An unexpected pang of homesickness for the city in the mountain suddenly struck her—not for the place itself, which she loathed, but for her lover Viyeki and the safety she had felt with him. The ache was so strong and sudden that she almost wept.

Viyeki—and my dear daughter Nezeru, my fierce little girl—where are you?

The early years of her child's life had been difficult for Tzoja, so difficult. *"Do not grow attached,"* Viyeki had warned her. *"She is not yours but the queen's and her people's. Soon she will go to Yedade's Box for her rite of passage, then to one of the order-houses. That is the way it is for the children of nobility—even half-mortals."* But even before the Sacrifices had taken her away, Nezeru had been a difficult child to hold, if not to love. Stubborn little Nezeru had crawled after her father whenever she saw him, following him even into his working sanctuary where she was not allowed. Time and again he brought her back to Tzoja, saying, "*She must learn patience. She must learn to live with solitude, to wait until it is time for her. That is the way of our people.*" But for Tzoja, who already agonized over how little time she was able to spend with her lover, it was a lesson she was not equipped to teach or even to understand. Eventually even Nezeru began to see her mother as different and weak, and soon afterward, at an age when mortal children were still at their mother's heels and under her feet, she found her way out of Yedade's puzzle-box and into training to become a Sacrifice officer. And although Tzoja had seen it coming—who could not have envisioned that future for such a determined child, so full of strength?—losing her daughter had almost destroyed her. For months afterward she had hidden in her room in darkness and silence until even Viyeki, despite not truly understanding her pain, had urged his mistress to fight for life.

"Our Nezeru was born to serve the Mother of All," her lover told her over and over, *"and to lift the honor of my clan, the Enduya, even higher. How can you not understand that?"* Another time he had told her, *"If it grieves you so, we can make another child for you."*

And then snatch that one away, too, she had thought. He would never understand. Men did not understand even women of their own kind, and Viyeki, with a lifespan of tens of centuries, could not see the horror that had overwhelmed mortal Tzoja as the child she had grown inside herself was taken away and taught to hate the queen's enemies. Because as far as the Order of Sacrifice was concerned, even Nezeru's own mother was such an enemy.

As the guard brought her back to the train of wagons she was distracted from her gloomy memories. One of the wagons had been pulled out of the train of carriages and brought to the front, where it stood not far from the queen's. Tzoja had seen that wagon before, and would have recognized its black-stained, featureless exterior even without the reddish light that seeped through the cracks. Tzoja had spent a horribly uncomfortable time in that wagon, face to face with the undead thing called Ommu the Whisperer.

"The dead cannot lie," the shrouded, tattered thing in the wagon had told her, a string of words that had flared in Tzoja's thoughts as though written in fire, *"and I tell you this—your line has a destiny that even I cannot see in fullness."*

Just being in the Whisperer's presence had made her feel ill, and she slept for hours afterward. She tried not to think about that day and had never mentioned it even to her blind friend Vordis. Just being near Ommu had been like standing in front of a window that opened onto ultimate, frozen emptiness. The experience had taught Tzoja that some things truly *were* worse than death, and that returning from death must be one of those things.

We will meet again before the end. The undead thing had told her that too, and the memory made her shiver.

Without realizing it, Tzoja had lifted her hand to slow the queen's guard on whose saddle she rode, and for some reason he had obliged, even bringing their mount to a halt while she stared at the featureless wagon. But soon he slapped the reins against the white horse's shoulder, and they started forward once more along the line of wagons, headed for Tzoja's own carriage. But even with the Whisperer's wagon out of sight, she could not shed the memory of that terrible emptiness in human form.

We will meet again before the end.

Although the light had now all but faded with the setting of the sun, long years in Nakkiga had made Tzoja's eyes sharper: she could see Vordis standing at the wagon's open window as they approached, eyes fixed on nothing, sweet face peaceful. In the midst of so much unhappiness and so many evil memories, Tzoja felt a wash of relief at the sight of her friend.

I think I can bear anything if I am not alone, she thought. *I have been alone too much in this life.*

"I hear that the wagons will be moving out again soon," Vordis said as she combed Tzoja's wind-tangled hair. "We are leaving."

"Leaving for where? And who told you?"

"The other Anchoresses were talking about it when we were last summoned to wait on the queen. As to where, that is more than I can say. If the others knew, they did not tell me."

Before Tzoja had a chance to respond to this new and unsettling idea, the door to their wagon swung open. Night had fallen, but even so she could recognize the serpent-shaped helmets of two fully armored Hamakha Guards silhouetted in the doorway.

"Who is there?" asked Vordis, startled.

"One of you just returned," said the nearest guard. "Which one?"

Tzoja fought to steady herself as she rose. "Me. I have just come back from gathering herbs to make simples for Queen Utuk'ku. I am one of her healers."

"You are to come with us."

"Bring the other too," his companion said. "His lordship will want both."

"Where are you taking us?" Tzoja demanded, trying to sound stern, though she was terrified by the sudden intrusion: mortal slaves had no rights among the Hikeda'ya.

The helmeted guard only prodded her out of the wagon. Outside a saddled horse and a two-wheeled cart were waiting; the cart was hitched to a silent, slow-chewing Nakkiga goat, a shaggy black creature as big as a plow horse. One of the guards lifted Tzoja under her arms and swung her roughly into the cart, then a moment later Vordis was set down beside her. One guard climbed into the saddle and the other onto the seat of the cart, then they set out along the track that ran beside the wagons, heading toward the front of the line.

Tzoja had not entirely given up hope. "Are you taking me to Her Majesty? If so, I will need my herbs and tinctures."

Neither of the guards replied or even glanced her way, and with their backs to her she could not even see their faces.

"What happened while you were out?" Vordis asked in a tremulous whisper.

"Nothing!" She could make no sense of it, which made it all even more frightening.

The cart creaked to a stop beside one of the biggest wagons Tzoja had yet seen, something with a dozen wheels, more like a high-roofed barn than any normal carriage. Its outer walls were covered with crudely painted symbols she could not read. For a moment, her heart sinking and her belly curdling, she thought it might belong to her master Viyeki's hated enemy, the arch-magician Akhenabi, master of the Order of Song.

They were lifted from the cart as unceremoniously as they had been placed in it, then forced up the steps and inside. The interior of the wagon was lit, but not brightly, by a single *ni'yo* sphere the size of an apple, which sat on a wooden tripod on the table. A wide bed stood against one wall, and she could dimly make out a pair of figures in it, then one of them sprang out from beneath the covers with the alacrity of a child finally allowed outside to play.

"Could it be? It is! Ah, what fun, but there is no one to share it with." The white-skinned figure was dressed in only an unbelted robe, so that Tzoja could see his naked loins and narrow chest, but it was his grinning face that held her eye as he leaned to examine the prisoners in the light of the sphere. "Still, they both have meat on them, as mortals do. Succulent. And they scream so unreservedly."

Lord Jijibo stood over them, robe flapping like a scarecrow in the wind. He had black paint smeared above and below his bright, black eyes, like a clown from a mummers' parade. The half-naked, wild-haired creature was the queen's descendant and the maddest of all the strange, ageless members of Clan Hamakha.

"Tell me your name," he said, his face almost touching Tzoja's. His breath smelled of something metallic. "Ah! Look at her, poor brute. Trying to think, trying to think! It is not hard, child. Just tell me your name."

"I am Tzoja, m-my Lord Jijibo," she stammered. "Slave to High Magister Viyeki and healer to Her Majesty the queen." Beside her, Vordis kneeled with her chin against her chest, silent and motionless as if her heart had stopped: she clearly recognized their captor's name.

"Oh, most excellent. Healer! Mistress of forgotten lore! But with just one of my sharp little knives I could carve that knowledge out of her, piece by piece, until even her own name was a mystery." He moved closer still—close as a lover. "You were seen just a short while ago, slave, spying on the queen's most important ally. Why? And for whom?"

"Sp-spying? I do not understand you, my lord. Spying on whom?"

"The Whisperer, of course." He reached out to touch her cheek, a gesture that seemed almost tender until something concealed in his hand pierced the skin just below her ear and made Tzoja cry out in pain. "Why were you spying on Ommu's wagon?"

"I wasn't! I only looked at it."

"But why? Oh, harken! Mortals are such terrible liars, even before the pain begins. I wonder if their hearts are smaller and more fearful than ours." He reached out again, as swiftly this time as a snake striking, and again something stung her face.

"Please, my lord, I tell you only the truth," she said. "I met her, the one you speak of. I spoke to her—not today, but another time. She . . . she said things to me I could not understand, and when I saw her wagon today, I remembered and thought about it." She hurriedly told him everything that happened before, when Ommu had ensorcelled a queen's guard and brought Tzoja into her sanctuary.

"Insolent little bitch." Jijibo's smile remained merry. "Here," he told the guards, "take up the other one. She looks a bit more delicate. Perhaps her friend will speak more freely when she hears her crying."

"No, my lord!" Tzoja cried. "I am telling you the truth!" But already the guards had grabbed Vordis and held her tightly as Jijibo produced a long needle from the sleeve of his robe. He probed first at the girl's neck, then at her ears, cocking his head as if measuring the quality of her weeping protests.

Tzoja threw herself down and crawled toward Jijibo until she could wrap her arms around the Hikeda'ya noble's cold legs. "Please do not hurt her, Lord Jijibo. She is one of the queen's healers, too. The queen will not like it."

For a long moment he stared down at her, his eyes so full of mad amusement that she had to look away. As she wept and pleaded, she saw for the first time that the other figure in Jijibo's bed was no living being at all, but a thing made of jointed wood like a string-puppet with no strings, its face blank and featureless. "Oh, please, please, my lord," she cried, trying to push this new, confounding horror from her mind, "I do not know what I have done wrong. I swear I have told you all the truth I know."

"Have you, then?" Jijibo turned away from sobbing Vordis, which was some consolation at least. "Perhaps she truly does not know," he said as if to someone—perhaps the wooden doll, Tzoja thought, and felt as if she would be sick. "But could that be? I should test it. But perhaps Great-Grandmother would indeed take it amiss if I carved this pretty little joint of meat into slices." He squatted in front of Tzoja, his pale, rootlike manhood dangling only a short distance in front of her. "Let us try again, creature. You see, I *know* you, Slave Tzoja, plaything of the Enduya. Many of us know about you. But why should deathless Ommu take an interest?"

She could only shake her head.

"I might almost believe it a coincidence," he said slowly, "but it is one coincidence too many, don't you think?" His words seemed offered to the air. "But perhaps the poor cow is ignorant of that, too." He extended his arm, held her chin with one of his chilly hands, then slapped her hard with the other. "I told you, *I know you*, mortal wretch. You fled from your master's house. You made your way to Suno'ku's lake and you met my children there. You have no secrets from me."

His children. The Hidden. Then Jijibo really was their 'Lord of Dreams.' Tzoja had guessed rightly, but now she wished fervently it had never happened. "I met . . . strange creatures there."

"Strange?" Again he slapped her, then caressed her face as if to make it right. "Not strange. *Beautiful.* The Hidden are so beautiful I can scarcely stand it. What right does a vile thing like you, a . . . *random* thing . . . have to call them such a name?"

"I am sorry, my lord. They were kind to me." *Until they betrayed me.*

"*Pfah.*" Jijibo abruptly stood. "They should have killed and eaten you. Then they would not always complain to me that they are starving. Still, I cannot help loving them. I made them, did you know?" He stared at her. "No, how could you? How could such as you even understand an art like mine? Neither Yedade nor his vaunted father ever managed such a thing, though they tried. Even the Mother of All does not know all I can do."

Jijibo began pacing now, as if he had forgotten Tzoja, Vordis, and the guards entirely. "But they all think to keep me from what I want. Except Great-Grandmother. She understands. And when the day comes . . ."

He broke off and returned to Tzoja. "Look!" His face again loomed close to hers. "She trembles—ah, see! She thinks her life is all she has to lose. Do I dare show her the gulfs she cannot imagine, the empty places beyond what she knows?" He giggled. "Ah, ah—what a sweet pleasure that would be. She has a certain faded charm that would be bliss to destroy. And the other—she is blind! All those other senses that could be exploited, nursed, caressed with so many kinds of agony—!" He stopped abruptly. "But still, all that talk of her line. All that talk of the last king . . ." He lifted a clawlike white hand and scratched absently at his belly and the pale, wispy patch of fur below it. "Perhaps I should consider more carefully. Yes! Never give in to the pleasures of the moment without looking to the future." He fixed Tzoja with his night-dark eyes, lips stretched in another dreadful grin. "You see, the only way to be certain you will not offend someone . . . is to birth your own victims."

Tzoja had lost the strength to do anything except crouch and silently pray.

"Take them back," he told the guards at last. "I will learn no more because she knows no more herself. But now I also must worry for my beautiful children back at home. Did I leave them any food? It is so hard, sometimes, when my mind is so full of ideas—!"

Jijibo turned his back on them then and went back to his bed, stretching his lean body beside the silent wooden manikin. After a few more moments had passed the guards decided Jijibo had finished. They hauled both women to their feet and shoved them toward the door.

When they had been returned to their wagon again and the Hamakha soldiers had locked them in, Tzoja and Vordis fell onto the nearest pallet, clutched each other, and wept, mostly in silence, until they fell asleep exhausted in each other's arms.

4
One Way Out

Nezeru held up her hand for silence, but the young mortal took a last step. The faint sound of his boot scuffing against the passage floor—*pif*—seemed as loud to her straining ears as a crack of thunder. She took a breath to calm herself. The youth was not even useful as a shield between herself and her enemies, as she had originally planned, because she had to make him walk behind her so she could hear what was in front of them. At least, unlike Jarnulf, this creature was not trying to make her doubt herself. Still, she thought, it might be a simpler and more merciful thing to draw her sword, Cold Root, and have the young fool's head off now, before he gave them away to her enemies.

Despite the mortal youth's noisiness, she could hear nothing except the deep, nearly inaudible groans of shifting rock common in underground places, but she could smell the resins that some in her Sacrifice Order used on their armor. Hikeda'ya warriors were somewhere close. She had known she would have no easy escape from Da'ai Chikiza, but she had chosen the abandoned city out of deadly necessity, not strategy.

"Do you hear anything?" the mortal whispered. Nezeru was concentrating so fiercely that his words seemed loud as a shout. She whirled on him in fury and her hand dropped to the hilt of the witchwood sword.

Whatever else he might be, the youth was not completely stupid: He recognized Nezeru's rage and quickly took a few steps backward, lifting his hands as if in surrender. Something about his expression abruptly drained much of her anger.

With those round ears and that tousled hair, he looks like Minku, she thought. The little brown stoat, whose name meant 'Slippery,' had been the only one of her father's wife's familiars that Nezeru had been able to stand. Her stepmother's other companion creatures had always reminded her of Khimabu herself, sharp-eyed and spiteful, but Minku had been a clown, knocking things off tabletops to chase them across the floor as they bounced away, or climbing into ridiculous positions and then chittering in dismay until someone helped him down. Like this mortal, whose thick hair stood up where it shouldn't, Minku had possessed a tuft of fur on the top of his narrow, brown head. When her father's wife had grown frustrated with the animal's misbehavior and had told one of her servants to take it away and drown it, Nezeru had felt her dislike of cold, beautiful Khimabu harden into something like hatred. Nothing since had changed that.

So you miss Minku, do you? she sneered at herself. *By the Garden, are you really sparing this clumsy fool's life because he reminds you of a dead animal? How many ways can you shame the teachings of your order?*

"Back," was all she said. "This way is guarded." This time she let him lead, half-hoping for a Sacrifice ambush that would solve the problem for her.

They paused in an empty storeroom so she could consider her next move. She could tell he wanted to ask her something, but that he had been sufficiently alarmed by her reaction to his most recent words that he did not want to chance it. Suppressing a sigh of frustration, she said, "Speak."

"Nezeru—that is your name, yes? I have that right?"

She only stared at him. At least Minku, for all his playful wickedness, hadn't asked questions.

"I wondered . . . I wondered where you learned to speak Westerling. To speak my tongue. Do they teach it to all Norn soldiers?"

"Norn?" It was a word she only dimly remembered.

"Hikeda'ya." He pronounced it as though he had a mouth full of sticks. "Your people."

"In my order, they teach us only war."

"Then how is it you speak my tongue?"

"My father knows some of that speaking. He learned from his—" She did not know the mortal word for *s'huo-gan*, which was the most fitting term for Viyeki's old teacher and superior, the former High Magister, Yaarike sey-Kijana. "He learned from his master. But also my mother teaches me."

Memories swam up as Nezeru spoke, like eager fish coming to be fed, of her visits home from the order-house during festivals and holy days, of her desperation to be with her father even when he was at work in his study. He had always seemed pleased to see her when she arrived but would fall into long silences as he perused his parchments and his old books. After a while she had usually surrendered to what felt like a shameful need, retreating to her mother's tiny chamber and climbing into bed with her, to be enfolded in Tzoja's soft arms. Sometimes her mother would sing to her, explaining the songs' mortal words, and though the tunes seemed almost bitterly discordant to Nezeru, the words, once explained, had always soothed her, songs of childhood and sleep and parents watching over their young.

She had lost something since those days, she realized, though she was not sure what it was. But for the first time she recognized an ache that had been with her for as long as she could remember.

"Why did your mother know Westerling?" he asked after a long silence.

Nezeru did not reply immediately, but her own hesitation annoyed her. What did she care what a mortal thought? "She is like you," she said finally. "Not Hikeda'ya."

The youth's eyes widened. "Your mother is a mortal like me?"

Nezeru shrugged, uncomfortable. "It is not strange, so. Mortal slaves make babies for nobles. My father is a noble." For a moment she succumbed to pride. "High Magister of the Builders' Order."

"Whatever that is," he said. "But is your mother really mortal? You say she's a slave?"

"*All* mortals in Nakkiga are slaves."

The one who called himself Morgan settled back against the storeroom wall. For the first time, she saw disgust in his expression. "So someone stole her from her own family, then your father raped her."

For a moment, she puzzled over the word, then as his meaning became clear, she found herself with one of her knives in her hand, its tip lightly touching the mortal's throat.

"She is a *slave*. My father does nothing dishonorable."

This time Morgan did not attempt to escape her anger. His face showed little expression. "Well then. Kill me because I told the truth."

She hissed between her teeth. What was this madness among mortals, this idea that they somehow owned the truth? "You do not know anything. My father is kind to her. He gives her everything. He cares for her more than his wife." She spat out this last, though she was glad of it, glad it was true. For a moment they remained that way, eyes locked, Nezeru's knife still pressing against Morgan's neck.

"Go on," he said at last. "You only mean to use me as a shield, anyway. What do I care whether you kill me or one of your Sacrificer friends does it?"

"Sacrifice," she said. "Not Sacrificer. And I told you—they are no friends. They want me dead."

"Hah." He scowled. "I just want to go home, then you can kill each other for all I care." Still, despite his bold words, the youth slowly leaned away from the knife; after a moment, Nezeru lowered it. "So," he said, "is there some way we can both get what we want and not let your Sacrificers—Sacrifices—get what *they* want? Because they may want you more than me, but I don't think they'll let me live if they catch us."

She looked at him with a flicker of admiration. He might be a mortal, with all the clumsiness and foolishness that meant, but he was not a coward. *Still, he cares too much about living. He would not make a good Sacrifice.*

"Here is a problem," she said at last. "Everywhere we go, I smell and hear them waiting. If we rest, when we move again they will be closer. But it is not me they are hunting—they do not know I am here. They search for the Zida'ya who lived in this city, the ones who escaped them."

"What do you mean, they'll be closer?"

"It is something we are taught in Sacrifice Order, a movement for searching.

It is called Funnel Net, and it is like what the fishermen use on rivers. Start very wide, then it goes more . . ." she struggled for the word, tried to show him with her hands, "more thin."

"Narrow," he said, imitating her gesture. "Starts wide, then gets narrower. In other words, they're closing in, but doing it slowly so we don't slip past them somehow and get away. But you said they're not even looking for us."

"But they will catch us, still. And then we die just the same."

They sat in silence for some time. Nezeru was still sifting the breeze for unusual scents, still listening for anything out of the ordinary.

"I have a little food," he said at last, and began to unroll his sleeve. "The Pure, the Sithi that live here, they gave me some bread and honey. I'm afraid I ate the honey already . . . and most of the bread." To her astonishment, he smiled as though a little ashamed.

Do these mortals show everything on their faces? How can they go through the world so naked? How can they give away so much to their enemies?

But then she saw the crusty end of bread he held out to her with an unsteady hand. She worried it might be a trick and reached out carefully to take it, her other hand on the hilt of her knife, but the one called Morgan remained stock-still, as though she were a horse that might startle. Nezeru sniffed the bread, then put it into her mouth, realizing only as she did so how long it had been since she had eaten anything. His offering felt and tasted strange, so soft that it did not seem bread at all, certainly not hard, chewy *pu'ju*, but instead as light as cloud-fungus and almost as sweet as the black honey from Nakkiga's lowest slopes, where the heather bloomed for only a few days in high summer. In fact, the bread was so light and soft that it seemed to disappear even as she chewed it, leaving her moments later with nothing but an empty mouth, an awakened hunger, and the faint taste of flowers on her tongue.

"Good," she said almost breathlessly. "You say the Zida'ya make that?"

"The ones who live here did." He looked up, as though he could gaze through stone. "The ones who *used* to live here. They must all be dead now." A look crossed his face, an expression of stark mourning she did not understand. Surely he could not have known the so-called Pure well enough to feel much about their deaths.

These mortals. Their moods may be complicated and mysterious, but they are also meaningless, from what I have seen. She was thinking about Jarnulf again. *They are like the roots of foxberry mats, broad but shallow.*

Still, even the brief taste of the Zida'ya bread had lifted her spirits, and the urge to dispatch this noisy mortal was at least temporarily in abeyance. "Rest," she told him. "I will watch. We must try again soon to find a way out before the Funnel Net is drawn too tight."

"Your kind don't sleep much, do you?" Morgan asked, but almost immediately yawned. "Must be nice. All that time to do other things." He had a sudden thought. "Do you drink wine? Your kind, do they drink wine?"

She was a little startled. "We do. We drink many things."

"And do you have anything to drink with you?"

She patted her drinking skin. "Water."

He scowled and stretched himself beside the rough-hewn stone wall, his scabbard scraping on the cavern floor as he made himself comfortable. "Not what I meant."

"Please forgive me, Kuyu-kun Sa'Vao," said Little Snenneq to the ancient figure in the tattered cloak, "but it seems my ears did not hear you correctly. It sounded as though you said, 'now we have come to the end of the world.' But this is not the end of the world, or even the outskirts. This is the great forest that men call Aldheorte."

The hairless head swung side to side in gentle negation. "You may call me Kuyu-kun. You may also call me the Sa'Vao if you wish. Both name and title are not necessary each time."

Snenneq tried to smile and nearly succeeded. Qina was impressed with her beloved's patience. "That is well. But what did you mean with your words about the end of the world?"

"Come, join us at our fire," said Kuyu-kun. "Share our meal—it is meager, I fear, for two such young and healthy Qanuc as yourselves, but you are welcome. Then I will answer your questions." He turned to the one who had brought them. "Tih-Rumi, you and the others give our guests room to sit."

Silently and with many a worried glance, Kuyu-kun's companions made space near the fire. Qina did not like being surrounded by so many larger folk, but despite their height and their massive hands, the delvers seemed as fretful and harmless as deer in a meadow.

The one called Tih-Rumi dutifully stirred the coals, then placed two more bundles wrapped in leaves atop them, near the edge and away from the flames.

"Give it a short time to cook," Kuyu-kun said. "Or do you take your food raw?"

"Cooked, please," said Little Snenneq. "You said we could call you 'the Sa'Vao.' What does that mean?"

"It means I am the memory of my folk, the Voice of the Dreaming Sea. In our tongue, 'Vao' means the great sea that birthed us. It is also what we call ourselves, the name of our people, but only one in each generation is the Sa'Vao. From my birth I was raised to remember, and I learned all that my predecessor knew of our people's tale. It is also our job to pass the tales along, and I hoped that someday Tih-Rumi would take my place when I was gone. But it appears that is not to be."

"How can we eat, how can we even speak calmly, when you keep saying such things?" Qina could not match Snenneq's apparent calm. "You keep speaking of the end of the world! You are saying that all our striving, all our plans, are without meaning?"

"Never without meaning," said Kuyu-kun. "In truth, those things may mean even more here at the end—only the stars are our judges." He smiled. "Ah, I think your food is ready. I hope it is to your taste."

Qina accepted the leafy bundle. She sniffed at it and was enticed by the meaty, slightly sweet scent of the steam. "What is it?" she asked.

"In our old mountains, we called it 'softfoot,'" Kuyu-kun said. "It is a mushroom that grows in many places, though. We have also seasoned it with forest myrrh."

Qina stared at the orange and brown flesh inside the bundle, poking it gently with her finger, but Snenneq had already started to eat. She broke off a small piece and placed it on her tongue. It tasted faintly of anise. She swallowed it and took another bite. After a moment, her caution evaporated, and she too began to wolf down the hot food. All around her, the delvers were pulling the other bundles out of the fire.

"Now, while all are filling themselves," said Kuyu-kun, "I will speak a little if I may. Do you know the history of the Exile?"

"Which exile?" asked Little Snenneq through a mouthful of mushroom. "The Sithi—the Zida'ya—speak of at least two—"

"There is only one Exile—at least for my people. The only true Exile was when the Keida'ya—the Sithi and Norns, as you call them, when they were still one people—brought the Devourer into the Garden and we, the Vao, were forced to leave the place of our creation. Not as a free folk, but as *slaves.*" Kuyu-kun made a gesture, hands crossed before his narrow chest, then closed his eyes, and sat in silence for long moments before he spoke again. "When it was seen that the Garden could not survive, the Keida'ya turned to Ruyan Vé, the Navigator, the greatest of our kind, and pleaded for his help. Ruyan did not love those who had enslaved so many of his people, but he knew he could not save the Vao without helping the Keida'ya to escape as well. So Ruyan, his daughters, and his sons worked to build ships that could flee the Garden, carrying all to a new land, a place beyond the Devourer's reach."

"What is . . . the Devourer?" Qina asked as she finished licking her fingers.

"The Keida'ya called it Unbeing." Kuyu-kun's wrinkled face was grim. "They created it, but they did not understand it. It was not a thing but an *emptiness*—a hole into freezing dark, a door that once opened could not be shut." He made another ritual gesture, this time with spread hands and gently bending fingers. "So Ruyan and his allies called on the wisdom of the Dreaming Sea and found a way to make ships that could carry us to safety. All the Keida'ya and all the Vao—Tinukeda'ya, as our masters called us—boarded these ships, then made their way, through many dangers and over many, many years, across the Ocean Indefinite and Eternal to this place. Eight ships landed here . . ."

"I know of those," said Snenneq excitedly, pausing from poking at the coals in search of another bundle of roasted softfoot. "The Eight Ships are known to all—"

"But the truth is known to very few, my clever Qanuc friend." Kuyu-kun did not seem pleased by the interruption. "Eight ships landed here in this new land, commanded by Ruyan Vé and his most trusted allies, for only the Vao could captain the ships that the Dreaming Sea had taught them to build. And that was the beginning of our exile. We lost not only the Garden, but the Dreaming Sea too—the place from which we came, the thing that we are—and arrived in a new world as slaves, little better than animals. And even the greatest of us, Ruyan the Navigator, who had saved the Keida'ya from their own folly, was to be punished for his generosity."

"Punished?"

"Betrayed and punished, yes. The one named Utuk'ku and her followers put Ruyan on trial for keeping the ships secret—the very same ships that saved them. He was chained and humiliated. He died a prisoner of the Keida'ya. And now they have even desecrated his grave at the fortress of *Ujin-do*—'the Trap,' as we Vao call it—dishonoring his sacred bones and stealing his fabled armor."

"What? This is all new to me," said Snenneq. "I knew Ruyan lived out his life as a prisoner, but I have not heard the rest."

"The desecration of his grave has only just happened. The Queen of the North ordered it." Kuyu-kun's head bowed as if in prayer, and the delvers began a chant from deep in their chests that sounded full of hopeless sadness. When the Sa'Vao finally looked up, tears trembled on his eyelids. "And since that terrible moment they desecrated his bones, I have dreamed every night—dreams that the prophetic blood in me, the essence of the Dreaming Sea—proclaims are real and cannot be changed; that this foul, unforgivable deed of Utuk'ku's will bring on the end of our world."

"The Sacrifice troops will slowly, carefully draw the net closed," Nezeru whispered. "We have no choice. If we wish to die with honor, we must choose where we will meet them, else they will take us like snowshoe rabbits in a burrow."

Morgan, who had been leaning close to hear her, was startled. "But I don't want to die with honor," he said. "I don't want to die at all."

Her look was stiff with contempt. "That is not a choice given to you or to me. What kind of warrior are you, to throw away even this last vestige of respect? Have you not sung your death-song? Have you not prepared for this moment?"

"Are you mad? Why would I prepare to die when there still might be some way to live? And what's a death-song? That sounds like something a grassland barbarian would do."

She shook her head slowly. "I cannot understand the words you speak. Are you truly a warrior at all?"

No, he wanted to tell her, *I'm a prince, and I've been living in the forest for months on berries and leaves, and I don't care one bit about a brave, honorable death. I just want to get home again and eat proper food and drink wine and see my friends and my family.* But looking at her stern, implacable face he sensed that a gulf of understanding lay between them that even their shared plight could not bridge. "Look you, Nezeru, if I have your name right, if the time comes when we really have no choice, I'll be happy to let you die in whatever way you wish. I may even start singing myself, though it doesn't seem likely. But I'm not ready for that yet. Yes, I'm a mortal. I'm not like you. We don't give up until there's no other choice."

Her expression softened, but not much. "I have met a few mortals and have heard many stories about your kind. That leads me to doubt what you say. But perhaps you are different from the others. Still, it does not change anything. I told you of the Funnel Net. If I know anything, I know my own order. The Sacrifice troops in the halls above us have only one goal—to sweep up, capture, and kill every living thing in this city."

"There must be some other way out. We can't just wait for them to find us."

"I do not plan to wait. I plan to kill as many as I can before they drag me down." She drew her sword from its sheath and took a bag from her belt, opening it to produce a whetstone and a jar of oil. "But Cold Root will drink deep before the end." She began to sharpen one of its edges.

Morgan sat back against the stone wall of the storeroom, overwhelmed. *It is my wretched luck,* he thought, *to have traded kind Tanahaya for this creature who thinks only of killing and dying.* Another thought came to him then: *If the rest of her kind are as fierce as her, how can men ever defeat an army of such cold-blooded killers?*

Thoughts of cold blood suddenly made him think of fishes and frogs. "Why don't we go down?"

"Down?" She barely glanced up before returning to her task. "I don't understand you."

"There are tunnels leading down beneath us. We passed many. Can't we go that way to escape them?"

She shook her head grimly.

"Well?" he asked. "Why? Or do you just want to die, no matter what?"

She set her sword carefully across her lap. "I will forgive you your foolishness because you are a mortal and do not know better. No, we cannot go down. I know—I am the child of the High Magister of Builders. I may have been raised in the Order of Sacrifice, but I am my father's daughter, and I learned a few things from him as well. We cannot escape by going deeper." She went back to sharpening her blade.

A part of Morgan could not help noticing that her command of his tongue seemed to be improving even as they spoke. "God's bloody Tree, Nezeru, *why* can't we go down?"

She lifted her eyes from the sword once more. "Because this entire city is built on a riverbank. *T'si Suhyasei* flows just beside us—the earth is full of water all around. Those who came before me could not have made a city here had they not built a cofferdam to keep the river out as they built."

"A coffer-what?"

For a moment her masklike expression softened a little, although it was still far from friendly. "A cofferdam. Think of it as a basin of stone sunk into the ground, if that helps you understand. It keeps out the water while something is being built—and then afterward, also. So even if we went down deep enough to find our way out of the city, we would only be stopped by the walls of the cofferdam itself. And if we somehow managed to break through those walls, the river would rush in, carry the earth away, and drown us."

Even Morgan had to admit that she had a point. He wracked his mind, trying to think of something, anything, that might help them survive. He had learned a little of war and sieges from his tutors and the Master of Arms, but those were not the same as true experience, and he felt it acutely. *Prince of Trees, that's all I am. Months on my own and all I've learned is how to climb and find nuts to eat.* But the beginning of an idea was making itself felt. "But the forest is all around Da'ai Chikiza, isn't it?" he asked. "It even grows in the city itself."

"It does." She tested the side she had been sharpening with her finger, licked off a thin stripe of blood, then turned the blade over so she could work the other edge.

"Are any of the city's towers still standing?"

She paused, staring at him as though he had turned into someone else, but still someone vaguely annoying. "What do you mean?"

"Come, you speak my tongue well enough to understand that. Cities have towers. I've seen the ruins of several of them along the way. Are there any still standing?" He thought for a moment. "Especially near the edge of the city?"

She seemed to think he had gone slightly mad, but she frowned and said, "I came in there, along the great thoroughfare, Gatherers' Way. I did see a tall ruin that stood beside what used to be the northern gate. The knot-runes above its gate called it the Tower of the Reaching Hand, but I could not see much of it because the trees had grown close around it."

Morgan let out a breath he felt he had been holding a long time. "That might work. Can we reach that tower from here without being killed?"

"I do not fault you for trying to think of a way to survive," she said, though he thought her tone suggested otherwise, "but your plan will not work. Da'ai Chikiza is a maze of collapsed passages and fallen ceilings. Even if the Order of Sacrifice was not hunting us, I could not find the way. This city has been deserted even by the Zida'ya since long before I was born, and I have never seen a map of it. We would be caught and slaughtered long before I found the tower again."

"But you think we're going to be slaughtered anyway!" Morgan had allowed himself a moment of hope, and now regretted it badly. "Why not try to escape?"

The Norn-woman's expression changed to out-and-out disbelief. "Why? Because if I am going to die fighting, I do not feel any need to cross most of the city first. I would rather save my strength for killing as many enemies as I can before I fall."

"I know you would, but I'm different—I'm a mortal, as you keep pointing out. I would rather save my strength for living. For escaping this place."

"It will not happen. Reconcile yourself."

Anger made his skin prickle. It was all he could do not to walk away from her, though he knew he would never evade the Norn soldiers on his own. "Reconcile myself to death, you mean? You're the one who wants to die. Still a Sacrifice to the very end, even when it's your old friends who want to kill you—noble Sacrifice Nezeru."

"Do not call me that." She would not look at him. "You have not the right—nor have I. The Order of Sacrifice has cast me out."

Morgan shook his head, horrified but almost amused. "So you're still loyal to them. That's the real and true difference between us, no matter what you say, and no matter how many hundreds of years older than me you might be." He scowled, shamed to be almost at the point of tears. "How old are you, anyway, that you're so ready to die? A thousand years? More?"

"I do not need to answer that." Her face had gone blank once more, but she was sharpening her sword with added vigor. "It will matter little when the end comes."

5
A Hut by the River

Hush little *one and hear my song,*

Jesa sang, her mouth close to baby Serasina's ear,

Crocodile is sleeping, but not for long
If we are quiet he will never, never hear us
Crocodile is sleeping.

Her own mother had sung the same words to her all those years ago in Red Pig Lagoon, when Jesa had been small and life itself had been no bigger than the distance to the banyans on the lagoon's other shore, trees bent and twisted like old people, their roots stretching down into the lagoon, as if they bathed their swollen feet in the brackish water.

Hush little one and hear my song
Ghants are sleeping, but not for long
If we are quiet they will never, never hear us
Ghants are sleeping.

She was no longer in the Wran, of course, but stranded somewhere in the far north of Nabban, or perhaps even across the border in Queen Miriamele's country of Erkynland. Jesa had survived the grasslanders' attack, but her friend Duchess Canthia had not; nor had Canthia's older child Blasis, whose throat had been slit by a bearded murderer. Now Jesa was alone with Canthia's baby, who was hungry and growing more so by the moment.

At least she's not frightened—she's too young to understand. But I am frightened.

Jesa had no idea if anyone was still hunting her, but the hungry baby, who now seemed more important than even her own life, would soon become a crying baby and Jesa did not want anyone on the nearby road to hear her. She also knew nothing about what she or the baby might eat in this foreign, hilly scrubland, so she decided to make her way downhill in search of water and worry about food later.

Serasina squirmed again. Her little hands had been scratched in their escape from the burning carriage. With no other idea of how to soothe her, Jesa took each tiny hand in turn and gently licked the blood away. Serasina made noises of unhappiness, but the animal simplicity of the remedy seemed to comfort her a little and the child's eyes soon closed again.

Hush little one and hear my song
Storm is sleeping, but not for long
If we are quiet he will never, never hear us
Storm is sleeping . . .

The sun had come up. Jesa could see the tree branches outlined in pink and gold, but the new light brought little warmth. She pressed the baby closer to her breast and tried to shield Serasina's delicate skin from twigs and brambles as they made their way down the hill, moving from the safety of one sheltering copse to another, though Jesa would have preferred to walk in the faint but welcome sunlight. Her own soft footfalls sounded loud as hammer blows, and the lullaby she had been singing suddenly made her wonder what hunting beasts might live in this place.

He Who Always Steps On Sand, guide my feet now. Guide me to a place of safety, I beg you. Help me save this blameless child. The gods of the Wran were distant, shadowy figures—never once in her childhood had Jesa heard anyone describe them, because even to try would be to insult them—but she had always felt their presence around her, just as she felt her ancestors and her spirit namesake, Green Honeybird, whose story she had heard so many times as a child.

Green Honeybird never gave up, she reminded herself. *Even when Tree Python stole her egg and swallowed it, the little honeybird went right into its mouth and down its throat to save her child.*

She now glimpsed a silvery, curving gleam of water far below at the base of the hill, and its resemblance to a snake gave her a superstitious shock of fear, but she could not ignore the needs of the sleeping baby. Serasina's mother was dead. Her brother was dead, too. Jesa was all that this little one had.

I will fly into the serpent's jaws if I need to, she told herself, and the realization brought her a kind of peace. *This child is mine to save. Queen Miriamele would not throw up her hands in despair, she would walk into Tree Python's mouth and down into its very bowels.* She thought of the queen taking Sir Jurgen's sword and facing down a band of killers. *The queen would not surrender to anyone. Oh, She Who Waits To Take All Back, I hope you have spared her from the Sancellan's fires! The world needs such women!*

Serasina was stirring on her bosom. Jesa was weary and sore, and her stomach was at least as empty as the baby's, but they had far to go before they could rest and begin looking for food. She took a breath and again began to sing.

Hush little one and hear my song
Buffalo is sleeping, but not for long
If we are quiet he will never, never hear us
Buffalo is sleeping.

Her lungs were burning from lack of air. Whatever was pulling Miriamele down into the river depths was stronger and heavier than she was. It also had an unbreakable grip on her leg. The lilies that dotted the river's surface were above her, trailing stems like broken threads, swirling as she thrashed helplessly against whatever held her. In some places the round green leaves made a solid roof that blocked the sky, in others they barely touched, breaking the light up into flecks and flares.

I'm going to die. The thought did not seem the most important thing to her. Miri only wanted whatever was gripping her leg so fiercely to let go, to let her float free so she could drown peacefully among the drifting stems in the dim green light.

Simon. I never had the chance . . .

Then she was yanked to one side and down again, toward a darkness that seemed as deep and impenetrable as mystery itself. The underside of the reed bed lay before her—a forest, a great and deadly forest—and she knew she would be tangled in the swaying canes and lost forever.

For a moment Miri had a glimpse of the creature that was pulling her as it passed through a slanting column of light, a huge, froglike thing, spinning as it pulled her down. It swam with its back to her, the smooth, manlike limbs churning bubbles, the head and shoulders so broad it was hard to tell where one ended and another began.

Something plunged past her then, too dark and too swift to make out, but as it passed, it sliced her skin in a white-hot line; her mouth gaped and the river rushed in. She tried to close her jaws but water filled her throat like molten silver, like fire, and she choked, coughed, then felt the world burst into white light even as blackness swept in on her.

Jesa knew the channels and lagoons of the Wran in which she had spent her childhood as well as scholars knew their bookshelves—which parts were safe, where hidden dangers lay, and how to make her way through both to do what needed doing. But she was in an entirely new place now, a place she had never seen and had hardly heard about. She had lived in Nabban long enough to have some idea of how the great city was shaped and the routes across it, but she knew almost nothing of the countries that surrounded it. She was no better off than a lost child who had wandered away from home into the deepest parts of the swamp.

She had left little Serasina sleeping in a nest made of long grass while she hunted along the riverbank for something to eat. What the child really needed was milk, but even with all the love she felt for the baby, Jesa could not conjure her breasts to produce any.

Thanks to They Who Watch and Shape that she has passed her first half-year. In her village on the shores of Red Pig Lagoon, that had been the point at which infants were first given other foods. Jesa had reason to hope she might be able to keep little Serasina alive, but only if she found something suitable for the baby to eat. *Please, They Who Watch,* she prayed as she foraged, *hold back the winter a little longer, that I may find food for the baby!*

It was late in the season and many of the plants were unfamiliar to her, but she found a few withered dandelions and a stand of brookstem that yielded a handful of leaves still holding a little juice. After bringing back this poor haul, Jesa made sure Serasina was still sleeping under her cloth, then clambered up the slope in search of other fare. She found some beech trees and hazels and gathered a solid handful of their nuts in the skirt of her already tattered court dress. On the way back, she stumbled across a prize—a bullace shrub full of small, plumlike, late-ripening fruit. She picked every last one and added them to the nuts before making her way back again.

The baby was awake and fretful, and Jesa gave her a finger to suck while she chewed up one of the bullaces, which had tipped over from sour to the beginning of sweetness. When she had reduced the fruit to juice and a little pulp, she spat some on her finger and then slipped that finger into Serasina's rosebud mouth. The baby's eyes widened a little at the introduction of this new thing and she stopped sucking, but a moment later she began again and even seemed to enjoy it. Heartened, Jesa continued to give the infant juice from her finger while chewing up some of the hazelnuts. When these were a paste in her mouth, Jesa added the juice from another bullace and induced Serasina to suck it off her finger. It took her what must have been the better part of an hour, but when she had finished Serasina finally seemed satisfied and drifted back into sleep so Jesa could concentrate on easing her own hunger.

Jesa could not think too much about Serasina's brother Blasis, or Canthia, the child's mother, but not because she did not care. *If you do not think of them, they will not haunt you,* she promised herself, but still the terrible memories came. *Do not haunt me, dear Canthia!* she pleaded. *I ache that I could not help you! All I can do for you is to try to save your baby.*

A brief rainstorm swept through the valley that night. Jesa found the thickest cover she could on the slope, then did her best to protect little Serasina with her body as the rain splashed down on them. She chewed up and fed the child with what was left of her day's forage, then rocked her as Serasina murmured and fidgeted, but at last the little one fell asleep again and Jesa was able to rest as well.

In the morning, Jesa had an idea. She had still not decided where she should go, but she knew it would likely be a while until they could sleep under a roof again. She did not want to build a permanent shelter since she had no idea of who might be looking for them, but she thought she might be able to make herself something almost as useful—a wide-brimmed hat. If it was sunny or rainy she could put it on her head to protect them both, but it could also be a cot for the baby as well, something more secure than the nest of grass she had built.

While Serasina took a late morning nap, Jesa gathered reeds for weaving, something girls and boys in the Wran learned to do almost as soon as they were old enough to sit up. The reeds that grew nearby were young and slender, and weaving enough of them together to make a good-sized hat seemed like it might take her all day or perhaps longer. She checked on Serasina, then waded out into a shallow backwater toward a stand of reeds that looked bigger.

As she pushed her way through the close-leaning stems, ear always cocked for any sound from Serasina, she gathered all the stems that seemed of a good size, wishing she had a knife or anything sharp. When her arm grew tired of holding the growing bundle, she wrapped a young reed around them all and threw them toward the shore, then stepped back into the depths of the reed bed in search of more. She saw a group of tall ones looming above the others like a picket and went to investigate, her skirts swirling heavily around her, but when she reached out to grab the nearest and uproot it, her hand touched something sticky. Her fingers were shiny with something as pale green as grass sap but thicker. She smelled her hand. The scent made her heart race.

It cannot be, she thought. *Surely I am too far north.*

Still, she moved with much greater caution as she continued, and before too long found another group of reeds stuck together with the same slightly frothy substance. It smelled like the phlegm of someone with the breathing sickness and looked a bit like it too.

Jesa heard a rustling in the canes and froze in place. Her honeybird namesake would surely have done something, flown away or attacked, but she could not make her legs move. Suddenly the sound of the wind in the reeds made it seem like things were moving all around her.

What if it's not the wind in the reeds?

Something splashed gently just on the other side of a bank of tall stems. She took a step back, stumbled a little and almost fell, but regained her balance and took another retreating step until she could feel the muddy bottom beneath her. Far above, the sun had burned its way through the morning overcast, and as rays of light arrowed down through the trees on the far side of the river, they revealed something she had not seen until that moment.

All around her sticky strands stretched between the reeds, some thinner than sewing thread, others thick as rough twine. In a few places the reeds even seemed to have been bent and then fixed in place by the slimy stuff.

There was no longer any doubt in her mind. Far north of the Wran or not, this was unmistakable evidence that ghants lived here.

Even as she thought it, a head rose out of one of the stands of reeds, tipped slightly to one side as if it was listening, though she did not think the fearsome creatures had ears. It was a ghant, and not a small one, either. She could not see its body, hidden by the waving reeds, or what it was standing on. Its head sat low on the rounded, hard-shelled shoulders. Its eyes were shiny, inhuman blobs of black like melted tar, and the front of its head was a face in name only, empty of anything except hungry interest as it slowly turned its body from one side to another.

Jesa stayed as still as she could, heart now bouncing in her chest like the dried beans in a Wind Festival rattle. The creature raised its arms as though it meant to climb over the reeds that separated them. Jesa held her breath. Then another ghant raised its head beside the first. This newcomer reached out and stroked a string of the greenish spittle that hung between one stand of reeds and another, like a fisherman testing his line with a finger. Somewhere behind them a third, still invisible ghant, let out a buzzing call. The two she could see hesitated for a moment, then lowered their heads.

Now that she could no longer see them, Jesa did not want to linger. After giving them a little time to retreat farther into the reeds, she turned and began wading as swiftly as she could without splashing or making noise, away from the stand of tall reeds and soon out of the backwater and onto solid ground once more.

A sudden, terrifying thought sent her dashing up the slope to where she had hidden Serasina, but the baby was still where Jesa had left her, stout little face peaceful in red-cheeked sleep. Jesa grabbed her up and squeezed her so hard in relief that Serasina woke and began to cry. Jesa carried her up the slope and then walked for no little time back upstream along the riverbank until she finally felt safe to stop and rest. She was still shaking badly when she seated herself against the trunk of a tall beech and held the baby close, whispering into her tiny ear to keep her quiet.

A ghant nest, she thought. *Surely they have never been so far north of the Wran before! But I heard people telling the duke that the kilpa were moving that way. Perhaps the ghants are moving too.*

She was still trembling all over, which made Serasina protest. Jesa stuck a wet finger in the child's mouth.

We must move on. I will never sleep again knowing those things are close.

She shuddered. The memory of that empty, inhuman face peering across the reeds would not leave her.

It seemed like a long time until the world came back to Miriamele, as though she floated down a different kind of river, a sluggish flow full of clinging grasses that held her back and whirlpools that threatened to suck her down into blackness. Wakefulness was the bank of the river, but every time she seemed to drift toward it the current seized her again and yanked her back toward unknowing, until she thought she must have died and the river was to be the whole of her afterlife.

I will drift here forever, she thought in a rare moment of clarity. *I will drift until the Lord Usires Aedon comes back to call me and claim me.*

When her eyes drifted open the next time, the smear of light gradually resolved itself into little flares of daylight. She lifted her head a little and saw that she was in a very small hut, the light leaking in through cracks in the wattling. She tried to lift her head, but it was an ungodly difficult thing to do and made everything ache, so she slumped back onto whatever was beneath her and tried to make sense of what her confused senses were telling her.

A bed? I'm on a bed? Her thoughts were slow, but the word seemed the right one. *Where am I? Sweet Mother Elysia, I think I might be alive.* It was an astonishing thought and went so strongly against what her dreaming mind had decided that she dared not trust it, lest it prove only another phantom.

Weariness was already pulling her back down, but she was determined not to be dragged away from this world and its bright and blurry but hopeful sights. Not very far above her she could see, not sky, but the beams of a ceiling made of rough-cut logs. She stared blearily at those logs for a long time, waiting to see if this seemingly real but confusingly unfamiliar vision would go away again, but the crude fact of it remained.

I was in the river, she remembered. *Not in a dream, but truly. I drowned.* But if she had drowned, why was she alive?

Suddenly her breath caught in her throat like a stick. A horrible gray-brown thing was dangling in the rafters a short distance away and looked ready to leap down on her. Miriamele's scream came out as little more than a terrified gurgle, then after several galloping heartbeats she realized the demonic thing was not alive but had been skinned and hung to dry. As she stared at the dead face with its tiny eyes and monstrously wide mouth, she suddenly knew that this was the creature that had caught her and tried to drag her down into the river depths.

Shuddering, she let her gaze slide down and finally saw the wide back of a dark-haired man sitting in the doorway of the hut, blocking the midday light. For a long moment Miriamele could only stare, trying to make sense of it all. Then, as if sensing her gaze, the stranger turned to look at her. His sallow face was that of a mortal man, for which she silently thanked God and His mother, Elysia. He had a wide brow, and his eyes were large, though they narrowed as soon as he saw she was awake and watching. A thin, wispy brown beard sprouted on his chin and a similarly sparse growth shaded his upper lip.

"So th'art waking," said the stranger in a low, rough voice. His Westerling sounded odd, as if it might not be his first tongue. "Long thou slept. Three nights did Agga sleep on floor for tha sake." He rose and walked heavily across the small room toward the low bench, the only article of furniture near the bed where Miriamele lay, then picked up a jar with a wide mouth and took a long drink.

"Who are you?" she asked, still too weak to sit up. "Where is this place?"

He eyed her for a moment, then lifted the jar for another swallow.

"God bless you for saving me, sir, if that is what has happened," she added hurriedly. "I don't mean to sound ungrateful, but I've only just come back to myself. Where am I? What happened?"

He wiped his mouth with the back of his hand before turning back to her.

"Thus many questions do weary us," he said. "Th'art saved from River Man." He gestured with his thumb toward the skinned monstrosity hanging in the rafters. "Kallypook, him's called sometime. See, him is barbed like the river cat." He moved toward the dangling corpse and lifted one of its skinned limbs, then waggled what was at the end of it, a hand with undeniable though misshapen fingers. "But him be handed like a man, see? River Man. Fell and wicked him be. Planned to take tha down to his nest for later, but Agga put a spear in and pulled him back up. Tha came'st with."

"And that is it? You killed that thing all by yourself?" Even as just a skin, the creature was dreadful.

"This 'un be's different kallypook." He indicated the gutted hide with his thumb. "Caught this 'un winter-last. Cleaned and cured now. Ready to sell. Him what catchet tha be caught too, but not skinned yet."

"Then I thank you from saving me from such a terrible beast," she said wholeheartedly. "I thank you and wish you all the blessings that God can bestow. When it caught me, I thought myself lost, and I would have been, that's sure."

"Sure, aye. Wouldst be meat in kallypook's larder." He turned then and abruptly walked out the door of the hut, leaving Miriamele staring in surprise. He did not come back for some time, but when he did, he walked to the table again without speaking and downed another swallow of whatever was in the jar. Her other senses had begun to speak to her, and now that she had noticed the hut's smell of sweat and old fish she could no longer ignore it, nor the even fouler stink of the flayed creature hanging in the middle of the room.

"I thank you again, sir. Is your name Agga? That is what I thought I heard you say."

"Agga. Aye. That be us's name." He surveyed her for a bit, and for the first time Miri thought she saw something else lurking beneath his curt, unmannered ways, a secret enjoyment that she did not understand. Her skin prickled in sudden fear.

"If you will help me to get back home, Agga, I promise you will be rewarded." Miriamele thought for a brief moment of telling him who she truly was but discarded the idea immediately: he would likely not believe her and might even be insulted, thinking she was trying to trick him. She again tried to sit up, but even lifting her head made the room spin. She tried to swing her legs off the bed, and for the first time noticed a heaviness on them, something that clinked and slithered like a metal snake. When she kicked in sudden fear a length of chain slid off the pallet onto the floor, tugging at a metal band that had been hammered into place around her ankle. Icy dread spasmed in her belly. "What is this?" she said, trying to keep her voice steady. "Why am I chained?"

"Tha did flail and flummet in tha sleep," he said. "Like River Man still held tha. Was to keep tha from doin' harm to tha own self."

She looked down. The other end of the chain that held her was attached to what at first looked like a miner's pick—a boat anchor, she realized.

"Take this off now, please," she said as calmly as she could. "I am no longer in danger of hurting myself."

He looked at her and nodded, then moved toward the bed until he loomed above her. He was as tall as Simon, but heavier in the belly and chest than her husband. The unnaturally long arms hung by his side as he looked down at her. Then, without touching her or saying another word, he turned and went to lift the skinned creature down from the rafters. He carried it out the door, leaving Miri squirming on the bed in dread.

Oh, God and His angels protect me, I am at this stranger's mercy. To think beyond that dreadful but inescapable truth would carry her into even more terrible places.

He returned later, smelling nauseatingly of the kallypook carcass, but said not a word about her chains or anything else. Instead, he started a fire in the simple firepit, then watched it for a long time as smoke drifted up and out the hole in the ceiling. The air became so thick that Miri coughed painfully, but he did not look at her. At last, as if he had been preparing the whole time, he began to speak.

"Agga does be summoned—see tha? The great lady what speaks to us in sleep hath told it all, over and over. Us be summoned to the north of the world, to join with all the others in honor of the lady. Her will have an army, and us, Agga, will be a great one in it."

Miri wiggled her ankle in the shackle while he was looking at the fire, trying to slide it off her foot.

"But long us has thought, what be honor worth without us has a son to share in it?" He spoke carefully, as if what he was saying actually made sense. "Us's Da did give us this place, deed of the river and use of all that do swim in it—or drown in it." Agga took a long, meditative swallow from his jar. "Long did us think on that, but nothing come of it. Then did us take the kallypook on our spear, and with the rope haul him out, and there come'st tha, dangling on hook-end like river maiden in our Da's stories."

"I am no maiden," Miri said tightly, but the shackle had defeated her attempts to slip free and she knew that for the moment at least she was helpless. "I am a mother and a grandmother, a good Aedonite woman, and my family is searching for me." But she could not believe Simon and the others had any idea where she was. "They will reward you if I am safe, but if you do harm to me, they will take a terrible vengeance on you."

He went on as though she had not spoken. "So it did come to us that this were meant, see tha? By her, the great one in dreams. Her has sent a wife to us, that Agga may stand before her in pride. You will be wife, and bear us a son, and stand proud beside us when the lady of the dream doth make great honors to us in the north."

She stared at the back of his neck in the dim light, the rough, almost scaly skin that covered it. Her fear was mixed with growing anger, that this creature should dare to lay hands on her and bind her, daughter and granddaughter of queens, mistress of the High Ward. "I cannot be your wife," she told him loudly, struggling to keep her growing fear hidden. "And God will curse you if you try to make me yours. I have a husband. We were married in the holy church."

"Church? Us never been at church. Church be nothing to the lady. Her speaks in dreams to us. Her shows us all things God never did think."

Sweet Mother of Mercy, Miriamele thought. *Holy Aedon and all Your angels, help me now! Because I am the prisoner of a madman.*

6

Arrow Bearers

The interior of the hillside cavern the Sithi called a hunting lodge was curtained with moving shadows. Aelin could hear Evan panting in discomfort as the healer cleaned the wound the young soldier had received in their last skirmish with the Norns. The leader of the immortal troop that had taken them—or rescued them—was waiting for Aelin to speak, but Aelin found it hard to calm his thoughts. *Uncle Eolair said that it is during the between-moments—between battles or between one dispute and the next—that it is easiest to miss things. I must pay attention. Even if I have only two of my liegemen left, those are two lives in my charge.*

"First of all, Lady Ayaminu," he said, "do I have your word that you mean us no harm?"

"If you mean you and your two companions," she said, "then yes. If you mean all your kind, then no—I cannot make such a promise."

"We will start small, then. A pledge for my men's safety—and mine—is ample." He looked over to Maccus, but the dark-bearded Hernystirman was watching Evan's suffering with his jaw clenched. Aelin knew the feeling. "You said you know my mortal kind well, Lady. May I ask how? I confess I do not recognize your name from my uncle's stories or from our people's history."

A small, sour smile pulled at the corner of her mouth. "I am not surprised. The only one of your mortal kind who spent much time with me was Duke Isgrimnur, and he found my company very trying during our time together in the last days of the great war against Utuk'ku and Ineluki."

"You knew Isgrimnur? The duke was a sworn friend to my great-uncle, Eolair of Nad Mullach."

"Ah." Her look became less guarded. "So you are Eolair's kin. That is good for you—and, I think, good for me. Count Eolair is well regarded by my people. Far more so than most mortals."

"I am proud to be of his blood." He was used to such reactions: his great-uncle had traveled widely and had friends—as well as respectful enemies—almost everywhere. But Aelin had never expected to have such an encounter in a hidden cave full of fairy-folk. *Still, what else could cap the madness of these last days?* he thought. *The Norns have conquered Naglimund. Great burrowing beasts rose out of the ground and threw down the walls. Giants and evil fairies killed most of my men.* "If you too hate the Norns, Lady Ayaminu, then surely fate makes us allies."

She showed a hint of a frown. "I do not hate the Hikeda'ya—the Norns, as you call them. How could I? They are flesh of my flesh. But I hate the path upon which Utuk'ku has led them, and I loathe the crimes they have committed in her name."

Aelin fought against a flush of anger. "The horrors done by your kin, the White Foxes, go far beyond mere crimes, my lady."

Her reply was stern. "And so did the sins of your own mortal kind, Sir Aelin. Some of them killed relatives of mine. Should I thus hate you all? If so, ours will be a short parley."

"Peace, my lady." He lifted his hand. "I take your point—if we stop to dispute causes and grudges the argument might never end. Count Eolair has many times made it clear to me that the Fair Folk, as we call your kind, were treated badly in the old days."

She nodded slowly. "Yes. But only remember, please, what are 'old days' to you seem barely past to me and many of my kind. My father, Kuroyi the Horseman, did not want to fight beside mortals in what you call the Storm King's War. Only his fury over Utuk'ku's attack on Jao é-Tinukai'i drove him to make peace with the mortals who had destroyed great Asu'a and so many other things dear to us."

"I do not know these names, except for the Norn Queen, as we call her. I should apologize for that and perhaps for the deeds of the ancestors they represent, but in my ignorance it would be merely courtesy." He gave her a hard look. "And I guess that you do not much value empty courtesy."

Finally she smiled. It was a very thin smile. "You are correct. Now, let us put aside the past and talk of the present. You are a problem for me, Sir Aelin."

"How so?"

"Because we are not planning to stay in this place, this hunting lodge, for long. A war is being fought all around us, but that is not the reason I am here. I await the arrival of some of our Zida'ya kin, then my people and I will leave this place to return to Anvi'janya, which is the home—and chief responsibility—of the clan I lead. But I fear you cannot stay after we are gone, no matter how unsafe the hills around us. We Zida'ya have few enough of these hidden places left that the Hikeda'ya have not already discovered. We cannot afford to lose another refuge to mortal mistakes."

Aelin's first response was irritation, but he thought of Eolair's famous patience and did his best to answer calmly. "I think you underestimate us, my lady, but what do you propose instead?"

"For now, nothing," she told him, rising to her feet once more. "We will continue to wait for our travelers—they may have something useful to say about this problem. But our time is short and they are late, so when they arrive at last we will have to make decisions swiftly."

"Your time is short?"

She looked him in the eye. "I suspect that everyone's time is short, Sir Aelin—mortals and immortals alike—but our people also have other, homelier needs. I will leave it to those we await to explain it to you . . . if they wish to do so."

With the icy wind whipping his face until he could scarcely keep his eyes open, Jarnulf looked down at an astonishing sight. A great Hikeda'ya army stood waiting on the wide road below the rocky hillside where he crouched, hidden. Just the wagons alone seemed to number in the hundreds, and Sacrifice troops swarmed around them in such numbers that Jarnulf felt dizzied.

Where have they all come from? Even after the queen arrived with her great company, there were nowhere near this many of them. Armored Sacrifices lined the roads as far as he could see, and more were streaming out of Naglimund's ruined gate, their torches turning the road into a flickering river of fire. He wondered briefly why so many of the sharp-sighted Hikeda'ya soldiers held torches, since the waxing moon was bright enough that night must seem like midday to them, but he was too overwhelmed by the sheer size of the army to ponder it for long.

When I failed to kill Utuk'ku, he thought helplessly, *I failed not only my God and my promise to Him, but mankind as well. Look at this! With such a host, the Hikeda'ya will carve their way through Erkynland like a knife through warm fat. And it is my fault.* He had actually had a clear shot at the Queen of the Norns, the author of so much terror, but he had failed to take it. Instead, Utuk'ku's ritual magicks had somehow clouded his wits and made him flee.

Like a child! I ran like a child who fears a whipping!

And now he could only watch as the queen—for that huge, many-wheeled carriage painted with the royal Hamakha sigil could only be hers—prepared to take her army south to enslave the mortals of Erkynland just as she had destroyed the towns of his Black Rimmersmen ancestors and dragged off the survivors as slaves.

If only I could have loosed that arrow . . .

But it was a long way to the Hayholt in Erchester, he realized. Even a fast-moving Sacrifice army would take some time to cover the distance. On such a long journey, might he not find another moment when the queen was vulnerable?

Jarnulf looked down at the columns as they assembled. *How could they ever have rebuilt their numbers so soon after their last defeat? How many are below me? Ten thousand? Twenty thousand? But how? In the year I was born, the Hikeda'ya nobles and warriors were so few that my mother once told me she heard talk in the slave pens of trying to overthrow the devastated Hamakha Clan. How did they go from that . . . to this?*

The halfbloods, he realized. *Nezeru and the rest of her bastard kind. Children of slaves, raised to love their masters and hate their own people.* He could not help thinking of the contempt that Nezeru and Makho and the rest of their Queen's Hand had shown him, as if a mortal were no better than the lowest animal, something to be hunted or slaughtered or, occasionally, made into a pet. *I half wish I had killed Nezeru when I had the chance. But the queen—the queen is the true enemy.*

Jarnulf turned and made his way carefully back along the slope into the shadows of the forest, where he found his horse waiting.

"Come, then," he said, stroking her neck before he swung up into the saddle. "You were my enemy's, now you are mine. I know a fight is what you were bred for, and I have finished feeling sorry for myself. God has reminded me of my purpose and my promise to Him. We will go to war again."

Tanahaya had found a place to hide, but it was only a momentary refuge and she knew it: hundreds of Hikeda'ya troops were searching through the ruins of Da'ai Chikiza. The Order of Sacrifice clearly wanted to empty the city of all living things except Queen Utuk'ku's soldiers. But why?

"Beware the queen's device." A dream-shadow had spoken those words to her, but even if the warning was real, she could not understand it. Had Utuk'ku's slaves built some terrible new weapon or war-engine, or perhaps hoped to find such a thing here in Da'ai Chikiza? Or did 'device' mean some dreadful trick? In the previous war, Utuk'ku and the Storm King had tried to turn back time itself and eradicate mortal men from the face of the world. Was Utuk'ku searching for some fateful weapon that would finally give her victory? Or had the dream-warning meant the witchwood seeds buried beneath the mortal castle? Tanahaya had only barely managed to pass that knowledge on to Jiriki before the thought-carrying Witness failed.

Enough, Tanahaya told herself. *I do not have the freedom to sit and wonder.* Lingering in Da'ai Chikiza would be a death-sentence—or worse. If she was captured, Akhenabi and his Order of Song would torment her until they knew of Himano's parchment, the presence of the mortal prince, and many other ruinous secrets. *I owe it to Jiriki, Aditu, and the rest of my folk to prevent that. I must escape—or, if I fail, I must take my own life. But I have other duties, and I cannot ignore them.*

With skill born of long practice under her master Himano, she calmed herself until her surroundings became no more substantial to her than the last wisps of a dream. She slowed her pounding heart and let herself drift down through inner silence until nothing else existed but Tanahaya and the memories that made her who she was.

"Find what is real," Master Himano always said. "Then consider only that." She imagined the dozens of fears clamoring for her attention to be as insubstantial as dust motes, her will a brisk breeze that blew all but the most substantial away, until she could examine what remained. *I have three possible paths,* she realized. *Three duties I owe to others. I must choose one, though all seem important.*

First—I swore to my beloved Jiriki and his sister, my dearest friend, that I would go to the mortal castle and be the eyes and ears there of our people. I left H'ran Go-jao to fulfill that pledge, and the pledge existed before I discovered the mortal youth and made him my responsibility. By the oath I swore, I am still their envoy, and that oath remains unfulfilled.

Second—I promised Morgan that I would take him home. He may be dead, but until I know that for certain, that oath, as well, remains unfulfilled.

Third—the "queen's device." That part of my dream torments me as much as any other concern, perhaps more. I have either forgotten something I should remember, or I have missed something I should have seen. Utuk'ku's malice threatens everyone. If she succeeds, there will be no Hayholt to accept my embassy, and if Morgan lives, he will not survive for long after his family is destroyed by the Hikeda'ya. But I do not know if a dream, no matter how striking, can be trusted in such desperate times.

Worst of all, if I linger and am captured here, I will fail in every one of my duties.

Long she floated in the depths of herself, trying to weigh every aspect of her dilemma, as Himano would have urged her. It felt as if she searched for something lost deep underwater, that she was groping in muddy depths with no idea what she sought.

At first Tanahaya resisted the distraction, as she had other useless thoughts that had drifted back during her long contemplation, but at last she could ignore it no longer.

Am I in danger? She opened herself to her senses once more, drank in all that they told her, and was relieved to detect no threat of immediate discovery. She was still hidden amidst a jumble of walls and broken pillars, in the stairwell below the collapsed ruins of the Place of Sky-Watching. She knew that the Hikeda'ya were all around, but they were still only a rumor to her senses. Most of the Sacrifices seemed to be scouring the passages and underground chambers below her. But one scent stood out more strongly from those of the Hikeda'ya troops, though it took her a few moments to recognize the crisp, cool tang.

Pine sap, she thought. *Morgan?* Though the mortal youth had washed himself and even his garments, the resinous scent had been ground so deeply into his clothes from living in the trees that he had never been completely free of it. This sudden recognition startled her. Could the body of the mortal prince be buried under the stones somewhere near her? Did she dare risk her own freedom to search for him?

But as she moved around in her confined hiding place, trying to get a stronger sense of where the scent came from, she was first puzzled, then surprised to realize it was drifting up from below her, from farther down the blocked stairwell beyond the fallen stones.

But how could that be? I last saw Morgan just a few paces from where I sit, when we brought the ceiling down—his scent would not be drifting up from below me.

Unless he survived, she realized. *Unless he somehow escaped and is in the city's lower depths. But an entire Sacrifice company is searching there!* Her contemplative calm dissolved in an instant. *If Morgan is alive, I must find him. I cannot leave him to the vengeance of the Hikeda'ya. I told Jiriki that I had found him, that I would keep him safe!*

But I also have a life growing inside me to protect.

For a moment she hesitated, almost perfectly balanced between two conflicting needs. *No,* she decided at last. *How could I give birth knowing I turned my back on one I had pledged to protect? It would harrow my child's destiny. It would make everything I believe of myself false.*

She turned then, though her heart was heavy and fearful, and began to worm her way downward between the close-leaning stones, following the faint odor of pine.

Aelin awoke from a deep, exhausted sleep into utter madness—choking fingers wrapped around his throat and a grimacing goblin's face peering down at him. He tried to cry out but couldn't: the nightmare thing straddled his chest and its powerful hands were crushing his windpipe.

Desperate and disoriented, he reached out for his sword but could find nothing but dirt, which he clawed up and flung in his assailant's face. The creature fell off him, barking in pain and rubbing at its eyes. Aelin rolled over onto his hands and knees, coughing, desperate for air, and at last gathered the breath in his bruised throat to cry out: *"Maccus! Evan! Help me!"*

A moment later the attacker leaped onto him again, but even as the clawing fingers once more reached for his throat he saw another shape appear from the corner and drag his attacker off him. Aelin crawled swiftly backward until he felt stone behind him, then lifted his hands, prepared to defend his life as long as he could.

What seemed another assassin lunged toward him. If Aelin had recovered his sword he would have used it, but a moment later he realized it was his comrade Maccus Blackbeard helping him to his feet.

"What treachery is this?" Maccus demanded loudly. Aelin had shouted his voice raw and his lungs empty: for the moment he could only stand swaying in the center of a ring of narrow, impassive Sithi faces. The closest two immortals were new to him, the flame-haired one who had attacked him, now crouched on all fours, and another who stood over Aelin's assailant. This second immortal had long, pale hair and his face was spare and stern.

"Are you sorely hurt?" the second Sitha asked Aelin.

"Your man tried to kill him!" Maccus cried. "We are here by guest-right!"

"Yeja'aro did not expect to see any of your kind," said the newcomer. "He thought we had fallen into a trap."

"I did not expect a death-struggle here in our lodge." Ayaminu now appeared from another part of the long, low cave. "And especially between my folk and those I invited here. I cannot say it pleases me. What is the quarrel?"

"No quarrel, *S'huesa*," the second Sitha told her. "We arrived only moments ago. Your sentries knew us and let us pass. Yeja'aro found the mortal and thought a deadly trick was being played on us."

Several of the glowing spheres, which had been dimmed so that Aelin and his men could sleep, now grew brighter. Aelin turned to the Sitha who had spoken. "Who are you?"

"We stretch courtesy somewhat, because my kinsman Yeja'aro was hasty and careless," the newcomer replied. "My mother named me Jiriki. I am of the Sa'onserei. This is Yeja'aro—though it seems you have two have already met."

"Is that a jest? If so, I am not much amused." Aelin's throat felt like fire and his words rasped. "Jiriki! But I know your name. My great-uncle has spoken of you often—and with affection." He looked at his dirty hands, turned them palms up. "I would have met you for the first time in a better way."

"Your great-uncle?" Jiriki leaned forward to peer at him. "It hardly seems possible, but I hear Hernystir in your speech. Do you speak of Count Eolair?"

"Yes. I am Sir Aelin of Nad Mullach," he said. "Eolair is my great-uncle."

Jiriki slowly shook his head. "Now that you tell me, I can see him in you, bones and flesh. How strange the world is! Do you know, it has been scarcely the turning of three moons since I saw Eolair myself."

Aelin's heart leaped in his chest. "Then you have more recent news of him than I do. Was he well? Do you know how he fares now, and where he is?"

"He was well when I saw him and I know of nothing that has happened to him since, but . . ." Jiriki shook his head. "I have just been given some strange news that bears on this and other matters. Apparently we all have much to speak about. But first, we who have just arrived must speak with *S'huesa* Ayaminu in our own tongue. Return to sleep if you can."

Aelin rubbed his throat. "Have I your pledge I will not wake again with—" he indicated the angry Sitha, who was now rising from the cavern floor, "—that fellow's hands around my neck?"

"I promise you," said Jiriki. "In fact," he said, staring hard at the red-haired one, "I am certain that Yeja'aro will ask you for your pardon. His mistake was an honest one, but his decision was . . . flawed." Jiriki turned and said something brief and harsh to his companion, who glared back at him for a long moment as if in disbelief, then answered him just as curtly in the liquid Sithi tongue. Jiriki's reply was not as loud, but Aelin heard something stinging in it, like the crack of a whip.

After a moment the one named Yeja'aro stepped toward Aelin. It was all the Hernystirman could do simply to stand and wait, because the Sitha did not look like he meant peace, let alone an apology.

"I did . . . wrong." If the red-haired Sitha's repentance was real, it had not entirely reached his voice or his heavily accented Westerling speech. "I dishonored Ayaminu's hearth. Grant me pardon, mortal."

"It is granted," Aelin said, ignoring Maccus, who was shaking his head.

"I apologize for poor hospitality," said Ayaminu. "I will send the healer to look at you, Sir Aelin. You will be glad to know we believe your friend Evan is healing well from his wound. Now, as Jiriki said, we Zida'ya must speak to each other, so after the healer looks you over, you should sleep again. Later, when you wake, we will eat and speak together."

Aelin woke again, this time without unwelcome surprises, and joined the gathered Sithi in a circle that nearly filled the limestone cavern. Beside Ayaminu and her grandson Liko, he recognized only the two newest arrivals, Jiriki and the flame-haired one who had tried to throttle him.

Ayaminu's people brought out bread that had been baked on rocks, sweet butter, berries, and other things gathered from the forest. Aelin and his companions had eaten nothing since they had snatched a bit of food from Baron Raynold's table in Naglimund just before the Norn attack; even Evan, pale but upright, set to the meal with a will. Seeing so many Sithi in one place gave Aelin a chance to observe the immortals more carefully, and he found himself fascinated and more than a little disturbed. In most ways they looked little different from mortals, though their faces seemed stretched and angular to his eye, their golden eyes large and uptilted. Their movements, though, were often as sudden and strange as those of birds, but still as elegantly smooth as the steps of a temple dancer.

Jiriki told them of his last meeting with Count Eolair and Prince Morgan. "I left them near the edge of the great forest, close to where they meant to meet their followers," he explained. "But things are unsettled all along Oldheart's edge and after I left them I heard rumors of deadly fighting there. We keep a close watch on our borders, as I think mortals also do."

"Which is how my men and I first became aware of the Norns," Aelin said. "Or the Hikeda'ya, as I believe you call them." He related the strange meeting they had witnessed that night on the storm-swept plain between the Norns and King Hugh's emissary, and of their subsequent escape from the king's Silver Stags. "It seems clear, though I am ashamed to say it, that the Hikeda'ya could not have crossed Hernystiri lands unnoticed without our king's assistance."

Jiriki did not frown, but his expression was unquestionably grim as he looked to Ayaminu. "This explains how they came to the mortal fortress of Naglimund with so little opposition," he said. "But if true, it is a dreadful portent. That one of Prince Sinnach's heirs should allow such a thing! It cannot be ignorance."

"Do not blame us all, I beg you," said Aelin. "It cannot be accident or ignorance on King Hugh's part, that is certainly true, but I doubt many at the court in Hernysadharc realize what he is doing."

"Even so," said Jiriki, making a gesture with his long fingers that Aelin did not understand, "it is clear that evil days are ahead—worse than even my darkest forebodings. And unlike the last war, I cannot see how we can help our mortal allies in Hernystir. Unless—" He fell silent, thinking.

Another figure now appeared from the back of the cave. She had jet black hair and the same lambent golden eyes as her fellows, but the look on her face was bright, not stern.

"Forgive me," she said. "I have been unwell today and could not join you earlier." She lowered herself in one smooth movement to sit beside Jiriki. "But I have listened with interest and concern."

"This is my sister, Aditu no'e-Sa'onserei," said Jiriki. "She too knows your kinsman Count Eolair."

"Eolair, King Simon, Queen Miriamele," Aditu agreed, smiling. "I know them and care for them all."

Maccus and Evan were both staring at her, forgetting for a moment the vigorous chewing they had been doing only moments earlier. She was quite lovely in the otherworldly way of her kind, but it was the simple grace of her speech and her gladsome manner that Aelin thought most captivating. She was also, it was quite obvious even as she nimbly seated herself, big with child. Aelin glared at his companions until they lowered their eyes to their food once more.

"You are most kind, Lady Aditu," he said. "My great-uncle Eolair has spoken of you as well. He said that you and your brother are the greatest friends of men among your people."

Jiriki made a low sound that might have been a snort of amusement. "Much to the horror of some of our own folk, it must be admitted." He turned to his sister. "But has something other than courtesy brought you to the fire?"

Aditu nodded. "As you told Aelin and his men, we have had unusual news from one of our dearest companions, Tanahaya of Shisae'ron. I think that news must be shared with them."

"All of it?" Jiriki did not seem angry, only hesitant.

"What use to us is keeping it secret when we cannot pass it to those who need it most?"

Aelin could only watch, sensing unknown currents beneath their polite words. Jiriki made a quiet humming noise that might have signified frustration or reflection or perhaps something quite different from either: Aelin was realizing that though both brother and sister Sitha spoke the Westerling tongue effortlessly, he still could not easily grasp the emotions behind what they said.

"Perhaps you are right," Jiriki said at last. He turned his nearly unblinking stare on Sir Aelin. "As my sister said, we have learned two things of late, both of great importance to mortals and Zida'ya alike. Our friend Tanahaya told us she has found Prince Morgan, the grandson of my friends Miriamele and Seoman—"

"He means King Simon," Aditu interposed. "Seoman has always been what he calls him."

"—and that Morgan is with her in the ruins of our ancient city, Da'ai Chikiza," continued Jiriki, smiling gently, "very close to where we found you and your companions fighting with the Hikeda'ya."

"Prince Morgan? Simon and Miriamele's heir?" Aelin shook his head. "I confess I did not know he was away from the Hayholt, but I am relieved to hear that he is safe. Is this Tanahaya with you here? Can we speak with her?"

Jiriki shook his head. "She is not with us. And even under her protection, Morgan is *not* safe—not nearly, I fear. But we will return to that. The other thing we learned from Tanahaya is that an object of power that your great-uncle spoke to me about, called the Witchwood Crown—something that Queen Utuk'ku of the Hikeda'ya apparently seeks—is real. Tanahaya learned that it is buried in the rubble of old Asu'a beneath the castle you call the Hayholt."

Aelin's heart sank. "That makes at least some sense of the Hikeda'ya coming into mortal lands."

"Yes, it does," Jiriki agreed. "And it also suggests that this attack on Naglimund is only the beginning of a campaign against Erchester and the Hayholt."

"Brynioch in his chariot!" swore Aelin. "That is foul news indeed, although I already wondered whether they planned some larger attack—Naglimund alone did not seem a prize worth starting up the war again." His eye was caught by the fire-haired Sitha, Yeja'aro, who sat near Jiriki and Aditu but seemed to still be watching Aelin intently, as if Aelin had attacked him instead of the other way around.

"So, this little snatch of good news—the prince's survival—is mixed with a great deal of dire circumstance," said Aditu, capturing Aelin's attention again.

"The high king and queen in the Hayholt must know of this!" Maccus declared around a mouthful of bread. "They must be told!"

"Finish chewing before you speak, man," Aelin said sharply. He did not want his own men slobbering like barnyard swine in front of these graceful Sithi. Maccus gave him a resentful look but had the sense not to say anything more. Aelin did not often insist on the privilege of his rank, but when he did, he was usually in a foul mood, and his liegemen knew he was better left alone.

"Then it seems that my men and I are returned to our original task," Aelin said. "We rode to Naglimund to bring news of the Hikeda'ya, but we arrived too late—the attack followed us by a mere hour or so. Now it seems plain to me that we must take this news to the Hayholt, to the High Throne. "

"I think not," said Ayaminu.

Aelin was startled. Did she and the other Sithi think mortals untrustworthy? "I do not understand, my lady."

"We have spoken while you slept, Sir Aelin," Jiriki explained. "And Ayaminu has convinced us that news of what happened at Naglimund will reach our friends, the king and queen, no matter what. The fortress and its defenders may have fallen, but not even the Hikeda'ya, with all their murderous cleverness, can silence an entire countryside. But there *is* important news that must be carried from here. First, though, we must ask a boon of you and your men, Sir Aelin."

"Of us?" Aelin was surprised. "We already said we would deliver any news that the High Throne needs to hear. What other task outweighs that?"

"Your own country." Where her brother's words had been grim, Aditu was sad and soft. "Any of us can carry the news about Prince Morgan and the Hikeda'ya to the Hayholt, but none of us except you can do what has to be done in your own land, Sir Aelin."

He was torn between resentment—he was not one of the Sithi, to follow their orders, but a landed son of Hernystir, heir to ancient Nad Mullach. But he understood very little of what was at stake here and of what was being argued, so after a moment's hesitation, he swallowed his angry words. "Explain, my lady, if you will."

"Our heart-sister Tanahaya told us that the Hikeda'ya are seeking witchwood seeds hidden somewhere in the mortal castle—or, more likely, in the old city of our people that lies buried beneath it," explained Aditu. "But what you may not know is that the Hayholt and its High King and High Queen are, at this moment, caught between two armies, the Hikeda'ya moving south and a great force of Thrithings-men who have crossed into Erkynland for reasons we do not yet know."

"Thrithings-men? Now?" Maccus said. "Those treacherous bastards! They are no better than animals!"

Aelin did not have the heart to reprove him again. "This is ugly news indeed. It is the first we have heard of it."

"It is fresh to us as well," Jiriki said.

"Then why do you want us to return to our own country of Hernystir? It seems that if ever there was a time when the High Throne needed loyal soldiers to rally to it, that time is now."

"There is no doubt of that," said Aditu. "You are but three men, though, however brave."

"That argument holds no water, my lady." Aelin was unhappy—the Sithi seemed to value mortals so lightly. "Perhaps we do not fight as well as your folk, but we are not reckoned lightly by—"

"You jump too swiftly toward conflict, as mortals often do," interrupted Ayaminu. "Wait until you hear the whole of our thought. If you still prefer to argue, there will be time enough for it then."

Maccus stirred beside him, but Aelin silenced him with a touch on his arm. Young Evan had sat quietly the whole time and looked as if he was thinking hard on something. "Very well," Aelin said. "Tell us your thought. We will do our best to listen without argument, though I cannot promise it will be with good grace."

Jiriki lifted his hands and made a gesture that Aelin guessed was meant to call for peace, or at least silence. "You and your men are of course free to ride south to the Hayholt, Sir Aelin, or even to join the fight against the grasslanders if you wish. But we think it is more important that you try to prevent your king from bringing his armies against the High Throne. An attack from behind, especially from a longtime ally, would surely lead to the fall of the Hayholt and the High Throne both."

Aelin was stunned. He looked back at the watching Sithi but saw nothing in their faces to suggest Jiriki was less than serious. "Surely this is a bad jest," he said at last. "I was the first to call the king of Hernystir a traitor, for traitor he must be to make common cause with our ancient enemies, and yours. And I do not doubt Hugh would be happy in the wake of Erkynland's defeat to swoop in like a carrion crow and make off with all he could, perhaps even throw off the rule of the High Ward. He is greedy and foolish and perhaps even imagines himself a conqueror like Tethtain the Great. But to attack his allies? What Hernystirman would follow him? No, no, I cannot believe that."

"Perhaps," said Evan quietly, surprising Aelin, "you are remembering the King Hugh that you knew, my lord. But rumor has painted him for a long time as greatly changed of late. Some even claim he has succumbed to madness—or witchcraft."

"You speak of the influence of that cursed woman, Tylleth." Aelin shook his head. "But that is still a step too far for me. I do not think so much of witchery that I believe she could change a man into betraying all his allies so completely."

"If you cannot take that step, then you may be left behind, to your sorrow," said Ayaminu.

"Enough talk." This came from Yeja'aro, the one who had tried to strangle Aelin only a short while earlier. "The mortals make excuses for their own kind. Always they do the same, no matter how many of ours—or their own—are murdered."

"Yeja'aro, please," said Aditu. "Those are old thoughts and old grievances. We need to find a better way."

"All I can do, Sir Aelin, is tell you what we see," said Jiriki. "We think we know what was given to Hugh when his man met with the Hikeda'ya on the night you watched from the tower. And we suspect we know what led to that meeting, as well."

"It is Utuk'ku, Queen of the Norns, who put all of this in train." As Aditu spoke she clasped her belly as if to protect what was growing inside her. "Everywhere we look at the chaos of these days, we see her pale hand behind it. I do not doubt that Utuk'ku also had something to do with the horrors we hear from distant Nabban. She has been laying her schemes for a long time, and in many places."

"And the mortals do not bother to resist her," said Yeja'aro.

"Enough with your complaints!" Ayaminu's grandson Liko the Starling had been silent until now, but had clearly lost his patience. "If you would help your people, Yeja'aro—*our* people—then let Jiriki and Aditu and my grandmother speak and keep your bitter thoughts to yourself."

The red-haired one stirred but saw the expressions of the other Sithi and fell silent.

"How could this Norn Queen spawn so much treachery in Hernystir from so far away?" Aelin asked.

"The Shard," said Aditu. "The Master Witness that is in the ruins of our once-great city of Mezutu'a, deep in the mountains behind Hernysadharc. Your great-uncle Eolair and Maegwin, the old king's daughter, discovered it during the last war. My brother and I think Utuk'ku has used it to speak to Hugh—perhaps even to offer him some great prize in return for his aid."

"I do not know what a Master Witness is," Aelin said. "Is it a place?"

"It is a thing," she said. "The one in Mezutu'a is a great crystal, part of the mountain's heart. In the old days, the Zida'ya and Hikeda'ya used such things to speak to each other across great distances."

"Ah," said Aelin. "Eolair did tell me about Witnesses. Magical things. But I thought they were small—'like a lady's mirror,' he told me."

"The ordinary sort, yes," said Aditu, nodding. "But the Master Witnesses are different. They cannot easily be moved, and they are much mightier than Witnesses that can be hidden, like the one my brother carries in his sleeve today."

"Sister, you breach a confidence," Jiriki told her.

"There have been too many secrets, my brother." Aditu spoke with a little quiet heat. "If the Hernystiri had been told of the danger of the Shard, they might have sealed away the Silverhome behind stone and Hugh would never have been poisoned with Utuk'ku's lies."

"You think she spoke to him with . . . through . . . this Shard?" Aelin asked.

"Witchcraft," said Maccus darkly; Evan made the sign of the Tree, then looked around quickly at the Sithi as if he might have offended them.

"A Witness is neither good nor bad." Jiriki patted the hilt of the blade sheathed at his hip. "It is like a sword that can attack or defend, preserve life or take it. But we have little doubt that Hugh found the Shard and somehow used it, and from that moment he was in Utuk'ku's snares."

"And then we guess that he bargained for a Witness of his own," Ayaminu said. "He wanted it enough to let the Hikeda'ya pass through his lands—thinking he was receiving a great weapon, no doubt. What he was truly receiving, though, was Utuk'ku's collar, and now he is her slave."

Aelin shook his head in wonder. "Black news, if true. But it does go some way to explaining things that puzzled me. Hugh was always mercurial, but I would never have supposed him to be a traitor to his own people."

"This King Hugh is not blameless," said Ayaminu in a dry tone. "Utuk'ku can sway weak minds or distracted ones, but even she must find fertile soil in which her seeds of corruption can grow."

"We lose our track a little, I fear," said Jiriki. "The reasons for Hugh's treachery are less important now than the fact of it. And what must be done." He turned his golden stare on Aelin. "We need you to go back to your country and find a way to keep Hugh out of Erkynland."

"And if we do?" Aelin asked. "If we manage to find support in our own land where, at the moment, every hand seems against us? We will still be useless to the High Throne at a time when King Simon and Queen Miriamele are most in need."

"Leave that work to me," said Jiriki. "Ayaminu and my sister go on to

Anvi'janya—that duty cannot be ignored—but I will go back to my people and gather a force to lead to the Hayholt. It will not be large, I fear. There are matters at stake here that I cannot explain now, and we cannot afford to leave our other positions undefended against Utuk'ku's assaults. But even a small company of Zida'ya arriving at the Hayholt in strength, and certainly in wrath, might make a difference. That will be my task."

"Then I suppose ours must be to return to Hernystir." Aelin turned to look at his companions. "But I am not sure how we will find our way there, with so many Norns between us and our own borders."

"There we can give you some help, I think." Jiriki rose to his feet. "Yeja'aro, you will go with Sir Aelin and his men to help them find a way through the enemy so they can return to Hernystir. After they are safely on their road west, you will journey on to the castle built atop ancient Asu'a's ruins and give our message of Prince Morgan's survival and the Hikeda'ya's coming attack on the Hayholt to the mortal king and queen."

Yeja'aro jumped to his feet so swiftly that Aelin leaned back, half-fearing the two Sithi would come to blows. The red-haired one let out a torrent of angry speech that Aelin could not understand.

"We agreed to speak the mortals' tongue," Jiriki scolded him.

It took a long moment before Yeja'aro could compose himself. "I will not do this! Aid mortals while leaving Aditu alone and helpless? No."

"I am never helpless," Aditu said. "You presume too much, Ember."

"Not to mention that Liko and I will accompany her to high Anvi'janya for the Year-Torch's appearance," Ayaminu added sharply. "Or do you doubt that we can keep her safe without you?"

"No. I will not do this," said Yeja'aro again. "There is no honor in it. Cousin Jiriki, you make these decisions as if your uncle *S'hue* Khendraja'aro was not the protector of the clan. As if *you* were."

"I will tell Khendraja'aro everything we have said and done here, of course," Jiriki answered. "He is the first I will go to in search of warriors to defend the mortal Hayholt. But as for you, who speaks so loudly of honor, have you forgotten the battle at Ma'asha already? It has been scarcely ten mortal years since you and I fought there in the hills. What did you tell me then, on the day we finally turned back General Ensume and his Spider legions?"

Yeja'aro's expression was hard, bitter. "You seek to humiliate me in front of mortals."

"I would ask you to remember your own pledge. What did you tell me after we survived that day?"

The other did not speak at once. At last, and grudgingly, he said, "That you were my *Hikka Staja*, Jiriki." He scowled, and for the first time, Aelin thought that he was seeing almost childish behavior in one of the Sithi. "That I owed you my life."

"That I was your arrow-bearer, yes," Jiriki said slowly. "And that you owed me a life. To me, that is a thing of great meaning. The mortal Seoman, the very king I would send you to, was *my Hikka Staja.* He saved me without knowing anything of our customs, purely from the courage in his heart. I cannot turn my back on him or his family . . . and I will not. Ayaminu is needed now in High Anvi'janya—as is Aditu, obviously—so you must be the one to go, Yeja'aro. This is no humiliation, but an act of great trust on my part. If I fail my mortal friends, I will not be able to live with myself."

Aelin was doing his best to take it all in but could only clumsily grasp what was being argued. Still, whatever the details of the dispute, it was clear that Jiriki somehow had the upper hand. Yeja'aro could only sit, fuming silently, knotting and unknotting his long fingers.

"So it must be, then," he said at last. "I am sent, so I must go. Jiriki's honor must overcome all else."

"I begin to lose my patience, Yeja'aro of the Forbidden Hills," Aditu said suddenly. "You are the father of our child, but you have not proved yourself a sliver of what my brother is. It is time to change that, I think, or I will have to admit I have misjudged you."

Yeja'aro darted a look at her so full of shame and longing that Aelin felt like a spy. "Enough," the fire-haired Sitha said. "You and your brother have stabbed me to the heart. Do not twist the blade."

Ayaminu ended the silence by getting to her feet. "We are settled, then, on our different roads. None of us must love the tasks we are given, we must only perform them faithfully. And if we do not all serve as we should, or if our best efforts come to naught—well, we may have a moment or two to regret it when we crouch in the ruin of our plans, but I think not for much longer than that."

7

A Meddlesome Priest

"Please, Bishop Boez, my heart is heavy and my head simply hurts." Simon had drunk too much wine the night before, and though it had blotted out thoughts of Miri that would have otherwise kept him awake for hours, it was playing hob with him this morning. And it was not just his head that ached, but all his bones and sinews too—he felt as though he was carrying the weight of another fully grown man on his back. "Tell me once more. You said money was missing from the exchequer—a substantial sum. What does that mean?" He was doing his best to concentrate because he knew he should: thin, serious Boez had not been a bishop long, but Tiamak thought highly of him. Still, it seemed odd that the new Royal Almoner should have been so set on a private audience in the king's own chambers.

"I do not feel confident I have found everything, Your Majesty, but my current count brings the shortfall to nearly three thousand gold thrones."

Simon was sufficiently horrified to forget his own misery for a moment. "*Three thousand gold!* Surely that is impossible! What, did old Gervis buy himself a country of his own?"

Boez had leaned back at the king's shout. He looked quite pale. "I do not know where the money went, or who took it from the Privy Purse, Majesty, but I am fairly certain Escritor Gervis is not to blame."

"Then who—and how? God's Bloody Tree, man, what are you doing about this?"

"Everything I can, my liege. But it is a more delicate matter than it may seem at first sight, so I beg you to keep your voice low. Whoever has managed to do this—and get away with it for some time—has also managed to cover his tracks very well. He has stolen enough to pay for a private army. We should not shout it up and down the corridors of the Hayholt—not yet. I have told only Tiamak."

Simon's anger had already turned to hopelessness. It took every ounce of his strength not to simply go back to bed. *Oh, Miri,* he thought, *it is worse than I ever could have guessed. Without you, everything falls apart.* "Well, if you have no idea of who's done this, what does Tiamak think?"

"The last time we spoke he was as dumbfounded and without ideas as I am,

Majesty. But I go to him now. When I have heard his latest thoughts, I will present you with my report on everything I have found and everything I have done about it. I beg pardon for bringing you such ill news, sire, but Tiamak said you do not like to be kept in the dark about important matters like this. I would have come to you sooner, but . . ." He broke off awkwardly. "Our great loss made me hesitate. The country's loss of its queen, but most of all your loss, Majesty. I waited as long as I could, but I could not forget what Lord Tiamak said."

At least Tiamak's learned something after keeping the news from me about that evil book John Josua found, Simon thought bleakly, but he was stunned by the chancellor's revelation. "How long has this been going on?"

"The thefts go back several years at least, though I have not finished all my work." Boez looked at a piece of parchment in his hand, squinted, then removed his spectacle-glasses and held the parchment close to his nose. "I apologize, Majesty. As I said, I believe Gervis was blameless in the theft, but he did not leave me the most well-ordered records, either. I have asked to meet with him. In any case, I am still discovering things, working my way backward through many thousands of entries. I will keep you informed, of course, of everything I find."

"You must." Simon could almost imagine that the morning sun was setting, not rising, because darkness seemed to envelop the chamber. "Bishop Boez, you must."

"My good lady Thelía is out," Tiamak told the bishop, "but I think I can find something suitably bracing to offer you—or is it too early? I fear the king's habits are catching. Even I have resorted to an occasional mid-morning draught to lift my spirits."

"Thank you, my lord, but I will not stay long enough for that." Tiamak thought Boez looked not just worried but also a little frantic. "I continue to discover more missing funds—the loss is now more than three thousand gold. I have spoken to the king. I told him most of what I have found so far."

Tiamak let out a breath. "I am surprised you did not bring me with you, if only for courage. How did he take it?"

"As you might expect—surprised, dumbfounded, more than a little angry." Boez reached into his tunic and produced a fold of parchment that he kept in his hand as he spoke, turning it over and over in his fingers. "But the king had to be told, as you yourself said—it was only a question of when. However, I have a more practical reason for asking to see you today."

"Which is?"

"Look at this, my lord. Tell me what you see." He handed the parchment to Tiamak, who spread it on one of the few clear spots left atop his cluttered table.

He squinted, then turned it over and examined the back, which was blank, before returning to the inked lines on the front. "I do not understand any of these symbols, although the one at the end looks familiar."

"We will come to that in a moment. The first ciphers you see are an old chancelry code that an earlier Chancellor named Father Strangyeard was wont to use."

Tiamak smiled despite himself. "I knew Strangyeard well. I can promise you that he was not the cause of the missing gold."

Boez shook his head impatiently. "I do not suspect him, my lord. The thefts took place long after his death. But others continued to use his code. It is simple enough, meant not to hide anything but merely to make things simpler for those who must write many figures every day. The first cipher means 'one hundred.' It is the two sets of characters after it that puzzle me. Because I can see why a cipher might be used to keep the writing of accounts simple, but there is no reason why the name of who is being paid or that the precise nature of one hundred *what* should also be kept secret—at least not that I can think of. After all, a record of an account is a record of all those things, not merely a number."

"But this does not look like a page from one of the chancelry books," Tiamak pointed out.

"It isn't. It was caught between the leather cover of one of the account books and the book's binding."

Tiamak stared at the jumble of ciphers again. "What was the date of the book in which you found it?"

"Last year's accounts. I confess, Lord Tiamak, that I have much to do before I can finish my report, but I could not ignore this. May I leave it with you, hoping you might find some answer to what it means? It could be only somebody's idle note to themselves, but two types of cyphers in the same notation—well, it struck me as odd."

"It strikes me that way, too," said Tiamak, squinting at the parchment. "And I think I have already made sense of part of it."

"Truly?" Boez leaned forward. He smelled of sweat and lamp oil. Tiamak did not think the bishop had found much time of late for sleep or grooming.

"Truly. You see, this mark after the 'one hundred'? It is not a cypher at all. It is another of Strangyeard's shorthand tricks, one I happen to remember because of the sort of things we used to discuss. He was a wise man, Strangyeard, and a scholar. This is an ancient Khandian rune for the word *'nebbu'*—gold. It was once used in many alchemical treatises and philosophical papers. The alchemists of old thought themselves the heirs of lost Khandia, you see."

"So it is a note that might mark the disbursement of a hundred gold pieces?"

Boez took off his spectacle-glasses to squint at the parchment. "No small sum. Yes, I would very much like to know what that last cipher might mean."

"It might only be someone's record of an ordinary debt owed to someone else and nothing to do with the palace accounts," Tiamak cautioned him. "We have enough true mysteries that we must be careful not to jump at every shadow and unexpected noise."

"I grant you that. But still, to find it hidden away as if it had been lost—well, I will eagerly await the results of your scholarship." He stood. "I hope I do not need to say this must be kept between the two of us."

"And the king?"

Boez frowned. "I think not yet, my lord, though I will bow to your judgment. Next time I would rather present the king with something more solid than the mere bundle of suspicions I have already burdened him with."

Tiamak sighed. "On this, I think we agree, Your Eminence. I will see what I can do to unpick this puzzle."

"I'm sorry to add to your burdens, my lord. I think they are many."

Tiamak shook his head. "I think if we survive these dreadful times, such burdens will seem no more than we were meant to carry. If not—" He broke off. There was no happy way he could finish that sentence.

He ushered the bishop out, then spread the scrap of parchment out on his table once more and brought the lamp close, examining it from many different angles.

Pasevalles was pacing back and forth across the top of Holy Tree Tower like a falcon tethered to its perch, his heart straining for release, his claws aching to clutch at enemies. He was stopped in mid-stride by the sight of Bishop Boez emerging from the Inner Keep's main gate with a small retinue of priests—returning to the Chancelry, Pasevalles had no doubt, after his royal audience.

And what precisely could Boez have wanted to share with grieving Simon? he wondered. Pasevalles had seen the appointment written in the King's book, along with the clear notation that it would be a private audience taking place in King Simon's own chambers. *And, judging by the door he used to leave the residence, Boez has been to see that infuriating little Wrannaman as well. I do not like the two of them talking together so much.*

As if someone had taken off his falcon's hood and released him into flight, Pasevalles suddenly turned and swept toward the stairwell. He could leave nothing to chance at this point, not with so many plans finally coming to fruition and everything tilting in his direction. As he swiftly descended the tower's winding stairway, he curled his hands into fists. Perhaps, he thought, it was time to take a more active role in the bishop's investigation.

"Let's pretend this is a castle," said Lillia, pulling the bed curtains closed. "And you'll be a dragon. A big fierce dragon living in a castle, lying on a pile of gold."

Her grandfather, the king, groaned. It did not sound like his usual playful groan. "We already live in a castle. No need to pretend. And I came in here to try to sleep, child." He rubbed his face. "Why are you here?"

"Because Auntie Rhoner sent me away. She said she had to talk with Count Eolair."

"And she sent you to me?"

"Yes." But Lillia knew that wasn't exactly true. "She said to go find something to do. She maybe said something about the nurses, but they're *dreadful*." Lillia had recently learned the word and was trying it out. "They never let me do anything. They never let me go outside."

"They are doing what they're supposed to do," said the king, lying back against a pile of pillows. "They are trying to keep you safe and out of mischief."

Disgusted, Lillia threw back the curtains. What good was it having a dragon if it wouldn't roar and breathe fire? "Why did Grandmother Queen Miriamele die? Was it like my mother? Did she fall?"

The king's groan was softer this time, more gurgly, and Lillia didn't like the sound of it. It took a while before he spoke. "No, child. Some bad men attacked her carriage."

"They were Fightings-men. Nurse Loes told me."

"If she told you they were Thrithings-men—*not* 'Fightings-men'—then why did you ask me?"

"Because I don't understand." She hadn't really wanted to talk about it because it bothered her and frightened her, but since her grandfather wouldn't play, the thoughts had all come back. "Why would someone hurt my grandmother? And is Morgan dead too?" Suddenly she was crying. "I don't want Grandmother Miriamele to be dead, and I don't want Morgan to be dead either!"

"Here now." Her grandfather reached out with his long arms and pulled her up onto the bed. He held her against his chest and stroked her hair. "Morgan is still alive. We're trying to find him, that's all. Don't cry."

"But why can't they find him? Is he hiding?"

"I don't think so." But the king didn't sound completely certain. "He went into the forest. It's a hard place to find someone, that's all."

"In the forest. With *bears*?" She was both horrified and fascinated. "Won't they eat him?"

She could feel the king's breath hitch for a moment. "No. They won't eat him. He's too thin and bad-tempered. Bears like things that are full of sweet juice, like berries."

She almost laughed, but her nose was running and her cheeks were wet. "That's silly. Morgan isn't like a berry."

"Exactly. That's why he'll be safe." But he tightened his arms around her until Lillia felt a little short of breath. "And so will you."

"Is Grandmother with my mother now?"

"They are both in Heaven," said the king. "And now they are both watching over you." Again she heard the catch in his voice and wondered what it meant. Was he telling her something that wasn't true? But why? Did it mean they *weren't* in Heaven, but everyone was afraid to tell her? That didn't make any sense, but lots of things happened around her that didn't make sense and nobody ever explained them properly. Almost everything about people dying and babies being born fit into that category.

"Have you stopped crying? Here, let me wipe your face." The king took up the hem of his coverlet and blotted her eyes, cheeks, and runny nose. "There. Much better. But your grandfather truly does need some sleep. Go back to your nurse. Tell her I said you have been very good, but now you need to be very good somewhere else."

Her kingly grandfather may not have noticed the flaw in the wording of his command, but Lillia was always keen to legitimately evade doing things the grownups wanted her to do, especially when those things were boring. He had said "go to the nurse" but hadn't told her not to stop on the way. A little part of her was gleeful at this omission, but her insides still felt heavy and sad. Was Grandfather really telling the truth—would Morgan be all right? And why did Lord Pasevalles always seem so strange and quiet these days when he used to be kind and funny? Sometimes he looked at Lillia so strangely. Did it have something to do with her mother and grandmother dying? Did he know they weren't in Heaven like everyone said they were? But then where were they?

Grandfather never said I couldn't stop along the way . . .

Halfway up the stairs Lillia had once again become a dragon-fighting hero like her famous great-great-grandfather King John, padding into the creature's lair as silently as she could, watching for danger on every side. By the time she'd reached the second floor there were so many people coming and going all around that although several of the servants looked at her and seemed to consider asking what she was doing, none of them did. She was keeping an especial eye out for Lord Pasevalles, who had almost caught her spying the last time. She did not want him upset with her, because he was one of the best grown-ups, but she had also begun to feel certain that he was keeping a secret from her, and secrets were one of the things she hated the most.

On the landing of the fourth floor, she crouched and listened for footsteps coming up behind her. When she was satisfied that she couldn't hear any, she ran lightly down the corridor to the room she had investigated before. To her pleasure—and a thrill of anxiousness—the door swung open with only a push. But she was disappointed to find that the chamber was quite empty and looked as though it had not been used for a long time. If ghosts had been haunting the room, they were haunting some other part of the castle just now.

As she turned to go, she noticed marks on the stone floor between the doorway and the carpet.

Footprints, she thought. *Those weren't here before.* She leaned closer, then got down on all fours until the light was striking at just the right angle, and she could see the shoe prints leading from the door to the far wall beside the fireplace. She got up and carefully followed them until they ended. Mysteriously, they only went in one direction; no footprints came back the other way. Someone had come into this empty room without leaving any sign of having walked out again. But how could that be?

Only a ghost could do that, she thought, and her heart began to beat very quickly. *Something is hiding here. Something really is. And nobody wants to tell me.*

She looked everywhere but she could see under the bed and in every corner: there was nowhere else in the room to hide. Lillia could not think of what to do next, but she was filled to bursting with what she had learned. This room really did have a secret—an *important* secret. And if the grown-ups were keeping it from her, then that meant she couldn't tell anyone that she knew. She would have to discover the truth on her own.

Her mind busy as a bumblebee, Lillia made her way out of the room, pulled the door closed behind her, then went quietly back down the stairs to rejoin the bustle of the royal household.

"I had hoped to welcome you home with proper dignity, my dear Brother Etan," Tiamak told him, clutching the monk's hand in both of his own. "You deserve a celebration! At the very least, I will do my best to bring you before King Simon for an audience so you may tell him everything about Josua you have discovered. But time and circumstance have made things very difficult here. Still, I am supremely glad to see you back and safe, my friend—come, let me embrace you."

When they had separated again, Brother Etan found his eyes grow teary. The Wrannaman looked bowed and compressed. Also, Tiamak's chin had never before shown even the trace of a whisker, but now a few curly strands of gray sprouted there, tangled and neglected.

"It is good to see you, my lord," he said. "I heard the terrible news about Queen Miriamele at Wentmouth when we took on stores. I have no words to describe my sadness—of course, I have prayed for her soul many times since we heard. I saw a little of the madness in Nabban—from a distance, mostly—but I never dreamed . . ." He shook his head. "In any case, my lord, you have no reason to apologize to me. And your lady wife is well, I hope?"

Tiamak nodded and took him by the arm—as much for his own sake as the monk's, Etan thought, because the Wrannaman's limp was more pronounced than usual. Then Tiamak led him into the working room, toward a table so full of precarious book towers that they looked like sculptor's models of a collapsing ancient city. "Thelía is in good health, I am very pleased to say, although like me—like everyone here—her heart is heavy with mourning."

"They say it was Thrithings-men who attacked the queen's carriage. Is that true? Does this Unver barbarian really mean to overthrow Erkynland?"

Tiamak shrugged. "It is possible. It is also possible that someone else paid grassland mercenaries to attack the queen's carriage." He seemed about to say more, but then pressed his lips tightly together and led Etan to a chair. "Let me get you something to drink, Brother. I doubt they gave you a proper welcome at St. Sutrin's."

Etan watched Tiamak's hand shaking as he poured. "And you received all my letters?"

"I think so, yes. Your last—the story of finding Lady Faiera in Perdruin—was painful to read. That poor, suffering woman! But it puts us no closer to finding Josua himself." He started as if something had stung him. "Ah! But you have not heard the news brought by Count Eolair, have you? Of course not—how could you? It was most unexpected. Prince Josua's wife Vorzheva has been found."

Etan was caught by surprise. "No, my lord, no, I had not heard. Found where?"

Tiamak related Eolair's adventures as a prisoner, first of bandits, then of the Shan himself. He finished with a grim laugh. "So we thought to bring her back into the fold, to embrace her with loving arms. Instead, she tried to murder the Count of Nad Mullach."

"That is all very, very strange," Etan said. "But everything I have read of Lady Vorzheva, or that you have told me, suggest that she has always been changeable as quicksilver. Still, how can she love being a servant of even a mighty man like this Unver so much that she would attack Eolair rather than return to Erkynland and be treated as a prince's valued widow?"

"A good question, but one which we likely must put aside for now."

Etan felt a heaviness, though he had been expecting this. "Are we to give up finally on our search for Prince Josua? The king must be disappointed in how little I discovered."

Tiamak shook his head vigorously. "The king does not even know you have returned. If we had definite word of Josua's fate, it would be different, but King Simon . . . well, he is in a black and miserable mood, as you would suspect. Later, when time has healed his heart a little, we will tell him what you have learned. But for now, I fear that I must turn you to another task."

Etan felt a moment of overwhelming weariness. "Of course, my lord, whatever you wish of me."

For the first time, Tiamak smiled. "Do not fear! I do not intend you should start this night! But while I have been busy with tasks of my own—important tasks, I hasten to say!—my wife, Lady Thelía, has been tending to all who are injured or ill in this castle both night and day, and your help would be most useful to her. But after you have rested from your journey, of course!"

Relieved, Etan nodded. "Of course. A few hours of sleep will cure all."

"Good," said Tiamak. "But I fear there is one last thing I must tell you." He went to the door that led to the passage, opened it, and looked both ways along the corridor before closing it again. His almost exaggerated caution made Etan uneasy. "Nobody about," the small man said. "I see you looking strangely, Brother, but when I tell you—well, you will better understand."

Although Etan's great, underlying weariness did not go away, as Tiamak told him about his conversations with Bishop Boez, the monk felt something else begin to crawl up from beneath the fog of his exhaustion—a growing sense of fear. And when he heard the vast sum that had been stolen by an unknown thief who had to be one of the king's most trusted nobles, he could not find any words at all.

Simon thought it was nearing middle-night, but he had slept part of the day away, and then slept again in the early evening, so he could not be sure.

"Avel?" he called. "Where are you boy?"

The door to the king's bedchamber creaked open and the young page looked in. "I'm here, Majesty. Very sorry. I just . . ." He trailed off, sounding a little flummoxed.

"What is the time?"

"The last bell I heard was for afternoon prayer, Majesty. But that has been some time back."

Simon frowned. Sleeping through the day meant long, sleepless nights. "What are you doing out in the corridor, lad?"

"You . . . you have a visitor, Majesty. Visitors, I mean."

"What are you talking about?"

"Countess Yissola of Perdruin is here," the youth said, making a helpless face. "She . . . I did not . . . she has come to speak to you."

"Good God," said Simon, sitting up. "What on earth? Give me a moment, I pray, before you bring her in." He looked to the Erkynguards standing on either side of the door, both busy looking professionally disinterested. Propriety, at least, appeared to be in safe hands. He glanced down at his rumpled, wine-stained night shirt and considered trying to find something cleaner, but instead pulled the covers up almost to his neck.

A moment later the door opened again. Countess Yissola entered, accompanied by a small Perdruinese woman of indeterminate age. Yissola wore a heavy wrap against the castle's winter chill, but Simon could see the hem of her nightdress and her slender ankles, bare above her slippers.

"Forgive me, King Simon," said the countess. "I have asked to see you several times, but Lord Pasevalles cannot seem to find a suitable time for us to meet. Thus, I decided to be bold and make my own audience with you." She smiled as though abashed by her own daring. Simon could not help reflecting that if such a handsome woman had smiled at him that way in his youthful days, he would likely have dreamed about it for weeks. "This is Peronella, one of my ladies," she continued, indicating the smaller woman. "I thought it might scandalize your household to have me walking the corridors by myself."

Lady Peronella made a courtesy to Simon but stayed silent.

"And I have young Avel there and several guards, as you see," Simon told the countess, amused despite the hour and his own grubbiness. "So both our reputations are safe." But there was still something strangely exciting about having this woman in his bedchamber in her night-clothes, even with so many others present. A moment later, he was filled with shame. *I'm sorry, Miri,* he thought. *I am a wretched dog for even noticing another woman with you so shortly gone.*

Something of his mood must have shown on his face. Yissola looked worried and came toward him. "May I sit on the edge of your bed, Majesty?" she asked.

He was not sure he wanted her that close, but he nodded. "What can I do for you, Countess?" he asked when she had seated herself near his feet.

"Two things," she said, "and neither of them require you to do aught but listen." She held up a finger. "Firstly, I thank you for amending the fairness of the harbor treaty."

He nodded, but he knew he would be castigated for the change by the merchants of the Northern Alliance. "Thanks for that go to Lord Tiamak, who looked into it at my request. A mistake does seem to have been made." Tiamak had seemed puzzled that Simon should have signed such a flawed law in the first place, but Simon could not remember the event.

"Still, I thank you for heeding my request." She slid a little way closer to him. He could smell her scent now, delicate and alluring. Yissola fixed him with her dark eyes. When she spoke, her voice was scarcely above a whisper. "And here is the second of my thoughts, Majesty. My heart breaks for you in your loss. Queen Miriamele was loved by many, all across Osten Ard, and I know you will mourn her long and painfully. I am so very sorry." She paused then, as if she expected Simon to speak, but he could not summon any words. "But that is not all I have to say." She hesitated, then seemed to muster her courage. "If there ever comes a day when your heart has healed a little, and you begin to think about a companion to ease your sorrows in the years ahead, I ask you to remember me." Yissola flushed, something that Simon did not think she did very often, and in his confusion and sorrow he was unexpectedly touched. "Please do not think me too forward," she said, still so quietly that only he could hear. "But I have met few honorable men, and of those, none who moved me." She seemed to realize she had been leaning closer, and suddenly sat up straight. "To protect my own honor, I cannot say more than that. But I ask you not to forget me, King Simon."

He was grateful for her kindness in trying to make him feel like a man again, but beneath that gratitude something dark and dreadful yawned, an emptiness that he knew could never be filled, not even by one as handsome and clever as Perdruin's countess. "I thank you, my lady," he said at last. "How could I forget you? I will remember your kindness until I am put in the ground beside Miri."

Her face changed a little then, before she could find her calm and disguise her feelings. Simon was saddened, and for the first time in many days, not just for himself.

"Then I will bid you goodnight, Majesty," she said, rising. "I have only a short time left before I must sail back to my home. I thank you for seeing me in such an informal way, and without notice."

She went out then, trailed by little Lady Peronella. When the door closed behind her, Simon let out a quiet moan of pain and fell back onto his pillow.

The flame of the last candle was guttering. Tiamak's eyes were weary. He knew he should put his work away but felt he was on the verge of discovery. The feeling had been proved false many times already that evening, but he was desperate to solve at least one of the questions plaguing him. He was concentrating so hard on the book of old Nabbanai ciphers that he had nearly forgotten where he was; when the loud knock came on their chamber door, he jumped.

"What is that? Who is there?" His wife's voice from their bed was muzzy with sleep. "Tiamak, is that you?"

"It is someone rapping at the door," he called to her, and closed the book with shaking hands. Then he set another volume on top of it to hide what he had been reading. Candle in hand, he limped across the chamber, the stone floor cold enough for him to feel through his slippers. When he opened it and discovered Lord Pasevalles looming against the shadows of the corridor, it startled him badly, jibing so completely with certain fears that had been running through his head that it was all he could manage not to slam the door closed again.

"My lord?" he said, trying to keep his voice steady. "What is afoot? It is nearly midnight!"

"I beg pardon for disturbing you, Lord Tiamak," said Pasevalles. "But Lord Captain Zakiel has asked to see the king immediately with grave news. I thought you would want to be there too."

"Of course, of course!" Tiamak, still a little confused and hesitant, set down his candle and took a shawl from over the back of his reading chair. "Lead the way, my lord." A cautious thought whispered in his ear. He raised his voice. "Thelía, my dear, it is Lord Pasevalles at the door. He and I are going to see the king. I will be back soon."

She acknowledged him in a drowsy way, but he had told her where he was going and with whom.

In the corridor, he asked, "Have you any idea of Zakiel's news?"

"None. But I fear it can be no good news, not if the Lord Constable is determined to wake the king." Everyone in the Hayholt knew how badly Simon was taking his wife's death, and how it had especially cursed his nightly rest.

When they came into the light of the hallway outside the royal chambers, Tiamak saw that several guards were there with Zakiel, all wearing black mourning ribbons. Their presence reassured him. "Thank you for waiting for us, Lord Captain," he said.

Zakiel only nodded, then opened the door. The king's young serving lad was waiting in the antechamber. "Beg pardon, my lords," the boy said. "His Majesty says he will be out to you directly. He was undressed."

"Dressed, undressed, it makes little difference," said Zakiel. "This tale will not wait."

Almost immediately the door swung open and Simon emerged from the inner chamber. His beard was pressed to one side, as though he had been sleeping on it, and his hair was tousled. "There you are, Sir Zakiel—no, I mean Lord Captain, forgive me," the king said, then nodded at Tiamak and Pasevalles. "And you two as well. It seems to be everyone's night for coming to see me. What brings you all? It cannot be good, I think."

"You are right, Majesty," said Zakiel. "Word has just reached me from Duke Osric's squire. His Grace was sorely wounded at Fellmere, fighting against the grasslanders, but is expected to recover."

"Well, that is certainly foul news." The king looked pale, almost ghostlike in his bedraggled nightshirt. "And I will pray for the duke's health, of course. But is his wound so bad that we all must be wakened and dragged from our beds?"

"We hope he will recover, but there is more, Majesty," said Zakiel. "The duke's men have had to retreat and the grasslanders have taken Fellmere."

"*What?*" Simon's voice was so loud in the small antechamber that it hurt Tiamak's ears. "Retreated to where? How could this happen?"

"I have not learned everything yet—the messenger was wounded and weary. All I can tell you for certain is that the Thrithings-men overran Fellmere Castle, and Osric and the rest were forced to flee. Had it not been for Earl Rowson, who I am told fought very bravely in the retreat, they might all have been trapped there and killed."

"Rowson?" The king sounded almost as astonished as he had at the news of Fellmere's fall. "Then perhaps I have wronged him, though God knows he tested my patience. But Captain Zakiel, this is terrible news! What are our losses? And where have our troops retreated to?"

"Many questions still remain, Majesty," Zakiel told him. "And I have sent messengers of my own to get better answers. But the wounded duke and the rest of the survivors have fallen back to Winstowe Castle in the Fingerdale."

"Winstowe!" said the king. "But that is only a day or two's riding from Erchester—from us!"

"Two or three days," said Zakiel. "But still far too close."

Tiamak shut his eyes for a moment. Dizziness swept through him, and for a moment he thought he might fall.

"Good God in Heaven." Simon looked up at the ceiling. "Have You deserted us entirely, Lord? Do You wish nothing now but our destruction?"

Pasevalles and the Lord Constable hurriedly made the sign of the Tree.

"We will not fall to barbarians, Majesty." Zakiel spoke forcefully, but Tiamak did not think he heard much confidence. "Do not fear, God will not desert us. Even twenty thousand grasslanders could not take the Hayholt."

"But it is not only the grasslanders we have to fear," said Tiamak. "Have you forgotten? An older and crueler enemy is also on the march."

Simon's face looked haunted. "Am I truly awake? Or is this some foul nightmare we are living? I have not dreamed in so long, perhaps I have lost my wits."

"If you have," Tiamak said, the dizziness gone but replaced only by hollowness and dry-mouthed fear, "then it is a nightmare we are all sharing, and *all* our wits are lost."

8

In the Heights

Morgan was increasingly fearful about being trapped in an abandoned storeroom under Da'ai Chikiza, knowing the two of them would eventually be surrounded and then killed by Norn soldiers, but Nezeru seemed to grow calmer by the moment.

"What is a mortal doing in the city called Tree of Singing Wind?" she asked him suddenly.

The question astounded him. "What does it matter now?"

"At the end, when nothing matters, everything matters," she said. "Fate has chosen you to share my death. I wonder why."

Angry and frightened, at first Morgan did not want to tell her anything, but after a long stretch of silence he cleared his throat. "I was on a mission to the Sithi who live in the great forest—a mission from . . . from the king and queen of Erkynland."

"Seoman and Mirmel," she said, surprising him.

"Miriamele. Yes. They sent me with some others to speak to the Sithi, to try to learn if our old alliance still held."

"They sent *you*." She gave him a long, searching look.

"I was part of the embassy, yes." Morgan was not so reconciled to his coming death that he was willing to open himself completely, and now that he knew she recognized the names of his grandparents, even less so. Perhaps she would decide that killing the Hayholt's mortal heir might be a splendid final act. "And we were also bringing back the Sithi envoy, Tanahaya. She was ambushed on her way to us and wounded with poisoned arrows. We thought the Sithi might be able to save one of their own."

Now her look turned to frank disbelief. "You and your fellow mortals sent one of the Zida'ya back to her own people to try to save her life."

"Yes, that's what I said. And they did save her, because later she saved me."

"She saved you? Do you mean this envoy, Tanahaya?"

"If you keep interrupting me, your people will kill us before I've finished the story."

A brief flicker of amusement crossed her ghostly features. "Continue."

He told her of his journey through the forest, his time with the Chikri, and his rescue by Tanahaya at the mouth of Misty Vale. To his surprise, Nezeru listened carefully, and questioned him when she did not recognize the Westerling words he chose. It was hard to deny that she had grown measurably better at speaking and understanding his tongue in just the short hours they had been together. He had heard about the immortals all his life; apparently they were just as ancient, clever, and strange as in every far-fetched tale he had heard.

His time in Misty Vale, and the little bits that Tanahaya had been able to tell him about it, seemed particularly to interest Nezeru: she had him describe every detail of the giant that had almost captured him and of how Tanahaya had rescued him.

"So the Sacrifice soldiers you saw were not in the valley but outside it?"

"Yes, and they tried to kill me when I was coming back out. Tanahaya said they must have been following me. But she said her own Sithi people weren't allowed to enter that valley, so perhaps the Norns—the Hikeda'ya soldiers—were also afraid to go there." He had a sudden thought. "Do you know what that giant was?"

"No. And even more strange, I have never heard of it—or of such a place, either. But then, our masters are careful not to tell us anything that we do not need to know to serve as good Sacrifices."

"To serve and die, you mean."

"True." For a moment her face again became expressionless. "Tell me more. You say this Tanahaya was leading you. Why did she bring you here to this abandoned city?"

Now Morgan became reluctant. He only had Nezeru's word that she was an exile from her own people, although if it was all a trick, it seemed overly elaborate. How could anyone have known he would be wandering in the tunnel where Nezeru had chosen to hide herself? And the Norns had certainly seemed intent on killing her and Morgan both. Still, as he told of their capture by the Pure, he kept to himself what seemed like the most important parts of the story.

"She brought you here in hope that the *Jonzao*—the Pure—had a Witness, so that she could speak to her friends? I do not understand her thinking. What could be so important, to risk so much?"

"I don't know." He avoided her night-dark stare. "But they finally let Tanahaya use a Witness. She spoke to . . . to her friends, and then something attacked her."

Nezeru frowned. "Attacked? Do you mean through the Witness?"

"That's how it seemed. We couldn't see anything but Tanahaya, but she was fighting with something and the leader of the Pure had to snatch the mirror away. Then the Norns attacked."

Nezeru had been sitting on her haunches. Now she got up and stretched and even paced a little as she thought. "Strange," she said. "But I warrant it was Akhenabi, the Lord of Song, who came for her. He is the queen's chief mage, and it is said he keeps a jealous watch on all the Witnesses."

As Morgan thought back on all that had happened to him and Tanahaya before the Norn attack, their capture by the Pure and the search among the ancient books and records of Da'ai Chikiza, something struck him. He turned to Nezeru, suddenly intent. "Before your people attacked us, Tanahaya and I were in the archives. Do you know what that word means?"

"I do. Why?"

"Because it's right in the middle of the city, and we might be able to find our way back to it. And if we do, we can likely find a map there. We might learn a way out, or at least a way to reach one of the outer towers."

She stopped pacing for a moment, then was silent for some time. "We would not reach it without fighting and killing many Sacrifices, I think."

"I think you're right."

A slow smile stretched her mouth. "Then that is a good plan, Morgan. It is always better to kill with a purpose—to die trying to achieve something. Then our death-songs will certainly be heard by our ancestors in the immortal Garden."

He laughed without mirth. "I don't have any ancestors in the immortal Garden."

"Then you will be part of my death song." She nodded in satisfaction. "Surely that is a better fate than dying as a mere mortal."

"If you say so."

"Where will you go now?" Qina asked the Sa'Vao.

"To the place where things end, to see how our story finishes."

"But where will that be, Kuyu-kun?"

"My heart tells me it is not far. To the east and north just a short journey from here. 'Tanakirú,' the Zida'ya call it—the Valley of Mist."

"I have never heard any of these names," said Little Snenneq. "Why will the world end there? What do your dreams see?"

"It is not something that can be explained with words," said the Sa'Vao, shaking his hairless head. "The valley I have dreamt of is not just a place but a time—a collection of possibilities. But every one of those possibilities I can see brings the end of our world."

Qina found herself shivering. "I cannot believe it. The world is so big! Nothing can end it. People cannot do it—even a nation of people could not. A battle that kills many and throws down great powers, yes, that could be true. Please forgive me, but maybe you see your own death and mistake that for everything ending?"

Again Kuyu-kun shook his head. "It does not feel so. But I did not invite you to our fire to bring you only sadness. Something good may lie beyond death—even the death of a world. Have courage. If you like, you may come with us to see what the truth is."

Qina felt an instant revulsion. "No. We want nothing to do with the end of the world, but if some great death must come, let it find us striving to keep our promises." She turned to Snenneq. "His words change nothing, beloved. We set out to find Morgan. If this world-doom is something more than just a dream, then that is all the more reason to find him, so that the prince does not face the end alone and fearful."

Snenneq looked doubtful. "But, betrothed! All the wisdom and history of the Tinukeda'ya race sits here beside us. When will I ever find the chance to have so many questions answered?"

Qina hissed in frustration. "If the world is fated to end, what does it matter?"

"Knowledge does not need to have purpose." Snenneq's tone was almost sulky.

"We already have a purpose—to find the grandson of my father's dear friend as we swore we would. Do you want your last act in the world to be a broken oath?"

Little Snenneq fell silent, poking at the small fire with a stick. Qina turned to the Sa'Vao once more. "We thank you, Kuyu-kun, but we cannot accompany you. And forgive me, but I hope you are wrong about your dreams."

"I also hope so," he said. "Because it is hard to think that this world will end without justice for my enslaved people. But in death, all will at last be made equal. Perhaps that is satisfaction enough." Tih-Rumi and the other delvers made quiet sounds of mourning; it was hard to tell whether or not they agreed with their Sa'Vao.

"It seems a grim sort of victory to me. But I wish you and your people well." Qina stood. "Come, Snenneq. A little daylight still remains. Let us get back to our work."

Her *nukapik* stood, obviously reluctant. "Will we see you again, Kuyu-kun?"

"If you come to Tanakirú," he said. "Before the end."

Qina bowed toward the Sa'Vao. "Thank you for sharing your food." She turned and made her way out of the clearing, looking straight ahead but listening with no little trepidation until she heard the reassuring sounds of Snenneq behind her.

"If we are to reach the archive safely, we must go as quietly as the breeze," Nezeru told him. "We cannot make you as silent as a Sacrifice, but we can at least make you sound more like one. Wait here until I come back. Stay silent." With no further explanation, she rose and left the storage room.

Grim thoughts pressed in on Morgan as he waited, followed by a flood of homesickness. Even though the idea had been his, he knew there was little chance they would escape the Norns, and that would mean he never saw his mother or his sister Lillia again, or either of his grandparents. He could think of so many things he wanted to tell them all . . .

Even though he was waiting for her, Nezeru's reappearance startled him. No pad-footed cat could have approached him more quietly. She set something down before him; a bundle that at first, in the dim cavern light, looked like a pile of clothing. It was only as he stared at it that he saw the dull glint of bronze fittings and realized she had brought him a suit of armor made from stiffened leather scales and metal rings. Sacrifice armor.

"Where did this come from?" he asked.

She pointed to the back of the armor shirt and grinned without mirth. Blood glistened on the scales. "Knife in the neck. Put it on."

"But why?"

She shook her head in disgust. "Even to get to the archive, we may have to fight every step of the way. You must have armor."

She had just found and killed one of her own kind for him, Morgan realized, as easily as he might pick an apple off a low branch.

He unrolled the bundle. The biggest single piece was a coat of plates held together with what looked like cords of woven metal wire. He lifted it and was astonished at its lightness. "By the Holy Tree, what is this made of? It feels like nothing."

"It is much more than nothing. But only high nobles possess witchwood armor, so these scales are made of *ki'tzi*—in your tongue . . ." She paused. "Bloodwood. It is strong, though not as strong as the witchwood. It will turn away a sword blow or a glancing arrow."

"How do I put it on?"

Her expression, though fleeting, looked like a smirk. "Start by taking off your ragged clothes, mortal boy. Then if you need help, I will help you."

He turned his back on her and stripped off his shirt, then his breeks, and for a moment stood only in his hose, staring down at the cluster of unfamiliar objects he now had to put on by himself, or suffer the indignity of being dressed like a child by this Norn. He heard a muffled noise of amusement and looked over his shoulder to discover that Nezeru was examining him, including his naked back and rump, with frank interest.

Morgan had seldom been inspected so openly, even by the women of Lady Strange's brothel, and he found it oddly uncomfortable. "Why are you staring?"

"Keep your voice down," she said. "I do not stare. I am interested to see how you mortals compare to the men of my own people. You are broader in the chest and shoulders, that is certain, but I think not so long of leg."

"What, you've never seen a mortal's backside before?"

"No. But the novelty is not worth a poem, as we say in Nakkiga."

Morgan could not help feeling outmatched. She could already fight better than he could ever hope to—would this she-creature soon use his native tongue better than he could?

To cover his embarrassment, he picked up the pieces of armor and began trying to fit them onto his body, but they were unfamiliar, and a few were also slippery with blood. At last, as the coat of lacquered plates clattered to the ground for the second time, he heard her voice just behind him.

"You hurry, but to no effect." She bent over and picked up a garment that looked like it was made from Khandian silk and handed it to him. It was indeed slippery as silk, though the weave was rougher. "Pull this on over your loins. Then your . . . *backside*, did you say? . . . will no longer be visible, and you will find it much more comfortable to don the other pieces afterward."

His cheeks so hot he might have spent the day in the sun instead of in the dark depths, he stepped into the breeks, then tied them tight at his waist.

"If you must keep wearing those dirty leggings," she said, "then the next thing to go on will be this." She handed him a padded, sleeveless vest. Her face was intent as she helped tie the knots, and he could see her strange, dark eyes up close.

"Why are you doing this?" he asked as she cinched the last laces.

"Your idea about the archives was a good one," she said, watching her own nimble fingers, not his face. She bent for the two armored sleeves and began attaching them to the vest. "It could be that you might produce one or even two more useful ideas before the Sacrifices kill us, helping me live long enough to kill even more of my enemies. So I have decided to keep you alive if I can—at least for a while."

"I'm honored," he said, sourly as he could.

She raised one of her thin white eyebrows. "So. That is good, then."

The armor of course was more confining than his own clothes, but still felt remarkably light. As he put his belt back on and settled his sheathed sword against his hip, he could not help wondering at the strange road God or fate had put before him.

First a Sitha scholar had to save me, now I've become little more than a squire to a Norn. How noble—how royal. He tried to remember the certainties of his life before the forest, before the nights living in trees, and the giant shadow in Misty Vale, but he could not. He could scarcely remember how wine tasted, or satisfying food. "We haven't eaten anything in a while," he said.

She peered at him over her shoulder. "And will not for a longer while, I suspect."

"Humans don't fight well when they're weak with hunger."

"Humans don't fight well at all, from what I have seen."

It stung. "And when was that?"

She took a moment to answer, as if she had realized too late it was a subject she did not want to pursue. "Once, when mortal soldiers had surrounded us. But they fell apart before our charge like a rotting curtain, and we escaped."

Morgan wondered whether this white-skinned killer could have been one of the Norns who had swept like a storm through the royal army near the North Road—the Norn band with the murderous giant. But he did not ask, uncertain of where such a conversation might lead. "You only saw mortals fight that one time? Those are strong words based on one skirmish. Perhaps the mortals you so dismiss were not trying to kill you but take you prisoner?"

She looked angry. "Ridiculous, if so. No Hikeda'ya Sacrifices, let alone Queen's Talons, would allow themselves to be taken alive. We are not weak. We are not afraid of death or even torment."

"But *you* escaped your own people, didn't you? Isn't that why they're chasing you? You didn't choose to die bravely instead of being captured."

She whirled, and the point of her sword hovered before his throat. He had not even seen her draw it. "I fought my way to freedom. I did not want to, but I had to, because the accusation was false. I killed one and wounded two of my own Sacrifice brethren to escape." Her face looked cold and hard as marble. "Do not think that you are somehow protected and can say whatever you wish to me."

Morgan chose the sensible course: silence. They stared at each other. At last, she sheathed her blade, then turned and led him out of the storage chamber and into one of the passages.

The mortal's words had infuriated her, but deep inside, Nezeru knew that what he had said was not entirely unfair. She was still repeating the code of the Order of Sacrifice as if she had just ended her test of worthiness in the Reach, but the simple, once-inspiring words no longer felt true to her. But had the truth changed, or had she?

It does not matter—not now. At least one of the Sacrifice Order's founding beliefs still held sway: *"Too much thought breeds defeat."* She had heard it first as a young trooper. *"For a warrior, the gift of thought is for strategy, not philosophy,"* she had been taught. "*Leave such idle things to the priests and celebrants. Your wits are used to defeat your enemy, not to question things above your place in the world. To question superiors or even to doubt them for a moment is to doubt the queen and your race, which is to give aid to our enemies. Too much thinking or doubt are both treachery to our people—to the Mother of All—and must be dealt with as such."*

The problem now was to make their way upward through several levels while avoiding those who searched for them, and somehow to reach the archive the mortal spoke of undetected. Then some form of escape might be gleaned from the maps and plans there.

But even if I escape, what then? I have no people, no home. My mother and father must be bitterly ashamed of me if they have heard of my fall, or at least of the lie that Jarnulf and Saomeji have told about me. Where can I go?

For a moment the beautiful simplicity of her early plan pushed away the complications of survival: *If I fight and die bravely, it is all taken from my hands. Others will decide what is remembered of me, what is said.*

But after all the unfairness, did she want others to tell her story when she was dead?

Stop, she told herself angrily. *This is what my teachers meant. Thought is a traitor and not just to the Mother of All, but to myself. Too much thinking and the mortal and*

I will be caught and killed. Something inside her wanted more possibilities, even though she could not imagine what those possibilities might be, or how they could even exist.

Enough. I must go forward until I die or I am free. If I manage to escape, there is time enough then to live among my treacherous thoughts.

Slowly, cautiously, they made their way upward through the labyrinth of Da'ai Chikiza's subterranean passages, avoiding sentries and search parties when they could; twice they could not, and Nezeru slit the throats of Sacrifice sentries. Morgan was awed by how easily and calmly she dispatched them—soldiers who had been her comrades not long ago.

"They are all death-sung," she explained as she wiped blood from her wrist and hand, replying not to something Morgan said but to the look on his face. "What matters it if their lives are taken by my hand or by the Zida'ya? They are no less dead either way and their sacrifice just as real."

Morgan had always thought of combat as something personal, something valorous, man against man, man against fate. Now he was watching something just as intimate, a knife in the dark spilling lifeblood, but much more difficult to conceive of as a contest. Yes, from what he had seen of her astounding prowess, Nezeru would probably have been able to best any of these nameless Norns in a fair fight, even two or more at a time, but they had been given no chance, dispatched by her sharp blade before they even knew their lives were threatened.

But the White Foxes have no souls, he reminded himself. *And they want to kill us—they want to kill all my people, and Tanahaya's people too. Even the beasts of the field just want to feed themselves or defend themselves. The Norns want to destroy everything.*

But how did he know that? *Wait until you have heard what several people you trust say*—that was a phrase he had heard from both his grandfather and father. What did he really know about the Norns? Here in front of him, walking with the silence and fixed attention of a stalking cat, was an actual Norn, but he dared not question her for fear of bringing her former comrades down on them.

Nezeru led them through passage after passage for what felt like the better part of a day, although Morgan had long since given up trying to imagine what time it was in the world outside the dark, damp tunnels. Sometimes they hid; other times they sprinted down corridors as if they were pursued by the demonic Nakkiga hounds, though Morgan had heard nothing behind them. It was strange to surrender oneself so completely to the competence of another, something he had never truly done even when Tanahaya led him. And as they made their way ever upward through the ruined city, digging their way through the fallen stones of blocked passages, clambering over obstructions too big to move, he found himself admiring his guide in a way he had not expected.

His first impression of Nezeru had been of a warrior, not a person. In their short time together, he had also seen flashes of other things—pride, yes, but a sort of humility as well. She was angry, but not at Morgan's own people as much as her own. How had that come to be? His grandfather the king had said the Norns were like demons, creatures with no thought but to destroy mortals; shadowy shapes with pale, corpselike faces that came out of the darkness to murder and then vanish once more. He was not surprised that Nezeru might be hunted by her own folk, but that she had decided to spare Morgan after she no longer needed to use him as a shield—*that* was surprising.

The walls around them were no longer just unfinished stone but were covered with scenes and figures, though mostly hidden by moss and dirt.

"I've seen these carvings . . ." he whispered, but Nezeru silenced him with a sharp gesture. She gestured for him to walk behind her, something Morgan was only too happy to do.

The corridor turned, then they mounted a short stairwell. Morgan saw a high wall full of niches in the chamber ahead, packed with scrolls and books: they had finally reached the archive. Nezeru reached back and halted him with a hand against his chest, then continued alone toward the doorway, crouching so low to the floor that she seemed more spider than two-legged creature. As she slipped through the arched doorway Morgan could hear faint sounds of speech, and although he knew he was defying his protector's wishes, he could not help moving up behind her to see better.

Three figures stood in the faintly lit chamber, one in a long, dark robe, the others clad in the wooden-plate armor of Sacrifice warriors. Morgan held his breath and stayed still, but the two soldiers both turned toward the doorway at the same instant. Nezeru let out a harsh syllable of fury, then her arm moved so quickly he could not follow it and a heartbeat later the hilt of a knife sprouted from one soldier's eye just beneath the rim of his helmet. The Norn warrior's mouth opened in a silent scream and his knees buckled, but Nezeru did not wait to see him fall. She leaped toward the second soldier, who sprang forward to meet her. Two swords, Nezeru's strange gray blade and her enemy's long teardrop of sharpened bronze, came together with a swift, muffled clank. Strangely, at least to Morgan's eyes, the black-robed figure backed away from the struggle until it reached the wall, then stood there in seeming helplessness as Nezeru fought the remaining Sacrifice.

The duel did not last long. The combatants took each other's measure for a few moments, being careful not to trip on any of the rubble littering the floor, jabbing and swiping at each other like snakes tongue-testing the air. Then they closed, grappling for a moment with their free arms, sword on sword, before breaking apart again. The Norn soldier feinted before twisting his wrist to jab suddenly at Nezeru's midsection, but she had already dropped into a crouch and his blade passed harmlessly over her shoulder. She knocked his legs out from under him with a single sweeping kick, and as the Sacrifice tumbled to the ground her blade slid between plates of his armor, piercing him just below the breastbone. He fell forward on his face, twitching, his lifeblood a growing puddle around him, almost black in the dim light.

Both Sacrifice soldiers were dead with hardly any noise and the robed one was cowering against the archive wall. As Nezeru turned, the hooded survivor even raised both hands in what Morgan thought was surrender, but Nezeru did not hesitate before springing forward to attack. The robed creature cried out once, a short, harsh, unrecognizable word, then the shadowy space between the uplifted hands suddenly spread outward, a billowing distortion that made everything Morgan could see seem to stretch and wobble, as a stone dropped into a pond would change a mirroring reflection into chaos. Nezeru stumbled, clumsy as a drunkard. The hooded one cried out again, a note of triumph in the shrill voice this time, and Nezeru crumpled to the ground, her sword clattering from her hand.

Ignoring Morgan as if he were not there, the Norn sorcerer took several steps toward Nezeru. The ice-pale hands spread above her, then the air in the archive room suddenly grew so cold that Morgan's gasp of shock spilled out as steam. Nezeru was squirming, panting for breath and unable to rise, though nothing visible held her. Morgan drew his sword, but for a long, terrified moment he could not force his legs to move.

Do something, you coward! His limbs felt like empty sacks. Was he under the spell too? *Grandfather said the Norns use black magic. How can I fight that?* It felt as if the invisible bonds that held Nezeru had gripped his own legs as well. *But if you don't, she'll die. You'll both die.*

In furious desperation, he drew back his arm and threw his sword like a spear, but Snakesplitter spun wildly, rang as it hit the floor, and bounced forward to strike the robed figure in the ankle. The hooded Norn only staggered back a step, then recovered and turned to stretch his arms over Nezeru again. But Nezeru was no longer beneath him.

The Norn magician froze for a moment in surprise, then Nezeru's head popped up behind the black robed shoulder. So quickly that Morgan could hardly follow, she yanked back the pale, narrow chin and swept her dagger across her enemy's throat. The long, dark line erupted into pulsing blood. The Norn fell back, perhaps trying to call out another spell, but nothing came out of the gaping mouth but dark bubbles. The robed figure took a single failing step before toppling to the chamber floor. When her enemy had at last stopped twitching, Nezeru bent forward, her hands on her knees, gasping for breath.

Morgan came forward cautiously and picked up his sword. He edged closer to the dead Norn and stared down at the blood-drenched robe and sightless, staring eyes. He could see now that the sorcerer was female. "What kind of creature is this?" he asked in a ragged voice as Nezeru straightened up beside him. "What was she doing to you?"

"It is one of Akhenabi's cursed Singers. They are sorcerers, the terror of Nakkiga. But she could have killed me when I was helpless. I think . . . I think she meant to capture me instead." Nezeru's eyes looked haunted. "But why would that be? Do they want me so badly, just to make me an example?"

"I don't know what any of that means," said Morgan, "but if others might be coming, we had better not stay."

She shook her head. "I cannot believe I am still alive after the Singer had me in her death-clutch. It makes no sense."

Morgan said, "I don't like it here. I hate this place, and if I don't see the sky soon, I fear I'll lose my wits. Please, let us do what we have to do so we can leave."

"Yes. You are right." Turning, she surveyed the shelves. "We seek a plan of the city. But where in all these books can we find it? I wish I were a scholar like my father, but I am not."

Morgan had grown used to relying on Nezeru's judgment as well as her ferocity. He looked at the daunting collection of parchments and leather-bound volumes—most of them stacked in niches that seemed more dust than books—and felt only despair. *No, think Morgan, think!* he chided himself. *You have been here before with Tanahaya. What do you remember?*

"From what that Lady Vinyedu told us," he said at last, "this city meant a lot to the Pure. She said they were going to rebuild the dome in the great chamber above us. They were trying to bring the city back to life, I think."

"Why should I care what the *Jonzao* wanted? We are losing time—"

"No, listen! They used their archive quite a lot, I think. Many of the Pure were already in here when Tanahaya and I came—and I think Lady Vinyedu, their leader, was a scholar, too."

"I still do not see where you are leading me."

"If they wanted to rebuild the city, make it more like it was in the old days, then it seems they'd want to use any maps or plans they could find."

She stared at him, midnight-dark eyes intent, lips tight-pressed. Then she nodded. "I think I understand. The *Jonzao* would have known where the plans were. But none of them can still be living, mortal. The Hikeda'ya have swept through this city like a fire."

"But look at the niches," he said, spreading his arms toward the surrounding walls. "Some are filthy. Like they haven't been touched in a hundred years—"

"Likely longer," she said. "Da'ai Chikiza was abandoned eight or nine Great Years ago—close to five hundred years as you mortals reckon it."

" . . . So we should search the ones that look like they've been disturbed more recently," he finished.

This time, Nezeru seemed almost impressed. "Ha! A good thought, mortal. Let us begin looking."

"Fine. And you can call me Morgan, not 'mortal.'"

"As you wish, Morgan."

He knew they were surrounded by enemies, and the search seemed to be taking a very long time, but at last Nezeru clambered down from one of the high shelves with a roll of parchment clutched in her hand.

"I have found something. It is an old plan of the city, but it should help us find a way to Reaching Hand Tower, as you suggested." She frowned as she studied it. "Then we must pray that the rest of your plan will bear fruit."

But she had no sooner begun to unfurl the parchment when the archive suddenly echoed with the sound of distant howling, a noise like the damned screaming in Hell, as if the sounds had been imprisoned inside the map.

"What . . . is that more hounds?" he said, his voice squeaking a little.

"Yes." She turned as the sounds grew louder, her head tipped to one side. "Coming from that passage." She turned again. "And that one. And that, too." She grabbed his arm and yanked him toward one of the remaining doors.

"Where are we going?" he asked.

"It does not matter now. *Run!*"

ERKYNLAND
KYNSLAGH
River Rd.
R. Ymstrecca
Cellodshire
R. Gleniwent
Gleniwent distributary
Meremund
Wentmouth
Goddinsborough
Eywick
Agga's Place
Coldwater R.
Wentmouth Rd.
NEARULAGH HILLS

9

The Man From Home

"You are going to live with rich people, little honeybird," her mother had told her. "It will be a wonderful thing for you." But her mother could not stop crying.

Since her breasts had begun to grow, Jesa had half-expected to be given in marriage to the chieftain's stupid son, who had been following her around since the previous rainy season like a piglet trying to stay close to its mother. She had dreaded the possibility and had prayed nightly to They Who Watch and Shape for a different fate, but she had never imagined being sold to drylanders like a bundle of silktail feathers.

"I don't want to go to Kwanitupul! I don't care about rich people!"

Her mother had wiped her eyes and tried to smile. "But generous Cousin Keleg is going to take you to be a companion to a rich man's daughter." Keleg was a trader. By the standards of Red Pig Lagoon, he was a rich man himself, and even had a large house in the Wran's only city. "Nobody in all our family has ever had such a chance. You will have fine clothes! You will have your choice of husbands!"

"I don't want a husband from Kwanitupul. That place is full of pirates and thieves—you always say it!"

Her mother had shaken her head. "Silly girl. Nobody is going to marry you to a pirate. And anyway, you are not going to stay in Kwanitupul. You will go to Nabban, the greatest city of all, and become a great lady."

Nabban. The very name had filled her with terror. All she knew was that it was a far-away place entirely made of stone and big as the Wran itself. "I won't go!"

"Of course you will." Her mother wiped her own streaming eyes, then wiped Jesa's. "You have the spirit of Green Honeybird. You can make a life for yourself wherever you go."

"You and Baba sold me for money."

Her mother grabbed her arm and squeezed hard. "Do not say that. Cousin Keleg brought your father a gift from the drylanders, but we did not sell you." Her mother burst into tears again. "Ay, daughter! We would never do that—never send you somewhere bad! How can you say that? We only want a good life for you. Nobody from our village has ever had such a chance!"

"Then give it to some other girl. I'm not going. I will stay in Red Pig Lagoon."

But in the end Jesa had gone with Cousin Keleg, crying so hard as his boat left the lagoon that her parents and family watching from the dock were only a shimmering blur. Keleg, who had once visited Nabban, talked endlessly about the glories of the great city during their journey to Kwanitupul, mostly of its size and bustle and endless crowds of people from all over the world. Jesa had thought it sounded monstrous and unknowable.

Before another moon had passed, she was living with a noble family in the terrible drylander city. Only the kindness of Canthia herself, who was less than a year older than Jesa and fascinated with her new companion, had eased the misery of being a stranger in such a strange place.

And now my sweet, kind Canthia is gone. Murdered. Jesa had the baby in her arms and could not wipe away the tears that suddenly returned. The trees that surrounded her were utterly unfamiliar, the landscape foreign. She only knew that she must save her friend's baby and herself.

But she had been finding it more and more difficult to find anything to feed little Serasina. *If only I could have been lost in Red Pig Lagoon, where every tree is like a relative, where I know the value of every plant and animal.* As it was, the only familiar thing she had discovered was the ghant nest—the part of her childhood home she least wanted to revisit.

Jesa had never felt the hands of the gods upon her before, but it was hard to ignore how they had brought only her and this little baby alive out of the terrible day when Duchess Canthia had died. If They Who Watch And Shape had not meant for her to protect this helpless infant, it would have been easy to end Jesa's life with Canthia's—clearly, the gods had wanted her to live. But despite her best efforts, she was failing in her one sacred duty: Serasina was getting thin and fretful, crying almost continuously, with dark circles around her eyes.

At last, on what must have been the fourth or perhaps the fifth day after their escape, with Serasina more unhappy every hour, desperation drove Jesa out of the wilderness. She took the child in her arms and began following the course of the river, hoping to find a village or at least a house where she could beg some milk for the baby.

After almost half a day walking, Jesa began to see signs of human life, though the small, rickety houses were few and far between, and all of them she passed were deserted. Hunger driving her, she even cautiously made her way inside a few of dwellings but could not find food in any of them. Either the inhabitants had little more than she did herself or the houses were simply not in use. She at last discovered a hut with a few signs of habitation, including a few dried fish hanging above the fire pit, and did not hesitate to take them. A part of her felt bad for stealing, but hunger silenced that inner voice, at least for the moment. But even as she chewed on the wonderful, salty flesh, hard as leather but satisfying, she knew that what she had found would be little use to Serasina. She put a little of the chewed flesh between the baby's lips, but the child did not even try to swallow, only shook her head in a fitful way until the morsel fell out again.

Morning turned into afternoon. As she made her way up the bank to avoid a steep, dangerous place along the river's edge, she caught sight of something that made her heart dance a little, a scattering of mud-and-wattle structures in the bend of the river in the valley below, modest huts mostly, with a few bigger farmhouses. For the first time she could also see people, a few on foot, others driving wagons or oxcarts as they made their way down the wide swathe of mud and ruts that served as the town's main road. Where the water spread and calmed a rope-ferry waited, and beyond it a road stretched away to the north.

The queen told us to meet her in Erkynland. That is north from here. If I only follow that road long enough, perhaps it will lead me to her. Jesa felt a powerful need to find Miriamele again. The queen was the first person who had made her feel safe since she had left Red Pig Lagoon.

A white stone manor surrounded by stout walls stood on the headland at the far end of the village, above the river bend. Cultivated fields stretched from the riverbank up the sloping ground and even into the hills themselves. At the end of the village nearest the manor house was a common, once green but now mostly brown as it waited for the winter rain. Around it stood the buildings most important to village life, the bakehouse and the smithy, both trailing smoke from their chimneys.

Blessings to He Who Always Steps On Sand for guiding my feet. She pulled Serasina closer—the wind on the hillside was strong and chill—then headed down into the village.

It was only when several of the townsfolk stopped in the road, not just to watch her pass but to turn and keep watching her, that Jesa realized she was not only unusual because she was a stranger, but because her skin was several shades darker than even the most sun-browned of the villagers. *Have they never seen anyone from the Wran?* she wondered. *Not carrying a pink-skinned baby, I suppose.* She could do nothing to change either of those things except to cover Serasina with a little of her own shawl to make the child's pale complexion less obvious.

Just a fortnight earlier the state of the muddy, pitted road would have made Jesa worry for her clothes and shoes, but she had escaped death and lived for days in the forest, wading in the river mud to pluck weeds and kneeling in the dirt to pound roots for the baby. Her slippers were ruined and her dress nearly as bad. Jesa had never been comfortable with the ways of Canthia's court ladies, who were raised from infancy to wear expensive gowns made from rich fabrics, with wooden pattens to protect their feet from mud, and expensive cloth draped on the chairs and couches to prevent their clothes from snagging. Still, she wondered if anyone would notice her gown, which even in tatters was still clearly something that had once been costly. She did not know for certain that anyone was hunting her, but their pursuers' dreadful, intentional murder of Canthia and little Blasis proved that the bandit attack had not been accidental.

On the main road just at the edge of the commons, she sat down with Serasina in her lap and spread her shawl on the ground beside her, as she had often seen beggars do in the markets of Nabban. The villagers who passed stared at her with unhidden interest and equally unhidden distrust. These folk did not look crushingly poor, but neither did they seem overly comfortable. Almost all of them were on their way to or from the well at the center of the commons, but none of them even met her eyes, let alone gave her anything, though she waited long enough that she heard a distant church bell ring twice. She heard a few of the townsfolk speak Westerling, though their accents were difficult for someone raised on the Nabbanai version. Several seemed annoyed to see her begging, and one even said something about "*dirty racksies,*" a word Jesa did not know but whose import seemed clear.

Not everyone was so standoffish. A farmer in clean clothes, with a prosperous-looking belly, examined her carefully for a moment, then tossed three coppers onto her shawl. A woman who did not look as though she could easily spare it—she had several children of her own scurrying around her like a waist-high thunderstorm—brought Jesa a half cup of fresh milk for Serasina. The woman even stayed and tried to make conversation while Jesa fed the milk to the baby bit by bit from her fingertip and then straight from the cup. The woman's children soon became bored and began playing a loud game all around them as the woman asked Jesa if the baby was hers.

"No. Her mother's dead."

The woman shook her head sorrowfully. Her hair was graying, though she did not look old. She had been pretty once, perhaps two or three children ago, though it was clear from her gnarled hands and slumped posture that her life had not been easy. "And th'art from Racksie or summat like?" she asked.

Jesa suddenly realized the word was the local version of "Naraxi," one of the islands in the Bay of Firannos. *She thinks I'm an islander. But surely this town is not so far north of the Wran that they've never seen one of my folk!*

"I am from the Wran, but I lived in Nabban," she said.

The woman made the sign of the Tree. "Us'd be going now," she said and stood up, though a moment before she'd seemed quite comfortable talking. She stuck out a hand. "Cup."

There were still a few spoonfuls of milk in the bottom, and Jesa tried to think of some way she could save the rest for Serasina, but the baby was now happily asleep, a bubble trembling on her heart-shaped mouth. Jesa downed it herself, and only at that moment realized how desperately hungry she was.

The woman hurried off with her cloud of squalling children, leaving Jesa to look at the sky and wonder whether she should start back or try to find a place to camp closer to the town. She didn't like to beg, but it was tempting to stay near a source of food and milk for the baby. Still, until she knew for certain that no one was searching for them, Jesa decided it would be best to stay in the woodlands near the river.

She had bent to retrieve her shawl and pick up the copper coins, and when she straightened up, it was to find herself face to face with the ugliest man she had ever seen. Jesa gave a little gasp and pulled the baby close.

"Will you come to church?" the stranger asked. He wore a black robe and had a nose so large, lumpy, and red that it looked like a ripe strawberry. His cheeks too were red, and his ears stuck out like the wings of a baby bird trying to fly, with tufts of hair growing in them. Only after staring in frank wonder at this apparition for a moment did Jesa realize that his shaved head and belt of knotted rope marked him out as a priest.

"To church?" she repeated.

He nodded. "My church, yes. It is a place of safety, and it is warm. The nights grow cold here, especially for one of your folk—or a little one like that." He smiled, which did not improve his looks much, because he had a prominent pair of front teeth, like a rodent. "Come, let me show you."

"I should not . . ." she began.

"I would let you follow in your own time," he said, "but my church is in the woods outside town. You might have trouble finding it, especially in the dark. Come, child, there is nothing to fear. God watches everything, but He watches His own house most carefully of all. You will be safe there."

Now keenly aware that she had eaten almost nothing in the past days because she had been working so hard to feed the baby, Jesa let herself be coaxed back in the direction she had come. Serasina, full of milk and contented, at least for the moment, sighed and broke wind.

As the priest led her out of town the harvesters were returning from the fields, and most of them stared at Jesa with unhidden curiosity. She cursed herself for having left the woods at all. Far too many people would remember seeing a dark-skinned woman with a baby following the village priest. But it was too late now, and to run away suddenly would only make her the object of more talk. Angry and a little afraid, she asked, "What is your name, sir?"

He smiled again. "Father Culby, I am called. And just like you, I came to this place as a stranger many years ago. The folk here are gruff and sometimes slow to embrace newcomers, but they are good people. You need not be fearful."

But Jesa *was* fearful, not least because they had left the village behind them now and were making their way up a wide and well-worn track into the wooded hills. She placed no great trust in drylander priests. Many of those she had seen at the Sancellan Mahistrevis had seemed to her just as intent on self-advancement as the rest of the courtiers, and very few of them had spared much courtesy for a Wrannawoman servant unless they hoped to use her to gain greater access to the duchess.

And all for what? she thought suddenly. *Now the Sancellan is burned to ashes and the duchess is dead. The duke, too.* She remembered one of her mother's favorite sayings—"*We are only loaned to the air, then the earth takes us all back.*"

Miri sat on the makeshift bed of river reeds and fishing nets, damp at its center and scratchy in the areas that touched her skin, staring around the single room, the tiny cottage that had become her prison. It was obvious only one person had lived here for a long time. There was only one bed, a pallet in the far corner from where Miriamele was shackled. A single cup and a single bowl sat on the trestle table, and a solitary wooden stool stood like a three-legged sentry beside the crooked stone fireplace. But the only detail that truly mattered was the shackle around her leg and the chain that fixed it to the heavy anchor.

Her captor saw her looking down at the chain. "For ox, that were—'fore him died," he said. "Did break down un's gate and tear up the byre. Sennight or more us had to work to fix all that him ruined, so went to town for a proper chain. Us traded a fine bronze cup found in weir for it."

Miriamele's first impulse was to respond to everything this Agga said with spite, but she did her best to swallow her bile long enough to ask, "To town? What town?"

"Eywick, her is called." He then gave her a long, hard look. "Why askest tha? Dost know it? Hast family nearby?"

For a moment she considered an outright lie—a family of powerful, dangerous sons and a vengeful husband—but that might only mean he'd move her farther into the wilds. "No. I told you, I am not from here. I am a married woman of good repute, though—a mother and a grandmother. You cannot keep me a prisoner."

"Not *prisoner*," he said as if the word annoyed him. "Th'art to be bride. The lady what speaks in dreams, the one dressed all in stars, her has said for us to come to place that is foretold. There us and tha will be married, right and proper."

It was all Miriamele could do not to scream. "But that cannot be! You cannot simply steal any woman you find and demand she become your wife! It's madness."

Agga's face was passive. "Did us not take tha up when tha fell into river and River Man caught tha, tha'dst be dead and drownded, certain. Thus it be proved the lady has gived tha to us."

Miriamele shut her mouth with a snap. *He's a madman*, she reminded herself. *No point arguing. Lived alone by the river for Heaven knows how long and he was probably simple even before solitude turned his wits.*

She watched her captor from the corner of her eye as he deftly mended a fishing net just outside the hut's door, his big fingers moving with surprising grace, placid face empty and fishlike mouth gaping as he concentrated. There was something about this Agga that tugged at her memory. Although she knew she had never seen him before, there was something familiar about the shape of his face, his large, wide-set eyes, even the roughened brown skin on his neck, crosshatched and bumpy as the armored back of a sturgeon.

A Niskie, she realized. *He looks like a Niskie.* A moment later she decided, *No, as if he has Niskie blood. Is that possible?* Dry now but still shivering after the previous day's immersion in the river, Miri stared longingly at the stone fireplace that lay beyond the reach of her chain. As she watched the flames, she remembered her visit to the Niskies in Nabban, in their deep chamber beneath the vast, curving Spar. *Hold a moment,* she thought, *what was it that the Niskie elder, Gan Lagi, told me? "The voices come to us in our dreams and always they summon us north. They come to many, including some folk of Nabban who have only a little Niskie blood in them."*

"Only a little Niskie blood," that's what she said. So they do make children with ordinary folk. And now that she considered it, Agga's babble about the woman who spoke to him in dreams sounded more than a little like what the old Niskie woman had said was happening to many of her kind. *So is that the answer here?* Miri wondered. *Is this benighted creature part Niskie, and having the same weird dreams as Gan Doha and Gan Lagi described?*

For a moment, her excitement at perhaps having solved this riddle made her feel better, until she realized that whatever Agga's motivations, her problem was not with his bloodline or the reasons for his madness, but with the heavy shackle that held her.

Still, she felt something that was almost pity for the brute who had captured her: he was clearly addled in his wits. *But I will kill him if I have to,* she thought. *If he tries to have his way with me, I will gouge out his eyes with my fingernails. I am a queen, by God and His Heavenly angels, and no man will use me against my will.*

While Agga seemed fixed on his mending, Miriamele carefully, quietly traced out the length of her chain, discovering with sad swiftness that her captor had already measured it out: she could get close enough to the fire to warm herself, but not enough to reach anything hot or heavy to use as a weapon. The shuttered window was also out of her reach, as was the door, though it stood temptingly, cruelly open.

From queen of all the lands to a slave with scarce ten cubits of freedom, she thought grimly. *But this will not be the end of me, I swear. I will find a way to loose myself, somehow, God willing.*

Agga glanced over his shoulder for a moment as her chain clinked on the packed earth of the floor. Miriamele retreated to her shabby bed, then hefted the chain that imprisoned her. It was far too strong to break, and there was nothing within reach hard enough to scrape through the links. The cuff around her ankle was a little rusty, but no matter how she pulled it or tried to bend it, it did not move a fraction of an inch. At last she gave up and lay back, closing her eyes against her prison as she forced herself to think carefully through every aspect of her situation. She could not see any way of escaping unless something changed, and Agga did not seem like the type who had many visitors.

But Simon must be looking for me, she told herself. *He will do everything he can to find me, I know that. Soon the roads in this part of the world will be full of Erkynguards, beating the bushes, asking questions. If I can only keep myself alive until then, someone will see me, or hear me, and then I will be freed.*

Heartened by this thought, she curled up and let herself sleep a while, though the bed was uncomfortable. Even through the threadbare blanket, the cords of the piled nets felt like a nest of eels.

"It is not far, now," Father Culby assured her. "Fear not, child! You are young and strong, after all. I am old and my bones ache, but I make this walk every day, rain or sun."

The jouncing was beginning to wake Serasina, who stirred against Jesa's breast. As the trees closed in and the town fell out of sight behind them, Jesa began to feel more and more uneasy. At one point, while pretending to fix one of her shoes, she picked up a stone as big as her palm in case the priest should prove to be less kind than he pretended.

The thick forest on either side of the road abruptly fell away, as though the trees had been commanded to make space, revealing a wooden church, its high spire protruding above the treetops. It looked old and more than a little disreputable: some of the fittings were in sore need of repair, and cobwebs festooned the upper reaches of the tower.

Jesa was suddenly uneasy. "I do not want to trouble you, Father. I should go on my way." She realized that there was no good reason she should leave after walking so far with him. "People are waiting for me," she improvised. "The baby's father." She felt bad lying to a priest, but she did not like the look of this forsaken spot and she did not want to be alone inside with him when the doors closed.

He looked at her in puzzlement. "Surely you would at least like to come in and rest before you go on your way."

"No, no. I thank you, but I have been too long in the town and the others will be worried."

He did not look as though he believed her, but he only nodded. "Very well, then. You must at least have some food to take with you. Come with me."

"I will wait here, if you permit it."

He smiled, a little sadly, and turned toward the church. "Goodwife Carpenter, are you there?" he called.

"Here, Father," someone shouted back somewhere nearby. "And I s'pose tha'll have thy supper now." A moment later a frowning, middle-aged woman appeared from behind the building. She looked quite surprised when she saw Jesa, and more than a little suspicious.

"We have a guest, Goody," the priest announced.

The woman wiped her hands on her shapeless dress and stared at Jesa. "Her is a darkling," she said, as if Father Culby had tried to hide that fact from her.

"We are all God's children, Goody Carpenter, and these children of God are hungry. Can you bring something to eat for her and her baby?" He turned to Jesa. "Are you sure you will not come in, my child?"

Jesa's fears had been allayed a little by seeing the woman, but not enough. "No, thank you, Father."

"Well, I should wait with you, but I am going to have a cup of something strengthening. Would you like a draught yourself? I'd be happy to bring it out to you."

She shook her head. Father Culby headed into the church, clearly eager for his reward after the long walk home.

The sun had only slid a short way down the sky when Goodwife Carpenter reappeared carrying a basket full of food. The woman who seemed so doubtful on seeing her had put together a surprisingly sumptuous meal, a heaping bowl of pottage made from beans and peas, a hunk of black bread, and even a little cold chicken. There was also a cup of milk, still cool from the larder, and when Jesa had finished wolfing her own food she began giving the milk to little Serasina, soaking a clean rag in it and then letting the baby nurse on it.

"Here," said Goody Carpenter, producing a parcel wrapped in leaves from somewhere in her voluminous smock and handing it to Jesa. "A bit more food for tha and thy little 'un to take with." She turned a stern stare first on Jesa, then the baby. "Tha couldst stay with us a bit longer, tha could. Fatten tha both up a bit."

It was very tempting, but though she felt more at ease now, Jesa also knew that bad people might be looking for her, and she did not want to put the generous priest and housekeeper in jeopardy. "I can't, but I thank you."

"Ach, well." The woman shook her head. "Keep the basket. Might do tha good—for carryin' yon girl, like."

"Oh! You are very good." Jesa was a little overwhelmed. She had not expected to meet such kindness in these cold, unfamiliar lands. "I must go, but I want to thank Father Culby."

Goody Carpenter waved her hand, half amused, half irritated. "Father's likely having a sleep now. Comes home, has a cup, falls asleep."

"Then please, thank him for me. I did not expect . . ." After a moment, the correct words came to her. "God bless you both for all you've done."

Now she saw a different look on the housekeeper's face—Goody Carpenter was embarrassed. "Say naught. Be's an old basket."

Jesa was much happier on her way back to the river. Now that she had a few days' worth of food—Goody Carpenter had provided a generous helping of cheese, milk, and bread—she could spend less time foraging and more time trying to decide what to do next. Even the woods seemed less hostile, more familiar, though she still could not name most of the trees. After her meal and long walk and so much time spent with strangers, she was looking forward to settling somewhere with the baby so they could both sleep for a while. Because of this, when she crossed the road nearest the river and began to descend into the valley, a little time passed before she noticed that the undergrowth had been trampled, as if some large creature had recently made its way down toward the water.

She stopped, her heart suddenly speeding. For a moment she wondered if it could be a large crocodile come up from the river. If ghants had traveled this far north, why not one of the biggest swamp monsters as well? But the more she looked at the broad swath of broken stems and crushed grass, the more she felt certain no single beast had done it, not even a crocodile, because the creature would have to be bigger than legendary Grandfather Sekob himself to make such a broad track.

She set down the basket, then clutched Serasina tightly against herself as she got down on her knees to look more closely. She could not help thinking of the times her father's brother had taken her and the other children out to hunt for birds and other small animals. Uncle Pok-Pok had always made a game of it, pointing at an almost invisible track in the sand and demanding to be told what it was. "River-strider or hookbill?" he would ask. "Quickly, younglings! Only one is good to eat. No use following a hookbill."

But whatever had left this trail of destruction through the grass was much, much bigger than any river-strider—even dozens of the birds traveling together could not have trampled down this much vegetation. Then she saw the clear print of a bootheel, and her skin turned cold with sudden fear.

Men, she realized. *At least half a dozen, and they were here not long ago.* Were they looking for her? She could not take the risk. She scrambled to her feet and stared around in terror, almost certain she would discover herself surrounded, but the woods were quiet.

Calm yourself. They have come up from the river and they look to have crossed the road here. It could be farmers looking for a lost animal. Even if they are soldiers, they may have nothing to do with you.

But they might be the same men who had pursued her and Duchess Canthia out of Nabban—the bearded grasslanders who had killed her friend.

Even as her racing blood exhorted her to hurry, Jesa took a moment to make certain which way the tracks were leading, so she could go the other way. If the ones who had made them were soldiers, they were not very stealthy. It was not only marks on the ground that told her: they had broken off so many low branches in their passage that she could have found their trail in the dark.

When she was certain that the tracks were coming up from the river and not toward it, she followed the river road downstream for a good distance. When she had walked a while without seeing further trace of human presence, she turned and headed down toward the water.

By the time she reached the riverbank the sun was dipping low in the sky. Jesa knew she had perhaps as little as an hour of daylight left. Her arm was aching from cradling Serasina, and she was exhausted and thirsty. She found a place of thick undergrowth a few dozen paces up the bank, sheltered from the slanting sun, then removed the food Goody Carpenter had provided and made a little nest for the baby in the basket, wrapping the blanket tightly around her. She straightened a few bits of fern to hide the makeshift cot more effectively from view, then made her way down to the river, staying close so she could hear if Serasina awoke.

After she had taken a long drink, she kicked off her shoes and wiggled her tired feet in the shallows at the river's edge, but the day was swiftly growing colder and she did not want to be away from the baby for very long. She had just put her shoes back on when she heard the loud sound—*ker-plunk!*—of something splashing in the water just a short distance away.

A big fish, she told herself. *But I have plenty to eat now.*

Still, she could not rid herself of her crocodile and ghant worries—she did not want something hungry coming up the bank while she and the baby were sleeping—so she went a little distance downstream and around a bend in the river to where the water widened and slowed to see what had made the noise. As she stepped past a patch of tall reeds, she came upon a man standing at the edge of the backwater with something in his hand. As she watched, he drew back his arm and threw it. The rock sailed through the air and splashed into the wide part of the river—*ker-plunk*. But it was not his mere presence that had startled and frightened her. She recognized him.

She might have made a noise of surprise, or he might simply have chanced to turn then, but he saw her immediately. He was dressed for a battle or a rough hunt, but though his eyes had at first widened in surprise, now he smiled as though he had been given a touchingly valuable gift.

"By the goodness of God!" he said, quickly making the sign of the Tree on his breast. "This is a fortunate meeting—heaven-sent, surely! Is it really you, girl? Can it be possible? I have been searching up and down and all through this country for days, but here you are."

Jesa waited, still as a startled deer.

"Do you not remember me?" asked the handsome, dark-skinned man. "I am Viscount Matreu of Spenit. I had the fortune to help you and your mistress that day when you were attacked in St. Lavennin's Square. After that, you brought me messages from her many times." He spread his hands in a show of harmlessness. "Come, you recognize me now, don't you?"

Jesa stared. "I remember you, yes." There were many reasons she should welcome a familiar face after so long alone, but her racing heart would not slow. She moved back a few steps as Matreu turned from the river and came toward her.

"Then you know I mean you no harm." His smile was a fine thing to see—or should have been. "In fact, I am seeking your mistress, Duchess Canthia—and her infant daughter, of course. I want to help them to safety. Can you take me to them?"

10

Blood and Poetry

Viyeki had been part of Nakkiga's intricate and treacherous Hamakha court his whole life. He had thought nothing could surprise him for more than a few moments. He had been wrong.

Being sent north by the queen was not something he'd expected, but Utuk'ku's machinations were seldom clear to those who served her. The fact that his Builders were far outnumbered by General Kikiti's Sacrifices was unusual too, since they seemed bound for the middle of nowhere. He knew better than to try to anticipate his overlords' military objectives, but nothing had prepared him for the unexpected presence of Hakatri on the expedition.

The revenant, or whatever he or it was, traveled in a wagon not unlike the queen's, a boxlike affair pulled by a team of eight huge black goats. Inside the wagon, his secretary Nonao had breathlessly informed him, the once-dead Zida'ya lay like a corpse in a witchwood sarcophagus, although Nonao had also told him that the Sacrifices intended to move Hakatri to a litter when they left the road.

Viyeki had no idea what any of this meant. Where were they going? Why so many of Kikiti's warriors? And why would they leave the road, except to strike out across the icy wastelands to the far north of the captured mortal fortress—lands all but uninhabited except for the troll-folk in their distant mountain retreats?

As the procession descended a long, sloping section of the road, he could see the shape of Hakatri's wagon. Other than a dark-clad group of Singers following just behind it, led by the rune-marked Sogeyu, the amount of space between the wagon and all the other marchers proclaimed that Viyeki was not the only one made uneasy by their silent, encoffined guest.

It reminded him uncomfortably of how they had retreated from the mortal Hayholt after the Storm King's failure, bearing the body of the fallen High Marshal, Ekisuno. But although Viyeki and his then-master Yaarike had disliked carrying the marshal's monstrously heavy casket on a dangerous retreat, he had never had to worry about what the body inside that casket was thinking, or what it might do next.

What have we become? We pull the dead back into the world as heedlessly as an angler yanks an eel from a pool. How can I keep my Builders safe, as well as the mortal slaves we brought with us, in the midst of such madness? Impossible tasks seemed to have been stacked, teetering, on other impossible tasks. How could a mere official like Viyeki, an outsider in the court, hope to maneuver over such deadly ground, operating as he was in a cloud of enforced ignorance? He was being sent to perform presumably important work in an unfamiliar land, in the company of the restless dead, but he still had not been given the slightest hint of what that task might be.

Calm yourself. Try to think. What would Magister Yaarike have done? Viyeki's mentor had always been the most practical of leaders, and chief of his lessons had been to expect confusing orders. The Maze Palace was a viper's nest of intrigue and had been so especially during the queen's long sleep. Many Nakkiga nobles had received conflicting orders in those years due to feuding factions in the ruling Hamakha clan. At least two nobles Viyeki knew of had only been able to resolve their dilemmas by suicide, which at least saved their families and estates. Several others had simply fallen from favor and been executed.

But I am not even being given a side to choose, he thought grimly, *so how would Yaarike have advised me to proceed?* His memories of his old master were still sharp—the long face so wry, so unsurprised by the mistakes and failures of others—and Viyeki suddenly remembered a moment during their journey together back to Nakkiga after the Storm King's fall. They had been trapped in a border fort by an army of vengeful mortals, facing what seemed hopeless odds. Viyeki had been preparing himself for the end that was surely coming, then Yaarike had asked him, *"But what if we do not die?"*

Back in that grim hour, Viyeki had not understood his master's words, not truly. He had believed it to be only the high magister's way of telling him not to give up. But now he recalled something else Yaarike had taught him and glimpsed a deeper meaning: *"When you discover a flaw in stone, do not examine only the flaw but how it formed, what it will do if left alone, and how the stone around it has responded."* Now, years later and in a strange land, Viyeki thought he finally understood what Yaarike had meant. His master's two thoughts were connected, like a worker, his hammer and chisel, and even the stone itself—all part of the same thing.

Perhaps I am not the one who is flawed. The idea was so startling that he looked around as if someone might have overheard his secret thoughts, but not even his secretary was looking at him. *Perhaps something is wrong with the way we live.*

It was terrifying even to think such a thing, of course. His distrust of those above him had grown steadily since the day he had set out on this confusing mission, and now it seemed he could not escape his own doubts any longer. Could his entire world—all his knowledge, his every belief—be founded on lies from top to bottom? Was the infallibility of the Hamakha and even of the Mother of All only a mask, like the queen's calm silver face, hiding ultimate corruption?

But this possibility was too frightening, and it had come far too fast. Viyeki recoiled from these new thoughts as if he had suddenly awakened to discover he had sleepwalked to the edge of a fatal precipice.

Madness, he scolded himself. *Nothing is perfect—nothing can be—but to lose belief in the meaning of everything you know will cast you down into chaos and despair. The creature in the wagon is a weapon, that is all. A weapon against the queen's enemies—our enemies.*

But though Viyeki pushed away the treacherous thoughts before they could overwhelm him, he still could feel something stirring inside him, a seedling whose ultimate bloom he could not imagine, and it frightened him badly.

The company of Sacrifices and Builders followed the river northward as it ran along the base of the rocky Yi'ire Mountains, the range that mortals called the Wealdhelm. The southern end was mostly low, rocky hills, but the farther north they marched, the higher the peaks became. To Viyeki's trained eye, the saw-toothed range looked to be part of a single granite mass, although by the dawn light he could make out greenstone belts pressed into the mountains' wrinkled hides, and a few signs that there might be seams of limestone running through them as well. But since he still had no idea what was expected of him and his workers and where they would be expected to do it, it was useless to do too much planning.

"Is it permitted to inquire yet about our destination, Serenity?" Viyeki asked when he next found himself riding beside Pratiki.

The prince-templar smiled as at a charming but slightly wearying child. "Certainly, you may ask—but I am still not permitted to answer. Only patience will bring you what you seek, High Magister."

Viyeki nodded. "I thank you for your honesty, Prince-Templar. I am certain you have the needs of many on your mind."

They rode for a little while in silence along the ancient road between the base of the mountains and the narrow silver strip of river mortal men called Nartha. Viyeki was faintly ashamed he could not remember its old, proper name. "It is sad to realize how long it has been since our people walked freely here," he said.

"All that is changing. The mortals will retreat from these places, then they will all regain their true names again."

"So is that what the queen intends—to push the mortals out of these lands?" Viyeki thought it much more likely that she intended to exterminate them to the last mortal child, but he wondered whether Pratiki would admit it.

"The plans of the Mother of All are not for us to wonder about, Magister." This time Pratiki's smile was colder. "I know you are wondering at certain things—certain unexpected facets of Queen Utuk'ku's intentions—but you must not try to make me talk about something that you know I should not."

A chill fell on him. "I apologize for letting my desire to prepare get the better of my good sense, Highness."

Pratiki relented a little. "It is a forgivable offense, of course. I know you wish to begin planning your work for our queen, and even I have been surprised by some aspects of our task." The prince-templar's face had become unreadable. "But you must never forget how much must still remain in shadow, and for good reasons. You are loyal, good Viyeki, I do not doubt that, but is everyone you know? Are all your Builders as loyal as yourself?"

Viyeki felt a flare of injured pride. "With all respect, Serenity, my Builders are as loyal as any order, and I say that with no fear of being proved wrong. There are always some in any group who are weak or troubled—even in the queen's service. Witness the deluded nobles who have been put to death over the years for treason, and whose ashes are scattered over the Fields of the Nameless. But I will hold my Builders up for loyalty against any other order, even the Sacrifices."

Pratiki gave him an odd look. Viyeki wondered if even his cautious mention of executions had gone too far. "Interesting," the prince-templar said at last. "I would follow this idea a little further." Pratiki turned to one of his clerics. "Ride ahead to General Kikiti and ask him if he would be good enough to join the high magister and myself."

Kikiti soon appeared. His carefully blank expression suggested his displeasure at being summoned to a conversation to which the High Magister of Builders had been invited first. "You called for me, Serene Highness?"

"Yes, General. I was having a discussion with High Magister Viyeki and thought I would ask your opinion as well."

"Of course, Serenity." But his slightly tense posture suggested that Kikiti could think of several more important uses of his time.

"Magister Viyeki and I were speaking of loyalty. I wished to know your opinion about it."

"It is the only thing that matters," Kikiti said immediately. "Without it, every other tie or connection is as frail as a cobweb."

"And by this, you mean loyalty to the Mother of the People, yes?"

Kikiti nodded, a single brief stab of his long chin. "Of course, Highness. I assumed that was what you meant. There are other kinds of loyalty—to one's order, to one's clan, one's family—but they are all wisps compared to loyalty to the queen."

"Ah." Pratiki nodded. "Of course. But what about loyalty to our race—to the Hikeda'ya?"

Kikiti almost smirked. "Loyalty to the race *is* loyalty to the queen." His eyes narrowed in his hard-boned face. "Did High Magister Viyeki suggest something different, Serenity?"

"No, no," said Pratiki, laughing a little as though he was enjoying the exchange, which was definitely not true for Viyeki. "Let me pose a question to both of you, then," he said. "I trust you will answer as truthfully as you can. Since we are discussing loyalty, let us pretend the queen says to one of you, 'I want nothing more of you. I do not want to hear or see you again. I command you to end your life now.' What do you do?"

"End myself," declared Kikiti without hesitation. "What else could I do, my lord? And I would do it gladly, because the Mother of All knows all ends, while I am but a plain soldier."

You say that with a little more pride than you realize, Viyeki thought. *Pride that goes beyond just being loyal.*

"High Magister?" Pratiki asked. "What say you? Does the general have it right?"

Even after his shocking thoughts earlier, he would not fall into such an obvious trap—so obvious, in fact, that he felt certain the prince-templar meant him to see it. "If the queen told me to kill myself? I would kill myself, of course. What else could I do? What else could any Hikeda'ya do?"

"So, you both agree on that," said Pratiki. "Then let me ask one more question. Let us say that the queen has given an order to you just as I said before, but as you kneel before her with weapon in hand, poised to end your own life, you see an assassin appear from the shadows behind her, though no one else has seen them yet. What do you do in *this* circumstance, General Kikiti?"

"Nothing," he said with flat finality. "Nothing but end my own existence, as the Mother of All told me to do."

"But what of the assassin?"

"It is none of my affair and it would not stop me from plunging my blade into my heart. Perhaps it is no assassin at all, but only a test of my courage, and the Garden would not receive me if I betrayed my debt to the queen, even in fear for her life. How could I be so foolish as to assume that I know more than our beloved mistress, the Mother of the People? No, even were the whole of Nakkiga to crumble down upon us, I would pay no attention. I would hasten to take my life, as I had been commanded."

"Interesting," said Pratiki. "And instructive. Viyeki?"

Viyeki thought he could discern something that General Kikiti, in his self-absorbed bravado, could not: Pratiki's questions had been shaped like tools, to serve some special purpose, though Viyeki could not discern it. "Do we speak of what we would wish to do, Serenity," he asked, "or what we think we would truly do?"

"A distinction worth noting, but why do you ask?"

"Because in all honesty, Serenity, my deep desire would be to selflessly and without hesitation carry out the queen's order. But I fear in such a situation, I might pause—to my shame."

"What? You admit you are disloyal?" Kikiti grimaced like a horse champing at its bit.

"Nothing of the sort." Viyeki spoke as carefully as he could. "But I am trying to be honest. If I were sentenced to self-slaughter and saw what looked like harm to the queen about to happen, I might indeed hesitate, my concern for her safety overwhelming at least for a moment even my desire to promptly obey her."

"Bah. These are weasel words." Kikiti seemed angry, as though he thought

Viyeki was trying to trick him or the prince-templar. "Loyalty cannot be measured. Either you obey your queen in every particular or you are a traitor."

"A forceful and gratifying answer, General Kikiti," said Pratiki with a graceful hand-gesture. "Thank you for your illuminating contribution. And I thank you, too, Magister Viyeki. You are both the kind of servants that our beloved queen needs, despite your differences."

It was perhaps the dozenth time that Tzoja had waited on the Mother of All and it still terrified her as much as it had the first time.

I will never grow used to this—never! The queen lay on her stomach beneath the silk covering as Tzoja, blind under her eyeless mask, let her fingers trail down the bumps of Utuk'ku's spine, which felt prominent as the links of a chain. *She has so little flesh on her.*

The queen was as silent as usual, her breathing so slow it was hard to detect. Tzoja went about her palpations just as quietly, knowing better than to make any comment without being spoken to first. Needing to ask questions had been terrifying, and she was more than willing not to repeat the experience. This time, she would cherish the silence.

It seemed that the queen, though, had other ideas. Her words suddenly dropped into Tzoja's thoughts, heavy as stones tumbled into a pool, sending ripples everywhere. *The tincture you gave me last time you came to us. What was in it?*

Tzoja was now full of apprehension. Had she made the queen uncomfortable, somehow? Even worse, sick to her royal stomach? "Agate mushroom, Great Majesty, mixed with a spirit made from maidenhair fern. I learned it from one of the Astaline sisters." She stopped herself before she began babbling about the woman who had taught her how to make it, a former nun from Perdruin who had looked far older than the immortal creature lying before Tzoja now, and who had taught her several tricks for making spirits.

Agate mushrooms. Maidenhair fern. Utuk'ku sounded coldly amused. *Who would have guessed? These things have been thought useless among my physicians. Perhaps they are, for those who eat of the witchwood fruits. But the last of those fruits are gone now, and even at this moment the last of the* kei-soma *leaves my body forever.*

Tzoja had heard of *kei-soma* before but was not certain exactly what it meant. She guessed it had something to do with the spirit or effect of the witchwood on those who consumed it. But the long silence that followed made it seem as though she should speak. "Did my tinctures make you feel ill, Majesty?"

No, little mortal. They did not. In truth, I feel stronger than I have in days, though I still feel my dreadful age in every bone and sinew. Still, your elixirs have brought me a little ease, and for that I thank you. Make more for me. Make me enough to last through the final weeks of the Moon of the Ice Mother.

Tzoja did a quick calculation—she would need three months' worth! "Forgive me, Great Majesty, I beg you, but I do not think I have enough of the elements left to make such an amount. It might be hard to find maidenhair fern at this time of the year."

You will find it, or if the weather is too harsh for it, you will grow it in one of the wagons. It was not a question but an order. *You have only a few days to discover some before I leave to travel south with my Sacrifice army. If you need help to find it growing wild, you will be given such assistance as you need.*

Tzoja was surprised, and for an instant forgot her self-pledge not to speak except in response to the queen's own questions. "Your pardon, Great Majesty, but I may have a better chance of finding it farther south, where the winter is not so advanced."

You are not going south with me, mortal. That is why you will prepare me an ample supply, to last me while I travel to the site of ancient Asu'a. I will not need you if the mushroom and fern spirit alone can suffice me.

And that, to Tzoja, sounded more than a little like a death sentence. Stunned and fearful, she busied herself tapping the queen's back above the lungs and listening to the sounds, but her mind was spinning.

Enough of this, said Utuk'ku, her thoughts now hard and sharp, jabbing into Tzoja's head like nails. *Enough with this pointless feeling and thumping. You have finally done something to earn your life, at least for a little while. You have been given a task, mortal. Go and do it.*

Fighting back tears of apprehension, Tzoja hurriedly picked up her few implements and knocked at the door for release. The tall Anchoress who opened it took her arm and steered her out of the queen's carriage-chamber. Tzoja was grateful for the Hikeda'ya woman's strength, because at that moment her own legs were neither strong nor steady.

The morning's light was growing brighter and brighter. After conferring with the prince-templar, Kikiti and his officers decided to make camp and wait out the worst of the day's glare. Viyeki, still reeling from the frightening uncertainty that had swept over him earlier, waited at the edge of the meadow, watching the Sacrifices erect a makeshift wall of sharpened stakes around the site. Unsurprisingly, only Sogeyu's Singers seemed willing to make camp anywhere around Hakatri's black wagon, which stood by itself on a knoll like a crouching black beetle. As Viyeki looked for Nonao and his other servants, he saw the prince-templar near a broad stand of pine trees, giving instructions to the pair of clerics that followed him almost everywhere, so he headed in that direction. When the prince-templar had dispatched his underlings, he saw Viyeki waiting and beckoned him over. "Come and get out of the wind a little, Magister."

"You are very kind, Serenity. I was hoping to speak to you again—"

Pratiki made a hand-gesture that Viyeki had never seen a Hamakha noble make, a crude swipe that the common folk of Nakkiga often used—*Needless apology.* "You are wondering why I called for that little show with the general." The prince-templar's voice was calm, even friendly, but Viyeki could see that he was looking across the meadow at the solitary wagon and the dark-robed Singers encamped around it.

"I confess that it did not seem as idle a bit of conversation as you made it appear."

The prince-templar smiled—a thin, surprisingly cheerless line. "General Kikiti is exactly what he should be, Viyeki, hard and sharp as an ax blade. Subtlety of strategy is useful in war, but subtlety in loyalty is not, Magister—not even in one of the queen's highest commanders."

Viyeki nodded but did not dare reply until he understood the prince-templar better.

"However, in times ahead," Pratiki continued, "it is possible that such simple, dogged, unthinking loyalty as Kikiti's may not best serve Her Majesty and the race of which she is the matriarch and the exemplar."

"I do not understand, Serenity," he said carefully.

"Of course you do not. That is not your fault." For a moment some of Pratiki's aloof manner seemed to fall away, and Viyeki saw something troubled in the prince-templar's subtle, cautious face. "These are strange days, Magister. Our holy witchwood is all but gone, and because of that, the oldest of our Hikeda'ya folk are in danger—including the queen herself." Even Pratiki, for all his high rank, could not suppress a swift look around to see if anyone was listening. "The Mother of All spent more than half a Great Year in the *keta-yi'indra*, the Death-like Sleep, and now she wages war against the mortals once more. Even more unusual, our queen has left the shelter of Nakkiga for the first time in the memory of any living being but herself. Yes, these are strange, strange times."

Viyeki took a small, calculated risk. "I still do not grasp what this has to do with loyalty, and with my debating General Kikiti at your behest, Serenity."

"I will do my best to be open, Magister, though my upbringing and my responsibilities both weigh against it."

Pratiki glanced around again, which only made Viyeki more fretful. If even the prince-templar was worried, how was the middling-noble leader of the Builders supposed to feel? "It may be," Pratiki continued, "that in the days ahead, those who wish to protect the legacy of the queen and the survival of our race may need something more than blind, unthinking allegiance to every ancient custom of our people. We may need thought that is more . . . versatile. And if our leaders cannot provide it, how can we expect our underlings, those of our race upon whom our survival depends, to understand a new world?"

Viyeki was doing his best to absorb Pratiki's words without stumbling into the dangerous terrain of too many assumptions. "Help me better grasp your thought, Serene Highness," he said. "You fear that we as a race are too hide-bound. You fear that those of more instinctive temperament, like General Kikiti, may not be best suited for what lies ahead."

"For the unknown future that lies before us, yes. For what change may bring to our people—and what change may demand from them. Yes, you have grasped a good part of my meaning, I think." Pratiki nodded, but he still did not look happy. "But there are many who would hear our speaking now and call it treason."

"Treason, Serenity?"

"You know it is true, High Magister. For the sort of whom we speak, like brave General Kikiti and very many others, anything that has not been repeated over and over and over is suspect, and any wisdom not found in the pages of *The Five Fingers of the Queen's Hand* is untrustworthy. But I suspect, like your honored mentor Yaarike, you are not quite so rigid in your certainties or inflexible in your methods. Is that true?"

Viyeki was filled with both exhilaration and sudden terror. Everything seemed balanced on a knife's edge. The distant black wagon was a mote at the edge of his sight. "I can only hope I am worthy of your confidence, Serenity."

But just as Viyeki had done earlier, the prince-templar seemed to have reached the edge of some inner cliff and was suddenly reluctant to take another step. "I should not repay such trust with danger," Pratiki said, frowning just a little. "I have not the right."

Viyeki could only wait.

"Let me at least share this with you," Pratiki said at last. "What I say may sound like something less than utter loyalty to our queen, but I assure you it is not. As you know, I am of the Hamakha. My own line is one of those closest in blood to the queen herself. Because of this, I have a particular duty to keep our people safe."

"Of course, Serenity."

"But to keep our people entirely protected, it is necessary to think about possibilities we would rather not consider. Unthinkable possibilities, many would say. Things that are treason even to imagine."

Now Viyeki's heart was beating very fast. "I am listening, Serenity," was all he dared say.

"Then I ask you, what would happen if, on some terrible, nightmarish day, we lost the Mother of All?"

Viyeki felt himself sway a little, as though the earth itself rolled in unease. "Lost?"

"As I said, the witchwood is now gone. No one has ever lived as long as our worshipful queen—but can even she live always? And in a world without Queen Utuk'ku—may it never come to pass!—what would happen to her people? *Our* people?"

Viyeki felt as if thick fog had suddenly surrounded him, though the midday air was frosty clear. "I cannot answer such a thing," he said, barely able to form the words.

"Of course not. I am her kin, member of her clan, and I can hardly speak of it either. But I ask again—if such a dreadful thing were to come to us, what would happen to our people?" He spread his fingers. "I do not expect you to reply, Magister. It was difficult enough for me even to imagine such a possibility. But in the end, I did. And once I began, I have never ceased to think about it."

It was what Viyeki had waited for—the prince-templar finally opening to him, taking a risk on Viyeki's loyalty. He was fearful, wondering how far the prince-templar would go, but he could not leave Pratiki to wonder whether he had betrayed himself. "You are very brave, Serenity, to take such risks for the sake of your people."

Pratiki stared at him for a long moment, then seemed to decide that the die had been cast. "In any case, good Viyeki, if such a day ever came, when the Hamakha had to rule without the justice and wisdom of our ageless queen, the world would be very different."

There was no need to reply to that.

"And so I have considered not just the practical things that would have to be addressed," the prince-templar continued, "but also matters of philosophy. How could our people survive in a world without their ageless matriarch? And it occurs to me that there are two ways to rule a people—blood, and poetry."

This seemed an abrupt shift, but Viyeki knew he was too far into dangerous territory to simply turn back. "Blood and poetry, Serenity? Please explain this to me."

"What I mean is that the ruler of many, of an entire people, must use both sorts of persuasion, both fear of punishment—the tool I call 'blood'—but also the exhortations of shared history and shared belief. I call that second tool 'poetry' because it is argument elevated to art, persuasive even to those who do not realize they are being persuaded. It does not call on fear or blind loyalty, but on that which is highest in all of us. Those like Kikiti respond to blood. Others—you are an example, Magister—must have poetry. They must live for something better than mere existence—than mere *loyalty.*"

"You praise me too much, Serene Highness. But I thank you."

"I doubt that I do, Magister Viyeki. You are known as a wise and practical person, a noble whose word can be trusted, and who calls out the best in others."

It was all Viyeki could do not to ask which nobles had said these kind things about him. *Even in such a momentous conversation, I feel the urge to leap toward flattery like a fish toward any shadow moving on the water's surface.* "I still think you set me too high, Serenity."

"Do not offer yourself in the market for a few iron drops, Magister. But I would say more, and also hear your thoughts." He fixed Viyeki with a long look. "Know that you speak only to me, and that anything you say will enter my ears but never pass my lips."

"Of course, Serenity."

Pratiki nodded. "Here is where I ask for your wisdom. First, I must tell you that there are some among the nobility of Nakkiga who are not entirely in support of this war against the mortals. They revere the queen, of course, as we all do, but they also fear that another such war could be dangerous, even unwise, especially when we are just regaining our strength after the disaster of Ineluki's failed scheme."

It was all Viyeki could do to keep his mouth from sagging open in astonishment. He had never heard a noble speak of opposition to any of the queen's directives, let alone of an undertaking as vast and serious as the new war against the mortals. As he stood, shocked and surprised, the sound of Sacrifices pounding stakes into the ground floated across the meadow.

"Now, since you are an honorable and upright noble," the prince-templar continued, "and one of the queen's high magisters, I am curious what you think of . . . such nobles as those. Of their ideas and fears."

There. After a show of almost unbelievable openness, Pratiki was asking Viyeki to condemn himself in return, or at least to put himself permanently in the prince-templar's power. If it came to dispute, nobody would believe a magister from a middling clan like the Enduya over one of the queen's own Hamakha kinsmen. But why else would he ask? Surely Pratiki didn't believe that even after his own admissions, Viyeki could afford to do anything but denounce these perhaps imaginary nobles? So that must be what he expected. He cleared his throat as unobtrusively as he could. "Anyone who would question the queen's wisdom, even indirectly by criticizing one of the queen's most important plans, would have to be a fool, a traitor, or both, Serenity."

The prince-templar smiled. "Just so, just so. But what would you recommend be done with such fools and traitors?"

"I would despise them, of course," Viyeki replied after a moment's careful thought. "But I would not execute them immediately."

Pratiki raised an eyebrow. "Truly? But you called them 'fools or traitors'—why should either be kept alive?"

"So our rulers could learn how they fell into such error. If they were merely foolish and not irredeemably treacherous, something might be learned from them that would protect other potentially foolish but otherwise useful nobles from tumbling into the same mistakes."

"Ah. Then you would not, as General Kikiti would no doubt advocate, destroy them at the first sign of mistaken thinking?"

"Not if they were otherwise no danger to the queen and our race." Viyeki could only pray that he had given an answer that Pratiki would find acceptable, since he still had no real idea what the prince-templar was trying to accomplish with this increasingly dangerous conversation.

"Interesting." Pratiki nodded slowly. "As I suspected, High Magister, you are more inclined to poetry than blood. I thank you for your honestly. I hope you have found our talk enlightening."

Enlightening? wondered Viyeki. *Staggering*—that was a better word. *Breath-*

taking and *bewildering* might describe it as well. But all he said was, "And I thank you, Serene Highness, for sharing so much of your time and thought with me."

"No Hikeda'ya noble who loves our queen and our people could give any less than his best, High Magister."

It is a high cliff indeed that I stand on now, Viyeki thought as he left the prince-templar beneath the tree and went to find his accommodations in the meadow camp. This time, he kept his gaze away from the troubling, solitary black wagon. He knew he would be lying awake for hours, thinking back over all the things that Pratiki had said. The harsh winter daylight made him feel dizzy, and he sped his steps to get out of the sun. *Yes, a very high cliff—higher and riskier than any place I have ever stood before.*

11

Cloudfoot

"The Year-Torch has kindled in the west," Jiriki said. "You must finish your journey, sister—and I must begin mine."

"I hate this parting, dear Willow-switch." Her voice had an unusual tang of bitterness. "Things have changed so swiftly and all for the worse. It is hard to believe that when the last Great Year ended, we were all in Jao é-Tinukai'i together—you and I, our mother and father and First Grandmother."

"May the Garden give them all shelter." Jiriki made the sign for deep mourning.

"Do not lament our mother Likimeya yet," said Aditu gently. "She still lives."

"I know that. But I fear we may never share her wisdom again."

The mortal Aelin, Count Eolair's descendant, caught Jiriki's eye from across the cavern. Jiriki touched his sister's arm, then went to him. *"Did you wish to ask me something?"* he asked in the mortal Westerling tongue.

Sir Aelin darted a glance toward Yeja'aro, who was lacing up his soft deerskin boots. *"Isn't there anyone else who can help us find our way through the hills?"*

"Yeja'aro is a skilled tracker and a gifted warrior," Jiriki told him. *"I can think of no one who would give you a better chance to get past the Hikeda'ya forces. They are all around us now. Our scouts say there are hundreds in Da'ai Chikiza, and many times that in Naglimund on the far side of the hill."*

"But he tried to kill me!"

Jiriki had no ready answer. *"Yeja'aro is fierce and sudden,"* he said at last. *"But he attacked you in a confusion of passion, unprepared for the presence of mortals in our secret lodge. It was simply a mischance of fate."*

"Perhaps, but he seems to hate our kind. That makes it hard to trust him."

"His uncle, as well as my mother, were both badly wounded by men of your people, so his grudge is not beyond understanding. Still, Yeja'aro may not like mortals, but he hates failure far more, and protecting you is now his sworn and sacred duty. Fear not. And heed well what he tells you."

Aelin did not seem much reassured, but at last waved his hand in a gesture of resignation.

Now it was Yeja'aro's turn to seek out Jiriki, and he did not wait long. "Are you so intent on shaming me?" he demanded, "that you make me the nursemaid of Sunset Children?"

"There is no shame in helping others," Jiriki replied. "Nor is there shame in giving aid to these particular mortals. Perhaps you are not aware, because your uncle has taught you only warcraft, that the Hernystiri were the first of their kind to ally themselves with our folk."

"Yes—but only to fight against other mortals," said Yeja'aro.

"Who else would they fight?" Jiriki's voice lost a little of its diplomatic calm. "In those days, the Hikeda'ya and we Zida'ya were not at war with each other. But this is beside the point. Sinnach and his Hernystirmen fought and died beside us on the killing field of Ach Samrath, as the mortals name it. Before that, just as many of the Hernystiri mortals fell with us at the Western Gate. Were those deaths without meaning? Strange to hear a warrior suggest such a thing."

Yeja'aro did not immediately reply. "You have never cared for me," he said at last. "You have always thought that I am not good enough—not good enough for your sister and not good enough to father a child for Year-Dancing House."

"There is much you do that does not please me, it is true," Jiriki admitted. "You have drunk too much at the spring of Protector Khendraja'aro's wisdom, which to me has a sour taste. Like him, you think that all problems have a single solution, and that solution is greater strength. But I have never scorned you, and I trust my sister Aditu's wisdom so much that I bow to it and set it above my own. If she sees in you a fitting father for her child, then I am certain she is correct."

It was plain that this answer did not much please Yeja'aro: he touched his fists together before his chest in a gesture of disagreement before he moved away.

"Aditu! Ayaminu! Liko!" Jiriki called. "Yeja'aro and the mortals are leaving. Come and say your farewells, for we never know when any of us may meet again in this world."

He watched his sister speak quietly and at length with the father of the child she carried, but when Yeja'aro and his mortal charges had set out, Jiriki did not question her about what she had said. Instead, he went to Ayaminu and her grandson, Liko the Starling. "I will be riding north with you until Red Campion Bridge," he told them. "But on the way here my steed went lame, and the horse-tenders in the far cavern say he is still halting and unsure. Do you have another mount for me? With so many Hikeda'ya now in these lands I will have a dangerous trip to the fortress in Wormscale Gorge."

Ayaminu nodded. "Then you must take my mare, Cloudfoot. She is the queen of Anvi'janya's stables—her bloodline goes back to Windrunner and his mighty clan. She will bear you swiftly and safely wherever you must go."

"I fear I will be taking her into great danger."

She laughed without much mirth. "Where can any of us take a horse these days—or ourselves for that matter—other than into great danger? Because the Garden is beyond our reach."

Jiriki nodded. "What you say is true, *S'huesa*. But that does not make it any easier to risk innocent lives."

"You fear for the mortals you sent with Yeja'aro?"

"I do, of course. But I also fear for the grandson of my friends, the mortal prince Morgan, and for my dear friend Tanahaya who accompanies him. In truth, I am tormented when I think of the danger they are in, and it pains me greatly not to rush to look for them. But I must give even more weight to the danger my friends Seoman and Miriamele face with Utuk'ku and her army. And I fear for my sister as well, though she will journey with you to the safest place our people still hold. Yes, you have seen rightly, my lady—I am almost torn to pieces with fear for those I love."

"That is too much worry for any one person to bear," said Ayaminu. "Even for one of great heart and greater responsibility. Your mother Likimeya once said, *'Carry only what you can and leave the rest beside the road. Either someone else will carry it for you, or it will still be there for you to pick up on another day.'*"

Jiriki managed a sad smile. "I miss her wisdom so. I miss her, and I cannot even mourn her because she is not dead, but prisoned in endless sleep."

"We all miss her. And you *can* mourn her, for absence is a kind of death, and that absence comes at a terrible time for our people."

Ayaminu's grandson approached, his two-colored hair hidden under a traveling hood. "All is ready, *S'huesa*."

"Not quite," she said. "Jiriki will be riding Cloudfoot. Make sure his saddle is on her and then prepare one of the other horses for me."

"As you wish, *S'huesa*." He turned and was gone.

"Your line seems to have remained strong," Jiriki said. "That is good to know in these diminished days."

"I wish my father Kuroyi could have seen his great-grandson grown." Ayaminu made a ritual gesture of regret. "Such a short time since we lost the tall rider, yet things are now so different! He would scarcely recognize the world in which we find ourselves."

"I fear I must disagree with you," said Jiriki. "It is a world of desperation, war, and a struggle against the destruction of our people. Your father would recognize it all too well."

"I confess, my lord," Evan told Aelin quietly as they rode, "that though loyalty forbids it, a part of me wishes I had stayed back at Earl Murdo's castle at Carn Inbarh with my fellow Aedonite, Fintan."

"Even Murdo's stronghold may not be safe for long," Aelin said. "And if we can make our way back to our country, he is the first we will ask for help against King Hugh. I do not doubt Murdo will give it, plunging himself and all his lands into a terrible war among our own people. But you chose freely to come with me, did you not?"

"Of course, Sir Aelin. It is a cowardly wish, and I am ashamed of it. I do not fear battle, or even the White Foxes." He looked about as though even mentioning the enemy's name might bring them out of the trees. "It is our guide who worries me. He hates our kind—he has made it more than clear. How can we trust him to lead us safely through these hills?"

"Honor, I think, is what we trust. The same honor that compels us to do what is right compels him to do what Jiriki has bid him." He looked at Yeja'aro, who had swung down from his saddle to crouch low to the ground, listening. A moment later he lifted his hand in warning and Aelin and Evan reined up, forcing Maccus to stop as well.

The red-haired Sitha rose, mouth set in a grim line, and gestured for them to dismount. He signed that they should lead their horses after him, into a defile lined with stubby pines. Aelin nodded to his men, then slid from his saddle and followed Yeja'aro down the narrow way between a pair of large, rounded stones that stood on either side of the track like gateposts. A few paces ahead, Yeja'aro had lifted his sword and was quietly chopping at branches, though Aelin was puzzled because they did not seem to be blocking the way. As the Hernystirmen caught up to him at the bottom of the defile, the Sitha motioned for them to stay silent. Birds called and crickets sang. Aelin moved his weight from one haunch to the other as his horse made quiet breathing sounds in his ear.

"What—?" whispered Maccus Blackbeard, but before he had finished that single word Yeja'aro's slender gray blade was at his throat. As Maccus stared, wide-eyed, Yeja'aro pointed to his mouth and gave a single, savage shake of the head.

Aelin realized that the birds he had heard a moment before had suddenly fallen silent. He could hear no noise at all on the twilight air—even his horse appeared to be holding its breath. Beside him, Evan's lips moved in soundless prayer. Yeja'aro was staring at a spot farther up the slope, his eyes as golden, even in dim light, as the painted halo of one of Evan's Aedonite saints. Aelin had stopped marveling at the differences between the Sithi and his own kind during the two days of being surrounded by them, but now he was fascinated again by the Sitha's odd, birdlike movements—fascinated and a little frightened. Evan was right: it was disturbing to think that their safety was in the hands of one so different from themselves, so . . . inhuman. But it was even more disturbing to realize that Yeja'aro could sense danger the rest of them could not. Like now.

We are like blind men compared to these immortals, he thought. *Including those that surround us. We must be led. We must swallow all our natural caution and trust a fairy stranger to lead us as though we were children.*

At last Yeja'aro nodded, then gestured for Maccus to turn his horse and lead them back up the ravine toward flat ground.

"What was it?" Aelin asked quietly when they had reached the top.

"A Hikeda'ya scout," the Sitha said. "She passed very close."

"One?" Maccus kept his voice low, but only with a clear effort. "One Norn scout—a female, at that—and we hide like children? There are four of us!"

"Four of us, but perhaps an entire company of Hikeda'ya Sacrifices close by," said Yeja'aro flatly. "Do you think you could silence the one before she gave the alarm to all?"

Maccus did not reply, but his expression was sullen. Aelin knew he would have to speak to his comrade soon to prevent an even wider rift with their guide. "Let us continue on," he said. "Can we make camp soon? I'm sure we are all hungry and tired."

"Camp?" Now Yeja'aro's scorn was clear to see. "The dark is coming down. We soon will pass through the Hikeda'ya lines, slipping between their camps and hoping they do not hear your loud footsteps and your loud breathing. Do you truly wish to camp in their midst, then try to cross their lines in the bright light of day?"

It was Aelin's turn to be taken aback. "But we can't travel at night. One of our horses will stumble into a hole and break a leg."

"Not if you follow me closely," said Yeja'aro. "The light from the waxing moon is more than enough for me. Understand, the Hikeda'ya have come in force to this place. They are all around us in the forest, in the hills, and thousands more lurk in the captured fortress nearby. We will be in their midst a long time. You must do only what I say, or you will die."

"Is that a threat?"

"Maccus!" Aelin turned to his liegeman. "Stop. If you love me, if you owe me any loyalty, Yeja'aro is right. We must trust him."

"Trust a fairy?" Maccus made a noise of disgust. "Did your parents never tell you stories of the Peaceful Ones? They are liars and deceivers who lure mortal men to their death."

Evan's voice was quiet. "My faith teaches me that Maccus is right, Sir Aelin. The Sithi may not be our enemies as the Norns are, but they are not people like us. They have no faith, no God—no gods at all."

Aelin entertained a brief hope that the Sitha's grasp of Westerling was not good enough to understand everything they were saying. That hope did not last long.

"So," said Yeja'aro, crouching by his gray horse. "You do not wish to be guided by me? Let it be so. I have been given another task by Jiriki, and it will be discharged all the faster if I am not lumbered by noisy, heedless mortals."

"Stop, please." Aelin struggled to keep his voice low. "All of you. Necessity has thrown us together. Maccus, Evan, you are angering me. Have you no faith in me at all? Has Nad Mullach done nothing for you? Does it not deserve your loyalty?"

"Of course we are loyal to you, Sir Aelin," Maccus said. "That does not mean we must be loyal to a creature whose purposes we do not know."

"Then you must fight me." Aelin tugged at his sword hilt, deliberately showing an inch of steel above the mouth of his scabbard. "Believe me, I would rather die myself than take up arms against my friends, but we cannot go on this way."

Maccus was clearly shocked—Evan even more so, to judge from his wide eyes. "Sir Aelin, no," said Maccus. "You wrong me if you think I could draw sword against you. You are my liege lord, as your father was to my father."

Aelin saw the immortal studying them with his imperturbable golden stare. *The Sithi must think us little more than animals,* Aelin thought angrily. *Dogs, growling over a bone.* "Be that as it might, Maccus, you and Evan cannot be loyal to me and still contest every step with our guide. I am trusting him with my life—is that not enough for you?" But even as he said it, he remembered the feeling of Yeja'aro's fingers around his throat, the seeming madness in his eyes, and hatred and resentment rushed through him so suddenly he almost felt dizzy. *Holy Mircha, Brynioch's gentle daughter, help me calm these angry hearts—especially my own!* Maccus and Evan were still staring at him, as though he had suddenly become someone else. He took a deep breath. "Swear you will follow this guide without question unless I tell you otherwise," he told them. "Swear, or we must fight."

Maccus pulled at his beard, worried and more than a little angry, but at last said, "Of course, my lord. Nothing is stronger than the bond between us. I will do as you say." He gave Yeja'aro a sour look. "I will do what *he* says."

"And you, Evan? Will your god permit you to follow an immortal?"

"No."

For a moment, Aelin despaired.

"But my God will permit me to follow you, my liege, and as long as you follow this godless creature, I will follow him too."

Aelin let out a pent breath. "Then we are decided, and I thank Heaven. You two are more than my liegemen, you are the hope of our country. We must go forward together."

Now Yeja'aro rose from his crouch and brushed his hands clean on his breeches, then stretched from fingertips to feet, slowly and luxuriously, like a cat. "If you have finished your arguing, let us move on. Often a Sacrifice scout is followed by the rest of a foraging party. More Hikeda'ya might be close behind the last one."

Jiriki swung nimbly into the saddle. The tall, sandy bay stood patiently, but as Jiriki settled himself he felt a tremble of anticipation in her lithesome body. "Your Cloudfoot is a rare beast, my lady," he said. "I can feel her eagerness to run."

Ayaminu smiled. "She has been like that since she was foaled. The old blood runs strong in her. Keep her safe—if you can."

"And by the Garden we love, keep yourself safe, too, dear Willow-switch," Aditu told him.

"Fare you well, Rabbit," he told her, gently touching her belly. "May the Garden protect you and the new life within you. You carry our parents' only grandchild."

Aditu laughed. "No one knows that better than I, Willow-switch. Even the strongest horse knows when it has a rider."

"May luck journey with you, Jiriki of the Year-Dancing," said Ayaminu. "Do you truly think Khendraja'aro will give you troops?"

"He will be lucky if his uncle gives him a meal," said Liko, riding close behind them.

"No jests, please," Aditu said. "The need is great, but I fear the Protector will not listen with an open heart if Jiriki admits our news of Utuk'ku's plans comes from Tanahaya. Our uncle is cautious and stubborn at the best of times. And these are not the best of times."

"What good to hold Wormscale Gorge if Utuk'ku throws down the Hayholt and seizes Hamakho the Dragonslayer's witchwood crown and its sacred seeds?" Jiriki asked. "What good our throwing so many lives away in Tanakirú if that selfish, murderous creature will live on forever? The Hikeda'ya now fill their armies with halfbloods—thousands of new Sacrifices since the Storm King's war ended. Given enough time, they will outbreed us and overrun us. And overrun the mortals, too, although I imagine you care little enough about that, *S'huesa*."

Ayaminu shook her head. "I do not hate the mortals. I spent time among them at the end of the war, as you know, though I would have done otherwise had your mother not directed me to go with them. And I saw things that both horrified and surprised me. But the mortal who commanded them, Duke Isgrimnur, had a good heart. He had many reasons to be vengeful and to wish the Hikeda'ya harm, but he did not give way to rage. In truth, I think he was relieved when the cliffs above the Nakkiga Gate fell, and not simply because it spared his own men the terrible task of trying to take the mountain city, but because he did not want to take more lives, not even the lives of Hikeda'ya."

"I had not thought to hear you praise any mortal," said Aditu, smiling. "Perhaps you are not as far from the beliefs my brother and I share as I had assumed."

"It is always wiser to assume nothing," Ayaminu told her. "The mortals were never my true concern, and they had never been my study before that time. I thought them little more than animals—but I discovered otherwise. Never forget, though, their race will likely outlast our own diminishing kind. Whether they mean it or not, they are still the doom of our people."

"I reject that," said Jiriki. "Our folk have always suffered from this sense of fatality, and that has been much on my mind of late. As First Grandmother

Amerasu warned, it has led us down many disastrous paths. But the future is not written. We can make of it what we will, if only we are strong enough."

"And lucky enough." Aditu spread her hands over her stomach as if to ward her child from any bad fortune.

"And there we will have to leave this debate," said Ayaminu. "Remember, I was born before the Second Exile. I have seen many more seasons than either of you, and nothing I have seen has changed my mind about our ultimate fate. The mortals will outlast us, and eventually they will forget us, too."

"Unless Utuk'ku destroys them as well as us," said Aditu grimly. "Then only the Queen of Nakkiga will decide who is remembered and whose names are lost. Her hatreds are eternal."

"There is always that possibility, too," Ayaminu agreed.

Jiriki watched his sister and her companions until their road led them out of sight beneath the leafy eaves of Oldheart, then he began the long ride to Tanakirú. As Ayaminu had promised, Cloudfoot was quick and eager, and she carried him swiftly across Red Campion Bridge and then north along the Forbidden Hills Road on the east side of the Coolblood River.

The settlements of the Forbidden Hills were empty now, the Zida'ya who lived there either gone away to war with their leader Khendraja'aro or fled to one of the settlements called "little boats," farther into the forest. Jiriki could not help remembering the days of his youth, when even long after Da'ai Chikiza had been deserted, the Coolblood Valley had still been home to many of his kind, its winding length ablaze with the colors of their boats, houses, and riverside pavilions. Jiriki's grandfather Hakatri had fought giants here, and poets had written odes to the region's beauty, naming the river "Oldheart's silvery soul."

But these days the valley held more than just old stories, Jiriki knew. At a league away from Da'ai Chikiza the forest was largely free of Hikeda'ya, and yet they seemed to be everywhere along the eastern side of the valley, in small groups and large encampments. It was all he and his lightning-footed mount could do to avoid them, or outrun those he could not avoid. As he sped north along the base of the hills, he saw an entire Sacrifice company marching along the river road on the far side and for the first time felt truly afraid. Such numbers! Heart chilled, Jiriki spurred Cloudfoot to even greater exertions. He had a dull, sick feeling about taking away any of the troops defending Wormscale Gorge and Tanakirú, but he knew they must protect the Hayholt as well. The witch of Nakkiga was clawing out in all directions, and the only sane hope was that she might somehow overreach herself.

At last, after many, many hours riding, Jiriki halted on a cliff top just before dawn. He and his mount had reached the gap he had been seeking in the eastern hills. As Cloudfoot waited with admirable patience, Jiriki stared down at the narrow entrance of Wormscale Gorge, which was seething with Zida'ya and Hikeda'ya warriors battling breast to breast, the Sacrifice troops trying to break into the narrow valley while Jiriki's own, outnumbered folk fought bravely to keep them out. After a dry winter, Wormscale Lake filled barely half the gorge, leaving dry land on either side where the Hikeda'ya Sacrifices were trying to force their way past into the Valley of Mist so they could reach their objective at the far end, the place called Tanakirú. Jiriki saw arrows sheeting down like black rain from the Sithi fortress atop the hill on the far side of the defile, but though each flight from the Hornet's Nest struck down dozens of the Hikeda'ya enemy, they were still far more numerous than the defenders. Jiriki saw that the Sithi line that blocked the gorge on the near side of the lake was beginning to shudder, like a cliff undermined by the sea. His eye was caught by a huge giant in war-gear leading the Hikeda'ya charge on the most threatened side of the gorge. This giant's pelt was darker than most of its kind, so even with the sunlight beginning to tint the sky it was hard for Jiriki see it clearly, although the devastation it caused as it smashed into the defenders was impossible to miss. Even as Jiriki watched in dismay, the armored beast swung its huge, spiked battle club and obliterated several Zida'ya with one terrible swing; a gap suddenly appeared in the line of defenders, like a tooth knocked from a jaw, and Hikeda'ya soldiers began to swarm toward the weak place.

Jiriki could watch no longer. He cried out and Cloudfoot reared, her whinny loud and sharp as the cry of a hunting bird, then he touched his heels to her ribs and she leaped down the steep, treacherous path into the gorge.

Though the half-darkness was as bright to the fighters as full noon would have been to mortal men, the upper rim of the sun had just crept above the eastern hills, peering out at the world as if it did not care to see what else the day would bring. Jiriki swept down from the heights, Cloudfoot leaping where there was no safe place to run, racing around bends in the ancient track so steep that Jiriki had to lean far to one side, then to the other. His witchwood buckler scraped against rock as he fought to keep the powerful horse balanced in her headlong flight toward the valley floor.

As they reached the bottommost slope, Jiriki drew his witchwood sword Indreju. *"For the Garden!"* he shouted, and the nearest Hikeda'ya turned in astonishment to see this unexpected phantom appear in their midst. *"And for Amerasu!"* he cried then, and the name of his ancestor, murdered at Utuk'ku's command, echoed above even the tumult at the valley's mouth. Many of the embattled Zida'ya looked up and saw him, and they shouted in joy.

Jiriki drove through the scattered Hikeda'ya who were trying to join their fellows at the mouth of the defile. Caught by surprise, they were mown down like stalks of grain. Cloudfoot raced so swiftly and dodged so nimbly that many of the enemy did not even realize they had been struck by Indreju's keen edge until Jiriki had thundered past and they tumbled to the ground in his tracks.

As he reached the thick of things, the Sithi who saw him coming lifted their voices in cheers and exhortations and threw themselves back into the fray with renewed vigor, charging so fiercely at the Hikeda'ya that for a moment it seemed they might actually throw the invaders back down the slope in front of the defile. But even as the Sithi found new life, the giant strode among them, knocking off heads with his great war-cudgel as though he waded through a field of dandelions.

"Now is the time, Children of the Sa'onsera!" Jiriki called as Cloudfoot reared again. "Push them back! Push!"

The armored giant heard him and turned, roaring out its own name, loud as an avalanche—*"Jun Dar Kran kills all! Come, little Zid-ja! Dar kill you!"*

As Cloudfinder sped toward it, the great gray creature swung its club, which was longer and heavier than Jiriki himself. He leaned sharply sideways; his foot in the stirrup was the only thing that kept him in his saddle as the weapon hissed past. Straightening up again, Jiriki hacked away at the clawing hands of Sacrifice soldiers who tried to pull him down. As Cloudfoot spun in a shower of muddy earth and turned back toward the giant, he knew he dared not get close enough to engage the monster with just his sword. The creature would break him like a stick if it ever closed its massive hand on him, or might rip the belly out of his horse with its claws. He saw no loose spears to be had, but one of the Hikeda'ya company banners stood crookedly in the mud nearby. Jiriki snatched it up as he and Cloudfoot thundered past. The distance between horse and giant closed quickly, and half a dozen Hikeda'ya Sacrifices flung themselves out of the way, fearing the giant's wild swings more than Jiriki and his strange choice of lance.

Jiriki stood in his stirrups, then with all his strength flung the standard butt-first at the giant, the banner trailing like the tail of a kite. Straight and true it flew and struck the giant on the breast so hard that the butt of the standard pushed the great curtain of mail a short way into the creature's chest. Surprised to feel pain, the giant looked down for a moment at the pole, then brushed it loose and looked up, baring yellowed fangs and red mouth in a roar of vengeful fury. Jiriki came sweeping in again and ducked a swing of the great cudgel. Indreju was a near-invisible blur of gray in the dawn light as it scythed through the great beast's neck in a single stroke. The immense body swayed for an instant, then collapsed to the ground.

Jiriki brought Cloudfoot around in another mud-flinging circle, hacking now at the astonished Hikeda'ya struggling to get out of his way, then slowed long enough to lean down and snatch up the giant's severed head by its shaggy fur. Holding the heavy thing above him, blood drizzling down his arm, he raced through the ranks of the attackers singing a loud song of triumph from the ancient days when the Keida'ya had fought the giants together.

"Heya! Ai! How shall they stop us? Heya! Ai! Free people never surrender! See us fight and conquer! Death to the servants of shadow!"

Heartened, the gorge's Zida'ya defenders pushed forward against the suddenly dispirited Hikeda'ya, who began to fall back in confusion. The Sacrifices were too orderly and well-trained to be routed, but they seemed to have lost hope for that day's fight, and began to retreat down the slope from the edge of Wormscale Lake and back toward the Coolblood Valley. Jiriki rode to and fro as the enemy fell back, waving his bloody trophy and singing. Several arrows buzzed past without harming him, but one stuck in the giant's immense forehead, and that made Jiriki laugh and sing all the louder.

"Run back to your heartless mistress!" he cried. "You are brave enough attacking from hiding, and your clan may have killed a few dragons in the old days—but the old days are gone!"

Many Zida'ya defenders rushed past him, chasing the Hikeda'ya out of the mouth of the narrow valley. Jiriki flung the giant's head away and turned back toward the center of the defending force.

Khendraja'aro was waiting for him there in the middle of his household guard. The terrible scar on the Protector's face made him look almost as fearsome as the giant Jiriki had killed, and his armor was so besmirched in Sacrifice blood that it was hard to guess its original color. "You arrived unlooked for, Jiriki," he said as Jiriki rode up.

"Someone or something has cast a pall over the Witnesses, else I would have warned you of my coming."

"Well, the Hamakha know of it now, to their sorrow," said Khendraja'aro, but he did not seem entirely pleased or relieved. "And since I doubt this sudden appearance of yours betokens anything good for our people, follow me up the hidden way to the Hornet's Nest where we will eat, drink, and speak of what brings you."

"As you wish, Elder," said Jiriki, wiping blood from his hands onto his breeches. "In truth, I would prize a cup of wine, be it of the humblest vintage."

"Yes," Khendraja'aro replied sourly. "Killing is thirsty work—even for those who arrive late to the battle."

A maze of steep paths led upward to the Hornet's Nest, a few of them true but many false. Some tracks were mazes open to the sky where besiegers would be exposed to a deadly hail of arrows from above. Other paths came to dead ends against walls of naked mountain stone, leaving those who entered to be killed like rats in a barrel. But for those who knew the safe way to the top, passage could be swift, and so it was that the sun had not even risen halfway to noon when the victors rode through a covered cavern and up the last slope, then out into the light of morning at the fortress gate, which swung wide to admit them.

Most of the Zida'ya inside came to meet them, hailing Khendraja'aro and the other fighters with joy and relief, but the Protector seemed to grow more hard-faced as he heard the loud cheers and cries of greeting directed at Jiriki.

After their wounds had been bandaged and they had washed away the dirt and blood of battle, the fort's defenders gathered in the main hall to share a midday meal. Jiriki greeted several of them for the first time.

"Ki'ushapo!" he said to the pale-haired one who came to embrace him. "My heart is full to see you, kinsman and friend."

"And mine delights to see you, Jiriki. Especially after such a timely arrival. We did not expect you."

Jiriki shook his head. "Some dark power—perhaps Akhenabi of the Stolen Face, perhaps the mistress of Nakkiga herself—has laid a silence upon all the Witnesses. Did you not know?"

"Only Khendraja'aro of all of us still has a Witness. If he knew, he has not told us." Ki'ushapo's expression darkened. "I wonder what else the Protector has not told us?"

"I did not come to drive a wedge between clansfolk," Jiriki told him. "I came out of necessity, so let us see what will come from this day's words. The Hikeda'ya fight fiercely, and I see, sadly, that they are numerous here at the gorge. How do you and the others bear up? Have we lost many of our own?"

"Not many, as history counts such things, but for our small force even a single death is too many, and we have lost far more than that—at least two hundred of our people since we last saw you here in this mist-soaked valley. We have lost some of the best among us, too. Niyanao of the Lake fell fighting in the defile six days ago, killed by General Ensume himself in single combat, and Selusana Moonhouse was struck by a Sacrifice arrow and tumbled to her death from these very battlements only half a moon before that. But despite so many deaths, we have kept Utuk'ku's warriors out of the Vale, although I wonder how much longer we can manage that trick."

"And the *Uro'eni*? Has the ogre been seen?"

"The mist-monster crushed two fighters from the Silver Fir Clan a short time ago but is just as likely to destroy the Hikeda'ya. Also, the thing does not range as far or stalk the valley as frequently as it once did. Some think it may be ill, or even dying."

Jiriki made a sign with his hand, then pulled Ki'ushapo to him for another embrace. "It eases my heart to see you, Flaxenhair. Come, let us go in with the rest. Fighting giants is hungry work."

After they had finished their meal, some of the clansfolk would have raised their cups to Jiriki's arrival and shared tales of the day's victory, for many of those present in the great hall had not been fighting down in the gorge, but Khendraja'aro silenced them with a gesture. "Enough," he said. "This is not the time for brave stories and songs. Jiriki, you come to us unlooked-for—though not less welcome for that." Some around the table exchanged looks at this, for in truth the Protector did not seem overly pleased to see his younger relative. "What brings you to us in this hour? Is there some threat to the little boats, or to one of our other remaining settlements? Does Anvi'janya still stand free?"

"It does, Elder. I saw *S'huesa* Ayaminu herself only two days ago, in one of our lodges near old Da'ai Chikiza. She now escorts my sister back to Anvi'janya for Year-Dancing."

"I do not understand why that farce of a ceremony should continue," announced Dunao the Gray Rider, his voice full of anger. He was one of the clan elders, and also one of Khendraja'aro's firmest supporters. "The witchwood is gone, the *kei-soma* is no more, and our cities are all thrown down. Yet Anvi'janya will host scores and scores of our people at this empty ritual—Zida'ya who would better be employed fighting Utuk'ku's minions here at our side."

"Better how?" asked Jiriki.

Dunao's look was cold. "I do not understand your question, Jiriki i-Sa'onserei."

"You said our people would be better employed fighting against Utuk'ku."

The Gray Rider made a gesture of disgust. "Would they not? Should we just step aside and let the witch of Nakkiga do what she wants, go where she wishes? Should we hand over Tanakirú to her—and all that is in it?"

"I did not say so," Jiriki responded mildly. "But I wonder what we are fighting for, if not for our heritage—for this 'farce' of a Year-Dancing Ceremony, as you called it."

"The ceremony meant something when the witchwood still grew." Dunao could barely restrain his anger. "Something important. But now it is a pointless travesty."

"If you think that the only purpose for Year-Dancing disappeared with the witchwood," said Jiriki, "then maybe you are right. But I cannot agree with you—"

"Enough of this," said Khendraja'aro from his seat at the head of the high table. "I do not think you came here to argue the worth of the Year-Dancing ritual, Jiriki. Or am I wrong?"

"No, *S'hue*, you are not wrong." Jiriki stood then and told the assembled clansfolk of the attack on Da'ai Chikiza and what he had learned from Tanahaya while messages could still pass through the Witnesses. The invasion of the mortal fortress at Naglimund and the incursion of Sacrifice troops into Da'ai Chikiza was news to many who had been fighting from the Hornets' Nest for several moons, and by the time he finished the hall was full of whispered talk.

"Be silent!" commanded Khendraja'aro. "Are you mortals or children, to mutter among yourselves this way? Jiriki, it is true the Witnesses have been useless to us in recent days, but I do not think you rode all this way and threw yourself into battle simply to give us this news."

"And I do not think you have missed the import of what I said, though you do not mention it, Elder." The air in the hall seemed grow heavier, as though a storm threatened. "Utuk'ku and a vast force of Hikeda'ya are marching on the mortal castle that was once Asu'a, our old home. They believe they can find witchwood there, seeds buried in honor of Hamakho, and I do not doubt that, to recover it, they would destroy the castle and the mortals who live there."

"Why do you bring this to me?" Khendraja'aro replied stiffly. "You have seen how hard-pressed we are here, how only the Hornet's Nest protects the gorge and keeps the Hikeda'ya out of Tanakirú. Surely you do not expect me to leave the Narrowdark Valley undefended because of a dubious suggestion from that troublemaker Tanahaya, and rush to the defense of mortals?"

Jiriki stood still and silent as a statue for several heartbeats. "Tanahaya of the Heart-Seed Clan has risked her life many times on behalf of her people—our people. But I will pass over your ill-chosen words, Protector, because the matters we discuss are more important than any discourtesies."

"I do not enjoy your sly speech, Jiriki," Khendraja'aro said. "If you think me wrong, say so."

"When you put the name of 'troublemaker' on Tanahaya, then you are certainly wrong, Elder. But that does not mean we must pit ourselves against each other. In truth, we must find a way to reach agreement."

"We must do nothing of the sort," said Dunao. "You must learn to obey the word of the Protector."

"I can speak for myself, old friend," Khendraja'aro told him. "Jiriki carries the blood of the Sa'onserei. He should not be silenced, even when he argues against the choices that I make for the good of all. But neither should his family heritage give his words any strength beyond their own merit." He wore a considering look on his terrible, scarred face. "Perhaps it is only the old ways that can unravel this knot."

"What old ways do you mean, Uncle?"

"In the Asu'a of which you speak so often, though it is home now only to mortals and memories, the most difficult questions were settled in a Song of Challenge."

Jiriki was surprised. "Truly, Elder Khendraja'aro, that is what you propose? Both of us to sing for our people's hearts, here and now?"

"If not, then where and when?" The Protector had risen from his bench. "Who else to judge this but your kinsmen here, those most at risk, those who have fought so bravely and so long—and at such hard cost—to give us this slender moment of safety in which to decide what we will do?"

Jiriki did his best not to frown. "I think you have begun trying to sway that judgment before we have even agreed."

"You may refuse the challenge. That is your right. Then I alone will decide."

Jiriki made a sign above his chest. "No. I accept."

"Then make your demands. Or your plea." Khendraja'aro looked grimly amused. "After all, you are the challenger."

Jiriki shook his head. "I have already made known my desire for warriors to take to the mortal castle, to thwart Utuk'ku's plan to snatch the last witchwood seeds. In a way, the challenge has already begun, so I ask your indulgence, Protector. You go first, then I will sing of my own . . . demands, as you call them."

Now the Protector smiled, the scarred side of his face wrinkling into something truly dreadful. "As you wish, young Jiriki." He spread his arms wide. "I call you all here to sit as judges. You have heard the challenge from my sister's son. I stand against it." He let his arms fall. When he began to speak again, his voice seemed at first ordinary. "Long we have fought, and nearly always with no help. Long it has been since our blood-kin, the Hikeda'ya, helped us. Now we fight against those kin and shed the blood we share. Mortals joined us once against other mortals. They joined us too when Ineluki rose from death and threatened all. But other help they have not given us, and often they have taken Zida'ya lives. Mortals drove us apart from the Hikeda'ya. Mortals broke those bonds. Nenais'u and Drukhi died to teach us hard lessons of loss, but also lessons about the danger of trusting mortals."

At first the cadence of Khendraja'aro's song was all but hidden, but soon the subtle rhythms of the chant became clear, the intricate and demanding art of thought-shaping called *sa'juya*—"weaveword." Jiriki was weary after his long ride and the battle, and also dismayed to think such an important decision should be put to this unexpected test, but if he left his uncle to decide the matter alone, he knew his suit would be denied. This way, at least some chance remained.

Khendraja'aro continued, his voice rising as he looked to each corner of the wide hall in turn, his mournful, angry words echoing beneath the rafters:

What do we have that this land has not sought to steal from us?
Once we had brothers and sisters, now they are enemies.
But our true enemies will never be brothers, those short-lived things,
And yet some of us would claim the rights of family for them.

Once we had true brothers and sisters, now they are enemies
That struck down our greatest wisdom and danced on her grave.
It is impossible now to claim the rights of family for them,
But it was the sunset-born who lit the forge-fire of that hatred.

Who struck down our greatest wisdom and danced on her grave?
It was the sunset-born who lit the forge-fire of that hatred.
The shadow in the silver mask laughs at our division, knowing
Who truly set the flames that will become our final pyre

The sunset-born lit the forge-fire of that deadly hatred
Now the shadow in the silver mask laughs at our division
Who truly set the flames that will become our final pyre?
But one stands here who would feed that fire with our precious lives

See how the shadow in her silver mask laughs! Our division
Will feed her fires with our precious lives.
She knows the pyres will be our final ending.
Their swirling smoke will be all of us that remains.

Khendraja'aro went on, spinning his skein of words, winding its length through endless loops to remind those in the hall of the many crimes that mortals had committed against them. As he elaborated on this grievous history, the hall grew more and more still, as if the moment between one heartbeat and the next had stretched to impossible length. The tale of Zida'ya woe at the hands of mortals was long and painful—even Jiriki could feel the power of the Protector's challenge, of the old words and ancient forms as they coiled around each other like the fabled World-Serpent itself, tail caught in its own mouth, its beginning forgotten, its ending unglimpsed.

It was impossible to guess how long Khendraja'aro sang. Beyond the windows the afternoon sky started to dim, but still he continued, shaping his words as carefully as a Tinukeda'ya stonecutter, until it seemed to nearly all those listening that he had built something that even time itself could not diminish or destroy. The ruination of the Lost Garden, the end of the sacred witchwood trees, and even the terrible wounding of Jiriki's mother Likimeya were all woven together like delicate strands of *srinyedu* cord into a picture of hopelessness, a darkness though which the only glimpse of light for their race was the chance to make an honorable ending.

If we help the mortals again, we only hasten our own end, declared the Protector's song. *This world despises us. It was never ours, and it will happily see the mortals supplant us. But the one thing it cannot do is take from us our own ending—the ending we choose.*

At last, with daylight now gone and the windows squares of blackness, Khendraja'aro finished his song of warning. The silence in the hall was absolute. Many of Jiriki's kin turned to look at him in curiosity, wondering less what he would say in reply than why he would even bother to dispute such terrible and inarguable truths.

For his part, Protector Khendraja'aro showed no pride at what he had done. He accepted a cup of wine from one of his supporters but did not seat himself. Instead, he stood where he had sung, a tired but confident warrior awaiting his enemy's surrender.

Jiriki sat for no little while staring at the fire that burned in the hearth, thinking of all that had brought him to this place in this hour.

"So?" asked Dunao the Gray Rider, with an expression that was almost a sneer. "Do you have no answer to the Protector's challenge, Jiriki i-Sa'onserei? Must we wait here in silence until the Cloud Children come climbing over our walls?"

"No, you need not wait, Rider. I have heard the song Khendraja'aro made and I cannot argue with any of it."

A silent shiver ran through the hall. There was surprise in it, and perhaps even disappointment from some, but it was easy to see a sort of heavy satisfaction on the faces of Khendraja'aro's supporters. The Protector had put Jiriki in his place, was their clear thought, and had proved that dividing their forces was madness, especially when those Jiriki wished to help were despised mortals, less like those in the hall than even their Hikeda'ya enemies.

"If you give up your challenge, then we proceed," said Khendraja'aro.

"Tomorrow Ensume and his Spiders will try to take Wormscale Gorge again, and we must—"

Jiriki lifted his hand. "I bid you hold, Protector. I did not say I had conceded the challenge, only that I could not argue with what you said. The great questions that our people have faced in their worst hours have never been as simple as you have tried to make this one—never only this or that, up or down, night or day. Yes, the mortals have treated us badly in the past—that is not in question. But just as Utuk'ku does not rule over our Zida'ya folk, though our people share her blood, neither do the mortals act with a single will. Protector Khendraja'aro did not know, so he could not add it to his account, but many of the Sacrifices we have been battling here came into these lands because a mortal king, Hugh of Hernystir, let them do so. I tell you that so you will know I do not hide the truth or hide from it. But other mortals, like the high king and queen in old Asu'a, have been our friends and allies. We cannot hold every member of their race to blame for what some mortals have done. Protector Khendraja'aro is not to blame because Utuk'ku sent murderers into Jao é-Tinukai'i and killed Amerasu Ship-Born on that terrible night, though like me, Khendraja'aro shares Utuk'ku's bloodline."

"Why does Amerasu's name come into this?" demanded Khendraja'aro. "It is too late to spread confusion, Jiriki. You know why we fight here. You know what we protect."

"But what good is there in fighting here, Uncle—what good protecting anything—if we lose our spirits by turning our back on those who helped us?"

"Do you speak of the mortal men of Hernystir?" said Dunao loudly. "You said yourself that their king has made a pact with Utuk'ku, may the very land beneath our feet curse the Hamakha Clan forever!"

"You have overlooked my point, Rider. The Hikeda'ya, people of our own blood, have turned against us, killed our best, and seem to want death for the rest of us as well." Jiriki had found his story at last. "Mortals, immortal—for once, the difference is unimportant. All that matters now is who will help us, and who we in return should help. I speak against turning our back on the good-hearted mortals who stood by us in the fight against Ineluki. I speak against turning our back on the living simply because they are mortals and do not share our blood. Instead of helping them, many of you would even choose death."

Several of the other Zida'ya now actively protested, but Jiriki raised his voice, purposely beginning his song with the somber, measured tones of one reciting familiar history.

I heard First Grandmother speak these words on the night of her death,
he chanted.

"We love Unbeing too much," she said. "It follows us like an abandoned lover."
She said we had not learned the lesson granted in the Garden's fall
We denied Tinukeda'ya and mortals both, withheld our secrets, scorned their lives.

"We love Unbeing too much," she sang—our Sa'onsera, born in exile—
"And in love's blindness, we do not see much that we should.
Tinukeda'ya and mortals both, our secret siblings, cry for aid
While, ignorant, we gaze into the night-dark eyes of our own ending."

Love's blindness is a mirror mask which hides what we should clearly see
And shows us only what we prefer, a silver face upon a skull
A face that scowls and mocks our ignorance, and knows
That we would rather die than live and lose those lies we have so loved

Rather we would live in those lies, lose our loves, lose our land
Ignore the Ship-Born's wisdom meant to teach us, all so that
Our much-loved darkness still will linger, love us, let us
Tell our tales of cruel fate, that took our Garden long ago.

Yes, ignore the words of our Sa'onsera! She never knew how sweet
It is to blame the fate that took our Garden, and long ago
Condemned us to this life in death. We scorn the mortal Sunset Children
Who never knew the Garden, who never had what we were given.

Many in the hall murmured in surprise as Jiriki wove his response, some even angry that he should call upon the name of the revered Amerasu, though he was in the direct line of her blood. But as he sang on, moving from one interlocking thought to the next like a spider carefully spinning a broad, ambitious web, many of the listening Zida'ya began to show a different kind of unease, as though they felt their fondest certainties grow less secure.

Jiriki was weary, deeply weary, but the mortal boy Seoman who had saved his life, his *Hikka Staja*, was now a grown man whose life and kingdom was in danger. Jiriki could not turn his back on that obligation, which had later become a true friendship. If Seoman and Miriamele fell, if the mortal High Throne fell, then the other kingdoms of men would crumble soon after—that Jiriki did not doubt. Already ancient, cruel Utuk'ku had sunk her talons into the kingdom of Hernystir, the first mortals who had ever fought beside the Zida'ya. So he crafted his reply around First Grandmother's words, spoken only moments before Utuk'ku's servant had murdered her. Then he built upon them, knitting together many old stories and many old sadnesses, but throwing a light upon them that had scarcely been seen since Amerasu's death.

But still we may save a piece of the Garden, still fulfill the lost land's promise
Not by mirror-staring, not by honoring the mask, but only by seeing ourselves whole
We fled Unbeing, Amerasu said that night, and thought we had escaped
Its shadow, but a piece of it came with us out of the Garden.
Came with us, hidden like a shameful stain, and always we knew it was there.
First Grandmother told the truth: "That stain, that shadow, is part of us."

He could not know for certain whether he had reached any of those most determined to resist his song, his attempt to overthrow his people's inbred desire for a surrender to inevitability, for the embrace of an honorable ending, but he could feel the hearts of others in the hall begin to turn toward him like flowers toward the sun.

"That stain, that shadow is part of us." So said our Sa'onsera, wisdom's heart
And though a darker shadow fell on her, stainless she went to her death,
Because she told the truth always. Rarest of blessings, rarest of sins.
All hail the truth-teller! For only truth can chase the shadows.
Only truth can cleanse the stain. Truth and a love that knows no distinction
Between worthy or unworthy, mortal or immortal, even between fallen and raised.
We cannot flee what has been. We can only turn our faces to what might still be.

He had subtly changed the form of his last stanzas, startling even those who had been swayed by what he had told them. Every eye was on him, wondering what he would say next.

"My challenge is over," Jiriki said. "I have already said that I agree with *S'hue* Khendraja'aro. We must protect Tanakirú from General Ensume and Utuk'ku's horde of Sacrifices."

The Protector had a strange look on his face, one that mingled anger with confusion. "Are no traditions sacred to you, Jiriki? You untimely end your reply, then as much as say there was never a point to it at all."

"Only someone who did not understand my song would say that, Uncle." Jiriki shook his head. "There is no simple choice of *this or that*. If we lose Tanakirú, mad Utuk'ku triumphs and there is no telling what she will do to us and to all who live. But if she finds what she seeks in the ruins of old Asu'a, her triumph is just as assured. If she finds and claims those witchwood seeds, the sacred trees will grow once more—but only in Nakkiga. No ancient bonds of shared blood will convince Hamakho Dragonslayer's tribe to share with us. Utuk'ku and her nobles will live on while the Zida'ya fade and pass away into memory."

Khendraja'aro was silent, his expression as tired and unhappy as Jiriki supposed his own must be. For all their rancor with each other, both knew their challenge had crowned no winner, nor could it have.

"So then, what would you have us do, Jiriki i-Sa'onserei?" demanded Dunao. "We are stretched to the breaking point and have no army to give you, even if we wished to save your mortal friends. Your own words weave a picture of inescapable doom."

"The only doom that is inescapable is the doom for which one helplessly waits," said Jiriki. "I choose to ride against it. Yes, we must continue the fight here, despite the odds. But we must also ride to the aid of the mortals. Tell me, Khendraja'aro, will you give me warriors to ride with me? Will you let me take half a thousand brave spirits to keep Utuk'ku from the witchwood crown?"

"Half a thousand!" cried one of the other Zida'ya. "You might as well ask to take the blood from our veins as well."

"Impossible," said Khendraja'aro. "That is almost a fifth part of our entire number. A twentieth of what you ask is still more than we can spare."

Jiriki shook his head. "If you had understood me, you would also have understood that to deny aid to our mortal allies is to harm ourselves as well. Shall we ask each one of us in this room how many we should send? Shall we ask each whether he or she believes in the words of Amerasu Ship-Born?"

Khendraja'aro was silent for a long time, his usually golden face now a pale ocher like sun-scorched grain, his long, terrible scar standing out like a flame. "I rule that you may take those who choose to go with you. But it can be no more than a hundred all told."

Jiriki spoke with deliberate care. "Such a small number will be scarcely noticed against a force as large as Utuk'ku sends against the mortals. I would be leading them to certain death."

"That is your choice to make—and the choice of those who may join you. Remember, each warrior you take away from our defense of the valley brings danger or even death to those who remain. I will not sacrifice our effort here simply because of a rumor—a rumor brought to you by one who has already flauted our orders."

Jiriki stared at Khendraja'aro, and for a moment it seemed he would speak out in anger. Instead, he bowed his head, then said in a low but firm voice, "Nevertheless, I put my trust in Tanahaya's discovery, and in the importance of our mortal allies. I will gather all who are willing to accompany me while respecting the needs of those who remain. Give me permission to take eight score and we will call these cold dealings a bargain."

"Do not put blame on me, who has the safety of all to protect," said Khendraja'aro. "But to spare the risk of more anger, I will grant your eight score. And now I leave you to your muster, Likimeya's son, for I am tired in my bones after a long day. Many of our folk have fallen, and my heart grows even heavier when I think of the days ahead."

As Khendraja'aro and most of his staunchest supporters left the hall, Jiriki turned to Ki'ushapo. "Have I dreamed it," he asked his kinsman, "or did the Protector actually compromise?"

"We still sit here in the waking world, old friend, but it happened as you say. However, I guess his decision to be less yielding than it seemed. We have had more than a little discord here and throughout the army defending Tanakirú, and the Protector is often the target. It is my guess that Khendraja'aro supposes those who go with you will be those who are most unhappy with his leadership, thereby shrinking the numbers of those who oppose him."

"You are wise, friend," Jiriki said with a weary smile. "I have no doubt it is just as you say. And are you one of those who will go with me, good, golden Ki'ushapo?"

"Without hesitation. I remember the mortal Seoman fondly. And the mortal castle is not merely the place where the last witchwood may lie, it is also the ancestral home of our family and our people. Honor and pride demand we go there, even if we can only bring enough fighters to die defending it."

"The Garden hears you," Jiriki said, pouring them each another cup of wine. "Now let us hope the Garden will help us, too."

12

Crow in the Rafters

Morning. Cruel morning, bringing it all back like a wave crashing against the shore. And Miri was still dead.

Simon pressed his fists against his eyelids, pushing until his eyes throbbed in their sockets as he tried to prevent himself from weeping or screaming with rage.

Why, God? Why would You let this happen? Am I so great a sinner? Is the kingdom such a wicked place, that you would snatch away its brightest light and leave us in darkness?

"Krawk!" Startling as a child's scream, the sudden, horrid noise echoed through the bedchamber and set Simon's heart pounding. It sounded so close it might have been inside his skull, and he sat up and clapped his hands over his ears, half-certain he would feel demons squirming and burrowing there.

"Rawk!" This time the shriek was slightly softer and was followed by a series of *clips* and *clops*, as if a tiny horse galloped upside down across the ceiling. Simon peered upward and saw a dim shape fluttering beneath the rafters. After a moment it landed on the sill of a high, narrow window and stood silhouetted against the gray morning light—a crow, not the biggest he had ever seen, but not small either. It stared back at him, black eye glinting, then took wing once more, beating along beneath the ceiling as if looking for escape, though the window it had just left was open to the sky. After a moment it dropped onto the canopy of his bed, out of his sight, though he could hear its claws scrape as it steadied itself on the wooden corner post.

"Carrion beast," Simon growled. "I'm not dead. I just look that way—feel that way. You've wasted your time."

"Wark?" The bird sounded as though it did not entirely believe him.

"Avel!" Simon sat up, tossed one of the cushions up against the canopy. The crow squawked in protest but did not leave. "Avel! Where in the name of the Bloody Tree have you gone?"

The door of the bedchamber swung open and the boy came in, barechested, hopping and stumbling as he tried to pull on his breeks. "Majesty? Are you well?"

"No, I'm damn well not. There's a crow in here—see it on the top of the bed? What's it doing here? How did a crow get in?"

Avel squinted at the offending creature. "The window, Majesty?"

"I know that. It was not a question I needed answered. I want it out." He scowled up at the canopy that temporarily blocked it from his sight.

"Should I try to catch it, Majesty?"

Simon shook his head, scowling. "No, boy, you should run and fetch someone who can use a bow and arrows. I imagine there must be at least one or two like that in all the Hayholt."

Avel hesitated. "It is bad luck to kill a crow indoors, Majesty."

"Truly?" Simon asked. "And is it bad luck to kill a servant indoors as well?"

The boy looked so frightened that the king's fury immediately cooled. "I did not mean it, lad. But that screeching is a horrid sound to hear on waking. Give me a cockerel any day. Now go and find someone who will drive this thing out of my chamber. Go!"

When Avel had hurried out, now trying to struggle into his shirt, Simon lay back against the cushions. The crow, apparently entertained by all that had happened, flapped down to the floor and began to pace back and forth, pausing occasionally to utter more of its harsh cries. Simon swung his feet to the floor and watched it.

"If you have something to tell me, some grim prophecy to share, you had better do it now," he said. "Go to. Utter your warning. Is the earth about to swallow up the castle? Or are armies of ghosts on their way to overthrow the kingdom? Speak. Otherwise, I will go off to the privy and you can stalk about the chamber by yourself."

When Simon returned, the crow was back on the windowsill again, perched high above his head and watching him like a spectator who was not entirely satisfied with the spectacle.

"The guards will be here soon to arrow you properly, you damned hopping, squawking thing," he told it. "If you have some dire warning for me, best give it now. But what can you tell me that I don't know already? The Norns are in our lands, killing our people? That good Erkynlanders lie dead at Fellmere and now are dying at Winstowe at the hands of grassland barbarians? That their king either does not sleep or when he does, cannot dream even of the wife he has lost or the son who died too soon?"

The crow leaned toward him and tilted its head.

"Go ahead, taunt me, you damnable bird," Simon said. "I've had more prophesies flung at me than you've had snails for supper."

The crow fluffed its wings. Simon realized that Avel was standing in the doorway. "Your Majesty?" the boy said. "Are you well?"

"Just talking to this bloody crow. Did you bring someone to drive it away? Is that him behind you? Step forward, man, and get to work."

Count Nial stepped through the doorway. "My king, I am sorry to . . . to interrupt your rest."

Simon was caught off guard. "Think nothing of it, my friend. I was . . ." He couldn't think of a way to explain exactly what he'd been doing. "What betides?"

"I seek your permission to travel with Eolair, Majesty. I think I can do more to help in Hernystir than I can here in Erkynland."

Simon felt a flare of anger, then a cold squeeze of fear. "What, are you all leaving me? Are things so woeful?"

"No, Majesty, no!" Nial dropped onto one knee. "My wife remains. Would I leave her here if I did not intend to return with help—with men at arms to defend the castle? I can find hundreds of men in the county around Nad Glehs that will fight for you."

"And in Hugh, you have a king who will hang you for it if you're caught." Simon lowered himself onto the bed, suddenly weary again.

"But I wish you would consider sending your granddaughter Lillia away, and my Rhona with her, Majesty. I fear for the safety of women and children here."

"And where would be safer?" Simon asked bitterly. "Your King Hugh is our enemy now. Nabban—only God knows what has happened there. Norns have taken Naglimund, and the barbarians have overrun eastern Erkynland."

"I am sure there is somewhere in Erkynland—Meremund, perhaps—where your grandchild would be safe," Nial said. "Perhaps she could go to her other grandmother's house in—"

"Avel, you are supposed to be finding me a crow-archer," Simon said sharply, cutting across the count. "Instead of listening to other people's conversations."

Avel's eyes went wide. He turned and trotted out.

Nial's gaze strayed to the ceiling. "As for the crow, I do not think you should shoot it, Majesty. They are birds of omen, everyone knows."

"I've heard. But I don't like omens," Simon said. "I'm not fond of crows, either, especially in my bedchamber." He waved his hands in frustration. "Enough of this. When does Eolair leave?"

"Tomorrow, Majesty. That is what he told me."

"Then go and make yourself ready. You have my permission. And I will think carefully on sending Rhona somewhere safe."

"Send her somewhere with young Princess Lillia," said Nial. "Please, Majesty. With Prince Morgan missing . . ."

"She is the only heir. Yes, yes, I know." Simon sighed. "Throw me those boots, will you? I am not going to sit here all day being stared at by a crow when there are things to do." He looked up at Nial suddenly. "Do you think I have lost my mind?"

"Majesty?"

"You heard me. I saw how you and Rhona looked at each other the night you came with the news about Hugh and the Norns. Now my wife is dead and the grasslanders have invaded us. The kingdom is a shambles—and so is the whole of the High Ward, in truth. Am I fit to be king, Nial?"

The count clapped a hand to his breast. "I believe that with all my heart, Majesty."

Simon smiled a weary smile. "Then pray for me to all your Hernystiri gods. And here's a piece of advice for you."

"Yes, Majesty?"

"Work to become a better liar."

"I thank you most sincerely for coming, my lord," said Tiamak. "I know you are busy preparing for your journey. The servants are busy with other tasks, and as you can no doubt guess, moving Aengas's chair is far beyond my strength."

Count Eolair waved his hand. "No need to explain. These are strange times—desperate times. Greetings, Viscount Aengas. I'm sorry I haven't had a chance to meet with you before now. It has been a long time since we last saw each other."

Aengas inclined his head. "It has, my lord. So long that I am no longer a viscount, but that is a story for another time."

They made a strange pair, Eolair could not help thinking, the Wrannaman so small, Aengas large to begin with but also prisoned in his immense chair—a wagon without wheels. "And how can I help you, my friend?" he asked.

"To be honest, you could help me best by not leaving the Hayholt," said Tiamak, but quickly raised his hand. "Peace, my lord. I know we have already talked much about this and your mind is made up. I wish you only luck with your journey, but all the same, I fear for the king to lose your wisdom at such a time."

Eolair shook his head, weary of the subject. "He has done without me for many, many months."

"And look at the state of the kingdom!"

"Tiamak," said Aengas. "Do you hear yourself, dear man?"

The Wrannaman clapped his hands together in frustration. "There! I promised myself I would not dispute with you, and I have broken my own promise. Forgive me, my lord, I beg you. This is *not* what I wished to discuss with you."

"Forgiven," said Eolair, though he felt a little nettled. It was hard enough to leave the Hayholt at such a time without others trying to talk him out of it at every chance. "And I think that sometimes you forget, Lord Tiamak, that you own a title yourself, one you have earned many times over by your service to the High Throne. Now," he said to forestall any more argument, "Why did you ask me to come to you?"

"What I show you and tell you next must be kept secret," Tiamak said, beckoning Eolair to sit at the table between the two of them. "From everyone, I must insist, except the king himself, who knows already, although not every single detail."

Eolair cocked his head at Tiamak's mysterious words. "You have caught my interest. What would you show me?"

"This," Tiamak said, waving a piece of parchment. "But first I must make some things known to you that have been discovered during your absence." He related the discoveries made by the new Almoner, Bishop Boez. "And he continues to discover more thefts. The total of missing gold has now passed four thousand, two hundred thrones, and Boez does not think that is the end of it."

Eolair could only blink. "Hands of heavenly Mircha," he said at last. "That is a dreadful sum. Do you suspect someone?"

"I suspect almost everyone," Tiamak said. "Not including those of us in this room, of course. And that is the problem. Whoever has done this has covered his tracks so carefully that it is hard to eliminate anyone but the king."

"You say you do not suspect me, but you are welcome to see any of my household records, or my books of accounts as Hand of the High Throne."

Tiamak waved away the offer. "No, I want something quite different from you, my lord. Look at this, if you please." He unfolded the parchment he was holding and set it on the table.

Eolair leaned close, frowning. "Forgive me, but my eyesight—"

"—is not the problem," Tiamak said. "It is written in cipher—one we puzzled over for a long time. Old Father Strangyeard used it when he was master of the Almonry thirty years ago."

"And Strangyeard is long dead."

"Just so. But there are at least a dozen or more nobles and perhaps five times that many counting-priests and other clerks that I cannot so easily eliminate. But what I want to share with you is what this particular parchment says, because I think it may detail not just a theft from the royal coffers, but the person who received it as a payment."

"Truly? What does it say?"

"Three ciphered runes. V-F-G."

"What sort of name is that? There is no such."

"It was made as a note, only. I expect it served as a reminder and was meant to be copied to some hidden record later, and therefore the one who made it had no need to spell out who received this largess."

"Well, I have now proved I am little hand at ciphering." Eolair tried to keep his tone light, but his hand was trembling on the tabletop. The idea that four thousand in gold could be stolen from the High Throne, perhaps by someone Eolair himself knew, had shaken and disturbed him. "If that is what you wanted of me, I apologize for disappointing you."

Tiamak leaned toward him. Even by lamplight, it was plain that the past months had not been kind to the little man. His skin was no longer a healthy brown, but rather the paler hue of riverbed clay, and all the lines on his thin face had deepened. "You have been the Hand of the High Throne for a long time, Eolair, and you were a trusted envoy even in old King John's last days. Search your memory, please. Is there anyone you can remember with a name that might match that cipher? Vifileg? Vindafrig? It might be a Rimmersman name or even old Erkynlandish, which many of the noble houses still use. It could be either a man's or a woman's. Can you think of anyone at all with a name like that—even a servant?"

Eolair shook his head in frustration. "No, nothing. I knew a Vilderig once, a baron out of South Erkynland, but that does not fit your scaffolding, and anyway he is many years dead." He sat silent for some time, doing his best to ignore the desperation in Tiamak's expression, but still nothing came. "My apologies. I cannot recall any that fit precisely." He shook his head, rising. "I beg your pardons, gentlemen, but I have much still to do before I depart. Trust that if I think of anything, I will write to you immediately." He made his way toward the door.

"No letter, please, and no note." Tiamak's voice was a defeated murmur. "Let us not make the same mistake our thief has made by committing anything to writing that might fall into the wrong hands. If you think of a name that fits, send it to me by your most trusted servant—have him learn it by memory. If the Thrithings-men can make do without written words, yet ravage halfway into Erkynland, then so can we."

Eolair stopped in the doorway. "Ah! You always were the cleverest man I know, Tiamak!"

"I beg your pardon?"

"He says you're a clever fellow," Aengas explained.

"The Thrithings," said Eolair. "You mentioned the Thrithings. While I was captive there I met Unver Shan's lieutenant, a man named Fremur. He ransomed me from the bandits who had captured me. But the man who delivered the gold was Unver's shaman, or at least so I understood. He was a tall, heavy man with a thick beard who seemed very certain of his own worth. His name, it has just come back to me, was 'Volfrag.'"

"A shaman you say?" Tiamak's stared at the cipher on the parchment, then back at Eolair.

"An important servant either to Unver's lieutenant or to Unver himself," Eolair said. "But I cannot understand why such a man's name would be in a note in the Hayholt's counting hall."

"Gold has a way of making borders disappear," said Aengas. "And it attracts all sorts of men. Like jackdaws, even the simplest minds like to see it shine."

"I do not understand all of this either," said Tiamak. "But I thank you, Eolair. You have given me something I can grasp, something to work with." He rose and hobbled toward the door, opening his arms to the count. "We have known each other a long time," Tiamak told him. "We have worked diligently together for Simon and Miriamele and the good works they have tried to do. I hope you have a safe journey and success in Hernystir, Count. And I pray that They Who Watch and Shape allow us to meet again one day."

Eolair was touched; he held the embrace for several heartbeats before letting go. "I hope for the same thing. You offer prayers to your gods, my friend, and

I will offer the same to mine. We will need the good will of all of Heaven in the days ahead."

It had been a long night's ride through wind and even a few snow flurries, and Porto wanted desperately for it to end. He feared for the covered carriage's wounded passenger, Duke Osric, but even more for his friend, Sergeant Levias, who sat huddled in a blanket on the bench beside the wagon's driver.

Porto nudged his borrowed horse closer to the carriage. After the disastrous fighting at Fellmere and now Winstowe, there were enough ownerless horses to take his pick, though he still mourned the loss of his fine charger in the Thrithings. He sighed and asked his friend, "How goes it there, Sergeant?"

Levias, whose face barely peeked from the blanket, tried to smile. "Shiversome, but God will keep me well if He wishes it."

Porto nodded. "We arrive soon, I think. And the sun will rise before we get there."

"I will welcome it."

"Sleep if you can."

Porto would have given much for a seat of his own. His old joints were all a-throb, and he felt as if he had aged a hundred years since he had last seen the Hayholt. But there was only room for one beside the duke's driver, so Porto rode with the handful of younger soldiers accompanying wounded Osric.

My third retreat in a matter of weeks, Porto thought. *This has been a catalogue of shame for all Erkynland's soldiers.*

The sky was slowly brightening from nearly black to a deep Naraxi blue, and the shapes of trees on either side of the River Road were becoming distinct. As Porto rode, half-nodding, the band of purple called Attara's Belt rose on the horizon, and a short while later he saw the sun's rays strike distant Holy Tree Tower, the castle's highest point, turning it as bright as if it had been gilded by the hands of angels. Porto reined up, waiting for the carriage.

"Do you see it, Levias?" he asked. "The Hayholt? See the towers glow?"

"Like the Heavenly City," his friend said, sighing. "But I fear our welcome there will not be as sweet as the one we will find someday in Heaven, God willing."

Levias made the sign of the Tree. Porto did too, but thought, *We cannot rely on Heaven because we are born full of sin. How can any man know for certain before the Day of Weighing Out what will become of him?*

Yet even so, the sight of the castle rising into the light atop the headland gave him hope—the first in a long time. *I must keep my faith,* he told himself. *That is what Levias has taught me, both by his survival and by his own steadfast belief. God has the final word, and His Son has promised us all redemption, if only we believe. Please, Usires my Ransomer, watch over me. Watch over all good people, for these are dreadful times.*

By the time they reached the Hayholt the sun had risen, but clouds had swept in and the sky was gray as lead. A dozen Erkynguards carried Duke Osric to his chambers. Porto stayed behind to help Levias to a bed in the barracks, where the wounded man quickly fell asleep. Porto went in search of linen to change his friend's dressings, but he was only a few steps past the door when one of the Erkynguard called to him.

"Are you the one that came in with His Grace, the duke?"

"I am, but—"

"You're to come now."

"What?" Porto was annoyed. A long, long trip, no food, and apparently no chance to find help for Levias, either. "Where? By whose order?"

The guard gave him a flat look. He seemed very young, Porto thought, but almost everyone seemed that way to him these days. "To the Throne Hall, by the order of King Simon himself. That good enough for you, Graybeard?"

Porto's heart sank. He knew exactly the question that the king would ask him, and his answer would inevitably reveal his shame and failure.

The great hall was surprisingly empty. A few guards in green tabards stood beside the doors outside and inside, but only three people waited beneath the famous ceiling and its upside-down hayfield of dangling pennants. Porto recognized the trio immediately—the king, Captain Zakiel, and Lord Pasevalles—and his heart sank like a ship's hull breached by unseen rocks. He half-expected that King Simon would simply call for his beheading on the spot.

The king frowned. "You—I know you."

His face was so much thinner that the bones showed, and his eyes were dark-circled and sunken. *He looks older than me*, was Porto's uneasy thought.

"You were one of Morgan's companions," Simon said. "Porto, that's the name."

"Yes, Majesty."

"You were with Duke Osric at Fellmere. Tell me what happened."

Porto savored a moment of relief that his personal failures were not going to be the first subject of discussion. He told of the arrow that started the disastrous battle along the Laestfinger, and the waves of angry grasslanders that attacked the camp over the following days, forcing the Erkynlanders to retreat west toward Fellmere Castle.

"But we are told the duke retreated once more, to Winstowe Castle," said Captain Zakiel.

"It is a much stronger fortress," Porto explained. "Osric did not think he could hold off the grasslanders from Fellmere. Or so I was told."

"Then how did our soldiers escape Fellmere?" King Simon asked.

"Earl Rowson led a sortie out through the gates by night. With a little luck, they might have split the besiegers and begun a rout—a second sortie had been readied—but some of the grasslanders were bathing in the river and raised the alarm. But while Rowson and his men engaged the barbarians, Duke Osric led the rest of the troops down to the riverside. They took the boats of the local fishermen and ferrymen and went up the river to Winstowe.

"Rowson?" The king shook his head. "Rowson led the sortie? I truly have underestimated the Earl of Glenwick, it seems. I owe him an apology." He stared hard at his counselors, as if they had all agitated for Rowson's harsh treatment. "Continue," he told Porto.

"We escaped to Winstowe, but Duke Osric was struck by an arrow there and fell from the battlements."

"From the battlements? How did he live?" asked Zakiel, astonished.

"He fell into a pile of dirt below the wall, which saved him, then he was carried back into the castle."

King Simon's annoyance had turned into confusion. "Then how is it that Osric has come back here to the Hayholt?"

"Somehow word got to the besiegers that Duke Osric was badly wounded. Unver Shan called Rowson and Count Aglaf, the lord of Winstowe, out to parley before the walls. We all stood on the battlements to watch, fearing some barbarian treachery."

"What is he like, this Unver?" asked Simon.

"A tall man—tall as me, I would guess," said Porto. "Tall as you, Majesty. Dark-haired but pale of face for his kind. Slender but strongly built, long-armed like a sea-watcher, and with a nose like a hawk. Moreover, he met with Rowson and Winstowe alone, leaving his men some hundred paces back from the walls when he came up to parley."

"Why would he do such a thing?" asked Simon .

"That I do not know, Majesty," Porto said. "But the truly astonishing thing was that the Shan said he would allow Duke Osric to be taken to the Hayholt to be healed of his wounds—that he wanted the king and queen of Erkynland to see how an honorable man pursued a just war."

"What a shameless creature!" It was hard to tell whether Captain Zakiel was angry or admiring.

"And he let Osric go? Just like that?" The king was clearly perturbed. "Tell me again what he said. About the king and queen."

"That he wanted the king and queen of Erkynland to see how a man of honor pursued a just war," Porto repeated.

"And those were his exact words?"

"Yes, Majesty. He spoke loudly. We heard him from the battlements."

"This is just boasting, Majesty," said Lord Pasevalles. "Do not take it to heart."

King Simon leaned back against his throne, shaking his head. "I wouldn't care if he called me a caitiff and a whoreson. He believes his cause is just. He thinks I sent soldiers to steal Eolair from him to avoid paying a ransom, and that Eolair stabbed one of his servants—the Lady Vorzheva, Prince Josua's wife. No, what troubles me is what this Unver said—'tell the king *and queen* of Erkynland . . .' Why would he say such a thing if he sent men to attack Miriamele on the road north from Nabban?"

No one seemed to have an answer for this.

The king turned back to Porto. "I thank you for your news, sir. If you have brought us more questions than answers, you are not to blame."

But he had an odd gleam in his eye, and Porto was not entirely comfortable. Was the king, like Duke Osric by the Laestfinger, becoming a little mad? *And who could blame him if he was?* Porto had only heard the dreadful tidings of Queen Miriamele's death while being escorted to the Throne Hall, and he was still shocked to his core.

"You may go now, Sir Porto," Simon told him. "You others, stay."

As he bowed to the king, Porto heard Tiamak say, "Let me go first to see how Duke Osric fares, now that I am reminded. I will only need a moment."

Unutterably relieved that his own failures had not been thrown in his face, Porto left the throne hall—slowly, because his legs were stiff from the night's riding. The pennants swayed gently as he passed beneath them, like new leaves on spring boughs, although the air in the hall was winter-cold.

"You must speak to him," said Odobreg. "He listens to you."

"Listening is not heeding." Fremur spat out the grass stem he had been chewing and rose to his feet. "Unver Shan is like a great standing stone deep in the earth. Push all you will, it will not tilt one way or another."

"Still, he gives more heed to you than anyone else, Fremur. And if you marry the widow Hyara, as you mean to, then you will be the Shan's uncle! Speak to him. It is time."

"His uncle." Fremur laughed sourly. "Yes, I am certain he will honor me like a parent then. No, you come with me, brother thane, and we will speak to him together."

The leader of the Badger Clan scowled. "You want more of us there to take the blame if the Shan grows angry."

Fremur could not help smiling a little. "You are right. I want something broad to hide behind, and you are wide and thick." He stretched. "We will take Anbalt and Etvin too. Perhaps he will try to kill them first so you and I can make our escape."

"Do not jest about such things." Like his clan totem, Odobreg was slow to anger but dangerous when finally roused, yet he was very cautious around the Shan. Fremur did not blame him much. Unver, never one to share his thoughts freely, had become even more remote since they had fought their way into Erkynland.

They found the other two thanes, then the four of them set out for the Shan's camp, which was on a low hill facing the castle, with the meadow valley stretching between the two. What had once been rolling fields and pastures now was trampled and pockmarked with campsites, cookfires, tents, tethered horses, and more clansmen than Fremur had ever seen in one place outside Blood Lake. Though they were a conquering army, at least so far, they seemed small beneath the walls of Winstowe Castle, a pile of gray stone that dominated the river valley. At times, looking at those high walls, Fremur felt like he and his fellow grasslanders were birds preening and strutting, all unknowing, beneath the gaze of a patient lynx.

But we are winning, he reminded himself. *Even if it does not feel that way.*

Unver sat by himself on a stone on the hilltop, far from the tents where the rest of his family, churls, and clansfolk prepared for another day. "Ho!" Fremur cried as they approached. "Great Shan! We are come to hear your words."

Unver did not look up. "What words do you hope to hear?" he asked, still staring up at the looming castle. "They will be the same words as yesterday."

Fremur took a breath. "If so, then tell us and we will be satisfied, Great Shan."

Unver gave him a sour look. "When I hear you call me that, Fremur, I know you are unhappy with me."

"I could not be unhappy with you, Unver Shan." And that at least was true. His choice to believe in his friend's destiny had been repaid in astonishing fashion. Only two moons earlier they had both been little better than outcasts. Now Unver was the leader of all the Thrithings clans and Fremur was his lieutenant and also thane of Clan Kragni. "But it is true that not all our folk are happy."

"Is that the Shan's task, then? To make all the clansmen happy?"

"No, nor to do anything but what the Shan thinks best," said Odobreg. "But hear us, please. You know we are all loyal to you. You know we will do what you say."

Unver turned back to examining the distant walls. "Have I not given you all horses and gold and honor?"

"We are grateful, Unver Shan," said Etvin of the Wood Ducks. "But today we wish for instruction more than gold."

Unver made a noise that might have been a grunt of displeasure or a sigh of regret. "Tell me what you want to know."

Although Etvin had brought it up, the thanes all turned now to Fremur, who scowled at them behind the Shan's back.

"The clans are restless," he said at last. "Like hungry wolves who cannot reach their prey."

"That is the nature of stone-dweller castles," said Unver. "They are hard as walnuts—they must be cracked and broken open before you can get at what is inside."

"But this thing you call a 'siege,'" Fremur said, "our men do not know it, do not understand it. All around us they see unprotected lands and villages ripe for plunder. Instead, they sit here—we *all* sit here—like cows waiting to be milked."

"You do not understand. I am waiting," said Unver.

For a moment all the thanes were quiet, waiting for him to explain, but the explanation did not come. "But, Shan—Unver," Fremur said at last, "what are you waiting for?"

"The king. I am waiting for the king of Erkynland to come out of his great stone city."

Fremur was appalled by this idea, and he could tell the other thanes felt the same. "But surely we do not *want* him to come, Unver! You have said yourself that there are more stone-dwellers than men of the clans. Why should we wait like crows on a branch until they send more soldiers? Should we not burn and break all we can reach, take their gold and cows and horses, and then go back to our grasslands? They come, we steer our wagons toward the sunrise, then after a while they give up. As always."

Now Unver finally took his eyes off the gray walls of the castle. His scarred, stony face seemed as alien to Fremur as a shaman's frightening mask. "As always. Yes, *as always*. And what will the king in his great stone castle say when we are gone? 'Those grasslanders are a nuisance. We must send more men to the border. We must guard against more of these raids.' That is what he will say."

For a long, silent moment Fremur tried to make sense of this. "And if he does, Unver?"

"None of you understand." The Shan's fists were clenched in his lap. "I am not fighting a war here. I am building a nation."

Odobreg and the other thanes exchanged glances. "A nation, Great Shan?"

Unver closed his eyes, taming his impatience. "Yes," he said. "I want the king of Erkynland to see that we are not children, living only to grab and run. That we can fight a battle like stone-dwellers or lay a siege if it is needed. That our honor cannot be cheated without cost." His gray eyes sprang open, startling as a sudden noise. "The king of Erkynland must come out and meet us, because otherwise things are no different than before. How do we answer the Nabbanai who build villages on our ancestral lands?" He leaned forward, and his voice was low and angry. "As always, we raid them. We send men on horseback to the outermost villages and set a few fires, stampede the livestock, kill some of their menfolk and steal some of their women—if any are worth stealing. And what is accomplished? Nothing. The stone-dwellers of Nabban are like rabbits, who know that a few of their young will be taken by hawks or foxes. Do they go to live somewhere else? No—they simply make more rabbits. It is what they know, and they have grown used to it."

This was more than Unver had spoken in the last sennight. It was also more words than Fremur could remember him ever saying at one time. He looked at his fellow thanes, who were trying as hard as he was to understand the Shan, but their expressions said they were not succeeding.

"But this is not Nabban," pointed out Anbalt of the Adders.

"No. And we will take our vengeance against Nabban one day, I swear to you by Tasdar's smoking hammer," Unver said. "But first, this—this siege, this small war. We came here to avenge a flock of insults. Count Eolair was stolen from beneath our noses when we were bargaining with Erkynland's king for his freedom, then the madman Osric ignored everything we said to him and attacked the Bison Clan at the river—again, as if we were unruly children. And you would have me set the men free to range about the countryside smashing and stealing, then flee back to the grasslands. Exactly like unruly children."

"What you want is for the king of Erkynland to take you seriously," said Fremur as the light of Unver's words began to dawn.

"No, Thane of the Crane Clan, I want him to take the *Thrithings* seriously. We cover a territory larger than other nations. We have thousands of warriors—hard, dangerous men. And yet the city-folk think of us as little more than children . . . or beasts. And as long as we do what we have always done, attack and run away, harry and then flee, that is all we will ever be to them. Do you know what the stone-dwellers call us? I lived among them, remember, and heard every insult. 'Barbarians.' 'Savages.' 'Animals.' They think we go naked, that we have no justice but the sword, that we lie with our own daughters. They think that we are stupid and backward." He was breathing heavily, his scars pale against his reddened skin.

"But how does *this*—" Anbalt made a swipe with his hand to indicate the valley, the castle under siege, the milling clansmen below, "—change anything?"

"It is only the beginning." The Shan's brief moment of anger was gone, and he had dropped back into stony indifference. "Since the waxing of the First Red Moon we have taken a great piece out of Erkynland—a long, cruel bite, like a Varn crocodile. But when the king of Erkynland comes to save the men hiding in that stone fortress, he will see that we do not flee but sit here waiting for him. He will see that Thrithings-men can change their ways—that they can fight together like stone-dwellers. And *then* he will fear us."

Tiamak went to the residence to look in on Osric. Though the duke was in pain and ill-tempered, Thelía and Brother Etan seemed to have his care in hand. By the time Tiamak returned to the throne hall, limping a little from climbing up and down so many stairs, it was clear that plans had been made during his brief absence. That worried him and also stung his pride.

"Duke Osric's leg wound is now clean and stitched, Majesty," he announced. "It is nothing too grave, though doubtless painful. His chest wound is worse and will take more time to heal, but I feel sure he will live. The duke is awake but not happy, as you may guess. He is most concerned that his men be saved."

"Of course," said Zakiel. "And it is not only for His Grace's peace of mind we must do so. Many hundreds of our Erkynguards are trapped in Winstowe Castle."

"We have decided we have no choice but to send more soldiers," Simon announced, but he would not meet his counselor's eye.

"Do we *have* more soldiers?" Tiamak asked.

"We can muster a few hundred to send to Winstowe and still have enough left to protect the Hayholt," Zakiel told him. "But I do not know how that will be enough to lift the siege."

"We have sent a thousand more home for harvest who have not returned," said Simon. "Beat the muster-drums. Send to every town and village between here and the River Greenwade, and south all the way to the coast. We will march out as soon as we have assembled enough men."

"We?" Tiamak asked.

The king scowled. "Don't be coy, fellow. If you want to ask something, then ask it. Yes, 'we'—I will lead them to relieve Winstowe."

Tiamak felt a sudden premonitory chill. "You plan to go against the grasslanders yourself, Simon?"

"Why shouldn't I?" The king waved for more wine and a servant scurried forward with a sloshing ewer. "After all, I was the one who sent Osric out on this mission." He snatched away the cup and took a long swallow before the servant had even finished pouring, so that wine spattered the floor. "It was on my word that he went against the Thrithings-men in the first place."

Tiamak did not like the heedless way Simon spoke. "But Majesty—"

The king abruptly sat up straight on his throne, staring past Tiamak as if the Wrannaman had abruptly ceased to exist. Simon's eyes had gone wide, and as he rose he seemed as shaky as a much older man. "How . . . How can . . . ?"

Confused and disturbed, Tiamak turned to follow Simon's stare and saw the doors of the hall standing wide. A woman was framed there with the light behind her, so that nothing of her face could be seen, only the glint of a gold circlet on her brow.

"I fear you make too much of me, Majesty," she said, and Tiamak recognized the nearly unaccented voice. "I have only come to say farewell, and to thank you for your hospitality in such a dreadful, sad time."

"Ah." Simon slumped back down onto his seat. His face, for a moment full of life and hope, fell slack once more. "Countess Yissola. Forgive me for my strange words. I . . . I mistook you."

As Perdruin's countess came forward, Pasevalles, Tiamak, and Zakiel all bowed. "Think no more of it," she said, but her face was sorrowful. "My ship leaves with the next tide, but I could not be on my way without wishing you luck and God's help in the difficult days ahead, Your Majesty." She bowed her head for a moment as the king kissed her hand; when she looked up, Tiamak thought her fine face had colored a little. "If better days come, and should you happen to think on the things we discussed . . ." She let the words trail. "I will always be your faithful servant, King Simon, and Perdruin will support you."

"Thank you for that, Countess. We much value your friendship." The king seemed a little awkward, and Tiamak could not help wondering why.

When Yissola had left to finish preparing for departure, Simon said, "Now, Zakiel, I can read an omen as well as the next man. God sent a crow to Saint Pelippa to tell her of the dying Ransomer's thirst, and God has sent one to me only this morning. Even now, our enemies are gathering—we have no more time to waste. If we are to relieve Rowson, Count Aglaf, and Winstowe Castle, we must begin this moment—."

"But Majesty!" Tiamak had not meant to interrupt, but he plunged on. "Putting aside the matter of whether you are in truth ready to lead, and whether such a small force is going to help at all or only expose you to terrible danger, how can you leave the Hayholt at such a time?"

Simon swiped at the air as though swatting away a bothersome insect. "The Norns are still mewed up in Naglimund, Lord Tiamak—we know that much at least—and unless they have all learned to fly like birds, this castle is safe for now, even with only a small force to defend it. But if they do attack us here, we cannot fight on two fronts, so we will need the men who are besieged at Winstowe."

"Your Majesty—Simon—this makes no sense to me." The king's recklessness frightened Tiamak in ways that went beyond strategy. *Does he hope to die in battle? Is life so meaningless without Miriamele that he cares nothing for what might happen to him?* "Your heir is missing, the Norns threaten, and Unver has shown he is no weak threat himself."

The king clearly did not want to hear these arguments. "Lillia is my granddaughter. She carries my blood and—thank God!—Miriamele's as well. If it is needful, she will be fit to rule one day. For now, her other grandfather Osric has come back to us—you said yourself that he will recover. And you and Pasevalles and Zakiel will also be here to help them rule if necessary." He saw that Tiamak was about to say something else and set his jaw. "Enough objections. You are my counselors, but I am the one who must make choices. I need you to tell me how to accomplish what I have ordered, not to tell me I am a fool."

Tiamak looked desperately to Pasevalles, but the Lord Chancellor seemed in a world of his own, his expression unreadable, though Tiamak thought he glimpsed something beneath the blank stare that almost looked like suppressed excitement, and it chilled him to the bone. *Pasevalles is no ally of mine, at least not in this fight.*

But he could not give in so easily. "And you, Lord Pasevalles—you too, Lord Captain Zakiel—what do you think? Am I the only one who dislikes this idea?"

"Do not push me, Tiamak," the king warned.

"You gave me my position to question as well as to obey, Simon."

Zakiel looked troubled, but all he said was, "It is not for me to gainsay the king's orders." Tiamak turned to look at the Lord Chancellor, almost daring him to remain silent.

"His Majesty is right," Pasevalles said at last. "We cannot do without the soldiers bottled up by Unver, and we cannot fight both Norns and the grasslanders at the same time. We must break the siege of Winstowe."

"But why must His Majesty be the one to do it?" Tiamak asked helplessly.

"Because I am the king." Simon's expression was colder and more distant than Tiamak had seen for a long time. "That is all the reason and the only answer, at the end of the day. Because I am the king and no one else is."

13

Fresh Wounds

The stone tunnels and echoing chambers enlarged the noise of the Norn pack into a nightmarish chaos of howls and barking. No matter how they ran, they could not seem to put distance between themselves and the pursuing hounds. Morgan's blood pounded in his temples as he followed Nezeru's flitting shadow through a maze of tunnels, some nearly as broad as Market Row, others so narrow he had to turn sideways to squeeze through them, all of them lit only by the dim glow of the ancient tiles.

"Where are we going?" he shouted above the din of the Norn pack. His legs felt like heavy bags of sand.

"To Reaching Hand tower," she called but did not slow so he could catch up. "Have you forgotten your own plan? We must come at it from beneath."

"But how do you know where to go?"

She stopped, hesitating at a five-way crossing as the terrifying sounds grew louder behind them. "Silence! Let me try to get the scent."

The scent of a tower? he wondered.

After sniffing the air for a long moment, Nezeru chose a passage and sprang down it without looking back at him. Already short of breath, Morgan hurried after her.

Nezeru finally slowed to a brisk trot, allowing Morgan to catch up once more. They were in a passageway lined with alcoves, many of which still held the remains of statues and massive urns, though most were little more now than piles of crumbled stone. She seemed to be swiftly examining the contents of each alcove she passed, but the cacophony of the pursuing beasts grew louder by the instant. Morgan was sweating profusely, and his lungs ached.

She pointed ahead to a right-angled turn in the passage. "Hurry on," she said. "Run and I will catch up."

"What are you going to do?"

"Kill you if you ask more questions! Go!"

If she meant to make a stand, Morgan felt he should join her, but the horrible, excited baying of the hounds sucked the courage from his bones, so he raced on ahead. When he reached the turning, he stumbled, bumped into the wall, and almost lost his footing.

Slowing to regain his balance saved his life. As Morgan swung his arms out for balance, he saw a darkness in the floor only a few steps in front of him—an emptiness. He barely managed to slide to a halt at the edge of a great rift in the floor. Monstrous cracks ran down both walls of the dim passage; the floor had collapsed into an emptiness half-dozen paces across.

He hastened back around the corner, looking for Nezeru. Now he thought he could hear the weird cries of Norn soldiers as well as the baying of hounds.

"What are you doing?" Nezeru shouted, though Morgan could not see where she had gone. At last he spotted movement in one of the alcoves, a shadow behind a stone urn taller than Morgan himself. "Stay away," she cried. "I told you to run!"

"There's a hole up ahead," he called. "A part of the floor is gone!"

"Jump across it."

"It's huge!"

"If you do not, you will die, because I cannot stop them all—!"

And then a flood of pale shapes and gleaming red eyes surged around a bend at the far end of the corridor behind them. With their quarry now in sight, the leading dogs were howling with what sounded like glee.

Morgan turned and ran back around the corner, then put all his strength into the last few strides and leaped just before he reached the edge of the hole. For a moment he was suspended in near blackness, and time seemed to slow as he stretched his arms before him, hoping to land on his stomach and slide forward. He felt his heart beat once, like a drumbeat in the center of his being, then an instant later something struck him in the chest so powerfully that the darkness exploded into whirling spots of light. He held onto his wits long enough to realize he had landed short, with only his upper body on the far side, and was sliding backward toward the endless dark. Morgan splayed his hands on the stone to slow his skid, then tried to find a foothold in the side of the pit but could not. All he could do was cling to the corridor floor like a lizard, though he knew his strength would not last long.

Suddenly he heard a great scrape and crash somewhere behind him, and the shriek of wounded animals. An instant later, Nezeru leaped over his head, so close that he felt the wind of her passage. As she landed on the other side the momentum of her leap carried her forward so that she fell and rolled. She sprang neatly to her feet and scrambled back to Morgan, then closed her cool, strong fingers on his wrist and started to pull. "Help me, you hapless mortal!" she cried.

Morgan lifted one of his bleeding hands and clutched her arm. Nezeru braced herself and kept pulling until Morgan could drag the rest of his upper body onto the floor. As he rolled over onto his back he saw the pursuing dogs charge around the corner, slipping and sliding against each other in their scrabbling haste, only to be suddenly confronted by the hole in the floor. Toothy mouths agape, eyes white around the edges with sudden alarm, the leading beasts slid as they struggled to stop. They might have succeeded had they not been so closely followed by the rest of the pack, but instead they were shoved yelping over the edge. Their panicked howls dwindled as they fell. The surviving hounds ran back and forth beside the gap in the floor, snarling and yelping at their quarry, so close but out of reach.

"Hurry," said Nezeru, yanking Morgan onto his feet. "The huntsmen will not be as quick as the hounds to get past the great urn I pushed over, but they will manage it soon and they carry bows." She turned and began to run again.

Morgan did not have to be told twice. He got to his feet and raced after her.

It seemed an entire day had passed when Nezeru abruptly halted and Morgan stumbled into her from behind. She rasped out a few words in her own tongue and pushed him back, then grabbed his arm to keep him in place while she sniffed the air again.

"If I have rightly remembered, we are deep beneath Gatherers' Way, near Da'ai Chikiza's northern gates," she said in a low voice. "That road, and the forest that surrounds it, lies perhaps three floors above us. We should start to make our way up, then I can listen for Sacrifices."

Morgan could think of nothing to say. With every moment that had passed during their lightless journey, he felt as if he had become less himself—as though he, a mortal, were now turning into one of the city's ancient ghosts, something that might drift for all eternity in shadows and bleak silence.

Nezeru led them down a new corridor. It was obstructed in many places by rubble and almost entirely dark, but at the end of the passage they found a stairwell, almost as if she had created it herself out of sheer will. Nezeru seized Morgan's arm as a warning to stay silent—Morgan did not have the breath after their long, hurried journey to do anything else—then listened.

"Nothing," she whispered at last. "We have lost our pursuers, at least for now. And see! There is some light here."

Morgan could hardly believe her at first—it seemed as dark as ever—but after a few dozen steps her slim silhouette began to take shape before him, and after only a little longer, he could see her clearly. Any other time, Morgan would have thought the glow dim and sickly, but at that moment, after so much darkness it seemed like the overwhelming radiance of Heaven.

At the top of the steps they found another crossing of five different corridors lit by a single tile, and again Nezeru paused to consider. She was covered with dirt and pale stone dust, and Morgan thought she looked like a phantom. He knew he must look much the same. *If anyone sees us, they'll think two statues have come to life*, he thought, which tickled his dazed, weary mind so much that he laughed out loud.

Nezeru turned to him in astonishment. "Have you lost your wits?" she hissed.

He shook his head but did not try to explain. She grimaced in disapproval, then turned and set off along one of the branching passages and into another stairwell before climbing the steps into increasing light.

For a moment Morgan found himself praying it was daylight, despite the dangers that would come with it, but as they emerged into a long, high gallery, he saw it was something stranger. The walls on either side of the passage were made from ornate reliefs of white stone, with what he guessed were more of the glowing tiles set behind them. Their light shone through the translucent stone of the inner walls like candles behind a screen, so that glow and shadow crisscrossed the entire length of the gallery floor.

Nezeru and Morgan both stared at the decorated walls. The carved reliefs were works of great intricacy and skill, the stone figures and symbols shaved as thin as lantern horn so that the light could spill through.

"I never thought to see such a thing," said Nezeru with an odd mixture of anger and reverence. Every movement made her face ripple in the uneven light. "The history of my people—but told by our enemies."

Morgan had no idea what she meant. He walked forward slowly, intrigued by the pictures lining both sides of the gallery. Many parts had faded into darkness, but where light still gleamed strong enough to illuminate the inner wall, he was stunned by the artistry of the carvers. He could make out crowds of figures in exotic dress, animals and trees, ships and waves, all rendered in sumptuous detail, as if a breath away from springing into life.

"Do you see?" said Nezeru bitterly. "They show the flight out of the Garden and the voyage of the Eight Ships, when we all were still one people. But the Zida'ya have carved the story as though all was good between the clans, when in truth they were already plotting to cheat our queen and steal Hamakho's legacy from us." The relief she pointed at was nowhere near so obvious to Morgan. He could make out odd, vast shapes that might have been the apparently famous vessels—Tanahaya, too, had mentioned a story of eight ships—but they had neither sails nor rigging that he could see.

"They always make us out to be the demons, the thieves, the destroyers of peace," said Nezeru in a harsh whisper. "Look, I see a picture of The Parting ahead. Do not doubt it will show my people as the evil ones." She stopped to look more closely at the frieze, her face twisted in angry disdain. Morgan could not make much sense out of these stone carvings either, though he could see what looked like some kind of ceremony. Still he was amazed by the skill of those who had made it. The walls were not in such good condition here—entire sections had fallen and shattered on the floor like sheets of ice—but the carvings that remained were so delicately detailed that he could see every scale on the armor of the nearest figures.

He turned to ask Nezeru how close they were to finding the way out but was struck by the strange look on her face. The anger he had seen before had not vanished, but it was complicated by a new expression, one of disbelief and confusion.

"This cannot be," she said. "Look, they show Queen Utuk'ku and her husband Ekimeniso leaving the Parting ceremony with the rest of my people, but the Zida'ya who remain, and even some of my own people, are shown mourning! See the dark-haired one there, that must be Jenjiyana the Nightingale—a name I was taught to curse as soon as I learned it—and she is portrayed weeping! Lies! The Zida'ya hated us—they drove us out of their lands! Why should they bother to pretend otherwise?"

Tanahaya's thoughts had been a mystery to a Morgan when they traveled together, but he understood this Norn warrior even less. "I thought you said the story in these carvings is all made up—that it's not true." He had at least recognized the name of Utuk'ku, the Norn Queen, and now he picked her out, a tall and dignified figure wearing the silver mask he had heard spoken of so many times. It was frightening to think that the infamous witch portrayed in these ancient carvings still lived. "If the Sithi are just telling their own side of things, what does it matter what the carvings show?"

Her whisper was strained. "Because they do not show my people, the Hikeda'ya, as monsters, but simply as those who left to go their own way. And it shows the Zida'ya-folk mourning that separation fiercely—see, Jenjiyana's cheeks run with tears! This is either the Zida'ya's cruelest deception or . . . or some of the things I was taught are not true."

Morgan did not understand why Nezeru seemed so upset, but the portrait of the silver-masked queen was a clear reminder that danger still surrounded them. "We should move on," he said.

For a moment Nezeru looked so angry that he thought she might even strike him, but instead she shook her head slowly, like a horse refusing to jump a wall. "Yes. You have it right, Morgan."

It was one of the few times she had called him by his name. "Shall we go, then?"

"We must. I will think on this strangeness later—if we survive." She turned away from the carvings with what looked like an effort of will, then led him toward the gallery's distant end.

Tanahaya had followed what she thought was Morgan's faint scent through many corridors and more than a few levels of the ruined city, but it was hard for her to feel certain she was on the right track. She passed through what she guessed must be the Welcome Hall and onto the landing of a ceremonial staircase. Many of the steps were cracked or crumbled, and several ribs of the vaulted ceiling had fallen, making the climb even more difficult.

Then, abruptly, the scent she had been following grew stronger, and Tanahaya felt a surge of hope. But by the time she reached the bottom of the stairs the scent had grown faint again, and for a moment she could only stand, disappointed and confused.

It occurred to her suddenly that she might have been following his traces in the wrong direction—that Morgan might have started at the bottom of the long staircase and finished at the top, or simply have lingered for a while on the upper landing without entering the staircase at all. She knew little of the underground labyrinth that lay beneath Da'ai Chikiza, but she did remember that there were several ways to move from any point to another.

As she wondered what her next step should be, she heard a noise from one of the adjoining corridors. A split-instant of hope—could it be Morgan?—froze into fear when she detected the subtle squeak of Sacrifice armor. A moment later she caught the scent of several Hikeda'ya soldiers.

She was trapped in the open, she realized, with nowhere to go but back up the obstructed stairway, an escape that would take time and make noise and perhaps still leave her helplessly exposed when the Hikeda'ya soldiers reached the landing where she now stood. She clambered as quietly as she could back to a fallen piece of vaulting that lay across the stairwell like a marble tree trunk, then flattened herself behind it. If they climbed the stairs they would find her, of course, but she had nowhere else to go. As she lay pressed against the broken rib of stone, she loosened her sword in its sheath, preparing to take a few of her enemies back to the Garden with her.

This is a trap I have built for myself, she thought in disgust. *I am a scholar and a failed envoy, not a warrior. I should have left this to others.*

She held her breath. The Hikeda'ya had paused somewhere near the landing below her: she could hear voices, the harsh consonants of Nakkiga speech, but could not yet hear what they were saying.

Unbidden but irresistible, a memory forced its way into her thoughts, a memory of another moment, another day, when she had faced death. But that time she had not been alone.

"Slow up!" she called.

Jiriki, as if startled awake, gave a gentle flick to the reins and his tall white horse slowed to a trot ahead of her. When she had almost caught up, she touched her heels against her own horse's side and they bounded past him. It was early spring, and though the sun was shining, snow still lay mounded in the blue shadows around the base of the cedars. A flurry of snowflakes festooned the air like tiny flecks of adamant, sparkling as they caught the daylight. "Are you in such a hurry to see me gone?" she called over her shoulder. "Was my visit too lengthy for you, Willow-switch?"

The brother of her dearest friend stared for a moment, caught by surprise, then smiled and urged his horse after her. "Wicked creature," he cried. "Is that how they teach the young in Shisae'ron to treat their elders?"

Too-serious Jiriki had a weakness, Tanahaya knew—a small twinge of vanity. He had changed the color of his hair again, using mushroom burned and mixed with alum for a golden glow. Tanahaya thought it made him look like a sun-crowned hero out of the early days of the Garden.

Her horse Bluejay was strong and swift, but Jiriki was already closing the distance between them, so she turned her attention back to the forest path. She was first puzzled, then astonished when a huge clump of snow just ahead of them began to move, shuddering as though the spring's warmth had brought it to life. Then the entire clump reared up, powdery snow flying off the snow-white pelt, and Tanahaya saw its huge eyes and gaping red and yellow mouth.

Uro'ye! *she thought—giant!*

The thing shambled forward, swiping at her with one of its broad, clawed hands. Her horse let out a snort of terror and reared up, legs kicking, tumbling Tanahaya to the ground. As she lay stunned, the horse collapsed on top of her, blood gouting from its torn neck. Only the thick snow saved her from broken bones, but her legs were trapped.

The face of the giant loomed above her, all gleaming eyes and teeth. She had only a moment to brace herself for its deadly attack—with her legs caught and her sword beneath her, there was nothing else she could do—when she heard Jiriki shout.

"Here, foul beast! Here!"

Jiriki swept past her then, leaning out from his saddle, his sword a dull gray blur. The monster threw up its arm or it might have lost its head; the blade bit deep into its forearm instead. The giant let out a bellow that shook Tanahaya's skull, then turned to follow its attacker.

It was a young giant, she saw as she finally pulled herself free of her dying horse—only a little taller than Jiriki, but vastly heavier and more muscled. Jiriki did his best to keep it at bay, hacking at it with Thunderbolt, his grandfather's sword, but the monster was canny: it ducked beneath his blade and lunged toward his mount instead, meaning to gut the horse and tumble Jiriki to the ground the way it had with Tanahaya.

It was pure luck that Tanahaya's own horse, in its dying moments, had fallen with its left side up, so she could reach her bow and quiver hanging on the saddle horn. The arrows had spilled, and were littered across the snow. When her fingers finally closed on one, she sat upright, lifted the bow, and in one fluid movement nocked, drew, and let fly. The shaft sped straight and true and sank into the creature's neck just above the shoulder, making the giant howl and swat at the wound. The distraction gave Jiriki an instant to recover, and he swiped a deep cut across the giant's forehead. Tanahaya had found another arrow, and as the bloody-faced thing roared in pain and thrashed blindly, she drew and loosed again. This one dug even deeper into the creature's neck, making it stagger. An instant later Jiriki split the giant's hairy head with a two-handed blow.

"Are you hurt?" he called. Even as the dead creature swayed and fell, Jiriki hurried toward her.

"Not badly. Are you?" With his help she slid out from under the carcass of her horse, a lively and trustworthy companion only moments ago, now just cooling flesh.

"I have never been so fearful," he said, and pulled her to him, wrapping his arms tightly around her.

"You have been in much greater danger," she said, but reveled in the embrace.

He let go of her. "You will have to ride with me now. Poor Bluejay." He looked down at her dead mount, the snow gone red around it. "But I do not understand why that creature was here. The uro'yei *do not venture so far south. Not for years."*

Her relief at surviving made her reckless. "You have faced and killed giants before. Why were you so fearful this time?"

He looked at her and recovered a little of his calm. "Did I say I was? It is not important. But you handle a bow well for a scholar, Spark."

"And you fight well for someone so unschooled, Willow-switch." But she would not let him off so easily. "You were about to explain why you were so affrighted by a mere giant, and a young, small one at that."

He looked at her then, and a host of subtle emotions rippled across his narrow face. "Do you play with me? With the one who has so many times showed you the subtleties of the game of Shent?"

"Oh, I would never dream of it. I simply wished you to finish something you began to say. Or has your recent fright tied your tongue? That seems strange in such a brave warrior."

He kept his mouth in a hard line, but she could see it was with an effort. "You are wicked, Spark. You tease and make light of me."

"When your sister is not present, it is my task to do so," she said. "Now speak. You have never been so fearful before, because . . ."

At last he surrendered. "Because it was you. Because I feared you would be hurt or even killed—that I would lose you."

"Do you think I did not feel the same?"

His expression was carefully neutral. "Felt the same fear for me, you mean?"

"Of course, you cautious, beloved fool." She laughed. "Forty summers and more we have known each other, and you have been like a brother to me—and more than a brother." She took a breath. "Can you not admit you care for me, Jiriki? And not just as another sister, but as more than that?"

"I do," he said simply. "But these are evil times, and I will be protector of Year-Dancing House after my father is gone. I did not think I had the right—"

"May Unbeing take your 'right'!" she said with some heat. "It is precisely in times like these when we must speak openly, must reach out for what we want. Do you want me, Willow-switch? Do you want me as I want you?"

He could not make himself smile, but he forced the other sorrows from his face. "I do, Spark. You know I do."

"Then that is settled. Help me up onto your saddle." She realized she was still trembling. "We will have to leave my good Bluejay here. I will mourn him."

The sound of Hikeda'ya speech startled Tanahaya out of the past. She held her breath and listened intently, trying to make sense of the whispering and the nearly silent shuffling of booted feet. She could still hear Sacrifice soldiers searching the hallway at the bottom of the stairs, but now she heard voices above her as well. She was caught between two roving parties of searchers. Huge pieces of fallen ceiling blocked much of the stairwell, hiding her for the moment, but she knew that Utuk'ku's Sacrifices were cautious and methodical. Sooner or later, a party of soldiers would decide to search the stairs thoroughly. She would have to chance a run for freedom.

She thought she could hear more Hikeda'ya above her than below, so Tanahaya decided that descent would be her best chance. She could quite clearly hear the murmur of T'si Suhyasei, the Coolblood River, and she hoped that meant that the river's edge was very near.

She waited until the whispering searchers at the bottom of the stairs had moved away. Those hunting above were still close, but they had not yet entered the stairwell, so when silence finally fell, she rose and made her way downward as quietly as she could. After an agonizing passage interrupted by several fearful stops and starts, she reached the mossy paving stones of what had once been a wide hallway. Beyond stood a crumbling arch, once a ceremonial entrance in a great wall but now a frame for the happy sight of the Coolblood, its waters shimmering dully in the winter sun.

Nothing seemed to stand between Tanahaya and the river except a single broad alder tree rooted deeply in the bank at the water's edge. For a brief instant she considered climbing into the tree to hide and waiting until the Sacrifice soldiers had moved out of this part of the city, but then she heard a shout of alarm in the Hikeda'ya tongue and knew she had been spotted. Hiding was no longer a possibility and neither was retreat into Da'ai Chikiza, so she sprinted out into the open and toward the river.

An arrow buzzed past her like an angry wasp. Sacrifice sentries were scrambling out of the ruins a little way upstream. She dodged blindly, first to one side, then another, as several more shafts whistled past. One struck the alder's dark gray trunk and stood there, quivering.

More Hikeda'ya voices cried out as she raced toward the tree, desperate to get something between herself and the flock of black arrows. She would be safe from Sacrifice darts if she leaped into the river, but she knew that a cascade of rapids began only a hundred paces or so downstream, full of sharp rocks that would break her bones if the current did not simply overwhelm and drown her.

An arrow ripped the shoulder of her tunic. Tanahaya saw no boats anywhere along the bank, and despaired. *If they do not kill me outright, they will catch me and give me to Akhenabi and his torturers. They will discover that I learned about the queen's plan to unearth the Witchwood Crown, and then all will be lost.* She could not let herself be taken.

The great alder loomed closer—a dozen steps away, then half a dozen. Tanahaya leaped for a large, low-hanging branch, but it broke away and she tumbled to the ground, rolling toward the river's edge as arrows dug into the muddy bank around her.

She snatched up the broken branch, long as a sword and thick as her calf, then threw herself into the river. She lost the branch in the shock of cold as she went under, but she stayed beneath the surface and swam with the rough, fast-moving current for as long as she could hold her breath, then lifted her head out of the water even as the river spun her in circles. The broken branch bobbed close by, so she pulled it to her. Arrows were still splashing into the water behind her, but she had been swept downstream a long distance before she had surfaced, and although several of the Hikeda'ya sentries hurried along the bank after her, the river hurried faster. She clung to the branch and kept her head low as the ruins of the city slid away and the misty forest closed in around her.

14

A Face Not Even God Could Love

"I cannot tell you how good it is to see you alive and well," said Viscount Matreu. "We—I—have been searching for all of you since you left Nabban."

Jesa had no clear reason to distrust him—he had saved her once and had been kind to her in Nabban—but the same instinct that had made her leery of the priest, Father Culby, warned her now not to venture within the noble's reach until she was certain of his intentions.

"Searching for us?" she asked. "For the duchess?"

"All of you, yes, but especially the duchess." He took a few steps forward. "Do not take it amiss. She is the duke's wife, after all, and important to many back in Nabban."

She edged backward. "What is happening there?"

Matreu sighed and shook his head. "What *isn't* happening? That is the real question. Anarchy, riots, fires. The gentlemen of the Dominiate and all the Fifty Families have more or less quit the city—vanished to their country homes or even to my own island home, where they would not previously have been caught dead. And Sallin Ingadaris in his fortified house lords it over the city, of course. Claims that his cousin Turia is carrying the child of Drusis, and that the dukedom should be his to hold until the baby is of age."

Jesa thought of Lady Turia, her old, cold eyes in a childlike face, the unperturbed way she had carried herself in the court of her enemies. "Sallin will not live so long."

Matreu gave her an odd look. "Perhaps not. But that is beside the point, since we know that there is already an heir—an heiress, to be more precise. The infant Serasina."

Jesa was confused, and with the confusion came a prickle of fear. *He speaks to me not like a servant, but like a friend, or at least an equal. He wants my trust, of course, but still, something seems amiss.*

"I see you are wary of me," he said, as if he could hear her thoughts. "I do not blame you. You must have hidden here for several days, hungry and afraid. But I swear I am your friend and a friend of the duke's household, may God grant him peace. Let me help you. Lead me to the duchess and Serasina and I will get you all to safety."

There. Now she finally understood. He did not seem to know Canthia was dead but he had not mentioned poor Blasis. How could he talk about little Serasina as the heiress to the duke's crown unless he also knew that the little boy Blasis was dead, throat slit and body cast aside in the road like an empty sack? Yet Matreu had said nothing about him.

"You want the baby," she said flatly.

"And to find the duchess, of course. I want to make certain all of you are safe," he proclaimed with a most winning smile. "I want to take you somewhere where you will not have to hide anymore, where you can live without fear."

"But is there such a place in Nabban anymore?"

"Likely not—at least not at this moment. Sallin's spies are everywhere, looking for Duchess Canthia. But I could take you to my father's house on Spenit. Nobody can harm you or the child on my family's island, so we can decide what to do next without fear or haste." He paused, watching her face. "You know, Jesa, I have always found you a very graceful and comely young woman. You would have a place of high honor in my family's house, a place worthy of your courage and beauty." Again he smiled, this time with just the right amount of humility and sincerity. How many dozens of young women must have gone weak in their knees before that smile!

But it had a different effect on Jesa. *He is no friend.* Her throat was suddenly tight, her stomach sour. *No, he is the Night Eater, the hungry ghost who stands outside in the dark and speaks in the voices of lost loved ones. To believe those soothing words would be to vanish into the blackness and never be seen again.*

And with that sudden certainty, a kind of calm spread through her. It felt like the moments before a great storm struck, when everything but the fight for survival dwindled and disappeared, when relatives who never passed a kind word to each other worked side by side to gather up the ancestor stones, and neighbors who had feuded for years helped each other's families into boats. *This man cannot be trusted. I cannot let him know where Serasina is, because as soon as he knows, he will have no further use for me.*

"Are you alone, my lord?" she asked with as much innocence as she could muster. "Is it not dangerous for you to be in the woods by yourself? Our carriage was attacked by bandits—grasslanders. Surely, it is not safe here for an important man like you."

He hesitated for the merest instant before saying, "I would risk the anger of a hundred barbarians to keep the duke's wife and daughter safe—and you as well, of course, Jesa."

I saw the tracks of many men. He has soldiers with him, likely close enough to come at his call, but he does not want to frighten me because he needs me to show him where

Serasina is. But as she thought of the baby, she recalled in sudden terror that the child was sleeping in her basket only a few dozen paces away up the slope. If Serasina woke now and began to cry, Matreu would find her in moments. Jesa had no illusions she could fight him off. She had to lead him away from the child's hiding place.

Jesa felt a terrible pang in her chest at the thought of leaving the baby alone for any length of time in a wild place, but she knew that the greatest danger to the child was this man and those who had come with him. "I will take you to the duchess," she told the viscount. "She is a distance away. I was just about to return."

Matreu's handsome smile returned. "Usires the Aedon bless you, young woman. Ah, the duchess is fortunate to have you as her companion."

"Servant," she said, growing a little weary of his incessant flattery even as her mind turned and turned, seeking a solution. "Follow me, my lord. But it is muddy, and there are thorns. I fear your nice clothes will be spoiled."

He waved it away. "Lead me. I would risk far more to save the duchess and her daughter."

Something in the easy way he said it made Jesa wonder for the first time whether Matreu was merely an opportunist, retrieving little Serasina as a useful bargaining tool to expand his own power, or if he had somehow aided in the murder of her mistress and Serasina's brother, little Blasis.

You are shallow and greedy, she thought. *Are you also a traitor? An assassin? What does someone like that deserve?*

As she led him along the bank of the river and away from the baby, this idea rolled back and forth through her thoughts, prickly as a thorn-studded toad-fruit. She needed to find some way to lose Matreu and lose him thoroughly, so that she would be able to get back to Serasina and escape with her.

"Come, woman," said Agga, startling Miri out of the half-doze in which she had blessedly, if only briefly, been able to forget her dire situation. "Come. Us will show tha something."

She was hungry and sore from being stuck in the same position all night by the heavy chain around her ankle. Agga had given her a bowl of gruel but she had barely touched it, thinking he might mean to poison her—not enough to kill her, perhaps, but enough to render her stupefied so that he could do with her as she wished. But the small amount she had eaten had done no harm except to remind her how famished she was. She grabbed the bowl up and began to shovel the remaining porridge into her mouth with her fingers.

Agga knocked the bowl from her hands; the last of the gruel splattered on her bare feet and the dirt floor. His face showed little expression, but his voice was harsh. "When us tells tha comest woman, then comest tha." He tugged the chain hard, almost pulling her off the bed.

Miri swallowed the curses that bubbled up in her throat. She was this man's prisoner—for now. It would do her no good to take a beating, perhaps to have bones broken. She needed to stay strong. *But my day will come, beast,* she thought. She struggled to her feet, heavy chain rattling.

Agga reached down and, almost without effort, snatched up the anchor. Whatever he was, part-Niskie or just an ordinary man, he was strong; she should not forget that. The muscles of his back were thick beneath his tattered shirt. This gave her an idea.

"If you treated me well," she said, "I might do things for you that a wife would do."

He gave her a speculative look. "What like?"

"Mend your clothes, for one thing."

He snorted but at least did not yank the chain again. Anchor dangling in one meaty hand, he led her out into sunlight. For a moment she was dazzled, but the brightness was only by comparison to the dark hut: the day was wintry, the sun hidden behind a veil of gray, a bright smear behind the clouds.

Miri looked carefully all around as she followed him out of the cottage and down toward the riverbank, studying everything without being too obvious about it. A rounded oven or kiln made of mud brick stood in the center of the clearing. At first she thought it might be for burning charcoal, though it seemed small for that, then she saw an anvil sitting in the dirt and a heavy hammer leaned against it.

So that is how he put the chain around my ankle. By our Ransomer, how I would love to put one around his—or wrap it around his throat! The rest of the dooryard offered little of interest—a crude sawhorse, a pile of nets awaiting mending, and a lean-to with a rack inside covered with gutted, drying fish.

"Faster, woman," he said, and gave the chain another rough jerk. Miri had started moving toward him at his first word and so avoided being pulled off balance, but now she was almost overcome by his scent—mud and fish and sour sweat. Disgust and rage mounted inside her like a storm, her heart pounding in her chest. If she had held something in her hand at that moment, something that could hurt him, she might have used it, beating or no beating.

Agga led her through a thicket and down toward the river. When they reached a shallow backwater at the bottom of the slope, she dropped to her knees and scooped up a handful of clear water in her hands and drank it eagerly. Agga laughed.

"Is it funny to you that I might die from thirst?" she demanded.

"Us'll not let tha die. Tha hast a calling—Her said so. Tha'll't be us's wife." He pointed to a spot a dozen paces farther upstream. "There be what's in yon water—water tha drinkst at, so thirsty. Here be what us brought tha to see."

She saw only the wind-rippled backwater and the more active surface of the flowing river beyond it. "What?"

He pulled at the anchor chain, tugging her along, careless of whether he made her walk with bare feet through a patch of sand nettles. She was so busy avoiding the stinging leaves that she did not look where she was going until Agga pulled back hard on her chain again, forcing her to stop at the edge of the riverbank.

The water looked much deeper here, but the color was strange somehow, at least in one place, as though a large gray stone lay just beneath the surface. She had only a moment to try to make sense of it, then the gray mass suddenly lurched up from of the water and Miriamele screamed in terror, slipped trying to scramble back from the water, and fell on her backside in another patch of nettles.

The thing splashed toward her, then jerked to a halt a few paces out from shore and loosed a deep, rumbling growl. It was a fish, but it was not a fish. Its head was huge, the mouth impossibly big—its gullet seemed wide and deep as a well. Strange, twitching horns wriggled on its upper jaw, and the tiny, expressionless eyes were somehow too close together at the front of its head. It lurched toward her again on bowed, froglike legs before being pulled up short, startling another gurgle of panic from her clenched throat.

Agga was amused. "Fear not! Him be spiked down good and proper—tha'rt not the only one chained, see?" He picked up a stick and poked at the gaping mouth; the thing snapped at it with a loud, wet *clack.* "Him be the one what pulled tha down and meant you for him's supper."

Half out of the water, but at the end of its iron-linked leash, the creature growled again, this time sounding as frustrated as it was angry. She could not stop staring at its close-set eyes, which gave the grotesquely broad head a weirdly human look. It reared up to strain toward her with flabby paws, and for the first time she could see its belly, white as marble except for something like a wide, dark star on one side of its chest, the flesh rumpled and raw around it. "See, there be barb of us's fish-spear what holds him," crowed Agga. "Gone right through him's chest, has. When him was tired, us made him fast to big rock."

"Blessed Elysia preserve us." Miri was breathing hard. She scarcely noticed the burning of her skin where the nettles were pricking her. "What in the name of God is it?"

"River Man," Agga said. "Kallypook is him's old name. Eat anything—fishes, birds, deer. Meant to eat tha, too. See yon gorge? Swallows all straight down."

"Why do you keep it this way?" There was a tiny sliver of pity somewhere in her revulsion. The thing was horrible, but the disturbingly manlike arrangement of its face made it seem almost human. *This must be what the damned souls in hell look like.*

"Not ready to do naught with him, yet." Agga tugged her chain, forcing her to clamber back onto her feet. "Keep him live and hide wet 'til market-time. Hide off big'un like him'll bring a few fithings, that be sure. Make a brace of boots."

"You're going to skin it?"

"Oh, aye. And meat smokes up nice, last us 'til spring."

The thought of eating the horrid creature's flesh almost made her vomit. "I can't eat that."

"Aye, tha will and be thankful. Take what river gives. Us's da teached us that." He pulled something out of his sleeve, and Miriamele understood why the smell of fish had seemed particularly strong: he waggled the large perch in his callused hand before the kallypook's face until the monstrous jaws opened wide and snapped shut. Agga tossed the fish into the water and the creature fell on it, sucking it down so quickly it seemed to simply vanish. "See? Him be's hungry. Can't catch much with us's spear in him." He pulled out another dead fish and tossed it into the water. Again, the creature inhaled it.

Miriamele shuddered as sour liquid rose into her mouth once more. The kallypook's maw was wide enough to swallow a child whole. Only a few days ago those gaping jaws had closed around her leg, then the thing had pulled her down into the darkness of the river depths. "Why are you showing me this?"

"Few be men on this river what can bring up kallypook with naught but spear and line," Agga said with more than a touch of pride. He had not spoken much before, but this seemed to be a subject he enjoyed. "Weighs twice a man. Teeth be small but get in you and them do hold fast and rip flesh. Us be only man 'twixt Wentmouth and Onestry what catch him as a rule."

Wentmouth. The word was like a sudden light in a dark room. She had never heard of Onestry, but Wentmouth stood at the ocean mouth of the River Gleniwent, on the southern bank, and she knew that city well. And across the river from Wentmouth, not half a league distant, lay Meremund, its richer twin—Miri's childhood home.

"Wentmouth," she said slowly. "I do not know that place. Is it far?"

For a moment he seemed about to answer, then his eyes narrowed beneath the hairless brows. "Far. Too far. Ask us no more questions now, or take a swim with River Man. Mayhap tha dost fancy him?"

"No." But Agga's response seemed telling. He didn't want her thinking about Wentmouth, which might mean that it was closer than he let on. And what had he mentioned the other day? Another town, a place with a market he had suggested was close by—Eywick? She did not know it, but it was a piece of information. Miriamele knew that you could never tell which pieces might fit together, like a puzzle, to show you a picture, to make sense of something—or in her case, to help her escape this horrid man.

Perhaps because her questions had annoyed him, perhaps because he wanted to remind her that she was in his power, Agga made her drag the anchor back to the cottage. They had traveled only a short distance to reach the pool, but it took her most of an hour to struggle back, and when she got to the hut, she collapsed in exhaustion onto her makeshift bed, ankle scraped raw where the chain had rubbed and her arms, shoulders, and back burning from pulling the weighty anchor. Agga laughed, then went out to his traps.

★ ★ ★

As days passed, the queen and her captor fell into a grotesque imitation of domesticity, Agga going out to do his various chores every morning just before sunrise, Miri sitting alone in the cottage for long hours. She found a broom, which Agga called a "besom," a word Miri had not heard since her childhood—her ancient grandfather had once compared his long beard to one. She employed the bundle of twigs as best she could, sweeping the worst of the rubbish into the corners of the hut and dislodging all the cobwebs she could reach, but otherwise had little to do. Her captor did not expect her to cook—no surprise, she knew, since he would not want her handling sharp things, boiling water, or fire—and fed her on what he ate himself, a diet that seemed to consist almost entirely of dried fish or the occasional fresh catch that he cooked on a stick over the fire. Miri had grown up in a seaside city, and soon grew utterly sick of fish flesh and begged him to bring in a vegetable or two, but though Agga sometimes plucked river plants and chewed them, he seemed remarkably ignorant about what might be growing around his cottage.

She was also left thankfully free of what might be thought of as other wifely duties, perhaps because she had made it clear that she would fight like a cornered animal if he ever tried. But Agga truly seemed to believe that they would be married one day, though in what kind of weird, otherworldly ceremony she still could not imagine, and he was willing to wait until that day for his husbandly privileges. Miri thought he likely knew almost nothing about women—he spoke often of his father, but never his mother, who seemed to have died or gone away when he was young—and she was more than content to leave things as they were. But to be safe, she did not question him overmuch on any subject that might lead him to think of her in a womanly way, and she deliberately left herself unwashed, though considering Agga's own smell and lack of cleanliness, could not believe that was what kept him off her.

She tried to escape, of course. The third day after they had returned from the kallypook's pool, when she knew he was going a good distance downstream to see what he might have caught in his nets below the rapids, she waited until she was certain he was far away, then heaved the anchor up from the floor and walked slowly out of the cottage and into the surrounding trees.

The anchor quickly proved too cumbersome to carry—not just its weight, which was considerable, but also because its arms kept snagging on branches, making it hard for her to move through the very places where she would be most hidden. But dragging it was even worse. She had managed to get only a few hundred exhausting steps from the cottage by the time the sun had risen past noon, and she collapsed soon after. When a cold rain began to fall, she did not have the strength even to get under the cover of a tree. Her captor said nothing when he returned near sunset and found her, only let out a single, brutal laugh, then threw her over his shoulder and carried her back to the hut with the anchor dragging painfully from her ankle the whole way.

Even if I find some way to kill this monster, she thought in despair as she lay throbbing and miserable that night on her lumpy bed of torn nets, *I will not be able to get very far.*

The forced intimacy of sharing the hut with him made her think often of Simon, although this togetherness was nothing like what she had enjoyed in her airy castle chambers, surrounded by servants and well-wishers, and with a companion who put her happiness above his own—sometimes to a fault, she had to admit. Every day she prayed that Simon would find her, though a stubborn part of her would have much preferred to effect her own rescue. *But he must be looking for me!* she reassured herself, again and again. *My good husband has likely turned all of northern Nabban and the south of Erkynland upside-down, searching for me. Surely it will only be a matter of time until the Erkynguard arrive at even this God-forsaken spot.*

But the days passed and the Erkynguard did not come. Agga's uneasy dreams became even more powerful, more disturbing. At night she could hear him thrashing in his bed on the far side of the cottage, mumbling, then listening, then mumbling again, as if conversing with invisible presences. A few times she heard him raise his voice to cry out, *"As tha sayest, Lady! So it shall be!"* and Miri would shiver. On such nights she could not get to sleep until he had fallen silent again, and the cottage was quiet except for the dull, incessant murmur of the river nearby or the occasional plaintive cry of an owl.

"Why did you stray so far from your mistress and the child?" Matreu had been following Jesa for no little time along the high bank above the river, and she could hear suspicion growing in his voice.

"I did not mean to," she said. "I was looking for a clove tree. The oil from the buds helps to calm babies when they are hungry or their gums hurt."

"I know clove trees from my own home," said Matreu, plucking burrs from the leg of his breeches. "But they do not grow here, I think."

"Oh! That is too bad!" she said, though in truth she had been looking for no such thing. "Little Serasina is often hungry. I am a maiden and have no milk in my breasts, and the poor thing had a wet nurse until the day we left Nabban."

Matreu fell silent, perhaps thinking about her maidenhead and breasts. If so, that was more than well with Jesa, who had not mentioned either by accident.

She led him on, through tangles of bracken and figwort, sometimes lower along the bank when the greenery grew too thickly. A light rain was falling, but the drops were cold, and Jesa thought worriedly about little Serasina, left behind in her basket.

They Who Watch and Shape, keep your eyes ever on the little girl, she prayed, *and protect her from serpents and fierce beasts. She has done nothing wrong to anyone. She has lost her mother and father, but her life still stretches ahead of her.*

"I begin to doubt we will find the child," Matreu said after a while. "This seems much too far for you to have gone."

An idea was in Jesa's mind now, but she had to keep him following her. She was terrified he would suddenly realize that she was leading him away from her young charge, like a mother bird that mimes a broken wing. While her back was to him, she undid the lacing on her kirtle. Finished, she pretended to drop something and threw her arms up in dismay, then dropped to her knees. "Oh! My locket! The chain has broken!"

Matreu came up beside her, looking down at her with irritation. "What are you doing?"

"My locket. It was a gift from my lady. The chain has come loose and I have lost it somewhere." She pretended to look, giving him a chance to see the upper part of her breasts in the loosened kirtle. It did not seem to mollify him, but it did keep him quiet for a score or so of heartbeats, then he grabbed her arm and roughly pulled her upright.

He leaned close. "If it fell and you do not know when, it is lost. You have left the child and her mother alone a cruelly long time. Keep moving."

"But it is dear to me!"

"So is your life, I think. We have wasted enough time."

As she pushed forward, she had a disturbing thought. *He will not be tempted because he thinks he will have me whenever he wants—perhaps as soon as the baby is found.*

A very short time later, when she stopped to look for sights she recognized, Matreu grabbed her arm again. "I think this is a bootless quest. I think you have lied to me."

"No, my lord! I swear it is just ahead—the place where I left the baby!"

Swift as the strike of a Wran salt adder, his knife was out and pressed against her throat just below her jaw, so that she had to tip her head back to keep the point from piercing her skin. Matreu brought his face close to hers, brows lowered as he scowled. "If it is not, things will go badly for you, girl. I need the duchess and her child—I do not need you. And you can lead me to them just as well with only nine fingers—or perhaps without a nose. And I can still make other use of you, though I may need to drape a veil over your face first."

Her heart was rattling and her breath was short. Just another hundred steps or so, that was all she needed. "I swear by God and Heaven!"

He turned her around, put his hand in the small of her back, and pushed so hard that she stumbled and almost fell. "Any more delays," he warned her, "and I will see if a girl from the swamp screams as loud as one from the islands."

At last she stopped on a high, steep bank beside the river, and pointed down into the reeds below. "There. They are hiding there, I swear it!"

Matreu looked past her but could see little from where he stood. "Why would they choose such a place?"

"So the reeds would hide them. Look! Can you not see them?!"

He stepped up beside her and peered down to the reeds and marshy ground a good distance below, gripping her forearm with one hand. "I see nothing—"

"Look closer." Even as she spoke, Jesa put both hands on his side and pushed as hard as she could. Her sleeve tore away in his fist, but Matreu was a large, strong man, and for a moment he swayed but did not fall, swinging his arms for balance as he teetered on the high bank. Jesa bent and snatched up a branch as thick as her wrist and shoved him with it. He slipped over the edge with a sputtering curse. She heard him fall crunching into the reeds below, then the noise of him splashing in the shallow, muddy water.

"*You are dead, woman!*" he shouted, so full of rage that his cry felt like it could wound her flesh by itself. "I will cut your heart out!" More sounds rose, splashing, reeds rattling, and the increasingly furious sound of his cursing. Jesa finally found the courage to look over the edge.

Matreu was thigh-deep in muddy water, his fine clothes soaked, in the middle of a forest of reeds whose feathery tops waved high above his head. The stems around him had been knocked down by his angry struggles but the sea of reeds extended in all directions. He stared up at her with unmasked hatred. "I will take your nose and both ears, you vile creature," he shouted, and spat up at her. "I will cut you open like a rabbit, from cunny to gorge!" He cursed again and tried to shake something from his hand. "What is this foulness?" In his sudden puzzlement he sounded as though he actually expected her to answer. "God burn me if I lie, I swear you will be . . ." He trailed off, and she could see him struggling to climb through the surrounding reeds toward the bank. "Aaah! What muck is this? It sticks to me and burns like fire."

As she watched him fighting his way through the forest of reeds, she suddenly realized she had wagered everything on a single long throw. Had she been wrong?

Then she saw the first of the ghants making its way through the swaying stalks, its stubby, dun-colored head gleaming like polished bone. Matreu was busily trying to free himself from the frothy ooze that clung to the reeds in pale, drooping strands. As he struggled to scrape it off his arms and legs and clothing, Jesa could see more heads on shell-covered bodies popping up in the reeds all around him, moving slowly inward.

Jesa had prayed she could find the ghant nest again. *Thank you, They Who Watch and Shape. Thank you for this salvation.*

Matreu heard the commotion in the reeds around him but had time only to pull his sword from its sheath before the first wave of ghants was upon him, shells rattling as they leaped from fallen trunk to fallen trunk or climbed over the backs of their fellows. Matreu was shouting now, a wordless, incoherent scream of rage and fear and disgust. His sword smacked against the nearest ghants and one or two fell backward into the shallow, muddy water, oozing pinkish-gray blood, but dozens had closed on him now, swarming like maggots on rotting flesh. He collapsed into the muddy water as more ghants hurried forward through the reeds to clamber onto the heaving pile. Some of the newcomers trailed long ropes of wet froth as if they meant to bind him like a spider's prey, but others must have bit at him or torn his flesh with their bony, clutching hands, because the silted water began to redden around the place where he had fallen. Matreu was now entirely invisible beneath a squirming carpet of child-sized creatures.

Jesa turned away. She did not need to see the last moments to know Matreu had received what he deserved, nor did she want to be there when the crablike creatures had finished with him.

She scrambled along the bank, headed back the way she had come. The only noises she could hear behind her now were the clicks and slurps of the ghants feeding.

She approached the spot as silently as she could, uncertain whether Viscount Matreu's men might still be nearby, though she had seen no further signs of them. Jesa could not hear any sound from Serasina even as she drew close to the hiding place, and her skin was cold with fear. But when she reached the spot on the hillside where she had left the basket, she found the infant girl just waking, eyes still gummy with sleep. Jesa snatched the baby up and clutched her to her chest.

"Ah, the gods are good to us," she whispered, and then wept, as much from fear and exhaustion as relief. As she held the baby close and kissed her, Jesa's tears dripped onto the child's precious head. "The gods are so good."

15

A Taste of Witchwood

Viyeki watched as Sacrifices and Builders hurriedly dismantled the sprawling camp beside the road, readying for the day's journey. Undead Hakatri's high-wheeled black wagon stood by itself in the center of the wide track. Even with all the bustle and chaos of breaking camp, not a single Builder or Sacrifice went near it, as if it were surrounded by an unseen wall.

He saw that Pratiki was also watching the proceedings, and called, "May the Garden keep you, Serenity."

"And greetings to you as well, High Màgister," called the prince-templar, then gestured for Viyeki to join him. The pair of clerics that generally trailed close behind Pratiki, like animal familiars, moved back several respectful paces as Viyeki approached. For a while he and the prince-templar simply stood, watching in silence as a good-sized village was folded up into bundles of sticks and cloth and loaded onto carts.

Viyeki thought Pratiki looked more careworn than usual, though it was always difficult to assess the appearance of one of the long-lived Hamakha Clan. Still, Viyeki felt more than a touch of unease to see weariness written so plainly on Pratiki's face: if something happened to the prince-templar, he knew, General Kikiti would be left in total command here. The general had made it clear many times that he considered the high magister of the Builders to be an irritation or worse—untrustworthy, insufficiently devout, and not even a member of an important family. Viyeki suspected that only the prince-templar's favor had kept him safe.

Am I being protected by Pratiki for some reason I cannot understand? And will I even know if that protection suddenly ends, or simply be dragged out and executed by General Kikiti's Sacrifices?

His anxious curiosity finally got the better of him. "Is there something my Builders and I can do for you, Serenity? Because you have only to ask and it will be done."

Pratiki showed him a narrow, official smile. "Very kind. In fact, I do have something to share with you, Magister. Something that may make your planning easier."

"I will be grateful for any help, Serenity."

"Do you play *shaynat*?" the prince-templar asked, catching Viyeki by surprise.

"A little, yes. But I would never claim to be an adept, only an interested novice."

Pratiki nodded. "We should play—but not during our next halt, because I fear we will not have any opportunity. Not only do I have something to share with you, but General Kikiti will be meeting with officers of the Northeastern Host, and I must at least make a brief appearance." Again, the careful smile. "I will be honest with you, Magister, if you will keep my secret—I do not much enjoy such meetings. The demands of protocol are wearisome, and the company is often boring, but of course I must represent the Mother of All and our clan."

The Northeastern Host. Again, they were speaking of an army that Viyeki had not even known existed until a short time ago, but which they were apparently meeting. As so often during these odd conversations with the prince-templar, Viyeki found himself with little he dared say in reply. "I am certain no one else could manage such a thing with as much grace as you will, Serenity."

Pratiki frowned, giving Viyeki an anxious moment. Had he offended somehow? Had he misread the situation? The problem with any kind of familiarity with a high noble was that the disparity of power never disappeared, even when the noble in question pretended that it had.

But the prince-templar only said, "*Grace.* That is a pretty word, good Viyeki, but it feels false. Let us say this instead: I am *m'shi*."

It was an old Hikeda'yasao word that meant both "water" and "watery," but also signified "that which fits where it is put," as water traveled quietly but swiftly to the first place that would contain it, then conformed to that place. The term could be both a compliment or gentle criticism, and Viyeki heard both shades in Pratiki's tone.

"I thank you for telling me what to expect, Serenity," Viyeki said after a long moment had passed.

"I would have to be as wise as the Mother of All to know *truly* what to expect, Magister," said Pratiki. "As you have doubtless noticed, we are at the very center—the crossing-point—of many, many possibilities." A moment later he signaled that he wished to be alone, so Viyeki retreated. Pratiki's clerics moved back to his side as quickly as baby birds, as though they had been shivering without his nurturing warmth.

To Tzoja's immense relief, even so late in the year, she could still find agate mushrooms for the queen's tincture, though she required the help of more than a few slaves to gather enough for her needs. She thought it was beyond strange to be giving orders to her own kind when only days earlier Tzoja had been the one scurrying to obey others.

I act for the queen now, at least for a little while longer. That is power. If I wished, could I claim one of these slaves had refused me and have her put to death?

The idle thought made her suddenly feel ill, so that she put her head down and breathed deeply until her stomach stopped cramping.

Tzoja found maidenhair ferns on the forested hillside north of the conquered fortress, in a gulley where a spring appeared from beneath the rocks and began its journey to join the Nartha River below. Maidenhair and other ferns grew all around the burbling spring, and although Tzoja could not ignore the Hamakha guard watching everything that she and the slaves did, she much enjoyed the time spent near the greenery and flowing water.

This one small place, she thought in wonderment, *only a few hundred paces from where the walls fell and so many people died, yet it seems another country.*

It was hard to return to captivity when the sun began to set, but she at least had the satisfaction of seeing several baskets of maidenhair ferns carried back toward Naglimund.

The queen had allowed Tzoja a small, precious cask of cloudberry wine to use in her work, the liquor that only the Hamakha Clan was allowed to possess now that the witchwood had all but vanished. When she was back in the wagon she shared with Vordis, Tzoja measured it out carefully into half a dozen clay jars stuffed with agate mushroom and ferns. When she had filled all the jars and stoppered them, certain that she had made at least three moons' supply of elixir for the queen, almost a full cup of the strong wine remained in the bottom of the cask. She sniffed it and was stunned by its many notes of flowers and spices and fragrant bark, as well as some bitter scents she could not identify, acrid hints of mineral and smoke.

"Here," she said to Vordis, pouring out a little into a bowl. "Drink this."

"Is it the queen's tincture?" the blind woman said. "I do not think I am strong enough to drink something made for the queen."

"It is better than any mere tincture—at least for you and me. It is cloudberry wine, and what's left is just for us. Drink! And I will drink some too."

Still worried, Vordis lifted the bowl to her lips, sniffed, and made a face. "It smells so strong!"

Tzoja laughed. "You may never have this chance again, dear friend. There is *kei-mi* in it—witchwood. This liquor is rarer than gold."

"I wouldn't drink gold, either."

Tzoja poured the rest into her food bowl and sloshed a little around in her mouth. The unfamiliar flavor struck her tongue like water on a hot rock. The first taste was harsh and hot like the brandy Valada Roskva had once shared with her back at the Astaline settlement. The shock of that had made her sneeze, which had sent Roskva into gales of laughter, but she had managed to drink it all and was soon glad she had done so. Cloudberry wine was both stronger and more subtle, and at first it was all Tzoja could do to hold it in her mouth and not spit it out. Then she began to taste the other flavors and to feel what seemed like a trail of molten honey trickling down her throat and into her stomach, as if a warm light was illuminating her from within. She almost felt she could look down and see it through her skin, glowing like a lantern. She laughed again, this time in surprise at how alive it felt inside her.

"Drink," she urged Vordis. "You must. It is quite wonderful." The wine's berry and blossom flavors and its stranger, more savory tastes combined in her mouth as she took her second sip. She detected a subtle breath of mint, and thought she also tasted fennel, thyme, and a different minty flavor that she guessed was birch bark, which the Astalines made into beer every spring. Then again, she thought, perhaps that was the hint of witchwood, since the Hikeda'ya said at least a drop was put in every jar. She poured half of what remained into Vordis's bowl—her friend was carefully sipping now—and the rest into her own.

"Oh," said Vordis reverently. "I feel it in my chest. It's so warm! Like drinking summertime."

"Enjoy it," Tzoja told her. "For a little while, we can be immortals, too."

Soon they were both swept up and carried on a balmy breeze of merriment. Everything that Tzoja said, even the most ordinary of stories about her girlhood or her experiences of later years, made Vordis giggle uncontrollably, which set Tzoja laughing as well. They embraced, telling each other that they had never had such a good friend before. Vordis suddenly began to weep. Tzoja put her arms around her and kissed the tears from her cheeks. "Here, here," she said. "What's wrong?"

"You. You had a family. I was taken from mine so young, I hardly remember them. And you had a brother, too."

"He was quiet and angry," Tzoja said, and found her own eyes beginning to fill. "Always angry. My mother blamed him simply for being a boy, because she said one day he would grow into a man and make women suffer."

"He sounds sad and lovely," Vordis said, then burst into tears again. "You have been so many places! But I have spent my days in darkness."

Tzoja could think of nothing to say, though the thought that someone could be envious of her fragmented, confined life astonished her. She held Vordis and kissed her cheek again. "All will be well," she said, over and over. "All will be well."

Sometime later, when they were once more in fits of laughter, the door to their wagon flew open. Two Hamakha Guards in their frightening serpent helmets looked in at them, faces set in grim disapproval.

"Do you have the queen's physic?" one of them asked.

Tzoja struggled to order her thoughts. "Yes. But the jars must sit for a while. Here, I have marked this one I made weeks ago. It can be used at once, but the others must be left until—" But before she had even finished speaking, the guards began carrying out the jars, handling them as cautiously as though they contained the blood of the Mother of All herself.

"Now, take your things," said the guard when they had removed the jars of tincture. "The Order of Sacrifice requires this wagon."

Tzoja was startled. "Now? But where are we to go?"

"Someone will tell you inside the fortress. Be swift and take anything you wish to keep."

She and Vordis had to scramble to pick up the remnants of Tzoja's herb-gathering and tincture-making, the tools and jars she had so carefully begged and borrowed to assemble her little workshop, then put everything in the baskets she used to gather plants. When they had finished, the guards prodded them out of the wagon and onto the hard, cold ground just inside Naglimund's outer gate, then led them across the torn earth and into the scorched and ruined inner keep.

"Go to the Residence," one of the guards said. "The celebrant clerics will tell you where you stay now." His message delivered, he turned his back on them, slammed the door of the wagon, then walked away with his snake-headed comrade.

The effect of the cloudberry wine was fading: Tzoja's thoughts cooled and hardened. The tears that suddenly seeped from her eyes felt like frost.

Now what? she wondered. The sky was dark, and the twilit hills loomed over the devastated mortal castle like stern, angry elders. Vordis seemed to grow smaller as she huddled against Tzoja's side in the cold wind—small as a child. *I am homeless again,* Tzoja realized. A wild thought came to her then. She looked around, but far too many soldiers surrounded them, dozens of armored Hikeda'ya busy with a hundred different tasks—but not so busy that they would all fail to see her running away. Also, she suspected, these hardened Sacrifice troops would see her and Vordis only as slaves and would not hesitate to kill them.

She put her arm around her friend's shoulder and led her deeper into the broken fortress.

Viyeki could not help marveling. Two large Sacrifice companies had just met in plain sight on a well-known road, deep inside mortal lands. An hour earlier, hundreds of Hikeda'ya soldiers from something called Fortress Stone Root had appeared beside the wide track as if from nowhere, part of the mysterious Northeastern Host. While General Kikiti and his underlings conferred with the officers of the new troops, the rest of the Sacrifices set up camp together in a meadow at the base of the hills.

The queen no longer needs to keep secrets—our power is displayed openly. Viyeki should have felt exhilarated by this sign of Nakkiga's resurgence, but what he felt instead was that long-held certainties were cracking and collapsing like spring ice.

"High Magister, your pardon!" He turned to see one of Pratiki's clerics bowing and making submissive gestures. "Excuse the intrusion, great lord. His Serene Highness, our master, wishes to speak with you."

Viyeki let himself be led through the encampment to the corner farthest from the road, where the tents were larger and squadrons of armed guards seemed to be everywhere.

"Ah, good." Pratiki stepped out of one of the tents. "Please join me, Magister."

As the cleric bowed and departed, Viyeki followed Pratiki inside. He had assumed the tent belonged to the prince-templar, but the interior was empty except for a heavy carpet spread on the ground and a scroll that had been unrolled atop it, edges held in place by stones.

"Forgive the crude surroundings," said the prince-templar. "I did not think you would be offended if we did without some of the usual luxuries in favor of haste. Come." The prince-templar pointed to a pile of cushions in a corner of the tent. "Take one of these and sit with me, Magister Viyeki. We have much to discuss."

The unfurled scroll was quite large, a pace and a half in width and more than twice that just in the length that had already been exposed. "I am quite amazed, Serenity," he said as he seated himself at the edge of the carpet. "This is the finest map I have ever seen!"

The prince-templar dropped a cushion beside Viyeki, then lowered himself in a single, supple movement, his robes spreading around him. "It should be—the Mother of All commissioned it expressly for this mission. It was made for the Order of Sacrifice, and Kikiti guards it jealously." He smiled. "Only the Hamakha blood I share with our queen has persuaded him to let me borrow it. As it is, it must go back to the general when the first watch ends, so give me all your attention, please."

Viyeki nodded, worried but also intrigued. The most important features dominating the center of the map were three mountain ranges, widely separated at their southern ends, but coming together at the northernmost extreme, like the tripod that held a household *ni'iyo.* The mountains and surrounding lands had been drawn with scrupulous care, the rivers and streams all clearly marked, along with what looked like every track and road, no matter how small. Viyeki had worked with charts and plans of many kinds, but he had never seen anything quite as detailed as this.

Although no features were named, he quickly recognized several landmarks. "Here," he said, pointing to the leftmost leg of the tripod. "These are the mountains we are skirting, the outermost range of what the mortals call Wealdhelm."

Pratiki looked annoyed. "Give them their old, proper name, please—the *Yi'ire.*"

"Your pardon, Serenity—the Yi'ire, of course." Viyeki slid his finger south along the base of the western-most range to a small, circular mark. "And I believe that must be the mortal fortress we conquered, so I guess we are now somewhere around . . . here." He touched a point about three-quarters of the way along the outermost spine of mountains.

"Precisely," said Pratiki, leaning forward. His finger touched near the northern end of the Yi'ire, where two valleys narrowed between three converging ranges. "And here is where your order's great task will be, upon the shoulder of this mountain," he said, pointing to a tall peak where the ranges joined. "Do you recognize it?"

In his acolyte days under his stern mentor Yaarike, Viyeki had been expected to know the name and composition of every significant range of hills and mountains from Nakkiga all the way down to the wastelands of Nascadu. "It is called *Kushiba*—the Beak—if I remember correctly."

"You do. And even farther north lies Lake Winterstone, the source of many great rivers—including the Narrowdark, which tumbles down the cliffs into the valley of Tanakirú." Pratiki's waved his hand. "But the lake is not important to your coming task. What matters is the peak called Kushiba—or at least the stone that it is made of."

Now he swung his hand to point at the lowland between the tripod's left and middle legs. "This is the Coolblood Valley, of course, where Da'ai Chikiza's ruins stand." Next, he pointed to the second valley, which stretched between the middle and rightmost mountain ranges. "And this is Tanakirú, the Valley of Mist. General Ensume and an army of Sacrifices are already engaged there against the treacherous Zida'ya. Your task will be to help them win that battle."

Viyeki was trying to understand, but also not to show too much surprise about anything, since he had no idea how firm the ground was beneath him. "So, to make sure I understand, we are at war in this Tanakirú—this Valley of Mists? And my Builders are needed there?"

Pratiki looked amused, but something more cautious swam beneath it. "It is not precisely *in* Tanakirú where your order will do their work." He used his finger to follow the road beside which they were camped, snaking north along the westernmost edge of the Yi'ire until it curled at last into the place where the three ranges joined. "Your work will be here, high on Kushiba's flank. The Zida'ya defend the northern end of Tanakirú jealously, and the peculiar terrain makes dislodging them very, very difficult, despite our superior numbers. But high Kushiba, which stands at the head of the valley, is riddled with caverns. The Mother of All wishes the Builders Order to connect those caverns into one descending tunnel, so that Kikiti can lead our warriors down from the slopes of Kushiba into Tanakirú below. That way, our Sacrifices will emerge behind the Zida'ya defenders, then the traitors will be crushed between this new force and Ensume's legions."

"We are to tunnel all the way down into the valley?" Viyeki nodded, trying to make sense of this new idea. "You said there are caverns riddling Kushiba, Serenity. I beg pardon, but I will have to see them before I can judge how long it will take to do what you want."

"Not what *I* want, High Magister," Pratiki reminded him. "It is what Her Majesty wants. What the queen *commands*."

"Of course. I hear her voice in your words." But Viyeki could not help feeling something was strange in all this. "I must beg your pardon once more, Serenity, but why am I hearing this in a private meeting, and not as part of a council with Kikiti and the other Sacrifice officers?"

Pratiki put a hand on his shoulder. It surprised him—generally Hamakha nobles did not like to touch those who were not of their clan. "Because you were not meant to receive this intelligence yet. I have . . . bent the rules, let us say, because I wish you to have a little more time to consider and prepare. When we reach the slopes of Kushiba, things will begin to happen very swiftly."

It was obvious that the prince-templar was worried, but Viyeki thought that unless there were terrible, unforeseen problems, his Builders should not have much trouble tunneling down through the soft limestone, connecting caves that water and time had already carved. The Mother of All was far away by now, journeying south with Kikiti's superior, High Marshal Muyare, and the bulk of the Sacrifice army to attack the mortal capital, so this new task should not be anywhere near as terrifying as excavating Ruyan's tomb under the threat of her immediate arrival. "As always, I appreciate your confidence in me, Serenity," he said out loud. "And your priceless assistance, too. But I fear I still have a few questions. I assume you will not or cannot tell me why our Sacrifices are fighting in Tanakirú, a seeming backwater."

"You assume correctly."

"Then I will ask only this—why have so many soldiers accompanied us on this journey north? With the new Sacrifices from Fortress Stone Root, there must now be at least a thousand warriors in train, likely more. Am I to build a tunnel large enough for them all to attack at once? There would be no mountain left!"

Pratiki shook his head. "Only a portion of all these soldiers will descend to the valley, in an orderly column. It is surprise that will give us victory in the Valley of Mists, not sheer numbers." He shook his head gently. "I see you still have more questions, High Magister. Let me anticipate you. We have brought so many Sacrifices because the Zida'ya enemy still holds Kushiba's slope, where the caverns wait and your work will begin. There can be no tunneling until we have driven out or killed them all."

Viyeki was surprised into silence. These mountains were riddled with caves, that was already clear; the Zida'ya might be able to hold out for many moons. "It sounds like a long and bloody task, my lord," he said, trying to keep dismay out of his voice and posture. "And my order's work will not even have begun until the fighting is over. Have the Mother of All and her advisors allotted enough time for driving out the enemy in this plan?"

"Leave the questions of planning to the queen, and of warfare to the Sacrifices," said Pratiki. "Your only concern is to see that Kikiti's troops can reach the valley floor and surprise the queen's enemies."

"How swiftly must we make this tunnel?"

"Quite swiftly," said the prince-templar. "We might have two moons—

three at the very most—but I do not know anything with certainty yet. Whatever task we are given, though, we must work together to ensure our queen's victory." Pratiki rose from his cushion and gestured at the map. "If you need to study this again, ask me privately and I will make it available to you. But be sparing in your requests, please, High Magister, and practice discretion at all times."

"Yes, Serenity. Thank you."

After the prince-templar had departed with the map, Viyeki was left alone in the now empty tent. His hands were trembling. *Two or three moons! I thought we would have half a year or more while the queen is in the south. A mere three moons to defeat an entrenched Zida'ya army and then hollow out an entire mountain!*

And, as he well knew, the Mother of the People had only one punishment for failure.

16

Blessings of the Aedon

"It's too tight," said Simon, frowning as the squire worked at fitting the king's armor. "I can scarcely breathe. This arming shirt does not fit well at all."

"Are you certain it is the shirt?" Lord Chamberlain Jeremias watched the king's fitting with a waspish, critical air. "Mayhap since you wore it last, you have grown a little thicker in the middle, Your Majesty. Certainly, you have drunk a power of wine and sack since then."

"I had it on only half a year ago!" Simon scowled. "By the Royal North Road in Hernystir—God as my witness, Jeremias, you were there! You saved me. Or have you forgotten? The Norns would have snaggled me with arrows like a porpentine's quills."

"I remember," said Jeremias, but hearing that heroic moment recalled seemed to bring him no pleasure. Simon paid his friend's change of mood little heed: Jeremias had always been prone to sudden and, to Simon, inexplicable bouts of sadness.

Simon tried to stand still while the squire returned with another padded doublet. "Better," Simon said.

"I wish you would be a little more patient. We could make the first one fit properly, and it is a better choice."

"Why?" Simon frowned at another squire, who was fumbling with the strings of the arming shirt.

"Because it is the color of your standard," Jeremias said. "This one is blue, and not even a blue that pleases the eye. It looks as though it has sat out in the sun for years."

"It is looser and more comfortable," Simon said. "If I must raise my arms and fight, I will care little whether my shirt matches my pennant."

"But you are the king," Jeremias said. "Your men will look to you. They will respect you the more if you are well turned-out. It shows confidence."

Simon made a noise of disgust. "Who has fought in a war here? Which one of us? I say the hue of my arming-shirt will mean nothing. You say it must match my hose and my underclouts and the color of my eyes." He shook his arms, which were beginning to cramp a little from being held out for so long.

"I am sorry, Majesty. I am a disappointment to you, I know." Jeremias turned away as if he would leave.

"Here, hold! Come back! What are you doing? You are no disappointment, nor should you take such offense to everything I say. You know full well I get cross when I have to stand still for too long."

Jeremias turned back, but his wounded expression seemed too profound for the scale of the disagreement. "As you say, Majesty."

"What troubles you, man? And do not deny it, for I have known you much, much too long to be fooled."

His friend shook his head. "It is nothing. But I suffer with my failings—I cannot forget them. I have . . ." He fell silent, as if it was too much to explain.

"You have done everything I asked from you, Jemmy." He ducked his head as the mail shirt was draped over him. "You are Lord Chamberlain and Master of the Wardrobe. Many is the time have you made me look like a proper Commoner King instead of just a commoner. And if I have nipped at you about it, like an old dog, it is only because . . . because . . . I hate *fussing!*" He wiggled his now gauntleted hand up and down. "God's Tree, now my fingers have gone to sleep." He beckoned back the squire, who had fled as the king's armored glove began flailing near his head. "Now, tell me why you are troubled, old friend, as I asked you already."

"No, no." Jeremias shook his head. "This is not the time—not when you must ride out soon."

"What better time?" Simon demanded. "While I am stuck here like a scarecrow in a field, I can do nothing else. Speak to me. Your face is a mass of gloom. You look like a marketplace thief who has discovered he can't get his hand out of a jar of olives."

Before Jeremias could answer, a guard stepped in and announced the arrival of Tiamak and Pasevalles.

"I will leave you to your duties, Majesty." Jeremias seemed grateful for the distraction. "I'll return to have a last look at everything, then the armorers will make certain your suit is well polished for the morning." He bowed, then turned and went out of the arming room without a backward glance.

"Greetings, Majesty," said Tiamak with a bow. "I hope you are well." The Wrannaman did not look any happier with him than Jeremias had been.

Simon did not want to hear Tiamak's complaints. He knew exactly what they would be and preferred to avoid the argument. "I am well, thank you, and I pray you are the same. Lord Pasevalles, how do you fare? Also well, I hope?"

"As well as can be," the acting Hand of the Throne said with a bow. "A little fearful of the responsibility you have put on me, Majesty, but I will strive to protect the kingdom and the castle in your absence."

"That is good to hear," said Simon, but he could no longer ignore Tiamak's look, as clouded as a gathering storm. He sighed quietly. "Is there aught else that needs my attention?"

"A thousand and one things, Majesty," said Tiamak. "As always. And they would all be better served by you being here and letting someone else go to Winstowe."

He should have known there was no escaping this struggle. "You know my reasons."

"To show strength before the grasslanders. To show our people in the eastern borderlands that they are not abandoned. These I understand, Majesty, but they could be done just as well by someone else. Every battle standard of Erkynland is the king's standard. Would you collect all the taxes yourself, too? Judge every disputed sheep or crooked wall in Erkynland?"

Tiamak was clearly not just unhappy—he was angry. Simon did not fully understand why the little man was taking on so, but he was not going to be talked out of what he knew to be the right thing. He might have been born a commoner, but he was as much a king now as anyone else in Erkynland's confused history: he could not be seen to hide in his castle while his country was invaded and his people menaced. "I have heard these arguments before," Simon said. "They did not convince me then. They will not convince me now."

"Like Lord Tiamak, I fear for you and your safety, Majesty," said Pasevalles, "but there is no doubt in my mind that seeing you riding to Winstowe will lift the hearts of all Erkynlanders—those who are under siege most of all."

"At least promise me you will not fight if there is any other way," Tiamak pleaded.

Simon was battling bad temper. However wise Tiamak might be in most ways, the Wrannaman had never truly understood how honor sometimes had to be placed above practicality. "I can make no promises," he said gruffly. "But I am not a fool. I will not throw away the lives of my men needlessly."

"It is not merely the lives of your men that worry me," said Tiamak. "Morgan, your heir, is still missing somewhere in the north. You know that the Norns may move on the Hayholt soon. And Duke Osric, who you leave as regent, is just recovering from what was nearly a mortal wound."

Simon flexed his gauntlet, then waved it in dismissal. "Osric will have both you and Pasevalles to advise him. And my dear Lillia is here too." He frowned. "Her grandmother, God and the Aedon treasure her soul, would not like to hear you talk as if Lillia could not take the throne simply because she is a girl child. If she has half Miriamele's quality, she would still make an excellent queen."

"That is not the measure of what I mean." Tiamak shook his head. "But at least promise me that you will give this Unver, this Thrithings king, a chance to parley."

"They call him the Shan," said Simon airily. "A sort of king-of-kings, like the old imperators. And if he wishes to parley, of course I will listen."

"There is every chance that he will when he sees you and your force appear behind his siege," declared Pasevalles. "But beware of tricks, Majesty. These barbarians do not have same code of honor that we do."

Tiamak made a sour face. "I must respectfully disagree. Perhaps not all Thrithings-men are trustworthy, but this Unver has given every sign he is seeking some sort of accommodation."

Simon's eyes narrowed. "What makes you say that?"

"Because, Majesty, he has crossed the border with a large force. To the mind of the grasslanders, he has every right to punish us—"

"Punish us?" Simon almost yelped. "How so? Because of a stray arrow on the Laestfinger?"

"No." Tiamak had once more taken on the patient air that so nettled Simon. "Not because of that. Because he tried to bargain with you over Eolair. I have seen the letters he sent! They came in with Osric's company. Unver said he did not have Prince Morgan but would surrender Eolair in return for an agreement on the border."

"Easy enough to say," Pasevalles commented. "But the fact remains, this Shan Unver is four days ride into Erkynland, and many of our soldiers have died at the hands of his riders."

"Soldiers, yes," said Tiamak. "But he has been careful—surprisingly careful—not to make it a broad assault on eastern Erkynland. He wants your attention, Simon—Majesty. He wants your attention and, I suspect, wants to make a bargain. He has a much greater problem with Nabban's encroachment on Thrithings-lands in the south than he does with Erkynland."

"Strange way of asking for a bargain," the king growled, "invading our borders. Besieging our castles. Why would he do that instead of just continuing to deal with us?"

"Because he thinks you are as subtle as he is, Simon—but it seems he is wrong!" Even Tiamak knew he had gone too far with that, and the small man immediately dropped to one knee. "I apologize, Majesty. You give me great freedom. Sometimes I misuse it. I will go now so you can finish your preparations." He turned and limped toward the door but stopped in the doorway.

"As my king—and as my friend," he said, "I wish you good luck at Winstowe and a safe return to us. Even if I have angered you, I beg you to remember what I have said. May He Who Always Steps On Sand guide you . . . and the Aedon defend you."

Then he was gone, leaving Simon alone with Pasevalles, the squires, and the pages who were still hard at work, armoring their king.

Levias insisted on walking from the barracks to the arming hall, though he walked like a man crossing hot stones on naked feet. His wound was largely healed, or so the physician's wife had told Porto, but Levias still kept one hand beneath his belly like a mother big with child.

"Don't fuss over me," he said to the old knight. "I have to do this. Just because I cannot ride with them does not mean I will let our men go without a farewell and a prayer."

"You cannot ride with anyone—not for half a year. And you should not be walking so far, either. That is what Lord Tiamak said."

"Bother Lord Tiamak. He is not a soldier. He does not understand."

Lord Captain Zakiel came out of the hall as they arrived. Both Porto and Levias, a little startled, hurried to salute him with fists on chest. "At your ease, fellows," he said. "Sergeant, should you not be abed still?"

"Yes, he should," said Porto before Levias could answer. "But he is stubborn as a cart-mule."

"I wish only to bid the men farewell," Levias told the captain.

"As I have just done." Zakiel smiled sadly. "We are king's soldiers, we Erkynguard, and we go where the king sends us, do as the king bids us."

"Can we drive the grasslanders back?" Levias asked.

"With the king himself leading the relief? Of course. But it will be hard going. The Thrithings-men are undisciplined, but they fight like cornered wolves." The captain made the sign of the Tree on his breast; Porto and Levias quickly did the same. "Keep our men in your prayers," said Zakiel. "The king, his knights, and the common guardsmen. But trust in the Lord to watch over them. They do God's work."

"Amen," said Levias fervently.

The great arming hall echoed with the sound of blades clanging against wooden posts as their edges were tested. Levias pulled away from Porto's supporting arm and tottered across the room to embrace one of his longtime comrades. Other soldiers came to join them, and after a few moments Levias was lost to Porto's view in a crowd of half-dressed guardsmen.

Porto looked around the long hall. The walls where the weapon had hung were almost bare now. Seeing the few crooked pikes and notched swords that remained, he could not help wondering how they would arm the provincial musters coming to help protect the castle.

God forbid that we must fight the White Foxes with nothing but hoes and hay rakes, he thought. For the second time in a very short while, he offered a prayer he had learned in childhood to the Ransomer and His Holy Mother. *Aedon without sin and Elysia without sin, look down on us, sinners all, and show mercy to us. Make our hearts full and our souls joyful in Your service even when we are surrounded by darkness and despair.*

He had never been much for prayer until he became friends with Levias, though he had been known to say one now and then, much to the amusement of his onetime comrades Astrian and Olveris. Prince Morgan had often chided them, saying God heard all prayers, but Astrian had delighted in pointing out that if a prayer for forgiveness was needed for every sin, Porto was already too old to be spared, even if he spent the rest of his life praying.

Now our Prince Morgan is lost, Porto thought, full of shame and sadness. *Be-*

cause the Erkynguard failed him. Because I failed him. And where are those other two, my drinking companions? Do they even live? But Astrian and Olveris, like cats, had a knack for landing with their feet on the ground. Porto's fear for Morgan's safety ran much deeper.

A voice rose in song on the other side of the hall, a little ragged at first but soon loud and clear. It took Porto a moment to realize it was Levias, singing one of the Erkynguard's favorite old songs.

In Nartha's dales I long to lie,
'Pon sacred soil, 'neath Heaven's sky.
Someday I will come home again
And take the rest God grants all men
In her soft grass, under His eye.

A few of the men standing near him joined in, some with surprisingly sweet and boyish voices.

Sing Ah-way-oh! Sing Way-oh!
Sing of all that's fair
And sing to me of Erkynland
All that I love is there.

At Martyr's Spring I love to kneel
And show the world my booted heels
While I in ecstasy may sip
The waters there that splash and drip
And turn a man's woes into weal.

A dozen more had joined in the pensive chorus, speeding up the familiar, sentimental song. Even those who did not sing, or whose hands were occupied with sharp, dangerous things, looked up. Some smiled a little, but others wore the sad, troubled expression of men reminded that they might not come back home again.

In Aldheorte wood, the graceful trees
Whose limbs do tremble in the breeze
And reach up toward the noonday sun
Or clutch the stars when day is done
Caress me with their tender leaves

Sing Ah-way-oh! Sing Way-oh!
Sing of all that's fair
Sing to me of Erkynland
All that I love is there.

The song drifted away at last somewhere after the second chorus. Several of the men said their farewells to Levias, and some wandered over to Porto, who still stood apart.

"Good luck to you," Porto told one. "Our thoughts go with you."

"You've done your part, graybeard," a guardsman replied. "Enjoy the quiet."

"It will likely not be quiet for too long," Porto said. "The White Foxes are in Erkynland."

"They would never attack this place again," declared the soldier, a husky young fellow with an exuberant beard. "Not after the thrashing they had last time. And we'll not be gone long, so if they try to lay siege here, they'll find us behind them. Surely even fairies are not so foolish!"

Porto did his best to smile.

When Levias had joined him again, the sergeant's shoulders a bit tender after receiving many comradely thumps, Porto pointed to a little dumbshow taking place in the courtyard outside the barracks.

"Is that Captain Zakiel?" Levias said. "What does he?"

"Says farewell to his wife, it appears. Likely sending her out of the city with the other women and children." As they watched, the lord captain stood helplessly as his wife held him tightly and cried against his chest. "Zakiel is a good man," said Porto. "Pray God he comes through this safely."

"I pray that for all of us—but I know God will provide. Our Lord punishes the wicked and all those who deny Him." Levias grinned. "Speaking of the wicked, have you heard aught from your friends, those Nabbanai knights?"

"Astrian and Olveris?" Porto shook his head. "Not since we left Winstowe Castle. I imagine they are still there."

"God will provide," said Levias again. "Keep them in your prayers."

So many people must be praying to Him today, thought Porto. *So much trouble in the world. He must be very busy listening to them all.* He sighed. *I will wait until tonight to add my prayers to the others. Perhaps He will be better able to hear then.*

The faces Pasevalles saw as he made his way through the Hayholt were almost uniformly full of worry. Outside the castle walls, a surprising number of people had already gathered along Main Row in Erchester to bid their ruler farewell, and more were arriving every moment. Pasevalles already regretted his errand, not because he did not want it completed, but because it broke his rule of not doing things himself. In perhaps an excess of caution, he pulled down the hood of his weather-stained cloak to better shield his features, but the people in the crowd were far too busy watching the castle gate to pay attention to a lone figure in shabby old clothes, and despite how much power as he wielded, Pasevalles was not well-known outside the Hayholt.

*Likely no one would recognize me even if I went bareheade*d, he told himself; even so, he hurried his steps a little until he had left most of the crowd behind. The district of the city called Little Thrithing was a long walk away, and he needed to get there and return before King Simon and the rest rode out for Winstowe.

Little Thrithing nestled on a high spot not far inside Erchester's eastern wall, not far from the fish market, as the smell in the air made clear. Many of those who lived there were traders who brought goods in from far-off New Gadrinsett or the other market villages along the edge of the High Thrithings, mostly hides and wool and wood. Most of the houses were imitations of grasslander wagons—without wheels, but otherwise built and decorated in much the same way as the rolling cottages they had left behind. But many of the grassland traders had simply brought their wagons into Erchester to live in, crowding for space among the painted houses. It was hard to tell which brightly painted conveyance would soon be leaving on another journey and which hadn't moved for years. With winter bearing down, the horses that pulled the wagons had reduced the once grassy commons to bare earth.

Because those wagons and most of the houses were either too small or too flammable for proper indoor fires, the residents of the Little Thrithings built their cookfires on the commons, and, as Pasevalles made his way across the uneven ground, he saw bearded men gathered around the firepits, dicing and drinking. Much of Erchester might be assembling to watch the king and his soldiers ride out at the city's other end, but Little Thrithing had more complicated feelings about such things, especially now that the enemy was rumored to be a true Shan of the grasslands, the first in generations. Even the most hardheaded and successful of the traders were beginning to feel torn between their profitable enterprises and the excited hopes of their people.

Pasevalles knew about this and exploited it when he could, but he was an outsider here and preferred to keep it that way. He kept his face hidden as he made his way through the settlement, and even affected a limp. He knew he was much too large to be mistaken for Tiamak by anyone who knew the Wrannaman, but it was always good to spread a little confusion.

Crossing the edge of the commons near one of the fires, he recognized a man throwing dice with several other clansmen, so he pulled his hood close and went to stand near him, careful not to intrude too obviously into their game of Dog and Eagle. When the young, much tattooed clansman finally noticed him standing by, Pasevalles beckoned him to one side, away from the others.

"Is that you, Master?" asked the man, trying to peer into the depths of the hood.

Pasevalles reflexively turned away. "It is who you think it is," he said. "I want Zhadu."

"I'll take you to him, Master." The self-appointed guide turned and called something to the others—his Thrithing-speech too swift for Pasevalles to make out—and was met with a roar of jibes and protests. He led Pasevalles off the commons, through many narrow passages between rows of wagon-like houses and house-like wagons, until they reached a ramshackle tavern nestled against a corner of the city wall. A few older clansmen were drinking on benches outside, greedy for the day's brief sunlight.

"He's in there," said the young grasslander.

Pasevalles unobtrusively dropped a silver coin into his hand. His guide nodded and hurried back to the dice game.

The tavern was little more than a hut, but it was one of the few places in this part of town with a sizeable hearth and a healthy fire burning in it. Slouched before it on stools sat half a dozen bearded men, all dressed more like traditional Thrithings-men than those he had passed outside, bones knotted in their beards and heavy silver and bronze ornaments clinking on their necks and arms. Pasevalles, who never stopped watching for trouble, was secretly relieved to recognize several of them as men he had hired—and paid well—in the past.

"Where is your thane?" he asked them.

"Here, Master," said a voice close to his ear.

Pasevalles spun, irritated at being approached from behind. The Thrithingsman Zhadu made a bow that seemed to contain a trace of mockery, irritating him further. The clansman was no taller than Pasevalles, but his chest was big as an ale cask and his arms were thick and heavily muscled. Zhadu also had one of the most hideous faces Pasevalles had ever encountered, though he was used to it now: a great scar transected the man's wide forehead, pushed his nose to one side, and ran jaggedly down his chin. The halves of his lips were poorly joined where they had healed, like broken pie crust. He looked, Pasevalles often thought, as if someone had tried to assemble a clansman from sundry pieces of the dead.

"Can we speak safely here?" he asked Zhadu.

The clansman glanced at the men by the stone hearth, then gestured for Pasevalles to follow him to the far side of the room. "Less who hear, less to fear," the ugly man said as they settled on a bench. "What does my lord need?" He grinned, which made his face even more disturbing. "And what does it pay?"

"Have I not already made you rich?" asked Pasevalles. "Fear not, this task will buy you many a bowl—nay, many a barrel." He lowered his voice. "And it is simple, at least if you wait until dark. It only requires pouring a little of this—" he produced a small, stoppered jar from inside his cloak and showed it to the clansman, "into an ewer of wine. And you must be out of the castle and far away before my enemy drinks it."

Zhadu gave him an amused look. "Sounds a bit complicated, my lord. Certain you wouldn't rather just have me put a dagger in his eye, whoever it is?"

Pasevalles was less amused. "How it looks is as important as what happens," he said. "Do nothing but what I say. Do you understand?"

The clansman waved his hand. "I only jested, my lord. Have I ever failed you?"

"There is always a first time," Pasevalles said, "and I do not like jests. Perhaps I should talk to your older brother instead."

Zhadu's expression turned cool. "Your doubts do not become you, Master. And in any case, Hulgar is far from here, at Unver's camp near the Fingerlest. He will not be back for several days, even if the weather stays good."

Pasevalles was silent for a moment, then pushed the small jar along the bench. Zhadu folded his large hand around it. "I will tell you the where and the when," said Pasevalles. "But it must be done just as I say."

"Have no fear," said Zhadu. "Your enemy is already a dead man. He just doesn't know it."

Simon could not remember the last time he had been in full armor on horseback. He felt heavy as a statue and almost as immobile. The streets of Erchester were lined with hundreds or perhaps thousands of people, even without counting those who leaned out and cheered from upper windows. A few of the wealthier had hung banners of their own family arms, the dragons of the royal household, and the Tower and Keys of King John's High Ward. Simon knew he should have been glad, and that much of the cheering came from his people showing that they loved him and mourned the queen just as he did, but it was hard to appreciate the noise and the bright winter sunshine. A gray cloud was on him, as it had been for weeks, and it was heavier than any armor. Seeing the banner with its scarlet and white dragons only made his heart ache, because one of the dragons was no more.

You can't let them see your sorrow. You are the father of the country—the only parent that Erkynland has left.

But it hurt. Tiamak was right, Simon realized—there was a part of him that would not mind dying. A brave end in battle would be the only honorable way he could leave his family behind and be free of the unending pain.

Yet would that not be self-slaughter? he wondered. *To know one wants to die and to let it happen—how is that different than if I put the blade against my own chest and rammed it home?*

"They love you, sire," said Count Pieres, who was the company's chief noble under Simon himself, since many of the men marching with them came from his Sistanshire holdings. Pieres was a sensible and experienced warrior who had fought with Simon, Osric, and others in the previous Thrithings war, as well as in several other skirmishes against the grasslanders when border clans had raided his territory. "Does it not lift your heart?"

"Of course," Simon said. "But it also reminds me that we must keep them safe."

"The clansmen are fierce." Count Pieres tugged at his long, well-groomed beard, which was a snowy white though he was several years younger than Simon. "I know them well, Majesty. My grandfather fought them in the first Thrithings War, when old King John was on the throne. And my family has lived on the border for longer than anyone can remember. We have been forced to cross swords with them often, but they are like wild dogs. When you stand up to them, they turn and run back to the grasslands, never fear."

"I wish the clansmen were our only concern," Simon said.

Pieres, who like many of the other nobles did not seem to believe the Norns would dare attack the Hayholt again, nevertheless nodded his head. "Fear not, Majesty. We will drive out any invaders, my lord, be they horsemen or fairy-soldiers."

Pieres' lieutenant rode up with matters to discuss, and as the count talked quietly with him, Simon took the chance to ride apart, craving silence more than reassuring words.

A gang of children running down the road beside the company caught the king's attention. They were darting in and out through the crowd and shouting to the soldiers, who shouted back at them. They looked unbearably young to Simon, thin and long-legged as crickets. One in particular kept catching his eye, a boy with hair as red as Simon's had been in his youth. The child was missing a few teeth and his face and worn clothing were dirty, but his eyes were bright and his voice was the loudest. He seemed to be the leader of the little group, and Simon thought he knew him despite never having seen him before.

He is the one who never stops, who never tires. The others follow him because otherwise they would do little but play the same old dull games. He could well imagine the flame-haired child leading his small army across the rooftops or on raids against the other gangs of children who crowded Erchester's streets at the end of the working day, in the hours before the gates closed for the night.

The red-headed boy appeared again, this time standing and teetering in dirty bare feet on the top step of a merchant's house, supported by some of his young comrades and tugged at by others. His perch was clearly a momentary thing, so before he lost it, he cupped his hands over his mouth and shouted. "*Hail the king! All hail the king! King Simon, take us with you! Make us knights! We'll show those grasslanders not to meddle with Erchester men!*"

Simon smiled despite himself and lifted a hand in salute. "Come and see me in a few years, lads!" he called.

The red-haired child, in a paroxysm of joy that the king had spoken to him, allowed the others to pull him down from his perch. His friends seemed so impressed that the only way they could show it was to pummel him and shriek like excited starlings. Simon laughed as he rode on past.

Something rose inside him then. It did not disperse the gloom that enfolded him but made it a little more bearable, as though a few rays of sun had pierced the clouds. *These are my people,* he thought, *and I love them. Even after all the mistakes I've made, all the things that have happened, they look at me and they see hope. I cannot fail them.*

The warmth quickly faded, not into gloom this time but apprehension. *But what if I fail?* he wondered. *What if I die at Winstowe without a proper heir to take my place? What if the Norns come and destroy every trace of the mortal kingdoms, as they have threatened for years? What then? What if I am the last king of Osten Ard, and after me there will only be suffering for these people, suffering and terror and death?*

He was only a man, he knew. And he was only one man.

It is too much. It is too heavy a burden, he thought as the banners flapped in the rising wind and the horses plashed their way down along muddy Market Row toward the city's eastern gates. *But God has given it to me and left me alone to shoulder it without my great love. Without Miri. So shoulder it I must.*

But a small, quiet voice inside Simon continued to remind him—promise him—that death always came at last. And when it came, all burdens would fall away.

17

A Bit of a Puzzle

"We have found it." Nezeru spoke so softly that Morgan had to lean close to hear. "The Tower of the Reaching Hand stands just above us."

He squinted up into the darkly winding stairwell, its steps half hidden by creepers, loose soil, and the crumbling remains of long-dead plants. He could see a tiny smear of indirect light at the very top, and for a moment hope battled caution. "Truly?" he asked. "How do you know?"

"Because that is where the plans in the library said it would be." Nezeru seemed annoyed by his question.

For a thousand-year-old Norn—or however ancient she was—Morgan thought she could be as peevish as a child sometimes. "And you saw all this in the few moments you had to look at it?"

"Yes." Her stare was hard. "Do you dispute me?"

"No, no." He reminded himself that he was caught in a very strange and very unfamiliar place with someone who could almost certainly kill him three or four different ways before he could draw his own sword. "In truth, I am impressed."

This seemed to satisfy her. "I passed through the gate beside Reaching Hand Tower on my way in," she said. "It is overgrown, with trees all around it, some of them standing much higher than the gate."

His flicker of hope suddenly flared into life. "Then let's start climbing! Let's get out of this place."

She gave him another stern look. "Have you any idea of whether it is day or night outside?"

Morgan had to admit that he did not.

"Then I suggest you let me continue to make the choices," she said. "We are trying to avoid being spotted by any Sacrifices. Just now it is mid-day outside and the sky is cloudless. My people see well in darkness, but they see even better in daylight."

"Very well, then," he said, conceding defeat. "What do we do next?"

"I am certain this will come as a great surprise to you," she said, "but . . . we wait."

"How do you speak our tongue so well?" he asked after they had spent a long, silent time huddled in the narrow stairwell.

"There is no need for us to talk, mortal," she said. "I sense no Hikeda'ya nearby, but there is no value in taking risks."

"I'll whisper," he said. "Unless you think the other Norns can sneak up on you without you knowing."

"Norns," she said. "It sounds an ugly word. What does it mean?"

Morgan shrugged, though he wondered whether she could even see him. They had climbed a little way up the winding stairs and left behind the gleaming tiles that lit the lower depths. Only a dull gleam from the tower top filtered down to them. For Morgan, it felt like hiding in a closet during a game of Holly King. "I don't know," he said. "'Norns' is what we've always called your people. Oh, and 'White Foxes.'"

"White Foxes I can understand, I suppose," she said, though he could hear the frown in her voice. "But Norns—?"

"I still want to know how you speak Westerling so well."

"I told you. My father learned it from his old master, and he practiced it on me when I was very young—before I was put in the Box."

"The box? What does that mean?"

He listened, appalled and fascinated, as she quietly explained the Hikeda'ya ritual of Yedade's Box, where children of the nobility were measured to see how their lives should be ordered to best help their people and their queen.

"You kicked your way out of a box, so they made you a soldier?"

A shadow fell across his face and he made a startled sound, then Nezeru's cool fingers clutched his nose and gave him a painful pinch. "Do not make light of things you do not understand, mortal. Yedade was a great philosopher."

"I'b cerdain thad's drue. Please led go ub by dose." He rubbed it. "It was just a question. No wonder you people are always at war—you are very short-tempered."

She laughed quietly, unhappily. "Always at war? No, always being attacked by mortals, you mean. These were our lands, once—everything from the far northern mountains to the southern seas. But your ancestors came and slaughtered and burned everything in their path, driving the Hikeda'ya and Zida'ya into the wilderness."

"Not my ancestors," he said stiffly. "That was the Rimmersmen when they first came across the ocean. Everybody knows that."

"Only mortals try to claim that one group of mortals is different from another. We who came from the Garden know better."

Morgan was angry. As if this was all the fault of his kind! "What about your queen?" he asked abruptly. "And what about the Storm King? We didn't attack him, he attacked us. He and your queen tried to destroy the Hayholt!" There had been other details, too, something about magical swords and powerful spells, but in truth Morgan didn't remember very much about it: the last hours of Green Angel Tower had been something neither Grandfather Simon nor Grandmother Miriamele had chosen to talk about. "A lot of people died, I know that much," he said. "A lot of *my* people. We didn't do anything to your folk, but first they tried to send a winter to freeze us all, then they tried to destroy our castle and bring the Storm King back to life."

"And then afterward your armies came to Nakkiga and tried to destroy it," she said, and now even Nezeru was speaking more loudly than was sensible.

Morgan did not answer at once, dimly aware, even in the throes of resentment, that this was a quarrel that could turn into something more dangerous, something neither of them could afford while surrounded by enemies. "We probably shouldn't talk about the past," he said.

"There is some sense in that."

Another long quiet stretch of time passed—for Morgan, a span of anxiousness curiously mixed with boredom. He was restless, but he also knew that he would undoubtedly live longer if he stayed right where he was and waited until Nezeru decided the time was right.

"How old are you?" he asked suddenly.

The question startled her. "I have not yet reached my first Great Year," she admitted.

"What is that?" he asked. "I've heard it, but I don't remember what it means."

"A Great Year is a Garden year," she said quietly. "The length of a year in our old home. Here in these lands, we mark the turning of that year by the appearance of the fiery star we call the Year-Torch."

"How often does that happen?" he asked, though he was not so much interested as seeking a distraction from his restlessness and worry.

She thought for a moment. "It appears once in ever sixty or so of your mortal years. Then it is the year's end for us and the beginning of a new Great Year."

As he did the sums, Morgan was surprised: if she had not seen an entire Great Year, that meant she was less than sixty years old, and might be no more than his grandparents' age. "You said you had not seen a new one."

"I will see one soon—if I live," she said. "It is almost time for the Year-Torch to appear again. Only two more moons or so, then a new Great Year will begin."

"You still haven't told me how old you are," he pointed out. "How many mortal years, that is."

"It does not matter. I am fully grown. I am a Sacrifice and a Queen's Talon."

He felt an urge to be difficult. "But how old?"

"Why do you want to know?" She definitely sounded annoyed.

"Because I do."

"Oh, if you must." She spent a moment calculating. "The last Drukhi's Day was my seventeenth."

The import of what she said did not immediately strike home. "And what is Drukhi's Day? When is it?"

"Why do you ask so many foolish questions?" For a moment, Morgan feared for his nostrils again, but she did not administer another pinch. "In the Stone-Listener's Moon," she said at last. "I think that is much the same as the midsummer moon you call *Tiyagaris*."

"Wait." He had finally realized what was saying. "You mean that last Tiyagar-month marked your seventeenth year? In *mortal* years?"

"Yes. What of it? I left the Sacrifice Order-house two summers ago. I am no longer a child."

"But you're my age!" Morgan was shocked, annoyed, and triumphant all in the same moment. "You're the same age as I am! More or less, anyway, because I'll have eighteen years in Decander. Wait—I'm older than you are!" He felt a sudden, powerful urge to tease her, but at the same time felt angry, as if he had been lied to: he had thought Nezeru was centuries old. But then another thought swam up to further muddle him. *By the Sacred Aedon, how did she become such a deadly fighter in such a short time?* Morgan felt as though he had carefully gathered all his ideas about the White Foxes into a pile, then this slender, deadly, difficult creature had kicked it over. "Your mother is a mortal. And you're no older than me."

"So it would seem," she said through clenched teeth. "Now it is my turn to ask something. Are we to spend our entire time of waiting here bandying questions? Is that what you mortals do? Talk and talk and talk until your jaws fall off your faces?"

He realized she was not wholly wrong. "I . . . I didn't mean to be discourteous," he said. "It's just surprise, that's all. Tanahaya, the last immortal I traveled with, never told me how old she was, but I know it was several of our centuries." He thought then of Likimeya and scarred Khendraja'aro. "And I have met others who were many times that."

He could not see her well, but he thought she gave him an odd look. "You seem to have spent many days with this Tanahaya," she said. "Were you lovers?"

"No!" The humiliating memory of his failed advances rose up before him like a murder victim's unquiet ghost. "No. We just . . . traveled together." Something else was tugging at him as well. "She saved my life. Saved me from your Sacrifices. And from a giant, too, the biggest one I've ever heard of—big as a house! But she called the giant something else—an ogre, I think. *Uro-inny*, or something like it."

"Uro'eni?" Nezeru sounded intrigued. She even moved a short distance closer, until her leg was against Morgan's and her ghostly face hovered only a hand's-breadth from his. "That is an old word from old Garden stories. I have never heard of one that lived in these lands. Tell me."

"Tell you what?"

"Tell me more about your time with the Zida'ya—and about this *Uro'eni*."

By the faint glimmer above, they had an hour or so until sunset, so it seemed a way to pass the time. *But don't give away anything important,* he reminded himself. *All I know for certain is that Nezeru says she's being hunted by her own kind.* Remembering the dozen or so Sacrifice soldiers she had killed, he had to admit that if she was trying to make him think her own kind was against her, she was certainly acting the part well.

He began his story, deliberately not speaking much about his original mission to the Sithi, concentrating instead on the attack by the Thrithings-men and his own escape into Aldheorte. As he slowly strung the pieces beside each other, one by one, he began to see that it made a strange and unquestionably interesting story, though not precisely crammed with examples of his own bravery and skill.

Other than the details of his time in H'ran Go-jao and Tanahaya's strange mirror-conversation with Jiriki, both of which he deliberately left out, he told Nezeru nearly everything that had happened since his first night in the forest. He had expected the details about Da'ai Chikiza would interest her the most, but instead it was the place Tanahaya had named Misty Vale that seemed to fascinate her. Even when he had moved on to other parts of the story, she kept asking questions about the ogre, the foggy valley and its queer animals, and what Tanahaya had told him about it.

"Why do you want to know so much about that place?" he asked after she had dragged his tale back to the valley for the fourth or fifth time.

"I am not certain," she said. "And your companion told you that the Zida'ya were banned from that place by Amerasu Ship-Born?"

He didn't remember precisely who Amerasu was, but it sounded correct. "Yes. So?"

"I just want to make sure I understand," Nezeru said. "If we manage to escape Da'ai Chikiza, we must know where we are bound—where we should go and where we should not go."

"Oh. Yes, of course. We truly, truly do *not* want to go near Misty Vale."

She nodded, or at least he thought she did but couldn't be sure, because the light from above was all but gone.

"It is time," she said. "Follow me."

"Qina! Qina, come here to me, please," Little Snenneq called. "I need your keen eyes."

"Again?" she asked.

"I must have done something wrong." Face and voice were both full of gloom. "I am a failure as a Singing Man."

"You are not a Singing Man yet," she reminded him, but gently. She leaned down to examine the tumble of small shapes in front of him. "I know this will make you unhappy," she said, "and I do not claim to know the knuckle bones as you and my father do. But that looks to me as if you have cast Unnatural Birth."

He groaned loudly and snatched up the bones from the circle of earth he had made. "It is true! Four times I have thrown the bones, and each time Unnatural Birth appears from nowhere, like a live maggot in a smoked ptarmigan."

She could not help smiling, though the idea itself was horrid. "A poetic image, my dear one, but perhaps this is no failure of your skill. Perhaps the bones are trying to tell you something you don't want to hear."

"But that cannot be," he said, though Qina thought that clearly it could. "Why would it come up again and again? I have even asked more specific questions, but each time it weasels its way in. It hovers over me like a storm cloud, making darkness wherever I look."

She shrugged as he gathered up the bones. They climbed back onto their rams, which had been cropping aimlessly at sparse shoots of dry grass on the steep hillside. "Perhaps," she said as she bounced her heels against Tipalak's sides and sent him ambling upward, "this Unnatural Birth that plagues you so *is* like a storm cloud."

He was struggling to get Falku moving, but the stocky ram was not happy about leaving the few last mouthfuls of grass behind. "What do you mean?"

"I mean, perhaps there is something *here*—" she swept her arm to indicate the rocky hill on which they rode and the forest behind them, "—that causes it. Something that belongs to this place, like a storm that comes down and will not blow away until it has emptied itself of all its rain and lightning."

"It could be," he said after a moment of frowning thought. "But whatever causes it, I must make sense of it. When the bones shout so loudly, only a fool would not listen."

Qina watched Tipalak's hooves as the ram picked his way down a narrow hillside path. After parting company with Kuyu-kun and his fellow Tinukeda'ya, she and Snenneq had spent many days searching the woods for any further trace of Morgan, but their search had been first inhibited, then cut short, by the presence of Norn troops. What had once seemed only a large, scattered party of scouts had quickly proved to be something much more vast—an army, centered around the ruins of Da'ai Chikiza, infesting that ancient place so thoroughly that she and Snenneq had not been able to approach it. They both felt strongly that the Norns might be holding Prince Morgan prisoner inside the crumbling city, but everywhere they had looked for a place to slip in and hunt for him they discovered more White Foxes. Da'ai Chikiza seemed to be completely infested with corpse-faced warriors.

At last, after several frustrated attempts, Little Snenneq suggested a different plan.

"Your father told us that there is a pass called the Stile that leads through the steepest part of the hills," he said. "And that the fortress of Naglimund stands on the far side. Perhaps we could find a path across the hills farther south, then come through Naglimund from the other side and make our way over the Stile to Da'ai Chikiza from there."

Qina had seen problems: the long journey would take days, and if the Stile led from the Erkynlandish fortress to the doorstep of the ancient city, it stood to reason that the Norns would have it as well-guarded as any other approach. Still, she could think of no better alternative, so they set out for the hills to the south of the ruined city. After crossing the T'si Suhyasei River on one of the fragile stone bridges the Sithi called "gates"—a crossing Snenneq managed only with extreme reluctance—they had spent the last two days climbing. The heights were not extreme to anyone raised on the steep, icy slopes of Mintahoq, but Hikeda'ya patrols roamed the hillside, so Snenneq and Qina spent almost as much time hiding as they did moving.

"Qina," Little Snenneq said in a sharp whisper. "Below us."

She looked down, and after a moment saw what he had spotted: a moving speck some hundred ells or more downslope, a single mote of dark color passing across a slope dotted with drifts of new snow.

"Norn," she said quietly. "But is he by himself?"

"Your question is a good one." Snenneq slid out of his saddle. "There is seldom only one Norn."

Qina jumped down and crouched beside her own mount, squinting. "We must wait until he is out of sight before we move again."

They watched, crouched and silent, until the speck disappeared. They stayed motionless until a second one appeared, following the first at a distance. Snenneq stroked Falku's neck to keep the big ram quiet until the other Norn had vanished as well.

"No wonder they are so busy in these hills," Qina said as they finally reached the crest. On their left, the Wealdhelm dwindled on its southern end into a rumpled mass of hillocks covered with grass so dry and old she thought it looked like shavings of bone. "By Kikkasut's greedy beak, what are they all doing here?"

The road below them, at the base of the hills, was packed with Norn troops, horses, goats, and many different wagons, a procession stretching beyond the visible distance. The pale winter sun glinted off thousands of spearpoints, and hundreds of black and white banners snapped and fluttered in the wind.

Snenneq shook his head. "I was a fool. I thought they might have been filling Da'ai Chikiza with their fighters to prepare an attack on Naglimund. But by the look of things, they have already attacked Naglimund and conquered it."

Before, Qina had only feared for herself, Snenneq, and lost Morgan, but now her fear deepened, making her feel hollow and sick inside. "How could this be? Where did they all come from?"

Snenneq stared but did not answer.

"We must hurry back to Erchester City." She fought to get her breath. Her chest felt as if someone had set a large rock on it. "We must tell Prince Morgan's grandparents what is happening here."

Snenneq wrung his hands in frustration. "How can they not know? Your own parents left days and days ago to take news to the castle. And if Naglimund has truly been conquered, those who escaped from the castle will have fled too. People must stop to eat and sleep, but news travels even on a moonless night, as your father says."

"But we cannot simply stand here and watch this vast force of Hikeda'ya marching off to slaughter our friends!"

"No, we should not stand here and watch," he said. "Else we may find more Norn scouts around us, and this time we may not be so lucky. Or one of those sharp-eyed creatures may simply look up and see us standing here on the hillside."

"Kikkasut!" she cursed. "But what can we do? We must do something!"

"Only what we came to do already, I think." Snenneq's voice was heavy. "Keep trying to find Morgan. But I think, for now, we retreat back into the forest. This is no place for two Qanuc, however brave and accomplished."

"But an entire army is on its way south. Where else would they be marching except to the Hayholt—to Prince Morgan's home? All his people are there! What if it is besieged? Destroyed?"

Snenneq sighed as he crawled backward, away from the precipice. "All the more reason, my dear Qina, for us to find him. It could be that soon poor Morgan will have no one else."

They made their way as silently as Morgan could manage up the twisting stairs. At the top, they discovered that the light came from an oddly shaped hatchway. The broken door that had once closed the hatch now lay in pieces in a pile of dead leaves and litter on the top step. Nezeru slithered up through the hole, then reached down to help Morgan climb.

Beyond the hatch they found themselves in the tower's wide bottom floor, more drifts of debris, and another coiling staircase that led upward. The stars in the dark sky glittered through the mossy ruins of several collapsed floors above them. "Stay here," Nezeru said. "I will climb up and see what awaits us outside the tower's top."

When she had disappeared up the steps, Morgan sat down on the uneven floor and began to rummage through the contents of his bag. He took out the climbing irons Little Snenneq had made for him, unused since he had begun to travel with Tanahaya, and tied them securely to his booted feet. Then, after walking quietly around to test the fit, he took off his scabbard and slung the belt over one shoulder so that he could carry his sword on his back.

Although it seemed quite dark to Morgan, when Nezeru came silently back down the stairs she saw his climbing irons immediately. "What are *those*?" she asked, as if he had put on something as pointless as a festival mask.

"For climbing. I'm good at it."

She looked doubtful, but only nodded. "As you say. I have been to the top. The roof is long gone, which is to the good. One tree is growing very near the tower—I think even you can jump to it."

He ignored this slight, though it did sting a bit. "What kind of tree is it?"

"I do not know the name in your tongue—we call it *xana*. It is broad and has green needles, which will be good for concealment. Most of the other trees nearby are losing their leaves now that winter is almost here."

Winter is almost here. The phrase, so simple, brought Morgan a stomach-swoop of horror. *Winter! I have been lost since the middle of summer. Everyone at home must think I'm dead.*

He did not have time to dwell on this, because Nezeru was already mounting the stairs again. Morgan did his best to match her swift, silent progress, but the steps were too shallow for him to manage easily with the blades on his boots. He had to turn sideways and climb that way, but still managed to scrape the metal on stone time after wincing time. At last, he stepped out onto the top landing. Nothing hung above him now but the evening sky: the top of the tower was gone, collapsed in some past age.

Nezeru had perched on the narrow lip of a stone window and was peering over the top of the wall. Morgan climbed up, then squeezed himself in beside her. The forest lay all around, the tops of the smaller trees a dark, frozen ocean just beneath them, the ground far below dusted with a recent fall of snow. Here and there taller trees stood above the others, and Nezeru pointed silently to the nearest. The hoary, ancient trunk was almost half as wide as the tower itself, and its branches spread out in all directions. One of the thickest limbs reached out to within five cubits from the tower top.

Yew tree, Morgan told himself, and his hammering pulse slowed a little. *A yew, thank the Lord. Couldn't be better.* He knew that if it was truly an old one, as its night-dark silhouette suggested, the trunk would be comprised of several ancient trunks grown together, and there would be lots of strong, horizontal branches. The distance he would have to jump still worried him, but no other trees stood as close on this side of the crumbling gate.

He was about to tell Nezeru what he was thinking when she waved him into silence with a violent flap of her arm. She was listening, he realized. She then made a careful circuit of the inside of the tower wall, climbing sideways and clinging like a lizard, until she had looked out in all directions.

She pointed to the spot where he stood on the windowsill. *Stay there,* was the obvious import. Then she clambered swiftly and gracefully onto the top of the wall and, with no obvious preparation, leaped outward.

He had seen squirrels jump from tree to tree and land with just as much calm certainty, but he had never thought to see anything with two legs do it. As she caught it, the thick limb barely quivered. For a moment she hung upside down, then she swung up on top of the branch and gestured that he do the same.

Easier said than done, he thought, but he gathered himself on the crumbling stone lip of the wall. He glanced down, then looked up again even more quickly.

I've done this before, he told himself. *With ReeRee and the rest of the Chikri creatures. Probably jumped farther. Certainly been up higher.* But his heart did not seem to be listening and continued to flutter.

Nezeru beckoned again. Morgan carefully got his feet beneath him so that his climbing irons would not snag on edge of the tower, then straightened until he was standing upright. A strong breeze staggered him. He knew he could not wait a moment longer, so he bent his knees and leaped outward.

He missed.

Nezeru caught his wrist as he fell past the branch, and the entire limb bent downward under his added weight. As needles showered his face and chest, he managed to get his fingers around the branch's rough bark. Grunting, pulling, and with much help from Nezeru, he struggled against the downward tug of his own weight until he could swing his legs upward and wrap them around the limb. He hung upside down until he managed to clamber onto the top of the branch, shuddering and panting.

"You said you were good at climbing," she whispered in his ear.

"That was jumping, not climbing," he whispered back after he had recovered his breath. "I never said I was good at that."

At last, when the trembling in his extremities had mostly stopped, Morgan followed her along the branch toward the rumpled mass of the trunk.

"Several other trees are close enough to jump to," Nezeru said. "Can you manage it?"

He wanted to say something that would soothe his wounded pride, but only nodded his head. "I think so. I hope so."

Nezeru abruptly stiffened beside him and gestured for silence. Morgan could hear only an occasional creak as the tall yew moved in the wind, but the concern on her face kept him stock-still.

"Sacrifices," she said in a soft whisper that still seemed far too loud. "A patrol, coming toward the gate and only moments away. We must move—we are too exposed here, and they will see us."

Morgan fought a rising panic. Now that she had said it, he could almost hear the tread of booted feet coming closer, though the Norns were famously silent. He desperately did not want to be hurried into another leap from tree to tree. Then an idea came.

"It's a yew tree," he whispered. "The trunk is likely hollow. We can crawl inside it. They won't see us."

"And the scent will help to cover our presence," she said in his ear. "A good thought. Come!" They searched in silence until they found a place where two parts of the trunk grew out in slightly different directions. "Yes, see," she said quietly. Her voice was calm, but there was an undercurrent of growing desperation Morgan could not ignore. "There is a hollow place beneath us."

"Climb in, then—I'll follow you."

"Are you mad?" she hissed. "Squeeze myself down there and then have you come smashing down on me with knives on your boots?"

"They're not knives, they're just—"

"Quiet. You go first, I will follow." She shoved him toward the place where the trunks diverged.

Morgan levered himself into the hollow, then began to work his way down. The inside of the tree was slippery with rain and occasionally crunchy with what might have been the remains of animal nests. When he had clambered downward a bit more than his own height, the way became a little wider. He called up to her in a soft voice, "I'm almost to a good spot. Just wait another moment and then you—"

Morgan did not know whether she had missed his quiet words or had suddenly seen the approach of the Norn guards, but a moment later she was sliding down the hollow trunk on top of him. He feared she would kick him in the head, but her booted feet scraped past his face and came to rest on his shoulders. For a moment they both stayed that way, like fairground tumblers in the middle of a trick. Then something gave way beneath Morgan and he suddenly lurched downward another cubit or two, letting out a muffled gasp of surprise. Nezeru slid down with him, but remained admirably silent.

They slipped until they could slip no farther. They were wedged tightly into the hollow trunk, neither able to move much, belly to belly and face to face.

"Well," said Morgan quietly after a few moments had passed, but then could think of nothing else to say. He could feel Nezeru's breath on his cheek, her slender form pressed against him from neck to ankles. He did not want to ask, but he sensed his Norn companion was not happy. "Well," he said again. "This is a bit of a puzzle, isn't it?"

18

The Graves of His People

Eolair rode west with Count Nial and a half dozen of Nial's men. As the Hayholt dwindled behind them Eolair's heart was heavy, his thoughts full of worry.

Nial, apparently, was no different. "King Simon asked me if I thought he had lost his wits," he said suddenly.

"Truly? That is not good to hear.' Eolair looked around. Their small company had stopped to water the horses at a stream. They stood a short distance outside a walled town called Clontub, and it seemed as though trouble could not be farther away. The fields were empty now that the harvest was over and the animals had been moved to their barns for the cold season, but though the land seemed deserted, he could see countless threads of smoke trailing from chimneys. On a hill at the far end, the manor house—with several chimneys of its own—looked down on the scene like a contented animal watching over its young.

"What did the king mean? Were you speaking of anything in particular?"

"It was when I asked him permission to return to Hernystir with you."

Eolair frowned. "It is hard for him to see his allies leaving at such a time, with Erkynland under threat from two directions. But he gave his permission, did he not?"

"Of course. I would not be here, else."

"Then the king understood that we can do greater good in our own country than we can in Erkynland." He laughed ruefully. "After all, I am not going to be much use defending the castle."

"I imagine you could still deal a few blows," said Nial. "You might have trouble staying on your feet after you swung your sword, though."

"I would be more amused if there were less truth in your jests," Eolair said. "I am feeling every bit of my age."

Nial had the grace not to say anything cheerful or reassuring, but only nodded.

Eolair was fond of Count Nial, although he had to admit that Nial's wife Countess Rhona was the cleverer of the pair. *Still, wit is not all,* he thought. *There is strength of arm and openness of heart, too—and honor, of course. Nial has all those things.* Nad Glehs, the seat of Nial's family since the days of Tethtain the Conqueror, was a broad, fertile valley nestled between two arms of the Fallaferig Hills. Its situation made it more self-sufficient than many of its neighbors, and its wide, gentle grasslands provided rich fare for sheep and cattle. By contrast, Eolair's own Nad Mullach was a smaller and less gods-gifted domain, but his family had held it as long as Nial's had held his, and the Mullachi were every bit as proud as any Glehsach.

They rode for several days across the western meads of Erkynland, but once they crossed the River Barraillean into their own land of Hernystir they guested most nights at estates and large manor houses, not only to soften the rigors of a long journey but also to sound out the other nobles they met, as a man might dabble with his fingers in a basin of hot water before plunging in his hands. Eolair let Nial guide him in these visits, since he had not traveled widely in his homeland for many years except as part of the royal visit to Elvritshalla the previous spring, a trip that had been more consumed with ceremony and protocol than anything else.

The Hernystiri nobles who hosted them were careful with their words, of course—Eolair would not have expected anything else after what Inahwen had told him the previous spring about the mood of the country—but he could not doubt that most of them were uneasy.

"It would be one thing if this was Lady Tylleth's father looking for more power for himself, or even King Hugh trying to move out of the shadow of the High Ward," explained one older clan leader, Tarn Aeth. The tarn—an old Hernystiri word for "chieftain"—was a liegeman of Count Larkin, an old comrade of Eolair's who was away at the royal court in the Taig. But Larkin was fretful, too, according to Aeth. "Those kinds of rivalries are as common as flies," the old man said as they all sat before the fire in his hilltop manor. "But some say this is different. It is Lady Tylleth, they say—she leads King Hugh on a path none can understand. He turns his back on old allies and embraces upstarts and ne'er-do-wells who support even his wildest schemes. Just this summer he and Lady Tylleth ordered the priests to leave the temple of Mircha and dedicated it to Talamh of the Land instead, Tylleth's favored goddess, though no one outside of the king's closest followers worships her." The old knight shook his head. "None can understand it, but the people don't like it when you muck about with the gods."

Eolair and Nial heard similar sentiments at several stops, and Eolair thought many others would have said the same had they not been afraid King Hugh. One baron's wife admitted as much, only approaching Eolair in the courtyard as he and Nial and the men prepared to set out after spending the night.

"You know my husband cannot say what he wishes he could," she told Eolair quietly, darting glances all around as though spies from the Taig might be lurking under the eaves of her own house. "Baron Curudan, master of the Silver Stags, owns the lands beside ours, and though our holdings are modest, he has long coveted them. He is Hugh's favorite, the one who rants most openly against Erkynland and the High Ward. If one whisper reaches the Taig that we spoke even a word against the king, then Curudan would march in here like a conqueror."

"I understand, my lady," Eolair said. "We will not mention your husband's name in any of our travels."

She looked at him with gratitude and pressed her lips to his hand. "May the gods keep you safe, Excellency."

He thanked her, offering prayers in return, but inside he was shaken and even a little sickened. *Is this what has come of all King Lluth's hopes for this kingdom? Is this what is left of his daughter Maegwin's great love for our folk? Nobles who are afraid to speak, and who fear that the king's friends may steal their lands away without law or the gods' blessing?*

Another sennight passed. The answers to even Eolair's most casual questions, when their hosts dared answer at all, were uniformly grim, and at last he and Nial stopped asking, worried that news of their inquiries might reach the Taig ahead of them. And not every lord who hosted them opposed the king's new ideas; some of them had already profited from supporting him.

"They are hidebound, all those who complain," declared one such noble, Tarn Garrad of Duncroich. He was dressed like a dandy from the Nabbanai court, Eolair thought, all in velvet and golden embroidery, and admitted he had only returned to his baronial hall for the Midwinter Rites, then would hurry back to the court in the Taig again. "Hidebound. You know that better than anyone, Count Eolair, surely—you have traveled the world! Some of these ancient barons have never even crossed the Baraillean, let alone seen the ocean. Like old trees, they moan and creak at every change of wind, with each new winter's chill, as if nothing so terrible had ever happened in the world."

Eolair looked him over carefully. Garrad was young, but surely not so youthful as to be utterly ignorant of the past. Had he never heard tales of King Elias, Prester John's mad son, who had also made a pact with the White Foxes, and whose dark reign had almost destroyed Hernystir along with the rest of the High Ward? But Eolair only said, "Still, people seem more unsettled than when I was last home."

Tarn Garrad laughed. "Change unsettles many, particularly the stupid. Since they cannot tell the difference between the sort of change that helps them and the sort that hurts them, they oppose it all equally."

Eolair nodded. "What changes do you speak of?"

Abruptly, the young baron's expression became guarded. "Oh, everything and nothing. I swear, the folk of this kingdom are becoming more like the Aedonites every day—everything new is suspicious, and they see Heaven's wrath in every thunderstorm." He stood and spread his arms. "Come, though, my lord, your company is an honor for my house and I would hate to spend all our time talking of dreary things. Let me show you and Count Nial my cellar. I am very proud of it."

As they rode away from Duncroich the next day, Eolair was troubled. "Did you see how quickly he stopped talking?"

"I was more struck by how well our young Garrad seems to have done from the changes he dismisses," said Nial. "In his father's day, Duncroich was one of the poorer baronies, with rocky pastures and sickly stock. But things have changed, at least for him."

"Is it only greed, then, that drives men?"

Nial laughed, but there was little heart in it. "Not all men, thank the gods, and for the weak, greed is not the only spur. Fear also plays a part."

"You are right. I saw a flash of it in his eyes just before he decided to shift the conversation to his collection of costly spirits." Eolair took a deep breath as if to clear his chest of the same air that Tarn Gerrard breathed. "There were wines there I have not seen even in the Hayholt or the great Nabbanai palace, the Sancellan Mahistrevis."

"It seems that knowing how to turn a blind eye and hold one's tongue is a well-rewarded skill these days."

"Yes, so it seems." Eolair adjusted himself in the saddle. Riding less than an hour, and he was already sore, but the ache in his lower back was as nothing to the chill in his heart. "Corruption requires silence to succeed. But the question that worries me more and more is, What else is going on in Hernysadharc that even those like Garrad are so obviously not talking about?"

"The fairy is bringing us right down on top of them," whispered Maccus Blackbeard. Maccus was almost as unflappable in battle as the legendary hero Airgad Oakheart, and Aelin had trusted the man with his life many times, but there was a quiver in his voice Aelin had never heard before. "He will get us killed!"

They were leading their horses down the hillside, along a path that only the Sitha Yeja'aro was able to see, if it even existed. Downslope, a scant bowshot away, stood a file of dark, armored shapes that the Hernystirmen could barely make out, but whom Yeja'aro had told them were Norn warriors.

"The White Foxes can see in the dark!" Maccus said, his voice louder this time. "We are too close!"

Yeja'aro, who was leading them, turned suddenly. With a single swift motion, he crossed several cubits and was standing in front of Aelin so quickly he might have flown there. "If you do not silence your man, mortal, I will do it with my knife," the Sitha whispered. Aelin did not doubt him for an instant.

Maccus's eyes opened wide, though it was hard to say whether anger or fear widened them, but before anything worse could happen, young Evan grabbed Maccus by the arm and pulled him a few steps back up the slope.

"All will be well," Aelin told Yeja'aro, placing himself between his men and the Sitha. "Just get us off this hill." He looked for the Norns where they had been on the hillside below, but to his alarm he could no longer see them. "By the Earthdog, where have they gone?"

The fury visible on Yeja'aro's angular face evaporated, leaving behind only a fine residue of scorn. "You are right to call upon your underground god," he whispered, "because that is where they have gone. They have retreated into their camp—a tunnel below ground."

"But why must we travel so close to it?" Aelin asked him.

"Because such outposts are everywhere in these hills." Yeja'aro's manner was calmer now. Like some mortals, the Sitha was quick to anger, but also seemed to recover his composure swiftly. "If we stay too far from one, we will be too close to another. Can you see them? No. So be silent and let me do what Jiriki tasked me to do. If we are caught, you will lose only your lives, but *I* will lose my honor."

Aelin opened his mouth and then shut it again. He could only hope Maccus and Evan had not heard their lives rated so cheaply. *And I like it little myself. But Yeja'aro is right—the White Foxes are everywhere. We could never have survived these mountains on our own.*

All through the twilight and then the evening, as the moon drifted through the sky, bobbing first upward then sinking down like a fat seabird riding the waves, Aelin and his men followed Yeja'aro down the wooded hillside, leading their horses. As the night wore on and the moon set, the going became harder and the Hernystirmen became wearier. Aelin found himself stumbling down the slope in a sort of blind stupor, tripping on loose stones or the gaping burrows of snakes. Several times he would have fallen had he not used the reins he was gripping to keep himself upright, though his mount did not like it much, and snorted its irritation.

With the last stars just visible above the horizon, Yeja'aro signaled them to halt.

"Stay here," he said, then vanished into the gloom as completely as water poured onto loose sand.

"Where is he going?" said Maccus. "Do you think he means to leave us behind?"

"Why would he? And why now?" Aelin knew it was hunger as much as fear that had sapped his men's courage. "No, stay strong. He will come back." He saw that Evan's lips were moving in prayer and decided the Aedonite had a sensible idea.

Brynioch Skyfather, he asked silently, *and Mircha, whose sign is the rainbow, watch over your servants. And over Evan, too, who may be an Aedonite but is still a son of Hernystir born and bred.*

They waited a long time in silence and increasing unease. Maccus wanted to light a fire against the cold—they were all shivering—but Aelin would not permit it. "We do not know what the fairy is doing, and we don't know what he might have found," he explained. "Try to take a little sleep."

They were seated back-to-back and Aelin was nodding when a noise brought him fully awake. A shape stood before him, silhouetted against the deep blue-black of the sky. Aelin let out a startled noise and in an instant he, Maccus, and Evan were struggling to stand and draw their weapons.

"You are like a nest of baby birds and just as noisy." Yeja'aro leaned forward and pulled Aelin upright with strength that seemed astonishing in one so slender. "Be silent and I will tell you what I have seen."

"We thought you had gone," said Maccus.

Yeja'aro gave him a look of disgust. "You do not know my people," was all he said. "You do not know me."

"Let's not waste time in argument," said Aelin. "What did you find?"

"A force of Hikeda'ya Sacrifices near the bottom of the hill." He dropped into a crouch so his whispers could be more easily heard. "Half a dozen fighters, armored and alert. But that is not the end of it. They have a giant."

Aelin's could not help remembering the huge, roaring, creature that had almost killed him as he carried a message to Eolair in the Frostmarch, and he was momentarily breathless with fear. "Holy Mircha watch over us," he murmured at last. "What do we do? Do they know we are here?"

Yeja'aro shook his head. "No. That is why I left you behind when I scented them. The smell of the giant in their camp likely covers the scent of mortals or they would have found us already."

"Can we go around them?"

"There are many Sacrifice camps in these foothills. I have walked far in these last hours. The one below us is the smallest."

"Why? Why are there so many of them here?" The darkness suddenly felt alive and malign. "They took Naglimund and killed its defenders. What else keeps them here?"

Yeja'aro shook his head again. "I do not know, but it does no good to talk about it. We must get past them or fail our trusts." For a long moment the Sitha simply crouched, staring down the hillside as though he could see even on this starless night.

And perhaps he can, Aelin thought. *Even after all this, I know so little about them. And I know less about their Norn cousins, except that they are fierce and deadly. What I would not give to have all my men with me. Half a dozen of us on horseback could at least give a good account of ourselves.* As he thought of his dead comrades scattered across Naglimund's keep, of loyal Jarreth buried under stones, some of his fear smoldered into anger. "We will kill them or die trying," he said.

Yeja'aro made a strange noise like the bark of a dog—a muffled laugh. "No, you will make your way as quietly as you can down the hill between that Sacrifice camp and their camp on the northern side. I will take their attention."

"Take their attention? How?"

"That is not your concern." Yeja'aro shrugged his bow off his shoulder and held it in his left hand. "But we have only a short time of darkness left. Get your horses and walk behind me in silence."

The hills were thick with oak, ash, and hornbeam, which provided cover as they descended, but it also meant it was nearly impossible to avoid making noise; each snapped twig or rustle of fallen leaves made the blood pound in Aelin's temples. From time to time they crossed a clear space with an uninterrupted view of the slope below. Far away, on the grassy lands to the west, he could see the first gleam of day as the sun rose past the hilltop behind them. It gave him a little hope, until he realized the growing light would make them even more visible.

They had entered a small copse of lindens when Yeja'aro suddenly lifted his hand, halting them, then pointed meaningfully to one side. When Aelin gave him a questioning look, the Sitha jabbed again, even more emphatically. Aelin led Evan and Maccus and their horses away in that direction while Yeja'aro stayed behind, silent and motionless. A moment later the three Hernystirmen were out of the trees and beneath open skies once more. The stars, bright as gems the last time Aelin had seen them, were fading as the sky began to lighten, and looked like cheap baubles spread on a peddler's blanket.

They had led their mounts only a short distance downslope when a sound rose out of the darkness behind them, a coughing grunt so deep and harsh it made the hair on Aelin's neck and arms rise and his skin tingle. A moment later the sound climbed to a rasping, inhuman snarl.

"The giant!" said Evan. "Is it coming?"

Aelin said nothing, only gestured for them to keep following him, but then a second cry rose from the hillside just above, a far more manlike cry of shock and pain. "By Murhagh," he said, "that is the Sitha!"

"Then we should run," Evan said breathlessly. "Or better, ride."

"No. We cannot leave him to fight and die alone." Aelin handed his reins to Evan, then turned and began scrambling back up the slope toward the source of the cries.

"What are you doing?" Maccus called, but Aelin did not stop. A thousand thoughts flew through his mind, most insisting he was a fool, but he could not stand to lose another companion, even the Sitha, in such a way.

It will be good death, he told himself over and over, though his heart was beating so swiftly it felt like it would leap out of his chest. *A noble's death.*

When he reached the stand of lindens, just enough light had seeped into the sky that he could see immediately what had happened. Four Norns in dark armor lay on the ground with arrows in back, chest, or neck, but the Sitha Yeja'aro lay on the ground among them, moving but apparently unable to get up. A huge, manlike figure loomed over him.

The giant wore crude armor, a chest plate of boiled leather and a skirt of hanging straps. In its clawed hand it held a long branch—a small tree trunk, in fact—that the monster had lifted to smash out the Sitha's life. Aelin leaped forward. He did not see any Norns other than the quartet who had fallen to Yeja'aro's arrows, but an instant later remembered that the Sitha had said there were six, and at that moment he saw a pale flash at the edge of his vision. Aelin jerked his head to one side, and though the Norn sword sliced him from cheek to ear, the blow was only glancing: Aelin did not even know he had been struck until blood began to run down his neck and onto his chest. By that time, he had reached the giant and slashed at the monster's near leg just below the calf. His sword bit deep. The giant staggered a step forward and let out a strangely muted cry, then sank to one knee, turning its weird yellow-green eyes on Aelin. An arrow wagged in the creature's broad neck, and its throat and upper chest were matted with dark blood.

Yeja'aro tried to silence it, Aelin realized, but that moment of distraction almost cost his life as the hairy thing lashed out with a clawed hand and though it only caught a little of his shoulder, the force of it smashed him face-first onto the ground, stunned, his sight full of flashing stars.

As Aelin tried to make his limbs do what he wanted them to, he saw that Yeja'aro was also struggling to climb to his feet, though one of the Sitha's arms was dangling uselessly. The giant was wounded but still standing, and two of the Norn Sacrifices remained alive and armed.

Then a shape as large as the giant came crashing into the clearing and the Norns had to dive out of its way.

This newcomer was Evan, mounted on his horse, and in the chaos that followed his sudden arrival, Aelin was able to struggle upright again. Only a moment later, Maccus rode in on his own mount, but his horse reared in terror as the giant lurched forward and snatched at it, and Maccus tumbled from his saddle. Aelin saw a spear lying on the ground and snatched it up. The giant was moving slowly and seemed confused, but Maccus was in immediate danger from one of the surviving Norns, who had attacked him before he could rise. Aelin ran toward them and drove his spear into the white-skinned warrior's back. The Norn staggered forward onto Maccus's jabbing blade, then fell. Though the Norn was clearly dead or dying, Maccus continued to hack at the fallen Sacrifice warrior as though at a venomous snake.

Aelin yanked the spear free and turned toward Evan, whose horse was kicking with its front feet as the one remaining Norn soldier tried to spear him. It was all Evan could do just to defend himself—the pale warrior spun and ducked and thrust so fast that his weapon was nearly invisible—but before Aelin could go to his countryman's aid, the hairy giant suddenly heaved back into his view, staggering toward him with its bloody muzzle stretched wide in pain and rage.

Yeja'aro suddenly appeared as if from nowhere and flung himself onto the monster's back. The Sitha wrapped his legs around the giant's neck, and began to jab at its neck and body with his sword. The giant made horrible, wet noises of anguish, but Yeja'aro kept stabbing until the huge creature swayed and then fell, its upper body a soggy mass of blood and torn, hairy flesh.

Maccus jumped in to help Evan, but the remaining Norn soldier now fought not to kill, but to escape, presumably to alert his fellows to their presence. He broke free of Maccus, dodged a sword-swipe from Evan (who was still struggling to master his rearing horse), then sprinted toward the edge of the trees. Aelin was crawling after the escaping enemy, dragging the spear with him, when it was snatched out of his hand. Yeja'aro flung the spear with his good arm and it hissed into the shadows of the outer trees. Scarcely an eyeblink later, Aelin heard a muffled grunt and the sound of a body falling to the ground.

"I told you not to come this way." Yeja'aro was breathing heavily, his injured arm twisted so badly that his palm faced out. "You made enough noise to wake Jakoya the Gatherer from her long sleep. Now we must run."

Aelin found his horse waiting just beyond the ring of trees and could not help marveling at the calm of the Sithi horses. Yeja'aro had vanished along the hill, but he reappeared a moment later on his own black horse to lead them down the slope toward the valley floor below.

He is like Murhagh himself, Aelin thought as he watched Yeja'aro ride, left arm bouncing uselessly and probably painfully at his side. *Even with but one arm, he killed the giant and speared a fleeing Norn, like Murhagh routing the gods' enemies at the Dubh Moinar.* Aelin felt half delirious, his head throbbing where the monster had struck him. *Legendary times have returned. Gods and men fight together against demons.*

They reached the Nartha and splashed along in its shallows until they could ride no farther. No pursuers appeared.

Hidden in the trees along the river's bank, the company took a moment to catch their breath. Aelin wiped blood from wounded cheek as he inspected his companions, but only the Sitha Yeja'aro had taken serious harm. "Your shoulder is out of joint," Aelin told him.

"Then put it back in. I cannot do it myself."

Aelin and Maccus laid hold of the upper arm and wrist, then lifted the Sitha's arm and pulled it forward until it rolled back into place. Yeja'aro did not make a sound, did not even grimace, though Aelin knew from experience that the pain must have been terrible.

"Is this a safe place to rest for a while longer?" Aelin asked.

"It is no worse than any other place when the Norns are hunting," said Yeja'aro. By the light of the morning sun, Aelin could see a thin sheen of sweat on the Sitha's brow. "But no better, either. If you need rest, then rest. I will keep watch."

Eolair's company of Hernystirmen crossed the river on the Drochbor Bridge but the local tarn was an ally of Hugh's, so instead of staying in the town, they made camp in a meadow south of the town. Eolair was just as glad, preferring the familiar rush and tumble of the swift Baraillean to being surrounded by people, even his own.

Soon I will see Nad Mullach again, he thought. *Praise Brynioch! It has been too long since I've touched that ground.*

"Will you take any men with you when we separate?" Nial asked.

"We are only a few leagues from my door," said Eolair. "I do not need an escort in my own domain."

"But what if you fall? You . . . you are not so young as you were, my friend."

Eolair looked at him sternly. "I have a little while left before I must be treated as a child who cannot go out without someone to watch over him."

"I did not mean it so—"

Eolair reached out and squeezed Nial's arm. "I know. It is my own unhappiness speaking. I cannot forgive myself for growing old."

They parted in the morning, Nial and his men to continue south along the river, Eolair to head west toward his family seat. "Remember, send no letters!" Eolair called after them. "Send only messengers who can remember what they have been told."

Nial waved. Eolair watched them until they disappeared over a hillock.

Frost had come during the night and the air was chill. The reeds and grasses had turned shiny white on either side of the river, as if carved from marble by a master sculptor. Eolair rode all that day, deep in thought, stopping only to water and feed his horse, eating his own provisions in the saddle as the cool, distant sun slipped by overhead.

Snow began to flurry in the middle of the gray afternoon as Eolair rode along the hedgerows that marked the edge of his family's land. The cypress and beech trees were mostly skeletal, only the laurels still holding their leaves, like misers clutching bills of credit. He realized that he was not far from the templeyard, so he left the main road to strike out across fallow fields until he reached the wagon track that would lead him there.

He reined up at the tumbledown wall of the burial ground, blinking snowflakes from his eyelashes. The death god's temple, sometimes called the House of Dunn, looked neglected, more than a few of its stones toppled and the roof fallen in on one side, but Eolair was pleased to see that the graves of his father and mother and nephew had all been tended. Flowers, though withered now by the winter, had been laid on each of them not too long ago.

Niece Gwynna has not forgotten her ancestors, he thought, relieved. It was hard to be so frequently away from home, and for such long stretches, though he trusted his sister Elatha and Gynna, both able, intelligent women, to take care of the family estate. Eolair had been able to visit the graves only a handful of times over the last decade, and he felt it acutely.

He kneeled beside his father and mother's barrow and murmured prayers to the gods, to bleak Dunn and sky-lord Brynioch and even to brown-eyed Deanagha, Rhynn's daughter, who took special care of those who had died of illness, like Eolair's mother and his nephew, Aelin's father. Prayers finished, he hoisted his aching body back into the saddle. The long avenue of leafless birches led him toward the house atop the hill, though the flurrying snow made it look indistinct and dreamlike. The birches waved at him as he passed, branches white and slender as the fingers of the dead, and Eolair had a moment of misgiving. The pastures were empty, and though that was perfectly reasonable at this time of the year, it added to his feelings of uneasiness.

You are an old fool, he told himself. *Everything is an evil omen. Every bird's cry or wail of the wind reminds you of death. It is the cold and your own weakness. The world is still just as young as it ever was, or at least the people who walk upon it are no different than those who came before them. And one day the world will go on without you, and you will lay in the same templeyard as your ancestors. What is there to fear in that?*

As he approached the house, he was heartened a little to see a servant carrying buckets to the pig's barn, but the man was too far away to hail, so Eolair rode on in silence. Nad Mullach had been built in the time of King Lluth's grandfather, more recently than some of the other great houses of Hernystir, but it was built on the foundations of a much older castle, a ring fort that had stood in that place longer than anyone could remember. Six generations of Eolair's family were buried around Dunn's temple, and it was said that the graves of at least that many earlier generations were lost somewhere inside the ruined walls that had once protected the house but had fallen into disrepair in his grandfather's day.

Will we need those walls again? If we take up arms against Hugh, will I regret the time I have spent doing the High Ward's work while my own house fell into ruin?

His gloomy thoughts were interrupted when a trio of dogs came streaking out of the dooryard and made their way down the track toward him, barking wildly, as though they had only just noticed him. He reined up and dismounted, soothing his horse as the dogs approached, then stood still long enough for them to range around him, sniffing and whining and yelping. He did not know any of the shaggy, bright-eyed hounds by sight—there were always a dozen or so running about the land and roving in and out of the manor house—but he knew the words to calm them.

"*Fa'sos!*" he cried—then, "Get down!" as one of them put its paws on his knees and tried to lick his face. "What kind of watchdogs are you? Do you even know me? I could be a murdering Norn for all you care."

Reassured to see the hounds running free, he led his horse up the long path toward the hilltop. Smoke was trailing from all three large chimneys and quickly vanishing, shredded by the winter wind.

Eolair dropped his cloak inside the bronze-bound front doors and scraped the mud from his boots, then made his way into the great hall. A slender figure sitting in one of the high-backed chairs looked up as he entered.

"*Bennach,*" he cried, falling back into his mother tongue without a moment's thought. "Elatha, my sister, it is good to see you!" The hall was just as he remembered it, the walls covered with ancient weapons and the straw-stuffed heads of deer and boar only slightly more recent, their polished stone eyes dulled by dust.

She raised her hand, but something in the hesitant way she did it made him hurry across the stone flags to her side. "Are you well?" he asked. "I am sorry

I have not written to you in so long, but—" Her expression arrested him in mid-sentence. "What is it?"

Elatha's familiar face was a little more lined with care than before, the cheeks a little more sunken. "I am sorry, Eolair," she said. "They have been waiting for you many days. The cursed dogs do not even growl at them anymore."

"What?" He could make no sense of what she said, and for a moment thought her wits might have been struck in his absence. Then a voice spoke behind him.

"*Bennach*, Count Eolair, and welcome back. I thank you for your hospitality, even if it was given without your knowledge."

He turned. The spare, hawk-faced man who had just stepped into the hall wore the colors and insignia of King Hugh's Silver Stags. As Eolair stared, trying to recognize him, a half dozen more Stags slid into the hall behind him. "Who are you?" Eolair demanded.

"I am Samreas, Your Excellency," the stranger said with a smirk, "and I come on behalf of your sovereign, His Majesty Hugh, king of Hernystir."

"Come for what?" Eolair looked to his sister, but Elatha only shook her head wearily. He turned back to Samreas. "Why have you made yourself at home in my family's house?"

Samreas gave him an arch look. "Do you begrudge a few meals and a few nights' lodging to the king's own messengers? What sort of loyalty is that?"

Eolair would not be cozened into the stranger's game. "I ask again, what is your business here?"

"Your king would have words with you, Count Eolair. He craves your companionship in Hernysadharc. You are too important to your country to be absent for such a long time."

"He is a liar," said Elatha. "They beat Gwynna when she demanded to see their royal warrant. She is in bed, covered with bruises."

In a sudden fury, Eolair reached for his sword, but Samreas flicked his fingers and all the Stags drew their own blades with a sudden screech of metal that made Eolair's heart rise into his throat. He cursed himself for being caught by surprise.

"Do nothing foolish, my lord," Samreas told him. "It will only cause more harm. It would be a shame if the Lady Elatha were to be injured because of a misunderstanding."

"Do you threaten my flesh and blood?" Eolair tried to calm his rising anger. "In our own house?"

"Do not fear for me, brother," she said in a grim voice. "I am old and not afraid. They have come to arrest you, Eolair, so do what you must."

He stared at his sister, then at Samreas and his men. Only Samreas seemed happy with the situation, a tiny smile playing about the corners of his lips.

Eolair sheathed his sword. "If you promise to leave my family and my people alone, I will come with you. I have words for Hugh, also."

"*King* Hugh," said Samreas. "Do not let the titles and honors the Aedonites have given you, exalted though they may be, confuse you, Count. King Hugh is your master, and His Majesty is not pleased."

Eolair closed his eyes for a moment, as if he hoped when he opened them again the strangers would be gone, the hall as he remembered it, familiar and welcoming.

"Well then," he said. "Give me your promise, and I will do as you say."

"We have no need to give promises to those who go against the king," said Samreas. "But I am no Thrithings barbarian. If you come peacefully and without tricks, we will depart Nad Mullach together, leaving your home no worse than it stands now."

Eolair felt an immense weariness. Just as his journey had ended, he must begin another. And this one, he felt coldly, dreadfully certain, would be his last on this earth.

19

The Eye of Gold

Miriamele did not know what day it was, nor was she even entirely certain what month, though she thought it must still be Octander. She had lived her life in courts ruled by the calendar, by saint's days and feast days and important delegations, first with her father and mother at Meremund, then at her grandfather's court and during her father's short, disastrous reign. Later she had ruled over a court of her own with Simon, and if the problems they faced and the solutions they pursued were sometimes different than their predecessors', the tyranny of the calendar did not change at all.

That had all come to an end on the day the Sancellan Mahistrevis had burned. After that, orderly time had come unstuck. Several days on the road, half a day or more insensible by the roadside, and then the endless, unchanging days of captivity in Agga's hut had left her adrift. She was a prisoner, but she should have felt at least a small sense of freedom at being liberated from the clamor for her attention from ministers and functionaries and petty lords, the need to put on a queen's face to observe both holy days and sad anniversaries. Instead, Miri felt as if the river had not surrendered her to the river-man but had kept her instead, pulled her down and drowned her, then swirled her away in its restless current.

Agga was testing the anchor chain that held her captive. He had secured it to one of the house's corner posts, because he was going into town, though he would not tell her what town that was.

"Never mind, tha—us is just going to sell the last catch now it be smoked and ready," he told her in his strange, flat way of speaking. "Time be come 'round at last. Lady of Stars came to us's dream yesternight with call to come now, come north, bide no longer but come."

"Who is this lady you keep speaking of?" Miriamele asked, but she had a horrible feeling she knew. When the Niskies had told her of their dreams, her first thought had been of the witch-queen Utuk'ku: who else could enter the dreams of so many? "And why should you believe her? She might be a demon, a servant of the Adversary."

"Na, na—her be's no demon. Her be Queen of Dreams and her has called us true and proper." He pulled on the chain so hard that the sinews in his long arms stood out like writhing snakes. The whole hut creaked, but the chain did not come loose. "Tha'll not slip that, not haply nor a-purpose." He gave the chain a last satisfied tug, then stood up, looming above her where she crouched on her uncomfortable bed. Agga's eyes seemed unusually bright, fierce as the eyes of a predator. Miri wondered if he might be imagining the wedding night to come, and her stomach heaved.

As if he understood what she was thinking, he bent and took her face in his rough hand, forcing her chin up until she looked him in the eyes. "Fear not, woman. Agga be not such a bad man, and th'art comely yet, though old. Mayhap the Lady of Stars will grant tha can'st still bear child."

She jerked her face free from of his hand. "Never! I am married already. No matter what you think this Lady of Stars is, God is higher, and He would not allow such a crime."

"Then had best spend tha time praying whilst us is gone. If God be listening." He gave her a gentle slap on the cheek, not particularly meant to harm, but it made Miriamele feel small, helpless, and even more furious than before.

"You will pay for this, Agga. You could have been rewarded. You could have been a rich man."

"Quiet, now. Us'll be at Lady's right hand when the Day of Weighing comes, and tha'rt meant for us's bride."

He went out then to finish loading his dried fish onto the back of his cart, then lifted the shafts onto his shoulders. He grunted with effort as he got the wheels moving across the muddy ground, pulling it across the dooryard and down toward the river road. Within moments he and the cart had passed out of sight.

Miriamele immediately rolled off her bed and dug out the single iron nail she had hidden beneath the nets and musty blankets. A prolonged inspection the last time Agga had been down at the river had revealed that most of the house was held together with wooden pegs, but in her exhausting search, pulling the heavy anchor across the packed earth of the cottage's floor, she had found a single iron nail which she thought Agga must have dropped without noticing. At first she had considered it as a weapon, but the spike beneath the square head was only as long as the first two knuckles of her finger; the only place it would really harm him would be if she managed to drive it into one of his eyes. Miriamele was angry enough that she felt certain she could do that, but knew it would be a very risky thing to try. If she failed to kill him outright, a furious, wounded Agga might murder her on the spot, star-marriage or no star-marriage.

Instead, she had begun scraping with it against one of the links of the chain nearest her ankle. That first day she had labored at it for what must have been the best part of two hours but succeeded only in scratching away the grimy surface of the link. When she heard Agga returning she had wiped a bit of dirt from the floor on the scratched place to hide what she'd done.

Now she resumed scraping nail against link, though she felt sure it would take many days to weaken the chain in any significant way, and Agga had just made it clear they might leave soon. More than a little panicked, she redoubled her efforts, scraping and scratching so hard that her fingers began to bleed. She tore a bit off the hem of her undergarment and wrapped the wounds, then went back to work. She scratched until the nail grew hot in her fingers and she had to let it cool a little, but she had made scant progress that she could see. She bent to her task once more, scratching the point against the surface of the chain link over and over and over.

No man rules me, she told herself. *No man rules me, nor ever has, nor ever will. Even my beloved Simon knows he is not my master but my husband. My father tried to make me do his bidding, may God rest his troubled soul. I ran away. Uncle Josua tried to keep me when I did not want to be kept. I ran away. The cursed Ingadarines tried to make me leave Nabban before I wanted to, and then tried to kill me when I did not leave, but they failed, too.* She found a sort of rhythm in the words, a tuneless song detailing all those who had tried to force their will on her and failed, and it lifted her heart a little. *This Agga will fail, too. I am my own woman—my own and God's. Nobody can make a slave of me. No man can own me. No man can own me.*

And all the time the nail in her cramping fingers continued to scrape—*skrt, skrt, skrt.*

Serasina wriggled and complained in Jesa's arms. It was nearing mid-morning and the baby was hungry, but Jesa did not want to stop. She had spent a frightened, fretful night in the woods with the baby after luring Viscount Matreu into the ghant nest, and had started awake several times at noises, the last time from a nightmare where Matreu had come shuffling through the trees with his head on backward, calling out for Serasina, saying he would rock the infant. After that she had not been able to sleep again and kept Serasina clutched tightly against her until dawn brought color back to the world.

Once up, she had set out northward beside the river, but was already regretting that decision. If Matreu had found her so easily, his men must be close by; if they were hunting for her, she would be far too easy to spot on the exposed river track. Years of carts and wagons had beaten down or broken most of the vegetation on either side of the wheel ruts, and Jesa felt as if she walked along the top of a high wall, exposed to all the world.

She hurried on, hoping to find an isolated house where she might be able to beg some food for the baby, then be far away before the householder told anyone about the curious visit of a dark-skinned young woman with a light-skinned baby.

At last she came to a crossing where a second road veered off from the river track and ascended toward the low hills. She guessed that the town where she had met Father Culby might be somewhere along that westward road, so she paused at the crossing, wrestling with the decision. From the town she might find her way back to the church and the good people there who had already helped her once. But she was also fairly certain that Matreu had picked up her track there, which meant that she might be walking into a trap if she returned, or at the very least, letting people see her who had no reason to keep her existence a secret, especially from a troop of armed men searching for their leader.

As she hesitated, she heard the rumbling squeak of wheels, and her heart began to pound. Looking around in sudden fear, she saw a stand of yew trees just off the road, growing among toppled stone ruins that might once have been a toll house or even someone's cottage. She hurried to the broken wall and hid herself behind it, peering through the drooping branches to see who might be on the road and whether they looked like someone she could ask for a little charity. Serasina squirmed in her arms and began to make the sounds that came before she started crying, so Jesa licked her finger clean and stuck it in the child's mouth, hoping to keep her quiet long enough to decide whether to stay hidden or not.

The figure that trudged into view was at first glance nothing exceptional—a man pulling a large, two-wheeled cart. She watched as it bumped along the rutted road, and a moment later smelled the strong, exciting sent of smoked fish, which made her mouth water. She was about to step out and try to beg a fish for herself when something about the man pulling the cart caught her attention. He was tall and darkly tanned, though not Wran-born like herself or an islander like the late Viscount Matreu, but something about him made her pause. He was talking to himself, which was not unusual—Jesa had done it more than a few times herself during her wilderness exile—but something about the way his head turned from side to side, as though he argued with someone invisible, made her worry that he might be mad. The stranger was big enough, with wide shoulders and great long arms, that the thought frightened her. As he came closer she saw that he had an unusual cast to his features that nevertheless seemed familiar.

Niskie, she thought. *He has something of their look*. She had never thought badly of the sea-watchers, though many in the Sancellan disliked them and even feared them, and she had no reason to distrust this man simply because he looked like he might have Niskie blood, but as the cart neared, she stayed in hiding.

". . . by the Lady," he said to himself when he was close enough for Jesa to hear. "And then all be well. The Queen will make all right. Stand at her good right hand, us will, and all the children singing, the ocean children all crying us's name. And them what hold us back, them will die."

The stranger said these last words with such calm satisfaction that Jesa sucked in her breath and held it, suddenly quite certain she did not want to give herself away. To her horror, though, the man stopped pulling his cart in the middle of the crossing, then left it and began to walk toward the broken wall where she was hiding. She ducked down and pressed her face against the fallen leaves and damp earth, praying to the gods of the Wran that Serasina would stay quiet.

The footsteps stopped not two paces from her on the other side of the wall. Her heart was beating fast, and she expected any moment he would reach down and grab her. Then she heard the patter of liquid on leaves and against the rocks and smelled the acrid odor of urine.

Jesa now had even more reason to hold her breath. The man seemed to take forever to void himself, mumbling about stars and ladies and glory. At last he turned away and she heard his footsteps receding. When she heard the wheels of his cart bumping along the ground again she risked another glance, and saw he had turned off the river track and was heading up the hill. She guessed he was bound for the town.

Now she was even more convinced she did not want to go there—something about the man's murmured words had deeply unnerved her—so though she sat up, she did not move for some time, doing her best to soothe little Serasina, who had grown tired of the taste of Jesa's finger.

I should keep on walking, she thought, though she had no idea where the river road would eventually lead her, whether she would find houses or another village, or simply carry on through the wild lands as another night fell and the baby grew hungrier. Now, with the immediate fear gone, Jesa could still smell the lingering odor of smoked fish, which made her stomach clench and gurgle with hunger.

Perhaps he dropped some, she thought with sudden hope. The cart had been piled high. It did not seem impossible that a dried trout might have fallen off, might even now be lying on the river road waiting for someone to find it. Someone hungry.

The battle between the urge to keep moving and the need for food was a short one, and hunger won. She got up, careful to keep the baby's tender head safe from scratching branches, then stepped out of the yews and returned to the crossing.

Very little had fallen off the man's cart. She found one tiny fish, scarcely as long as her hand. By the time she had chewed it to a sticky pulp, there was barely enough of it to quiet Serasina's hunger pangs.

She was tired after walking all through the morning and part of the afternoon, and the sun, though winter-dim, glared through the branches and made her head ache. She found a place out of sight from the river road and sat down to rest as Serasina slept in her arms.

It is so cold here in the north, she thought. *I cannot keep the baby in the wilderness for long. But where else can I go?* She was alone in a land she did not know, a place more foreign than Nabban had ever been, since there Duchess Canthia had shielded her from hunger and dangers. *Until the end,* she thought, and shuddered again. *Even Canthia could not keep so much evil away.*

As she distractedly rocked the baby, a noise began to intrude on her thoughts.

She ignored it at first, thinking it was just the wind, which was rising as the sun slipped lower in the sky. But after a while she noticed that whatever caused the sound, it rose and fell in a way that was not like wind or even the rush and murmur of the river but was complicated by breaks and starts.

It's music, she thought. *But from where?*

She stood and moved closer to the road, but the rutted track was empty in both directions, and now the sounds seemed farther away. She carefully retraced her steps to where she had been sitting, and now she could hear the movement of melody above the sonorous muttering of wind and water.

Slowly, with a worried heart but a still empty stomach, she followed the sound up the hill and through the trees. She whispered to Serasina as she walked—placatory, wordless sounds to keep the baby quiet. It felt as if she was in one of her grandmother's stories, the one about a wandering child who stumbled into the lair of the *mukah,* fairy creatures who sang or sent flickering lights to lure unwary travelers off the safe paths and into the sucking mud, but at the same time the music was so sweet that she could not help moving toward it. It sounded more and more like the voice of a woman or a young boy, and even as she feared supernatural trickery, Jesa could not help hoping she would find safety at the other end—a kindly cottager singing as she took down clothes that had been drying, or even better, as she prepared a hearty kettle of stew. Jesa's mouth watered. *I have been hungry so long.* Her night of food and safety with Father Culby and his helper already seemed years in the past. *They Who Watch and Shape,* she prayed, *help me keep this child safe. That is the most important thing. But if there is food to be had, please let me eat!*

The trees gave way to a slope covered with undergrowth and a knot of scrubby oak trees. As she reached the edge of the spinney, she saw a cottage made from wattle and daub perched on a hillside a short distance above the river. The music had stopped for a moment, and she was not certain that it had come from the small, rustic hut, but as she stood staring, hesitating, her stomach aflutter with both want and fear, she heard the voice again. It was sweet but not loud—someone singing to themselves instead of to others—and it eased her fear a little. But Jesa thought she heard real longing in the person's voice, as though it were more than something to pass the time, and she wondered again who was singing.

Come back, my love, come back,

the singer lamented.

From out the waves and wrack
I wait for you my captain dear
Though you have gone for many a year
And I shall bide here 'til you do
Come back, my love, come back!

Jesa looked carefully in all directions but saw no other sign of life. The dooryard was a shambles of broken benches and tangles of rope that she thought might be fishing nets. To one side of the open space stood a makeshift shelter covered with split timbers and old blankets, and this froze her in her tracks with the sudden fear that someone else might be inside it, a husband or son who would think her a robber and chase her away. Or might there be dogs, as she had seen in some of the houses of Nabban, she wondered—some snarling beast that would snatch the baby from her arms and savage it before she could do anything?

As she stood, uncertain, the voice rose again.

My love he was a captain who sailed out from Jinnsennee
He swore he'd find the world's lost edge and then sail back to me
So here I stand upon the strand, a-waiting by the restless sea
And through each day I stand and pray that he'll come back to Jinnsennee . . .

Nothing else moved, and Jesa was certain now that the singing came from the tumbledown cottage. What was strange, though, was that something in the voice seemed familiar, though Jesa knew that could not be. How could it, here in this alien land?

Nevertheless, the mournful song drew her up the hill toward the cottage.

His ship, the Eye of Gold, it rode the waves just like a gull,

Miriamele sang, suiting the rhythm of her scraping to the measure of the song.

And a hundred men stood hand to hand to measure out its hull
But the sea is cruel and old, and all her thoughts and loves are cold
And though she is Green Mother called, our mother is not merciful.

Come back, my love, come back,
From out the waves and wrack
I wait for you my captain dear
Though you have gone for many a year
And I shall stand here 'til you do
Come back, my love, come back!

They say the Eye of Gold sailed far from home and comforts fair
To World's End and the biting rocks that waited for them there
Then passed the Horn of the Angry Sun, where men have tails and dogs have thumbs
But no word came to Jinnsennee of where they next did fare . . .

I've seen much of the world, Miriamele thought suddenly, *but I've never heard of Jinnsennee. Is it made up?* Distracted by the idle thought, she sucked on her bloody fingers and examined the bit of the chain she had been scraping. Agga would be back soon, she felt wretchedly sure. It was already late afternoon, and she had dug only a hair's breadth or two into the iron link. Agitated and angry at herself, she wrapped her sore fingers in a fold of her tattered dress and went back to scraping, singing even louder to cover the noise, though she was exhausted and her wrist and hand ached.

Come back, my love, come back
From out of the waves and wrack
I wait for you my captain dear
Though you have gone for many a year
And I shall stand here 'til you do
Come back, my love, come back!

And then my heart returned to me, for I did see a gleaming sail
By moon's bright light it came to me, and loudly I did hail
But like a vision or a ghost, it turned from shallows and from coast
Though once I thought I saw my love a-standing at the rail.

And now I know he sails the seas, and he shall sail them evermore . . .

She broke off at a sudden noise and looked up. A face was peering into the cottage window. Miriamele let out a shriek of surprise and alarm.

"Usires save us! Who are you? What do you want?" But a mere moment or two passed before she saw that it was a woman with dark skin holding a baby, and as her fright subsided, she felt an astonishing and unlikely certainty. "Sweet Elysia, Mother of God—*I know you!* You are the nurse, the child's . . . is it Jesa? What are you doing here?"

The face at the window looked as startled as Miriamele's must have, but though the eyes stayed wide with surprise, the young woman nodded. "Yes, Queen Majesty, it is me. But what are *you* doing here?"

Miriamele had dropped the nail in her momentary fright, and after so long scraping with it she could not at first help looking down for it in the tangle of chain, as if it were a part of herself she could not survive without. "Oh, praise Heaven. Do not ask me to tell the tale now. You are in danger. The man who has captured me may be back at any moment."

"Then come with me," Jesa said. "They Who Watch and Shape have truly led me! Come with me and we will run away!"

"I can't—I am being held here. Wait—that baby in your arms—is it little Serasina? Oh, God is so good! Is Canthia somewhere nearby too? The duchess?"

The young woman's face twisted. "She is dead, Majesty—the duchess is dead. So is the boy Blasis. I could only save the little one."

Miriamele's heart sank. She made the sign of the Tree upon her breast. "Oh, merciful God, what happened? No, don't tell me now. I need your help. Go into the yard outside and see if you can find a chisel. I have a chain to cut that holds me here."

"A . . . chisel?" Jesa clearly did not recognize the word.

"A tool to chop through metal, like a blunt knife. This big. You pound it with a hammer."

"Ah—*panuk*," the girl said, almost to herself.

"Go look, I beg you! And be quick! The man who lives here is very strong and he is mad in the head, too."

Jesa disappeared from the window. Miriamele could only sit and wait, heart beating swiftly, like the wings of a bird trying to outrace a hawk. After a painfully long time she heard a rumble and thump from the front door. Thinking it was Agga returning, she despaired, but when the door opened she saw it was Jesa, still cradling the baby in the crook of one elbow as she dragged something long and obviously heavy with her other hand.

"There was a rock against the door," Jesa said. "A big one. I had to roll it away."

"Did you find a chisel?"

Jesa shook her head. "No. But I found this." She lifted the long handle up so Miriamele could see. It was a maul, with a flat hammer-head on one side and a blade on the other.

"Bless you, girl," Miri said. "Come here and let me have it. Now, stretch the chain out and hold it with your foot. There." Miri could not lift the maul by the end of its handle—it was too long and heavy—but she gripped it about halfway down from the head and managed to raise it up to shoulder height. She swung the blade down onto the chain, but the blow only pressed the link into the earthen floor.

"Help me get this chain to the fireplace," she said. Together, they managed to drag the chain flat on the stones at the fireplace's edge, then Miri swung the maul again. The blade rang loudly against the stone and the cutting edge of the maul chopped through one side of the chain link. Miriamele's heart rose in exultation, but even as she lifted the maul to finish severing the chain, she heard a loud, angry voice from outside the cottage.

"Here! What trick dost tha play?"

It was Agga. Miri turned and cried, "Get out, girl!" but Jesa instead ran to the far corner of the cottage and pushed herself back into the shadows as the baby in her arms let out a hitching, wailing cry. An instant later the door crashed open and Agga stood silhouetted against the afternoon light, his face flushed and contorted into an angry demon's mask. He looked around, distracted by the sound of Serasina's distress, but then saw Miriamele crouched by her bed, where she was trying to hide the maul. The half-split length of chain still lay in the middle of the room, and as he saw it, Agga's eyes widened and his face purpled with rage.

"Witch!" he cried. "Deceiver!" In two steps he was looming over her. He dealt her a hard blow with his open hand that knocked her down onto the makeshift bed, her head ringing and her eyes unfixed, as though she had fallen back into the river to sink into blurry darkness. She saw his hand come up again, then something landed on him from behind and he let out a grunt of surprise.

As Jesa grappled with him, shouting and scratching his face, Miriamele felt for the maul. When her hand closed on it, she slid her fingers up just below the heavy iron head, then swung it into the nearest part of Agga, which turned out to be his belly. Gurgling in pain, he doubled over, dumping Jesa heavily to the floor. Miriamele got both hands on the maul, lifted it, and swung again, this time with all her strength. The iron head cracked against Agga's skull and knocked him sideways. He staggered one step, then crumpled to the dirt floor and did not move again. His breath rasped in and out of his throat as though he had taken an arrow in the lungs, but Miri saw only a trickle of blood from his ear and a white dint in his temple where the head of the maul had struck him.

Jesa ran to pick Serasina up again from the place she had set her. As Miri's captor lay insensible, his breath sawing in and out in a painful, shuddering wheeze, Miri bent to her fetter again. It took three more blows because her hands were shaking so badly, but at last the chain fell away, leaving only the loop still fastened to the iron shackle around her ankle.

Silently, as if they no longer needed to speak to understand each other, she and Jesa ransacked the cottage, snatching up anything that looked useful. They found a pile of flatbread wrapped in leaves, stale but edible, and a knife sheathed on the back of Agga's belt, though taking it from him, even in his current state, made Miri's heart speed again. She was half-certain he was only shamming, that he would grab her and drag her down and choke the life out of her, but the knife came out of its sheath as easily as a worm plucked by a robin. A moment later they were outside, gathering up the few remaining smoked fish from the drying tent and from Agga's cart, which stood deserted on the slope a few paces away.

"Now we must run and get as far away as we can," said Miriamele. "He might wake up and come after us. He is mad. He thinks I am his bride."

"Should we tie him?" Jesa asked. "Or kill him?"

"I don't want to go near him," Miriamele said. "In any case, I think he's dying. Now, run!"

Jesa turned and began to hurry down the well-worn track between Agga's hut and the river road; Serasina howled as she jounced up and down in her protector's arms. Miriamele followed, aching and already breathless because of her long confinement. But before she had gone a dozen steps after her, another noise drowned out even the baby's wails.

"Woman!" It was a hoarse bellow from the hut, a shout of rage and pain that echoed along the wooded hillside. *"Cursed be! Kill tha!"* A scant heartbeat later, the door of the hut flew open so hard that a hinge was torn from the jamb, and

a bloody figure shambled out into the dying light of the afternoon, still roaring, but now without words.

Miri saw the open, empty road along the riverside at the bottom of the hill. She looked back to see Agga stumbling a little as he came after them, but he did not lose his footing and seemed to be gaining strength with each step. Miriamele doubted they could outrun even a wounded madman on the open road, with the river blocking their escape on one side, and no one else to help them, perhaps not for leagues.

"Jesa! Into the trees!" she cried, then turned and began to run parallel to the river, hoping she could lose him in the crowding pines. *At least I must lead him away from Jesa and the child,* she thought, but already she was having trouble getting enough air, and felt as if she was still dragging the anchor behind her.

Agga continued to make bizarre, unintelligible sounds as he flailed through the trees after her. She ran, dodging trunks, brambles clawing at her legs and her tattered skirt. The river was near, its voice loud. Miri did not want to get too close for fear of falling in and being swept away, but her strength was fading quickly. The rush of exhilaration that had come with Jesa's unexpected appearance had nerved her to beat down Agga and flee, but that febrile strength was fading quickly now, and she kept stumbling, each time terrified that she would fall and Agga would catch her. There was something dimly familiar about the pine spinney, she realized, but she had no time to consider it.

Miriamele's headlong flight had led her close to the river again. She slowed for just a moment to look back at the bellowing thing behind her. The huge man was smashing his way through everything before him, like some ogre out of a nightmare, his face crimson with rage, his roars incoherent, animal. Terrified, she tripped, and just managed to grab at a trunk to keep from falling. By the time she could get her feet beneath her again he was only a few paces behind her.

The river's edge lay just before her now, a broad backwater surrounded by waving reeds. For a moment she thought she might hide in them, but the stand was too sparse. Agga was just behind her, breathing heavily and harshly, like a winded horse. Miriamele saw a broken branch lying near the water's edge. She grabbed it up and straightened, ready to sell her life as dearly as possible.

Agga's head was visibly flattened on the side where she had struck him, and his eye on that side wandered beneath the jutting brow like a slowly spinning wheel on an upended wagon. Blood dribbled from his ear down his neck, and from his nostrils as well, so that his face was a mask of red and white, but his good eye was fixed on her. He took a clumsy step forward, then another. Miri backed along the edge of the eddying water, heart rabbiting in her chest, and lifted the limb above her head.

"Don't come any nearer!" she cried. "I'll kill you! I will!"

A scarlet-tinged bubble bloomed on Agga's lips, swelling and shrinking like the throat of a courting frog. His big hands reached toward her, his face a horrible grimace in which she could see nothing human.

"Stop!" she cried—but he did not stop. She swung her makeshift weapon and hit him across the chest, but it hardly seemed to slow him at all. He tried to twist the branch out of her hand, but even as his fingers closed on it, he flinched and cried out, then reached up to feel the back of his head.

Another rock struck him, this time in the neck. Agga turned to look back. Jesa was a dozen paces behind him, little Serasina still clutched in one arm as she bent to pick up another stone. This time Agga was ready, and though he seemed more than a little dazed, he tilted his head and let the rock fly harmlessly past, then turned back toward Miri. Jesa bent and grabbed an even bigger stone and flung it. This one hit him in the back with a hollow *thump*, and he took an off-balance step toward the edge of the water, but his one good eye was still fixed on Miri. Then something heaved up behind him, and Miriamele fell backward as water fountained up and over her. The chain on the kallypook Agga had captured kept the creature from escaping the pond, but Agga had wandered close enough for the thing to spring out and suck his foot and ankle into its gaping, monstrous mouth. Agga only had time for a single wordless cry, then the gray thing dragged him backward into the water, then beneath it. Within moments, nothing remained on the surface but diminishing waves and ripples.

Jesa hurried to Miriamele's side. They did not say a word, but only scrambled up the bank as fast as Miri could go. Little Serasina was crying, but otherwise the backwater had gone silent but for the sundown wind strumming the reeds.

20

The Open Door

What fools these *so-called immortals are.*

Pasevalles climbed out of the dark, cobwebbed depths and into the understory of the Granary Tower in the Hayholt's Middle Bailey. His anger was sharp as a knife, but he could do nothing with it—could neither slit throats nor stab hearts. He was used to pushing down such rages, though sometimes they felt so powerful he feared they would overwhelm him, that he might wrap his fingers around the neck of some idiot courtier or a meddling fool like the Wrannaman Tiamak, then squeeze until he heard something crack. This was such a time.

Rule yourself, he thought in disgust. *Who is the master, you or your anger?*

He did not know exactly who among the Norns' Order of Song spoke to him when he held the Master Witness called the Mooncloud, but he knew it must be someone important in Nakkiga just by the power of their presence. But that did not make being treated as a lackey by one of Queen Utuk'ku's minions—or worse, as a gullible peasant—any easier to take.

Do not seek to understand the great plan of the Mother of All, the chill, rasping voice had told him. *You will receive all you have been promised, but only if you do what you are told and hand the mortal king over to us. And you must not flee the castle too early.*

How he had struggled to keep his thoughts silent, his outrage hidden. *Of course not,* he thought now as he opened the doors and took a careful look outside. *I'll sit here waiting until your death-pale soldiers knock the walls down, just to make certain everything goes as the Mother of All wishes. I'll hand over what she wants, then wait like a wagging dog to be rewarded by the treacherous fairy-queen who hates my kind. Why would I not?*

Pasevalles did not trust the Norns at all—not the least bit. In truth, he had stopped trusting anyone at a very early age, when he realized that no one else thought in the way he did, with a depth and craft completely unmuddied by sentiment. But sometimes bargains had to be made, and that was the case now. If a ravening wolf wanted something from him, then he had to decide how to give it over without having his hand bitten off.

Outside the tower, the expanse of muddy ground between the castle walls was full of servants and workers, but they were all hurrying somewhere or other, heads down, as if the Norns might appear outside the gates at any moment. Pasevalles put on a mask of deep concentration, meant to discourage anyone from approaching him as he made his way toward the heart of the castle.

"No, damn it all!" Duke Osric was once more struggling to rise. "The king needs me at Winstowe!"

"You are not going to get on your horse, Your Grace," said Lady Thelía sternly. "Not for a long time still. And you will be no good to anyone, least of all King Simon, if you thrash yourself into an apoplexy." She looked up and saw Pasevalles in the doorway. "My lord, would you be kind enough to help me give him this draught? I am afraid he's going to break my arm."

Pasevalles could see the shadows of weariness on Thelía's face. He manufactured a smile of sympathy. "Of course. What can I do?"

She rolled her eyes. "Talk to him, Lord Chancellor, please. See, Your Grace, it is Pasevalles, come to confer with you about important matters." She looked meaningfully at Pasevalles. "I am certain it is important, yes?"

Arrogant bitch, he thought. *Am I your servant?* But his resentment did not alter his blandly reasonable expression. "As it happens, it is, my lady. Greetings, Duke Osric, first I must apologize for not having come to see you in the last few days. We were all very worried for you, but I know you have been getting good care from Lord Tiamak and Lady Thelía."

Osric's bleary eyes fixed on Pasevalles; the duke struggled a little higher in the bed.

"Don't do that, Your Grace!" Thelía said. "You will open your wound again!"

"Don't do that!" Osric repeated, mocking her. "God's Blood, I have been war-wounded more times than I can count. Do not flap over me like a hen, woman!"

His caretaker shared another look with Pasevalles. "Now, listen to what the Lord Chancellor says, I beg you," she told the duke, "and while you are listening, drink this cordial." She held out a spoon. Osric looked at it with suspicion.

Like some monstrous, hairy infant, thought Pasevalles, but said, "She is correct, Your Grace—we have important matters to discuss. You know that the king rode out this morning for Winstowe."

Thelía's spoon was near his mouth, but Osric did not unclench his teeth until she had taken it away again. "I'll not have it," he said. "I need no physic from a jar, I need to find . . . to find . . ." His lips writhed, as if he might indeed cry like an angry infant. "God in Heaven, where is my grandson? Where is the heir to the throne, Pasevalles?"

"As it happens, I have some small news, though his true whereabouts are still unknown. If you swallow what Lady Thelía offers, I will tell you."

Osric looked at him from beneath his bushy brows for a long moment. "Very well. But if you are lying, I will cuff you up and down, wound or no wound."

He opened his mouth and she put the spoon in then watched carefully to make sure he swallowed.

"God grant you health, Duke Osric," she said. "That should help." She turned to Pasevalles. "At least it should make him less troubled. He will sleep soon."

"Do not speak of me as though I am dead or witless," the duke growled.

"You may go now, my lady," said Pasevalles. "I am sure you have many other matters to attend to, and I have a few more things to discuss with the duke. I will stay with him until he sleeps."

She gave him a grateful smile. "Thank you and God bless you, Lord Pasevalles. I will avail myself of your kind offer." She rose and carefully packed several medicaments into her bag, then went out.

"Well?" said Osric. He slurred the words a bit, but his reddened eyes were still fiercely intent. "You said you had news of my grandson, man. Out with it!"

Pasevalles patted him on his broad forearm. "I have had information from some of my sources, Your Grace, that your grandson is still alive."

Osric again tried to sit upright but gave up after a moment. He was breathing hard, and despite the cold day, beads of sweat had sprung up on his forehead. "Tell me, man! Would you torture me like that physic-woman? What do you know?"

"Very little. But I have heard that Prince Morgan was sighted in the western Aldheorte forest and that he was apparently well and unharmed." He did not bother to inform the duke that his informant had been the sepulchral voice from Nakkiga.

"Sighted!" Osric did not seem to know whether to bluster or weep, and for a moment threatened to do both at the same time. "Who told you this? Who told you?" He was having difficulty now with his words: Thelía's potion seemed to be taking effect. "Go to, man, spit it out!"

"It is news from an informant, and though he did not see Morgan himself, he swears the information is trustworthy. Also, this informant of mine has no reason to lie to me, since I was not asking about your grandson."

"The Wes . . . Wessern Aldheorte." Osric's lids grew heavier; he had difficulty holding Pasevalles' gaze. "I will go . . . go there as soon as I can m-mount a horse. I will take a hundred men—t-t-two hundred!—and we will scar the forest. *Scour.* We will scour . . . the forest."

"That task does not need to wait until you are well enough to do it, Your Grace," said Pasevalles smoothly. "You know my men Astrian and Olveris—the ones who found Count Eolair and freed him from the barbarians. I can send them a message at Winstowe, and they will go out to search for your grandson. I think they will have better luck than a whole company might—the tangled trees of the great forest are not friendly to armies. Have you not heard of Tercis, the Nabbanai Imperator's son, who led an entire company into Aldheorte in search of the fairies' castle and never came out again?"

Osric was looking at him now with almost complete incomprehension. "Fairies?" he said. "The fairies have my grandson?"

In fact, the fairies *did* have Morgan, at least according to the cold thing on the other side of the Witness, but that struck a little too near the mark for Pasevalles' liking. "No, Your Grace, I but reminded you of an old story about them. I think you need rest. Be easy in your heart. I will not give up until we find your grandson and bring him safely home again."

"Bless . . . you . . ." The duke's eyes closed.

When he heard the first heavy breaths and felt Osric's arm twitch beneath his fingers, Pasevalles rose and left the chamber. He put on an appropriate expression of calm command, then told the guards to inform Lady Thelía that Duke Osric had peacefully fallen asleep.

Auntie Rhoner had been talking to the tall woman in the green dress—one of the noblewomen who used to wait on Grandmother Queen Miriamele—for a long time, and Lillia began to feel annoyed. It was not that she needed Auntie Rhoner's help, because she was being forced to read a terribly long, terribly boring book and she had been barely glancing at the pages as she turned them. But as usual, everybody was rushing around and whispering and none of them were telling her *anything.*

"Lillia? Will you come here, please?"

Groaning deeply, though she was secretly happy to leave the book, she rose and went to her. "What do you want, Auntie?"

"That is neither the way a princess should talk nor the way a princess should walk," said Auntie Rhoner in her singsong way; Lillia usually loved the lilt of the Hernystirwoman's voice, but just now she was too cross to appreciate it. "But that is beside the point, dear child. I am needed in the Chancelry. Lady Gytha is going to stay with you for a little while until one of your nurses can be found. I told her you have your book of animals to read and that will keep you content."

"The pictures are terrible," Lillia said. "They all look the same."

"You do not learn from looking at the pictures, you learn from reading the words. Did you read about the unicorn?"

Lillia had been particularly unimpressed with the picture of the unicorn, which she thought looked like a goat with a tree branch growing from its head. "Grandfather Simon—the *king*—said that unicorns aren't real."

Auntie Rhoner sighed. "Well, then learn about cows, my honey-lamb. I am fairly certain cows are real."

"How long will you be gone?"

"I couldn't say for certain." Lillia's Hernystiri auntie lost her look of distraction and even smiled a little. "But I promise you we will have time together later, before bed. I could even read to you from the other book—the one you like so much."

"Truly?" Lillia considered. *A Compendium of Stories of Aedonite Women*, unlike any of her books about saints, talked about women who fought with swords and bows, or who held besieged castles against marauding enemies while their husbands were gone. She was especially fond of Ardith of Cellodshire, who had famously ridden onto a battlefield and killed a bad knight with an arrow to save her wounded son. "Very well. But don't forget your promise or I will be very angry."

"Ah, I'm sure of that, *mu' harcha*."

When Auntie Rhoner had gone, Lady Gytha came and perched at the edge of the bench. "Carry on with your book, dear," she said, fluttering her hand as if "book" was someplace she wanted Lillia to go.

She sat down and picked it up, but though she lingered for a moment on a picture of a wolf with a dead sheep in its jaws and a look in its eye that suggested it might jump off the page and see what a Lillia tasted like, she was already bored.

"Lady Gytha," she said. "I want to talk to Nurse Loes. Go and find her. Please." She added the last, mindful that grownups sometimes needed a little coaxing to do anything useful.

Her temporary caretaker looked startled. "Oh! But I . . . are you certain?"

"Of course I'm certain. I'm a princess, remember?"

"I don't know where she is."

Lillia was amused. Lady Gytha didn't know how to argue very well. "She's probably down on the bottom floor, talking to the Mistress of Chambermaids. I saw her there just a little while ago." Which was a wicked lie, Lillia knew, but she *had* seen Nurse Loes there the day before, talking to the Mistress of Chambermaids, so it wasn't completely untrue.

After all, Lillia told herself, *she might be there again today.*

Lady Gytha wavered a bit, but Lillia was not worried. She knew what kind of people could avoid doing something they didn't want to do, and Gytha was not one of them. At last, the lady-in-waiting got up. "You'll stay right here, won't you?" she asked, but more in a tone of hope than certainty.

"I'm a princess," Lillia said again.

That seemed to answer Gytha's question, because after she made a courtesy, she went out. Lillia promptly dropped her book and stood up. She had been held prisoner all day and she was restless. Auntie Rhoner had said that Grandfather Osric was going to bring Morgan back. Osric had returned but her brother had not, and Lillia felt cheated.

Where has everyone gone? Why won't they tell me? They say my mother's dead and in heaven but that she's still watching me. They say Grandma Queen Miriamele died too, but they wouldn't let me see her being dead. And now Morgan's gone and nobody will tell me where.

Lillia was feeling more and more strongly that something mysterious was going on, something all the grownups knew about and wouldn't tell her, and she was tired of not knowing things. *Mother went up the stairs to the top floor, then she was dead. And Lord Pasevalles keeps going back to that room. What's in there?* She could almost believe that her mother and grandmother and maybe even her brother were all hiding from her somewhere, like a game of Holly King, though she didn't really believe that. But what was the secret they all seemed to be keeping, and more importantly, why was she—the only princess—the only one who didn't know?

It took her but a short time to slip from her family chambers and out into the hallway. The second floor was strangely deserted, but Lillia could not have asked for anything better; within moments she was racing up the stairs. She passed the third floor and heard a few of the chambermaids talking in one of the rooms that were empty now after the Perdruin woman had left. Lillia still wasn't sure what to think of the Perdruin woman, Countess Yissola. She had been very tall and beautiful and wore lovely clothes, but she had hardly spoken a word to Lillia, even when Lillia politely explained that she was a Princess and that was higher than a Countess. Also, soon after the countess arrived at court, Auntie Rhoner had come to Lillia, crying so hard she could hardly speak, and told her that Grandmother Miriamele had died. Even if Yissola had not been responsible, Lillia still didn't think she liked her much.

When she reached the top of the stairs, she crept down the hallway toward the room, half-afraid someone would throw open one of the closed doors and leap out. She listened again outside the door, then pushed it open. The room was empty, the bed was made, but the floor was dusty and scuffed in several places with footprints. Lillia felt a sense of triumph. Somebody *was* coming here, at least Pasevalles, and maybe others! What would cause someone as busy as the Lord Chancellor to keep coming to an empty room?

Lillia carefully closed the door behind her but was immediately plunged into darkness. A little afraid, though she didn't like to admit it, she quickly opened the door again and stepped out into the passage. She didn't want to leave the door open in case someone came, but trying to explore the room in utter darkness was silly (and frightening), so she stood, sucking her finger, trying to decide what to do. Then her eyes settled on a candle burning in a wall sconce two doors closer to the stairs.

Lillia tried to reach it, but even jumping as high as she could, she fell short. After a moment's frustration, she returned to the room, this time leaving the door open so she could see, then dragged one of the chairs out into the hallway. She climbed onto it and stood on the seat, and though it swayed a little from side to side, making her catch her breath, she at last managed to reach and take down the candle.

Back in the room, she walked around with the candle held high. Many of the footprints seemed to cluster just to one side of the fireplace, where a strange, long shadow ran down the wall like a piece of string. When she held the candle closer, she saw that the shadow marked a place where the wall did not quite fit together. She slipped her fingers into the narrow crevice and pulled. Nothing happened at first, but then she thought she felt something—a slight movement. She put the candle down on the hearth and squeezed the fingers of both hands into the crack. This time when she pulled, it suddenly swung toward her—not just a door but an entire section of the wall, a massive wedge of bricks and mortar that pivoted outward as silently and easily as the turning of a seamstress' spinning wheel. Beyond, all was darkness.

For a moment Lillia could not catch her breath. She had wondered for so long why people kept coming to the room, and now the secret was in front of her. It was like one of her dreams where she could walk across the castle's roofs or through its solid walls.

She picked up her candle and cautiously poked it through the gap, revealing a passageway like others that could be found all over the ancient Hayholt. But as she stood in the opening, she had a moment of deep misgiving: who knew how many spiders and other things might be hiding inside, just out of sight? Also, Auntie Rhoner would be back soon. If she found out Lillia had gone out without permission, there would be trouble.

But the secret door is right here! How could she walk away from it? What if it was never left unlocked again?

At last, after bouncing up and down on her toes in fretful indecision, Lillia made up her mind to explore at least a little way into the secret corridor. She stepped through, then carefully pulled the door shut behind her, leaving it just a little open, as she had found it. Then she began to walk slowly forward, candle gripped in her fist and eyes wide open, in search of Mystery.

He kept knocking, louder and louder, until Tiamak opened the door.

"Brother Etan?" the little man said. "I am glad to see you! I have just made a most astounding and distressing discovery—" He gestured to the book in his hand, but Etan could not wait. He pushed his way into the Wrannaman's chambers and yanked the door closed behind him.

"I fear this is no time for books, my lord," he said, "no matter how astounding. Bishop Boez is dead. Poisoned, or so it seems. Father Wibert found him in the Chancelry. Froth spilled from his jaws like a mad dog."

Tiamak stared, wide-eyed and suddenly pale. "Truly?" He shook his head and put the book down on the table, then moved a pile of other books on top of it. "Of course, truly," he said, answering himself. "Why would you come to me with anything else? By the gods of my people, why did no one else tell me? When did this happen?"

"He was found but a short time ago, I think." Etan's heart was still racing. "The surgeon of the guards is with him."

"So they sent you to fetch me," Tiamak said.

"No one sent me, but I thought you would want to know."

Tiamak paused, obviously caught by surprise. "How long ago was he found?"

"Wibert told me only a short time ago, but the surgeon had already been called. The priest stopped me because he was searching for Pasevalles, but I didn't know where the Lord Chancellor was." He was troubled by Tiamak's expression. "Have I done something wrong?"

"Why would they not come to me?" Tiamak limped to the window, looking down from the residence at the crowd of people gathering at the Chancelry. "I do not like this at all."

"What do you mean?"

Tiamak did not reply but took up a piece of foolscap and his pen and sat down at the desk. "I must write a letter and write it now. There is no time to waste. Please go and get Lady Thelía. She will be tending Duke Osric. Tell her nothing of what has happened, but only that I said she must come *this moment.*" Then he bent to his parchment, writing swiftly and intently, as if Etan were no longer present.

Brother Etan hesitated. "I do not understand . . ."

"But I believe I do," said Tiamak without looking up. "And every moment has become precious. Please, Brother, hurry to Thelía and bring her back as quickly as you can. Talk to no one else. No one! Now, go, please." At last, he met Etan's eyes. "Haste!"

Puzzled and frightened, Etan hurried out, leaving Tiamak writing as though his quill was on fire and he had to finish before it burned his fingers.

"Do not ask me, please, my lady," Etan said to Thelía. "I beg pardon, but I know only what he told me. Come now, he said, ask no questions, and speak to no one."

She wiped her hands clean on a wet cloth. Duke Osric was grunting and twitching in his sleep like a dog that dreamed of running. "Then we must go," she said. "My husband would not say such a thing lightly."

She found one of the chambermaids and sent her in to watch over Osric, then they made their way to the chambers she shared with Tiamak, who was writing out the last lines of his letter. He blotted the ink with fine sand and carefully folded the parchment, then dripped wax across the closure and pressed his seal onto it.

"I fear I must send you on another mission, Brother," Tiamak said. "I owe you an apology, but for your own safety I cannot tell you what is in this letter. You must deliver it to King Simon."

"But the king rode out for Winstowe Castle days ago."

"I know." Tiamak met his wife's gaze and nodded. Thelía immediately departed to the bedchamber. "Now take it, please, Brother. You can ride my donkey, Scand. He is slow but steady, and you will receive less notice that way, both leaving the castle and as you travel—just another itinerant friar on the road."

"The road? You want me to go to Winstowe? Where the Thrithings-men are besieging the castle?"

"It is likely too late to catch Simon before he gets there," Tiamak said. "So, yes, I suppose it is Winstowe." He had begun searching through the clutter of objects on his table as if he had lost something important. "Do you trust me, Brother?"

Now Etan was the one caught by surprise. "Trust you, my lord? Of course I do. Utterly."

"Good. Because events may give you cause to doubt that trust in days ahead. But I swear to you, Brother, my wife and I have only the good of the kingdom and the High Ward in our hearts."

"I am confused, my lord."

"Just as well. The less you understand, the quicker they will realize you had nothing to do with this. Now listen carefully." He held the letter out but did not immediately let Etan take it. "You must deliver this to King Simon *and no one else*—no servant, page, or other intermediary, no matter what anyone tells you. If you cannot put this straightly into his hand and you see no chance of doing so, then it must be destroyed. Do you understand?"

Etan had never seen the little man like this, and his own fear was mounting. "Yes! Yes, I understand," he said. "I swear on my faith, I will give it to the king or destroy it."

"Good." Tiamak seemed a little easier, but he still held Etan's gaze. "If something terrible happens and this falls into someone else's hands, and you are asked how you got it, you must say I gave you the letter before you had the chance to tell me about the bishop's death."

"But that would be a lie," said Etan.

"Yes, a lie to preserve you from being tortured or at the very least put in shackles. Remember—*you told me nothing.* Say that, before you could inform me about Boez, I gave you the letter and ordered you to leave at once to follow the king. I beg you, for the sake of your life, admit nothing else."

Etan felt as though he had walked into St. Sutrin's only to hear the cathedral's ancient stone floor tremble and crack beneath his feet. "This frightens me, my lord."

"As it should." Tiamak opened a drawer beneath his table. He took out a pouch and shook it once to make the coins clink, then handed it to him. "This will help you with food and lodging if you need them."

It felt like a substantial weight. "May God protect us all," Etan said.

"I can only echo that," said Tiamak. "I fear we have been far too confident about far too many things." He did not explain what he meant, saying instead, "Go, Brother Etan! May your God lead you safely to King Simon. Go now. And know that you are doing nothing but your duty for your monarch and your faith."

"My lord Tiamak, I—"

"I know. This is a terrible way for us to part. If Heaven allows, we will see each other again one day and I will make all clear, but for now—make haste!"

Pasevalles was on the stairs leading to the second floor of the Residence when Father Wibert found him. The counting-priest's hood was crooked, his habit disarrayed, and he was waving his arms like a man who had only discovered he could not swim after falling in.

"Oh, praise Usires," cried Wibert, "there you are, my lord! A terrible thing has happened!"

Pasevalles put on a look of concern. "What is it?"

"It is Bishop Boez. He is dead—poisoned, the surgeon says!"

Pasevalles altered his expression to one of appropriate shock and surprise. "Mother of God, no! How terrible! Are you certain he's dead?"

Father Wibert was panting with the exertion of having run across the keep. "The surgeon . . . he says that the body was cold and stiff when he was brought in. They think he must have died in the night."

"Dreadful. May God grant him peace in Heaven." Pasevalles made the sign of the Tree, then hesitated. "I apologize, old friend, but I must give you another errand."

Father Wibert looked as though he would rather go lie down in a cool place and catch his breath, but he did his best to appear willing. "Yes, Lord Pasevalles?"

"Find Lord Captain Zakiel. Tell him to meet me here as quickly as he can with at least a half dozen Erkynguards."

"Are you not coming to see Boez?" Wibert was still fighting for breath.

"I fear there is nothing I can do for the bishop," Pasevalles said. "But there is still something I can do to save the kingdom."

Wibert's eyes widened. "The kingdom?"

"No time to explain, I fear. Go and find the lord captain. I have something I must do, but the safety of the throne itself may rely on you telling Zakiel I need him, and swiftly."

Wibert nodded, clearly wanting to ask more questions, but also suitably affrighted by Pasevalles' grim words. "Yes, my lord. I go now. God watch over you."

"And over us all," said Pasevalles and once more made the sign of the Tree.

As soon as the priest was gone Pasevalles sprang up the stairs as quickly as he could. He dispensed with his normal caution and reached the uppermost floor in a matter of a few dozen heartbeats.

He was annoyed that Zhadu the grasslander had taken so long to remove Boez. He had hoped that the bishop would succumb while the king was still in the Hayholt. He had wanted to be able to witness what would have happened next, but Pasevalles had always prided himself on his ability to adapt, to keep his goals in mind while bending to circumstance. Having the king gone might not be such a bad thing after all. With Osric in bed healing from his wounds, and Eolair departed for the west, there was no one in the castle who stood high enough to interfere with him.

He threw open the door of the room—*his* room, as he often thought of it, since he alone knew all its secrets—and went immediately to the hidden door. Just a short while earlier he had remembered that although he had returned through Granary Tower after his last sojourn beneath the castle, he had come through the door here. He had not expected to spend so long with the Master Witness and had quite forgotten about the door he had used to enter the castle's secret places.

The crack between the door and the wall stones was clearly visible, and Pasevalles was annoyed with himself that he should have been so careless. What if someone had come in and seen it—even opened the hidden door? It could have been particularly disastrous if the Wrannaman had discovered it.

But whatever *might* have happened hadn't, he reminded himself—and Lord Tiamak would not be a problem much longer. He pushed the door closed until he heard the latch that held the great wedge of stone and mortar in place fall shut. Now even if someone stumbled into the room, they would not find it. Only Pasevalles knew the hidden devices that would allow the door to open from either this side or the other, and now the secret was safe again.

He left the chamber, descending as swiftly as he had climbed, and reached the bottom just as Zakiel and a half-dozen guardsmen came hurrying toward him, armor clanking.

"My lord, have you heard the news?"

"I have, Lord Captain. I had feared something like this might occur. I will curse myself forever for not better anticipating what he might do."

"He? Bishop Boez?" Zakiel shook his head, puzzled.

"No, the bishop is but an innocent victim—a martyr to a treacherous plan that has already meant death for many, I fear, and might have eventually seen the king himself assassinated."

"What?" Zakiel looked stunned, which was just as Pasevalles wished it. "Whose plan? Are you saying we have a traitor among us?"

"We most certainly do," said Pasevalles. "Terrible as it is to realize. Come, follow me upstairs—there is no time to lose."

As the guardsmen followed them, all quite agog, Pasevalles clutched Zakiel's elbow and pulled the captain close until they climbed side by side. "I had suspicions," he said quietly into Zakiel's ear. "No, not just suspicions—fears, I may fairly call them—when Boez first came to the king. Someone has been stealing money from the privy purse for several years. And not a small amount, but thousands of gold pieces."

"By the Good God!" said Zakiel, then sketched the Tree on his breast. "Forgive me for taking Our Lord's name in vain, but I am astonished. Do you know who did this?"

"I fear I do, and I should have seen it sooner. Boez told me that he had examined everyone who had access to the money and could find no evidence that any of them had done this terrible thing. The only one he did not investigate was Lord Tiamak, because he was so close to the throne, and because Boez feared to upset King Simon—especially after the queen's death."

Zakiel stopped on the stairs. "Are you saying that the little Wrannaman did this? Stole all that gold—and killed Boez, too?"

"Who else could it be? Boez was beginning to think Tiamak was the thief, and I fear he may have confronted him. You know that the Wrannaman and his wife are masters of herbs and potions—and poisons, too. Small wonder if they decided they had no choice but to silence Boez for good while the king was away."

"I admit I have never much liked the fellow," said Zakiel, hastening upward again. "But I would never have guessed him to be such a monster." The guard captain looked pale, but set his jaw in a determined line. "We must arrest him at once."

"Yes. Do not let him or his wife destroy any parchments or books."

"You think his wife is a traitor, too?"

"I cannot say for certain yet, but I fear she must be."

They reached the top hurried along the corridor toward the rooms that Tiamak and his wife shared. A pair of chambermaids who were shaking out a bedcover in the hallway saw them coming and shrank back against the wall.

"Stand beside me," Pasevalles said when they reached the door. "We must not give him a chance to destroy anything that might show his guilt. When I give the sign, Lord Captain, your men must break in the door."

Zakiel nodded. Pasevalles reached up and rapped sharply on the door with his fist. "Lord Tiamak!" he called. "It is Pasevalles. I need to have words with you!"

They listened but heard no sound from inside. Pasevalles pushed and the door swung inward. The guards stumbled through, pikes and swords at the ready.

The chamber was in disarray, books and parchments strewn everywhere, but there was no sign of Lord Tiamak or his lady. Two of the guards hastened to the bedchamber and Pasevalles heard them opening chests and moving the bed as they hunted for the fugitives, but they returned a moment later, empty-handed.

"Where could they have gone?" Zakiel asked.

"Anywhere." Pasevalles was furious with himself for having misjudged the timing. It was one thing to have the Wrannaman in chains and under a charge of murder, but quite different to have him running loose somewhere, knowing more than he should and capable of doing mischief to Pasevalles' careful plans. He turned to the youngest-looking guard. "You—hasten to the gate and tell the sergeant there that no one must go in or out of the keep without my approval. And to especially watch for Lord Tiamak and his wife. If they are found, bring them to me with no delay."

The guard saluted and hurried off down the corridor.

"A spy and traitor." Zakiel shook his head. "The king's close friend and counselor. Who would have believed it?"

"It is a wicked, fallen world, Captain," said Pasevalles as he began to gather up the pieces of parchment scattered across the table. "It is dangerous to trust anyone too far. But we will find those two and they will pay for their crimes—I swear it."

Lillia had found the first stairway at the end of the corridor and had even gone down it a short distance. She could hear things in the darkness, faint voices, odd sounds. She thought it must be people in the residence nearby, the voices changed and made strange by distance, but she could not entirely convince herself.

She sat on the steps, trying to work out whether she was brave enough to go any farther. Even though her candle was made of fine beeswax, it was nearly half-burned, and she had a sudden, horrifying thought about what it would be like to be here in this dark, strange place if it went out. She had no way to light it again.

Her heart racing now, she got up. She would figure out how the door opened and closed, she told herself—there must be a handle or a latch somewhere—and then she could come back when she wished. Her next trip she would be better prepared, with more than one candle and perhaps even flint and steel. She had always wanted to try lighting a fire with flint and steel ever since Morgan had proudly showed her how to do it after accomplishing the feat himself.

I'll bring something to eat, too, she told herself. *That way I can spend as long as I want down here.*

But she would have to make certain that she wasn't missed by Auntie Rhoner or the nurses, of course—planning for that would take thought. *I've done enough for today,* she decided. *And it is so dark and dreadful down here.* She didn't want to admit it even to herself, but she was beginning to lose her nerve. She had never been so separated from the other people in the castle before. *If I fell and hurt myself, no one would even know.*

That decided her. Lillia got up and made her way back up the stone stairs, then down the winding length of the corridor until she arrived back at the door. It seemed different than she had left it, and she stared at it in growing confusion until she realized what had changed.

It's not open anymore!

Suddenly very frightened, she tried to reach into the crack between door and wall, as she had from the outside, but the gap was now too narrow for even a child's fingers. She pushed, hoping the door would swing outward, but she might as well have been pushing on a wall of solid rock.

Her panic growing, Lillia pushed and pulled and scratched at the door until her fingers were scraped bloody, but it would not move. At last she began to shout, then to scream, calling for help over and over until her voice was ragged and her throat hurt, but no one came.

21

Needle

They mounted the crest of the hills in late morning of the second day's riding. The valley called the Fingerdale stretched before them, still bottomed in fog though the sun was in the sky. The Laestfinger was a wide, curving smear of pewter at the valley's center, and the pale stones of Winstowe Castle could just be seen above the mist, on a prominence at the river's bend. Simon was relieved to see Count Aglaf's standard—an image of a chimerical creature, part river-pike and part lion—still rippling defiantly above the tallest of its square towers.

"That is a gladsome sight, at least," said Baron Snell, whose Brockfordshire levy had joined the king and Count Pieres that morning. Snell had brought nearly a dozen of his household knights and ten times that many foot soldiers. The baron was a veteran campaigner who fought bravely in the last Thrithings War, so though his pikemen were mostly farmers, Simon felt confident they had been well trained. Surrounded by other, richer landowners, Snell believed in being prepared at all times.

As the sun rose higher and the royal guard and levy-men made camp on the hilltop, Simon peered out over the valley floor below the castle. As the fog burned away, he could still see the rising smoke of hundreds of fires scattered in the valley, countless red spots like the eyes of rats, and he knew every fire marked the presence of at least a few grasslanders.

"How many would you guess they are, my lord Snell?" he asked.

"Hard to say for certain, Majesty. Perhaps two thousand or more. And most of them mounted." The baron shook his head. "That is where they are fiercest—on their swift horses, loosing arrows as they ride."

"I remember." Simon had thought more than a few times of the last battle he had fought with the grasslanders, two decades past. He and the Erkynguard captain Sceldwine and a few hundred men had held the high ground against half a dozen times their own numbers. Sceldwine had died at Simon's side, and Freosel of New Gadrinsett had taken an arrow in the fighting that, although not immediately fatal, had taken his life within a few months.

If only I'd had Tiamak and his wife on that field, he thought, *we might have saved that good man Freosel and dozens more. I wish I could have them here now, but praise*

God they are back home instead, watching over Osric. We will need him badly in the days ahead, or I miss my guess.

It seemed strange even to think about the future. Since the moment the sun had come up, waking him from a shallow and, as usual, utterly dreamless sleep, Simon had been haunted by a strange feeling, as though just for a moment he had been given a presentiment of his own death. He had thought he no longer feared dying, not with Miriamele gone on before him, but now he felt ashamed. *Too many are counting on their king for me to waste my life.* He also felt a flush of anger. *How did this happen? When I was the poorest of the poor, ordered about from dawn to dusk by Rachel and the scullion-master and nearly everyone else in the castle, I was still more free than I am now. If I wanted to risk my life, I did—and more than a few times.* When he had been young, exploring the Hayholt, especially climbing to forbidden spots like Green Angel Tower, had been his fondest pursuit. *Now if I sneeze, a dozen surgeons leap to my side. Thank God for Tiamak and his sensible natural philosophies, though I understand not a morsel of it.*

He looked down on the mass of Thrithings-men now materializing as if by dark magic out of the fog that had blanketed the Fingerdale. The sun was high now, almost at its noon peak, but the sky was slate gray with a wide blanket of cloud. On the hilltop, Simon shivered. *Another day of death,* he thought. *Fighting and dying, but for what? Unver's pride? Mine? These are only mortal men, like us. What a horror, that we should fight while the Norns stand by, ready to war against all of us. And if they do, this Unver Shan's horsemen will fare no better than those of us who live in stone castles.*

The weight of the day seemed to press down on him, thick as the clouded sky. He turned away and walked back to the tent that had been raised for him.

The king, Count Pieres, and Rightmark Obed, deputy of the Erkynguard captain Zakiel, were breaking their fast and downing a few cups of watered wine when they heard loud voices outside. One of the guards appeared at the tent flap; after making his salutes, he said, "Two Erkynlandish knights from the castle have come to speak with you, Your Majesty and my lords."

Simon turned to Pieres and Snell, but the nobles also looked surprised. "Erkynlanders? Come out of the castle?" Baron Snell asked, clearly baffled. "Out of Winstowe—the castle that is under siege?"

"So they say, my lord." The guard's expression suggested that he did not feel he should be held responsible for such an outlandish claim, but worried that he might be.

"Send them in, but let us keep a close watch on them," Simon said. "It seems there's a bit of a mystery here."

He recognized the pair when they came in, one short, the other taller even than Simon, so that he had to duck low to get into the tent. The small one had the sly, narrow look of a fox that had just discovered an unguarded henhouse. The big one might have been carved from wood for all the expression he showed, but they both bent their knees before the king.

"I know you two," said Simon. "Your names—what are they? You were Morgan's friends, though I might have wished him less unruly company." The small one's name came to him. "Astrian. You are Sir Astrian. And the other . . ."

"He is Olveris, sire," proclaimed the shorter knight. "And that is more than enough to know about him, because though useful in a fight, he is otherwise as boring as a rainy day in the company of only ugly women."

"You like to hear yourself talk, don't you, fellow?" said Count Pieres. "How is it you claim to come from the castle, and what is your news?"

"We claim it because it is true, my lord." Astrian looked almost comically indignant. "There are ways in and out of Winstowe that few know, sires, and that the barbarians and their Shan cannot even guess. We have come through a set of tunnels in the hill under the castle, then had to walk a great distance to reach you. Would it be too forward of us to ask for a little of that wine, Your Majesty, while we tell our news?"

Simon waved to the cupbearer. Within moments the two knights had been supplied with their own rations.

"Now," Simon said, "if you cannot think of anything else you need, gentlemen, perhaps you will tell us what you are doing here?"

"That was always our intention, Majesty. We bring you greetings from Count Aglaf, who is hale and well, and Earl Rowson, who is not."

Simon felt a pinch of shame. "I heard that Rowson was wounded. Is he likely to live?"

"Oh, most likely," said Astrian. "At least he would be if he would only rest and let his wounds heal. But he is determined to ride out again, though the surgeon raged at him and even the count thought it a bad idea."

"Ride out again? When?" Baron Snell was angry. "Does he know that we are here—with the king himself, no less!—to relieve the siege?"

"Oh, he knows," said Astrian. "Scouts brought news of your approach last night, after dark fell."

"Going in and out through the tunnels you mentioned?" Simon asked.

"Yes, Majesty. But Rowson says it is almost certain that the grasslanders are growing restless after so many days camped before the walls. He thinks that an attack from two sides might split them and begin a rout."

"Slow, slow," said Snell. "From two sides?"

"Yes, my lord. Rowson is determined to ride out when the church bells ring for the dawn prayer—out from the sally-port with a sizeable portion of the castle's defenders. He says that if you attack the barbarians first—but only just—we can cut their army in half."

Simon turned to the nobles in surprise. "Did you hear this too? Am I mad? Has Rowson decided on his own to make a sortie and is now telling us what we are to do?"

Baron Snell looked grim and Pieres the same. Rightmark Obed, a lean, leathery man, looked dumbfounded. "It seems so, Majesty," said the count.

"Could you get back to Winstowe in time to tell him no?" Simon demanded.

"Likely," said Astrian.

"Not likely," said Olveris, the first time he had spoken.

"My comrade does not like exertion," Astrian explained. "Those long legs mean he must walk farther to go the same distance as a more modestly fashioned creature like myself."

"That is exactly backward," said Olveris wearily. "Smaller legs mean more steps."

"Yes, but my steps are much swifter and more nimble—" began Astrian.

"Enough!" Simon bellowed, startling everyone in the tent. "Enough of this infuriating babble! Could you two get back into the castle in time to tell Rowson that I said not to do it?"

"Yes, certainly," said Astrian. "Though it is a goodly distance and climbing back up the hidden tunnels will take longer than it did coming down."

"And we might encounter foraging companies of grasslanders," added Olveris.

"Hmmm," Astrian said. "My tall friend is right, I fear. We saw almost none in the early hours, but for days they have been ranging through the local countryside like locusts, taking any food or game they can find and lopping trees right and left."

"So if we send a message to Rowson, but you do not get there in time, he will make his sortie without us. He and his men will be surrounded and butchered by the Shan's riders." Simon thumped both hands against his thighs. "That damnable Rowson! I admit I wronged him before, but he has put me on my back foot now, for certain. What are we to do?"

"Risk all on the messengers getting back in time," said Snell in a gloomy tone, "or else ride out to try to protect him."

"I do not like it," said Pieres. "We have scarcely had a chance to see how the enemy is arrayed."

Simon turned to Sir Astrian. "Rowson will bring more than our almost-a-thousand with him, won't he?"

"I think so," the knight said. "But I am only the messenger."

"All by yourself, eh?" said Olveris. "Then what am I?"

"A buffoon," Astrian replied quickly. "But useful for snuffing candles hung high overhead or getting things off top shelves."

"Enough," Simon growled. "If I wanted a pair of jesters, I would have hired real ones. It seems we must be prepared to act as part of Rowson's foolish sortie. Do you two need a place to rest before you ride out with us?"

Astrian raised an eyebrow. "Ah. Did we give you the idea we would be riding with you? We cannot join you, I fear. We have made a solemn promise to His Grace, Duke Osric, that we would continue the search for his grandson—your grandson too, of course. Your Majesty may overrule him, of course.

However, we also brought one of Count Aglaf's guardsmen along with us. He waits outside—we thought his company might be a bit too untutored for the royal presence. But do not fear, Majesty. He is a bit dull but still should be able to carry your message back to Aglaf and Rowson."

This nettled Simon, but other than his dislike of the Nabbanai knight's annoying self-absorption, he could think of no reason to countermand Osric's order, especially after the duke had been so badly wounded fighting to defend Erkynland. And what difference could two fewer knights make in the battle to come?

"You have my leave," he said, but he could not make himself sound happy about it.

Etan had decided by the middle his first afternoon on the road that he and Scand the donkey had to part ways. The creature was so unhurried, so willing to explore every patch of anything vaguely green beside the muddy road, that Etan knew it would take him ten days to reach Winstowe unless he changed mounts. He found a free farmer with a spread of land outside Erchester and gave the man one of the coins out of the purse Tiamak had given him. It bought the use of a decent horse and a place for Scand in the farmer's barn until Etan returned.

Scand did not seem to mind being retired, especially since the day had turned cold and had started raining. The last Etan saw of him, the donkey was contentedly chewing straw with the air of someone who had bravely given his all for the cause and was now taking a well-deserved rest.

"You are a liar and a cheat," Etan called to him, but the cutting remark did not diminish Scand's satisfaction with his new circumstances.

The farmer helped him climb onto the much higher saddle of his new mount, no swift charger but a draft horse as tall at the shoulder as Etan himself. "Her name be Hollyhock," the landsman said, "and don't let them thick legs fool you. She's half grassland pony and can go fast enough if she wants to." Etan wasn't much concerned with her pace—he didn't plan to gallop to Winstowe—but he was glad to have any steed that didn't halt to crop weeds by the roadside every fifth step. Hollyhock was also calm and easy to ride. Etan was no horseman, although he had been forced to ride more than a few times on his journey across Nabban and Perdruin, so he was grateful for her equanimity.

He stopped at an inn in Flintwall the first night and passed over a bit more of his silver to the innkeeper for a bed in a common chamber on the second floor, filled with snoring peddlers. The pallet was suspiciously full of little creeping things, but Etan did his best to be grateful in his prayers.

. . . And thank you, Lord God my Ransomer, for not sending Madi with me on this journey as a guide, like the last time. At least I know whatever money I have will not be spent on drink or gambling.

Flintwall Town was even less prepossessing by early morning light; there seemed little evidence of the village even being inhabited beyond the smoke of various fires. Bernet, the next little town over, was no livelier.

If the villages were deserted, the roads were not. Etan met quite a few carts laden with whole families and their meager household goods, likely people from the Fingerdale fleeing ahead of the invading grasslanders. Many others he passed were driving herds of animals to Erchester—lowing cattle, drifts of swine, and straying companies of pugnacious geese, bound for the yearly St. Granis's Fair market. Most folk who passed him were on foot, but some rode on carts drawn by donkeys or sad-eyed oxen. He saw peddlers, tinkers, and the occasional man of God like himself, though Etan doubted any of them were engaged in as unusual an errand as his.

Etan had hoped to reach the Fingerdale by the second night and perhaps take his rest in the king's camp after delivering Tiamak's message, but as the light fled and the road emptied, he found himself in an unfamiliar valley. As night thickened around him, he worried that his borrowed horse might break a leg, or that the bandits who stayed away from the king's road in daylight might be emboldened by the dark, so he stopped at a deserted homestead, where he tied Hollyhock to a tree and bedded down on the earthen floor of the hut. His long day of riding meant that even the scratching and chittering of rats could not keep him awake for long. He pillowed his head on his saddlebag, pulled his cloak over his face to keep the rodents off, and slid into an uneasy sleep. He dreamed he was surrounded by tiny, noisy demons arguing over the best way to cook a monk.

As the hour of daybreak approached, Simon, Count Pieres, and several other nobles and knights huddled in the king's tent, staying out of the rain.

"It will be terrible footing," said Baron Snell, watching the downpour.

Simon shrugged. "No better for the grasslanders."

"But their horses are smaller and more nimble," said Count Pieres. "And the new muster from Wentmouth has not arrived yet."

"Then we must ride by ourselves, and try to break their line quickly," Simon said. "That means heavy lances. And we must stay close together." He had fought against Thrithings-men before and knew that their ability to quickly counter a mounted charge was one of their greatest strengths. "But we will not ride until we know with certainty that Rowson is coming out. We must stay close together. How many horsemen have we got?"

"Three hundred," said Snell. "But Rightmark Obed should be here to hear this. The discipline of the Erkynguards will help hold those on foot together."

"Fetch him." Simon turned his helmet over and over in his hands. "The hour to ride creeps closer and closer."

* * *

Even though Simon had been waiting impatiently for more than an hour, the sound of Winstowe's distant bells ringing for dawn prayer still startled him. "Ware!" he called.

"Hold, men, hold!" cried Baron Snell. Simon's war horse Silvershod snorted and pranced, sensing the moment.

As they watched, a line of mounted men rode out of the castle's sally-port in the south side of the wall and charged downslope toward the Thrithings camp. The first casualties were grasslanders bringing up newly built siege ladders. The attack caught them unprepared, and many were cut down on the slope beneath the castle's outwall.

"That is Aglaf's Lionfish!" shouted Pieres, seeing the count of Winstowe's banner. "And Earl Rowson's Falcon is with him. *Hoy!*" he bellowed. *"Hoy! Aglaf and Rowson for Erkynland!"*

The attackers out of Winstowe kept coming. Only the first few score were mounted, but Simon thought the foot soldiers looked to number in the hundreds, perhaps as many as a thousand, all shouting as they raced down the embankment. The Thrithings-men were slow to adjust, and though the horsemen directly in the path of the onrushing riders quickly mounted to defend themselves, many of the other grasslanders scattered before the attack, falling back toward the main mass beside the river.

Simon saw that Count Aglaf had aimed his sortie to cut across the nearest corner of the invading force. Winstowe's lord obviously planned to separate that part from the rest, and it seemed equally obvious what he hoped the contingent from Erchester would do. Simon called out orders, and Rightmark Obed and Snell rode up and down the line.

"Together, stay together!" Simon shouted as the riders moved into place. "Now, upon my call . . . *charge*!"

The rumble began softly, outshouted at first by the blare of war horns, but within moments the noise of their hoofbeats filled the air like thunder. The king and his knights became an avalanche of steel and horseflesh that sped downslope and struck the segment of the Thrithings besiegers split off by Aglaf's sortie. Simon saw bearded grasslanders turn in despair or rage as they heard the approaching horses, then his own lance took a Thrithings-man under his arm and pierced him all the way through, so that as the man fell, he almost pulled the lance from Simon's hand. All around him Erkynland horsemen clashed with grasslanders, steel on steel, and the screams of the suddenly wounded spiked the air. Simon saw a Thrithings-man running toward him, swinging an ax with the intent to hamstring his horse. Simon had a moment of indecision, not certain if he could lift his lance fast enough to pierce his attacker, but even as he decided to drop the lance and try to draw his sword, his attacker was struck in the gut by an arrow and fell, skidding on the muddy ground to lie still only a few paces from Silvershod's hooves as Simon thundered past.

There was ease, even a dark joy, in letting go of everything but the moment. Simon had spent too much time in troubled thought, too much time helplessly mourning, but now all but the battle before him flew away like wind-plucked leaves. Arrows were speeding from all directions, from Simon's own supporters on the hillside and from the mass of Thrithings-men encamped along the riverbank. *The grasslanders don't understand real war,* Simon thought with something like relief. *Nothing has changed. They have cut off their own retreat—they'll have to fall back along the line of the river.*

He saw a tall figure in a dark cloak and simple steel helm riding back and forth along the near bank of the Laestfinger, directing the clansmen with loud cries and broad sweeps of his curved sword. Simon wondered briefly if this might be the Shan himself, but the man seemed too plainly clad to be anything but the lowliest barbarian chieftain.

Well, we will find out when we put them to flight, he told himself.

But any idea of a grasslander retreat was premature, the king quickly realized. The remnants of the Thrithings front line, scattered by Count Aglaf's surprise attack, now drew together again, with the obvious aim of getting between the count's troop and the sally-port, preventing his escape back into Winstowe.

An arrow struck through the chain mail under Simon's right arm, rocking him in his saddle. It had barely grazed flesh, but every time he moved his arm the point dug into the skin above his ribs. He tried to pull it out, but his fingers were wet and he could not see well through the slit in his visor. After a moment's futile struggle, he tore the helmet off his head. Then, as the rain poured down, soaking his hair and beard and running into his eyes, he finally found the arrow and tore it loose from the curtain of mail. Before he pulled his helmet back on, he saw that several hundred mounted Thrithings-men were now in pursuit of Aglaf and his soldiers, who had turned and were spurring back toward the walls.

"Erkynlanders—to me!" Simon shouted, then called to his standard bearer, Sir Finias, to lift the royal dragons high. The king's company had carved off one side of the grasslanders' force, and now he and the other mounted knights left the foot soldiers to keep the barbarians occupied while they charged across the field, arrows snapping past them from both sides, the cacophony of war so loud and so continuous that for a moment the battlefield almost seemed to grow still. Aglaf's herald was blowing the retreat, and Simon did not want to be left on the field in the middle of thousands of angry grasslanders, but he still couched his lance and led his horsemen into the Shan's newly reformed line. The speed and sheer force of the armored war-horses shattered the lighter Thrithings cavalry, leaving them in disarray, and Simon finally dropped his lance to his standard bearer so he could use his sword on as many of the confused grasslanders as possible.

"Now back, Majesty!" Snell shouted from somewhere behind him. "Aglaf and Rowson have reached the gate. Back up the hill!"

Simon called for the closest pikemen and knights to follow him, then turned, awkwardly ducking a thrown ax before turning his charger back toward the high crest overlooking the valley. The heavy horses slowed as mud churned beneath their hooves, and for a moment it seemed the Thrithings-men might manage to surround the king and his troop, but a volley of arrows suddenly leaped from the hilltop, falling among the grasslanders like deadly hailstones.

As Silvershod struggled up the slope, Simon saw several score of Erkynland archers crouched at the edge of the hilltop camp, loosing shaft after shaft down onto their pursuers, tumbling dozens to the sloppy ground. The foot soldiers retreating behind the horses slowed just long enough to finish any downed barbarians who were still moving.

Once back on the hillcrest, Simon let his squire help him out of the saddle. His muscles ached, especially his thighs, and his limbs trembled with weariness.

Scarcely an hour in the field and I am as shaky as a colt, he thought.

The unexpected arrival of Lord Sherwyn's Westfold bowmen—the last arrivals of the muster—had ensured their safe retreat, and Simon saluted them and their leader as he crossed the camp. Back in his tent, the king downed a cup of wine. "What are our losses?" he asked Snell and Pieres.

"Hard to say for certain until we count heads," said Snell.

"I can tell you one thing for sooth, Majesty," the count said. "We killed many more of them than they did us."

"I mourn every man fallen," said Simon, but he was lighter in his heart than he had expected. War simplified things.

Simon's second day at Winstowe was even rainier. The king and his men fought several skirmishes against grasslanders trying to overrun their position on the hilltop, but with the skillful aid of the Westfold archers, the Erkynlanders held their ground even without another sortie from Winstowe's defenders.

Afterward, Simon and his officers dispatched a message to Count Aglaf that the next day they would expect him to sally out again a short time before dawn, and that the king's company would once more attack down the hill, trying to break the lines of the besieging clansman and put the barbarians to rout. The leading knights could then curl back toward the castle and drive whatever grasslanders remained back toward the castle, where the archers on the walls could do mortal damage.

As Simon laid himself down to sleep, exhausted, with several small wounds freshly bandaged, he could hear the chaplain singing the *Mansa sea Cuelossan* over the day's dead. The exhilaration of the first evening, when he had been delighted simply to find himself alive, was gone. He wondered, as sleep took him, how the Lord God could love mankind even after watching them do such violent harm to one another.

When Etan reached the hilly pass that led down into the Fingerdale, it was already growing dark. Beacons blazed on every wall of Winstowe Castle, and campfires burned on a hilltop beside the castle, and also along the Laestfinger, where he guessed the Thrithings-men must be camped. As he made his way down into the valley, he could see warriors from both sides of the day's battle gathering up their dead, of which there seemed to be many. He was worried about being mistaken for a spy and killed, so he held his wooden Tree before him and made his way up the slope toward the king's camp loudly singing the *Cansim Felis.*

As he reached the song's ending and began again, something abruptly sprouted in the earth before his feet. Etan stared. It was an arrow, still shivering.

"Wait! I come in peace!" he cried. "I am Brother Etan, sent from the Hayholt with a message for the king!"

A moment later a trio of shapes unpeeled themselves from the shadowy trees and approached him, two of them with their bows drawn. At first Etan could see nothing of their badges because they had draped themselves in leafy branches, but as they drew closer, he thought he could see the badge of the Erkynguard, which calmed him, if only a little. Etan was not used to having arrows loosed at him.

"Look!" said one of the sentries. "A pretty grass-ape what has learned to sing like an Aedonite."

"Learned to dress like one, too," said a tall soldier whose bow still hung on his shoulder, who seemed to be the leader. He was thin, unshaven, and missing almost all his upper teeth, which made the moonlit grin he showed Etan even more memorable. "Ho, fellow, are you a monk in truth? Are you trying to save souls or steal one—like the king's, perhaps? We have feathered more than a few grasslanders trying to sneak into our camp and murder our good King Simon."

"No, no," Etan said hurriedly. "I am one of the king's loyal subjects, I swear by my faith! I am a man of God, and I bring a message to King Simon from the Hayholt."

"Oh, aye?" The leader moved closer. The light was almost gone, and the thin soldier stood so close to the monk it seemed he might be sniffing him. Etan could not help wondering how an assassin would be expected to smell.

"So tell me, then," said the leader. "Does Archbishop Gervis still rule over St. Sutrin's Cathedral?"

Etan almost smiled. "You know well he does not, though he still abides in Erchester. The lector in Nabban granted Gervis an escritor's golden robe several months past, but Gervis dares not travel there to be invested because of the murders and uprisings. But His Eminence is still a loyal king's man."

The leader chuckled. "More said than needed, but that is the way of you monks. Methinks it be the silence you must live with so often."

"Perhaps. Can you conduct me to the king? Lord Tiamak said the letter is an urgent matter."

"No, we cannot," the leader told him. "Not so far as that. We are bound to stay near our cold and lonely spinney." His guardsmen seemed to be enjoying the distraction from their routine and had gathered close. "But we can guide you to the edge of the camp and tell you how to find the rightmark of the Erkynguard. If he judges your errand to have merit, he will take you to the king."

He was as good as his word, and soon enough had led Etan to the edge of the camp. The leader asked him to bless them before they went back to their post, and Etan gladly accommodated him, then the scouts melted back into the gloaming like phantoms fleeing the arrival of dawn.

Etan's loud approach kept him alive until he reached the guards at the perimeter of the camp. After they had inspected him, a groom took his horse and Etan himself was led to one Rightmark Obed, but there it seemed his errand would end, at least for the day. The guard captain looked at Etan as though he carried not a sealed letter for their king, but a pocketful of annoyance.

"His Majesty sleeps," Obed informed him, as though that should end the discussion.

"But the message is very, very important. Lord Tiamak said so."

"His lordship the Wran-fellow?"

"Yes."

"Is it aught to do with the battle—with the siege of Winstowe?"

Etan searched his memory, trying to remember the Wrannaman's precise words. "I know not," he admitted.

"Well, doubtless your Lord Tiamak's message must be delivered, but the king must rise early tomorrow, and he has been asleep for some time." The captain leaned forward and fixed Etan with a hard stare. "You know the king does not rest well these days."

"I have been traveling across much of the world of late on King Simon's business," said Etan with more than a touch of anger. "I freely admit that I was not kept apprised of how the king slept while I was gone." *Still, small wonder if His Majesty sleeps poorly. He has lost nearly everything that he loves and might still lose the Hayholt as well if Tiamak's worries about the Norns are right.*

"Well, the point is not where you have traveled, Brother," said the frowning captain. "The point is that you are not going to wake him up when there will be fighting at first light tomorrow, or nearabouts. But if you leave me the letter I will give it to his squire, who will see that he gets it when he rises."

Etan shook his head. "I was told to put it in no other hands but the king's. That was my lord Tiamak's clear order."

The captain shrugged. "Then you must wait until His Majesty wakes and give it to him yourself. It seems we must find a bed for you." He sounded unhappy about this, though Etan did not think it could be such a terrible burden in a camp of at least a thousand men. Obed waved over another Erkynguard. "Go with this man," he told Etan. "He will hunt you out a place to lay your head, then you may attend the king in the morning."

Etan reached into his purse to make certain the letter was still there, though he had checked it a score of times already today. He was not happy at the delay in discharging his promise to Tiamak, but the little man had been very straightforward: the letter must be given directly to the king and to no one else.

The guardsman led him across the camp to a place where the camp cooks lay sleeping, squeezed as closely as newborn puppies beneath the victuals wagons to shelter from the rain. Etan found a spot beneath one of the wagons, beside a pot-boy half the monk's size, who immediately turned in his sleep and poked his head into Etan's armpit, letting out a mumbled grunt of pleasure, perhaps remembering his infancy in his mother's arms. Etan rolled his eyes, but the long day's journey had left him with no strength to search for another place. He clumsily patted the sleeping boy on the back and then let himself be tugged down into darkness.

Simon's first thought was that something had fallen on top of him. In his confused state, an instant after waking, he thought he was caught in crumbling Green Angel Tower—that he had plunged back to the last hours of the Storm King's War.

Miriamele is in here somewhere! Where is she?

But then he realized that it was not tower stones that had tumbled onto him but a thrashing human shape. With a roar of sudden realization and alarm, he began to strike his attacker with both fists, little caring what he struck so long as he kept whoever it was from stabbing him.

"Majesty, Majesty! Don't beat me! It's me, Orvan—your squire!"

"Good God, man," Simon said, shoving the young man away. "What are you doing, trying to frighten me to death?"

"There are Thrithings-men in the camp, Majesty! I came to wake you, but I fell in the dark." Orvan was the son of Lord Feran, the Hayholt's Master of Horse. Like his father, he was stolid and not overly imaginative, and thus unlikely to throw himself on top of his king by mistake.

"Thrithings-men?" Simon scrambled up from his pallet. "How many? What are they doing? Why am I just now being awakened?"

"Because they tried to murder Baron Snell, but he was awake and killed one of them instead. There were only two more, and the guards have been hunting them all over the camp."

"By God's faithful Mother," said Simon, puffing like a bellows as he tried to wrestle on his armor. "What madness . . . ? Orvan, help me with these cursed things!"

Simon made his way to Baron Snell's tent in time to learn the other two grassland assassins had apparently escaped. The third man lay in a pool of blood on the ground just inside the tent-flap—he had fallen backward in his death throes and partly collapsed the tent, so it took a moment to straighten things enough to examine him.

"Well, he looks a Thrithings-man sure enough," said Simon, observing the dead man's thick beard and tattooed neck.

"Even if he hadn't been," said Snell, "he could hardly complain of his treatment after stealing into my tent an hour before dawn."

"Where is his weapon?" asked Rightmark Obed suddenly.

They looked carefully everywhere nearby, but found no sign of knife, sword, or ax. "That makes no sense," said Snell. "Did he think to kill me with bare hands?"

"Did he even think to kill you?" Simon was more disturbed by the attack than Snell was. *That could have been my tent,* he thought. *Could it have been me he was looking for? But why would a man go weaponless to kill a king?* "Ask the guards whether any of them have picked up a stray weapon," he told Obed.

As he stood with Baron Snell, staring down at the corpse as though the dead man might suddenly speak and give them the explanation they craved, Simon heard a bell ring, high and distant. It took a moment for the import to strike him. "God's Bloody Tree, is that the morning bell in the castle?"

The baron turned to him with a look of growing horror. "I can see dawn outside. By our Lord, even now Aglaf and the others must be riding out!"

Simon could hear Count Pieres outside, calling for them in dismay, and he shouted for Orvan. "The rest of my armor, lad! Hurry!" He turned to Snell, queasy with their failure. "Do you think that was the purpose? To cause confusion and distract us when Aglaf needs us?"

"If so, someone has given away our plans, because the grasslanders chose just the right time. Do you think we have a traitor?"

"Only God knows, and we don't have time to find out." Simon beckoned angrily to his squire. Orvan was carrying the rest of the king's armor across the wet grass with the help of two young pages. "We must ride, Baron, and we must ride now, or Winstowe's soldiers will be cut down before the sun is past the hills!"

Simon's sword had no name. For a while in his youth he had carried the black blade, Thorn, the fabled weapon of Camaris, and then had borne King John's own Bright-Nail through the final days of the Storm King's War; but having felt the terrible power in both of them, he had never wanted to name the blade that replaced them. Nor had his new sword been forged by the Tinukeda'ya smiths who had crafted those two blades and so many of Osten Ard's other important treasures, and had also carved the cities of the immortals out of solid rock. Instead, this blade, a present to Simon from the late and generally unlamented Duke Varellan of Nabban, had been forged by the finest mortal craftsmen in Palano, a southern city where sword smithing was the chief art. The steel was exceptional, made by precise heat and shaped by thousands of hammer-blows, each stroke timed by smiths chanting the Precentor's Hymns from the Book of Aedon, just as they had done for hundreds of years. The blade was lighter than either Bright-Nail or Thorn, and best of all, it had no complicated history and no will of its own, as Thorn had often seemed to display. It was just a sword—Simon's sword, nothing but clean Palanesian steel. The king's sword.

He realized that his thoughts were wandering. Snell and the rest of the knights had formed up around him, and his standard bearer Finias held the Tree and Dragons banner high. The fog swirled around them, but the sounds of battle came through it, and even in the dullness just after dawn he could see knots of warriors seething in front of the gate, spears piercing upward through the mist and brief flashes of color from waving pennants.

"Count Aglaf and his men fight to push the invaders out of Erkynland!" Simon shouted as helmeted soldiers opened the barrier of thorns around the camp so they could ride out. "We can do no less! Blow the horns, trumpeters! Forward, men!" Simon pressed his rowels against Silvershod's belly and the charger leaped down the slope.

"*Rowson, Aglaf, we are coming!!*" shouted Baron Snell. "For Erkynland!" The men around him took up the cry until it echoed down the valley. The clansmen at the base of the hill looked up, eyes wide, then those who were nearest spurred their ponies up the slope to meet the king and his men. Simon couched his lance and took aim at a large barbarian, judging the angle carefully, dropping the tip of the lance so that it fell to chest level just as the two riders met. A tremendous shock almost threw Simon from his saddle, and his lance caught in his enemy's boiled leather armor and broke off halfway down its length, but the Thrithing-man was flung out of his saddle to tumble over and over, then lay still.

Simon tossed aside the broken lance and drew his nameless sword. Snell and the rest had also pushed through, although a few were still fighting against mounted grasslanders.

"On, men!" Simon called. "Ride for the gate!"

Baron Snell hurried his knights forward to surround the king; together they galloped down the slope. It was sheer luck that the mist parted for a moment and one of the other knights saw what lay before them. "'Ware!" he shouted. "Wolf traps!"

A moment later Simon saw them too: a series of trenches the grasslanders had dug along the base of the hill, and though he could not make out the bottom of any of them, he did not doubt that they were full of sharpened wooden stakes. He echoed the warning cry even as Silvershod neared the pit, then they were soaring over both trap and steeply sloping ground. For an instant it felt like something out of a fairy story, as if his mount had sprouted wings. Then they crashed down on the far side and the jolt almost flung him out of his saddle.

Simon looked back and saw that the hillside beneath their encampment was almost clear of grasslanders, and his archers were leaning on their bows on the hillcrest, watching the battle. "Tell the archers to come a ways down the hill so their flights can reach the Thrithings-men where they are thickest!" he shouted to Snell. The baron relayed the order to a mounted soldier who turned and sped back up the slope.

The royal herald Sir Finias had been spurring hard after Simon, the Tree and Dragons flapping in the wind. "Sire!" he shouted as he reined up, "Earl Rowson is hard-pressed! Look, near the gate—the Falcon-banner of Glenwick is wavering. He is surrounded."

Simon squinted but could not make much sense of the melee, but saw the earl's standard sway and then fall. He raised his voice. "Forward, men. Follow me to the gate!"

Now it was hard, ugly sword-work as they rode through the thickest part of the Thrithings forces. During the night the grasslanders had dug man traps in many places, and only a few moments passed before a horse carrying an unwary Erkynlandish knight plunged over the lip of one and fell in. The horse was skewered by sharpened stakes and the knight screamed as the creature rolled over him in its pain and terror, but both quickly fell silent.

Now Simon could see the knot of struggle before the gate more clearly. Many of the Erkynlandish knights were now on foot, their mounts downed by Thrithings arrows. In the middle stood Rowson and his household guard, trying to hold the slope above the trench against superior numbers, and Simon spurred toward him.

"Rowson, I am coming!" he shouted, though he doubted anyone there could hear him through the chaos of sword on shield, shrieks, curses, and shouted orders. "Trumpeter, blow the attack!"

A horn lifted a long, ragged note, then a series of short bursts as the king's armored knights sped toward the gate.

"Earl Rowson is down, Majesty!" shouted Finias.

Simon was already dealing blows, thanking God that most of those he fought were on foot or riding smaller Thrithings horses. The grassland mounts could turn faster than the Erkynlandish chargers, but they were several hands shorter, and Simon valued every inch. He stood in his stirrups, mowing with his sword, and his enemies fell like hay. With every swing Simon moved closer to the castle's defenders as they were pressed back up the slope toward the gate.

This is certain hell, he thought as he took off a Thrithings-man's arm above the elbow. The man stumbled back, eyes wide in disbelief, the stump pulsing blood. *Hell for the living. Hell for the dying.* He could no longer see Rowson's standard, but a knot of soldiers from the castle were clumped in one place, as though defending a fallen leader, and Simon urged his horse toward them.

"Oh, sweet God," he said as he drew close. Several men had gathered around Earl Rowson, who lay on his back with his helmet off. A priest in a black robe crouched beside him. "Is it dire?" Simon asked a soldier wearing Glenwick's Falcon badge. "Will he live?"

The man looked up and his eyes widened beneath his pot-shaped helmet when he saw the king. He saluted, then said quietly, "I think not, Majesty."

Simon surveyed the battle as it eddied around them; then, with help from the guardsman, he dismounted and crouched at Rowson's side. Someone had unbuckled the earl's armor, exposing his blood-soaked gambeson. A long spear lay on the muddy grass beside him, its iron head wet with blood. The kneeling priest spoke his prayers more swiftly now, as though hurrying after something that might otherwise escape him.

The guardsman pointed at the spear. "Lord Rowson pulled it out himself. He was already bad wounded from before, but he wouldn't stay behind."

Simon leaned over. The earl's face was as white as a Norn's, his eyes wandering. "Rowson, I wronged you," he said. "Will you forgive me?"

The earl's eyes tried to find Simon but couldn't. "I . . ." He pushed a froth of blood from his lips with his tongue. "I . . . do not . . ."

Simon felt it like a blow. His head, already dizzy from the exertion of battle, throbbed like someone was squeezing it. "You will be remembered as a hero," he said.

"I . . ." Rowson was trying again. "Do . . . not . . ."

"Ho, is that the king?" shouted a voice from a little distance away. *"I think you have my spear!"*

Simon looked up in fury to see a tall, black-cloaked figure riding toward them, slipping nimbly through the seething mass of warring soldiers. For a confused moment Simon thought this was another priest, until the man on horseback threw back his hood to reveal an iron helmet.

"Unver?" Simon said it as a question, but already he knew, and he picked up the spear that had given Rowson his mortal wound and threw it as hard as he could at the approaching figure. It fell several cubits short and stood quivering in the mud.

"Well, you are a gentleman, at least," called the rider.

"God curse it, get me back on my horse and hand me my shield!" Simon shouted at the men around him. Two of the soldiers helped him into the saddle and he turned toward the man in the black cloak. The tall warrior did not ride forward to pick up his spear, but instead drew his long, curved sword and waited for Simon's approach.

"Are you a fool or a murderer?" Simon cried as he spurred toward him. The knots of fighting men between them loosened; the combatants, grasslanders and Erkynlanders alike, hurried to get out of the way as the king's heavy, armored horse came thundering toward them. Simon raised his sword. "There was no need for all this killing!"

"What? You blame *me*?" cried Unver Shan in angry mockery. As the king came down on him, he warded Simon's attack with his shield as Silvershod swept past. "You stole my prisoner even as we bargained," Unver called as Simon's charger turned for another pass. "Your men loosed arrows at the Bison clan camp and killed one of their headmen. Heaven calls for vengeance!"

"Then fight me, damn you!" Simon shouted, so angry that he could barely think. "If you think God favors you, fight me like a man, not like an animal."

It was hard to see the Shan's expression through the slit of his helmet, but his voice had lost its tone of sour amusement and now seemed as furious as Simon's. "Animal, am I? I think you will learn a hard lesson, stone-dweller."

Simon charged again, but in a deep part of his thoughts he could not help noticing that Unver spoke very good Westerling for a clansman. As they closed, he caught the grasslander's stroke on his own shield, then rammed his horse sideways against Unver's, so that the Thrithings horse had to quickstep to keep from falling.

Now they traded blows in earnest, steel on steel. Unver was as tall as Simon, or nearly, and Simon guessed that his enemy might be only half his age, but with the rage of battle in his blood, he could think of nothing but hammering the mocking grasslander out of the saddle and trampling him into the mud.

"Majesty!" Count Pieres called from somewhere nearby. "Fall back!"

"Keep the others away," Simon shouted. "This is my fight."

"So greedy, like all your kind!" said Unver. "But fear not—there is much of me to share, and I will gladly save some of my blade for all your knights." But even as Unver finished his boast and managed to slip Simon's scything attack, his horse stumbled in a hole and lost its footing. For a moment it seemed the clan chieftain might keep his balance, but the horse tangled its own legs and fell with a thump like the beat of a gigantic drum and Unver vanished beneath it.

Simon stared down, gasping for breath. Only a few heartbeats later the black-cloaked figure crawled free of the broken-legged horse and stood, apparently unharmed, though he had lost his shield. He lifted his curved blade before him, finding his balance and turning as Simon's horse cantered a little to one side.

"May the good Lord preserve me," Simon said, half-aloud. "This barbarian must have some angel watching him."

"Majesty, get away! Let the archers finish him!" Count Pieres called. Simon could hear Snell also urging him to retreat, to let others complete the task of taking the Thrithings-lord. But there was something strangely calm about Unver as he kept pivoting to keep Simon and his horse before him. "Ride him down, sire!" shouted someone else.

Instead, to immediate cries of horror from his knights, Simon slid out of the saddle and landed heavily on the ground, then dropped his shield by Silvershod's feet and strode toward Unver. "If I am wrong to call you animal," he said, "then it would be wrong to ride you down like one. Defend yourself, man!"

The combatants on all sides had scrambled out of the way, and almost all had stopped to watch the king and the Shan fighting. Simon waded in, hacking hard, knowing even as he did so that the strength animating him, born of anger and fear, would fade quickly. But every blow he made at his enemy's head, neck, or legs was countered—though not always easily, because Unver's own blade was heavy, meant for fighting from horseback. Still, though the grasslander had no shield, Simon could not pierce the other man's guard. Unver had much lighter armor, and though it offered less protection from a solid blow, Simon also knew that the Shan would tire more slowly than he would in his heavier plate.

They fought on as the rain returned and the torn, muddy ground grew ever more slippery. There were moments when they both failed to land a blow and then fell against each other almost like partners in some strange dance, grappling and sliding, face to face, until they could get their feet beneath them and draw apart again. Soon Simon was cursing the foolish courtesy of discarding his own shield. It was all he could do to keep his weary arms up, and he found it harder and harder to defend against Unver's brutal counterblows. He received a hard buffet that dented his helmet and crumpled part of his visor. Blood began to run into his eyes, though he felt no pain from the wound. He snarled in frustration, then tore the helmet from his head and cast it away. Surprisingly, Unver did the same thing the next time they broke apart from each other, so that at last they were truly face to face.

The Shan showed little expression, teeth clenched in a grim line as his breath sawed in and out, his gray eyes slitted with effort. The Thrithings leader had scars all over his lean, tanned face, both old wounds and horrendous newer ones. Simon had a nagging thought that something about his enemy seemed familiar, but he had enough to do simply trying to stay alive. He could feel his strength ebbing as remorselessly as a retreating tide, but though Unver was clearly weary too, Simon knew the other man would outlast him.

Miri, I'll be with you soon, he thought. *Morgan, Lillia, it's yours now, all yours. I pray God will make you strong.*

Sensing his chance, Unver leaped forward, slashing with the great curved sword, hammering at Simon's blade and armor until the king was forced to give ground. As he stepped back, Simon's foot slipped and he went down on one knee. Unver had already committed to the stroke, which hissed past Simon's naked face so closely he felt its wind. Simon had desperately flung out his own sword, hoping to block the blow, and though his stroke not touch his opponent's blade, the edge of his sword sliced Unver's knuckles through his gauntlet. The grasslander cursed in his own tongue, his fingers suddenly running with blood, and Simon brought his sword around in a backhand swipe that caught the crosspiece of the Thrithings blade and yanked it from Unver's wounded hand. Without thinking, Simon took a step forward and brought his heavy, booted foot down on the blade, meaning only to keep it from his enemy's grasp, but instead the Shan's iron blade snapped.

In that instant, as Simon stood with one foot on the broken sword, time itself seemed to slow. Unver looked down, then looked up again, but if there was fear in his heart it did not rise to his scarred face.

"You do not want to be called an animal," Simon said, holding his own sword out before him as he struggled to keep it steady, each breath now like fire in his lungs. "Do you wish to surrender, then? Or fight on like a beast, using only your hands?"

"*No!*" The unexpected cry did not come from Unver. It was a woman's voice, and it pierced Simon's ear like a knife. "Take this and live! Take your father's sword!"

He turned and saw someone riding toward them through the rapt crowd watching their combat. The rider was a woman, though her hair was cropped like a boy's, and she waved a slender sword. Simon's head and chest were aching so badly he could hardly stand, and his breath would not fill his lungs. Did this madwoman mean to attack him? Had the grasslanders all lost their wits? A few arrows leaped from the Erkynlandish solders, but none of them struck her. The Thrithings warriors parted to let her through, and as she raced toward them Simon stared at her with growing astonishment. Surely it was . . . it had to be . . .

"Vorzheva!" he cried. "For the love of God, woman, *what are you doing here?"*

She ignored him, guiding her horse near enough to Unver that she could fling the blade she carried. It winked in the dull, winter light as it spun, but Unver did not catch it, letting it fall instead to the torn earth at his feet.

"No," he said. "Not that."

"Take it up!" Vorzheva cried. "It is all he left you—all he left us!"

As Simon stared, completely befuddled, Unver at last bent and plucked the sword out of the mud. It was no two-handed great sword, nor was it one of the curved Thrithings' blades. In truth, Simon thought he had seen it before—in a dream, perhaps, in the days when he still dreamed. He stared, still struggling for breath. The blade was slim but sharp, long and wicked as a shining silver needle.

"Naidel." As he said it, he fully expected the sky to rattle with thunder and lightning to flash. Instead, the rain continued to hiss down, splashing on his face and in his eyes. "God's Bloody Tree—*I know that blade!* It is Naidel, and it had belonged to Prince Josua himself—

And suddenly he understood—Vorzheva's presence, her shouted words about Unver's father, everything. He looked at the Shan, who stared at the blade as though he still had not decided whether to wield it.

"Deornoth!" Simon cried. "You are Deornoth, Josua's son!"

"Deornoth is dead," the other snarled. "I am Unver. I am Nobody."

"No. You are the son of my dear friend, Josua." Simon took a few more steps, so close now that Unver lowered the tip of the slender sword against an attack, but instead Simon let his own blade drop from his mailed fist onto the ground. The watching Erkynlanders cried out in dismay, but Simon held up his hand. *"Let no man come nearer!"* he cried, though it hurt his chest badly to shout, and he felt like a great fist had closed on his lungs. He looked up at Unver, who was watching him in undisguised astonishment, then Simon reached out and took Naidel's thin blade between his fingers. "I would rather die than raise arms against you, now that I know," Simon told the scarred man. "I owe your father everything. I have searched for him all these years." He fumbled loose the buckles and pulled loose his armor, then set Naidel's tip against the padded coat, just above his heart, which was beating swiftly and painfully beneath his arming shirt. *Lord, what is this mystery?* Simon asked his god. *Why have You brought me to this place?*

"Finish him!" Vorzheva cried. She sounded more than half-mad herself. "They lured your father away! They turned their backs on us!"

"We have hunted for him since the day he vanished," said Simon quietly, and Unver seemed to hear him.

"Majesty!" Snell shouted, but the baron seemed so far away that Simon barely noticed. He looked around. The field had grown unnaturally quiet but for the muted drumming of rain. All around, Thrithings-men and Erkynlanders had stopped fighting to stare at the spectacle of a king on his knees. Simon caught up the point of Josua's sword, which had drooped a little, and placed it back over his heart.

"It is a trick!" Vorzheva cried, but even she sounded unsure.

"Do what you will," said Simon, and fixed Unver—*no, Deornoth,* he reminded himself, *my dear Josua's lost child*—for a long moment with his gaze. It was impossible to read what was in the other's face. Simon closed his eyes.

What will come will come, he told himself. *Lord, I commend my soul unto You.*

And then he felt a thump of impact as the thin blade drove into him and pierced his heart like a tongue of fire. Behind the murderous shock of pain came a great pall of blackness, rolling over him like a thunderstorm, and Simon surrendered.

PART TWO

Dance of Sacrifice

I have seen the Sa'onsera.
I would know her with my eyes closed
Because where she walks, silence surrounds;
I have heard the Sa'onsera,
But were I deaf, I would know her still,
Because where she stands, light bends and bows its head.
Still, I need neither eyes nor ears
To know she is the Highest
Because when her thoughts touch mine, my spirit cries out in joy
And in that quicksilver moment I dwell in the Garden,
The love that we all have lost,
The love that is precious beyond anything.
And that is all I need to know
Of her or of myself.

—BENAYHA OF KEMENTARI

RIMMERSGARD
OSTERDYR PLAIN
Kushiba
Tanakiru
Anvijanya
COOLBLOOD VALLEY
Narrowdark River
Hornet's Nest
WORMSCALE PASS
THE WEALDHELM
COOLBLOOD VALLEY
NARROWDARK VALLEY
Coolblood R. (Ts'i Suhyasei)
to the FORBIDDEN HILLS
Naglimund
Da'ai Chikiza
THE STILE
Himano's House
FLOWERING HILLS
Aelfwent
Geloë's Lake

Hakatri

Second Interlude

Time had begun again, and its touch was agony.

The Word of Command had summoned him from the blessed, eternal emptiness in which he had floated for so long, and now it flung him back into the prismatic, nightmarish instant when the great witchwood stake had pierced the dragon's heart and the boiling fountain of black blood had changed him forever. He felt its dreadful essence course through him once more, scalding away his spirit and leaving only dragon-life. As he burned, he changed—an agony of death and birth. The burning black tide scorched away all time and distance, so that in a single moment he perceived everything that lived in the spinning world, and much that no longer existed.

He saw his wife weeping, tears glittering on her cheeks like frost.

His daughter appeared before him too, face daubed in the ashes of mourning. She was a child no longer but had grown into someone he could recognize only by her fierceness. Then came his brother's face, stretched in a terrifying rictus of madness so dismaying that if he had possessed a body, he would have recoiled.

His brother's crazed mask melted into nothingness, but more shapes followed it, one after another, like mourners in a funeral procession. Some he dimly thought he recognized, but others were utterly strange to him—a slender Hikeda'ya female carrying a long witchwood blade, a shaggy giant pursued by a scarred, pale-haired mortal man, and a child-sized figure standing alone on an empty beach. But these visions were only billows of rotting gossamer, faint as shadows or streaming mist, and he sensed they were not truth but only possibility. And over them all, above and behind them, and even somehow *in* them, loomed a great, pale shape, a pillar of stone that towered above the world like a gigantic pointing finger, and around it he could sense the swirling winds of countless destinies.

He tried desperately to turn away from these grim or confusing phantoms, but he could not escape them. He had been called out of his long sleep by a Word of enormous, almost incomprehensible power, and with that summons had been dragged back into the endless horror that the burning black blood had forced upon him so long ago.

Once again, he was time's prisoner.

"The hour has come." The strange, multiplied voice came from nowhere and everywhere, reverberating like the tolling of a gigantic bell. *"You have heard the Word that summons you. Now is the hour come for you to truly awaken—for you to serve your race."*

He fought, but his resistance was useless, doomed before it began. Time had encircled him like a strangling serpent, like a cruel rope, like the sucking rings of a whirlpool, and with it had come the pain that had blighted his life, the dreadful, black burning.

"You have been drawn back because you alone can do what must be done," the voice declared. *"You alone of all our kind have the blackness in you. You alone have bathed in the fiery, elemental blood, have drunk from the treacherous Dreaming Sea."* Strangely, he seemed to sense two more voices speaking in concert with the first, like the simultaneous chanting of celebrants, but he was equally certain that all three spoke with only one thought, one will. It was all too much for his confused spirit, so raw, so newly returned, and he drifted toward exhausted surrender as the voice spoke on. *"Now those who destroyed all that you cared for will be punished. Together we will find a victory they could not imagine."*

He could not remember how to speak, but somehow his thoughts became words: *"Why? Why have you brought me back? Why have you returned me to this horror?"*

"Because only you can make things right," declared the threefold voice.

"I don't understand!"

"But you will, child of the year's end. And when you understand what the mortal beasts have done to your kind—to our kind—you will also know what you must do. You will understand. And you will punish."

22

Quarrel

Sisqi had spent a long morning foraging for green things to eat, because a steady diet of fish felt too much like winter in Yiqanuc, and this part of the vast forest was full of interesting plants. As she returned to the campsite beside the lake, she was alarmed to see no sign of Vaqana. The white wolf had spent much of the last fortnight guarding Binabik as he slept through the worst of his fever, and she could think of no good reason Vaqana would have left him now. She hurried down the slope, heart racing, but to her relief, she found Binabik open-eyed and awake. He even smiled when he saw her. "Greetings, wife," he said quietly.

"Daughter of the Mountains, that frightened me." She knelt beside him and lifted off the bandage of leaves so she could examine his shin. The skin around the twin holes was raw and the wounds were still deep, like tiny ponds, even after they had started to heal. Her husband would have scars the rest of his life, but the bite had finally stopped weeping. "I saw Vaqana was gone. I could think of no reason she would leave your side," she said, "except . . . except because of something bad."

"She saw I was better. Then she saw a rabbit."

Sisqi laughed a little, though she had not entirely recovered from her sudden panic. "Here. I brought back some snow daisy leaves—I think that is what they are called, at least."

Binabik studied the leaves carefully. "Yes, I believe you are right. But am I to eat them? A man recovering from being poisoned should have food for strength. Could you not catch a pigeon or two?"

"I am glad to see you have regained some of your appetite but that does not mean you should simply begin inhaling birds willy-nilly."

"The man who eats well, sleeps well," said Binabik solemnly. "The man who sleeps well *stays* well."

"I believe that is another wise old saying that you have made up yourself." She leaned down and kissed him. He still had the smell of sickness about him, but the yellow color was gone from the whites of his eyes and all his appetites were clearly returning. "And you may stop fondling my *nuluk*, because I cannot prepare any food if I am distracted."

"But when I am well, my Sisqinanamook—and I am feeling much better today—you are always a distraction to *me.*"

"Flattery from a Singing Man?" Sisqi gently removed his hand from her backside and sat up. "I am sure you know some old saying about how untrustworthy such a thing must be."

"I cannot think of any such saying," he replied, his round face all innocence.

"Then invent one of those, too." On a sudden impulse, she bent and kissed him again. "Oh, my beloved, I cannot tell you how good it is to hear your voice, even when you are being silly and difficult. I so feared to lose you."

Binabik sat up, not without huffing and puffing. When he finished, his forehead was damp. "When I brought you here to Geloë's lake, dear wife, I did not think we would still be here when Sedda had waxed and waned once more."

"You did not think you would be bitten by a viper—nor did I."

They were interrupted by the reappearance of Vaqana, who had apparently been making free with the local wildlife, or so the spatters of blood on her muzzle suggested. When she saw Binabik sitting up she bounded up the slope and nearly knocked him to the ground again, then stood over him with her paws on either side, licking his face.

"Save me!" he cried. "She will take off all my skin like a pumice stone. And her breath smells like mice!"

"Well, you said you were hungry. Perhaps she will bring you the next one."

He scratched the wolf's chest vigorously. "I would not scorn a mouse, nor anything with blood and meat. I feel as weak as a weasel kit her first time in the snow. But surely it would be easier for us to catch a bird or two than to go digging for mice. If Vaqana could jump high enough, she would have emptied the trees of birds all around before deigning to eat a single mouse."

"You will get soup, and you will finish it all," said Sisqi, feeding fresh deadfall to the fire and putting a stone into it to heat. "When you are strong enough to dart a few birds yourself, then you may eat your fill of winged creatures."

"Have I told you that you are a cruel woman?" His voice was light, but Sisqi gave him a knowing look.

"Yes, frequently. And I see you are tired already, despite your brave show. The poison nearly killed you, so lie back down and I will feed you like a baby."

"*Pfah,*" he said. "Snow daisy soup. Even baby birds are fed worms."

"Fine. I will chew up a few of those for you as well."

In a winter forest full of hungry bears and wolves, the last thing either of the trolls had thought to worry about were snakes. But on the day when they had planned to leave Geloë's lake, Binabik had stepped on a necklace viper hiding in a pile of fallen leaves, and the creature had sunk its fangs into his leg.

At first it had seemed nothing dire. He made his way back to Sisqi and enlisted her help in treating the wounds, but as he rooted through his bag Binabik had suddenly begun to have trouble breathing and complained that his tongue had grown larger in his mouth. Sisqi saw that his lips and neck were also grossly swollen and that his eyes were as red as an eagle owl's, and it terrified her. She had seen more than a few bad snakebites at Blue Mud Lake, so she quickly slashed the wound with her knife and sucked out as much of the venom as she could, ignoring the dreadful, bloody bitterness and the loss of feeling in her own mouth, which did not go away for hours. While Binabik could still talk, he bade her take several packets of herbs out of his bag and crush them before feeding them to him. The last thing he told her which she could understand was to make a tea of beechwheat and wild licorice and pour as much into him as she could get him to swallow.

For days after that, Sisqi had watched him slide in and out of a dreadful fever, and though she carefully bathed his wound and bandaged it several times each day, she saw little improvement and began to despair. The place by the lake had now become her permanent camp, and every day she had to find food as well as care for her husband. Her ram, Ooki, seemed perfectly happy with the new situation, wandering happily along the lakeside cropping on what growing things he could find. Vaqana, though, seemed as worried as Sisqi herself, and spent hours sleeping by Binabik's side, sitting up anxiously to watch him when the fever was strong, licking sweat from his face and whining at him as if to convince him to stop his foolery and get up.

Only the night before his awakening, he had been so feverish and his breathing so weak that Sisqi had put her own mouth over his and forced her breath into his chest, as though her love for him could save him even in the form of insubstantial air. She had wept afterward, though he seemed a little better, and had slept with her head beside his, still listening to his uneven breathing long after the moon had slid down the sky.

Three more days passed after the fever broke before Sisqi would consent to Binabik riding on Vaqana's back again; even then, she only allowed him to do so for an hour before she insisted they stop for the night in the foothills of the southern Wealdhelm.

"But we have lost so many days!" he complained. "Before the snake stung me, we had news to take to our friends Simon and Miriamele. Now more than ever we must hurry!"

"If you hurry, you will only make yourself ill again," she said flatly. "And that I will not allow. Remember, you are the friend of the folks in Erkynland, but you are also a father, as well as the Singing Man of your people. You have no right to be careless with your life."

He grimaced. "My life means little when set against the dangers we face, and more than the folk of Erkynland will suffer if the Norns attack. But it is my friends' suffering that I most wish to ease. That is why we must take the news that Morgan still lives to the Hayholt."

"Perhaps. But that news is now almost a month old." She could not meet his eye. "Perhaps it is no longer true."

Binabik sat up and thumped a fist against his chest. "Pray to the ancestors that it still is!" he said. "Do you mean that something bad has happened to Prince Morgan?"

"How would I know?" She made him lie down again. "I have been nowhere but by your side through all your suffering, hunting for yarrow and licorice and other hard-to-find things even as autumn chills all this forest. I mean only that you are in a hurry now to deliver news that is very old, and that is no good reason to bring back your fever."

In the end, Binabik surrendered, though not with the best of grace. "But I will be quite well enough to ride when the sun comes back," he declared.

"We will see. Until you are completely well, though, *I* am your Singing Man, and I will say what you may or may not do." But though she did not agree with him, and sometimes wearied of his stubbornness, Sisqi could not help loving him for the loyalty he felt to his friends.

At her insistence, they rode slowly, though Vaqana was obviously frustrated at not being allowed her usual bounding pace. For two days they crossed the foothills of the Wealdhelm, now thoroughly in the season's chill grip. Snowflakes flurried in the cold wind from the north and mounded on the branches of evergreens.

"This is more comfortable weather." Sisqi brushed snow from the fur of her hood. "This is like Blue Mud Lake at the season of return. We might even find a ptarmigan!"

Binabik smiled at her jest, but it was clear from the droplets of sweat frozen on his brow that the leg was still giving him much pain, and Sisqi ended their riding early that night. They chose a spot to camp by one of the streams running noisily down through the hills, then she built a fire and made him sit next to it while she went to hunt for food. Vaqana stretched out beside him, tongue lolling from her wide, toothy grin, so Sisqi did not need to worry about leaving her husband alone.

She was only short ride from the camp and had just begun foraging around the edges of a small pond for snow daisy and nettle leaves when she heard the unmistakable sound of voices. She caught up Ooki's reins and led the ram a little way up the hill so they could hide behind a tangle of thorn bushes and watch. She clutched her crook-handled goad tightly—it had a sharp spearpoint on one end—ready to fight or flee.

The first of the newcomers was so small and the color of its skin so like her own that for a moment Sisqi almost believed it must be some kind of forest troll, some long lost part of her own tribe. As half a dozen more figures followed it to the edge of the pond, she saw that the first was small because it was a child: within moments, she recognized the long arms and sloping shoulders of the adults.

As she watched, larger members of what she now felt sure was a family of Niskies—though she had no idea what those people could be doing so far from any ocean—stood watching carefully as the four small ones splashed in the pond. Sisqi was so fascinated by the sight of Niskie children swimming and playing in the chilly water like fish that she did not realize she had lost track of the third adult until she heard a voice just beside her.

"Is the pond yours?" someone asked in the Westerling tongue.

Sisqi jumped, startled. A slender figure stood just at the edge of the thorn bushes, watching her with large, calm eyes. She lifted her goad to defend herself, but when the one who had surprised her made no movement, she lowered it again.

"Is the pond yours?" the Niskie man asked again. He had a fringe of pale gray hair and the leathery, wrinkled skin of one who had spent many years under the harsh sun, and seemed older than the other two adults.

"Not mine," she said, struggling to remember the Westerling words after a month or more of speaking only Qanuc.

"Ah." The Niskie nodded. "Good. The young ones are tired and thirsty, and we have traveled far today."

After another long moment of watching the children frolicking in the pond, Sisqi took a calculated risk. "If fresh water you want, my man and I have camp by a stream. Better for drinking."

The Niskie nodded again. "You are kind." He lifted his head and called out to the others in a wheezing voice. The children in the pond paid him no heed, but the other two adults turned to look, eyes widening when they finally noticed Sisqi and her ram crouched by the brambles. They called to the children, who still did not hurry to leave the water, but at last came out, dripping and shy, wet hair straggling down over their faces. The biggest of them was scarcely more than half the size of the elders; the smallest had the chubby limbs of a child just out of infancy.

"I am Han Goda," said the oldest one to Sisqi. "This is my family. Well met."

"I am Sisqinanamook of Mintahoq," she said, still not entirely certain she had done the right thing. "My husband has sick from snakebite. Come in our camp and drink. The stream is sweet."

Binabik had pulled up the leg of his breeches and was rubbing yarrow paste into his wound. He was surprised but apparently unworried to see her return with the newcomers. When she had introduced him, and Han Goda had introduced his grandson, Yem Suju, and Yem Suju's mate, Yem Gili, they all gathered around the fire. While the children drank from the stream and splashed each other with cold water, laughing and squealing, Sisqi put what roots and leaves she had been able to find in a pot. Yem Gili produced a handful of small, dried fish from a sack and shyly offered them to Sisqi, who tossed them into the pot as well. Han Goda examined Binabik's wound and said, "You have been well cared for. Many others would have died from that bite."

"I know. Always I have been gifted with good fortune, but you are seeing my greatest luck sitting right beside you—my wife."

"Where are you from?" Sisqi asked carefully. "Do I speak right—you are Niskies?"

Han Goda nodded. "We come from Melcolis, a small port on the northern end of Emettin's Bay. We are backfish."

Sisqi looked at him, mystified. "Backfish?"

"My wife is not being so comfortable with your speech as I am being," said Binabik. "But I confess I do not know this word either."

Han Goda smiled, showing only gums—he was as toothless as a turtle. "It is a word we use to describe ourselves—the fish so small you throw them back. We do not serve on the big ships, but only on the small fishing boats, and only during the season when the boats must go far out to sea to catch the tunny."

"Is that why you were leaving your home? For having too little work?"

The old Niskie looked at him with honest surprise. "No, no. My fathers and mothers and their fathers and mothers and generations before that have lived that way. No, we left because the Lady called us."

His son and daughter-in-law both nodded. "She has called us to a better life," said Yem Gili in a small but firm voice.

Binabik looked at Sisqi, then back to Han Goda. "I do not understand. Who is this lady who calls you?"

Han Goda told them of dreams that he and his family had all shared, though the children had not been able to describe theirs very well. "And always she tells us, 'Come north! Follow my call!' And so we have traveled far from our ocean and our home."

"Whoever calls to you," Binabik said, "we are wishing for you and your family safe and fruitful journeying."

"That is kind," said Han Goda. "We have met many perils already. Who knew that the meadows and the forests could be as dangerous as the sea itself?"

"We saw a great army traveling south," said his grandson. He leaned forward to sniff the pot. "Ah! I am getting very hungry."

"Explain, please, this army-seeing," said Binabik, his expression darkening. "In a moment the soup will be ready for eating, but first please tell us of this army."

"We saw them almost a fortnight ago," said Han Goda. "It was an army of the Norns. We have no doubt of that—the whiteskins were our old masters, and we remember those days with bitterness. We were very afraid when we saw rows and rows of their soldiers coming down the great road by night, so we hid. We had to hide for a very long time as they passed, there were so many of them."

"Let me be sure I understand," said Binabik. "This army of Norns was traveling south?" He pointed. "Or north?"

"South," said Han Goda. "They filled the whole of the road as far as we could see in either direction, many riding, but many more walking. They had many large wagons, too. One of my great-grandsons said he saw the Queen with the Silver Mask riding atop the largest, but I do not think that can be true. Everybody knows that the Norn queen does not ever leave her mountain."

"Tell to me more of this, please," said Binabik, his brows creased in concern. "You say there were being many Norn soldiers?

"More than I could ever hope to count," Han Goda assured him. "More than there are sprats in a sea-cloud."

"Have you anything else about this in your memory?"

"I saw something," announced Yem Suju. "I saw a wagon that seemed to be on fire but did not burn."

"But how could that be?" demanded his wife. Her voice was small, but it seemed clear she did not hesitate to speak up when she felt it necessary. "How can something be on fire but never burn? You were tired. We all were."

"Be telling more of this, please," said Binabik.

"It is as I said. One wagon, far back from the others but ahead of the leaders of the Norn soldiers, spilled out a strong red light, as of a forge-fire. It was no mere lantern that made it—it glared out across the night through the wagon's windows and door, and even through the cracks between the boards."

"Ah." Binabik sat back. "Some foul magicks, I am not doubting. This makes me even more fearful for our friends in the Hayholt."

"Foul magicks," said Yem Suju, almost in triumph. "Just as I said! This fellow knows what I saw is true."

His wife shook her head but did not argue.

Sisqi took the pot off the fire, and when it was cool, passed it around. She did not take much herself, wanting to make certain Binabik got a good share.

Han Goda and his family stayed in the trolls' camp that night and slept piled together in a heap near the fire. The Niskies did not even seem to have cloaks, and after they bid their hosts farewell in the morning and continued on their way north into the forest, Sisqi shook her head gravely.

"I fear for them. Winter is close now, and they are hardly dressed for it."

Binabik had been quiet since he woke up and had broken his silence only to bid their guests a good journey. Now he reached out and took his wife's hand. "I worry for them too, but they at least hold their destiny in their own hands. But their news is fearful indeed. A Norn army! Perhaps even the queen herself leading it, and they are headed south toward the Hayholt—toward Simon and Miriamele."

"That was many days ago," Sisqi pointed out. "And even in such force, the Norns move quickly. We could never hope to get to the castle before they reach it. Especially with your leg still healing."

"Perhaps." Binabik climbed to his feet. It was hard for him, and Sisqi moved to take his elbow, but he pulled away. "I cannot treat myself like a sick child any longer. You are right, my beloved, we cannot hope to beat them there, but we must follow as quickly as we can."

"Why?" she asked. "My husband, I know you love Simon. We both care much for him, and for Miriamele. But what could two Qanuc like us do against an army of thousands?"

"Not defeat them, of course. But there might be something else we could do, and we will not know unless we are there. We cannot stand by, knowing such doom is coming to friends, and do nothing."

Sisqi was silent for a long time. "And our own child?" she said at last. "She still travels these woods with Little Snenneq, hunting for Prince Morgan. What of them?"

"They are both of them clever and brave," Binabik said. "We already made our peace with leaving them. And we likely could not find them now if we tried—it has been almost a month since we parted."

"So, we leave our own blood-kin in the forest to follow an army we cannot hope to defeat?"

"Tell me of another choice," Binabik said, already looking weary despite the early hour. "Tell me another and we will consider it together, my wife."

But Sisqi could not think of one. They were silent as they packed up their few belongings and readied the ram and the wolf for riding.

T'si Suhyasei's brisk current slowed as the river widened, and Tanahaya could finally swim to the bank. When she reached it, she stretched out in a patch of weak winter sun to rest and to dry. She was far from having accomplished either when a feeling of vulnerability drove her to sit up and look around. Anyone passing on the river would be able to see her, she realized, and she was only a half a league or so away from Da'ai Chikiza and its occupying Sacrifice soldiers. She forced herself to get to her feet and look for a better place to rest.

It was hard for her to believe her own kind had once lived in this wild and desolate place. She made her way deeper into the green shadows until she felt safe, but even so far from the heart of Da'ai Chikiza, she saw bits of broken tile gleaming in the moss beneath her feet.

Fewer than ten Great Years have passed since the city called Tree of the Singing Winds emptied, she mused sadly, *but without looking closely, no one would ever guess that my people lived here, that they loved and feasted and made poetry that still echoes in our thoughts today.*

She stripped off her clothes, wringing out as much water as she could before putting them back on, but left off her boots to let them dry. It was growing dark, which meant the soldiers from the captured city would be out on patrol soon, and she was weary in every muscle and sinew. She decided to find a secure, hidden place to rest in until morning. Also, a thought had been troubling her all through the last day and night of hunting for Morgan, but the danger then had been too great to allow her to consider it properly.

Tanahaya had been trained to think methodically, first by her troubled but clever mother, then by her father's sister, who had studied with Master Himano in her youth. This had led to Tanahaya's own apprenticeship with the esteemed scholar of the Flowering Hills, and her first steps on a path that had felt so unplanned at the time, but now seemed inevitable.

Himano's method of careful consideration began with making one's body and thoughts as still as an undisturbed pond. Only when such quietude had been reached—he called it, "the Peace of the Gatherer"—was it truly possible to follow any single thought. Tanahaya herself had come to think of these elusive thoughts as tiny fish swimming through the pond's tangled greenery, moving in and out of shadow.

But it was difficult to find such crucial stillness, especially after one had just escaped death by arrows or drowning. Tanahaya was deeply troubled over the fate of young Morgan, and wished she could keep searching for him, but she also had to consider what would be best for the child that was growing inside her, the rare and sacred life that she and Jiriki had begun. Even more worrisome, she had become uneasy about Himano's parchment and what it said about the Hayholt and the Witchwood Crown—news she had shared with Jiriki just before control of the Witness had been snatched away from her. With so many needs to be addressed, old and new, it felt as if impatient voices were calling to her from all sides, demanding her attention.

Stillness, she reminded herself, *find stillness. Let the ripples diminish, Master Himano always said. Until you do, you cannot see the bottom.*

Her teacher had been the first person to suggest to her that simply thinking was as important as anything else she could do, as important as fighting, as finding love, as giving birth. It seemed particularly poignant now that a child was growing inside her, but her master's lesson still held, difficult as it might be to achieve.

Still. Let the waters go still.

She had found only odd moments to contemplate all that had happened in recent days, and a small, distracting *something* was hidden in that mass of unconsidered experience, an uncomfortable piece of grit, like the sand grain that spawns a pearl. It had irritated her even as she dug her way out of the fallen columns of the Place of Sky-Watching, and it had stayed with her as she followed Morgan's scent through the ruins of Da'ai Chikiza, hiding from Sacrifice patrols. But though it had troubled her for some time, she still could not say what it was. Still, Tanahaya knew herself: she would not find true peace until she discovered what that grain of discomfort was.

Why had the Hikeda'ya killed Himano? To silence him, that seemed obvious—why else murder one who was no warrior, whose eminence was in his wisdom. Certainly, the burning of all the books in her master's house suggested that silencing him was the reason—it was fortunate he had managed to save the parchment about the Witchwood Crown before they killed him. Was that knowledge what Utuk'ku feared? But even if the mistress of Nakkiga did not want the existence of witchwood seeds revealed until she had seized them for herself, it did not explain why so many Sacrifice soldiers had been sent to

Da'ai Chikiza, to capture a city that was all but abandoned. Or was Da'ai Chikiza not the object of Utuk'ku's design, but only a waystation?

The fish she had been following through the waters of her memory had again lost itself in a group of similar swimming things.

I am failing to find stillness, she decided sadly. *I must leave the puzzle alone until its right time has come.* She sighed and took Himano's parchment out of the oilskin in which she had wrapped it while in Da'ai Chikiza, and thanked the watchful stars of the Lost Garden that she had been carrying it during the Hikeda'ya attack. Otherwise, it would still be in the rubble of the Place of Sky-Watching, lost as certainly as Vinyedu and so many of the Pure had been lost there, buried beyond reach under broken stone.

Tanahaya had not spent a great deal of time studying Hikeda'ya chronicles, but Vinyedu had said that the seal was Utuk'ku's own, meaning that the ruler of Nakkiga had seen this document and then ordered it sent to the archives.

She held the parchment up to the late afternoon sun, searching for hidden writing, then made a systematic observation of every mark that had been added, starting with the queen's own rune and continuing through each barely legible annotation made by the clerics who had assigned it to the Nakkiga archives. Vinyedu had confirmed that it was real and came from the long-gone era of the Tenth Celebrant.

Something caught her eye then, something she had looked at several times, but which suddenly made her wonder if she had approached the entire matter backward. As she examined it again, she felt a stir of memory, followed by a deep shock of concern. It seemed unreal. Could Tanahaya, an apprentice scholar, be the only one who had noticed this small oddity, which both her teacher and the famed scholar Vinyedu had missed?

So many terrible possibilities hung on whether her new suspicion could be correct that the question of where she should go next now seemed even more momentous. She was desperate to share her concerns with Jiriki, but she had no idea where he was, and Vinyedu's Witness was buried under a mass of fallen stone. Could she find some other way to speak to him?

Anvi'janya. *With Da'ai Chikiza overrun, that mountain city is my nearest and best hope.* The ending of the old Great Year was close now—the scents on the wintry air told her the appearance of the Year-Torch could not be much more than a score of days ahead—and because her people had deserted Jao é-Tinukai'i, the celebration this time would be held in Anvi'janya. The ancient Year-Dancing ritual did not mean as much these days, with the witchwood all but gone, but Tanahaya knew that many of her kind would be there, scholars and celebrants among them. More importantly, Anvi'janya held one of the last unspoiled archives of her people's history, where she might find answers to the questions that were troubling her.

But Anvi'janya also lay many leagues north of where she was, and she had no horse. Tanahaya thought fleetingly about trying to steal a mount from a Sacrifice patrol, but the idea seemed so foolishly dangerous that she soon gave it up. Overwhelmed, she wrapped Himano's parchment back in its oilskin.

Tanahaya had not snatched a full hour of sleep since before the attack on Da'ai Chikiza. She found a place for herself in a fold of earth well away from the riverside, then picked up a deadfall branch plumed with yellow leaves. After wrapping up in her cloak, she lay down and pulled the branch over herself. No one would see her unless they ventured very close.

Still deeply troubled, her mind full of confusing, frightening thoughts and oppressed by the heavy weight of her own inadequacies, she at last succumbed to exhaustion, and slept.

When she woke, the sun had risen, wintry and distant. Tanahaya went down to the river to drink. She had spent much of the previous day being yanked along in the Coolblood current and did not need to wash, so after a careful survey of the banks on both sides, she kneeled and drank her fill. She was about to climb back up to the spot where she had slept when something caught her attention. The muddy bank was pockmarked with deer tracks—clearly it was a frequently used trail—and though marks had been left by several different animals, the tracks that looked most recent were surprisingly wide and deep, the spoor of a very large buck, the twin hoof crescents and heel spurs of each track as long as her hand from fingertip to wrist.

This gave her an idea, and she went back to retrieve her bag. She quickly brushed all traces of her stay from the ground, then returned to the deer track and followed it deeper into the woods.

After a little while she found fresh droppings, which heartened her, then continued until she discovered a clearing dominated by an immense oak tree. Its bark had been recently scored with the rubs of a buck's antlers, and the marks were far enough off the ground that she felt sure she had found the animal she sought, and that it would be big enough for her purpose. Tanahaya climbed the great tree, made herself comfortable on a branch some six or seven times her height above the ground, then waited with all the patience a Zida'ya scholar could employ, which was considerable.

Finally, as the sun climbed toward noon, she heard something large moving through the bracken at the edge of the clearing. She gathered her coiled rope in her hand and held her breath. She was still less than two leagues outside the ruins of Da'ai Chikiza, so the noise might be a roving Sacrifice patrol. She did not scent soldiers, though if she was wrong she would be in terrible danger. Still, she needed to reach High Anvi'janya more swiftly than she could travel on foot, so it was a risk she had to take.

At last, and to her great relief, she saw a huge buck emerge from the trees and onto the track. Its reddish pelt was winter-long and touched with gray, and it had a magnificent sweep of antlers. Tanahaya silently rejoiced.

The stag may have smelled her, or it was simply cautious after coming out onto comparatively open ground: it froze, ears flicking, and Tanahaya chose that moment to drop a loop of rope over its antlers. The startled creature let out a loud snort and immediately tried to spring away, but as soon as the rope had settled around the broad sweep of horn, Tanahaya belayed its other end around the trunk, then quickly clambered down to the ground while the great buck pranced and struggled. Faced with an enemy it could see, it did its best to kick at her, but Tanahaya stayed well out of reach. She knew she had to act quickly: it was late in the year and the big buck might be ready to lose its antlers, so they were likely fragile. She hadn't spent several hours in a tree just to see her quarry escape, so she cautiously moved closer and managed to get another loop of her rope around the animal's hind legs. This she pulled tight, so that the buck's leaps became smaller and smaller though no less frantic. After a short but wearying time, she managed to tie the rope around the trunk of another tree, then held on while the buck continued to struggle.

Tanahaya began to sing. Her song was nothing too powerful—not a Word of Command nor even something crafted for use with animals—only a calming melody she had learned from her father's sister, and she sang it over and over. At last, either because of the song or because it had simply grown weary, the stag eventually stopped fighting so violently. She tied off the other end of the rope, then began to walk around the captured animal, still singing in the ancient language of the Garden.

Leaves are shuddering, branches grow
The roots twine upward from below
And this is all we ever know,
Who live between, in life's brief glow

Who live between the day and night
Whose hearts grow weary from the fight
That sees the lonely stars take flight
We are, and when it ends, we might

We are, and so the skies roll on
While we below, who wait upon
The eyeblink turn from dusk to dawn
So soon are we, and so soon gone

So soon are we, who sing the song
So late are we, who live so long
So weak are we, but yet so strong
Who sing so all may share the song

Who sing so all the branches grow
And roots twine upward from below . . .

She slowly circled the unhappy stag, and each time she finished the chant, she began again. She did not know how many times she had sung it when the exhausted animal finally gave up and sagged in its bonds, tongue lolling and sides heaving.

Tanahaya approached it slowly, keeping her gaze fixed on its hooves and the huge spread of antlers in case it began to fight again. The stag's eye only rolled in weary desperation as she reached out her hand and laid it on the creature's brow. It shuddered at her touch, still frightened, so she began a new song, a quieter song with words so old that even Tanahaya did not know what they meant. She covered its eyes with her hand and kept singing until the great stag finally stopped struggling.

The beast was one of the largest red deer she had ever seen or even heard of, its shoulder as high as Tanahaya's head. She did her best to sense its thoughts, and as she quietly continued to sing, she began to feel a bit of its mood, too—angry and fearful—and to sense a bit of its history as well.

"You are old but still strong," she whispered into its ear between verses. "Fear not—I will not harm you. I only need your help. Help me and I will set you free again." She felt something push back at her—nothing like words, but a shove of stubborn resistance, and she could not help admiring the animal's determination.

"You have fought many battles—I can feel it," she said quietly. "You have never given in to anything, and you are always quick to anger. Under the binding of my song, I call you Quarrel, and while you travel with me that will be your name." She sang a little more, keeping her hand on the beast's head between the wide antlers. At last, shuddering, it dropped to its knees beside her. She freed its back legs from one end of the rope, then carefully fashioned the part that had tangled its antlers into a makeshift harness, with a loop around its wide neck and another behind the front legs. She climbed onto the stag's back, the big chest swelling and contracting beneath her as it breathed.

"Up, Quarrel." She gave a gentle pull on the new harness. The stag let out another snort, but it sounded more like exhaustion than resistance. "Very well," she said. "Rest a little more."

She sang her calming song again. When she felt she had given the stag enough time to regain its strength, she told it to stand. It did, and she was lifted swaying to a height she might have seen from the saddle of a war horse.

"Now I will show you which way to go." She gave a gentle tug on the harness and the great stag turned a little to that side. "Good," she said, and softly touched her heels against the barrel of its chest. "Run, Quarrel!"

The great beast sprang away through the woods with Tanahaya clinging to its back, north toward high Anvi'janya.

23

A Lesson and Its Aftermath

Morgan could sense more than hear the stealthy tread of feet just outside the yew trunk where they were hiding—Norn soldiers searching for survivors of their attack on Da'ai Chikiza, of which Morgan was one. But he was finding it very difficult to give that danger the attention it deserved. That was because he and the Norn deserter Nezeru had slipped down the inside of an old, hollow yew tree, where they were now wedged very tightly, face to face and body against body.

Morgan knew that the two of them could not have been more vulnerable if they had nailed themselves into a barrel and rolled it into the center of an enemy camp. At the same time, although his heart was racing with fear, Morgan was all too aware of Nezeru pressed against him, of her breath against his cheek—she smelled of wild licorice—and of his fear that if he tried to ease the tight fit by moving, he might send them both sliding even farther down into the trunk.

We could be trapped here, he thought. *We might stay in this old yew until we're just bones.*

Finally, she whispered, "I do not hear them now. We must try to get out."

They struggled but could not find enough purchase on the inside of the crumbling, largely dead trunk to lift themselves out of their predicament, and the rubbing and slipping only caused Morgan more distraction. Nezeru was slender, but her muscles felt hard as wood, and he was reminded again of her prowess in battle, her speed and nimbleness.

"Stop," she said in a harsh whisper. "We are making too much noise. And you are giving me a strange feeling."

"I thought you said you couldn't hear them anymore."

"Yes, but their hearing is as sharp as mine, and if we make enough noise *someone* will hear it."

He suddenly caught up to what she had said. "What do you mean, a strange feeling?"

"All this rubbing. It makes me want to couple. Now, be silent and do not move."

Couple? Did that mean what he thought it did? Now Morgan could not stop thinking about that, and as he did, the results drew Nezeru's attention.

"What is this?" she whispered. She sounded angry.

"I don't know what you mean," he said.

"*This.*" She slid her hand in between their bodies and squeezed him.

"Oh. Oh, my sweet Ransomer." The extravagance of the sensation was made even stronger because the yew trunk held him firm and he could not move away. "Don't do that!"

"Why?" She sounded genuinely surprised. She squeezed again. "Does it hurt?"

"Aaah!"

"I told you to be quiet."

"Then don't do that!"

She slowly withdrew her hand. "All that fuss over a *nei*," she said, but she sounded more mocking than upset.

"What does that mean—*nei*?"

"I think you can guess. But the word means "root."

He was silent for a long moment. "I thought you said your sword was named 'Cold Root.'"

"It is."

"That is . . . very strange."

She laughed, a nearly silent flutter of air against his ear. "Keep your voice low, mortal. The name of the sword is a different meaning of the word, that is all. Do not words sometimes mean more than one thing in your mortal tongue?"

"Yes. Let's not talk about it anymore." The problem caused by their continued contact and her aggressive root-handling had not gotten any better after she had stopped. "If we're still allowed to talk quietly, tell me why you left the Norns."

Now she was silent for a long time. "I wish I could say that they left me," she said at last, "that my good intentions were betrayed—because in part, at least, that is true. But what is more important is that I was blind when I thought I could see everything clearly."

"I don't understand."

"Then count yourself lucky, young mortal, and pray to the Garden that you do not discover the same thing someday."

Morgan ignored the insult of "young mortal"—now that he knew she was no older than he was, it had no sting. He knew what the Lost Garden was because Tanahaya had talked about it, but he still could not quite grasp Nezeru's meaning. *Blind when I think I can see?* Then he considered how many certainties he had lost, or which had been outright stolen from him since he had left the Hayholt, and decided he might have glimpsed a little of her regret. "We all learn," he said. "There isn't any shame in that."

"No, but there can be shame in knowing what you did while you were still denying the truth."

"What truth?" The distraction seemed to be working. His excitement was passing, and he was eager to hear this Norn warrior reveal her hidden thoughts.

"The truth that I was encouraged not to think for myself. That I was given the same simple answers for every doubt from the time I was a child, and that it never occurred to me that simple answers are often bad answers."

"Your masters tricked you."

"But my masters may have been tricked in turn. We were all raised to believe our queen's will is infallible, and a part of me still thinks that might be so. But I have come to realize that no matter the wisdom of our immortal queen, her underlings are certainly capable of error. Some are interested only in their own advancement. Some are so terrified of being wrong that they would kill to protect their ignorance."

Morgan thought that sounded like any court in Osten Ard, even his grandparents', though he doubted any of their courtiers would be capable of doing murder. Why should they? All the nobles had everything they wanted—land, servants, glory. What else did anyone need?

It was almost pitch dark in the tree. Nezeru had gone quiet, and he wondered whether she regretted sharing her doubts with him.

"Why do mortals kiss?" she asked.

It was a question he had not expected. "Kiss? What? Don't Norns kiss?"

"If you mean Hikeda'ya, yes, we do, but only between lovers. From what I have been told, mortals will kiss anyone at any time, old, young, male, female. Some of them even kiss dogs and horses, I have heard." She laughed silently again.

He felt her chest move against his ribcage.

"Have you ever kissed someone?" she asked.

"Good God, yes, of course."

"Lovers?"

He took a deep breath. Just when he had regained control of himself . . . ! "Yes, lovers. But also grandparents, parents, friends. There are many kinds of kisses. Some are just greetings, others are marks of respect, like when you kiss the ring of a bishop."

"Ring?"

"It is just as it sounds," he said, a little cross. "Or does it have another meaning in Norn language? I mean a ring around the finger."

"No, no, I understand." She paused again. "Can you show me how mortals kiss?"

Now it was Morgan's turn to stay silent for a while. His grave error with Tanahaya still shamed him. "You mean you want *me* to kiss *you*?"

"Is that wrong? Are you promised to another, or do you prefer to kiss other males? Or are Hikeda'ya simply distasteful to you?"

"No! I mean, I don't know. Yes, I find the members of your race who tried to murder me and kill my family *distasteful*, as you say. But you saved my life, and I . . . I suppose we are allies, if not friends."

"No," she said quickly. "Not friends. But allies, at least for now."

He didn't much like the sound of that, but he was in no position to pick a fight. "But why? Why would you want me to kiss you?"

"Because I am curious. I kissed another mortal, and it was . . . strange."

"So, I am not your first?" He amused himself with his twinge of jealousy. *You are truly mad, Morgan,* he told himself, *to have such a feeling at such a moment.* "Why were you kissing a mortal? God save us, you weren't killing him, were you?"

"No. Don't be foolish. That would be a waste of time." But she didn't explain why. "I traveled in company with a mortal for a while. He upset me with his many questions and made me doubt the things I had been most sure about. I was drawn to him in some strange way, I suppose, though I should have hated him." She hesitated, and when she spoke again her whisper was harsher. "I *do* hate him—but not because of his questions." She shook her head, something he could sense but not see. "But I do not wish to speak of him. He kissed me, but his heart was not in it, as we say."

"We say that too. But why do you find it surprising that a mortal, your enemy, would not enjoy kissing you?"

"Because it did not seem like he would be that way. I thought I sensed something in him . . ." She trailed off. "I was wrong, as is obvious to me now. But I cannot help wondering if something I did put him off. So you see why I am curious."

In so many ways it seemed like a terrible, foolish thing to do, but Morgan knew he was in a unique position, facing an opportunity that might never come again.

How bad could it be? he wondered. *If she wanted to bite me to death, she could have done it a dozen other times.* "Bring your face nearer to mine," was all he said.

She did, and for the first time he sensed hesitation in her usually brisk movements: She leaned toward him far more cautiously than she had grabbed at his manhood. She smelled not just of licorice but of pine sap and other things he could not quite distinguish, though none of them were unpleasant.

"Show me what you did with this mortal." Morgan spoke even more softly now that their heads were so close.

"I told you, he did not seem to like it—!"

"Hush. It is a mistake to talk too much when you are kissing someone. It is a distraction. It also might mean someone gets bitten by accident."

"If you bite me, mortal boy, I will bite you back!"

He ignored this. "Nearer." And then he pressed his lips carefully against hers.

In the first moments, it was as if he kissed a shy shepherdess or an inexperienced chambermaid. Her mouth received his as though she expected him to feed her like a baby bird. But this slightly distasteful thought only lasted a few moments; her mouth began to soften and her lips to move beneath his. A moment later he felt her tongue push past his teeth, and he only just avoided laughing in surprise: Nezeru had not come away from her previous encounter completely unschooled, it seemed.

And as the kiss went on it deepened into something more than merely instruction, though no words had been spoken. She pushed her body closer against his, when their situation had already brought them almost as close as two people could be, then began to rub her belly up and down against his in a sleepy, almost dreamlike way. Soon she was shoving her loins against him and he found himself responding.

What does she want? he wondered. *Does she not understand what she's doing to me?* Still, the taste and feel of a soft mouth against his was something he had not experienced in some time and had not realized until this moment how very badly he had missed it.

Nezeru had worked herself into a regular rhythm, using all their confined space to drive her hips against his. *If not for my breeks and hers,* he thought, *I would have to warn her about the perils of raising a prince's bastard.* She seemed to reach a shuddering pitch then, and for a moment her mouth fell away from his and he heard her breath rasping in her throat, then felt a convulsion travel through her as though she fought against a fever. As the throes died away, she reached her hands up and took his face between them, kissing him again with a thoroughness he could not help enjoying. Then her fingers touched something behind his head and she suddenly leaned back.

"Your sword," she said in a quiet, almost breathless voice.

"We have no room," he pointed out.

"No, you fool, your sword. Your real, true sword. It is hung on your back."

More than a bit overwhelmed by what had just happened, Morgan could not make sense of her words. "What?" he asked at last.

"It is helping to wedge us in this trunk." Suddenly she was crisp and serious again, as if nothing unusual had just happened. "But unlike all the other things holding us in place, we can remove your sword and scabbard from behind you. It might give us enough room to climb upward again."

He finally grasped what she meant. "If you do take it from behind me, be careful. That is my father's sword and it means much to me. If you drop it, it will fall to the bottom of this tree and I will never recover it."

"It is not the sword that matters, it is the wielder," she told him. "You should not attach yourself to mere things. Now, brace your feet and elbows so you do not slip down when I take it away." And so saying, she unbuckled his sword belt where it crossed his chest, then grasped the scabbard with her two hands and began to lift it slowly upward as Morgan dug his climbing irons even deeper into the interior of the yew trunk. It made for a strange sensation—the space behind him slowly growing wider. A bit of bent metal decorating the end of the scabbard tore his shirt and scraped his neck as it slid upward, but at last she had it free. Maneuvering carefully, she buckled the belt again so that the sword hung down one side beneath his arm.

"Push upward," she said. "Slowly."

He did, rubbing against both her and the inside of the trunk. He managed to lift himself a few fingers' breadth, lifting Nezeru with him, and was surprised by how light she was. She kept herself braced as well, helping with elbows and knees and feet until they stopped, still in the same position but slightly higher up the inside of the trunk. She surprised him then by leaning in and kissing him, a sweet and swift nuzzling of her lips against his that lasted only a few instants.

"Now again, my mortal ally," she said. "Bit by bit until we lift ourselves to the top."

Morgan set his feet and pushed back against the yew's interior, then lifted himself a little farther. Nezeru did her best to move with him.

They inched upward this way for what seemed the better part of an hour, stopping after each movement to listen for noises beyond their woody prison. At last Morgan could see a wash of blue moonlight on Nezeru's pale face and knew they were near the top. He was exhausted, his legs trembling and aching.

Nezeru looked around quickly, then grabbed the ragged top of the dead trunk and dragged herself out of it and onto one of the yew's still-living branches. She helped him until they were both sitting side by side on a heavy branch.

"Are you strong enough to climb?" she asked.

"Climb?" His limbs were all a-quiver.

"It was your idea, mortal. We do not want to travel across the ground where the Sacrifices might see us or come across our tracks. And we cannot sit here in plain view. So it is time to climb—first to that wide-spreading tree there, I think."

And without waiting to hear his reply, she scrambled along the length of the branch like a squirrel—or a Chikri, Morgan could not help thinking—and then leaped to another good-sized branch on an oak whose boughs almost reached the yew tree's. Morgan took a deep breath, made the sign of the Tree, and then jumped after her. It was not far, but only his months of climbing allowed him to reach it without an embarrassing and perhaps dangerous fall; he had to cling to the branch with both arms until he could get a leg up onto it.

"You climb like a bear cub," she said, then began to make her way through the spreading oak. Morgan sighed and followed her.

They continued moving from tree to tree through the middle hours of the night. When a weary Morgan sometimes grew careless, Nezeru let him know it without ever raising her voice, goading him on until they had put at least half a league between themselves and the ruins of Reaching Hand Tower. When she decided they were finally safe from Sacrifice patrols, she waited for Morgan to catch up, then pointed down to a rocky outcrop that reminded him of the place he had first encountered ReeRee.

"There is a hole in it," she whispered. "Perhaps big enough for us to take shelter."

"Big enough for snakes," he said, though it was too dark for him to make out anything much. "Or leopards."

"There are no leopards in this forest," she said. "Nor anywhere north of the great southern desert. I have never been here before, but I know that. What do they teach you in your mortal cities?"

"What makes you think I was listening to my tutors?" he said, but his irritation was eased by the idea that they might finally get to rest. He followed her, but one of his feet slipped several times on the way down. When he reached the ground he sat on a bulging root and quickly discovered the reason.

"I've lost one of my climbing irons!" He stood. "I have to go back and find it."

"You would be a fool," she said. "Unless you know where it fell."

He shook his head. "No. I only just noticed."

"Enough, then. Forget it. Let us have a look at this hole—or cave. I am very hungry."

Morgan allowed her to lead him through to the outcrop. Nezeru, who he knew had better eyes than he, got down on hands and knees and peered in. "Something was here once," she said. "But not for some time, I think." She crawled in.

Morgan was relieved to discover that the crevice was larger than it had seemed from the outside, high enough that he could sit up if he bent a bit. He could see nothing except a patch of dark blue night sky at the top of the opening. He spread his cloak out on the ground, preparing to lie down and sleep. Then he felt a cool hand on his neck.

"You are thoughtful," she said. "I would not have believed it of a mortal."

"Huh?" It was not one of his wittier responses, but he had left his wits far behind, somewhere near the outskirts of Da'ai Chikiza. "Thoughtful?"

"I would have laid myself down on the ground without a thought. We are trained that way. But if we are to feed my hunger, this is better."

He was still trying to catch up. He wanted to eat something, but at this moment he wanted to sleep more. If she wanted to share the blanket, he would not object, but he hoped she would sleep without too much thrashing. It had been a confusing day and he could barely think. He was about to explain this to her when he felt her hand slide down the side of his chest until she reached the laces of his breeks and began untying them.

"What are you doing?" he asked, although even in his weariness that seemed fairly clear.

"I told you—I am hungry. Your kissing and your rubbing have given me a fierce, fierce appetite." He heard her shucking off her clothes, the dull clack as she tossed aside her armor. A moment later she was finishing with the ties of his breeks.

Traveling with a mortal enemy was turning out to be more complicated and unpredictable than Morgan would have ever guessed, but as Nezeru pushed herself against him and he felt the smooth coolness of her flesh against his side, he began to feel less tired.

"Ah," she said. "So not all mortals flee from the touch of a Hikeda'ya woman."

"Don't handle me so roughly," he said, wincing. "You have already convinced me."

She went about it at first with a military stiffness that might have been learned from a master-of-arms instead of a lover—and perhaps it had been, he thought—but soon began to find her own way, accommodating herself to him with what seemed like genuine enjoyment. She was only a pale, moving shape, sometimes below him, sometimes above him, and he found it easy to forget who she was and who he was.

After their coupling was completed and they both lay gasping, damp with perspiration in the close confines of their hiding place, she insisted on trying it again—two more times. At the end, when they lay tangled together in such a muddle of naked limbs that an exhausted Morgan could barely tell in the dark where he left off and Nezeru began, she kissed him one last time, a soft and lengthy exploration that she ended with what seemed like reluctance.

"It has been," she said—very quietly, perhaps because she spoke to herself or because she feared that Sacrifice troops might still be somewhere nearby—"a very interesting day."

Morgan would have agreed if he had the strength. Instead, he fell asleep a scant few moments later with his head upon her breast and the soft murmur of her heart against his ear.

Qina made them stop so Tipalak could graze on the sparse grasses. The most recent snowfall had all but melted, and the ram happily picked among the few remaining white patches. Falku, Snenneq's larger mount, never missed an opportunity to fill his stomach, and was ripping yellow grass from the ground before he had even dismounted.

He made his way to where Qina still sat on Tipalak's back. She let him approach, struggling with an anger that she knew was not really her betrothed's fault.

"Why do you give me those dark, unhappy eyes?" he asked with more than a touch of complaint. "They are like pissholes in the snow."

"As usual, you know how to use flattery to reach a woman's heart."

His smile was cursory. "I did not mean it, dear one—not quite—but you look at me as though you wish you could set me on fire."

"We have searched for days, Snenneq! We have walked far around the outskirts of this old Sithi city, hiding from Norn sentries and almost caught more times than I can count. When do we admit that we will not find Morgan here?

If he is in the ruined city itself, we cannot reach him—not with so many enemies there. And we have been through the woods from one end to another without seeing any more trace of him."

"But you were the one who said we must search for him!"

"No, I was the one who said we should take the news of what happened here south. You were the one who said we could not leave poor Prince Morgan alone."

"But how can we? He has no one else to care for him, no one else to help him."

Qina took a deep breath. "You are clever and strong, my dear Snenneq. No one could think more of you than me—not even yourself, and that is saying something. But you are as stubborn as a sledge-ram with scald in its hoof. When you set your mind to something you will not be pushed or pulled away from it, even when it is clear it will not work. You think that you and Morgan are destined to be companions, like my father and his friend King Simon. That is well and good, but you cannot ignore all else."

Little Snenneq tossed aside the stick and appeared ready to say something truly unpleasant. Qina felt her eyes well with tears, though she felt more anger than sadness. A moment later, though, Snenneq's round face turned sorrowful.

"I *am* stubborn. You are right, as you often are," he said.

"As I always am," she replied, but softened her voice to make it more of a jest. It was a rare man, she thought, among her own people or any other, who would ever admit his own mistakes. "You know many things I do not, beloved, but you live on the mountain of Might-Be, as my father likes to say. I am down here in the valley of Must-Be."

He helped her off Tipalak's broad back and they sat down on the ground, facing each other. "What do you propose?" he asked.

"I wish I had something to propose. I only know we cannot go on this way, hiding from our enemies but staying near them, all in the very thin hope of discovering Morgan. And we saw the great Norn army heading south—where my mother and father went."

"So you wish to go south, to Erchester and the castle?"

"I wish to go home." She held up her hand before he could protest. "I know that we cannot—not yet. We have made promises, some spoken, some only understood. But, in truth, what is all this to us? We were on our nuptial journey, but somehow instead found ourselves in the middle of a war. Yes, I wish with everything in me that we could turn our heads back toward Yiqanuc, that we could ride our rams home to beautiful, tall Mintahoq and have the life I wanted." She shook her head. "But that would be a betrayal of what we set out to do here. Also, I cannot go home without knowing that my mother and father are safe."

"Of course." Snenneq's brow wrinkled in thought. "Very well. I will offer you a proposal."

"You already did that. That is why I am in such a situation. I do not think Yutu, the jacket-maker's son, would have led me so far from home."

He winced. "Ugly Yutu. He did not deserve you, and your parents never liked him. But if you wish to wound me, I will be forced to remind you that there were many others beside you who would have been proud to call Little Snenneq their 'nukapik.'"

She laughed, genuinely amused. "Skinny Merewa? The one who looks like a bundle of sticks? Good luck staying warm at night with her sharing your cave."

Snenneq swallowed another retort. "Let us declare a truce. And let me make a proposal—no, a *suggestion*."

"Go on."

"We have not gone all the length of the city. Most of the ruins at this northern end are gone, lost in a flood—you have seen the great stones in the river—but we may still go a little farther before we have looked at all ways in and out of the city. Let us ride a little farther north, past the last gates of the city, and if we still find no trace of Morgan there, then we will follow your parents south."

It was what she wanted, but it still felt like defeat—like giving up. "What else can we do?" she said at last.

"Hope," he said. "So join me for a little while, my love, on the mountain of Might-Be."

Later that day they covered much of the area Snenneq had suggested without learning anything new. In the cool, wintry air, both rams and riders were growing thirsty.

"Let us take them down to the river," Qina suggested. "We should be far enough beyond any sentries for it to be safe."

They had gone scarcely a hundred ells down the slope toward the river when Snenneq's huge ram balked, shaking his head, his nostrils huffing air. Qina's own mount would not pass him.

"He is frightened of something," she said.

"Nothing frightens Falku!" But Snenneq looked concerned. They tied the rams to a tree in a deep thicket and crept down the slope in cautious silence. Near the bottom, Snenneq put his hand on Qina's back. "Down," he whispered.

"Do you see something?"

"Hush." When they were both on their hands and knees they crawled forward down the slope until they could see the bend of T'si Suhyasei gleaming like old silver. They moved to a great oak with roots knee-high above the ground—knee-high for trolls, at least—and peered carefully over them.

Below them, something was digging at the mire close to the river's edge. They could see bits of mud being flung into the air. But nothing visible was doing the digging.

"What is it?" Qina whispered.

"I am not sure," Snenneq said. "We watch."

Within moments something appeared from the hole. At first Qina thought it was a rat or vole or some other burrowing creature, small and covered with mud. Then the thing turned back toward the hole and moments later several other small, soiled shapes followed it out onto the riverbank. Most of them crouched, but some actually stood upright, and what she saw made Qina gape. Some of the little creatures were wearing what looked like bits of ragged clothing.

"Qinkipa of the snows, are those *boghanik*?" she said in a small, shocked voice. "Do I truly see them?"

Snenneq covered his mouth with his hand, suggesting silence. Qina, who had never encountered *boghaniki* before, realized he was right to be cautious, because it soon became clear that there were more than a few. The tiny, man-like creatures that the mortals called *bukken* or sometimes "dirt goblins" were swarming out of the hole now. The hollow in the soft riverside mud became a little wider each time another group emerged, until it was as wide as the mouth of a large cooking-pot. The manlike creatures swarmed along the riverbank, and to judge by the chittering sounds they made, which were almost too high-pitched for Qina to hear, they were having a fierce argument.

As she watched she felt a wave of revulsion pass through her. It was not that they were small, ugly, and dirty that disturbed her so, although they were all those things. It was not even their history of swarming to attack and kill human travelers. Rather it was how much like people they were, with hands, feet, and even bits of tattered clothing visible beneath the muck. A few held weapons, crude spears made of sticks and stone chips. Some were so much smaller than the others that she could not doubt they were females or perhaps even children.

As she watched, one of the *boghaniki* turned to look up the hill toward the place where she and Snenneq hid. She could see the glitter of eyes in the grimy, tangled mat of hair and beard, and unlike the other goblins, this creature held a long metal blade clutched in its arms, something that looked like the corroded remains of a dagger.

Snenneq tapped her on the arm, then made a motion to indicate they should retreat. They did, crawling slowly back up the slope. Every moment Qina thought to hear the skitter of tiny feet behind her, or a shrill squeak as one of them spotted the trolls and raised the alarm, but she heard neither. After long, fearful moments they were back in the thicket with Falku and Tipalak.

"What are they doing here?" she demanded quietly as they untethered the rams. "They never leave the north." She knew that the *boghaniki* had been driven away from the borders of their own land, Yiqanuc, many centuries earlier, in a famous struggle the trolls called "The Battle of the Hollows." They were now remembered mainly in cautionary tales that Qanuc parents told to straying youngsters.

Snenneq nodded but did not reply until they were back on their rams and had traveled some distance up from the riverside. "Kuyu-kun, the Voice of the

Dreaming Sea, spoke to us of dreams that had troubled all his changeling people, remember? That they had been called here for the end of everything."

"Yes, but his people are Tinukeda'ya."

"I am beginning to wonder how many creatures are *not* Tinukeda'ya," he said. "Remember the ghant? And we saw kilpa in the river too, headed north like Kuyu-kun and his delvers. Kilpa are utterly unknown in this area—but now they are here. All drawn, it seems, by the same thing.

"So you think that the dreams Kuyu-kun spoke of have called these goblins, too? But that would mean . . ."

"That they, too, are Tinukeda'ya." He shook his head. "It is all more than I can understand. How I wish your father were here!"

"No more than I do." She guided her ram toward a line of tall old trees that crowned the top of the gentle slope. "I am wondering whether we should turn back now and get as far from this place as possible. From the old tales, those nasty things can appear anywhere, especially if they hear footsteps on the ground above them."

"More even than your father's presence," Snenneq said, "I am wishing we had his wolf Vaqana with us. My Falku is brave and loyal, but he would not be much use against *boghaniki*, except perhaps to fall on some and crush them. But Vaqana would make short work of that entire troop, I think, and enjoy it greatly."

"Perhaps," she said, "but that is . . ."

He waited for her to finish, but she remained silent as their mounts made their way upslope toward the line of tall trees. "Qina?" he asked at last.

"I see something." She slipped down from her ram's woolly back, then went forward on foot. When she reached the nearest trees, she bent and plucked something out of the underbrush before turning to hurry back toward Snenneq. "I saw it shine," she said, handing it to him.

Snenneq lifted the bits of metal tied with leather thongs and held it up to catch the fading daylight. "Daughter of the Mountains!" he breathed. "Qina, you have the eyes of a snow-owl! You are a prize beyond measure!"

"Your flattery is improving," she said drily, but in truth she was flushed with pleasure. "It is Morgan's, is it not? The ice-shoe you made for him?"

"It is, so it is!" He turned to her with a wide grin. "He has been here!"

"Yes—but going which direction? Toward the old city, or away from it?"

"We will know that only when we have climbed some trees," he said. "He was not wearing it for walking on ice, that is plain. It could be he has been climbing trees, as we saw before. We need only find which trees and follow the marks—the likelihood is that he approached them always from the same direction, so the marks of these blades should show us his direction." He rubbed the mud off the ice-shoe, then dropped it into his bag. "Will he not be surprised when I hand it back to him?"

Qina thought this was perhaps looking a little too far ahead, but she could not help feeling relieved. They still knew little about where Morgan was or what he might be doing, but at least they had something now besides questions. "I do not have the strength to climb any trees now," she said. "Let us find a place to rest. I do not want to be stumbling around these woods in the dark with Norns and goblins and only all-seeing Sedda-knows-what-else roaming around."

For a moment, Snenneq looked as though he wanted to argue, but then he nodded. "Your sharp eyes have brought us the first hope in days. And what you say has sense. We will do as you suggest."

"Now you are learning how to be a proper *nukapik*," she said, squeezing his hand.

24

Breaking the Seal

For a very long time he did not know who he was, or where he was, or whether he was anywhere at all.

A field of inconstant, shimmering light stretched before him, and above it hung an endless mist of gray. It was only after an indefinable length of time had passed that he realized he was looking out across a great expanse of water. It should have been familiar—he could feel that—but it was not. He watched it apprehensively, still without a name of his own, still without any certainty about where he was or how he had come here.

He suspected he might have died.

Am I to cross all this water, then? It seemed impossible without a boat or bridge. *Is Heaven on the far side?* He had a powerful but inexplicable feeling that he hoped to see someone again, someone he loved and needed. *Is she waiting there, across this endless deep?* In that moment he conceived of a God that had brought him here, and wondered, *But why would He leave me without word, without understanding? Why would He leave me alone?*

You are not alone. The voice spoke in his thoughts, but if it was God, then He was a She. *Look down.*

He looked down. Earthly reflex, still strong, expected to see legs and feet beneath him, holding him up, but instead he saw only that which lay beneath him, a shining, polished sweep of amber-colored wood, shot through with streaks of gleaming gray. It seemed clearly something made, not grown.

Turn, now, the voice directed him.

He turned, not as a creature with a body would turn, in an ordered movement of limbs, but as a flame would turn with its wick when the candle was moved. Before him loomed a gate unlike anything he had ever seen before, set into the face of a dark but not entirely substantial extent of stone. Two vast, curving lengths of the same golden-and-gray wood that stretched beneath him also marked the gate's dimensions, as if two recurved longbows stood side by side, leaning together at their top ends. Above this beautiful, monstrous arch—it seemed a hundred times his own height—the rocky wall rose until it met a great eruption of brilliant white stone looming against the gray sky. It seemed too large and too bright for his eyes to properly see or his mind to understand.

The Gate of the Fifth Ship, the voice in his thoughts said. *Made from two pieces of its great stern. Enter.*

He did, aware in a distant way that he was not walking but drifting along the jetty that stretched outward from the vast, shining arch. As he passed beneath the twin curves of amber and gray, he felt a shock of astonishment at the sheer size of them. If this was the gate of a castle, it was big enough for another, smaller castle to be dragged through it without touching either side.

Where am I? he asked.

In my dream, she said. *In my memories. Here were the moments of greatest beauty and greatest horror I ever knew.*

Beyond the immensity of the arch, he found himself in another astoundingly large space, and though he could never completely fix his gaze on anything around him, he perceived that he was inside a huge rectangular hall with immense staircases in each of its four corners, the farthest end so distant that he thought it would take a very long time to reach it. Figures moved all around him, the first signs of life beyond the voice that spoke to him, and though they seemed like familiar things—two arms and two legs, some hurrying, some standing in pairs or larger groups as if in conversation—each and every one of them was as translucent as a ghost from a midwinter tale, and all of them seemed to shudder in and out of fixity, as though seen through moving water.

The Hall of Five Staircases. The words came with a weight he had not felt before, heavy like a rain-sodden cloak. *Someone I love died here. See!*

As if his head turned by her command, his gaze shifted to the nearest staircase. A shadow lay across its lowest step. He could make out nothing beyond its rough shape, the limbs at strange angles, as if it had tumbled down from above. The shadowy figure also appeared black and twisted like something burned, and it sent a shiver of terror and loss through him to see it. *Who was it?* he asked.

I do not know, the voice said. *Only that she was important to me, and was felled by an arrow in the back—an arrow loosed not by enemies, but by her own kind.* He felt bitterness in the words. *Why can I so clearly remember the terror and infamy of it, the pain, but not her name?*

Can you remember anything else? he asked. *I can't remember my name, either.*

These are my memories, but they are incomplete—mere fragments. I think we may be somewhere that names are not allowed. Or at least where they are not easily gained or remembered.

But you have told me the names of the gate, the hall—

Yes, it is a mystery, was all she said. *I do not know the answer. Come up.*

He left the shadowy thing on the floor and drifted up the staircase as it angled along first one wall, then another, climbing toward the distant ceiling. He emerged through another arch, decorated with intricate carvings that blurred before his eyes, and onto another level place. But if the gate and the first hall had astonished him with their size, this new space made the others seem like something children had built in hopeless imitation. Though his memory was all clouds, he knew beyond doubt that he had never been inside anything so large—a massive circular hall as wide as a city, or so it appeared. It stretched so far above him that as he stared up at the fiery glint of light at its highest point, he thought the great rotunda must reach all the way to Heaven itself.

Or is this *Heaven?* he wondered.

That does not feel right, the voice told him, and he thought he heard—or at least felt—a dry laugh at the idea. *I believe it is the Hall of the Great Circle.*

He could not look away from the brightness above but could sense that he was now surrounded by people, or the shadows of people, though none seemed to take notice of him.

Why are you showing all this to me? he asked. *Why have you called me to this mad place?*

I did not call you. You are simply here with me, little spirit—that is all I know. Now, come. I am waiting for you on the Tan'ja Stairs.

The Tan'ja Stairs. He knew that name, though he could not say why. He saw only one stairway in that impossibly huge, cylindrical chamber, a great spiral that followed the outer wall upward, through tier after tier. As he moved toward it, he found his gaze drawn upward. The walls along each staircase tier were carved from beautiful white stone. Some had been shaped like frothing ocean waves; others like the eaves of forests, all the trees and undergrowth created with loving accuracy. But even in the forests of white stone, real plants and trees grew. Each tier was bursting with greenery, a spiral of living vegetation entwined with the marmoreal carvings, all rising together in a tightening spiral that closed at the top in a burst of light too bright for the eyes this dream had given him.

Heaven. A faint, faceless, and nameless memory of his lost love came to him again. *Does she wait for me there*? Even the idea of her, though without name or face, pierced him like a blade in his heart. *But I do not belong with God,* he said to the voice guiding him. *I do not belong there. I have failed all those I loved.*

You mean you lived, she told him. *Now, look, mortal. Here I am.*

And there, on the wide, bottommost step of the great stairway, he saw her at last, a shadow marginally more real than the others moving across the monstrous circular floor below. He had expected something grand, a glorious, angelic figure, but the shape that stood waiting for him was small and slender, wrapped in bands of what looked like cobwebs, though he could only glimpse them here or there, as if a faint light played across her and dispelled the shadows for mere instants at a time.

Ah. I know you, she said. *Or so I believe.*

I do not know you. But if you know me, tell me my name!

Again came the laugh, dry and dusty as an ancient book. *I told you, this is an untrustworthy realm for names. But I believe I met you in the old world, the solid place, where truth takes strange shapes. You are the mortal boy. You came to our home in the forest.*

Something drifted to him then, a blurry thought that might have been a memory—a glowing disk the color of an autumn moon; a kind voice; words that gave him hope in another time, when hope had been hard to find—and with that memory, a name returned. *Are you the one born on the ship?* he asked. *The one who lived in a hollow tree? She was kind to me.*

Ah! she said, and a shudder seemed to pass through her spectral form. *No, I am not her, but now I remember her. By the Garden, I loved her too, as I did the one who lies at the bottom of the stairs. Perhaps that is what this place is—a place for memories of love lost long ago to return. That would be good, I think. That would be enough.*

She turned back toward the rising steps, beckoning him to follow. They did not walk but floated up the stairs like tufts of thistledown, around and around the great atrium, ever higher above the vague, foggy gray below them. But if the floor receded, the shred of memory that had come to him did not, entwining inside him like a swirl of smoke, shifting, eddying. *That beautiful old woman. In the forest. Among the Fair Ones, the immortals.* He had stayed long with them, though it did not feel as if it had been by his own choice. He had stayed with them until . . . until something terrible had happened.

They killed her, he said suddenly, or thought it. In either case, his spectral companion heard him.

Yes, she said. *I feel that too. The one with the silver mask reached out into our home and killed her.*

Fire. Fire and shouting and arrows. And hounds baying. As it came back to him, something tore through his thoughts and left anger and sorrow behind. First Grandmother had been kind to him. She had been ancient, so old that she had been born before the great ship at last came to rest. The Ship-Born, they had called her.

First Grandmother. As he said it, he knew it was true. *The Fair Ones called her First Grandmother.*

The shape beside him stopped, billowing like a filmy scarf in the breeze. For a moment he thought she would do something terrible to him for saying the name, strike him or dismiss him from this place. But when she spoke, she sounded relieved.

First Grandmother. Yes. My father's mother. And it was my mother who died in the Hall of Five Staircases. For a moment he thought he saw a hint of his companion's face beneath the cobwebs and shadows, features proud and fierce, eyes gleaming like those of a hunting cat in the night. *But I still cannot remember their names. I cannot even recall my own name. It is hidden from me.*

A moment passed in the timeless silence, then he heard or felt her say, *But I thank you, mortal child. You have given me back a little of what I had.*

But I don't remember anything of my own, he told her. He was nothing but a phantom—a lost, wandering soul. *All I remember is that I had everything—and then I lost it.*

Brother Etan watched in silent horror as the killing went on and on, not guessing that the worst was yet to come.

Philosophers and poets had likened a battlefield to Hell itself so many times that it had become a mere platitude, but he could think of no other comparison. All across the slope below Winstowe Castle and along the broad ditch that surrounded the curtain wall, men murdered each other in a hundred different, terrible ways. He heard the screaming of the wounded, both men and animals, saw bloody soldiers staggering with missing arms or other dreadful wounds, and was all but deafened by the clamor of men shouting in desperate rage and the clash of metal on metal. Even his nostrils were filled by the commingled smells of war, of blood and human waste, of iron, salt, and shit.

As the sun rose higher, Etan caught occasional glimpses of King Simon in his bright armor, wielding his sword like a hero on a tapestry come to life, scattering Unver's men, riding them down. Then the fighting would close around the king again, like fog shrouding a mountain peak.

As the battle dragged on, Brother Etan began to see patterns in the fighting, subtle as the way stones on a riverbed shaped the current on the surface. Unver Shan kept sending in his supposedly uncontrollable warriors from different angles, as if he were playing a game of *Kunsbort*—King's Table. A hundred grasslanders would sweep in to engage with the Erkynlanders; then, just as both sides began to tire, the clansmen would fall back and another force of Thrithings-men would charge in from another angle, forcing the Erkynlanders to turn and fight again without a chance to rest.

The battle roared on, surging here, falling apart there, active and unpredictable as a living thing—which, Etan thought woefully, in a way it was, and bigger than any of its combatants.

He felt rather than saw the change that took place shortly before the midmorning bell rang high in the castle's tower: the cries of the fighters lost some of their individuality and rose together in waves of excitement, and the knots of struggling warriors began to move toward the center. But it was only when a circle formed in the middle of the battle around two mounted men that he understood what was happening.

"The king!" someone shouted. "The king and the Shan go against each other!"

Startled, Etan picked out the tall figure of King Simon, and thought Simon's dark-cloaked opponent must be the grasslands' new chieftain. It was hard to see with so many men rushing forward to watch, as if the slaughter had abruptly turned into something more like a tournament, but even Etan knew that this was more deadly than even the wildest mêlée. If either Simon or the Shan fell, the winner's men would sweep in and do their best to put the loser's army to flight. The battle, after hours of blood and horror, now swayed in the balance, the fate of uncountable thousands to be decided by the strength of two men's arms.

Forgetting his own safety now, Etan pushed forward with the rest of the Erkynlandish camp—grooms, pages, camp followers, and cooks—but the crowd around the two warriors was so thick that even from the hill above the battlefield, he could barely make things out. Each time something important happened, Etan tried to guess which side was cheering loudest, but the fighters were so close together and the tumult so overwhelming, it was impossible to be certain of anything.

Then, as the last of the morning mist burned away beneath the climbing sun, a series of heavy blows that Etan could hear but not see suddenly stopped, and in the silence he heard cries of alarm. Now someone new was riding across the field toward the place where the king and Shan fought, waving something—a sword. The slender figure flung the blade to one of the opponents, but Etan could not see which one. As he jumped up and down, struggling desperately to discover what was happening, a huge groan swept through the crowd, rippling outward.

"The king!" someone cried in astonishment and fear. "King Simon is down!"

"The barbarian has killed the king!" shouted another. "God curse them all!"

"Everything is lost! The king is dead!"

The chaos at the center of the field abruptly resolved into broad movements, Erkynlandish knights rushing forward to surround King Simon, the Thrithings-men, instead of pushing their advantage, drawing back as though from a grisly accident. Etan thought he saw Unver Shan, still standing, trying to wave his men back, and though it made no sense, that was exactly what seemed to happen. As the grasslanders withdrew, Erkynlandish knights came down from their horses and bent over what must be the body of the king.

As if some other spirit animated him, he found himself running across the field, holding his wooden Tree high in the air as he cried, "Let me through! Let me through in God's name!"

Later, he could not remember anything about his trip across the muddy, bloody field, though he must have passed hundreds of people, many of them Thrithings-folk who cared little for the Tree of the Aedon and could easily have spitted him with sword or spear. But the grasslanders seemed almost as confused as the Erkynlanders. Still shouting God's name, Etan pushed his way into the circle of men and horses that had formed around King Simon.

"He does not need you, monk!" said a knight as Etan struggled past. The man's gauntlets were covered with blood. "The chaplain is saying the *Mansa*."

And indeed, a priest in a clean white robe had already knelt beside the king. Simon's face was turned to one side, but his skin was so wan and white that Etan's heart lurched.

The chaplain broke off his prayer as Etan pushed his way through the last of the surrounding knights and threw himself beside the king's body. "What are you doing, Brother?" the startled priest demanded.

"Have you even looked to see if he is breathing?"

The chaplain ignored him, beginning the ritual again, but Etan leaned forward to tug a knife out of its sheath on the king's belt. Several knights and other soldiers reached down to restrain him, but at least one of the nobles recognized what he was doing and called for the others to let him alone.

Etan gave the knife a quick swipe on his own cassock, then held it before the king's pale, bluish lips. He lifted it to look at it and saw nothing but wiped it again and this time held it for a longer moment. When he pulled it away once more, he saw a film of vapor that swiftly vanished.

"He lives!" said Etan. "He is breathing, but only just." He stared down. The king had several minor wounds on his arms and legs, but his dangling breastplate and mail, though both were damaged in several places, showed no blood. "What happened to him?"

The nobleman who had protected Etan from the others said, "His Majesty was struck down by Unver Shan. The savage stabbed him to the heart, and he fell."

Etan saw the striding badger on the noble's surcoat and knew this must be Baron Snell, one of King Simon's most loyal allies. "There is no deadly wound, my lord. I see nothing. Please, take off his helmet."

The first knights at his side had opened the king's visor, but now they removed his casque entirely. Etan checked Simon's damp red and gray mop of hair but found no wound there either. "He is not pierced. He has had an *apoplexis*. He may yet live."

Baron Snell stood and cried, "Bring a litter. We must take His Majesty back to Winstowe!"

"No!" cried Etan, and the men all turned to look at him, as if a dog had suddenly begun human speech. "No. He must have better help than any they can give him there. You must hurry the king back to the Hayholt. Only Lord Tiamak and his wife can save him. I swear to you it is true. I am their helper and I know."

"It is two days' journey, even on fast horses," said Snell in amazement and anger. "How can he survive that?"

"Don't be foolish—it is the only way he *will* survive." Etan had never spoken to a noble that way in his life, but in that moment he felt only desperation to save the king. "Lord Tiamak can save him. No one else but God can. I swear on my immortal soul it is true!"

Baron Snell scowled, but he was thinking. Several men ran up with a litter and began to lift the king's apparently lifeless body onto it. "We need Count Aglaf's fastest carriage," the baron said. "Hitch a team of four strong horses and send the king back to the Hayholt with an escort of Erkynguards. Hurry! His life may yet be saved!"

Etan sank back on his heels as Simon's limp form was lifted onto the litter. Four large soldiers hurried it back toward the camp as others raced toward the castle to get Count Aglaf's carriage.

But to the monk's great distress, when the carriage rolled out of the gate, several knights insisted on accompanying the king's insensible body. Though Etan protested that he could help care for Simon, in fact might be essential to keeping the king alive, he was not granted a place and could only sit and watch forlornly as the team was whipped to speed and disappeared along the road toward Erchester.

Disconsolate, Brother Etan sat in the remains of the Erkynlandish camp, head in hands. The battle, which only an hour or so earlier had been at its bloody height, had now apparently ended. The Thrithings-men under the Shan had retreated to their own camps along the riverbank, and even seemed to be preparing to withdraw. Winstowe's defenders still lined the castle walls, but no more arrows were loosed.

Etan felt for the letter in his pocket. What was the point of his errand now? The king was dying, and if he lived, he would be reunited with Tiamak, who could presumably tell him whatever had been written in it. *If you cannot deliver it*, Tiamak had told him, *it must be destroyed.* Etan got up, the letter now clutched in his hand, and walked toward the nearest campfire as Erkynguards trudged past him, carrying away the important dead or groaning wounded on makeshift litters. He reached the fire, where he was regarded without interest by a foot soldier still bleeding from a wound on his head, eyes as seemingly lifeless as Simon's had been.

"Can I do anything for you, man?" Etan asked. The soldier only stared at him.

Brother Etan held the letter over the fire, staring distractedly at Tiamak's seal on the wax. Then, in a moment of indecision, he turned away from the flames. It was a crime against Tiamak to read a letter meant for the king—in fact, it was a crime against the king himself, and a grave one. But to simply consign it to the flames seemed senseless. He felt hollow, except for a nagging, painful belief that he had not done enough, that he had failed his mission. He knew he could have slipped the message into Simon's tunic in case the king woke, but then someone else might have taken it, something Tiamak had been utterly clear should not happen.

Brother Etan had walked a short distance from the campfire and the wounded soldier, but now he stopped, hesitating. Was he really thinking of opening a letter meant for the king's eyes only—a letter entrusted to him by his friend and mentor Lord Tiamak? He could not help remembering the last time he had looked at something forbidden. The memory of finding Bishop Fortis's cursed book, the *Aetheric Whispers*, still haunted both his waking and dreaming hours. But things had changed so much since that day, and all which had seemed true had turned upside down in the last few months.

He moved to an isolated part of the hillside; then, in a fit of frightened resolution, he broke the seal. He read the words Tiamak had written, then read them again to make sure he had understood them, but no amount of re-reading changed the import.

"God the Father and Aedon the Son, watch over me now," he murmured, then made the sign of the Tree on his breast, turned, and began walking across the field toward the Thrithings camp.

"But why should we retreat now?" Fremur demanded. He had never spoken so brusquely to Unver, but nothing about the day's events made sense to him.

"You have killed the king of Erkynland! I know I was one of those who doubted the wisdom of this fight, but I was wrong. And it was you who said we should never again strike and flee, as our fathers and grandfathers did, but instead show the stone-dwellers that we are more than that. So why retreat?"

Odobreg and the other chieftains nodded, though none dared to speak up as Fremur had. Like him, they had all worried about continuing the siege, but now saw the prospect of rich plunder lying open before them. "Fremur speaks the truth," said Odobreg. "This retreat does not seem wise, great Shan. Especially now that you have killed the Erkynlanders' king in a fair fight."

"I did nothing!"

Fremur wondered at the anger in Unver's words.

"I did not touch him after he dropped to his knees. As I stood over him, he fell—god-struck, as though I had stabbed him!"

"It matters not," said Vorzheva, whose presence disturbed the thanes, but who was generally given much latitude by Unver, and took advantage of it. "He and his wife and nobles stole the throne from you. Now is the time to take it back."

Unver turned toward her. Now his anger was fronted with a grin of disbelieving mockery. "What now, my lady? This is a new tale from you. Stole the throne of Erkynland?"

"Your father defeated his brother, the mad king Elias. I know—I was there." Her own fury seemed to mount, matching Unver's. "The throne should have been his, but instead it was given by that beast Isgrimnur and the others to the callow boy you just killed. They even married him to Elias' daughter to make the barons happy. The throne was stolen. It should have been ours!"

"Ah." Unver scraped at the ground with the tip of his father's sword, which he still held. "It should have been ours? It sounds to me as though your ambition outstripped my father's, Lady."

"I am still your mother. Speak to me with respect."

He looked at her for a long, silent moment. "All of this is nothing to do with where we stand. Even if I were to covet Erkynland's crown—which I do not—it would take a long, deadly campaign to claim it. As you saw, we would have to teach our men how to fight stone-dweller wars, because that is the only way to defeat them."

"They are soft," said Thane Etvin.

"Perhaps," said Unver. "But their castles are hard, and our siege-craft is like that of children. Do you know how many men we lost to stones thrown down from the walls by their engines? Dozens—a hundred or more!—and each one leaves mourners behind. We could never have taken this castle. We do not have the experience or the tools. And before we attack stone-dweller lands again, we must learn those ways of fighting." He shook his head. "No, we came to avenge an insult, and we have more than succeeded. The city-folk will fear us now in a way they have not for a long time."

"Avenge an insult?" Vorzheva spoke in a whisper so harsh it seemed louder than her earlier words. "Is that what you call it? The stone-dweller Eolair tried to kill me, and nearly killed my sister, Hyara. She is still weak and cannot walk!"

Fremur felt a twinge of fear at Vorzheva's words. He had thought Hyara was almost healed. Was the Shan's mother only trying to push Unver in the direction she wished him to go, or had Hyara, who had become dear to Fremur, truly grown worse?

"We will speak about that another time," said Unver slowly. "Just you and I, my lady. It is a conversation I have been putting off until the siege was over." He turned from her, leaving Vorzheva looking surprised. "Where is Volfrag? The Blessing of the Horses must be given before we leave. We should also send some kind of terms to the Erkynlanders, or it will seem as though we are indeed retreating from a lost battle."

"Terms?" Odobreg was confused.

"That is the way the stone-dwellers do things," Unver replied. "We will send them a written message to say we have achieved our ends, avenged our slights, but will come back if we are mistreated again."

Fremur was frustrated. "Unver, will they not see that as a sign of weakness?"

But Unver was looking past him, to the field that had so recently been full of death and dying. "Who is that? Is he a madman?"

Fremur followed his gaze. A man in a dun-colored monk's habit had been caught by some of the clansmen on the outskirts of their camp. He was struggling and, as Fremur watched, one of his captors gave him a cuff on the head.

"Go and rescue him, Fremur," said the Shan. "He may bear a message from the castle's defenders."

Fremur had soon retrieved the short, stocky young monk from his tormentors and escorted him back to Unver's campfire. Itinerant monks were not unknown on the Thrithings, but they were not protected as they were in the towns and cities, and Fremur had never been so close to one before. He seemed clean, which refuted one tale told about them on the grasslands, but he also kept saying that he had to speak to the Shan, which suggested that either he truly did have a mission from the castle's defenders or he was not very sound of mind.

"Tell him your words straightly and do not waste the Shan's time," Fremur warned him. "He is a lord of the grasslands, powerful as any king."

The monk only nodded.

When they reached the Shan, the monk spoke clearly and simply, though Fremur could see the man was trembling. "I am Brother Etan, of St. Sutrin's in Erchester. Lord Tiamak, King Simon's counselor, gave me this letter to carry." He held it out for Unver to see.

"The seal is broken," said Unver in a flat voice.

"It was not meant for you, but for King Simon," the monk explained, but his trembling increased. "I was told to give it to him or destroy it, but then the king was . . ." he stared at the ground for a moment, working up his courage. "The king was struck down with an apoplexy in the middle of battle—as you know."

"That does not explain why the seal is broken," Unver said, still without a trace of human feeling in his voice.

The monk colored, cheeks and throat going red. "With the king ill and perhaps dying . . . well, I took it upon myself to decide whether to destroy it or not."

"And?"

"And I am giving it to you." He held out the folded parchment. "Take it, please, Unver Shan."

Unver reached out. All his thanes watched as he slowly read it. When he had finished, he looked up at the monk. "And what do you want me to do with it?"

The monk let out a pent-up breath. "Whatever you think fit, my lord. I ask you only to remember that you hold my life in your hand. Should you hand it over to the nobles of Erkynland, I would doubtless go straight to the headsman's block for the treason of reading it, by my gentle God—let alone for giving it to you!" He bowed his head. "But I did what I think is right."

Unver put the letter into the purse on his belt. "And what reward do you seek, priest?"

"I am a monk, only, my lord—a humble monk. And I seek no reward except peace between our peoples."

"That is a steep price for your reward, do you not think?"

"No price for peace is too great for men of good hearts," said Brother Etan.

Unver turned to Fremur. "See that this man crosses the field safely, back to his own side. He is not to be harmed by any of ours."

"Of course, Unver Shan." But Fremur was puzzled, and from their expressions, he could tell Vorzheva and the thanes were bewildered too. Still, he had learned to trust Unver's strange ways, and Odobreg and the others would also continue to follow him, no matter how little they understood his thoughts. If the gods themselves had made Unver the Shan and given him this great victory, then mere mortals must abide by his seeming whims.

It took Etan three and a half long days to get back to the Hayholt, slowed by returning his borrowed horse and retrieving Scand the donkey, who seemed to prefer his new home. At last, he made his way up the long, hilly road until he saw the rooftops of Erchester and the spire of St. Sutrin's in the distance.

I have done what I could—what I thought best. Why do I feel that I have betrayed something—perhaps everything?

When he reached the Hayholt, he soon discovered two terrible things that made him even more uncertain about his own choices.

King Simon was dead. Etan guessed it even before he had gone much past the Nearulagh Gate—people were weeping and draping black bunting and ribbons everywhere. More surprising and far more frightening, Lord Tiamak and his wife, Lady Thelía were both gone, vanished from the castle with most of their possessions left behind, and both were under suspicion of poisoning the Lord Almoner, Bishop Boez.

"Captain Zakiel and Lord Pasevalles are looking for you," a guard at the castle stables told him when he returned Scand the donkey. The helmeted guard stared at Etan with what the monk thought was open suspicion. "They have questions for you, Brother—perilous questions. It might go better for you, I'm guessing, if you went straight to see them. This very moment."

Oh, my good Lord, Etan prayed as he trudged toward the residence, *watch over our Erkynland, because I fear the days of darkness have fallen upon us all.*

25

The Cursed Air

It was one thing to decide to try again to murder the oldest living creature in the world. Finding the right place to do it was another.

Jarnulf rode south day and night for many leagues, and at last caught up with the Norn army in the hills at the southern edge of the Wealdhelm. As soon as he saw their columns marching silently through the darkness ahead of him, he turned aside into the forested hills beside the road and passed at a distance that he hoped would prevent even their sharpest scouts from scenting or hearing him. He was light-headed and muddled from lack of sleep as he led his stolen mount through the woods, grateful for its soft-footed, Hikeda'ya-bred stealth, though he still missed his own horse.

The Norn-girl Nezeru does not know what a gift I gave her. I pray she has taken good care of my poor Salt. That animal carried me faithfully for years after I took him from his dead master. And that was not all I took after I killed him. He was suddenly overwhelmed with remorse and sorrow. *Oh, God, my Father, I have done it all for Your glory and the defense of Your people. I have tried always to serve You. I pray You still think me worthy to complete my quest.*

Autumn had turned bleak. Even the hilly lower reaches of the Wealdhelm were powdered with snow. The sky was mostly a memory—even when the sun shone, the air was full of low, thick clouds, as if the world were trying to hide itself from some celestial hunter. Jarnulf was inured to cold by his upbringing, and the Nakkiga horse had also been raised in a chillier place than any Erkynland could provide, but Jarnulf still shivered as he rode. The longer he was forced to wait, the more impossible his task seemed, and his shameful failure at Naglimund still whispered to him during the dark nights, sucking away his strength more quickly and certainly than even the bitterest winds.

After a few days and many leagues spent searching through the hills, he found the spot he had been hoping for—the almost invisible ruins of an ancient hill fort on a high slope above the Wealdhelm Road, a circular array of crumbling walls only barely visible through waving grasses, wild rosebushes, and ivy. He guessed that he must now be about a day and a half ahead of Queen Utuk'ku's great army, which would give him time to prepare.

As Jarnulf led his horse upward beneath the shrouded late afternoon sun, through tangled trees and clinging thorns to the hillcrest and the center of the ruins, he wondered who had built the place and whether it had been the immortals or the first tribes of men who had labored here before Erkynland had its name. The size of the fallen stones showed that it must have dominated the lands beneath it. He could only pray that it would serve that purpose one more time, giving a defender—the defender of the entire mortal race, as Jarnulf considered himself—a chance to punish a deadly invader.

He found a gnarled fig tree growing out of one of the tumbled inner walls and tethered his horse to it, then followed the half-hidden stones until he found what appeared to be a perfect site overlooking the road. The slope beneath was steep: the distance to the ruts that marked the once-busy track beneath him was significantly less than two hundred paces. The surrounding hills were empty but for a herd of sheep a quarter of a league away to the south, gamely searching for grass between patches of snow. If the flock had a shepherd, Jarnulf could not see him. The wide road, built centuries earlier during the Second Nabbanai Imperium, had been empty all day, and he could see no sign of any of the farmers and fisher-folk who had lived nearby. The few cottages he had passed had been deserted. News of the advancing Norn army had obviously spread swiftly.

Jarnulf took his bow from its covering and warmed it with his hands, then strung it and loosed a few practice flights before scrambling down the hill to recover his arrows. The distance down to the road was at the outside range of his certainty, but he relied on God to keep his arms strong and his eye sharp.

He loosed shafts until his arms and back grew tired, trying to learn the winds along the hills, then clambered down again and gathered all of them up again, a little more confident now that he could hit his target with enough force to pierce any armor that the queen of Nakkiga might be wearing.

God only grant me my moment, he prayed. *Give me one clear shot, O my Ransomer, and I swear on my soul that this time I will not fail.*

He lit no fire, but instead made his evening meal from a handful of dried meat and a single wrinkled, undersized turnip he had kicked up in a fallow field; then he rolled himself in his cloak and bedded down near his tethered mount. As he lay waiting for sleep, he watched the stars, the gems on God's dark mantle, and tried not to think too much about the coming moment.

Jarnulf turned his mind instead to the things that had happened in the months since he had joined the Queen's Hand on their journey to Urmsheim—the storm of *Furi'a* in which he had found them, the immediate hatred their leader Makho had shown him, and most of all, the fury of Nezeru as he poked at the armor of her belief. It was not her resistance that puzzled him, but his own determination. Why had he spent so much time trying to convince a sworn enemy that she was wrong? What weakness in himself had led him to separate her from the others and tie her to his own mount to send her away? Even as Salt had thundered off with Nezeru tied to his back, Jarnulf had not entirely understood his own choices. Was it affection for her? Was it something like love?

No, he told himself. *It could not have been*. Just thinking of it, he felt a kind of revulsion, like a mother bird finding a cuckoo's child in her nest. No, he had no such soft feelings for the Hikeda'ya woman, nor ever had for any female, mortal or immortal. He was the Lord's weapon, forged by suffering and slavery and then honed to a deadly point, and that point was coming closer to its ultimate target every moment. The Norn army would travel through the night and rest their animals in daylight, since their creatures were not as tireless as the Hikeda'ya themselves. Soon, though, that great force would come down the road, and Jarnulf would be ready. He could not fail again.

His struggle with shame reminded him of a time when he had been someone else, someone with more certainty but without a holy purpose. As he drifted down into sleep, he remembered the night he had taken Salt from an enemy—the night his sacred quest had truly begun.

It was bitterly cold on the edge of the Nornlands—the coldest night he could remember. After years among mortals, most of them spent wandering errantly with the nameless once-priest he called Father, he had lost his mentor. Father had walked off one night into the dark and never returned. After weeks of searching for the older man, he had been forced to give up, and forced also to admit that his life was without purpose, animated only by rage against the creatures who had stolen Father's family and also his own—the corpse-skinned Hikeda'ya, who had raised him like an animal, but treated him with less kindness than they gave even to their hounds and horses.

Anger was all that he had left, and it had led him steadily through the cold, mostly empty lands of Rimmersgard, closer and closer to the borders of the place he hated so deeply that it never left his thoughts. He was untethered, blown like a leaf—a leaf that drifted ever northward.

He had learned to live off the land in the time he spend with Dyrmundur and the pagan outlaws of the Skalijar, *but even so the journey was a hard and hungry one, made worse because he knew that unless something changed, it must end for him in either death or a return to slavery. But Father had taught him that God did not make men without a purpose, and did not guide their steps without a destination.*

After weeks and weeks of solitary travel, he reached the borders of the Norn lands. When a Queen's Huntsman spotted his small fire during his first night back in the land of his birth, the armed rider's arrival seemed a sign from God Himself.

The huntsman was tall, the skin of his face burned brown by sunlight on snow, but even without the ruddy coloring, the young man crouched by the campfire would have known he was another mortal. Almost all the Queen's slave-hunters were men, and the rider's bulk and graceless way of moving—at least compared to the catlike Hikeda'ya—had proclaimed his race long before he lifted the visor of his helmet.

"Who are you to trespass in the queen's lands?" the rider demanded.

The youth's heart was beating fast, but he rose slowly and said in a voice as unconcerned as he could make it, "Who wants to know?"

The rider stared at him, then his mouth curled in an unpleasant smile. "Jarnulf am I named," he proclaimed. "Huntsman of Queen Utuk'ku. Answer me or I will spit you where you stand." He brandished his long lance. His white horse stood stock-still beneath him, but the muscles bunched beneath its birchbark-pale coat suggested it could move very swiftly when it wanted.

Despite his racing heart and his justified fear of this large, well-armed man, he could not help being amused at God's intention for him being shown so clearly and so quickly after he had reached Nakkiga's border. His younger brother's name had been Jarngrimnur, and Jarngrimnur's death had been one of the first tally-marks that the cruelty of the Hikeda'ya had made on his heart. He knew now what he must do with as much certainty as if the Blessed Aedon Himself had descended to whisper it in his ear.

"You are a traitor to your own people," he told the huntsman calmly. "Ask God for His forgiveness and perhaps He will welcome you into Heaven, because you will meet Him soon. My name is Gilhedur. I was born in a barn at White Snail Castle."

"So, as I guessed, you are a runaway slave," the huntsman said with heavy satisfaction. "And a slave with a sharp tongue—even worse. If you lie down on the ground, I will shackle you and you will live. But any more of your insolent prattle and I will kill you where you stand. I will still be paid a bounty at one of the forts, though it will be disappointingly smaller."

"Things will go differently than you say," he told the huntsman. "I will kill you, and then I will take your horse, your armor, and your name."

After that insult, the huntsman spoke no more but flung his lance with a speed and strength that should have pierced his enemy through. But the youth had already been poised to spring out of the way, and his days with the Skalijar *had taught him the foolishness of any kind of fair fight, especially against a creature like this, a mortal who would treacherously hunt his own kind in the service of the ageless witch-queen Utuk'ku. The lance flew, missed him, and pierced the trunk of a tree. As the huntsman drew his long sword, the youth sprinted toward the armored man's unprotected side and, instead of attacking directly, grabbed at the huntsman's leg and swung himself up behind him onto the saddle of the rearing white horse. The long, thin blade he had been given by Dyrmundur before he left the* Skalijar *was already in his hand; before his enemy could even turn, Gilhedur had yanked back on the man's helmet and driven the slender length of steel into his throat just above his gorget. A moment later he slid off again and watched as the Queen's Huntsman swayed in the saddle, eyes wide and throat burbling blood, then turned as pale as one of his Hikeda'ya masters before falling heavily to the ground in a puff of disturbed snow.*

He removed the dead huntsman's helm and armor, then dragged the body to a ravine. As the horse watched with what seemed very little interest, he dumped the one who had been Jarnulf down the slope, then rolled stones on top of him to help hide the body until the snow could cover it over again. He put on the huntsman's armor, then climbed into the huntsman's saddle. He stroked the dead man's pale horse behind the ears. "I guess that your old master did not treat you well. You will find things better with me." Snowflakes were already beginning to mound on the horse's shoulder, but its coat was no less white. "I will call you Salt," he said, "for the Lord God says in the Book of the Aedon, 'To he who worships Me and thirsts, I will give water. To he who worships Me and hungers, I will give bread and salt.'" It had been one of Father's favorite passages from the Book of the Aedon. Then he added the final words of God's promise. "'And he who would triumph in My name, I will make new.'"

"Gilhedur is no more, and will not live again," he cried, voice raised to the sky. The land around him was white and empty—no one would hear him but the One to whom he spoke. "Not until the Hikeda'ya are defeated and God's children are released from their captivity. Now I am Jarnulf, the Queen's Huntsman, and I will kill as many Hikeda'ya as I can find, until I become a story of terror in every part of the queen's enslaved land."

When Jarnulf woke, the sun was climbing toward noon, and he felt a clutch of alarm that he might somehow have missed his opportunity. But full awareness made him certain that even the stealthy Norns could not have marched an entire army so close to where he lay without waking him. He set about filling his stomach with the bits in his saddlebag—mostly *pu'ja* bread and the tiny cache of dried fish that had been in Nezeru's saddlebags. Afterward, he spread dry twigs across all the approaches to his hilltop redoubt so that no Hikeda'ya scouts could approach without his knowing, then he settled in for the long wait.

Thinking of his lost horse Salt brought memories of Nezeru and the strange moments they had shared even before he had risked so much to send her away from danger. Why had she thrown herself upon him that day in the cave? What had she hoped to accomplish? In dreams afterward he had seen her as a naked demon, whispering as she tempted him with her body, though the sight of her pale skin had filled him with horror instead of lust.

These are the doubts the Adversary has put in your head, he told himself. *Thus does the Great Betrayer seek to confuse the Lord's soldiers and thwart His will.* He prayed until his heart was calm again, then began to prepare his ambush.

He unwrapped his bow and arrows, then took out the little pot containing the precious dragon's blood. God, he knew, could not have led him to such a prize on the high slopes of Urmsheim by accident. What else could it be meant for, except to destroy Aedondom's greatest and most terrifying enemy?

When he had done all that he could to prepare, he composed himself and began to pray again. He recited the soothing words over and over until his thoughts seemed to slip away from him and fly free as birds, even to the borders of Heaven itself.

Your will, my God, he silently reminded his Maker. *Your heart. Your arm. I am Your servant, and I act in Your name.*

Jarnulf awoke again to rain splashing on his face and the murmur of distant thunder in his ears. Night had come, and the moon, though just past full, was little more than a hidden gleam behind heavy clouds overhead. At first, he simply listened. A flash of lightning illuminated the sky. For a brief instant the clouds looked like billows of smoke from a burning building, shot through with flames, then the light faded. But the thunder remained, a continuous low rumble.

Suddenly alert, Jarnulf sprang to his feet and hurried to the nearest of the fallen walls. Directly below him the road was empty, but he could make out a vast, moving shadow a short distance to the north. He feverishly re-strung his bow and set his quiver beside him so that he could snatch an arrow and have it on the string in a heartbeat's time.

The roll of thunder continued, but a weaker glare of lightning revealed a line of distant white faces and writhing pennants whipped by the wind. The Hikeda'ya army had arrived.

Their line moved strangely. The Sacrifice troops did not tramp in unison like trained mortal guards, nor wander in straggling chaos like an ordinary army of men. Instead, their long lines moved at a staggered pace, like some immense, many-legged insect.

Jarnulf could see the eyes of the Sacrifices in the vanguard now, reflecting bright as cat's eyes from the slits in their helmets, and he could make out the bulky shapes of a score of massive wagons just behind them. His heart sped. The rain was slackening a little, and he prayed that Utuk'ku was not sheltering in her royal carriage.

One chance, he told himself. *One chance only . . . !*

The vanguard of the Hikeda'ya forces flowed past with its strange, muffled cadence, and he saw brief flashes of legion flags—Catamounts, Vultures, and even the feared Night Moths. Then, to his startled surprise, in another lightning flare he saw hand-chieftain Makho seated atop the first wagon—dragon-burned Makho, whose resurrection from the Tebi Pit Jarnulf himself had witnessed. The hand-chieftain's expressionless, ruined face was unmistakable, his one remaining eye staring at the road ahead.

I am glad I stole your sword and gave it away, monster, Jarnulf thought. *But I have a greater quarry than you. Still, God willing, you and I will settle our differences on some other day.*

Two more large wagons followed close behind Makho's, the first glowing brightly out of every crack and space in its frame—a smoldering, reddish light, as if it the interior were on fire. Behind it, with a deep rumble and squeak of wheels Jarnulf could hear even through the thunder, came the queen's long, linked train of wagons.

Jarnulf's heart was beating so fast he could feel his blood coursing through his veins. On top of the first of the tethered wagons, beneath an awning that rippled in the wind, flanked by two tall, white-helmeted guards, sat a slender figure dressed all in white—Queen Utuk'ku herself. A train of men and smaller carriages followed her, an army so immense that the wide roadway could barely contain them all. Even from his high vantage point, Jarnulf could not see the end of the procession.

By the Sacred Wounds of Usires, he thought in horrified surprise, *a generation ago the Hikeda'ya were almost destroyed. How can they mount such an army now—ten thousand Sacrifices? More? I never dreamed it possible.*

But he could not let himself be distracted. The moment was upon him. God Himself was watching.

He nocked his arrow and waited until the vanguard was passing just below him, then he dipped the iron arrowhead into the jar of dragon's blood; when he withdrew it, the metal was already smoking. He steadied his bowhand atop the tumbled wall, then lowered the arrow's smoldering as rank after rank of armored Sacrifices passed below him, all ignorant that, had Jarnulf wanted a different victim, any one of them was an instant from death. But Jarnulf had only one target.

He found her thin, pale form again, then calmed himself with slow breath until the head of his arrow stopped quivering. He felt a strange tightness in the air that reminded him a little of the weird spell that had gripped him on Naglimund's outwall, and it made him hesitate, but this time the grip of terror was less and his fear of another shameful failure far greater. When the thin white shape was almost below him, another flicker of lightning blanched the clouds and gleamed on the queen's silver mask. He expelled his breath, then loosed the smoking arrow.

In the dying gleam of skyfire, he saw the shaft fly toward her, straight and true, and for a triumphant moment he was sure he had pierced the Queen of the Norns through her black, century-shriveled heart. But to his horrified astonishment, she did not waver or fall, and her wagon trundled on as though nothing at all had happened. By the time he had set a second arrow on his bowstring, the queen's carriage was past him, its upper bulk blocking her from his sight.

As Jarnulf stared in stunned disbelief, trying to understand how he could have missed when he had been so sure of his arrow's flight, and wondering what kind of dark magicks the queen might have used to make the cursed air itself into her invisible armor, he saw a flurry of movement among the mounted nobles just behind the queen's carriage, and heard several of them cry out in their high, cruel voices: Utuk'ku herself might be oblivious to his attempt to kill her, but her minions had clearly noticed. A moment later several Hikeda'ya riders began racing up the hill toward his hiding place, and others threw open the door of one of the long, low wagons, releasing a horde of white hounds who came boiling up the hill behind the Sacrifice officers, belling and howling.

Jarnulf snatched up his bow and few belongings and leaped onto his horse, spurring it out of the ruins and up into the hills. Already the noises of pursuit were growing loud behind him.

Has my luck simply deserted me? he thought miserably as he hunched low over the horse's neck. Trees flew past, grabbing at him like merchants trying to restrain an escaping thief. *Or is it You, O Lord, who has found me unworthy?*

At last, many leagues north of the captured mortal fortress, the marching column of Sacrifices and Builders left the ancient river road and turned east into the mountains. Viyeki was relieved to be off the great track, though he knew his fears were foolish. Simply marching so confidently through mortal lands still seemed dangerous to him, a complete inversion of many years of caution, but he also knew it was unlikely any mortal force in this part of the north could threaten them. The mortals of Rimmersgard were skirmishing with the mortals of Hernystir all along their southern borders, and they were also fighting against raids by the queen's own Sacrifice troops. But Viyeki had lived most of his life within a much more cautious Hikeda'ya strategy of isolation and self-protection, the only deviation being the brief but violent aggressions and eventual deadly failure of the War of Return. The current crop of Sacrifice officers seemed to have forgotten or dismissed the misery and death the queen's last war had brought to their people, of how close Nakkiga itself had come to being conquered.

I suppose Sacrifices only see the task before them, he thought, *as my workers do not think of the mountain's birth or early centuries when they dig in its stony outer hide. But is it not the duty of magisters and officers to remember what others do not, to think not only of what they hope will happen, but also of what might happen instead?*

His old master's words kept coming back to him. "*Do not examine only the flaw but how it formed.*" If there was a flaw in his people—or in the way they were ruled, though he quailed at even entertaining the thought—what could be learned from considering its origins?

But does it even matter? he wondered. *I am likely the only one foolish enough to question what we are doing. Even Pratiki, for all the privilege of his blood and the independence of his mind, never questions the queen or her closest counselors.*

His worries had been increased by the troubling spectacle of the undead thing called Hakatri being helped from his wagon when their company left the road. Hakatri's crystal tile armor had glittered even in the dim twilight, but his movements seemed precisely what would be expected from something recently dead, and it was clear from watching the stolid Sacrifice troops marching past that this was a companion they feared. As Hakatri was helped up into the curtained litter for the next part of the journey, the entire line of Sacrifices marching past shifted a measurable distance to one side, disturbed by his mere existence. Many of them even looked away from the weird spectacle, which stretched marching discipline to its utter limit. It was apparently more difficult for the soldiers to forget the phantom thing they had brought with them when it was staggering around out in the open.

Just as the litter's curtains shut and darkness swallowed the figure, Viyeki had the disturbing sensation that the gleam of eyes in the round, fishlike eyeholes of the helmet had swiveled toward him to meet his gaze, and he had trembled as if gripped by fever.

Why make us travel with such a disturbing, unwanted ally? Viyeki wondered. The queen's *shaynat* strategy seemed to rest on a game piece none of her servants could understand or even bear to look at.

As they wound higher into the mountains, snow flurried and the wind blew fiercely. For Viyeki, the cold and the swirling whiteness reminded him of home, but he worried a little for the mortal workers—slaves, to name them truthfully—brought out of Naglimund. They were underdressed and poorly shod for walking in the cold heights, but he could do nothing to help that. At least, he reflected, the prisoners' forced march was no longer being overseen by General Kikiti's Sacrifices, who had commandeered the front of the column for their journey into the heights to defend against ambush. If the general's warriors had been in charge instead of Viyeki's own builders, he guessed that fewer than half of the slaves would survive to their destination. As it was, he hoped for something closer to four fifths, and he would need every one of them.

But if they were not needed for the great work, he told himself, *they would not be worth so much concern. After all, our peoples are at war.* But despite the obvious sense of the thought, Cuff the Scaler's hapless face tugged at his memory. He should have felt contempt for such a faulty mortal creature, but something prevented it, though Viyeki could not say what the obstacle was.

The Yi'ire Range had grown steadily steeper as they traveled north, until the hills of its southern reaches were replaced by true mountains capped with snow. Now their company of Sacrifices, Builders, and prisoners climbed into the highest peaks of what mortals called "the Wealdhelm."

And the mortals call this land "Osten Ard," Viyeki thought. *So why do we, who were once masters of all of it, have no single name for this place, where we have lived so long? We Hikeda'ya call it so many things—"the new place," "the land after the Garden," "the place the queen found for us," or even, simply, "Landfall," but those are descriptions, not names.*

As his horse labored up the steep track, in and out through stone outcroppings as singular as ancient statues, he came upon Prince-Templar Pratiki. He could not help wondering whether the prince-templar had deliberately slowed to wait for him. *If you want my friendship, my lord,* Viyeki thought, *you had better ask for it straightly. I dare not step out of my place, especially with such a high-ranking member of the Hamakha Clan.*

"There you are, Magister," Pratiki said as Viyeki caught up. "I wonder what you make of the strange shape of the mountains here. So angular, so . . . artistic."

"Indeed, Serenity. This sort of limestone is like a good servant, my old master taught me. It shapes itself to the strength of its betters. Wind and rain carve it into these shapes."

"And create caves, I am told. Is it easy to dig?"

"Dig? 'Carve' might be a better word—it is stone, after all. But it is easier to shape than basalt or granite, for what that is worth."

Pratiki nodded slowly, as if carefully considering this. "We are fortunate to have you with us."

Viyeki allowed himself a cautious shake of the head. "Any of my gang chiefs could have told you the same, Serenity, and I am certain you knew that. Our work will be hard, I am sure, but I will give my all."

"Of course, of course. We owe the queen no less. But your work here will be important as well as hard—perhaps the most important thing you will ever do."

Which was a slightly odd thing to say after Viyeki and his order had just exhumed the remains of fabled Ruyan Vé so that the Mother of the People could use the Navigator's armor to bring the Storm King's brother Hakatri back from the dead. However, it was an ancient truism among the Hikeda'ya that things were never learned by questioning, only by listening patiently to one's superiors, so Viyeki only nodded and said, "The Builders Order exists only to serve Her Majesty."

"Of course," said Pratiki.

After that, they rode a while in silence up the winding track. At the outer edge the cliff face dropped away in many places, so that Viyeki could stare straight down into foggy emptiness. The great company was now almost a quarter of the way to the summit. He did not mind the cold himself, but he hoped for the sake of his mortal workers they were not expected to climb all the way to the top.

"After the Mother of All could no longer trust our Zida'ya kin, she withdrew our people into our mountain," said Pratiki, as if sharing a sudden, idle thought. "The governance of all this area was left to our onetime allies, now become our enemies." He shook his head sadly. "Do you think there could ever be a rejoining of our people, High Magister?"

Viyeki had to take a sudden, surprised breath. The offhand way Pratiki said it made him certain this was another test of some kind. He mulled his words carefully but swiftly; even a too-long moment of hesitation could be seen as proof of insufficient loyalty. "Who can say, Serene Highness?" he offered, a lateral move even a novice player of *shaynat* would recognize, a comment on the game itself. "Only the queen would know. Only the queen could make such a thing happen."

"True. And our queen has told us the Zida'ya are now our mortal enemies," said Pratiki. "That is clear enough, is it not? Sometimes I think too much about things that are beyond my poor wisdom. It is a failing of mine, I admit with no little shame."

Viyeki took a calculated risk. "I am certain that thinking about matters that might help our people in the days ahead can only be a good thing, Serenity, and you are clearly someone who tries to do so. But of course, even you and the other leaders of the Hamakha Clan must wait for the queen's wisdom to show the way."

"Of course. Yes, of course."

And that seemed to end the conversation. Pratiki rode ahead once more to discuss making camp for the day with General Kikiti and his staff. Viyeki sent his secretary Nonao to find his overseers and tell them to be ready to assemble the tents for the nobles and also to begin feeding the mortal workers as soon as the great train of wagons, horses, and goats stopped.

But inside he was still considering the things Pratiki had said. *His complaints become bolder. Is it because he trusts me now? He is worried about the future, or he pretends to be, and he seems to be sounding me out as to whether I am concerned as well.*

But I still cannot trust him, of course. Viyeki looked down at the mist-hung gulfs to his left, an emptiness into which someone like him might fall and simply vanish forever. *As my father used to say, "The company of the Hamakha makes any spot a high and dangerous place. A single false step can bring death . . . or worse."*

The Builders, along with all mortal slaves healthy enough to work, were setting up camp on the slopes of Kushiba, amid stark outcrops and clusters of pines. But to Viyeki's surprise, General Kikiti and his Sacrifices did not join them in the new camp but continued up the mountain to drive out the Zida'ya enemy and secure the place where the Builders would begin excavations. Viyeki had been relieved to see the Sacrifice troops carrying Hakatri's curtained litter with them into the heights.

"I am sorry I cannot tell you how long we must wait here," Pratiki told him. "War does not follow anyone's plans for long."

That first night Viyeki heard a few faint cries echoing eerily from far above them, and once the urgent notes of a war horn cascading down the mountainside and raising the hairs on the back of his neck. They were the first sounds of conflict he had heard since the mortal fortress of Naglimund fell.

"It will be silent fighting up there, for the most part," Pratiki said, as if to reassure him. They stared up at the dark bulk of the mountain, which blotted out half the sky. "The Zida'ya are our kin. They do not shriek and howl in combat like the mortal animals."

"Some of the mortals can fight silently too—almost as silently as Night Moth Sacrifices," said Viyeki.

Pratiki nodded slowly. "Ah, yes, I forgot that you battled them in the south and also when they besieged Nakkiga itself."

"Half a Great Year ago, Serenity, but it seems longer. And I did not, myself do much fighting." He lifted his gaze from the shadowy mountain to the plenitude of stars in the cold, midnight-blue sky. They seemed unimaginably distant—as far away as the Lost Garden. "In truth, Prince-Templar, I thought those days spelled the end for all of us."

"I remember that time well," said Pratiki. "But I was safe in the Temple of Martyred Drukhi, inside Nakkiga. The mortal soldiers did not chase me across the wild lands as they did you and your master, Yaarike."

Viyeki was a little surprised—he had never discussed that dreadful siege with Pratiki. Still, he supposed it was only natural that a high Hamakha noble, the queen's close relative, should know something about what the High Magister of the Builders Order had done during the terrible days after the failure of the War of Return. "If the mortals had broken down the gate, Serenity, as they tried so hard to do, you would have fought too. We would all have resisted to the last Hikeda'ya life."

"With certainty. But tell me, now that we speak of mortals, how are your slaves holding up? I saw more than a few of them working today. You have done well to keep them healthy enough to contribute."

"They are a resource, so they belong to the Mother of All. It is criminal to waste anything that belongs to her."

Pratiki nodded. "I hear the queen's voice in your words."

The prince-templar's clerics now appeared, clearly anxious to have the prince-templar put his stamp on some important messages, so Pratiki took his leave.

This is certainly a drawn out flirtation, Viyeki thought. *The prince-templar clearly has something he wishes to confide to me. Unless I have misunderstood him. Unless I am making a terrible mistake.*

They waited three days in their camp at the base of the mountain, and though messengers from General Kikiti brought regular dispatches to Pratiki, the prince-templar did not share any of them. Left to his own pursuits, Viyeki did his best to prepare for the task of burrowing through the mountain. It would have been comparatively easy to create a tunnel down to the valley floor for the Sacrifice troops if his Builders could have used a few of the monstrous rock-borers that had brought down the walls of the mortal fortress at Naglimund, but the creatures were too large and too dangerous to be dragged for miles up a mountain. The Sacrifice engineers also guarded them jealously. Even in Nakkiga, it was hard for the Builders to get permission to use them, as if the creatures were small and delicate as lacewings instead of weighty monstrosities covered in near-impervious shells, with mandibles that could crush stone to powder. But it was no use lamenting what he could not have.

It will be brute force digging here, he thought. *Fracturing and collapsing seams as we go, with no time to spare. I'll put Overseer Gayu and her stonecrackers to work clearing the way, with Oroji One-arm and his props-and-pillars troop behind her to make it as safe as they can manage in these conditions.*

Making a plan before seeing precisely where his Builders would work, and without testing the site's rocky bones with his own eyes, fingers, and tongue, felt a bit like trying to seduce someone he had not met nor even seen. Digging through solid stone was always tricky work, and every mountain was different, each with its own foibles. Viyeki never felt he truly knew stone well until he had almost finished a task.

Is it possible we learn best about something by destroying it? he wondered. *That is a sad thought. If the queen wipes the mortals from the land, will we wish afterward we had not done it?*

Another, even grimmer idea followed that one: *And if we are the ones who lose this war, as we lost the last one, and we are the ones destroyed, will the mortals someday mourn us and wish they had known us better?*

Kikiti's deputy, Legion Commander Hezidri, came swaggering down the mountain and into camp the next morning with a company of Sacrifices who were finding it hard to keep their emotions properly hidden. Viyeki thought it obvious that they were very pleased with themselves, and when he was called to the prince-templar's tent an hour later, his suspicions were confirmed.

"We have won a great victory!" Pratiki announced to a crowd of officers and overseers after leading a prayer of gratitude. "All praise to General Kikiti and the troops, and of course to our guiding spirt, the Mother of All. Our Sacrifice warriors have routed Kushiba's defenders, killing many Zida'ya and at last driving out the rest. The caverns are ours! And now your work can begin, High Magister."

Viyeki was relieved that the waiting was finally over. Much work would be needed simply to assess the task, plan it, and organize his Builders to perform it. And several of the days Pratiki had promised him, to complete this life-or-death work, had already burned away while they waited. When the brief celebration was over, he sought out the Prince-Templar. "This is excellent news, of course. When do we go there, Serenity?"

"Now, High Magister, now!" Pratiki seemed relieved too, as though some great fear he had been hiding had now proved false. "That is why Commander Hezidri and his troops are here, to escort your order up the mountain."

"Do we need an escort? You said the Zida'ya had all been driven out."

"General Kikiti has sent the soldiers purely as an excess of caution—and, in honesty, likely because of me." Pratiki smiled. There was no question his mood had improved. "Our general would not want anything to happen to one of the high Hamakha, even by accident. Now, hurry, Magister! We will depart as soon as the animals can be hitched to the wagons."

Viyeki, with his trained stoneworker's eye, could not help wondering at the old track that led them farther into the heights. It had been crudely hacked out of the mountain and looked as if it had never been properly finished. It was also surprisingly wide and flat, as though whoever had begun it had anticipated it would be much used. He knew a little about Zida'ya builders and could not imagine any of them would have been satisfied with such a hastily constructed track, but he could not otherwise make much sense of it.

They planned something they never finished, he decided. *But though they did not finish it, they kept a garrison here to protect Kushiba—or did, until Kikiti and his Sacrifices drove them out. But was it really the mountain they were defending, or even the valley below, or are the Zida'ya protecting something else entirely?* Every time he wondered about the ultimate purpose of this strange offensive, he ended with more questions than when he began.

Viyeki had already done everything he could to make sense of Kushiba, chipping away samples all around the base camp, testing the chips with scraping-stones and vitriol and the other methods which his master Yaarike had so rigorously taught him. As he had guessed, the mountain was mostly limestone, and as his Builder company followed the Sacrifice company up the wide track, Viyeki could see that stands of wind-gnarled oak and birch became extremely sparse in the heights, and though the evergreens grew straight and seemingly defiant, they were huddled together in isolated groves, like troops under siege.

In late afternoon, almost halfway up Kushiba, Viyeki's horse finally clambered off the steep track and onto a wide plateau that he had not been able to see from lower down the slope. The rest of the Yi'ire range spread away into the eastern distance, vanishing at last in a smear of fog. The plateau was a wide horizontal gouge, as if someone had taken a monstrous ax to the middle of the mountainside, then quit after chopping out a single massive wedge. Sacrifice soldiers were busy all about the plateau, laying out a long-term camp beneath a sky lively with flurrying snow. The greatest concentration of armed men were centered around a group of tents on the northern edge of the plateau; Viyeki guessed that was where General Kikiti and his officers had their headquarters, and that the gouge in the mountainside was the entrance to the caverns, where Viyeki and his Builders would work.

As his order set up camp, Viyeki made sure the mortal slaves were penned in a spot where they would be sheltered from the worst of the winter weather. Mortals were fragile things, he had learned: they grew sick or died in conditions that would not harm even a Hikeda'ya child. Busy with such arrangements, he did not notice Pratiki's approach until the noble was almost upon him. This time, the prince-templar was accompanied by Kikiti. The general wore an expression of barely hidden distaste, as was usually the case, but Viyeki saluted them both. "And congratulations on your victory, General," he added.

"You must mean 'our victory,'" said Kikiti. "Surely this is a triumph for all our folk, not just the Order of Sacrifice."

"How true, General. I stand corrected." Viyeki found Kikiti easy to loathe.

"Do you have a moment to come with us to see something, High Magister?" asked Pratiki.

A polite request from a Hamakha noble was not actually a request. "Yes, with certainty, Serene Highness."

Three of Kikiti's Sacrifices and the same number of the prince-templar's Hamakha Guards accompanied them across the plateau, although Viyeki could see little reason for so much protection. Did they fear wild animals? He rather pitied the bear—or even the smallish dragon—that decided to attack Kikiti. The tall, hawk-faced general was one of the most dangerous handfighters in all the Order of Sacrifice, and was wearing his witchwood armor. Or could it be that the Zida'ya had not been as thoroughly subdued here as Viyeki had been told?

A dozen Sacrifice soldiers with pikes stood guarding the wide hole in the mountain's face but quickly stepped aside to let the prince-templar and the rest of their small company pass through into the cavern's entrance.

"By the Garden!" said Viyeki in stunned surprise.

"Is it so different than what you imagined?" Pratiki seemed mildly concerned. "I have great confidence in you and your Builders, Magister."

But though Viyeki could now see the interior of the large cavern, it had not been the task ahead of him that had startled him into speech, but the bodies of many female and male Zida'ya fighters lying scattered about the plateau and piled beside the cave's mouth. Most of the golden-skinned corpses lay in their own blood, sprawled and open-eyed, as if they had died only moments earlier.

In contrast to the monotonous dark colors worn by most of the Sacrifice soldiers, these dead Zida'ya were dressed in many different hues—even their armor was extravagantly painted. Viyeki thought it looked like a flock of colorful birds had been frozen in midflight, then plummeted to the ground, and for some reason this thought deepened his unease. He was no stranger to dead bodies, whether of immortals or mortals—no one who had survived that escape back to Nakkiga could be—but he had not expected to find the mountain's protectors still lying where they had fallen. He watched with a sense of unreality as Pratiki stepped around the corpse of a blue-haired Zida'ya who, at least in shape of body and face, could have been the prince-templar's close kin.

Kikiti saw him staring at the dead. "Waste no mourning on those traitors." He spat. His contempt seemed to encompass the High Magister of Builders as well as the fallen. "They are a failed, vanishing race."

But they are the same race as us. Viyeki could not help being disturbed by how much like his own folk these dead Zida'ya appeared: only a difference of skin color distinguished their features from those of the Hikeda'ya victors. But of course, he did not say so.

They snaked their way through the tumble of bodies and deeper into the cavern, which stretched some ten cubits high and four or five times that far across. Viyeki looked back as they reached it, and now that the shock of seeing the dead Zida'ya had passed, he was struck by how comparatively few bodies the cavern contained. *Kikiti must be right,* he thought. *If they valued this place enough to defend it, they must not have many warriors left who are able to fight.* Aloud, he asked, "How many died here?"

"Very few, praise the Garden and the Mother of All," said Kikiti. "But the traitors lost several hundred. We could have extinguished them the first day—the first few hours, even—but most of them hid in the caverns below and it was difficult to force them out. We used fire, in the end." He glanced at Viyeki. "Do not worry, Magister, you will not have to dirty your hands. My Sacrifices will drag out the bodies when they have cooled. The stink may linger a bit, but I'm sure your Builders have worked in worse conditions."

Viyeki made his face as blank as sanded parchment.

"So here is the place where you will perform your great task for the queen," announced Pratiki as they reached a jagged hole in the cavern's back wall. "I would like you to observe it carefully. Do you carry a *ni'iyo*?"

"Always, Serenity." Viyeki produced the sphere from the interior pouch in his long winter cloak. "Should I go in?"

"I cannot tell you your work," said Pratiki with a smile. "But, yes, I would assume that to be a good beginning."

"Make it swift," said Kikiti. "My officers are awaiting me."

"Patience, General," Pratiki told him gently but with a subtle hint of reproof. "I have questions for you, too, while we wait here for High Magister Viyeki to return."

Viyeki ignited the sphere and ducked through the gap, then continued forward cautiously into the smaller space until he could lift his head again. To his surprise, he found himself in another cavern almost as large as the outer one, its carbuncled roof several ells above his head, though it was lower farther on, just as the sides of the cavern also narrowed at the back. He squeezed the *ni'iyo* until it brightened. A broad, almost empty trough of stone, worn by years of water, wound across the cavern floor to disappear into darkness at the rear of the cavern. A stream of meltwater ran toward the rear of the cavern, leaving behind only a thin, musical murmur as it disappeared into a wide crevice in the floor. The water had clearly been carving away at the limestone for a very long time, and also forming the caves he had been told waited below. For the first time, Viyeki could smell something strange, the faint but pungent odor of scorched flesh.

And the Zida'ya tried to escape Kikiti by climbing down into this trap, he thought. *What a horrible end they must have had.* The faint keening of the wind outside the cavern might have been the echo of their last cries.

Viyeki could not stand the smell or the place any longer, so he retreated toward the front of the cavern and the clean mountain air.

"I have seen the water channel," he told Pratiki. "The top end is narrow, but if we are lucky, it will be wider below."

"We cannot rely on luck, Magister," said the prince-templar. "Our time is short, and General Kikiti's Sacrifices must be able to reach the valley floor of Tanakirú soon."

For a moment, Viyeki was too surprised to reply. "Serene Highness, we must be at least half a league above the valley's bottom—perhaps a good deal more!"

"I told you to leave it to my order's engineers," said General Kikiti. "*They* are not afraid of a challenge."

Pratiki ignored him. "Can you do it, High Magister? That is all I want to know."

Viyeki struggled for calm. "Can we dig our way down through the limestone, following whatever caves have already been carved by water? Yes—yes, of course we can. But it will be hard going, and dangerous for my Builders. We will have to cut steps in many places, and at some point we may find we cannot dig any farther with the tools we have brought with us."

"We will deal with such a problem if it happens." Pratiki gave him a significant glance that Viyeki could not understand. "Can you do what the queen has commanded, High Magister?"

This is not a matter where my misgivings have any place, or will be listened to, Viyeki realized. "Yes. Given enough time." He did his best to ignore Kikiti's grunt of anger.

"And how much time is that?" Pratiki asked.

Viyeki tallied up the Builders he had with him and the mortal slaves, who were much less useful, then made a few rough calculations. "With the tools and workers I have," Viyeki said at last, "we can perhaps finish in four moons if we encounter no significant obstacles."

Pratiki shook his head. "Impossible. We have been given two moons to finish it. The Mother of All has declared that the Sacrifice Order must be able to reach the valley by year's end. There is no changing that."

Viyeki felt as if a strong hand squeezed his heart. "I . . . I can only try, Serenity. But I do not think it can be done in such a short time. I apologize, but I can only relate what my experience tells me. I will do everything I can to fulfill Her Majesty's desire, but—"

"Perhaps one of his overseers can do better," suggested Kikiti with a hard stare at Viyeki. "I am certain we could find one who would not immediately begin complaining this way."

"The High Magister of the Builders is giving us the gift of his experience, General," replied the prince-templar. "And the task has been a secret from him until this moment. Very well, Magister—go to it with all the haste you and your Builders can manage. And do not despair. It could be that I will find you some unexpected help."

As their little company made their way out of the cavern and back across the plateau, the peaks surrounding Kushiba seemed to look down at Viyeki in cruel amusement. He could only guess what they would think about a tiny, frail creature like himself, condemned to hollow out an entire mountain or die.

Jarnulf's doomed flight toward freedom did not even last until dawn.

His Hikeda'ya horse was game, but at least a dozen mounted Sacrifices hunted him, and every time he thought he had escaped, a pack of snarling, ghostly Nakkiga hounds cut him off, turning him back toward his pursuers.

Even as he galloped across the forested hills, trying and failing to find a hole in the net of armored soldiers, he was devastated by his latest failure. He was certain his aim had been true, but somehow the witch had protected herself from the arrow. His fear of her now outstripped even his hatred. How could mortals hope to defeat such a creature, who could not even be touched and who ruled over such an astonishingly vast army?

In a long valley between two hills, he splashed along the length of a narrow streambed, dry only a few months earlier but now filling with the runoff from the season's rains. A handful of mounted Hikeda'ya crested the hill and came galloping down the slopes; but even as he yanked the reins to turn his mount toward the other side of the valley, a company of mounted Sacrifices appeared on that slope as well. He heard the baying of hounds from the valley's mouth behind him and knew he had only one chance—to ride as swiftly as he could and hope he could get past the Hikeda'ya hunters before they reached the bottom on either side.

This was not to be, and it all ended suddenly. His horse threw back its head in fear as the first group of riders crashed into the stream in front of him. As he tried to turn away from them, the second group caught up to him. Strangely, though many of his pursuers had bows slung on their saddles, they did not loose even a single arrow at him. Jarnulf drew his sword and managed to wound one of the first riders to reach him, but a moment later something hit him hard on the back of his head. As if the lightning itself had struck him, he saw one great burst of light, then tumbled from his saddle into darkness.

He woke, still in the dark. His head throbbed, and it took him more than a moment to realize he was trussed and draped belly-down over the back of a Sacrifice saddle. He struggled, but the slippery cords were knotted tight around his wrists and ankles—he could not even squirm hard enough to slide off the saddle and onto the ground, though he tried. When his Hikeda'ya captor noticed what Jarnulf was doing, he turned and drove a gauntleted fist into his captive's face, bringing back the lightning, sending everything else away.

Jarnulf had no idea how long he had been insensible, but when he woke again it was to dawn light in the sky and the road bouncing beneath his head. His hands were securely tied behind his back. Strangely, he seemed to be the prisoner of a very small company—he had expected to be dragged back to the marching army to be tortured and executed as diversion for the Hikeda'ya troops. Instead, as he craned his neck—carefully and slowly, to avoid being noticed and beaten senseless again—he saw a vast shape to one side of the road, slowly looming nearer—Naglimund's ruined curtained wall. His Norn captors, for some reason, had brought him all the way back to the captured and nearly obliterated fortress.

His cautious movements had not been cautious enough. "He's awake," called a rider behind him.

"Just as well," said the one on whose saddle back Jarnulf was painfully jouncing. "The Lord of Song will want him awake and alert.

"He'll want him in one piece, too, so he can carve bits off him, I'll warrant," said the first Sacrifice.

"Oh, this one will be a *very* long time dying," said the second. "This mortal vermin tried to kill the queen."

"We should kill him ourselves," declared the trailing soldier.

"Be silent!" said the other, and Jarnulf could hear real fear in his voice. "If we did, we would take his place. Have you ever seen Lord Akhenabi angry? Trust me, it would shrivel your heart in your chest."

Jarnulf turned his bruised, aching head to see the broken pillars of Naglimund's great gate as they rode through. The rider carrying him said, "Awake again? Stop squirming," and struck him. They carried him through the castle's outer rings, past the remnants of its destruction, tumbled stones, scorched beams, and the disheveled earth of mass graves. The Sacrifice soldiers stopped at a storage building and carried Jarnulf to it. They unlocked the heavy door, then flung him into the darkened interior, where he landed on an earthen floor, the wind punched out of him.

He lay for some moments trying to get air back into his lungs. As his breath returned, he became increasingly aware of a stench in the enclosed space, a fierce, sour musk with a tinge of rotted meat about it. He could also hear a deep, rumbling sound from the other side of the dark storehouse.

"So." The impossibly low, growling voice rattled his bones, startling him so badly that he nearly pissed himself in sudden fear. He could see nothing, but he could hear his monstrous companion's heavy movements and the sound of chains dragging as it shifted position and leaned toward him. "You come back, eh? You come back to where you began—slave to the white queen. Are you to be my supper, little mortal man? Because old Goh Gam Gar is very, very hungry."

26

Black Banners

Jesa was amazed by all the things that had happened to her since she had fled Nabban, but strangest of all was the exalted position that had been thrust upon her. Not only had fate given her care of Duchess Canthia's orphaned child Serasina, but she had also become companion to the queen of all the nations, a woman Jesa fiercely admired. It was as if one of the storms that often wracked her childhood home in the Wran had snatched her up and whirled her away to an entirely magical place like one of her grandmother's stories, just as the great vine had lifted Aponi to the clouds where she met and married the sun.

It had not all been glorious, of course—not by any means. The death of Canthia and her little son still haunted her, and she and the queen were not out of danger—as Miriamele kept reminding her: "Yes, Jesa, we are in my own country of Erkynland now. But even with that madman Agga dead, we are far, far from safety, and that witch Turia is likely to have men hunting us still."

When Jesa had told the queen about Viscount Matreu's wretched fate, Miriamele had only nodded her head in tight-lipped satisfaction. "I have no forgiveness for traitors," she said. "That is why we must reach Erchester as swiftly as possible. An even greater traitor is still hidden there in plain view, and only I can bring him down."

After escaping Agga's hut, they had walked east for days, sleeping rough and begging a little food where it seemed safe, until they reached the ocean. Now they followed the coast northward.

"We will be safe when we get to Wentmouth, which cannot be far ahead of us now," Miriamele explained. "I was raised across the river in Meremund, second greatest city of Erkynland, and I have many allies there, many friends. But we must not be caught along the way." Casting a look over their once-fine, now filthy and ragged clothes, the queen said, "We will only attract notice dressed in these ragged court dresses. We must find more suitable, less memorable garments." They passed through many villages as they followed the coast road northward, Jesa often begging for food on the main thoroughfare with little Serasina in her arms, but none of these settlements were large enough for Miriamele's purposes.

"We need a town that has a good seamstress, and is also big enough that the arrival of two strangers, one of them a Wran-woman, will not be the only thing people talk about for days afterward."

"But we are far north of Nabban now," Jesa said. "Why do we still go in secret?"

"Because of that monster, Pasevalles." Miriamele's lips curled, as if she drank spoiled milk. "He became one of our most trusted servitors, and I doubt not his power has spread more than any of us can guess—remember, he even got his claws into old Envalles—a member of Duke Saluceris's own family! No, I will not underestimate his treachery or his reach again. We will go quietly and attract as little notice as possible until I am certain we are safe."

As they followed the Wentmouth Road, the weather grew colder every day. They slept in abandoned barns or empty, tumbledown huts when they could, traveling north for almost a sennight until they reached Goddinsborough, a substantial market town where the Wentmouth Road crossed a lesser arm of the Gleniwent over a high bridge lined with buildings. Miri wrapped herself in a blanket and sat with the baby on the steps of a church while Jesa went searching for more clothes. The marketplace was mostly empty so late in the year, but a fascinated farmer, who despite living near the coast had clearly never seen a dark-skinned woman before, told her of a tailor's shop only a few streets away. Less than an hour had passed before Jesa was carrying a pair of new (but far more ordinary) dresses back to the queen.

Miriamele was still waiting in front of the church, the baby held close against the chilly wind. A few cintis-pieces and one silver fithing lay beside her, left by pitying folk as they passed. Serasina was crying in a cross, scratchy way, but quieted a little when Jesa took her back.

"Let us go and buy her some milk," said Miriamele. "Then let us find someplace we can put those clothes on. I am tired of these rags. They remind me of nothing good." She got up, wincing after having sat so long. "Did you ask about the mourning banners I see all around here?"

"Yes, Majesty."

"Ssshhh! Someone might hear you call me that. Well? Is it someone I know?"

"It is. They are mourning for you."

For a long moment Miriamele only stared at her. "For me?" she said at last.

When Jesa related what she had learned in the shop, the queen made the sign of the Tree. "Sweet Elysia, Mother of God, watch over us," said Miriamele. "They must have found your mistress Canthia's body—you said she was badly burned. It hurts my heart to think of her. But why would they think it was me?" Her eyes narrowed, then widened. "By Our Lord, my ring! Oh, no. Oh, my poor Simon!" She began to cry, which almost unnerved Jesa. "My poor, dear husband must think me dead! And what of Morgan and Lillia? They already lost their mother—now they must believe they have lost me too! They will be in despair." Miriamele stopped suddenly, tears still glistening on her cheeks. "And this woman said my husband has gone to war against the grasslanders?"

Jesa nodded.

"Then, by our beloved Ransomer, we must hurry ourselves. Oh, that poor man. He will take terrible risks if he thinks I am truly gone." She made the sign of the Tree again, then folded her hands and looked up past the church roof toward the heavens. "Protect him, O Lord, please!"

And straight away, as if they could walk to the Hayholt in an hour, the queen set out for the town's western gate at so fast a pace that Jesa, with baby Serasina in her arms, could barely keep up with her.

Just because I have lost my country and my order is no reason to abandon discipline. Nezeru was angry with herself. Her nakedness felt dangerous. The fact she had let herself fall asleep, even after many days of hiding from the Sacrifices who had overrun Da'ai Chikiza, felt like a betrayal of her training. She rolled herself free of Morgan and rose, then strapped herself back into her armor, a routine whose beginnings in the order-house when she was a child she could not precisely remember. At the beginning of each day the great ordinal bell would toll, warning them out of their beds, and she and the other Sacrifice acolytes would dress in the nearly complete darkness, their huge sleeping room lit only by a single lantern above the door. Then the door would fly open, and they would troop out in file to the Knacker's Yard, as the older Sacrifices called it—the wide parade ground where each day's training began, and where useful meat for the queen's wars was separated from the useless offal. Once she had been more than proud simply to be part of her people's greatest order. *But what was it all in service of?* she wondered now. *The queen, the race—now, because of a mortal's trick, I am the enemy of both. I am cast out. I have no comrades.* Her gaze slipped to the mortal youth, still deep in sleep, his face hard to see in the darkness even for Nezeru's sharp eyes. His slumbering expression, so uncomposed, seemed like that of someone much younger, and for a moment Nezeru found herself oddly moved.

He is as old as I am, yet his life must have been so much different. What nurtured him? Is he a soldier? She discarded this possibility quickly—a soldier as unskilled as Morgan would have died a long time ago. *Then what? The child of wealthy merchants?* It was hard to know for certain because any life of leisure he might have led had been all but erased by the several moons he had spent living wild in the forest. She could still feel the rough touch of his hands on her skin, fingers callused by tree-climbing. The strength in his arms had been surprising for a mere mortal.

Staring at him she felt a sudden ache of sorrow—not for this sleeping youth, but for herself, who had never known the life of careless ease he must have had to be so open, so willingly foolish. And yet, she would not have traded it for her armor—either that which she now finished buckling into place, or that which held her together within, the years of cold, remorseless training by the Order of Sacrifice.

But now I am no longer a Sacrifice. What am I? More to the point, what do I do next?

And so, as Morgan slept, Nezeru pondered.

He woke at last, groaning loudly and stretching. Nezeru, who had already ranged far from their cavern hiding place, knew that no Sacrifices were nearby, but she still crouched beside him and put her hand near his mouth.

"Quiet," she said briskly. "You do not know who is outside, but still you bellow like a buck goat in rutting season."

He stared at her for a moment as he became fully awake, then a grin slowly spread across his face. "But it is—or it was, anyway."

"What are you talking about?"

"Rutting season." He reached up to pull her down, but she shook him off, frustrated and annoyed. He did not seem to realize that they were still in danger, still on the run from a vast, hostile force.

"What, will you not even give me a kiss?" he asked.

She stared at him. "What? A kiss? What nonsense are you talking?"

For a very brief instant he looked astonished. "Are you telling me that nothing happened? That we did not make love?"

"We coupled. It was good, if perhaps a little strange." Still, the touch of him, even as it irritated her, had reminded her of some of the previous night's intimate moments, and she feared she might have flushed a little. She did not want to give him the wrong idea. "But now is not the time for anything like that," she said as evenly as she could. "Now we must move. We are still within a short distance of Da'ai Chikiza, and still within the likely rounds of Sacrifice patrols. We must keep moving."

He sat up and swung his bare legs toward her, then yawned broadly. He seemed in no hurry to cover his own nakedness, which bothered her, though she could not say precisely why. He seemed to be taking liberties—liberties unearned. Coupling was one thing, and their situation was obviously unusual, but he was still a member of an enemy race. She might be an exile from the Order of Sacrifice, but nothing had truly changed between them, so why was he acting so careless?

Morgan was now rooting around in his bag, searching for something to eat, no doubt. Whatever else his time in the forest had done for his strength and hardihood, he almost never seemed to stop thinking about food. "Come," she said. "Dress yourself. We will find provisions as we travel."

He had found a rind of bread and begun to chew it. The motion of his jaw slowed and stopped. "Travel? Travel where?"

"We will speak about it when you are dressed. Put on your sword. We are still on discipline."

"On discipline?" But he slowly got up and began dressing, starting with his dreadful linen smallclothes, which she guessed must have been white once upon a time. As he tied them in place, she watched the muscles moving in his back and shoulders with a certain wistfulness. He was not bad to look at, though much bulkier in the chest and arms than the male Hikeda'ya she was used to. She wondered if all mortal men had such strong sinews, or whether it was strictly the effects of his life in the trees.

"You said put on my sword," he asked suddenly as he reached for his tunic. "Which way?"

"I do not understand your meaning."

"Are we climbing? If we're going to be in the trees, I'll hang it on my back. If we're going to be walking, I can wear it in the ordinary fashion."

"Walking, I would guess. But we may have to climb suddenly if we hear Sacrifice scouts."

He made a noise of dissatisfaction, a kind of snort, but then hung the belt so that the sword and scabbard bumped against his back.

Nezeru was pleased that he did not dwell on what had happened the previous night. Already she was beginning to think of it as a sort of accident, an aberration that did not need discussing. It had felt good, though, that she could not deny. Her body felt warm and comfortable in a way it hadn't for some time.

"So where do we go now?" he asked, then turned and pointed. "If this mad forest hasn't confused me again, my home is that way. You'd be safe there."

Nezeru could only stare at him in astonishment. "Your home? Do you truly think I could go into a nest of my mortal enemies without being taken and killed?"

He shook his head. "It's actually rather nice—I wouldn't call it a 'nest' of anything." His eyes narrowed. "But that's where I must go, in any case. I've been away for months."

"Then I wish you well, Morgan. I release you." She said it without hesitation, which belied her sudden pang of disappointment—something she would have to consider later, since too much attachment to anyone or anything but the Mother of All was a long step toward failure, capture, and death. Her teachers in the order-house had beaten that into her over and over.

"Release me?" This time his irritation was clear. "And where are you going? Or am I not allowed to know that? Is it some kind of Norn secret?"

"No." She could not understand his bad temper. She had taken him prisoner, and they had survived several bad moments before escaping Da'ai Chikiza. Then they had found a night's refuge in each other's company. Now she was releasing him. What more honorable parting could a onetime prisoner want? "No, there is no secret. You yourself gave the idea to me. I will go to the Vale of Mists—*Tanakirú*."

"You'll *what*?" He stared as if she had begun to prophesy like a fume-drunk templar. "Misty Vale, whatever it's called—didn't you listen to what I was saying, Nezeru? There's a giant living there as big as a cathedral tower! And things with too many legs, and the Good Lord alone knows what else!"

"Exactly." He still did not understand her. "You said that the Zida'ya have been commanded by their rulers not to go there, and that they keep the Hikeda'ya out as well. Even if the tale you told me about this biggest of giants is true, and you were not tricked somehow by the light and fog of the valley, what better place could there be for me, whom both sides wish to destroy? I would rather try to hide from one giant than a thousand soldiers."

That should have ended the discussion immediately: Nezeru could not imagine a more compelling reason than the one she had given. But instead, the youth set off on a long and frustrating litany of disagreements, none of which made any sense to her. "And if you're not stamped flat by the giant, then what?" he finished. "You'll just spend the rest of your life hiding?"

" *'When death is close,'*" she said, quoting the poet Zinuzo, a favorite of Sacrifices, "*then life must be lived breath by breath.'* I will think about the future if I ever have one."

As they stood outside the rocky shelter where they had slept, Morgan continued to argue, but Nezeru countered his every thrust with ease. She could not be dissuaded because she knew she was right; and because she was right, she would never surrender. That was what discipline gave to her.

"Then go!" he said at last, almost shouting before he realized how loud his voice had become. "Run away! Leave me alone in the forest again."

She looked at him curiously. Did he think she owed him protection? "You were alone when I found you."

He glared at her so furiously that she half-expected him to lunge at her, and she tensed her limbs. She was suddenly fearful, not of the mortal youth, but that he would do something so foolish that he would force her to hurt or even kill him. Even in her exasperation she did not want to harm him.

Another odd thing to consider, she told herself.

But Morgan only clenched his fists and stared at the ground. After a short time had passed, Nezeru decided there was nothing more to do here. "Farewell," she said, and turned to begin heading west toward the valley he had described.

She had only gone twenty paces or so when she heard him walking behind her. His pace sped until he was tramping along at her elbow, his steps heavy enough to wake every burrowing thing within a long stone's throw.

She did not look at him, even when he spoke. "I don't want to be alone again." He sounded angry. "And I don't think I can find my way back by myself—not with your Norn comrades running around all over the hills."

"They are no longer my comrades."

"That's not the point." He walked for a while without speaking, but she thought his weighty tread must still be shattering the sleep of any nearby woodland creatures. "And . . . and I don't want to leave you alone," he finally added.

That was such an unexpected thing for him to say that Nezeru did not immediately respond, which he seemed to take as a form of assent because he continued.

"I mean, it's not as though . . . don't misunderstand." He scowled. "You are fierce, I've seen that. An excellent fighter. But I don't want you to . . ." The scowl still hung. "I find you . . ." Again he fell silent, and this time he said no more.

They had traveled a long way onward when he finally spoke again. "Misty Vale. Sacred Usires and God the Father protect us! We're going to die, you know."

"Almost everyone does," she reminded him.

They approached the western gate of Goddinsborough, which was guarded by a small contingent of disinterested men-at-arms wearing black ribbons on their helmets. A hundred paces from the gate, the supposedly extinct queen abruptly stopped short and reached out a hand to squeeze Jesa's arm.

"Oh, God forgive me, I am an utter fool," said Miriamele. "We have spent all of Agga's coins. I should have asked for a few fithing-pieces back from the tailor's shop as well as the clothing—that ring was more than worth it. Then we could have bought some proper food for the baby and ourselves."

"Please, do not call yourself names, Majesty." Jesa shook her head. "You are good and clever."

"Good and clever won't buy a cup of milk." Miri was too cross with herself to be much soothed by the young woman's kindness. "We had best keep moving. If we must stop to beg for food all the way to Wentmouth, the going will be very slow indeed. In fact, I'm afraid we must consider outright theft just to fill our stomachs on the journey if we wish to keep our secret until we're safe."

Jesa's eyes went wide. "But if we are caught stealing, we will be hanged!"

"I will not let that happen, child."

And then Jesa remembered something, and let out a little cry of despair, apparently at her own foolishness. "Wait, Majesty!" Jesa carefully handed little Serasina to her, then sank into a crouch to begin searching through her bag. "I forgot! I think I have something that will help!"

"If it is food, I promise I will forgive you your lapse of memory." Miriamele shielded herself with her hand from a flurry of cold rain. "By Our Lady, girl, how much do you have in there?"

"My grandmother told me to always have a run-away bag ready for bad times." Her fingers closed at last on what she had been seeking and she drew it out. "Here."

"What is it?" Miri stared at the leather pouch with an almost superstitious reluctance. "I feel I have seen it before."

"It belonged to the man who captured you," Jesa acknowledged. "I saw it on the floor as we were getting ready to leave. He must have dropped it when we fought him." She opened it, looked inside, then handed it to Miriamele. "Look, it is his money."

Miri looked around quickly, then poured the coins out into her hand. "Coins, and more than a few. Oh, praise Usires, see?" She held out her palm where something glittered like the sun. "A few silver fithings, and even a gold throne! Look, there is my own likeness on it—and Simon's." She stared at the somewhat crude likeness for a time and found her eyes beginning to fill with tears. "Forgive me. It has been sometime since I have seen his dear face, even on a coin." She began counting the coins. "You are a wonder, Jesa. This is scant payment for all the indignity that creature piled upon me, but it makes us a great deal better off than we were. That foul man must have been saving for the journey he kept babbling about. Now we can afford food for the baby and for us, and I think we might even be able to purchase a horse."

"Oh, Majesty," said Jesa. "I have never ridden a horse. It would frighten me!"

"Said the young woman who saved the duchess's child from armed horsemen and then helped save me from a madman. There is nothing to fear. We do not have so much money that we can afford to buy a swift horse if we also want to eat on our journey. More likely it will be some old, swaybacked farm nag."

Miri had not been far off in her estimate. At the cost of a significant portion of their riches, she was able to talk a Goddinsborough farrier into selling her a horse, saddle, and bridle that had been left by a previous customer for an unpaid debt, as well as a basket of food and a jug of milk supplied by the farrier's wife. The bread was freshly baked, and for the first time since she had fled Nabban, Miri was able to eat a great hunk of it without a thought about saving some for later meals.

They made their way out of town in much more comfort than they had entered, with clean clothes and a steed to carry them. For a while, despite the strangeness of passing so many signs of mourning for herself along the road west, Miri felt more hopeful than she had for some time. All they had to do was reach Wentmouth, where it would be easy enough to take a ship for Erchester, though she wanted to do so without revealing her identity. She had no idea how thoroughly Pasevalles had spun his webs, what minor officials or paid killers he might already have in his employ. If Simon was away from the Hayholt, she did not want to reveal herself until she knew the traitor was in shackles.

As they rode through the countryside, she spent more time thinking about how to safely secure Pasevalles' arrest than she did about seeing her husband again, although that had been her greatest wish for months. If Simon was truly off on campaign, she prayed that Count Eolair would be back from the journey he had taken with Morgan. Perhaps by now her grandson had returned, too. And she would see her granddaughter! But what she really needed was someone loyal whom she could trust to arrest Pasevalles as soon as she ordered it. If Eolair had not returned, the most obvious choice was Tiamak, but though she would have trusted the Wrannaman with her life, she knew he was viewed with resentment by some of the Erkynlandish nobles, who did not like having a man of his color and background as one of the kingdom's most important counselors. Could Pasevalles convince some of them that she was lying or had lost her wits? Worse, if he got the news of her survival before she arrived, could he convince the other nobles that she was an impostor?

That is why I must get back to the Hayholt, she told herself. *I dare any of them to look me in the face and try to tell me I am not who I am!*

To Jesa's almost childlike pleasure, the queen permitted her to name their horse, and so she called him "Bonog" after a long-faced cousin from back in Red Pig Lagoon. Every night when they would stop for the night, while Miri gave little Serasina milk squeezed from a rag, Jesa would groom the horse carefully, never entirely without fear—she had never had to take care of any animal so large—but with growing pride as Bonog came to know and trust her.

With the queen at the front and Jesa seated behind her with the baby, they traveled the winding coastal road, past village after village, and leagues of fallow fields now turned to spilled cream by drifts of early snow. Jesa could not help marveling at how big the world outside the Wran truly was. Yes, Nabban might be the most populous city in the world, and she had finally grown used to its staggering size and its crowded, noisy streets, but here the farm fields stretched all the way from the road to the distant horizon. It intimidated her in a way that even the busy thoroughfares of Nabban had not, because the Five Hills always seemed protective, looming over the city like grandparents keeping a close eye on the family fortunes.

Here, though, the sky seemed almost infinite. Even when cobweb-gray clouds filled it, it seemed to stretch away forever. *How can these people live with their gods—or their God—staring down at them all day long?* she wondered. *And to think I longed to get away from my village, where everything I did was watched and noticed by family and neighbors. Here it is Heaven itself that watches all day—and judges us too, if the Aedonites speak the truth.*

The days of their journey turned into almost half a month as they made their way northwest toward Wentmouth, one of the two port cities that stood sentry at the mouth of the Gleniwent River. Jesa and the queen rode each day from early in the morning until oncoming darkness made the danger of bandits too great. Jesa spent at least part of each day wondering what would happen when they were finally safe again. Would the queen take Serasina away from her? It seemed inevitable: What right did a servant have to raise the child of a duke and duchess? The baby girl would be taken into the royal household, to receive the kind of education and training a child of high nobles should have. But even to think of that made Jesa's heart clutch: if Serasina was taken away from her, she feared she could never be entirely happy again.

You are fortunate simply to accompany the queen, she scolded herself—*the queen of all the known world! Do not plague her with your selfish worries.*

But when she took the baby back from Miriamele at sleeping time, she sometimes thought that the queen handed the child over reluctantly, and Jesa was reminded that the queen had lost her only son. At those moments, with the sleeping child again clutched to her bosom, Jesa was sometimes so fearful of losing Serasina that she even thought of running away with her.

But I cannot. That would be betrayal of the queen—and of my mistress Canthia as well.

Each night she fell asleep with these almost equally strong urges battling inside her—to trust the queen or to protect her own happiness. Most nights she did not sleep well.

The last miles into Wentmouth reminded Jesa more than a little of traveling down from the duke's family manor on the Antigene Hill. The road descended through a long, winding valley, following one of the Gleniwent's minor tributaries, past market towns that grew closer together as the port city drew nearer. When they could finally see the spires of the city atop its promontory above the river, Miriamele was heartened and Jesa was soothed by the queen's improving mood.

It was late morning, nearing noon, when they entered the gate and joined St. Rumen's Way, the main street through the center of Wentmouth. "We must get to the docks to find passage," Miriamele told her. "Our journey from here will be much faster by river."

The city reminded Jesa more than a little of Kwanitupul. Like that trading port on the edge of the Wran, Wentmouth seemed to have happened without ever once being planned. Fine stone houses stood beside clusters of smaller wooden shacks, and even the walls around the city were patched like old clothes. In contrast, as they reached the market near the river docks, Jesa could see across the wide river to Meremund, whose walls and tall towers looked so venerable and sturdy that they might have been built by gods of old, proud structures built from granite the color of a roasted pig-flesh.

"Meremund is where I grew up," said the queen, and Jesa heard sadness in her voice. "Before the Storm King's War. Before my father went mad." She shook her head. "But I have decided we will not visit it this trip, but go straight on to Erchester. We can find plenty of ships to suit our purpose right here in Wentmouth."

As they reached the far side of the wide square, the smell of the docks and the lively fish market growing ever stronger, they saw a group of soldiers setting up a sort of stand decked in black bunting. A man the queen did not recognize, but who was clearly a royal herald of some sort by his white surcoat bearing the Tree and Dragons arms, waited to address the crowd that had begun to assemble.

"Oh, for the love of our Lady Elysia," Miriamele said with a sigh, "I do not have the strength to hear the official rules for mourning my death announced again. It is too dreadful." She handed the baby back to Jesa. "We need more milk for Serasina. I will go to that cook-shop and buy some. I smell pies, too—good, plain mutton if my nose tells me true—and I will get one of those for us to share as well. Wait for me by that leather-worker's stall."

The cold rain had stopped. People were emerging from beneath the awnings that surrounded the open marketplace. Jesa stood uncertainly for a moment after the queen had gone, listening to the cries of hawkers and peddlers pulling their carts, wondering yet again at the strange turn her life had taken. She found herself caught up by the growing crowd, nudged forward toward the now-finished platform at the edge of the market. She looked across and saw Bonog's head and shoulders across the marketplace. The queen was leading him but had not yet reached the bake shop.

Jesa was now within a few dozen paces of the platform, where the royal herald was being helped onto it by several soldiers. His fine hat had been disarranged in the process, and he set it back in place with an angry flourish before unrolling a parchment that dangled almost to his feet.

"Be it known," he began in a hearty voice, though some at the back cried for him to speak even louder. *"In this twelve-hundred and third year of the Founding, a great calamity has come upon us."*

Many in the crowd began to whisper or even call out questions, and the folks on the outskirts of the crowd shouted again for the herald to raise his voice.

"Know all that as he rode to the defense of Winstowe Castle, which was besieged by barbarians from the grassland, our good King Simon was sorely wounded and carried from the field."

Some cried out in concern. Others looked to their neighbors as though not certain what they had heard.

"Despite the best help of surgeons and apothecaries, and the prayers of many priests and bishops of Mother Church, the king died on his way back to Erchester. May he rest forever in the loving arms of Our Ransomer, Usires Aedon, in the court of God the Father."

A woman near Jesa cried out in astonishment and terror, and immediately afterward more voices rose in cries of disbelief or in loud, hoarse prayers. Others were openly weeping, and mothers with children ran from the marketplace as though an armed conflict might begin at any moment. Some of the men near the front had begun shoving each other, and a fight quickly broke out, though Jesa—badly shocked herself, and feeling as if her bones had turned to ice—could see no reason why.

The herald continued, declaring that King Simon's grandson and heir had not yet returned to Erchester to be crowned, but soon would. He also proclaimed that the heir's other grandfather, Osric, would serve as regent until Prince Morgan could take the throne. The rest of his message was lost in the growing cries and shouts of misery. Some called out, "Who killed our king?"

and "God Bless Simon the Commoner!" but others simply mourned loudly and cried out to the heavens.

Jesa could only stand, clutching Serasina tightly as the noise and confusion washed over her. The people who had not fled at the first announcement began to fall into smaller groups, many of them kneeling together to pray, others perhaps to make plans for mutual protection. Jesa turned away. She felt scoured and empty inside. *What now?* she wondered. *And how can I give the queen such news?*

But that dreadful chore did not fall to her. Jesa saw Bonog coming toward her through the milling crowd, led by Miriamele, who was otherwise empty-handed and walking like a drunkard in a high wind. When the queen at last met her gaze, Jesa took a step back in alarm. Queen Miriamele's face was so pale that it seemed to glow even in the winter sunlight, an unholy white mask. Her eyes were empty, as if the reports of Miriamele's own death had all been true and this was her revenant.

Jesa rushed toward her, but Miriamele would not be touched or comforted. All Jesa could do was walk beside her as the queen crossed the market and headed toward the docks.

With a host of swaying sails visible before them and the waterfront only a few dozen paces ahead, Miriamele at last stopped and looked around, as though she had only now realized where she was. Then she sat down on the ground, ignoring the people who eddied around her, and covered her face with her hands for a long time. No one paid any attention. Many of those coming from the market seemed to be wandering aimlessly, and a good number of them were also crying.

Jesa crouched beside her. *What if the queen loses her wits?* she wondered. *She loved her husband the king so much. What if this has broken her—what will happen to the baby and to me?*

Miriamele at last looked up, her face no longer deathly white, but mottled pink from weeping. "Jesa, child, is that you?"

Her face was so close to the queen's it seemed impossible for Miriamele to mistake her, but she said, "Yes, Majesty, it is me."

"I know that monster Pasevalles has arranged this somehow, may God send his soul to eternal suffering. And I do not doubt he has Osric under his thumb, but whether the duke was tricked or treacherous, it matters little until we can reach the Hayholt."

"Will we still take a ship, Majesty?"

"I don't know. I don't know." Miri gasped as though trying to lift something too heavy for her, then got unsteadily to her feet. She seemed to have aged ten years in less than an hour. "I can scarcely think." She closed her eyes again, and for a moment Jesa thought the queen might faint. When she opened them, though, her look was hard—hard and sharp.

"It must be Meremund, after all," Miriamele said. "At least there are people

I trust there, and I cannot go back to the Hayholt without soldiers. But I promise I will have vengeance for my husband—for my lovely Simon. Pasevalles will die, and his death will not be swift or comfortable."

Now Jesa too began to shudder as the queen led her toward the docks. As if sensing that something had gone badly wrong, even little Serasina began to cry.

The king is dead, Jesa thought helplessly. *Gods of the Wran protect us, the king is dead and the baby has no milk.*

27

Girl in Darkness

Lillia banged her fist against the locked door over and over, though it made only the smallest, most disheartening noise. She shouted for help, first demanding that someone let her out, then pleading for someone to hear her, until her voice was hoarse and her throat sore. She cried, angry and frightened, but when she had cried out all the tears and nothing was left but dry, hitching sobs, she was still alone, still in the dark.

The candle had begun to drip wax on her hand as it burned down, so she carefully set it on the floor. Soon that little flame would be gone and then she would be in true darkness. Even as she thought of it, the shadows seemed to stretch long, spidery legs toward her, as if just waiting for that light to die before they pounced.

More, she thought. *I need more light.* Her heart was beating so hard that she felt dizzy. *Why won't anyone come for me? I'm the princess! Don't they know I'm gone? Isn't anyone looking?*

Grandfather King Simon had once taken her for a walk in the Kynswood. He had told the guards to stay far behind because he said he wanted to hear the noises of the woods without the clanking of armor and the thumping of boots. Later in that same day he had told her that the first rule of being lost was to stay in one place.

"When you realize you're lost, stop moving." His familiar bearded face had been so serious that it had frightened Lillia, who had never even considered the possibility. "Stay where you are. Let us find you."

But if she did that now, she thought, the candle would burn away and she would be alone in complete, true darkness. Alone except for whatever creatures lived down here—snakes, bats, rats, spiders, and maybe other things, too.

Ghosts? It was unpleasant even to think it. She had come here in part because she did not understand what the grown people were hiding from her. Her mother had died and gone away, and nobody had managed to explain it to her in a way that made sense. Now Grandmother Miriamele was gone, too, and the king said she was dead. She knew he must be telling the truth because Grandfather King Simon had barely been able to speak for crying when he said it. He had held her so tightly afterward that she could scarcely breathe.

And Morgan? Where was her brother? Why was everyone going away?

Everything was wrong. Nothing made sense. And now she was lost too, and nobody seemed to be searching for her. Was that what had happened to Morgan? Was that the reason nobody could tell her where he was? Was he lost somewhere in the dark here as well, maybe searching for the same answers that Lillia herself had been seeking?

The candleflame dipped and threatened to go out, then recovered a little strength. Her heart was speeding again.

Maybe I could find another candle.

She went to the closed door and pounded on it once more, but her fists barely made any noise. She might have been a bird beating its wings against the chapel's windows while the choir sang loudly inside. Nobody would hear her.

I'm hungry, too, she realized, then a cascade of other fears slid down on top of her. *If I don't find food, I'll be hungry and sick and maybe die. And I'll be in the dark. And nobody will hear me.*

After she had cried a little bit longer, she clambered to her feet and shouted again, though her throat was already raw. Nobody heard her. Nobody came.

As she sat staring miserably at the candle, which had burned almost halfway, another idea suddenly came. *Maybe there's another way out.*

That sudden thought felt nearly as good as another candle. She stood up from where she had slumped against the hopeless door and wiped her face with the sleeve of her dress, exactly the way Auntie Rhoner always told her not to do.

If you don't like it, Auntie, come stop me. Please.

She carried the candle to the back of the bleak, empty chamber, toward the stairwell, a deeper darkness that she had instinctively turned from. When she looked back at the locked door, her own shadow loomed and quivered. She bit at her lip and turned back and turned to the stairwell.

It's steps, she told herself. *It's steps that go down. They have to go somewhere!*

Are we dead, then? he asked her.

The Tan'ja Stair was a cataract of steps that twined upward through the phantom Asu'a, a misty emptiness of raincloud shadows and inconstant light, a place of ghosts and memories. His companion might have been either one.

That is hard to say, she told him. Her dim, gray presence continued to move upward, and he, as if connected by some unseen tether, moved with it. As they wound upward, the huge circular well of the hall stretched above them and most definitely below them as well, an immensity he could barely grasp.

Where are we? he asked.

In great Asu'a, I believe, she said. *But it is not entirely true, this likeness of my old home—my people's old home. Perhaps there is something in it of the wonder I felt about the place as a child.*

I was a child here, too, I think. Not this place, but the castle on this headland.

The mortal castle, she said slowly. *Yes, I remember it. I could not bear to regard it when I lived, though I saw it many times. It seemed like a child's toy made from the bones of a noble ancestor.*

He was silent, thinking not so much of what she had said as the idea that life was beyond his reach now. He wondered if he might spend all eternity, not at the feet of the Almighty as he had been promised, or in the company of all those he had lost, but alone with this fairy-phantom. What if the Book of the Aedon was wrong? What if, instead of being reunited in Heaven, those he had loved were only wandering specters now, as he was? And why couldn't he remember any of his loved ones' names—or his own?

I want to go back now, he said. *I want this to end.*

He could sense the other's dismissal as clearly as if he could see her shake her head. *That is not mine to grant,* she said. *I too am lost. There are many folds in the Veil—the barrier between life and death. The Dream Road is but one of them.*

The sense of loss and emptiness that swept through him then was enough to bring him to a halt, but the gray figure turned back toward him. *Come with me,* she said. *If this is eternity, there are worse ways to spend it than in the Yásira of my people.*

Is that where we're going? The . . . Yásira? The word seemed familiar, but when he tried to grasp the memory, it escaped like windblown smoke.

There have been many Yásiras. They are always at the center of anywhere we live. The one here in Asu'a was perhaps the greatest of any after the Lost Garden, and it is the one I remember best. Love makes the strongest memories.

Something cold touched him. *My wife died,* he said, remembering. *I was not there to protect her.* A deep horror hovered somewhere just beyond his reach, he realized. He was afraid to bring it closer. *I hoped we would meet again so that I could tell her how sorry I was for failing her.*

So too did I lose my husband, his companion told him. *He was killed at the orders of the queen with the silver mask*—At that, her words stopped, and for a moment he thought she was gone. *Utuk'ku,* she said, and a ripple ran down the stairway and seemed to pass through them both, as if great Asu'a itself had shivered. *That is my enemy's name, the enemy of all living things. But even after my death—if I have truly died—I cannot loose myself from her grasp.*

What do you mean?

She and I have been joined in the Three Who Are One, and Utuk'ku is the strongest of us. She still holds me somehow.

He felt quite lost. *The Three . . . ?*

The Three Who Are One. An ancient and perilous song—or spell, as you would call it. Three must be brought together, and while they are linked, they wield unequaled power. For the song to harness such might, a triad of strong spirits must be linked, One Who Will Not Go, One Who Returned, and One Who Waits Between. The first is she who refuses to die, Utuk'ku of the Silver Mask. The second, who died and then returned . . . ah, I remember now, that is Ommu, a sorceress who was the smoldering heart of the Red Hand.

He waited. *And the third?* he asked at last.

Yes, she said, *that is me. Neither dead nor alive, unable to return to the world or to go onward. I am the One Who Stands Between. Or at least I was.*

The heavy hopelessness of her words silenced him again.

Utuk'ku and I have been enemies since long before I became my people's Sa'onsera, she continued. *But though her power was always greater than mine, she could not force me to do her will. But under the binding of the Three Who Are One, I could not . . . cannot . . . resist her. As the one who sang that deadly song, she can call on the strength of both myself and Ommu the Whisperer.*

He was having trouble keeping up. *Ommu? I don't know that name, or at least I don't think I do. Could this Ommu help you fight back?*

He felt her quiver of angry disdain. *The Whisperer? She wears a living body now, but she is little more than a phantom, held together by rage and twisted memory, as was Ineluki, the Storm King.*

Faint but terrifying memories swam up from deep inside him, lightning and fire and a swaying tower, the sound of impossibly loud bells. He did his best to push it away, but even the slightest touch of it sickened him. *I remember the Storm King,* he said.

Not as well as I do, now that my memories are returning to me. Ineluki was my father's brother. As they drifted up the long spiral of stairs, her words seemed to trail in the air like a funeral scarf.

My mother was Briseyu of the Silver Braids, she said. *She gave me the names of things and made sense of them. My father was Hakatri, the Protector's heir. He and his younger brother fought the black dragon when I was only a child, and though they slew it at last, my father was terribly burned by its blood. In the end, because pain filled his every moment, waking and sleeping, he left us in search of healing—or so my mother said. But whatever the cause of his leaving, he never returned.*

Her thoughts felt as harsh as a winter gale.

Ineluki grew apart from the rest of us after my father left, perhaps because of what happened when they fought the cold-drake, perhaps because of something that was always in him. He turned strange and silent, and lost himself in dreams of what might have been. He seemed to think about nothing except undoing the damage that our people, the Gardenborn, had suffered since escaping to this new land. Though I begged him, the only stories he would tell me of my father were angry ones, chronicles of loss. And when the mortal warriors from the north at last came to lay siege to Asu'a, Ineluki grew so fell that he slew his own father, Iyu'unigato, and would have slain my grandmother Amerasu as well, had she not fled Asu'a with many of our people.

Ineluki, my uncle, or at least his living form, was destroyed when his great song failed to defeat the mortal invaders, and Asu'a—our home—fell into their hands.

Her thoughts seemed more than just painful now, as though she had been pierced with a barb that tormented her but could not be pulled out.

By the Heart of the Gatherer and by our Lost Garden, the burning legacy of the worm's blood went on and on! At the moment of his death, nothing was left of the Ineluki we had known, only hatred and the lust for vengeance that had so twisted his life. But he would not find peace even in death. Utuk'ku discovered him on the far side of the Veil and plotted to bring him back.

I . . . I remember this. I remember! He thought of the spire that had stretched toward the sky like a pointing white finger. *It happened in the tower. Yes, and my wife's father was at the heart of it all. He and the red priest Pryrates.*

My wife! He could not summon her name, but the truth of her now returned to him, sudden and startling as a blaze of trumpets—his wife, his lost love. It felt like a blessing, but it also brought a terrible stab of despair that for a moment threatened to pull him apart.

The mortal king, the red priest, they were only tokens on a painted map, all of them, his companion said. *Pieces in a mad game that could never have ended other than badly. But the dead who cannot let go do not think as living things do. They are spirits entirely made of passion, of despair, of longing.*

Is that what we have become? he wondered.

I cannot say. Some sense of her unformed thoughts drifted to him—an acknowledgment of limits, a helpless shrug. *It is true that I still feel angry. Perhaps there is nothing else left of me.*

But you said that Utuk'ku still has you in her power.

The gray figure shimmered a little, and for a moment he was frightened that she would vanish altogether, leaving him alone and still nameless, but the moment passed. *She does. She holds the three of us in a delicate balance—the three faces of the Dark Lady. It is a conjunction that can shake a world—or rebuild it. But I do not think that Utuk'ku, ancient and bitter as she is, plans to make the world green again. Certainly not for mortals, and likely not for her own folk, either.*

They were still drifting up the murky, seemingly endless spiral of stairs. The mist that obscured the far side of the great well, and hid its ornate carved balconies, had grown thicker. Everything but the stair was now a ghost-land of swirling gray.

It comes back to me now—my name, she said abruptly, and there was both wonder and sadness in her thoughts. *My mother named me Likimeya. And with my name, I remember all of my losses, the long decline of our house from peace into anguish. But even with so much sorrow, I think it better than remaining nameless.*

Her words stirred his own memories, but at first they were only fragments, bits of spinning flotsam. *But why am I in your dream?* he asked. *Can you remember my name, too?*

Your name? I never knew it, young mortal. But you have been in so many of my dreams of late—there must be some reason for that. He could barely make out her spectral form, but her voice still came as clearly as if she whispered in his ear.

But you did know me! I was in Jao é-Tinukai'i with you—don't you remember? Amerasu brought me to the butterfly place when she spoke to you all that night. The night . . . the night she died.

And suddenly he could see his companion clearly again, or at least the gray outline and the shadowy face returned. *Hold,* she said. *Jao é-Tinukai'i, you say? Then you are not who I thought you were.*

What? What do you mean?

The smear of face turned away from him as she began to drift upward once more. Within moments she had melted into the growing white emptiness that was now filling the dream-Asu'a. But her voice, still strong, echoed through his thoughts. *It must have been kin of yours, I see now. Possessor of the same blood, touched in the same way by the Dream Road. He was in many of my dreams. I spoke to him.*

For a moment he was overcome by wonder and by a kind of terror. *Was it my son? Have you met my dead son on the Dream Road?*

No. No, I do not think so. This one had the feel of someone still caught in the coils of life. But he was of your line, and I sensed him near me as I wandered through this nowhere. He was lost and confused. I was astonished that he could perceive me when my own flesh and bone and blood could not.

Lost? And then it came to him. *Was it my grandson?* he asked. At first the name would not come, just as he could not remember his own, but then he clutched at it, felt it, and remembered. *Was it Morgan? My grandson?*

Perhaps. He was certainly much like you. Yes, I believe it could have been him who spoke in my dream. And now I begin to see everything more clearly. Her voice, which for so long had been full of the calm of endings long foreseen, of defeat gracefully accepted, now grew sharper and stronger. *Yes, that must have been more than happenstance. And so must this be. All of this. It must be. It . . . must . . . be . . .*

Her words grew faint, as though whatever stood between them was stretching, pushing them apart from each other.

Likimeya? Don't leave! Tell me my name if you know it! And what about my grandson? Did he need help?

At first only silence answered him. Then he heard her again, but this time from such distance that it was barely a whisper.

I must think. I must try to understand what this means. Forgive me—forgive us all . . .

And after that he did not hear her again. The whiteness slowly closed around him, obliterating everything.

If Lillia had disliked being in the chamber behind the door, the stairwell was worse. Cobwebs hung from the roof in trailing, clotted strands or in tattered nets, waving as she passed beneath them. She squinted up into the darkness before each step, looking for spiders. Lillia did not like spiders.

She almost dropped her shrinking candle when a wafting cobweb brushed her cheek, making her jump and squeal. She batted at it, but it wound around her fingers, and she did a little dance of disgust until she managed to wipe it on the stones of the stairway wall; even with it gone, her heart did not slow its rapid drumming.

Why hasn't anyone come? How long have I been missing? She didn't know, couldn't tell. Time usually meant the bells of the chapel spire or the louder, deeper tolling from St. Sutrin's, marking out the times of prayer, summoning her back to supper, or sending her to bed. Why couldn't she hear the chapel bells tolling the hour?

I've been here hours. It must be hours!

She continued to descend as carefully as she could, always aware of the wax running down the candle and hardening on her fingers. How long did a candle burn? It was the sort of question with which she often pestered grownups, but now that she really, truly wanted to know, there was no one to ask.

"Hoy!" she cried, suddenly desperate to hear a voice, even her own. "Hoy! I'm down here! It's me, Princess Lillia!"

But though the echoes rattled away in all directions, they died without an answer.

A little while later she heard a scraping sound. It sounded very near, and Lillia stopped, half-frightened, half-hopeful. Had someone heard her? Were they coming to get her out? The memory of the sweeper's son who had become stuck in the kitchen chimney one holiday came back to her. Three Erkynguards with ropes had climbed onto the roof of the Throne Hall; several more soldiers had gone to the kitchen to poke the handles of their pikes up the chimney, as if to dislodge a noisy bird, but only loosed great spattering drifts of soot. All the kitchen workers had gathered around the great fireplace to offer advice while Lillia had stood watching from the edge of the crowd. She could still remember the small, hopeless sound of the boy's voice, saying "That be me, milord! That be me!" every time a pike handle poked him in a sensitive spot.

They had freed him at last by taking off the chimney cap and pulling him up and onto the roof. The boy, so black with ashes that he looked like a wingless crow, had been carried down to the kitchen and then—to his deep shame—stripped naked and scrubbed clean by the kitchen staff as he cried and said over and over that he couldn't help it, it hadn't been his fault, that they shouldn't scold him.

Lillia first thought was that if she was offered that kind of rescue, she would refuse it. The idea of such a public shaming made her feel angry and mistreated. But only a few moments later, as her candle's flame wavered once more and almost died, she decided that was a silly way to think and she would be happy to be found and saved, even if it meant being scolded and even scrubbed in front of the servants and soldiers and everyone.

But they wouldn't do that to me. They wouldn't dare. I'm not a chimney sweep's boy.

She did not take much pleasure in the distinction, though. *Better to be a saved sweep than a lost princess,* a voice in her head suggested.

After the first scraping noise, nothing else broke the silence but the shuffling of her own cautious footsteps. When she reached the bottom, she found that she had a choice of two ways. She chose the least cobwebbed of the two, but within a few dozen steps the corridor ended in a wall, so she turned back and tried the other direction. It bent first one way, then another, in a series of angles that made no sense. As she crept ahead, she did her best to avoid brushing against the abandoned spider's webs, but never took her eyes off the candle for long. It was now much less than half of its initial length.

I have to get back to the room where the door is before this goes out, she thought. *If I don't, I'll be lost down here in the dark.*

She turned back, but only a few score of speeding heartbeats later, she again heard the scraping sound. When she turned a corner she found the passage blocked, though another corridor led off at a right angle.

Lillia's hand was shaking so hard she could barely hold the candle. *It wasn't like that before!* She was certain of it, certain that the way back should continue straight ahead. The corridor had changed, somehow—but how could that be? She sniffed the air of the unfamiliar passage and smelled something that she only recognized after taking a few more breaths: it was the sea, or at least the Kynslagh. She remembered her grandfather telling her that there were caves at the bottom of the Hayholt's rocky hill, along the shores of the bay, and that several people had entered the castle that way during the Storm King's War. She thought he had even said that Uncle Timo was one of them, but that didn't seem right. Surely little Uncle Timo with his limp and his worried face wouldn't be climbing into the castle to fight the wicked Norns! She decided to ask him, then remembered that she couldn't ask anyone anything because she was lost under the castle.

What if they never come? The idea, which she had pushed down until she could almost pretend she had never thought it, came rushing back up. *What if they don't know I'm down here?*

These fearful thoughts, which seemed all around her in the darkness, like the powdery ash that had turned the sweeper's boy black, were suddenly blown from her mind when she turned another bend in the passage.

Before her, on a broken stone block, sat a serving tray with two plates upon it. One plate was empty except for shiny smears of what looked like grease, but a hunk of bread and piece of cheese stood on the other, as if they had been dropped down from Heaven just for a hungry princess.

And she *was* hungry suddenly—starvingly empty. But how could this be?

The light of the candle seemed to shrink until all that she could see was the lump of brown bread and the waxy shine of the cheese, but her thoughts had exploded into chaos. Some of those thoughts warned her, *"Trap, trap, it is a trap!"* but she also felt a slow-dawning fright as she realized that she must be somewhere different now, somewhere she had not passed through on the way down—because she would have seen the tray, she would have!

Lillia stood, frozen with indecision, then reached slowly out and curled her fingers around the knob of bread. She lifted it to her nose and sniffed, fearful of poison, though she had no idea of what poison smelled like; but she could detect only the scent of wheat flour. She held up the front of her dress and dropped the bread into it, then reached out for the cheese. As she took it, she heard another noise—not a scrape this time, but a near-silent padding—and she immediately retreated down the corridor. As she did, holding the food in her dress with one hand and the candle in the other, something caught at her sleeve. In a panic, she yanked away from whatever had caught her, then she was free and walking as fast as she could in the direction she had come, heart knocking like a woodpecker at the trunk of a tree.

Two bends more and she stopped, panting. She stood in silence until she was certain nothing was coming down the passageway after her, but she was still too frightened to eat anything. Instead, she leaned against the wall of the corridor and tried to make sense of what had happened. She had only come a short distance from the end of the stairwell, but now she was in a strange place, and the way back had disappeared. How?

Even as she struggled with this frightening, unanswerable question, she heard a strange slithering sound, then something brushed her face and shoulder. She squeaked in surprise and leaped away from the wall just as whatever it was slid past her and hit the floor with a quiet slap. It was a cord—a loop of slender rope that someone or something had dropped from above. The noose only lay there for the length of a heartbeat, then it was yanked back again. Lillia held her candle up and saw a flicker of movement in the shadows in the narrow space at the top of the wall, and broken cobwebs waving. The shape was only there for an instant, a suggestion of dark red robes and a flash of pale, bare legs as thin and disturbing as the limbs of the crippled beggars in Market Square. An instant later it had vanished.

It's hunting me, she realized, even as terror squeezed her throat until she feared she would never get her breath again. Whatever had just tried to catch her was hiding somewhere in the cobwebbed shadows overhead. From there, it could follow the light of her candle wherever she went.

In that moment of terror, Lillia blew out the flame. The darkness leaped up all around her, gathering in everything.

Likimeya's gone. I'm alone again. Alone and nameless and nowhere.

Everything around him had turned white, white as the heart of a blizzard, white as a skull tumbled for years in a river, and he felt no desire to continue with this dreary imitation of life. He still did not know his own name, but he could remember enough to understand how completely he had failed. His beloved was dead, his only child was dead, his grandson was lost, and his land overrun. Nothing was left that tied him to his life. Nothing mattered.

But as he stood, a stubborn part of him sang a song of rebellion in his ear. *Then why stop? Climb up! What is being hidden from you? What is it that you think is beyond your reach? Climb up and find out!*

But it would be so much easier simply to merge with the white. To *become* the white, to let it flow into every part of his being until it had turned all his passions and memories into colorless swirls. *Surrender . . .*

You can always surrender later, the childish, hopeful, and painfully foolish part of him urged. *Surrender is the last move, when all else is exhausted.*

But I am *exhausted.*

You are mortal, that's all. Mortals weary, then they sleep, then they grow strong again. It almost seemed like Likimeya had returned to chide him, but he knew it was his own impatient nature that pushed at him. *You are sleeping now, in a sense. You are in a dream, but someday you may awaken again . . .*

Slowly and almost unwillingly at first, with thoughts so muddled he could barely believe he was doing it, he began to drift upward once more. And to his surprise, as he rose the emptiness began to thin into . . . something. He no longer saw the endless steps of the Tan'ja Stair beneath him, but rock. Rock and snow. The whiteness that only moments before had covered everything now shrank into flying streaks of white that he could feel on his face like the pinprick touch of tiny thorns.

Snow. It's snow!

And almost instantly, even before the first voices floated to him, he knew where he was—on Urmsheim, the great, icy peak, searching for the lost sword Thorn.

"Here, boy," cried someone ahead of him in the snow. It was Haestan—poor, doomed Haestan. "Watch thy step, now!"

"I am with him." He recognized the calm tones of the Sithi prince, Jiriki. "I will not let him fall."

Up they all struggled, as the wind snatched at them like a furious child determined to fling away these small, unsatisfying toys. The snow swirled, the sky that showed through was dull as lead, and the cold gnawed at him like a living thing. His fingers felt like lumps of ice, and he could not feel his feet at all, but he knew he must keep going, must keep climbing.

Because he was frightened now. *They don't know! They don't know what's waiting at the top. The sword, yes, but the dragon too!* He could see the monster as if it already loomed before him, the bristling white back, the hateful, pale-blue eyes like the sunken orbs of a corpse. *It will kill Jiriki!* He redoubled his efforts, but as he did, the invisible earth far below seemed to increase its downward pull, tugging backward on every part of him so that each step was an exhausting struggle.

I can't let it happen. But trying to save himself and Jiriki from the dragon would mean that the creature's burning black blood would splash him again, marking him forever—and not just on the outside. Never again would he be able to live in peaceful ignorance of the spinning world and the Greater Worm that girdled it. Never again would he be able to retreat into the innocence and irresponsibility of youth.

But I can't give up.

He staggered on, knowing that the monstrous white worm waited for him above, that he would fight it and either die or be forever changed. Upward. What else could he do? The whiteness gathered and the snow blew harder. Ice stung his face until he wanted to scream. Even the voices of those climbing with him were swallowed by the wind's triumphant howling.

Now the white had once more spread everywhere. The wind still blew, but below its angry howl he heard a deep rumble broken by intermittent crashes, like great stones being split. A momentary flash turned the whiteness as bright as the disk of the winter sun, and he saw that there were steps beneath his feet once more, an orderly procession winding upward.

It's the Tan'ja Stairs! His thoughts shifted, changeable as if he dreamed. *The Yásira! I will reach the Yásira!*

But when the lightning flashed again, he saw that the steps were not the crisp white blocks of Likimeya's dream-stairway, perfect as the carved facets of a gem. These stairs were old and had been worn by many footsteps. They might have been beautiful once, but now they were chipped and flecked with ash, and the spiral of their upward progress was much tighter.

Where am I? But he kept climbing even as he struggled to understand. Lightning flared, turning a window above him into a blazing rectangle before it faded to darkness once more. Thunder followed, rolling and booming until it seemed to shake the very stone beneath his feet, and he remembered where he was.

Green Angel Tower. I'm in the tower, climbing to the bell chamber. I have to hurry! I must take the sword there, before the Storm King's spell is complete! He could feel Bright-Nail in his hand, heavy as shame, though he could see nothing of it but a stripe of shadow through the mists that filled the tower stairwell. *The king's sword—John's sword! It wants to go up!*

But he knew what no one else did, that the sword wanted only to join its brothers, and that Pryrates and the Storm King were waiting at the top of Green Angel Tower to complete their terrible spell. Time would roll backward on itself, then mortal men and all their works would vanish from the world and the dead would rise and rule over all. He was desperate to stop it from happening, but he also knew what was in store: Elias, the mortal king, would die, killed by his own daughter. The spell would fail, destroying all that the Storm King had built, and leveling the tower as well. And for him, his own life would be changed forever, beyond anything he could have imagined.

Why can't I remember my name when I can remember so much else?

If he kept climbing to the top of the tower, he would become king. But then everything he loved would be taken from him—every person and every belief, stolen away by mischance and death and time, until he had nothing else.

But still he climbed upward as the Storm King's clouds turned the sky black and the heavens raged and flung their bolts at the cowering earth. The thunder roared with the triumphant rage of Ineluki Storm King himself. *Mortal! You can do nothing!*

I can try.

And as he thought this, still pushing grimly upward through the blinding mist and the monstrous noise and buffeting of the storm, the whiteness closed on him again.

No, he thought. *I cannot turn back. I am needed. I promised—!*

The clamor softened, until it was only the rush of wind across the cliffs above the Kynslagh. It battered him and chilled him, but as the fog drifted away again, dispersed by wind and the pallid sun of an Octander morning, he could see the trail beneath his feet and the drying grass that grew beside it. Far below, at the bottom of a great open expanse of air, the waters of the Kynslagh splashed against the Hayholt's docks.

But the mildness of the day, the thinning of the mists, did not lift his heart at all. He could see the oblong shape of his beloved's bier just ahead of him on the winding track, carried slowly toward the burial ground by four strong Erkynguardsmen. And what was in the coffin was barely even his wife's body. He had not even been left with a cold cheek to kiss in farewell or cold hand to clutch, only a charred insult, a blackened thing.

They took everything from me!

He turned and looked down from the hill track, down the rough rock face to the booming, sunlight-painted swells of the Kynslagh, and knew that if he took but a single step in that direction, it would all end—all his care, all responsibility, everything that had weighed him down for so long, all gone in a moment of free flight. It would end with green darkness and quiet.

All over. The story finished.

A hand touched him, lightly. He could feel someone beside him.

"Majesty? We must go up."

It was Tiamak. His counselor and friend had seen something in his face, perceived a danger that no one else had. For a moment he stood, balanced between the step into freedom and the horrible farewell he would have to endure at the end of the path, atop the windswept hill. Cairns and headstones and emptiness forever. Or a swoop through the air like a bird taking wing. Either way, life would go on—with him or without him.

He felt Tiamak's hand tighten on his forearm. "Can you hear me?" the Wrannaman said. "You must keep climbing."

Weary beyond expression, he turned back to the steps, mounting slowly beneath the great weight of his life and losses, but still climbing. For all the other things that were familiar, his name still floated somewhere beyond his reach, so he kept climbing. And as he did so the deadening whiteness swept in again, as if a great bank of fog had rolled across the Kynslagh at tempest-speed, covering everything, even the path, even the last moments above ground of his beloved. Of Miriamele.

Miriamele! It was more than a name that came back, it was a door into the life he had lost. *How I miss you, Miri. Oh, God, there are no words to say it.*

The whiteness that surrounded him began to harden into something more intricate, more complicated, until he found himself standing once more on the airy uppermost steps of the Tan'ja Stair, which were bathed in light and color beneath a dome of white stone filaments. Far above, the sky spread cornflower-blue beyond the lacy, carved stone, but something else had caught his eye and made him stare upward.

Every inch of the dome's open fretwork was covered with moving spots of color. Butterflies.

The silent creatures were everywhere, crowded on every strut and crossing, crawling along the white marble walls beneath the dome or fluttering around him as he slowly made his way through the galleries circling the base of the vast domed roof. Butterflies fanned their wings slowly on every surface, every possible perch—grass-green, orange as flame, purple, pink, black, blood-red. The sun streaming down out of the cloudless sky met their wings and flew apart in a thousand different rainbow hues. Spots of color moved and mingled on the unstained whiteness of the gallery floor as if the light had fallen in radiant drops straight from Heaven.

He shuffled forward between the flares of winged color. Butterflies lit on his shoulder. Others eddied up from the floor at his approach like powdery gouts of jewel-dust, flickering and glinting.

Someone was waiting for him just ahead, a small, upright figure seated beneath the immense canopy of light and color. He did not recognize her at first, only saw that she was someone high and strong and fair, with a face lit by a deep, calm love. She might have been a woman of thirty summers, she might have been some ageless spirit, or even Elysia herself, the Mother of God: he only knew that he wanted to be near her. But as he drew closer he at last saw her amber eyes, kind and patient, and he realized he had seen her before.

First Grandmother? he said. *Lady Amerasu?*

So you have made your decision. He heard her words clearly, though her gently smiling mouth did not move. *I am not surprised.* She lifted her hand and made a gesture that seemed both a blessing and a farewell. *The end of things is not known, Seoman Snowlock. Do not doubt yourself—you have always done what you needed to do.*

Seoman! He felt as if his heart had been abruptly returned to his body. *That's me, Seoman—Simon the kitchen-boy, Simon the mooncalf. I am Simon. And I am the king.*

Remember those who went before you, she said, but she was already fading into white. The spiderweb roof of the Yásira, the bright, shifting gleam of the butterflies, and the arrowing rays of sunlight, all began to blur together into a single, indistinct glow. *When you are weak, remember them. When you are frightened, let them help you. And trust in . . .*

And then she was gone. Everything was gone, and he was falling as slowly as thistledown through vast, empty spaces.

"So," said a new voice. "You have decided to survive. I should thank you. It will make many things sweeter for me."

Heavy-headed, chest and lungs aching, and his body weak as a newborn calf, Simon struggled to make sense of his surroundings but could not. It was dark and he was on his back; for a moment he thought he might be in his bed again, waking into the simple misery of another dreadful day after another empty, dreamless night. *But my wound!* he remembered—the sword in his chest! He tried to touch the place he had felt it pierce him, but something rattled and held him back.

Chains. He was chained.

"Not surprising that you are a little confused," said the voice. "You have been sleeping like a dead one for days."

Simon sat up, but a wave of dizziness nearly felled him in the middle of the exercise. He lay on a pile of rags, surrounded by damp, straw-covered flagstones, and the only light came from a barred window at one end of the very small chamber. Simon lifted his hand toward the window and finally realized that he was shackled to the wall behind him. Someone was peering in at him from the barred window, but the only light was behind them, and the face was in shadow. "Who is that?" he said. "Where am I?" More memories of the fight came back to him. "Unver?"

The shape in the doorway laughed. "The son of your old friend has left you for dead and gone back to his grasslands—yes, I know who he truly is. You are going to learn a few more unfortunate things as well."

Finally, Simon was able to put the sound of the voice and the shadowy silhouette together. "Pasevalles? Is that you? What happens here?"

"Much and much." The head shook slowly from side to side. "I will explain it all to you, never fear. But you must learn two hard facts."

"What are you talking about?"

Pasevalles went on as if he hadn't spoken. "The first is that you are no longer the king. The second is that you are no longer the king because you died at Winstowe."

28

The Bowman's Answer

"Why the sulky face, Count?" asked Samreas. "Is it such a hardship to share a mount with Sir Gurryn? And we did not even tie your hands! Remember, we could have thrown you across the saddle and carried you to the king arse-up."

"I would almost prefer that," Eolair said. "At least then it would be clear to all who see us that I am being taken against my will."

Samreas laughed. "Your sensitivities are too refined, my lord, and out of step with the time. The good folk of Hernystir are weary of nobles who take a share from everyone and give nothing back. They will see you as the king's prisoner, which you are, and it will please them."

So much for the thin fiction of being called to a royal audience, Eolair thought, not that he had ever believed that. But he also knew it was useless bandying words with Samreas: the hawk-faced knight took a positive pleasure in the knowledge that the prisoner was not enjoying the long trip west to the capital.

This is likely the last time I will see any of these places, Eolair thought, not without a touch of self-pity, but it was a minor voice in a much larger chorus. *I have spent so much time away that I had almost forgotten the beauty of my own land.*

It was many leagues' journey from his family lands at Nad Mullach to Hernysadharc. For the greater part they had ridden through the meadowlands known as the Fearanthar, following the winding course of the River Cuihmne, which ran down from the mountains to join the greater flood of the Baraillean on its way south to the sea. The winter grasslands were largely empty but for a few wandering, unshorn sheep; other than the occasional shepherd, the only signs of life were trails of smoke from some of the local cottages. But in the last few days they had reached the hills and begun the long upward trek to the base of the Grianspog Mountains where the city lay. Here the landscape showed less of what men had built and more of what wind and rain had accomplished; steep river valleys and high tors like abandoned ancient forts, their tops dusted by snow. They rode past ancient quarries, long abandoned and indistinguishable from the rocky slopes except by the widening of the roads where great stones had once set off on their journeys across the countryside, most to wind up in defensive walls or manor houses, or—in a much earlier age—to stand on isolated hilltops as mute symbols of the gods.

It was a beautiful land, and though Eolair did not greatly fear death, it saddened him to think that he would never again hear the birds of the high, lonely moors, or the ringing cascades that filled some of the steeper river valleys with noise and glimmering light.

The Blue Top Hills, Curath Tor, the snowy heights of Rhynn's Beacon, they all line up and then slide away, like old friends come to say farewell. And I still labor to fix all that I see in my memory, though it is likely no one will ever share it. I might as well be a monk in a forgotten temple, copying manuscripts for no one.

He did not have much choice, of course. Not only was he forced to ride like a child on the back of one of the Silver Stags' saddles, but he was surrounded by a dozen more of the king's elite horsemen, not one of them above half his age. After all the indignities he had suffered in the last year, he knew he could barely run at all, and in these open meadows and high, barren hillsides there would be few places to hide. In fact, the idea of escaping was so ludicrous that even though he cared not a whit for his dignity, he did not think it even worth considering.

So instead I will smell the heather and watch the crows scudding across the clouds. There are worse things to do while waiting to die.

Eolair was surprised when the company did not take the wide road to Hernysadharc, but instead continued westward along the edge of the mountains. As they climbed higher, he had a momentary glimpse of the Taig, the ancient wooden palace on the city's highest hill, but could make out only its verdigrised copper roof and a sprinkling of colorful pennants visible through a gap in the hillside trees.

"I thought I was being taken to Hernysadharc," he said.

"I never told you that." Samreas spoke flatly, but his expression showed suppressed amusement.

"You said you were taking me to the king." *Am I to be executed in the middle of nowhere, in secret?* But if so, why had Samreas and the Stags bothered carrying him all this way through Hernystir? They could have slit his throat and dumped him anywhere outside his own lands and nobody would ever have known.

"And that is what I am doing. It is you who assumed King Hugh was at the Taig." Samreas smirked, as though he had proved something important. "As it happens, the king is elsewhere, and that is where we are taking you. Elsewhere."

Eolair did not want to give Samreas the satisfaction of sneering at him again, but he could not help being curious. "If King Hugh is not in Hernysadharc, who rules there?"

"His Majesty Hugh, of course. But Count Curudan acts as his regent until the king returns. You know Curudan, do you not?"

"I did not know he was a count." Eolair shrugged. "It seems the king rewards his lackeys well, even as he mistreats those who truly love their country."

One of the Silver Stags snarled and rode closer to where Eolair sat behind Sir Gurryn, but Samreas waved the man back with a stern look. "Curudan has always been one of our king's staunchest friends. But you need not be envious. Both of you will not hold the same title for very long."

Eolair ignored this but could not help puzzling. Why was King Hugh not at the Taig? Did he fear an uprising—or even assassination? Could resistance to his misrule have already begun?

It was only after a long days' riding, when the walls of Hernysadharc were several leagues behind them, that things became clearer. They turned off the main road to follow a steep, narrow track upward. Now, no matter how they turned, the granite peaks of the Grianspog loomed always above them, staring down like unhappy ancestors contemplating the failures of their descendants. Eolair began to understand then and felt a chill that went well beyond the fear of his own death. "Hugh is in the old Sithi city inside the mountain, isn't he?" he said at last. "The place the immortals called the Silverhome."

"You should know it well, since it was you and the old king's daughter who discovered it anew," Samreas said. "But like a child who finds a gold coin and can think of nothing better to do with it than chew on it, you left it behind without discovering its most important secrets. King Hugh is wiser than you. He has found *power* there—the power to free Hernystir from its years of servitude to the Erkynlandish throne."

"Your sort always mistakes power for freedom," said Eolair in disgust.

Samreas laughed. "And your sort always mistakes your own satisfaction for the way the world ought to be. But that is changing here in our land, mark my words."

Eolair fell silent again, overtaken by memories of the ancient settlement that the Sithi had named *Mezutu'a*—the Silverhome. He would not cheer Samreas by revealing it, but secretly he was more than a little fearful of seeing the dead city again. It had been while they explored that almost-abandoned place that the old king's daughter Maegwin had finally slid over into the madness from which she had never recovered, and Eolair had realized how much he cared for her even as he understood that it was too late for the two of them to find any happiness.

So much for hills and valleys and birds, he thought. *So much for collecting memories to soothe me in the long darkness. Now I shall think of my poor, sick Maegwin and how little I did to save her.*

Eolair's silence lasted so long that Sir Gurryn called to Samreas, "By Murhagh's one good arm, you shut him up properly that time, Captain!"

For Aelin, Yeja'aro was a puzzle that he could not solve.

The young Sitha—for however many years he might have lived, Aelin felt certain he *was* young by the measure of his own people—seemed a mass of contradictions. He had once tried to kill Aelin, but now would awaken him with a touch so light and careful it might have been the brush of a moth's wing. Yeja'aro's concept of honor also confused Aelin. The Sitha did not seem to think of it as something to be protected or defended, but as something completely inseparable from himself, like his body. The words "my honor will not permit it" meant, as far as Yeja'aro was concerned, the end of any discussion, as if he had said "I cannot fly" or "I am not that tall"—simple, irrefutable facts. In the past days Yeja'aro had led them through many dangerous situations, down narrow tracks where even Aelin, with his weak mortal eyes, could see Norn warriors encamped barely a stone's throw away on either side, and yet had somehow got them past the Norn troops safely. At the same time, it was obvious that Yeja'aro was too rigid, too angry and full of himself, to be any kind of true leader. The immortal was a natural follower, but he did not have enough respect for mortals to follow one.

Leadership was much on Aelin's mind as the little company made its way across the abandoned farmlands west of the upper Westfold, putting distance between themselves and the Norn soldiers. Aelin's men, Maccus and Evan, were in an almost constant state of revolt against their Sitha guide's aggressive, impatient demands, and though the two Hernystirmen held to different faiths, their distrust of Yeja'aro led them to side with each other far more than with their leader, Aelin, who had no choice but to straddle every disagreement in the hope of conducting all of them to safety.

"A noble cannot show weakness, either in war or diplomacy," his father had often said. *"Once he has reached a decision, it must be as Heaven itself has ordered it. Otherwise, his command of his liegemen will become a thing of conversation and argument, which is death in a time of need. Show no weakness!"*

But after his father died, Aelin's own mother had told him, "It is when you are most certain that you are right—that your cause or belief is beyond question—that you must ask yourself why." She had smiled as if to soften her words, which had nevertheless filled the young Aelin with confusion and even anger. "That was your father's greatest mistake—may Holy Oymos lead him safely to Heaven's peace." She touched three fingers to her mouth in the Sign of the Knot. "He was so determined to lead by his example that once he decided on something, nothing could change his mind. He lost friends that way, and a few battles as well."

Disbelieving but hopeful, the younger Aelin had asked, "Did Father fight, then? I know he took our household guard to the Thrithings War, but I heard he wasn't in the battle—that King Simon had ended it by the time Father and his men got there."

"There are other kinds of battles than the kind fought with spears and swords," his mother had said. "The life of a landowner and a king's counselor is full of them. Your father was known for rectitude, for principle and bravery, but he lost some fights he could have won if he had been a bit more willing to bend."

At the time, his mother's words had seemed like an attack on the things Aelin held most dear—his father's legacy, the honor of their rank, and the duty of a nobleman to lead others—but over the years he had learned more lessons from his great-uncle, Count Eolair, and from the High King and High Queen as well. Sometimes it was best to bend. Sometimes it was the only way to succeed.

But still, each day with Yeja'aro guiding them stretched Aelin's leadership to its utmost. The Sitha spoke to the Hernystirmen as though they were children, something that drove Maccus in particular to fury. Blackbeard, as he had been called since the first inky whiskers had sprouted on his chin, was an able fighter and unquestionably brave, but his inability to rein in his anger was a continuing liability. Several times Aelin had barely been able to keep the younger man from challenging Yeja'aro to fight, or from leaving the company entirely.

Evan was a different animal, thoughtful and cautious, full of clever ideas, but Aelin thought Evan's Aedonite faith sometimes got in his way. Despite their complete reliance on their Sitha guide to bring them through the Wealdhelm hills safely, Evan had a superstitious fear of the young immortal and would not go near him unless it was absolutely necessary. Aelin cared little about what people chose to believe as long as it did not interfere with what must be done, and so far, Evan had not crossed that line. But it had been a close thing too many times.

In fact, Aelin was so consumed by these ongoing struggles that he was caught by surprise when Yeja'aro waved them to a halt in a driving rain on the banks of the Baraillean and announced that the time had come to part ways. "You are only a short way from your destination," he said, face as usual devoid of any emotions Aelin could recognize. "And I have tasks still to perform, promises to Aditu and her brother."

Maccus and Evan hung back, as usual, uncomfortable with the Sitha and unaware that he was leaving them. They sat on their horses in the sheeting rain and watched Aelin talk to Yeja'aro, murmuring back and forth as they tried to guess what the immortal had found to complain about now.

"And where will you go?" Aelin asked.

Yeja'aro was silent for a long moment, as if deciding whether the Hernystirman, with whom he had traveled for many dangerous days, and with whom he had fought several skirmishes, could be trusted. "First to the mortal High King Seoman, Jiriki's friend, to tell him the news that his lost grandson was heard to be alive and traveling with Tanahaya of Shisae'ron. Then afterwards I will ride into the Hernystiri mountains to deliver a message to *S'hue* Yizashi at Skyglass Lake."

"Skyglass Lake? I know of it, though it has a dangerous name among our folk. And what will you tell this Yizashi?"

Yeja'aro frowned. "That is not my secret to share." His look made it clear there would be no compromise.

Aelin shrugged. What could a communication between two chieftains of the Sithi mean to him, anyway? He had more than enough to think about.

"Then if we are to part here, Yeja'aro, I thank you for what you have done to keep me and my men alive. We would never have got this far without you."

Now Yeja'aro shrugged, a fluid ripple of movement that Aelin had learned to recognize during his brief time among the Fair Folk. "I did what I promised. I could do no less with my honor held captive against it. Your men are badly disciplined, Sir Aelin but you, at least, are not a fool."

Which was the closest thing to a kind word, let alone a compliment, that Aelin had yet heard from their Sitha guide. "Ride well, then," he said.

Yeja'aro nodded once, then gave a low whistle, and his horse began to trot southward.

Aelin watched as the fire-haired Sitha reached the bend of the river and followed its course back toward the east.

Maccus and Evan rode up to join him. "Did he finally lose his temper with us?" Maccus asked.

"Not at all. He rides on to fulfill his other obligations. As we must, too." Aelin had to conceal a sudden grin. "He said that you two lacked discipline."

Evan said nothing, but Maccus Blackbeard narrowed his eyes. "If he had said it to my face, I would have showed him discipline—a heavy weight of it."

"Oh, be quiet, Maccus," Aelin said, but not unkindly. "You had plenty of chances. Let us ride on. The weather will get no better today, and I am already soaked through. A few more hours and we will be back on my family lands." He turned his horse north toward the ford.

As they rode through the woods that covered the skirts of the homely Blue Tops, Aelin soothed himself with thoughts of Nad Mullach and how good it would be to see it once more. The dogs would rush out, of course, roaring and romping with excitement, and soon his sister Gwynna would come out to see what the fuss was about. His grandmother would be waiting in her accustomed chair, and it was even possible that Eolair would be there as well. It would be a happy meeting, even if most of the news he was bringing was foul. For one night at least, he and Maccus and Evan would warm themselves at a proper fire, eat heartily, and all would at least *seem* well. After months of being away, that would be gift enough.

But as they rode through the rain, through ancient trees that swayed and waved their limbs like hungry beggars, he realized that the sound that had been growing louder was not thunder, but hoofbeats. For a moment he thought it might be Yeja'aro returning, but the noise came from the wrong direction. Someone else was riding after them—and riding swiftly.

The others heard it too. They drew together to face whatever was coming, swords drawn, as a lone rider burst into view around the forest's edge. Their pursuer was hooded and cloaked against the downpour, so it was not until the rider looked up, saw the three men waiting, and threw back her hood that Aelin realized it was a woman.

As he stared, the words to the old prayer came back to him:

Holy Mircha, clothed in rain, sky-lord's daughter and the sun's shy sister . . .

But there was nothing shy in the way the rider whooped loudly when she saw them, then stood in the stirrups, waving her arm. "Aelin!" she cried. "Sir Aelin! Wait for me!"

He recognized her as she neared. "Isleen? Isleen of Carn Inbarh? By the Holy Cauldron, is that you?"

She reined up, her white horse rearing and kicking at the air as though it could not bear to stop running. "Of course it is! I can see how you might have mistaken me, wrapped up as I am, but did you not recognize Swiftwing?" She patted the horse's shoulder. "I rode like the very wind to catch you."

Aelin turned to his men. "This is Isleen, Earl Murdo's daughter." He turned back to the young woman. "And what are you doing out in this storm?"

"Give me a moment to catch my breath," she said. "You always were impatient, Aelin."

She had changed, that was certain. The last time he had seen her, some three years or more ago, the earl's youngest daughter had been scarcely more than a child, though sharp-tongued and self-assured beyond her years. "I missed you when I was last at your father's house," he said. "He told me you were with your aunt and uncle at Lismoor."

"And so I was. But I thought you were going to let me catch my breath."

Aelin smiled. "True."

At last she straightened up in the saddle and brushed her damp, curly hair from her forehead. "I should not be so short with you. My father sent me to you with news, and the news is not good."

"Tell, then."

"First, you must not go any closer to your house at Nad Mullach. The king's Silver Stags are waiting for you there. A company of them took Eolair the moment he arrived home, then carried him away to Hernysadharc at Hugh's orders."

"What? Took Eolair?" For a moment, despite all his foreboding and all his fury over the things King Hugh had already done, it seemed impossible. "They took him out of our own house?"

She nodded. "We had a messenger from Lady Elatha. She could scarcely write clear letters, she was so full of anger and grief."

Aelin could only shake his head, overwhelmed. *Hugh must be confident beyond all understanding,* he thought. *Or completely mad.* "You said your father sent you? I beg pardon, my lady, but why you?"

Isleen gave him a look of disgust and her pale cheeks colored a little, though not with embarrassment. "Because Swiftwing is the fastest horse in our stables, and she will let no one else ride her. But do not fear, Aelin, if you are already weary of speaking to a mere girl. My father rides close behind me with many men. They should catch us up before dark."

"Does Murdo think to attack the king's men here at Nad Mullach?" A part of him wanted nothing more—the idea of Hugh's Silver Stags making themselves free with the ancestral home called up a deep rage. Surely even Hugh understood that the other nobles would not ignore such a heedless, brutal display of royal power. Even during the ancient kingship of Hern himself, a chieftain's home had always been a sacred, inviolable place.

Hugh has not just stepped over a line—he has obliterated it. But fighting the king's soldiers had been one thing in a distant border outpost like Dunath Tower. If Silver Stags had now taken Eolair under king's arrest, and planned the same thing for Aelin, then fighting back would be a clear declaration of war against the Taig and the throne.

"As always," he said with a sigh, "Heaven does not wait for man's convenience, and the gods move in their own time. We will make camp in the woods while we wait for your father, Lady Isleen."

Jiriki was riding far more than he was sleeping, but on those few occasions when exhaustion overcame him and he snatched an hour or two of half-slumber, the Dream Road seemed to have become an ominous place.

All his visions were dire, but the one that troubled him most, though he could not guess why, was of an egg that had dropped and shattered. As its essence dripped out onto the ground, a host of ants swarmed over it.

He awoke to find his kinsman Ki'ushapo riding beside him, a look of concern on his usually amiable face. "You cried out, cousin."

Jiriki shook himself awake and looked out at the moonlit forest. It was strange to see the green fastness of the Oldheart around him. In his dream entire swathes of the great wood had been reduced to blackened stumps and barren ground.

"I slept. The Dream Road is showing me things I would rather not see, but foremost among the messages it gives me is one, and that is 'Be swift!' But I also fear that we have not found enough fighters to make a difference."

"Both things are doubtless true," said Ki'ushapo. "But we can do little about them. All those who are with us are brave fighters. And likely we will find a few more to join us we before we ride to the Hayholt."

"But not enough, I fear, and the longer we seek, the later it will be before we can bring aid to the mortals."

Ki'ushapo smiled. "Such grim thoughts, old friend. Perhaps you would find better dreams if you slept somewhere other than in your saddle."

They broke their fast while riding, racing south along the Coolblood Valley, but swinging widely around Da'ai Chikiza, which the Hikeda'ya now held. Six score volunteers from the Hornet's Nest fortress followed them, nearly all blooded in battle, all willing to risk their lives under Jiriki's command. But not all his folk would be persuaded to join him so easily, he knew, and he badly needed to find more help.

Once beyond the valley, they sought out the Little Boats, gathering more warriors at each settlement, though never enough to satisfy Jiriki. Most of these exile communities had been driven out of Jao é-Tinukai'i after Utuk'ku's treacherous attack and the murder of Amerasu. They all despised the Hikeda'ya and their silver-masked mistress, but many had already followed Protector Khendraja'aro to the defense of the fortress at Wormscale Gorge. Still, two or three joined him from one forest settlement, half a dozen from the next, until the Little Boats had gifted him with another three or four score of willing fighters, male and female, old and young. Jiriki's company now numbered almost two hundred, but he knew from reports that they were facing a Sacrifice army of many thousands, so he continued to follow the ancient forest roads out to the furthest settlements, all but pleading for their help to defend the mortal castle from Utuk'ku and often meeting with more scorn than welcome.

In ancient Peja'ura, the Redstart Clan leader Ba'atigasa was one of the scornful. "Why do you come to us now?" she demanded. "We have already sent our tithe of warriors to Protector Khendraja'aro, to defend First Grandmother's secret valley."

Jiriki did his best to explain his need, but he only angered her. "Send help to the creatures who stole Asu'a from us?" she said, her narrow face set in stern lines. "No, Jiriki e-Sa'onserei, your clan's love of the Sudhoda'ya is well known, but the mortals who live on the forest's edge in ever-greater numbers have discovered our cedar groves and are already hewing down our trees as swiftly as they can. By the command of your mother and father we may not harm them, though they take what is ours and leave behind only stumps and stones. That is hard enough, but now you want us to send some of our few remaining folk to fight for the mortals again?" She shook her head. "Remember, only half a Great Year ago we sent ten dozen riders to follow you in the war against Ineluki Storm King—also on behalf of mortals—and only a handful those ever returned."

"I regret every lost life," Jiriki said as calmly as he could. "But we did not join that war simply to help the Sudhoda'ya, but because Utuk'ku had murdered our Sa'onsera, Amerasu Ship-Born, in our own home. Surely you remember that."

Ba'atigasa ignored this. "And now you want us to help them again, but meanwhile these very mortals steal our beloved cedars. Like rats, they gnaw at our means of living, but you want me to risk my people's lives for them. No, Jiriki. I honor your high house, but not this pointless errand."

Another of the other Redstart Clan stepped forward then, an old male that Jiriki recognized as Shen'de the Bowman, a fighter of no little repute.

"You know me," Shen'de said to his clanfolk. "You know that I have always honored my family and my house." He turned to Ba'atigasa. "I was honored to serve both your mother and your grandfather. And when House Sa'onserei called us, I went and was one of the few who returned."

Shen'de was one of the last of the Landborn, perhaps the oldest in all the eastern settlements, born in the first generation after the Eight Ships had brought them out of the destruction of the Garden. He had fought in many skirmishes against encroaching giants, and against the mortal Northmen in the terrible battle called *Ereb Irigú*—the Western Gate. His bravery was known to all present, and Jiriki waited patiently to hear what he would say.

"I have no great love for mortals," Shen'de declared. "In fact, I have no love for mortals at all. But that does not mean I will ignore what Jiriki i-Sa'onserei has said. For too long we have allowed the self-styled queen of the Hikeda'ya, to do as she pleases—but I say, *no more*. It is clear she means to destroy all her enemies, not merely the mortals. What good will it do us to live hidden away here in the forest deeps when she finally decides to bring the might of Nakkiga against us?" He turned to Jiriki. "I followed you before, son of Likimeya and Shima'onari, to the M'yin Azoshai and the grave of Asu'a itself. I will follow you again, even if I am the only one of my folk to do so."

"Not the only one." A young female Sitha stepped forward, her wide eyes bright. "*S'hue* Shen'de, I hear your words and I feel their truth. I know they speak from the heart of our clan, and so I will come too." She turned to Jiriki and Ki'ushapo. "My mother named me Rukayu. Others have called me Crow's Claw. I cannot wield a bow as well as my great-grandsire, but no one else here can match me."

"What she says is true," said Shen'de with obvious pride. "And she can also speak the mortal tongue."

"She cannot leave!" said clan leader Ba'atigasa. "Who else will bargain with the mortals who claim our cedars?"

Rukayu ignored him. "Will you give me leave to join you, Jiriki?" she asked. "I am young, but I have learned warfare from venerable Shen'de and could have had no better teacher."

"Of course, brave Rukayu," said Jiriki. "You are welcome in our number."

But even after Shen'de and Rukayu had declared themselves, no others came forward. "Better two brave hearts than a dozen of thinner blood," Jiriki said quietly to Ki'ushapo. Though Jiriki's company were all hungry and tired, they declined the offer of a meal from the Redstart leaders and continued on their way. Jiriki was fretful. Time was growing short, and if this was the sort of greeting he received in the rest of the ancient Zida'ya territories, he would be taking a very small force to face Utuk'ku's vast army.

May the Garden honor this consecration and nurture the fallen, he thought. *Because I see little hope of victory.*

The road to Silverhome was steep, and in Novander-month—the Pine Tree Moon, as it was still called in the Hernystiri countryside—it was also bitterly cold. As snow flurried around them, Eolair found himself shivering despite his thick cloak. He expected no comfort from Samreas and the Stags, nor did he get any.

"Only a little farther, old fellow," the captain called as they mounted yet another winding mountain path, the horses walking in file with a sheer drop beside them. Eolair was now tied to the saddle to make certain he did not throw himself over the edge and spoil King Hugh's plans. "Then you will be out of the wind—and may never have to suffer it again."

"I thank you for the words of comfort." Eolair's teeth were clenched against his shivering. "May Brynioch of the Skies take equally good care of you if you live to my age."

Samreas let out a hiss of amusement. "Old Brynioch can do as he pleases. The King and his lady have found gods that take better care of their worshippers, as all our land now acknowledges."

"Ah. So has Lady Tylleth made her Morriga devil-cult the duty of all Hernystirmen?"

Samreas's lip curled. "Do not dare to speak badly of the king's lady or I will deliver you to His Majesty with more than a few bruises on your ancient hide, Count."

Eolair thought he detected a twitch of unease beneath the officer's words and wondered if Samreas favored the king's mistress or feared her. His response had been faster and more severe than seemed ordinary. Or perhaps it was the Morriga herself that Samreas feared, the three-faced goddess of woe and war.

As the sun rose high in the sky and gray clouds briefly retreated, the riders made their way up a final series of switchbacks—each turn opening up views increasingly familiar to Eolair—until they arrived at an opening into the side of the mountain, a cave that looked as if it had been freshly hacked into the mountain's rocky skin: bits of rubble were still being cleared away by sweating, silent peasants under the watchful eye of armed soldiers.

"Welcome to the Silverhome," said Samreas. "I believe you have been here before, but now it has been reclaimed for our folk."

Eolair had entered the hidden city almost three decades before, searching for Maegwin, the old king's daughter. That time, he had made his way downward through the ancient mineshafts that pierced the mountain in many places, only to find not just Maegwin, but the lost Sithi city of Mezutu'a, hidden deep inside the rock.

This new entrance was lined with pennants that flapped and tangled in the wind, and Eolair saw stonemasons hard at work, decorating the rocky edges around the cavern's mouth—creating an entrance more befitting Hugh's sense of himself, Eolair guessed. A small force of royal guards stood on either side, watching without expression as Samreas, his Stags, and their prisoner approached, doing their best to make this gouge in the mountainside seem like a royal entryway.

But this is no door—it is a wound, he thought in disgust. *It is where the kingdom has begun to rot, as an untreated gash soon turns putrid.*

Eolair was untied and helped down, though not particularly gently, then Samreas led them into the cavern and down the first of a series of rough passages that turned first this way, then that, but always downward, until Eolair's legs, so long unused, began to ache.

It was a long journey down to the great chamber at the center when I first came here—

what was that place called? The Site of Witness. Yes, that was it. As he trudged on, with Samreas in front and guards at either side of him, he felt a moment of strange irritation. *Typical of Hugh to make a man walk so far to his execution. It is a clumsy and unplanned kind of cruelty, the act of someone who cares nothing for what is not directly in front of him.*

They descended deep into the mountain, and at last reached the outskirts of Mezutu'a, the ancient Sithi city which had been carved entirely out of the living mountain. The long-deserted streets were powdery with stone dust, and silent but for the sound of their footsteps. He thought of Maegwin again, how full of hope she had been as she had led him through this empty place. She had been so certain that the Sithi still lived here, that if only she, the king's daughter, could find them and tell them of her people's plight, the immortals would emerge and rescue their old Hernystiri allies. Instead, they had found only the Dwarrows, weird and awkwardly formed cousins of the Sithi and Norns, who had been brought out of the legendary Garden as little better than slaves. *Tinukeda'ya*, was the name the Sithi gave them. And though in the end the Dwarrows had indeed provided help, it had come far too late for the king's daughter. Maegwin had crossed over into madness and eventually into death, leaving a hole in Eolair's heart that had never been filled.

My poor, lost love. You could not escape your own sadness, he thought. *Then again, can any of us?*

They finally reached the wide corridor that led to the Site of Witness, the great circular hall at the center of the city.

Soon I will feel the god Dunn's cold hands, he thought, *and then lie long in this self-same earth, either in dark unknowing or something worse. Gods of the water and sky, I wish they had cut my head off back in Nad Mullach! At least there I could lie beside my forebears as my father and mother and grandparents do. At least my kin could come and set lilies on my grave.*

His guards took Eolair's elbows and dragged him stumbling through a carved doorway into a place he recognized. The Site of Witness might look like something he could only visit in a dream, but he knew he had truly been there. The chamber was round and high, its floor a great shallow stone bowl that had once been filled with stone benches, now fallen to pieces. At the center, casting a guttering, phantom glow, stood the huge crystal called the Shard, the Master Witness of ancient Mezutu'a. Eolair felt certain that the shining stone—with the silver-masked Norn Queen as its wielder—was what had led Hugh out of mere capriciousness into outright madness.

Only when the light of the great, jagged lump of pale crystal faded for a moment did he become aware that the walls of the chamber were lined with torches, and that at least two dozen armed Silver Stags stood silently watching. With the Shard momentarily dark, he also saw for the first time what had been hidden by its glare—two high thrones set beside the tall crystal, both occupied.

Captain Samreas took his elbow and urged him forward, then shoved him to the floor in front of the thrones. Broken tiles bit at his knees and shins like teeth, and a sharp edge cut his hand, so that he stared at his own blood for a moment in dull surprise.

"So. The Hand of the High Throne favors us with his presence."

Eolair looked up. Hugh was staring at him, the king's expression full of contempt, but Eolair thought he saw something else as well—a sneaking sort of triumph, as if this humiliation of an old friend and mentor was something Hugh had long imagined. The king was dressed all in black and gray except for the silver crown his grandfather Lluth had worn. Something was odd about the king's garments, but at first it eluded the count's weary understanding.

"Your Majesty," Eolair said, "why do you treat me this way? I helped raise you. Have you forgotten those times entirely?"

"You have no right to question the king!" cried the woman beside Hugh. Though her voice was loudly imperious, she had not yet learned the trick of sounding as though such a commanding tone came easily to her. Lady Tylleth was dressed all in white, with a white scarf draped over her dark hair, so that she looked like a bride being taken to her marriage ceremony.

"All is well, my dear, and more than well," said Hugh. "Count Eolair is right. He has some small claim on me—or at least on my childhood. But as you can see, old friend, I am no longer a child."

"I will withhold my judgment on that." As Eolair spoke, he saw that the king was wearing, not Hernystiri armor, but plates of polished wood, though its color was more like stone. "I see you wear the witchwood armor of a Norn noble, Majesty. Is that what you gave up your people for? A place in the court of the Norn Queen? I must say that you sold your birthright very cheaply."

Hugh laughed, if not entirely easily, but Tylleth sprang to her feet, face pale with anger. She stood over Eolair for a moment, then slapped his face so hard he almost fell over, despite already being on his knees. "You—you swine of a Mullachi! You are always so full of yourself. But all your learning and all your practiced words are useless now."

"I know your father, too, Lady Tylleth. He must feel ashamed to see his daughter turn her back on the gods of our people." He suddenly understood the import of her white robes. "And do you imitate the Norn Queen, then? Do you even know why she is said to wear only white? That mad creature has mourned her dead son for more centuries than Hernystir has existed. And she has sworn the death of all mortals in payment for Drukhi the White Prince. Do the two of you truly think she will spare you after she is victorious?"

"The Norn Queen is only one face of the goddess!" declared Tylleth, almost spitting it out. She looked as though she might strike Eolair again, but instead returned to her throne. "You know nothing, old man," she said. "Turn my back on our people's gods? The Morriga is our people's oldest protector."

"You are both fools," was all he said.

Hugh stood up, his armor clicking at the joints. "You may expect me to tell you all the things you don't know, what the Norn Queen has promised us and what will happen to your beloved Hernystir when we have helped her in return." He smirked. "But I will not. Instead, I will tell you that you will spend some few nights in a cold cell here beneath the mountain, and then you will be taken back to Hernysadharc, where your execution will serve as an example to any of the population who still harbor traitorous thoughts. Take him away now."

Samreas and the guards sprang forward and heaved Eolair onto his feet. He could taste blood in his mouth from Lady Tylleth's blow. But before they could lead him away, Hugh raised his hand.

"One moment. In the pleasure of this reunion, I almost forgot—someone has been waiting to see you. Bring out the other prisoner."

Eolair heard the muffled tread of booted feet, then a moment later two Stags appeared at one end of the chamber with a third figure held between them. She seemed so weak she could barely stand, and Eolair felt a moment of horror and anger that she should have been treated so badly. "Inahwen!" he cried. "My queen, are you well?"

She looked up at him with an expression of such hopelessness she might have already been one of the weeping dead. "Eolair," she sighed, but seemed to have the breath to say nothing more.

"How could you do this to your own stepmother, Hugh?" he cried. "Have you lost all human feeling?"

"Yes, I suppose I have." Hugh waved his hand airily. "But I thought the two of you might like to see each other—are you not grateful? Because the next time you are in each other's presence, you will be meeting the Withy Crow, and I fear you will not be talking then, but screaming." He pointed. "Take them back. But set Eolair far from her. I do not want them plotting together."

The guards grabbed his arms again and led him out of the Witness chamber behind Inahwen and her captors, then down into ancient shadows.

29

A Little Jar of Pain

Unver took another long swig of *yerut*, then handed the skin back to Etvin, thane of the Wood Duck Clan. He wiped his mouth with the back of his hand, then gestured for Fremur to accompany him back to his wagon.

The camp on the eastern bank of the Laestfinger was teeming, but the clansmen were confused. Though the battle was over, they were not pushing deeper into Erkynland or heading back to their homes in the grassland. It was strange, because the Shan had defeated—and, so rumor said, killed with his own sword—the High King of all the stone-dweller lands, yet the clans neither advanced nor retreated.

"How many of the Cranes are here with us?" Unver asked.

"Most of the fighting men, and a good number of others," Fremur told him. "I think our clan has the greatest numbers in all this army."

Unver nodded. "And is old Burtan the shaman among them?"

"He is."

"Good." Unver gave him two directives, the first of which merely surprised him, the second of which startled him greatly. Unver did not explain either and Fremur knew better than to ask—the Shan would give his reasons when the time was right.

When Fremur had finished the first errand he returned to Unver's wagon, which sat on a hill above the river, its tall wheels chocked with stones. Inside, the walls were covered from floorboards to ceiling with tapestries featuring the Black Bear clan emblem. The wagon had belonged to Rudur Redbeard, but Unver, with his usual unconcern for anything that did not directly affect him, had left them in place, though Rudur was months dead. "Keeps it warmer in here," Unver said when he saw Fremur looking at the hangings. "After all, someday soon I will need a wife."

Fremur was not certain whether Unver was jesting or not. Taking a wife and growing out his beard would be a reasonable thing for any ordinary Thrithings-man to do after surviving a major battle, but Unver had never been either ordinary or entirely reasonable. "Do you mean it?" Fremur asked. "Who?"

"I have not met her yet. Nor laid eyes on her, nor even dreamed of her face. But one day I will take a bride."

Fremur could only nod. Sometimes the Shan spoke in riddles. This seemed one of those times. "You said Odobreg would meet us. Do we wait for him?"

"He will come in his own time. Did you do all I asked?"

"I did."

"Then sit. Have a little of Rudur's wine. He must be missing it now—I hear that Hell is a thirsty place."

As Fremur lifted the cup to his lips, heavy footfalls mounted the wagon's steps. He expected Odobreg to come through the door, but instead an even larger man loomed in the doorway.

"Ah, Volfrag," said Unver. "Come in. We are just sampling a little of Rudur Redbeard's wine. From the Commeian Hills, I think, and quite good. Will you have some?"

The shaman bowed his head and his beard bent against his wide chest like a wedding robe being folded into the box beneath a wagon seat. "I thank you, Great Shan, but no. I must keep my mind clear, so I may better understand the gods' wishes."

"Of course. Of course. And Rudur showed us why you must be careful about drinking wine from a cask that has already been opened."

"Shan?" Volfrag seemed puzzled.

"A mere jest. Sit. So, have the gods made their wishes known to you, shaman?"

The bearded man hesitated for a moment before speaking. "It is not possible to know every whim of the gods. Sometimes they do not speak clearly. Other times they seem to say one thing very forcefully, but the student of their ways can divine a different meaning hidden inside the first."

"Then we must be grateful that we have a clever shaman like yourself, eh? Tell me, what do the gods seem to think about what has happened here? Please, sit."

Fremur remained standing by the door as he had been told to do. Volfrag settled onto the stool, his size and heavy robes making him look like a tent someone had half-erected inside the wagon. The shaman carefully ran the fingers of his large hand through his whiskers. "As I said, Great Shan, it is hard to discern the gods' will exactly—"

"Come, come, man," said Unver, mock-sternly. "This is not some stone-dweller market. We do not seal a contract here. I only ask for your best opinion, your clearest advice."

"Then I think I must say that the gods do not seem to approve of your current course."

Unver raised an eyebrow. "Truly? What course is it that has troubled them? For I have done many things since they gifted me with the rule of our people."

"This planned retreat from Erkynland, Great Shan. It seems odd that we should triumph over the city-men so utterly and then fall back to the grasslands. All around us their villages and cities lie ripe for plunder. Their king is dead, and the stone-dweller nobles are in disarray. The gods wonder if you might be squandering the gift they have given to you."

"Ah. I see." Unver nodded. "But if the gods know what I plan, they must also know of the coming invasion by the white-skinned fairies from the distant north—the Norns, as they are called. Surely the gods would not want to put our free people in their deadly path simply for the sake of plundering a few Erkynlandish towns?"

"As I said, I cannot tell you the gods wishes as clearly as I am able to understand your own, Great Shan. They do not speak that way, but instead send their messages in dreams and . . . and signs. They speak to me in the flight of birds, the shape of smoke from a sacrifice, the pattern of blood on a hot rock . . ."

"Let me understand you, Volfrag." Unver leaned back, tipping his own stool until the front two legs left the floor. If it had been another man Fremur might have feared he would lose his balance, but he had never met anyone surer on either horseback or solid ground than Unver. "You believe that the gods do not want us to leave Erkynland yet, that they would prefer we harry the retreating troops and plunder the lands now open to us."

"That seems to be their will, yes—as far as I can tell." Now Volfrag appeared a little uncertain. "Remember, the gods are not—"

"Straightforward, yes. You made that plain. And I admire straightforwardness." Unver tipped his stool forward again and reached into his shirt. "Perhaps you would examine this and give me your honest, straightforward answer as to what you think it is."

Fremur recognized the parchment the Aedonite monk had delivered to Unver on the battlefield, though, like everyone except the Shan, he had no idea what was written in it.

Eyes wide, and perhaps even with lip trembling slightly—it was hard to tell in his great thatch of beard—Volfrag took the letter and unfolded it. He glanced at the broken seal and Fremur would have sworn that he went pale. "What is this, Great Shan?"

"You can read Westerling writing, can't you? Or should I read it to you?"

Volfrag stared at the letter. "I . . . yes, I can read it . . . a little. But I don't understand why . . ."

"It is a letter meant for the dead stone-dweller king, from one of his headmen. Apparently, someone in the king's inner circle has stolen a great deal of money from the king's coffers. And in the letter, this headman is telling the king he has found a record of a payment made with the stolen gold. Do you see the letters of the name? *V-F-G.* Now, can you think of someone who might have those letters? Someone who might have received some of the stone-dweller king's gold from a traitor in his court?"

Volfrag's eyes were wide. His hands trembled. "Surely, Great Shan, you do not think that it could be *me*?"

Another heavy tread made the wagon's steps creak, then someone knocked loudly on the door and a startled Volfrag jumped halfway off his stool. At the Shan's signal, Fremur—who had been waiting—drew his sword. "You are too fretful, Volfrag," said Unver. "It is only Thane Odobreg. *Come in*," he called.

Odobreg entered and looked from the shaman to the Shan. "Just as you said, Unver Shan. I found it under the floorboards of his wagon." He came forward and passed a small wooden chest to Unver. Fremur let the tip of his sword touch Volfrag's spine, which made the big man start again.

"Sit until you are told to rise, shaman," Fremur said quietly.

Unver spent a moment admiring the box, which was of red Aldheorte cedar with mother-of-pearl inlay. "Fine work," he said. "Perdruinese, or I miss my guess." He lifted the lid and took out a black leather purse, then poured a shower of golden coins into the box. "Erkynlandish crowns. Quite a few!" Unver smiled at Volfrag, but the Shan's eyes were as cold as a serpent's. "And what else have we here? Some fine jewelry—is this for a woman? Volfrag, you old dog, do you have a sweetheart, or are you merely hoping to find one?"

The shaman said nothing, only stared at Unver with fear in every line of his face.

"And look—a pile of letters, tied neatly with a string. I wonder who they could be from? That sweetheart of yours?" He squinted. "If so, she writes a very masculine hand, it seems."

"Great Shan, I will tell you all!" Volfrag said. "I have no secrets from you!"

"You may not, but the floorboards of your wagon seem to think differently. Did you find anything else, Odobreg?"

The thane of the Badger Clan carefully handed him a small, cut-glass jar. Unver removed the cap and sniffed it. "Smells like enough to kill quite a few men. Wolfsbane, of course, but there is something else in it I do not recognize." He turned back to Volfrag. "Is this what you put in Rudur Redbeard's wine cup?"

"That jar belonged to Rudur!" the shaman said. "I found it after he died, but I did not know he poisoned the cup! He betrayed himself. If he had told me, I would have kept better track of which cup was which!"

"Meaning you would have killed me instead."

Volfrag's lips pulled back from his teeth in a snarl of animal helplessness. "No, Great Shan! I did not—!"

"Or perhaps you poisoned both cups. Perhaps this "Dominis"—"*master*" seems a strange name for a friend to give himself—who signed the letters hidden in your wagon, wanted us both dead."

"I swear it is not true! My friend wanted you to live!" Little flecks of spittle now decorated Volfrag's beard.

"You really must learn to keep your lies straight, shaman," said Unver. "But I think for once you have told the truth. This "Dominis"—and what is his real name—?"

"Lord Pasevalles, Great Shan. He is a high noble in the Erkynland court. I swear that is the truth!"

"This Pasevalles, then, may well have wanted me to win out over Rudur. Because nothing could have driven Rudur to make war against the stone-dwellers. By all the spirits, Redbeard would not even fight the Nabban-men who overrun our lands every day! So, this king's trusted noble, this Pasevalles, wanted someone who could bring the clans together, and even take an army of clansmen against Erkynland . . . if things could be arranged that way." Now for the first time Unver put off his pose of mockery and leaned forward, his gray eyes like the heads of iron nails. "Tell all the truth, Volfrag. Tell it all, and there is a good chance the gods will have mercy on you."

As Fremur and Odobreg listened in stunned surprise, the bearded shaman poured out the story of Rudur Redbeard's long alliance with the Erkynlandish noble Pasevalles, how in exchange for gold and other favors, Rudur had found men to serve Pasevalles; mercenary clansmen who would carry out the noble's bidding. Volfrag maintained that he had been only a go-between at first, but that as time had passed, he had developed his own relationship to the king of Erkynland's counselor.

"And then?" Unver asked. "Come, now. When I was young, the Aedonite monks I met in Kwanitupul told me that confession eases the soul. Your soul must need a great deal of it, shaman. And then?"

"Pasevalles told me that Rudur was too old-fashioned, that he wished to see someone else take Rudur's place as thane of thanes—someone who would not be afraid to fight against the stone-dwellers. But I did not try to harm either of you, I promise! It was Rudur's own plan to poison you. I knew nothing!" Volfrag seemed on the edge of tears now, eyes red around the rims. Fremur felt a surge of disgust at the shaman's complete surrender. *May the Sky-Piercer forbid that I ever fall out with Unver,* he thought. *But if I ever do, I will tell him straight to his face and take what he gives me. Who could live with anything less?*

As the shaman spewed out every secret Fremur could have imagined, and a few more that surprised him, they were interrupted by another knock at the wagon door, and Burtan, ancient shaman of the Crane Clan, stepped into the now-crowded wagon. Volfrag looked at the newcomer with a mixture of confusion and fear.

"Shan, I heard your call and I am here," the old man said.

"I thank you, Grandfather," said Unver with ritual courtesy. "Tell me, are you strong enough to take on a few more responsibilities?"

Burtan considered this carefully. "I am honored by your concern, Great Shan. It is true I am nearly blind now, but I feel strong in my body, and I believe my heart can still hear the songs the gods sing."

"And is there someone who can take your place as shaman of Clan Kragni?"

"My helper has learned all that is needed and proper. I think he is ready."

"Good." Unver sat back again, as though all the day's business had been resolved. "Then you are my shaman, now, Burtan—shaman of all the people of the grasslands." He turned to Fremur and Odobreg and flipped his hand at Volfrag. "Take that one's head off."

The shaman let out a choking noise of despair. "Great Shan," he cried when he could speak, "you said you would be merciful if I told you all!"

"No, fool. I said *the gods* would be merciful. And they may be. But if not, you are welcome to return and tell me your complaints." He stood. "By Heaven, Fremur, not in here. Take him outside."

Odobreg dragged Volfrag toward the door of the wagon. Though he was even larger than Odobreg, the shaman seemed boneless, unable to resist.

"And here." Unver took the sack of coins back out of the box and tossed it to Fremur. "When his head is off, set it on a post. Then hang this on the post, too."

"But, Unver," Fremur said, hefting the bag in surprise. "This is a great deal of gold. What if someone steals it?"

Unver looked at him and his mouth curled in a mirthless smile. "Ask yourself, my friend, would *you* steal gold from me? Gold still wet with a traitor's blood? No? Then neither will anyone else, I think."

Fremur followed Odobreg out. The thane wrestled Volfrag down to his knees, then put a foot on the shaman's back, forcing him to bend the until his forehead almost touched the ground. Volfrag was openly weeping.

"Make it fast," Odobreg said. "I cannot bear to touch this pig of a traitor any longer."

Fremur accomplished the execution with one swift sword-blow, then picked up the head by its hair, long beard trailing, and went looking for a suitable post.

"You might as well eat me, giant," Jarnulf said into the shadows. His head was throbbing. His hands were still tied behind his back, so that when the guards flung him into the dark room, he had been unable to avoid landing on his face. But he suspected that was the least of his problems. "Do your worst. There is nothing else left for me."

Jarnulf could feel a slow, rhythmic rumble in his ribs and the bones of his skull: Goh Gam Gar was laughing. "You make me not want to eat you after all, small man. Your meat must be very sour."

"In truth, I would rather be a meal for you than a plaything for thrice-cursed Akhenabi." He was not exaggerating. It would be far better to die quickly, even to be devoured alive, than to suffer the near-endless torments practiced by the Order of Song.

"What thing is this, man?" the giant asked. "It fell out when the guards brought you."

Jarnulf could only shake his head, and even that felt like a waste of his last moments before the Order of Song came for him. "I don't know what you're talking about."

"This. Little jar."

A bit of fading daylight seeped in from a small, barred window high in the back wall. Jarnulf could just make out Goh Gam Gar holding a tiny object in his huge fingers, like a tax collector examining a single pea.

"Don't break it or you will regret it," he told the giant. "It is dragon's blood and it will burn you. It came from the dead worm on the mountainside, on the cliff where Hand-chieftain Makho nearly killed us both."

"It smells strange," said Goh Gam Gar. "I do not like it in my nose—or my head. Dizzy! Take it."

"I can't. My arms are tied behind me."

The giant leaned toward him with a clank of chains. A massive hand curled around Jarnulf's wrists, then, with a single flick of the beast's fingernail, the ropes binding his arms parted. He gasped in pain as the blood rushed back.

"Now tell," rumbled Goh Gam Gar. "Why do you still carry this thing?"

Jarnulf felt something bounce off his chest and heard it fall to the hard-packed floor beside him. He was feeling so defeated, so finished, that he almost left it there. Instead, groaning, he bent and picked it up with prickling fingers. "I was going to use it to kill the queen," he said. "I smeared the blood on an arrowhead."

"Silvermask?" He heard something new in the giant's voice—interest, perhaps even a sort of respect. "You try to kill the *Higdaja* witch?"

"Ever since I learned she still lived. But I failed. Twice. Her craft is too strong for me." He clutched the jar in his fist. *I could throw it at Akhenabi and hope for better luck than I had with his mistress.* But he doubted that the stout little jar would break.

"Tried to kill her? That is why you are here?"

"Yes. But something kept my arrow from striking her." *I could swallow the jar,* he thought, *but if it didn't simply choke me, my ending would be slow and horrible, on fire from within.* Still, even such dreadful, fiery suffering would likely be a better death than being sent back to Nakkiga and the Cold, Slow Halls. Still, his faith told him that God did not want him to take his own life. "But why are *you* here?" he asked. "Why are you not with the queen's army, marching off to attack the mortal castle in the south?"

Another rumble, this time empty of amusement. "Does Goh Gam Gar know what the white-skins do, or why? They are mad, all of them. The queen's madness is in them like fever. Nothing they do makes sense. Capture dragons alive, raise dead brother of the Storm King—all mad." The giant growled. "But I swear old Gam will kill more than a few of them before he dies, though this collar burns off my head."

It was almost alarming to discover that the giant's murderous hatred was so like his own. *That is what that ancient witch Utuk'ku has accomplished,* he thought. *But it is not just the giant and me caught up in it—not just her slaves. She spreads her madness across the entire world.*

The latch clanked, then the door of their prison abruptly swung open and late afternoon light spilled in. Now Jarnulf saw that their prison was a stone-built storeroom of some kind, and that the giant Goh Gam Gar wore chains ten times as heavy as his own that were fixed to a huge iron loop set directly into the wall.

Two figures wearing the dark, hooded cloaks of Akhenabi's Order of Song stood silhouetted in the doorway. "The Lord of Song summons you, slave," the nearer figure announced. Before Jarnulf could react, the other Singer leaned forward and touched him on the arm and Jarnulf's muscles suddenly drew tight in terrible, cramping pain. As he fell to the floor, gasping, a foursome of Sacrifice guards followed the Singers in. They saw the ropes the giant had cut and quickly bound his wrists once more but did not notice the jar clutched in his fist. His arms secured, they heaved him upright like a sack of grain. Bruised and beaten, Jarnulf could only hang in their grasp, limp as a butchered carcass, as they carried him across the ruined courtyard through the dreary winter sunlight.

At the far end of the courtyard, Akhenabi's large wagon stood just inside one of Naglimund's ruined inner walls. Dangling upside down, limbs twitching, Jarnulf stared at it without understanding. Only as his nerves and sinews finally ceased jerking did he realize that it looked different than when he had seen it last, in the camp where Akhenabi and Saomeji had resurrected Chieftain Makho. The painted symbols and words were gone and the surface of the large wagon was now all black, so that it seemed more like a deep hole in the world than an object within that world.

As they drew closer, cloud-filtered sunlight played across the wagon's side and he saw that the marks were not gone but had instead been carefully repainted in a different shade of black, only a faint sheen revealing their presence. As he stared, the letters and signs seemed to throb and move, crawling like serpents, and Jarnulf was filled with an uncomprehending horror that roiled his guts and made his eyes blur. He let out a moan of protest, and one of the hooded Singers touched him again, sending a sizzle of torment through his shoulder and neck. In that agonizing instant, the spells stopped squirming on the wagon's side. When Jarnulf could see again, the runes were nothing more than black paint on black paint.

Pain, he realized. *Pain distracts. It overwhelms even the power of their foul songs.*

Not wanting the Singers to touch him again, Jarnulf did not struggle as they dragged him up the wagon steps. The deceptively ordinary wooden door swung open and the soldiers set him down, then hurriedly shoved him inside, as if even standing in the wagon's doorway was dangerous. He fell to the floor, eyes squeezed tight shut, but after several moments passed without anything happening, he risked opening them. What he saw astonished and sickened him.

It could not be the same wagon. He was being tricked, somehow. The Lord of Song's carriage had been long and tall, but not like this—not like *this.* The interior of the wagon seemed to have no walls or ceiling: it stretched away above and beyond him into shadowy nothingness. Nor was it a mere trick of the light: he could feel the moving air of a high, isolated place pimple his skin, gusts of chilly wind that clawed into his bones and made him shiver uncontrollably. An abyss of icy emptiness stretched before him into some unimaginable distance, as though he stood on a high promontory staring out into a sea of fog. But the semi-darkness around him was also full of moving, hooded shapes—members of the Order of Song, bustling here and there through the misty dimness like laboring ants, some carrying things whose shapes he could not discern, others huddled together and conversing in silent hand-signs. None of these spared even a glance for Jarnulf, which brought him a moment's unlikely hope. He scrabbled backward across a wooden floor that he could feel but not quite see until he reached the wall behind him, but the wagon's door, which had only been a pace or two behind him, now seemed to have vanished.

Nothing here made sense. Lights flared in the emptiness, briefly illuminating some of the Singers—here, a half-hidden face covered in runes, lips moving soundlessly as its owner stared at an old book; there, a funereal mask peering from a hood, its features dead but for the glittering eyes. Robed figures swirled out of the shadows and then swirled away again. Disturbing scents assaulted his nose, hot metal, noxious herbs, and the oceanic tang of blood. Sounds with no visible sources drifted to him as though across great distances, incomprehensible chants and muffled, heart-twisting screams. But despite all this activity, the hurrying figures did not even seem to see him. The moments stretched and stretched, and Jarnulf could only crouch against the wall of this new and maddening prison, bewildered and fearful.

Surely this is what Hell must be like, he thought. *So must the damned busy themselves until the arch-demon himself, the Adversary, appears to command them.*

And then, as if his thought had summoned it into being, a vast, robed figure took shape before him, assembled mote by mote out of the very darkness—Akhenabi, the queen's dreadful arch-magician. Jarnulf tried to turn his face away but could not, as if cold fingers had clamped around his skull and held it. The face that peered out of the depths of the dark hood was a strange and wrinkled thing, the stolen, dead flesh of another sewn to that of the living Lord of Song. But even as Jarnulf stared helplessly at this fearsome apparition, he wondered why it looked so tremulous and inconstant, like the bottom of a pond seen through rippling water.

"*So,*" rasped the creature in the corpse-mask, and his harsh voice did not settle in Jarnulf's ears but thrust directly into his thoughts. *"I remember seeing you now—your ugly, animal features. I am told you are a Queen's Huntsman."*

Jarnulf's mouth was so dry with terror that he could not make words.

"Silence is a useless tactic, mortal," declared the Lord of Song. *"Either you give me all that I ask for or I will simply pluck it out of you. Tell me, and do not bother to lie—who sent you to kill the Mother of All?*

Jarnulf felt cold fingers of despair clutch at his innards. Akhenabi knew he had loosed an arrow at Utuk'ku. Soon the powerful Lord of Song would know everything else as well—about Jarnulf's one-man campaign against the

Hikeda'ya as the White Hand, and how he had subverted and then kidnapped the Talon Nezeru, even about the treacherous message he had sent while Makho's company had been surrounded on the hillside by the mortal king's army.

"N-no one sent me, great lord," he stammered. "I . . . I was angry that I was not rewarded properly." Even to his own ears, the excuse sounded lamentably unconvincing. "I helped capture the living dragon that you and the queen wanted so much. But Saomeji, the Singer, treated me as though I was only another mortal slave."

"Lies," said the Lord of Song, and the flat malice of it was like a brutal slap. *"Saomeji assures me he paid you what was promised—and he would not dare lie to me. And not even a mortal would be foolish enough to try to assassinate the queen over the matter of a few iron drops."* Akhenabi leaned forward. Despite the strange, unreal shimmer that surrounded him, the dry and crinkled skin of his mask became even more horrible as it loomed closer—Jarnulf could even make out a transparent mole on what had once been a living cheek. *Akhenabi of the Stolen Face,* he thought, trembling all over. *A thousand years old or more. I am a child compared to him. He will drag everything out of me. Then the Slow, Cold Halls . . .*

The black eyes fixed him, shiny and expectant as a carrion-bird watching something die. Jarnulf tried to look away as the Lord of Song began to pry at his thoughts but could not. Everything else in the dim chamber began to fade, until he could see nothing but those glittering, remorseless eyes. Akhenabi began to pull things out of him—old memories, arbitrary thoughts—and then discard the unwanted scraps. Jarnulf could do nothing to prevent it, and he knew that soon the Lord of Song would unearth the secrets that would doom him to the halls of torment.

Abruptly, and without warning, he felt the controlling strength of Akhenabi's thoughts pull away, and a moment later the dreamlike image of his inquisitor turned as if someone had approached him, though Jarnulf could see nothing except the dark, robed shape of his captor. Akhenabi's hands moved in swift, confusing gestures, until Jarnulf realized that some acolyte or other Singer must have momentarily distracted the Lord of Song's attention.

He is not even here with me, Jarnulf realized. *Who knows if he is even in this wagon—this country? And he continues to pursue his other works even as he interrogates me. I am only another minor task.* Even through his horror, he felt the sting of humiliation. *The White Hand! Would-be killer of Great Utuk'ku! I believed myself such a threat to them, but they think no more of me than they would of a scullion who stole from the queen's larder.*

As the brief moment of respite hurried past, Jarnulf realized that the jar of dragon's blood was still hidden in his fist behind his back, though he could not think of any way he could use it, short of dropping the jar on the floor and then trying to turn and swallow it, in defiance of God's condemnation of self-murder.

An instant later the Lord of Song finished with whatever had taken his attention, and Jarnulf felt the chief magician seize his thoughts once more. He did his best to resist, to throw up barriers before Akhenabi's cruel and careless intrusion, but each time he did they were tossed aside, as a grown man might break the clinging grip of an infant.

Memory by memory, his life was being dragged out of the depths of his being and examined—testing the wind from his perch in the hill fort; his young sister shivering in the cold and crying herself to sleep as he held her in the slave barn, trying to lend her some of his own warmth. After that came an image of his own hand, red and wet with blood against winter white. Soon, he knew, some clearer remembrance of him marking one of the many Hikeda'ya soldiers he had killed would be pried loose from the panicky mass of his thoughts. Jarnulf's head felt like a pot boiling with its lid on, as though only instants remained before everything inside his throbbing skull must come frothing out. Without realizing it, he squeezed the hidden witchwood jar so hard in his desperate agony that he dislodged its seal and the black blood inside touched his fingertip. A thunderbolt of pain lanced up from his hand, through his arm, and scattered his memories like leaves. Gone with them, at least for that moment, was Akhenabi's hold on his thoughts.

Pain, he recalled in his agony. *Pain overwhelms even Akhenabi's songs.*

"If you continue to fight me this way," declared his inquisitor with a hint of impatience, *"it will be too much for you and you will die—but even then, your suffering will not end."* The Lord of Song was angry—a victory of sorts, if a hollow one. *"I will only bring you back to life the same way I did for your companion Makho, then torment you until I learn what I wish to know. Now give me what I want!"*

He suddenly knew what he must do. Already the Lord of Song had begun digging roughly through his memories again, so Jarnulf shoved his finger into the neck of the jar until it sank into the black blood.

A monstrous flower of pain bloomed inside him, so excruciating that it took every bit of his will to keep himself from shrieking and yanking his finger out of the jar. It grew and grew until it seemed to fill the whole world with fire, until he felt nothing else, until pain was all and everywhere and forever. It felt as though his entire arm was burning away, his body blackening and shriveling in hellish flames. He could still dimly feel the Lord of Song ransacking his memories, but the sensation was disappearing rapidly, scorched away by the hideous, unspeakable torment of his hand.

A kind of gray pall settled over him, though it did not lessen his suffering. He surrendered himself to it, letting it cover him over, until he was without will or understanding. Light faded. The wagon had long ago vanished, and even Akhenabi himself had become only a dim memory. The terrible, indescribable suffering was all that existed.

He did not realize how much he had been thrashing and writhing until he pitched forward and his face slammed against the floor of the wagon. It jarred loose a tooth and filled his mouth with blood, but against what he was already suffering it felt like the gentle slap of a teasing lover. He had struggled so desperately he had broken the loosely-tied ropes around his wrists. His fall had pulled his finger out of the jar, but the horrid burning did not end—would never end, as if the dragon's fiery blood had charred him all over, leaving his red meat exposed and screaming.

But Akhenabi was no longer in his thoughts.

Silence fell, but for his own tormented, gasping breath. Jarnulf sensed rather than heard the door of the wagon open, and then he was seized by the rough hands of Sacrifice soldiers. He had pissed himself, he was dimly aware, but nothing mattered except the continuing misery of his blazing nerves and ruined flesh.

He felt rather than heard Akhenabi's faint words, a last tendril of their connection. *"Someone has taught you a cantrip against giving up your thoughts, I see. I will think on this, then next time you will surrender everything, and your suffering will be even greater for daring to contest with me."*

Next time. It was both a promise of horror and a dream of relief. He was dragged across the muddy snow of the yard, then flung back into the storeroom. He heard the giant's voice after the guards were gone, a question that contained hint of mockery, but Jarnulf could not understand it, could barely understand anything but the misery of his ruined flesh.

At last he rolled over and extended an arm that he was surprised to discover was still attached to his shoulder. His hand fell into the thin sheet of light leaking under the storeroom door, and he could see what he had done to himself.

His hand still existed, which astounded him, and he still held the little jar as tightly as the grip of a stiffened corpse. But the tip of his pointing finger was gone, reduced by the length of its first joint and ending in bubbled, blackened flesh.

Is that all? he thought, and would have laughed if he could, but he was far beyond anything like that. As he stared, both his ruined finger and the light under the door grew blurry, then he tumbled into blessed nothingness.

Tzoja watched Hikeda'ya guards drag the new prisoner back to the storeroom beside the cell she and Vordis shared. She had heard his screams echoing from the wizard's huge carriage in the inner keep—dreadful, agonized cries, like the straying donkey she had once heard being devoured alive by wolves in a forest outside the Astaline settlement. As she peered out of the doorway, she saw the prisoner was a mortal. His limp feet scraped along the muddy, rain-pocked ground, as though the black-clad Hikeda'ya guards were fishermen dragging some monstrous catch to shore. They opened the doorlatch with a key, then shoved him inside. After locking it up again, they left without a backward look.

"Poor man," she said. "That poor, poor man. They tortured him."

"Come away from the door, Tzoja," Vordis urged her in a quiet, tight voice. "What if they see you?"

"They're already gone. They threw him in with the giant again, then marched away. We are nothing more than animals to them." As she watched the retreating guards, something like hate kindled in Tzoja's heart. She had lived much of her life among the Hikeda'ya, and though she had learned the trick of silence, the catechism of downcast eyes and quiet, respectful replies to any who questioned her, she had never thought much about the things the Hikeda'ya actually did. During her time as a slave, then as Viyeki's concubine, the treatment of her kind had been like the ever-present stone tunnels, like the incomprehensible weight of the mountain above them—simply things that *were*, like sun or snow. Now that she was living among the mass graves and the charred stones of Naglimund, she had for the first time begun to think of the Hikeda'ya army as a sort of engine, a great device created for destruction and murder—an engine utterly under the control of the witch-queen, Utuk'ku.

Where will this end? No, that is a foolish question—it will never end. It will continue until all mortals, even the privileged ones like me, are ground beneath the engine's wheels.

And at that moment Tzoja came to a decision—only a small one, though in the private depths of her self-understanding, she could sense that it would lead her to larger and more dangerous decisions in days ahead. Out loud, she said, "I'm going to bring that poor man some water."

Vordis was beside her in a moment, pulling her back inside and shoving the door closed with her foot. The blind woman held Tzoja's wrists as if beginning the steps of a dance, but her pretty face was distorted with fear.

"I beg you, do not! You said they had thrown him in with the giant. You saw that horrible, monstrous creature when they put it there! There can be nothing left of that man by now."

"Perhaps. But there is a window on the far side of that storeroom, out of sight of the rest of the keep. It will not harm anything to look."

"Please, Tzoja, if you love me, do not! What if the guards see you?"

"There are no guards. They have gone back to the inner keep. We are beasts as far as the Hikeda'ya are concerned—no, less than beasts. At least they feed their horses and hounds properly." She and Vordis had been hungry since their wagon had been taken and they had been forced to live in the ruins of Naglimund. They had only been saved from starvation by threatening the Sacrifice quartermaster with the queen's wrath if he let two valued mortal servants die for lack of food. The Hikeda'ya soldier had acceded with bad grace, and every day allowed them each a few sticks of pu'ja bread and a little pottage, barely enough to keep them alive. Tzoja's stomach had not rumbled so much or so loudly since she had subsisted on pollwags and watergrass beside Lake Suno'ku.

She pulled on her heavy cloak, then took her own cup and dipped it into the bucket of water they carried back each day from the well in the inner keep. Vordis had fallen silent but her face was full of despair.

The rain had stopped. After a swift inspection of the courtyard, Tzoja sloshed her way across the bleak wasteland of mud and broken stones. She stepped over the ruts left by the prisoner's dragging feet, then made her way around the back of the storeroom until she could look up and see the single barred window set high in the wall of mortared stone. It was much too far above the ground for her to reach, so Tzoja searched for something to help her climb high enough. After picking through rubble and debris, she found a great round of tree-trunk, wide as a serving plate and standing as high as her knees. The top was crisscrossed with the scars of sword- or ax-blades, and she thought she could see dried brown blood in the deeper crevices.

From animals, she told herself. *Slaughtered for food.* It was partly a prayer.

She rolled the log back and set it against the storehouse wall, then climbed onto it. Now she could peer over the stone sill. On such a dark day, the small window allowed little light into the storeroom, but she could make out a human figure stretched on the muddy, damp straw that covered the floor. She called softly in Westerling, *"Hoy! Hoy, can you hear me?"* but the figure did not move. She tried again, and this time saw a stirring of limbs so slow and painful that she thought the tortured man must be dying. At last, he lifted his head, but she could make out little more of him than the dull gleam of eyes and a pale smear of bared teeth. *"I brought you water,"* she said, and tapped the lip of the cup against the bars. *"Here. Can you come to me?"*

The shadowed face seemed to stare at her for a moment without understanding, then the head shook slowly from side to side before sinking once more to the filthy straw.

As she stared, helpless and frustrated, something massive rose into her view on the other side of the bars—a huge, hairy gray hand, with fingers as big as rolling pins, ending in broken, clawlike nails. Her heart leaped into her throat, and she swayed and almost lost her footing, but the hand that she felt certain would reach through the bars to seize and crush her did not move. Then a voice came, an impossibly deep rumble like the purr of a cat as big as a barn.

"Give me the water," it said in Hikeda'ya speech.

Tzoja's pulse began to race so swiftly at this surprise that she felt lightheaded. She swayed on her makeshift stool and almost tumbled to the ground, but she knew she had not been mistaken. She hesitated, but despite her terror, something would not let her run away. Her entire body quivered as she stretched her arm through the bars again, but instead of ripping it out of her shoulder-socket, the monstrous hand only extended its fingers and took the cup with the delicacy of some noblewoman's pet ermine being fed from her hand.

As Tzoja watched in disbelief, the vast, shaggy arm reached out and prodded at the mortal prisoner's arm with the rim of the cup until the man at last lifted his head and his eyes fixed slowly on the offered vessel. He took it from the giant, then immediately forced the whole of his left hand into it and rolled over onto his back, holding the cup upright on his chest as he began to weep.

"It was for you to drink!" Tzoja said in surprise and confusion.

"Bring more," said the deep, rumbling voice from beneath the window. "Old Gam is thirsty too."

She returned to the storeroom she shared with Vordis, but their bucket was now almost empty; Tzoja cursed herself for not leaving it outside while the rain had been falling. "I must get more water," she said. "Vordis, come with me to the well."

Her friend shook her head. "I do not know what has happened to you, Tzoja, but I think you have harmed your wits. We have already been to the well today."

"Yes, but I need more water. I need you to go with me because we always go together. If I go by myself, one of the Sacrifice soldiers is likely to notice and wonder."

Convincing Vordis took a long time. Tzoja decided to wait out the last hour of the rainy, bitter cold afternoon and go to the well after evening fell. When twilight had reduced the broken buildings to silhouettes, she led her friend out, both women cloaked and hooded despite the evening's clearing skies.

A few female Hikeda'ya were gathered by the well, tall and graceful and dressed much better than the two mortals. These were nobles the queen had left behind, and though they watched Tzoja and Vordis approach like herons looking down their beaks at the ugly pointlessness of frogs, Tzoja for once did not feel inferior.

You are all monsters, she thought. *Beautiful monsters that think you are something better. But you stand now in the midst of all the destruction and murder your kind has done here, and try as you might, you cannot keep the filth from the hems of your gowns.*

She could sense Vordis struggling to stay calm, so she led them quickly to the well and drew enough water to fill their bucket. As they retreated toward the outer keep, the liquid voices of the Hikeda'ya nobility filled the air behind them.

Whoever or whatever greets me when I die, Tzoja thought as she listened to the whispers, which were deliberately pitched loud enough to be heard, *at least they will not ask me why I stood by and did nothing while countless folk suffered. But what will you creatures say when you are asked the same, you high-living ladies of Nakkiga? What excuse will you give?*

Tzoja let Vordis retreat to their shared room as she carried the bucket to the back of the place the man and giant were imprisoned. She set the log in place again, but even before she climbed onto it, she could see that she would have trouble lifting the water up to the window, and that the bucket itself would never fit between the bars. As she wandered through the wreckage of another storeroom, now only mounds of shattered rock, she found some flat paving stones that might once have formed a path. She dragged three of them back, piled them atop each other, and then—wheezing and groaning—set the blood-seamed tree stump on the very top. She then carefully lifted the heavy bucket and clambered onto the block, steadying herself against the wall as she went, until she was able at last to lift the bucket onto the stone sill.

The rainclouds had blown past. A sliver of moon dripped light through the barred window. The tortured prisoner still lay on his back in the straw, hand still crammed into the cup she had brought him.

"I have more water," she announced softly.

"Pour," the giant growled from below the window, his voice so deep it might have come from the throat of some ancient thunder god.

"What about him?" she said, and though the giant could not see her, he seemed to understand what she meant. One vast arm reached out, chains ringing, and the hairy fingers clamped on the mortal prisoner's shoulder to drag him closer.

"Pour," said the giant again.

Tzoja stood on the tips of her toes until she could tilt the bucket far enough for the water to splash over its rim and down onto the hairy giant and the man. The giant leaned back, his jaws yawning open to show his massive yellow teeth, and let the water splash into his great mouth. A little of it cascaded down his broad gray breast and into the parted lips of the mortal. Then the giant lifted the man up onto his huge belly, like a child being cradled by his mother. As Tzoja poured the water down on them, monster and man gulped it down together.

30

Into the Narrowdark

"Quickly," Nezeru whispered. "Follow. We must climb."

They were making their way down a long slope toward the river, which wound between the trees like a silver-gray snake. "What? Why?"

"No questions—now!"

"But I don't have my climbing irons!"

"No need—this tree will not tax your skills." So saying, she scrambled up into the nearest oak as swiftly as a squirrel. Cursing under his breath, Morgan pulled out his rope and clambered up after her.

"There, do you see?" She pointed down to a place where the river bent. The afternoon sun had sunk below the trees, and the water had turned the same dull color as the darkening sky.

"The river?"

"No, beside it." She leaned a little farther forward. "There, on the near bank. *Furi'a*."

Morgan didn't recognize the word, but after long, squinting moments he last he made out a collection of small moving shapes on the bank. From such a distance, they could have been rats or crabs or any other small, creeping things. "What are they?"

"*Furi'a*—goblins."

He nodded, finally understanding, and with that understanding came a shiver of fear. "*Bukken*, we call them." He made a noise of disgust. "Horrible things. My grandfather was attacked by them on the Frostmarch. But they're so far away! Why are we up a tree?"

"Because where a few are, many are. That is the way with *Furi'a*. And they are swarming at the very place where we must cross the river."

This was entirely new knowledge, and Morgan felt a twinge of anger. Nezeru was only a soldier, after all, while he was the grandson of monarchs. Why should she make all the decisions? "Then we should cross somewhere else."

"Fool." She said it without heat, but it still stung. "The fords and bridges are all guarded. The Order of Sacrifice occupies all the lands around Da'ai Chikiza and much of this valley. We can only get out by crossing where they would not expect us to cross—like here, where the water is fast and would sweep away anything that enters it."

She was right about the fast water. The river narrowed here as it passed through a stony gorge, leaping and splashing in a way that would have been lovely to contemplate if he hadn't just realized that she meant to cross it. "How would we even do that?"

"There. That alder tree at the top of the bank on our side. From up there I can toss a rope to the tall pine on the other side of the river."

"And then?"

"And then we cross."

"What—hanging from a rope?"

She gave him a flat look. "Would you prefer to try to convince a troop of Sacrifice soldiers to let us use one of the fords?"

As if this ended the conversation, rather than just silencing Morgan for a moment, Nezeru began to climb upward until she found a long horizontal limb. She crawled out on it until it bent, then leaped to a branch on the next tree. "Come, follow," she said. "But quietly. The *Furi'a* can climb."

Which, Morgan thought, was one of the most unpleasant things anyone had said to him lately.

As cautiously and quietly as they could manage, they sprang from branch to branch, tree to tree, until they had almost reached the alder at the edge of the gorge, a few dozen cubits above the goblins swarming along the river's edge. Neither of them spoke, and as Nezeru pondered the best way to reach the last tree, Morgan stared down at the small creatures, who also seemed to be intent on crossing the Coolblood River. Even after months of unmatched strangeness, it was one of the more unusual sights he had encountered.

It was not only that the goblins were horrifyingly ugly things, misshapen and filthy with mud, but also how much they looked like people. Their little faces were grotesque but manlike, and some even seemed to be wearing rags of clothing, though it was hard to tell since they were almost all covered in muck. Some of the goblins rode on muddy steeds that he finally decided must be moles; others clutched little spears or axes made of what looked like chipped stone. But most disturbing of all was the way they huddled in small groups, chittering and squeaking.

They are arguing, he thought, fascinated and sickened. *They are trying to solve a problem, just as men do.*

Perhaps Bukken are Tinukeda'ya too—the changelings that Tanahaya talked about so much. As this thought came to him, one of the tiny, mud-spattered things on the bank glanced up and seemed to look straight at him. Morgan froze in place. The little creature stared up at the tree for the length of several heartbeats, then turned away to resume squeaking at another goblin as Morgan finally let out his breath.

"We should hurry," he whispered. "They're going to spot us soon."

"I think I see a way," Nezeru replied. "Follow me. When we reach the tall tree beside the river, climb swiftly."

Morgan followed her along a nightmarish path from tree to tree. He had lost the knack of climbing quickly without the boot irons Little Snenneq had given him, and often felt as if he was just barely able to keep his grip and avoid falling. The trees that flanked the river were mostly evergreens, hard going for Morgan at the best of times because their trunks were all but invisible and their close-set branches made it hard to see which limbs would best hold his weight. He was also shamefully aware of how much noise he made in comparison to Nezeru, but he did not dare look down to see if the Bukken had noticed their presence.

A rising hope that they would manage to reach the river's edge unnoticed was flattened when Morgan heard the high-pitched murmurs below suddenly swell into a frenzy of squealing cries.

"They've seen us!" he called, but Nezeru only continued leaping from one branch to the next as he struggled after her. He risked a downward glance and saw a swarm of goblins following them along the ground, leaping and screeching.

Nezeru reached the alder, which stood alone on a spur of earth that jutted above the edge of the river, and clambered high into its branches. Morgan followed, slipping down a foot's length for every two he managed to climb. The Bukken had deduced where they were going, and were gathering around the base of the tree, some of them already scrabbling their way up the pale gray bark. He could hear their small, clawed fingers digging in and the angry chirp of their voices, but to his astonishment Nezeru simply stood on her branch staring out across the river to the far side of the gorge.

"What are you doing?" he cried. "They're coming up after us!"

"They hate fire," she said, but her attention was clearly on something else.

"If you can think of a way for me to climb and light a fire at the same time," he said in rising panic, "then tell me!"

She pulled one of her knives from some hiding place in her armor and calmly began to tie the thin rope she carried around the cross-guard. Morgan heard a noise and turned to see that the first of the climbing Bukken had reached the limb on which he was crouching. The little monster crawled along the branch toward him with surprising speed, a little stone ax in one hand and a horrible grin on its hideous, muddy face. Without thought, he kicked it off the branch and had the minor satisfaction of watching it fall screeching down through the yellow leaves, but he could not enjoy his victory for long: already a dozen more goblins had reached the limb and were swarming toward him.

Morgan pulled Snakesplitter from its sheath and swept the first of the creatures away, but several managed to swing themselves beneath the branch, and kept crawling toward him, now upside down. More goblins leaped from the trunk onto the branch like two-legged rats, and at least half a dozen others were hurrying up the trunk toward Nezeru's perch as she spun the weighted rope and then cast it toward the far side of the gorge, over the surging river. The knife knotted at the end fell a few paces short of the tree she had chosen, and she began reeling the rope back in. Morgan knew he had to keep the goblins at bay. His father's sword was too narrow for this kind of work, and he was also afraid he would drop it, so he used it instead to chop loose a large limb above him, one that forked into a dozen or more leafless branches. He used his new weapon more as a broom than a blade, flailing it at the oncoming Bukken so that they fell off in a chorus of whistling shrieks. He did his best to sweep the underside of the wide branch as well, knocking loose a few more. He looked up and saw Nezeru whirling her weighted rope again, but then was distracted by a sudden, bitter pain in his ankle. One of the Bukken had got past his defenses and was clinging to his woolen hose, jabbing a small, sharp piece of stone into Morgan's unprotected ankle. With a cry of disgust, he reached down and snatched up the squirming creature, then flung it as hard as he could at the trunk of the tree. The limp corpse bounced off and tumbled out of sight.

"Quick now," Nezeru called. "Climb to me."

Morgan did not have to be told twice; he swept away another wave of goblins, then discarded his branch-broom. He scrambled up until he stood beside her, but unlike the Norn, who perched on the slender limb like a bird, he had to put one hand on the trunk to steady himself. This time, her cast had been true: anchored by the knife, the slender rope had wrapped around an upright limb on the distant pine, spanning the river gorge.

"It will hold," she said. "Go. I will keep them off this branch until you have crossed."

Morgan's eyes widened. The gorge was some twenty or thirty paces across, and it was two or three times that distance down to the rushing water. The rope sagged like the back of an ailing, overworked donkey. "Climb across on *that?*"

"Yes, foolish mortal—unless you want to become a feast for the *Furi'a*!" She abruptly leaned past him. Her sword darted once, twice, three times, almost too fast to see, each time transfixing another goblin. She waved the blade violently, sending the tiny bodies hurtling out into the growing darkness. "Go!"

Morgan crawled past her until he could bend down and grab the rope with both hands, then commended his soul to God and slid off the branch. For a sickening moment he was falling in space, then he felt a burning tug in his arms and shoulders. He bounced in the air, dangling from the rope with arms fully extended.

"Make haste, mortal!" Nezeru said from behind him. "I must use it as well!"

He began climbing hand over hand along the swaying, sagging rope. His months in the trees had much strengthened him—he would never have managed otherwise, not for such a distance—but he had never dangled so high above river rocks and dangerously swift water. Once he risked a quick downward glance, but the yawning gulf beneath him made his stomach lurch and his heart seem to stop beating.

Don't look down again, he told himself.

It took a horribly long time to cross, and several times Nezeru begged him to go faster. The roar of the river, so loud and fierce that it seemed like a monster waiting to swallow him, and he dared not hurry too much for fear of losing his sweat-slippery grip. At last he saw the far edge of the gorge, and when he finally reached it, he dropped onto the top of the embankment, praying that none of the Bukken had made it across the river behind him.

As he sat up, he saw that Nezeru was already swinging across hand over hand, moving as quickly and nimbly as an island ape. The branch from which she had come was thronged with goblins, and several of them were sawing at the cord, while others attacked it with their teeth.

"They're cutting the rope!" Morgan cried. "Quickly!" He scrambled to his feet, ignoring the burning misery of his shoulder joints, and began to pull the rope tight to keep it from swaying.

Then, as Nezeru passed the halfway point, the rope snapped and she plummeted out of sight.

Morgan immediately backed several steps up the top of the bank, digging in his heels as he went, trying to brace himself for her weight on the rope—if she did not simply tumble down into the foaming, rock-filled river. The rope pulled tight, but the weight was so much less than he had expected that he almost despaired, thinking she could not still be on the other end. But he kept his grip, and after a few moments he could feel a rhythmic tugging on the tightened cord. He backed farther away, and after a few more moments, Nezeru's head appeared above the rim of the gorge.

With one last heave from Morgan, she scrambled up onto the bank and finally let go of the rope. She got to her feet, looked at Morgan, and nodded once, as if to say, "Well, that's done." On the far side, the enraged goblins leaped and chittered on the alder branch, unable to follow.

Morgan helped Nezeru unwind the rope and anchoring knife from the pine tree. As she examined the end the goblins had cut, a little flower of frayed fibers, he grew increasingly angry.

"You might at least say 'thank you,'" he said.

She gave him a puzzled look—not hard, not angry, but not grateful, either. "Why?"

"Because I helped save you, didn't I?"

She made the gesture he had come to recognize as a shrug. "We do not think that way. Those are mortal ideas."

"It's a mortal idea to be grateful that someone helped save your life?"

She considered this for a moment. "More or less. We use words of gratitude when a noble has done a favor for a person of a lesser clan or rank which must be acknowledged. Or a child might say it to a parent. But between a Sacrifice soldier and a mortal?" She shook her head. "That is not our way."

"Your way is stupid, then."

"It is far older than any customs of your own folk."

"Besides, I *am* a noble." He had not meant to say it, but his anger at being taken for granted by her had overwhelmed his good sense. "I am a prince. I am the grandson of the High King and the High Queen. Someday I will rule all these lands!"

She stared at him for an uncomfortably long time. "So then, Your Highness," she said at last, "perhaps you would like to follow me as we continue on our journey across this land of yours. And perhaps when we meet the *Uro'eni*—your monster in the Vale of Mists—you can explain to him that he should not crush us because he is one of your loyal subjects."

As she walked away, Morgan stared after her. *She doesn't believe me. All this time I kept silent, but she wouldn't have paid any attention even if I'd told her.*

His anger made him want to kick something, but his legs were far too tired for kicking. He followed Nezeru away from the clamoring river and up the slope into thick forest.

They had climbed for perhaps an hour up a wearyingly uneven hillside when Nezeru called him to join her on an outcrop of rock. Morgan was now aching in a way he would have complained about bitterly if his companion had been anyone else; so, hoping that perhaps she finally meant to make peace, or at least suggest that they stop for the night, he hastened up the rise. But when he reached her, she only pointed back toward the river, now a good distance below them.

"There. Do you see it?"

He squinted, but the evening light was fading fast and he could make out nothing but a mass of trees and the river. "No. What?"

"That broad place on the valley floor just beside the ruins of Da'ai Chikiza. That is one of the Moorings—the place where *Sacred Seed* found its landing."

"Sacred what?"

She gave him a stern look. "I thought you said you knew of the Eight Ships. *Sacred Seed* was the eighth and last ship, and it came to its mooring there. You will never see a place more hallowed—unless you someday travel to Nakkiga itself."

He had heard enough about Nakkiga to already know he had no urge to visit it. Instead, he asked, "But how could a big ship sail on so little water?"

"The river was larger then, I am sure. It must have filled the whole valley from side to side." She wore such a strange, bright-eyed expression that Morgan did not want to ask any more questions. "But soon after Da'ai Chikiza was built, the first of the mortal folk came into this land. And that began the downfall of all that was good."

"That's not true," he said, nettled. "God made everything here—the land, the sea, the sky, and all the animals and people too—standing on the summit of Mount Den Haloi. It says so in the Book of the Aedon."

She gave him a look he could not immediately unpack. "Does it, then?"

"Yes, it does. Look, I'm glad we saw the Mooring or whatever you called it, but when can we rest and find some food?"

"Soon, perhaps." She leaped down from the outcrop, then headed up the slope once more, a slender figure already moving so quickly that Morgan had no choice but to follow, grumbling to himself.

They finally came upon a limestone cavern in the hillside, and after being assured it was not already home to a bear or a wolfpack, Morgan gratefully entered and stretched out on the ground. Now that he had stopped moving, he never wanted to move again. His stomach, though, was empty and letting him know it.

"Are you willing to go out and hunt for something?" she asked. "Or are you expecting me to do it?"

Morgan stifled a groan and sat up. "I'll do it. Although I don't know how much luck I'll have in the dark."

"I still have a little *pu'ja*," she said. "It is old but has been wrapped in leaves. It should still be good."

"What is it?"

"Bread. Soldier's bread."

He accepted a piece, and although he questioned her use of the word 'good'—he thought it tasted like a charred stick of particularly flavorless wood—it did help fill the hole in his guts, and he accepted two more pieces from her before she put the leaf-shrouded packet away again. "It is more filling than you think," she said.

He was beginning to realize that she was right: in fact, he was already feeling so much restored that he crawled over to her on his hands and knees and put his arms around her shoulders, then pushed his face against her neck and smelled her scent, which was far more familiar than it had been before their time in the yew tree two nights earlier.

"What are you doing?" There was no hint of any double meaning: she did not seem to know.

"I am trying to kiss your neck," he said. She still sat like a stone statue. "It is a form of love-play."

"Love-play?" She shook herself free of his embrace and turned toward him, her pale face stern. "I thought you were dying of hunger and exhaustion."

"I feel better now."

She stared as if seeing him for the first time. "You wish to couple? *Again*?"

"What do you mean by 'again'? It only happened once."

"And that should be enough for you. We are surrounded by enemies. Yes, it happened. But I told you, that was a moment of foolishness."

He reached out and touched her hand. She did not pull away, but she closed her fingers into a fist. "It was a nice moment of foolishness," Morgan said. "Wasn't it?"

She let out what he felt certain was a sigh, though it sounded more like the hiss of an irritated serpent. "As I said, it was . . . interesting. But it will not happen again soon, I think—if ever."

Half insulted and half sad, he let go of her hand. Ever since that night he had seldom stopped thinking about it, but it seemed to have meant nothing to her. "What are you?" he demanded. "An ebur?"

"Ebur? What is that?"

"A great, huge animal with legs like tree trunks. My tutor told me of it. It was big as a whalefish and twice as tall as a man, and it had an arm growing out of its face. He said the kings of Khand used to ride them into war."

"And why do you call me such a thing?"

"Because my tutor told me that they lived so long that they only mated—coupled—once every hundred years."

"Hmmm." She gave him a very dubious look. "I think it was more likely your tutors who only coupled once in a hundred years." And with that she turned her back on him.

Their climb into the range of hills that separated what Nezeru called the Coolblood Valley from the Narrowdark—the place that he knew as Misty Vale—was longer and a great deal more arduous than Morgan had expected.

The trees became sparser as they climbed, but despite the greater ease of movement, Morgan missed the cover they had provided. Here in the heights, the winds blew fiercely, with a heart of ice that he could feel even through his Norn armor. He was grateful that at least it was not snowing.

In fact, no new snow had fallen in the upper hills since they had begun climbing, though the higher they went, the more old snow there was—great white meadows hidden in the folded landscape, and shining caps of white on the peaks. Morgan was discovering muscles in his legs he did not know he had and had not known could ache so miserably.

In truth, they seemed to have entered into an entirely new world, one with no signs of either mortals or fairy-folk ever having lived there, only hares, deer, and the cautious goats, as well as an occasional falcon skimming past overhead. And if the land had seemed welcoming in the lower reaches, the heights did not. Great natural walls of pale limestone edged the almost invisible tracks Nezeru chose, or stood out from the ground in strange, elongated shapes like ancient barrows.

They made camp the first night in a cluster of large stones. The mountain wind nipped at Morgan's hands and nose all night. They were moving again with the dawn.

As the morning tipped into afternoon, and afternoon collapsed gently into twilight, the variety of trees that grew in the valley and on the lower slopes shrank to only pines and spruce, which held their ground on rocky hillsides like soldiers wondering where the battle had gone. As they climbed ever higher, Morgan was struck by a profound and frightening sense of loneliness. Neither mortals nor immortals meant anything here. The hills belonged to the cautious goats that watched them from the heights, and the skimming raptors that carved the gray sky into pieces above his head.

I didn't know much of anything about the world before this. This new thought was both shameful and liberating. *And it will all go on without me when I'm dead. The mountains don't care about princes. They were here before me, and they'll still be here after I'm gone.*

More than anything else, it was the emptiness of this land that had seized him. *If there had been a few crofter's huts here,* he thought, *I would have noticed none of this, only seen another place where people live. And back in the forest?* he wondered. *It was the same, but I was too busy trying to stay alive to think about it. If I had found even a deserted cottage, a tumbledown wall, things would have seemed different. But the forest, the valleys, these peaks—they don't belong to people.*

Nezeru had said nothing all day about his claim to be a prince, and he was just as glad of that. She had been far too intent on finding safe paths through the hills to talk, and Morgan could not have explained the things that he was thinking in any case, not without exposing himself as a fool—or so he felt sure his companion would judge him. He followed her dutifully, foot up, foot down, now sliding on a scree of lose stones, then moments later grabbing a jutting rock to help himself mount a difficult slope. He was, he thought, climbing the skin of the hill like a flea on a horse's hock, living in two worlds at the same time while understanding neither—or so it seemed.

Nezeru finally found a place to stop on a high slope, shielded from the worst of the wind by a limestone scarp that stood up straight as a castle's outwall.

"Can we light a fire?" he asked.

Nezeru shook her head. "In such weather, even by night, I would see the smoke from at least a league away, and we cannot trust the Sacrifice soldiers camped in the valley below us to be any less skilled. There may be patrols here in the high places, too. We will eat *pu'ja* and speak in whispers." She pointed at the scarp towering above them. "That is like the inner wall of a great temple—it will throw sound a long distance. No, quiet and dark, that is how we will spend the night."

After another meal of the Norn bread—less satisfying tonight, though he was no less hungry than the night before—they huddled against the limestone wall as a brief flurry of cold rain passed over them. As the clouds swept on the rain stopped; a few stars smoldered into life at the edges of the wide sky. Nezeru did not speak, but only sat in an attitude of deep stillness, staring into the middle distance at nothing Morgan could see. It was frustrating to have her so close and yet so distant: he felt as if they had lost something important. He finally broke what seemed an hour's silence.

"You don't believe that I'm a prince, do you?" he said quietly.

She did not look up. "I do not know the lands of mortals well, Morgan. Perhaps you truly are the prince of some small kingdom. It matters little. I was once a Sacrifice and a soldier in a Queen's Talon, but that also matters little out here."

He badly wanted to explain how important his grandparents were, that they ruled all of the known world. But here in the heights, with the lands of men so far away, it felt worse than pointless. Still, he could not entirely silence his pride.

"Why don't you believe me?"

She finally looked at him. "Because I have seen princes. They go nowhere alone. I saw Prince Pratiki once, and he is only the many-times-great grand-nephew of the queen, yet he was surrounded by soldiers and courtiers. The whole of the Avenue of the Fallen was closed off so he and his company could pass. But you I found wandering alone in Da'ai Chikiza, Morgan. Why would a prince of men be alone in a ruined city?"

"I told you, I lost the rest of my company. They were attacked."

"Perhaps." She did not seem very interested. "But you must admit it seems unlikely."

He swallowed an angry reply. She was right—it did seem unlikely. Everything that had happened to him seemed unlikely. *"You don't know you're in a story until someone tells it to you afterward."* How many times had his grandfather Simon said that when relating his own adventures—adventures which, when Morgan thought about them, were no more terrifying or dangerous than what he had already gone through himself? *Am I in a story then? And if I am, how does it end?*

"I will not sleep this night," Nezeru announced, her pale face just barely visible. "You might as well."

Morgan curled himself in his cloak and watched her for some time, but she did not once look at him. He thought her expression was the oldest thing about her, jaw set as if in an argument she did not want, eyes fixed on things he couldn't imagine. Their moment of passion seemed long in the past, as though it had happened to someone else, and Morgan had only heard about it.

"Good night, then," he said, and closed his eyes. He heard no reply.

The next day they mounted higher and higher. Far below them, the forested depths of the valley looked like an ocean, flecked with whitecaps of snow. The cold bit more deeply now; he felt it in his lungs as well as his extremities, a gnawing want of air that never entirely went away. By mid-morning they left the hill on which they had sheltered and climbed to another, this one topped by a great, long crest of hard stone that jutted like an ax-blade. For the first time Morgan could see no other peaks looming in the distance, only dull sky.

"What is on the other side of this ridge?" he asked.

"Tanakirú, of course," said Nezeru. "What you would call the Vale of Mists—the place that you warned me away from." A hard smile appeared, then quickly vanished. "It is a long valley carved out by the River Narrowdark." She looked around. "The clouds certainly seem thicker there. Let us start walking again. I do not think you would enjoy spending the night this high up."

He groaned a little, but the chill on his bones and the frosty sting in his throat and lungs suggested that she was right.

They reached the top of the hill in mid-afternoon and clambered up onto the narrow limestone crest. Finally able to look down into the far side, Morgan found he could see almost nothing. The wide valley Nezeru called Tanakirú was so full of floating white mist that it appeared to be filled to the brim with washed wool, great pallid masses of fog that covered everything lower than their high perch and the distant peaks on the valley's far side. Nezeru lifted her hand to point down the valley to his right. "In the south, there, is where you entered into the vale before. If your story is true."

"Of course my story was true. Why would I lie?"

Nezeru shrugged. "Pride. Shame. Or merely because you were misled by weak mortal eyes. Perhaps even by a brief madness. There are as many reasons as there are untruths." She gave him a serious look. "I do not say you told a deliberate falsehood, Morgan, only that your story might not have been entirely true. There is a difference. Now, let us find a way into the valley. This great outcrop is too steep to climb down. We should avoid doing so." After surveying both directions for a moment, she led him north along the top of the bladelike scarp. She stopped abruptly—it was all he could do not to run into her—and brushed a clump of snow from the stone at her feet.

"Do you think this is your Mount Den Haloi?" she asked him.

He could only stare at her. "What?"

"The place where you say that your god made all the world—the animals, the birds, the fishes, and mortal men."

He shook his head in irritation. "Of course not. That's far to the south, on the other side of the Nascadu wastelands."

"Ah." She pointed to the bare patch of stone she had uncovered. "Then I wonder why your god chose to put fish so high up in the mountains?"

For a moment Morgan thought she had lost her wits, but when he bent forward, he saw that what he had first taken for flecks of lighter stone were actually the skeletons of strange, tiny fish.

Her hard smile had returned. "Perhaps this was where your god learned that fish need water."

Morgan ruminated unhappily as he followed her. If she didn't believe he'd really been in Misty Vale, and if she thought the truths of his faith were laughable, no wonder she doubted he was a prince as well. A chill seeped into his heart as they made their careful way along the top of the great stone barrier, which narrowed in places until it was scarcely wider beneath Morgan's feet than the span of his shoulders, and where the teasing pushes from the wind suddenly became deadly threats. *But how can anyone prove they are who they say they are? Only when someone who knows the truth says that it's true. And even then, some will doubt it.*

They began to make their way down from the hillcrest at last, following the lightly worn tracks of goats or deer that Morgan could see only intermittently but whose spoor Nezeru never seemed to lose. They were soon joined by a rivulet of snowmelt, which then gathered to itself several more small but fast moving streams. Soon they were descending into the foggy valley beside a loudly chiming river. Each time they heard its splashing turn into the louder roar of a cataract below them, they chose another way downward to avoid steep drops.

Morgan chose a gurgling pool at the bottom of one cataract to drink and splash water on his face, because even though the valley's fog cooled the air and the journey down was much less strenuous than the journey up had been, he was still sweaty and tired. The water tasted clean and sweet, and revived his spirits.

"So where are we going?" he asked as he wiped his hands dry on his woolen hose.

"Who can say? But we still have a long way to climb down before we start looking for shelter."

It was a long, arduous journey. By the time the afternoon sun had sunk out of sight behind the heights, they still could not see the valley floor. If the same odd trees and trickling Narrowdark River waited for them that he had seen the first time he entered the place, Morgan thought, they were entirely hidden by the mists.

Anything could be down there—giants, dragons, things there aren't even names for.

"We should stop," he said. "I know you can do this for days—Sacrifice training, all of that—but I can't. It's getting hard to see and I don't want to fall the rest of the way down, even though it might be a faster way to get there."

For the first time in more than a day, Nezeru showed him something like an ordinary smile. "You are jesting, but I understand you. We will look for a place to stop. If we build a pit carefully, and hedge it round with stones, we might even make a fire tonight. I think the mists will hide us from anyone who might be looking."

This was the best news he had heard in some time, and Morgan had a bit of bounce in his step as he followed her down the slope. The hill's rocky bones were covered with a snow-spotted layer of earth. Leafless shrubs and increasing numbers of evergreens filled the slope.

They had stopped on a relatively flat part of the slope so Nezeru could consider it as a site to make camp when they heard the first distant rumble. "Is that thunder?" Morgan asked.

Nezeru stared up at the sky. "Likely. If there is a storm coming, we would not see it through this murk. Then again, if a storm is approaching, I think we should feel more wind here." She waved her hand; a faint trail of mist swirled around it. "Whatever the cause," she said, "I think we should search for some more protected place—"

Another rumble came, louder this time but less drawn-out, more like a single, earth-shaking impact, as if the hills themselves had begun to wake and one of them had just dropped something. Morgan's heart began to speed. "No. No, I've heard that before," he said. "May Holy Aedon save us, that's not thunder! We have to hide!"

"What are you talking about?" demanded Nezeru, but as a third great thump shook the ground, her eyes went suddenly wide.

"The ogre!" He looked around in growing terror. The mist no longer made him feel sheltered but blinded. Where should they go? The thunderous noises now seemed to fill the entire valley, and Morgan and Nezeru glanced around in desperate confusion.

"Which way?" he cried.

Nezeru shook her head. For a moment he thought she had frozen in panic, but then he saw that she was slowly turning, listening. Another vast drumbeat followed; the ground jumped beneath Morgan's feet, the mist swirled, and the trees around them shivered.

"This way!" she cried. "Run!"

The monstrous footfalls grew closer, each one shaking the ground hard enough to make Morgan stumble as he raced after her. *DOOM.* A pause, tree branches still rattling, then: *DOOM.*

Morgan could see something angular showing through the mist a little way ahead of them, a wide shelf of rock like a broken plate half-buried in the hillside. He turned toward it, scrambling up the slope, falling and then struggling to his feet again before being knocked to the ground by another echoing *DOOM.*

"Here!" he shouted. "Here! We can hide up here!"

But when he reached the shelter and looked back, he could no longer see Nezeru. He called her name and thought he heard her voice farther down the slope, but the space between them was full of swirling fog.

DOOM.

And then he saw it—something impossibly large, an upright shadow in the whiteness, looming as tall as a cathedral spire. Trees splintered. Massive branches flew into the air and then fell back into the mist again. Morgan, his heart swollen inside him until he thought it would choke off his breath, scrambled back down the slope, searching desperately for Nezeru.

He found her, but only after he had almost stumbled over her. She lay on the ground, teeth clenched in a fixed grin of agony. Half a large tree had fallen on her, part of a smashed and splintered trunk, and it was pinning her legs and hips. He kneeled beside her, trying to lift it away, but the tree trunk was too large, too heavy.

"Leave me," she cried. "You cannot help."

He ignored her words and began scrabbling at the dirt, trying to dig enough of it away that he could pull her out. The monstrous footfalls were so close now that the ground seemed to leap up and fall back with each thunderous impact, as if a titanic, drunken lord pounded on his supper table, making all the crockery jump in unison. Nearby trees were toppling, great ripping sounds followed by booming crashes as they fell and pulled other trees down with them.

Morgan could not think. He could not afford to think. The worst thing in the world was almost on them, and all he could do was dig. He grabbed Nezeru's arm and pulled as hard as he could, and though she let out a muffled cry of pain he kept pulling until he finally felt her weight begin to move. He sat on the ground and pushed at the broken tree with one foot while straining to drag her out from beneath it, managing inch by inch to pull her toward him. At last, just as Morgan was certain a gigantic foot would smash them into jelly in the next instant, Nezeru's legs slid free from beneath the trunk. He picked her up and considered trying to reach the overhanging rock he had chosen for shelter, but at that instant a monstrous shadow fell upon them. He flung himself a few steps down the slope and rolled, clutching Nezeru so tightly that as the world spun around them, he could not tell what was her and what was him. A tree-trunk stopped their fall, Morgan half on top of her. He pressed his face against her shoulder, unwilling to see the thing that was likely reaching down to crush them.

DOOM.

Then, long moments later: *doom*.

The monstrous, hill-covering shadow slid past them. The twilight returned. The deafening noise of footfalls gradually faded until once again they seemed nothing but a rumor of thunder.

Morgan rolled off Nezeru. She was breathing, but he could not tell if she had broken any bones. He picked her up as gently as he could, then staggered up the hillside through a waste of ruined, splintered trees toward the stone shelf. When he reached it, weariness finally overcame him. He did his best to set Nezeru down without dropping her, then his legs folded, and he slumped to the ground.

He might have slept; he could not tell. All he knew was that when he heard Nezeru's voice and opened his eyes, it was utterly dark outside their shelter.

"I was a fool, Morgan," she said.

He crawled to her side. "Are you badly hurt?"

"Only scraped and bruised, thanks be to the Garden. And sore. But it is my pride that has done me the most harm."

"Your pride?" He squinted, but he could barely make out her narrow face in the darkness.

"I did not believe in your ogre. I thought you had seen one of the bigger, older giants, the sort that I have seen myself many times. 'The mortal has let terror convince him it was some monstrosity never before seen on this earth,' I told myself. But I was a fool."

He did not even have the strength to enjoy being proved right. "It doesn't matter," he said. "It truly doesn't."

"Will you hold me?" Her question caught him by surprise, so that he did not immediately answer. "Not to couple, my brave mortal," she said. "But I do not want to lie alone, either. Will you put your arms around me, and we can lie together? Be not alone together?"

He did not need to speak, he realized. He stretched himself out beside her instead and pulled her to him. She made a little sound of discomfort as she rolled onto her hip, but quickly squeezed his hand to let him know the pain was not too bad. He did not need to speak at all, and that was a relief, because at that moment nothing existed except the small place where they hid. Words had become too small to explain anything. He folded his arms around her, her head against his chest, his head resting against the top of hers, and that was the way they fell asleep.

31

Pirates, Priests, and Martyrs

The galley knifed out from the dock and into the roiling waters of the Gleniwent River and the lights of Wentmouth began to shrink behind them. Jesa could hear cursing as the boat pitched and rolled. Men strained at the oars to keep the bow pointing toward the distant bank as the current tried to push them toward the sea. The river was shrouded in fog, and Jesa could see nothing of the far shore. She had never been on a proper ship before, never anything bigger than the dugout her uncle used to navigate the waters around Red Pig Lagoon, and she was terrified.

"Why does the boat go up and down so much?" She tightened her grip on little Serasina.

"Nothing to fear," said the queen. "These men make this crossing every night." Her words would have more been reassuring if she had sounded like she cared whether they survived or not.

She has lost her husband, the king, Jesa chided herself. *You are being selfish, girl. She has troubles far greater than yours.* But knowing that did not make her heart or her stomach any easier.

"Why are there no lights?" she asked a little later. "What if another boat comes upon us in the dark?"

"As I said, do not fear. Nobody travels this part of the river at night—it's too dangerous. We will meet no other ship."

This did not soothe Jesa's worried heart. "But our boat has no lanterns, no lamps!"

"I suspect they do not like to be noticed, as a rule. They are likely smugglers."

"Smugglers?" To Jesa, the word meant the same thing as "pirates," and she immediately began to fear that they would be robbed, ravished, and thrown overboard. "Why are we on a smuggling boat?"

"It was the first crossing I could get to Meremund—otherwise we would have had to wait until daylight, maybe until afternoon. And I do not dare to wait so long, or to cross Meremund in the day. Someone might recognize me."

Jesa was still confused—surely the queen *wanted* to be recognized, since everyone thought she was dead. But a glow on the headland behind them had caught her attention. As they moved out farther into the river, she could see it was a great billowing flame, the only bright thing beneath the clouded sky. "What is that?" she asked, pointing. "That fire-mountain?"

Miriamele turned to look. "That is the Hayefur," she said. "It is a beacon, lit on the hill to keep ships from striking the rocks at the river's mouth."

"Men made it?"

"Must have, but it has been there a long time." She sounded weary.

"I thought it was a fire-mountain, like Ya Mologi in the heart of the Wran," Jesa said. "They say that sometimes flames and smoke come from that peak, and burning mud runs down into the trees." She realized she was talking a great deal and very loudly, and likely squeezing the queen's hand harder than she should. "No one lives near it because it is holy," she said, but lowered her voice. "And because of the fire."

"That's nice," said the queen, staring at nothing.

The first pink of dawn lightened the eastern sky as the galley nosed its way to a dock at the outermost edge of Meremund's main port. The city looked bigger than Jesa had expected, much more substantial than the one they had just left. If Wentmouth was a sailor, ragged and tattooed and looking to earn a coin any way it could, Meremund was a merchant, large and prosperous. Beyond the port with its tall warehouses and tax stations, the towers of the city loomed even higher, as though keeping an eye on all their ventures. And highest of all, stretching far above even the tall, fortified mansions of the wealthy, stood a single spire.

"That's where we're headed," the queen said. "St. Tankred's. Unless everything I know is wrong, we will be safe there. And if we're not safe in the cathedral . . ." Her voice trailed off.

They disembarked down a flimsy gangplank over choppy green water. The oarsmen, stretching and grumbling after the long passage, watched them go without expression. The queen led Jesa to a place she called the Cornmarket, a great cobbled expanse against the outside of the city walls, already full of people despite the rain and the earliness of the hour. As Miriamele bought some milk for Serasina, Jesa watched the vendors and peddlers setting out their wares, grain and vegetables and flowers and fish. Except for the wide black bunting draped along the walls and black pennants flapping on many of the nearby towers, it could have been any market in any prosperous city. Jesa, who had not slept at all during the trip from Wentmouth, suddenly felt safer, and with that relief came a tremendous weariness. But Queen Miriamele had plans, and within a short time they had left the Cornmarket and entered the tall city gates.

It had begun to rain, the drops chilly and hard as little stones. Jesa wrapped

Serasina even more closely, so that only the baby's wide eyes stared out from the blanket, but she had finished her milk, so they did not stay open long.

"We are not walking all the way in this weather," Miriamele said. "We'll find someone to carry us to the cathedral."

"Will we take a carriage, Majesty?" Jesa asked. Her last experience had made her reluctant ever to get in such a thing again.

"Don't call me 'Majesty,'" said Miriamele in a stern whisper. "And Queen of Heaven, no, we will not be in a carriage. We might as well announce ourselves to anyone who might be interested. No, we will find some farmer's wagon to take us."

The queen quickly located a crofter who had not done as well with his geese as he had hoped and was more than willing to earn a few extra coppers. They climbed into the cart and huddled beneath a tattered cloth, surrounded by large, damp, disapproving birds. The farmer clicked his tongue and the ox strolled out with the air of someone who intended to go no farther than the next warm, dry spot.

They wound slowly up the cobbled main street, past houses of increasing size and improving decoration. The queen was leaning forward as though trying to make the cart go faster by sheer will. "It is hard," she said quietly. "This was the city of my birth and my childhood. When we lived here, my father still had his kindness and all his wits—he had not met that serpent Pryrates, the priest who corrupted him."

"You were happy here," Jesa said, thinking of her own childhood in the lagoon, surrounded by siblings and cousins and other children, all of them left largely to their own pursuits as long as they did not stray out of sight of their houses, which stood on stilts at the edge of the water.

"I was lonely here," Miriamele replied. "But I suppose there was happiness, too. It never lasts long, does it?" The queen blinked, and Jesa saw a gleam of tears. "I do not know what I will do now. Without Simon." She took a deep, shuddering breath, then wiped at her eyes and forced herself to sit straight. "But I can't think of things like that. Not when the entire kingdom is in danger." Her jaw was set, the moment of weakness replaced by cold anger. "If I find that Pasevalles has connived at my husband's death, he will not be given the release of death himself for a long time. A very long time."

Jesa could not help shivering a little, though everything she had heard of this Pasevalles made it clear the man deserved to suffer. But she had not seen the queen so hard, so chilly in aspect even when they had been confronted by armed men in Nabban. This cold new Miriamele unnerved her.

They had to pass another gate to enter the hilltop precinct, but the queen produced her haughtiest manner and the guards decided it was less dangerous to let her in than to argue with her. Miriamele told the farmer to stop, then paid him off.

"Come, Jesa," she said, scraping her shoes clean on the cobbles after their ride among the geese. "It will be faster to walk from here."

Jesa saw no ordinary houses around them, or at least nothing that she could easily identify as one. Instead, as on the Sancelline Hill back in Nabban, the structures clearly belonged to rich merchants and nobles, each one a little fortress with its own towers and walls. The queen took a turn carrying Serasina, to Jesa's silent relief, and as the bells for mid-morning prayer rang from the cathedral spire in melodic thunder, they reached the front of the great church.

Jesa had seen cathedrals before—Nabban had several—so the size of St. Tankred's did not astonish her, but it was still a very impressive building. The beautifully ornate lantern and belfry loomed high over the city, topped by a slender openwork spire like an arrow aimed at the sky to threaten Heaven itself.

Jesa was holding Serasina again, and as the queen led them through the great doors, she feared the baby would start crying. There was something about the echoing heights which made her feel out of place, as though this great church did not want to welcome her but to remind her of how unimportant she was.

Miriamele found a verger tidying the altar and spoke to him while Jesa waited, but the man seemed reluctant to do whatever the queen had asked. At last, and after some heated words from the queen, he went out and came back with a priest. Now the priest and Miriamele spoke, but Jesa thought from the queen's expression that she was still not getting the results she wanted. At last, as Jesa wandered closer, Miriamele took a ring from her hand with a gesture that was almost violent and handed it to the priest. "Take it to His Excellency," she said. "He will recognize it. Tell him I am waiting to speak to him."

The priest shook his head, then vanished into the curved *ramis*. The verger watched the queen for a short time, as if waiting for her to try stealing some precious relic, then he wandered away and pretended to be polishing the seats in the choir stall.

Time seemed to pass excruciatingly slowly while Jesa waited, but at last the priest returned, and this time his attitude was completely different. He bowed deeply, hands folded, then gestured for Miriamele to follow him. She in turn summoned Jesa. The priest looked more than a little surprised to see the baby in Jesa's arms, but forced a smile and a nod, then led them back through the corridors behind the *ramis*.

The smell of rain-soaked earth floated to them as they walked through a covered gallery to a pair of tall wooden doors. The priest hastened forward and pulled them open. Half-fearing he might try to shut her and the baby outside, Jesa hastened after the queen.

The walls of the high-ceilinged room were covered with paintings and embroidered hangings. Jesa suspected the pictures were from the Book of Aedon, but she did not recognize the scenes portrayed in any of them. An old man in heavy clerical robes was waiting for them in a gilt chair with velvet cushions, but he rose as soon as Miriamele entered. He held something in his hand, fumbling it nervously with his fingers—Jesa guessed it was the ring. He came toward them on silent, slippered feet, then lifted a glass circle to his eye and peered at the queen as though at some unknown and slightly worrisome wild animal. A moment later his face went slack with surprise and he dropped awkwardly to his knees.

"Your Majesty," he said. "How can this be? By God Himself, this is the answer to all the prayers of Aedondom! Are you truly here, or have I been carried out of life and into Heaven?"

Miriamele laughed, but without much enjoyment. "I assure you, Archbishop Orvyn, I am alive and here in front of you. It was not me who died in the burning carriage. But before I tell you the story and what brings me here, tell me quickly—does Earl Durward still live?"

"He does, Majesty," said the archbishop. "But His Lordship is very ill and has not left his bed for the better part of a year." He shook his head. "Forgive me, but my heart is beating so fast! So strange, all of this! I must sit down. Father Swidelm, fetch a chair for the queen." He finally noticed Jesa. "And her lady-in-waiting as well. Then you may go."

"No, Your Grace." The queen's voice was unexpectedly hard. "No, I will take a seat with thanks, and so will Lady Jesa, but Father Swidelm must remain here with us for now. No one else must know I am in Meremund, and that means the secret must be very tightly held."

"Of course, Majesty, of course." The archbishop tottered back to his own chair as the priest brought out seats for the queen and Jesa. "But how can this be?" the old man kept saying, half to himself. "How can this be?"

Jesa hardly heard him, though she was hugely relieved that they seemed to be safe at last. *The queen called me 'Lady.' As if I were one of her noblewomen—as if I were her friend. Who would ever have dreamed such a thing?*

I have seen this place before, Simon realized. *I know it.* He stared at the damp stone walls, the moldy straw, the rusted shackles. *Dear God, this is where King Elias imprisoned Prince Josua all those years ago.*

Memories came flooding back like a rain-swollen river bursting its banks, drowning fields and houses, carrying everything before it in a slurry of mud. *That day, that mad day—the day everything changed.* That had been the day his first life had ended. By freeing Prince Josua, he had begun everything that came after—his own exile into the wilderness, Josua's declaration of war on his brother the king, and all the war and death that followed.

Miriamele. That day brought me Miriamele, too, though it took a while. And now she's been taken from me.

He was a prisoner in his own castle. His hand-picked chancellor, Pasevalles, was a traitor.

And it seems I didn't die at Winstowe either, though it might have been better if I did.

He was wearing only his underclothing, hose and the same pair of linen trews he had worn beneath his armor at Winstowe. This did not surprise him so much as his own chest, where he could find no trace of a wound.

But I felt Unver stab me! He put his sword right into my heart.

Perhaps he had been god-struck, like old Shem Horsegroom—one moment telling a tale, laughing at his own story, the next moment dropping to the ground like an arrow-pierced grouse, never to move again. *Apoplexy. That's what Tiamak called it. But I suppose it hardly matters what I thought happened.* He sent up a half-considered prayer. *What do You expect me to do for my kingdom, Lord, locked up in a dungeon and with everyone thinking I'm dead?*

The worst part of it all was that a man he had trusted had proved a villain. *Miri never thought as much of him as I did—she said we should give his place to an Erkynlander, because the barons were restless about all the other foreigners we had raised to powerful positions.* But even Miri had not dreamed of anything like this.

Still, it was almost impossible to believe such evil was possible, though he had heard it from Pasevalles' own mouth. What could drive a man to such measures? Why would he steal from those who had lifted him up and would have given him even more riches and responsibility? And why would he pretend Simon was dead? Surely, he did not believe he could actually take the throne—Duke Osric, however headstrong and temperamental he might be, would not allow himself to be ruled by a mere advisor, especially one who was not even an Erkynlander. No, Osric was too old-fashioned, too stubborn. So what could Pasevalles be thinking?

Simon tugged idly at his chains, but they were heavy and strong, secured to an iron ring in the cell's rear wall. He saw no one beyond the door's barred window, so he called, "Hoy! Is anyone out there? Help me—it's the king!" The echoes seemed to die within an instant. He was deep, deep beneath the castle. It seemed unlikely anyone other than Pasevalles would ever know he was there.

But I helped Josua get free from this place, he told himself, *so it isn't impossible the same could happen for me.*

He bowed his head and prayed, more carefully this time. *God, Father of All, I am deep in troubles. The High Ward is in terrible danger. If you still love me—or at least love the people of the kingdom we have tried to rule well in Your name—send someone to help me as I once helped Prince Josua. Please, God, send me a friend. Or at least an ally.*

He had nodded off again. The blessed nothingness of dreamless sleep was followed by the first moments of waking and the brief possibility that it had all been a nightmare. That possibility vanished quickly.

"Wake up, Your Fallen Majesty. You cannot shirk your duties. There are people here you must meet."

Simon shifted position, feeling the ache in every muscle. He knew before he opened his eyes whose mocking voice had woken him.

"Go to Hell," he said.

"Oh, eventually, if there truly is such a place." Pasevalles sounded just the same as he always had, measured and confident.

How long has this been going on? Simon wondered. *How long did I stare into this damnable liar's face while he plotted against me?*

"In fact, I flatter myself that I will rank high among Hell's citizens," Pasevalles said, "with Crexis and your predecessor Elias and other great sinners. But until then, we both have things to do. Rouse yourself."

Simon groaned as he straightened up. Two shapes stood outside the barred window, one large, one less so. The smaller figure spoke. "As I said, I wish to introduce you to some people. They have all been instrumental in my work—as have you, yourself, my dear Simon."

"Just because you talk doesn't mean I have to listen."

"Of course not—although I could force you, I suppose. But what would be the pleasure in that?" Pasevalles sounded disturbingly cheerful. "First, meet your jailer. You will not recognize him, but he has been earning gold out of your treasury for some time." The smaller shape stepped back and the torchlight revealed more of the other, who was not much taller than Pasevalles but a great deal thicker in the neck, shoulders, and chest. The head of this second man was hairless, and what Simon could see of his eyes was like meeting the empty stare of a reptile. "This is Zhadu Split-Jaw. I met him in the part of Erchester called the Little Thrithing. Do you know it?"

"I know my own city." What little that Simon could see of the clansman by torchlight was disturbing—this Zhadu looked as though he had once taken an ax-blow directly in the face.

Pasevalles chuckled, honestly amused. "Well, you *think* you know it, at least. Zhadu here has helped me many times. He knows many other clansmen like him, unhomed by their own clans and willing to fight or to kill for gold. *Your* gold, as it happens."

Simon shook his head. "So, this is what you've done with what you stole. Three thousand crowns to hire a few sell-swords, hoping that would bring you the throne."

"Three thousand?" Pasevalles laughed again. "Oh, Simon, I must have taken at least three or four times that amount from your coffers and sent it to more places than you could imagine, all with the single goal of ruining you."

It seemed like madness—it *was* madness. "But why, curse you? What have I ever done to you? I gave you a place in the court, lifted you to high rank—"

"And for all that, I thank you. In truth, Simon, you gave me the most important gift of all—trust. I could not have done what I've done without that."

"But why, man? Why?"

"Because I hate you. Surely that is reason enough."

Full of pain and confusion, Simon had only just realized what Pasevalles had said. "Hold, traitor. You said this Thrithings brute hired your sell-swords. Is this the animal that killed my wife, then?" Fury swept over him like a spill of burning oil. "Give him to me! Give him to me and I will break him with my own hands. Damnable, cursed beast!" Even as he strained at his chains, Simon's eyes filled with helpless tears. "The devil take you all for murderers!"

"Save your curses for a better target, Simon Once-King," said Pasevalles, laughing. "Yes, Zhadu spread the coins that brought that band of sell-swords onto your wife's trail, but his villainy is minor compared to what others have done. No, you have not asked the right question yet."

"What madness are you talking, traitor?"

Pasevalles shook his head. "Oh, poor, foolish Simon, someone is only a traitor if his gambit fails . . . and I have won, not lost. But since you will not ask the question that should be asked, I will do it for you."

"Shut your lying, cursed mouth!" Simon cried. "Kill me now, go on! God save me, I am sick of your talking."

Pasevalles continued as if he had not spoken. "The question that should be asked—*must* be asked—is: How did I manage to take so much of what was yours without your knowing? How, Simon? You were surrounded by a company of painfully, annoyingly honest men and women, your many foreign advisors—all of whom, by the way, are much disliked by the Erkynlanders in your court. The unimpeachable Eolair, of course, and self-righteous little Tiamak of the Wran—all pagans! Count Nial and his wife Countess Rhona, too. They were too much your slaves and worshippers for me to have any hope of them being useful to me. They would have smelled the odor of crime no matter in what fair clothes I dressed it. So I needed another ally, one close to you." Pasevalles turned from the cell door and shouted. *"Gum me nu, Hulgar!"* Simon heard a door creak somewhere down the passage. "I speak some of the Thrithings tongue," Pasevalles explained. "One of my nurses when I was a child at Chasu Metessa was a Thrithings clanswoman. The little of her speech she taught me has proved very useful."

Simon could hear steps in the hallway outside. He waited, his chains weighing on his weary limbs.

Zhadu Split-Face had dropped back a little way from the cell door. The figure that moved up to take his place was even bigger, three whole handspans taller than Pasevalles and wide as a double door—a second Thrithings clansman, his face covered with crude tattoos. Simon knew that Thrithings mercenaries liked to decorate themselves for every man they killed, and this man's face had as many black lines as the thorns of a thistle-crown.

The huge man squinted in through the cell door at Simon and laughed. The teeth that glinted in the man's thick beard were a jagged ruin, like broken crockery mortared onto a wall to keep out trespassers.

"Hulgar is Zhadu's brother," said Pasevalles. "I see you admiring his unusual smile. Yes, both brothers have suffered from ill luck. Hulgar's injuries came when a stallion kicked him in the face. Then he strangled the horse. Hulgar is very strong. But it is the person Hulgar has brought that I truly want you to see." He snapped out a command in the clansmen's tongue.

The huge grasslander reached to one side and dragged a small, round man-shape out of the shadows, then shoved it face-first against the barred window.

"Oh, Simon," said the whimpering figure. "Oh, Simon, I am so sorry. I am such a fool!"

Simon had thought himself beyond surprise. "Jemmy? *Jeremias?* Good God, man, what are you doing here?"

"I suspect that the Lord Chamberlain has come to beg your forgiveness," said Pasevalles. "But I suspect just as strongly that he will not get it—not when you hear what he has done."

If all had seemed nightmarish before, now Simon felt as though he had fallen into some pit in the Adversary's bleak fortress, haunted by impossible things, unimaginable betrayals. "What is he talking about, Jeremias? Did you do something?"

"Did he *do* something?" Pasevalles leaned in close and patted the Lord Chamberlain on his cheek as if he were a child. Jeremias's face was swollen and tearful, his usually immaculate clothes disarranged by rough handling. "Only the most important thing of all! He gave me access to your royal seal, King Simon—the symbol of your rule. I used it in a hundred different ways to smooth your path to ruin. Look at him! Look at your friend."

"Is this true?" Simon asked, though Jeremias's misery seemed to confirm it. "Tell me it's not, Jeremias."

"He tricked me!"

"Give me a straightforward traitor every day." Pasevalles twisted his voice a little to sound sober and sad. "Not these weaklings with their attempts to shift the blame, to claim they were misled. It always disappoints me."

"Lord Pasevalles told me that he needed my help," Jeremias said through his tears. "He said I could help him get his work done and make less work for you, if only I let him use your seal from time to time. I thought I was doing something good."

"Liar," said Pasevalles. "Hulgar, shake him." As Jeremias shrieked in the clansman's grasp, Pasevalles took the torch from its bracket, then turned back to Simon, light gleaming along one side of the noble's face. "Your childhood friend knew what he did was wrong—of course he did. But he is an unhappy little man with a small soul, full of jealousy that his friend was king and he was nothing."

"No! That's not true!" Jeremias struggled to get free, but Hulgar grabbed his head and struck it against the window bars. Both Thrithings-men held him up when he swayed and would have fallen.

"Why?" Simon asked. "I have loved you like a brother. Why would you do something so foolish?"

Jeremias, his lip and nose now bleeding, said, "You were always so *busy*, Simon. You gave me a position, but then made fun of it." Something else crept into his voice, a shadow of grievance. "I thought I could be useful. Pasevalles told me I could, that I would help him do great things, even if no one ever knew. But *I* would know, you see. That's all I wanted."

Simon felt sick, his thoughts in chaos. "But I still don't understand. *Why*, Jeremias? If you were unhappy, why didn't you tell me? I would gladly have given you more—."

"You would have *given* me," Jeremias cried. "Given! Like a rich man tossing coins to a beggar! *I* wanted to give something for once."

"Oh, but you did, Lord Chamberlain," said Pasevalles. "You gave me what I needed to destroy your friend. By handing me the royal seal, you gave money from the exchequer, and laws that angered and confused our allies—oh, Jeremias, you gave and gave." He lifted his hand. "Zhadu, Hulgar, take this pathetic creature back and lock him up again. You will be pleased to know, Simon, that this crawling villain is not walking free while you are confined. No, for who would trust him? Certainly not me, not with Erkynland and the High Ward now my sole responsibility."

"You will never keep any of it!" Simon said, pulling his chains nearly straight in his desire to reach Pasevalles's throat. "There are others who will take my place—!"

"No, no." He shook his head in mock sadness. "There is no one to rule but me. Duke Osric is half-dead. Your grandson Morgan is gone, and if he happens to turn up—well, kingdoms have faced usurpers pretending to be heirs to the throne before. Some of them may even have been the true heirs, but once those who rise against the throne are dead, the lie is all that remains."

The clansmen had dragged Jeremias away. Simon heard a door in the corridor open and slam closed. Pasevalles still stood behind the barred window, lit by the single torch, still half an angel, half a demon. "I will kill you myself," Simon said.

"I have heard that before," said Pasevalles. "Yet here I stand." He stepped back from the door, then paused. "I had not planned to keep you alive, at least not for long. But I find myself enjoying our conversations. It is hard to keep so many secrets for so long with no one to share them, so I think I will return so we can talk more. After all, when you are dead, it will all be secret again."

"God will know!"

"Ah, yes. God will. But God has known about me since I began my quest twenty years ago, and yet He has done nothing to stop me. Think on *that* if you grow bored here in your new royal residence—which will also be your last." He returned to the door. "But fear not, Simon—I have enough stories to tell that your death is still a distance away. Next time we meet I will tell you about your beloved Josua, for whom you have searched all these years." He grinned. "If I may spoil the suspense a little, it ends with me killing him." He made a mocking bow, then set the torch back in its bracket and walked away.

Simon heard the door open and close one more time, then silence swept in.

As Miriamele described her escape from Nabban, Archbishop Orvyn kept interrupting to exclaim in horror, to assure the queen of his outrage, and to wonder, with shaking head and fierce frown, what had happened to the world.

"Yes," said Miri in growing frustration, "it is all terribly shocking, Your

Grace. But I have a more practical need this moment than to decry how bad things have become. I must see Earl Durward as quickly as possible—within the hour. Not just Erkynland but all the High Ward are in danger."

"Of course, of course," said the archbishop. "But you will get little help from Durward, I fear. He has been failing for a long time. He never leaves his bed, and I am told his mind wanders—."

"I still must see him." Miri looked at Jesa, who at the queen's request had told the archbishop about the deaths of Duchess Canthia and her little son Blasis. Jesa's voice had quivered a few times during the telling, but otherwise the young woman had spoken clearly and carefully. Miriamele could not help wondering if one of her own court ladies would have done half so well. *She has already helped save me once. I must not underestimate her.* "Who is caring for the earl?" she asked out loud.

"His daughter and son, of course. The boy is his heir."

By his expression, the archbishop seemed to have thoughts he was not sharing, but Miriamele did not want to waste any more time. "Then take me to them," she said. "We must all go to Prince's Hall, quietly and without being noticed."

"But, Your Majesty." The priest, Father Swidelm, was startled into speech. "I have many tasks still before me today. And the archbishop, too—!"

"You both have perhaps the most important task of your lives in front of you." Miri was exhausted and angry and struggling to keep the unfathomable horror of Simon's death from overwhelming her. It was all she could do to remain civil. "That task is to save the High Ward and the kingdom from a murderous usurper. What else calls more loudly for your attention?"

The priest could not meet her eye. Another day, Miri might have felt sorry for being so harsh, but this was not that day.

"Nothing more?" she asked. "Then let us go to the castle. And, Father Swidelm, perhaps you might find Lady Jesa and myself a pair of cloaks that will hide our faces."

Prince's Hall had been built just over a century earlier by a self-styled king who had ruled the city in the years before Miri's grandfather John had brought all Erkynland under the sway of his High Throne. It sat on a tall rock called the Peck, overlooking Meremund's great harbor. It had three concentric moats, and by the time the archbishop's carriage with its two overworked horses had reached the innermost gate, the sun had begun to set, painting the square white towers with fiery color.

For Miriamele, everything was becoming more and more dreamlike. She had spent so much of her childhood in this place that no corner or wall was simply a thing of stone, but the center of some memory instead. Here stood a wall where she had hidden from her guards when her mother died; there was a courtyard where she had played lonely games in the garden because her father did not think a princess should be seen behaving like an ordinary child. Some sights even reminded her of lost loves: She had formed a deep romantic yearning for her horse's groom when she was only nine years old.

She had grown up in Meremund, but Prince's Hall had always felt like a waystation to her. She had known since early childhood that one day she would go to the Hayholt with her father, but her grandfather had lived so long that the day hadn't arrived for years and years, until she was almost a woman. During those in-between years, she and her father had grown further apart, so that by the time they moved their household to the Hayholt, Miriamele had wanted to be somewhere else—anywhere that she was not just Elias's daughter, not just a playing piece to be moved around a board at will until she was given to some man in marriage, to benefit the crown.

I stood on that very rampart and watched a seagull with a broken wing trying to fly, she remembered. *And hid from my nurse in that culvert over there, then received twice the punishment for coming back wet and dirty.*

As they reached the keep, guards and servitors sprang from the gatehouse to meet the archbishop's carriage and escort his guests inside. Miriamele kept her hood low even after they were under a roof again, waiting impatiently while Orvyn whispered with the earl's chamberlain. She had forbidden him to name the guests he was bringing, and it seemed obvious that despite the power and respect the archbishop enjoyed, the chamberlain was reluctant to let them into the family residence.

Miri was only a few moments away from revealing herself to the chamberlain, if only to wipe the annoyed look from his face at these unwanted visitors, when he capitulated at last.

"He did not want anyone but me to go to the earl," explained the archbishop as they were led through the courtyard outside the residence. "But I said that I could not leave you behind."

"You did not tell him—"

"No, Majesty, I told him only that you and the other lady had important information for the earl and his family. I swore upon my ring and my reputation that you were trustworthy." The archbishop's wrinkled face showed his worry. "You will not do anything to make me a liar, will you, Majesty?"

Miri made a noise of disgust and shared a swift look with Jesa. "By Holy Elysia, no. Do not be foolish, Your Grace. And forgive me for pointing this out, but if I *did* need to do something drastic, the necessity would outstrip even the need to protect your reputation."

"Oh. Of course." But her answer clearly did not make Orvyn feel any better. "But remember, the earl is very ill."

Miri sighed but said nothing.

It took no little time to make their way through the throngs of courtiers, servants, and guards that seemed to crowd every hall of the residence. Several of them tried to prevent Jesa bringing the baby into the suffering earl's presence, but at last the door of the bedchamber closed behind them, leaving them alone with Durward, his family, the stubborn chamberlain, and a pair of suspicious guards, who only eased their martial readiness when the Archbishop Orvyn went to the earl's side and offered his ring to be kissed.

Earl Durward was not an old man: the archbishop, Miri guessed, had twenty years on him. Still, to see them side by side, it would have been hard to guess which one was the elder. Durward's long hair was white and sparse, his face sickly pale, with the strained, distracted look of a man with one foot already in the next world. Miri remembered hearing that he had suffered a fall while riding and that, although his broken bones had healed, his wits had never fully recovered.

"Is that you, Father Timmas?" asked Durward in a faint, quavering voice. He did not seem to see the ring, and Orvyn at last withdrew his hand.

"No, my lord, this is Archbishop Orvyn," the chamberlain told him.

"Are the nuns and monks praying for me, Timmas?" he asked.

In quiet despair, Miri turned her attention to the earl's two children. The younger, she knew, must be Dregan, the heir. He was perhaps twelve years of age, fair-haired and thin, with a serious, fretful face. The earl's wife had died birthing him, and to the frustration of the Prince's Hall courtiers (and Miri and Simon as well) Durward had never remarried, dedicating himself to hunting and other out-of-doors pursuits like a man who no longer cares for his own home.

"Come, Father," said the boy, impatience clear in his voice. "You know the archbishop. Greet him properly!"

Durward's daughter, Lady Dorret, was a young woman several years past the first bloom of youth. She had a handsome face but was stocky and tall—in no wise what would ordinarily have been thought lovely in an Erkynlandish court. Miriamele remembered occasional talk about the duke's desire to find her a suitable husband but did not recall such a thing ever coming to pass before she herself had left on her last trip to Nabban. Something in the daughter's posture, though, a sort of quiet watchfulness, made Miri think that this might be the most important ally to cultivate. *Someone is making decisions here,* she thought, *and I doubt it is the son. He looks as green as spring grass.*

She took a breath, considering, then threw back her hood.

"It is time for truth," she said. All eyes except the earl's turned toward her. "I am Queen Miriamele and I am alive, despite what you have heard. I need your help. Without it, Meremund and all of Erkynland may fall."

Almost an hour had passed by the time all the questions had been answered. As Miriamele had suspected, Durward's daughter Dorret had asked the most pertinent ones, though young Dregan had done his best to sound like the earl's heir, mostly by saying over and over, "We will not stand for this!"

"We will go to war against this Pasevalles," he announced when Miri had finished. "We will take a thousand men to the Hayholt and drive this traitor out."

"Perhaps we should call the council to session, my lord," suggested the chamberlain. "With all respect, your father is still the ruling earl."

"My father is very ill," said Dregan. "He does not even know what we are talking about." And that at least was true—Earl Durward had given up on what was going on around him and had slumped back into his pillow, staring at the ceiling.

"We do not have a thousand men, Dregan," his sister said gently. "We sent twice that number to the Hayholt at the last muster. They must be still at Winstowe Castle, fighting the grasslanders."

"Then we shall levy men from the houses that have not yet filled their tally."

His sister smiled, but there was strain in it. *This sort of thing has played out many times before*, Miri recognized. "We cannot draw water from a dry well. We have perhaps three hundred men we could spare—all the rest are necessary to hold Prince's Hall against a siege."

"Siege?" Dregan was irritated. "There will be no siege. Not if we strike before this Pasevalles has a chance to tighten his grip on the throne."

Miriamele thought it was time to intervene. "I thank you for your bravery on my behalf, Lord Dregan, but Pasevalles has been planning this a long time, I think—years. He will not be so easily unseated, and the last thing we should do is try to besiege the Hayholt, however many men we can find, since it is my own subjects who would suffer. Also, from everything I've heard, there is a Norn army moving down from the north. Surely you do not want to see your soldiers caught between the walls of the Hayholt and the wrath of the White Foxes."

Dregan's eyes widened. "Truly, Majesty? White Foxes? We heard rumors, but—"

"I cannot speak for all rumors," Miriamele said. "But those about the Norn Queen and her army seem true, and both my husband and myself tried to prepare for it in the last year."

Dregan's youthful bluster seemed to have dried up. "Then what do we do?"

"I think your chamberlain has made a good suggestion," she said. "Convene your council—but in secrecy. Do not tell them who will speak to them. Does Baron Norvel still live and serve the crown?"

"He does," said Lady Dorret. "A most faithful noble. The largest part of those who went to Winstowe were his, and only a hunting injury prevented him from leading them."

"Good. I hope he has recovered. We will need him." Miriamele ignored the brother's hurt look. This rivalry would have to be dealt with at some point, but now was not the time. She needed resolve and unanimity from Meremund's nobles, as well as from those of the surrounding shires. "Please send for him immediately." She turned to Orvyn. "Archbishop, have you brought a Book of Aedon with you?"

The old man looked surprised but gestured to Father Swidelm, who hurriedly produced a copy.

"My father has one beside his bed as well," offered young Dregan.

"One will do," Miri said. "Everyone in this room must now take an oath on the Book, in front of Archbishop Orvyn and God, that they will not breathe a word of my presence to anyone—*anyone*—until the council has met." She looked around. "Is there any objection?"

Nobody spoke until Dorret said, "Of course not, Majesty. It is a blessing from God Himself to find that you live."

After they all had sworn on the Book of the Aedon, Miri felt her tension ease a little—but only a little. She gave Jesa what she meant to be a reassuring look. "All is well, then," said Miri. "At least as well as it can be in these dreadful days. I want a room for myself, my lady-in-waiting, and the baby. Nothing large or grand!" she added as the chamberlain stood. "I do not want anyone to wonder about the secret guest being treated like royalty." She took a deep breath. "Ah. I have one more question."

This time, it was Archbishop Orvyn who spoke. "What is that, Majesty?"

"Are the black banners and bunting I saw on the walls and Prince's Hall false mourning for me, or true mourning for my beloved husband?" For some reason, the distinction seemed important to her.

Dorret answered again. "In truth, it is hard to say, Majesty. Some signs of mourning were already up for you, then we heard the news of the king's death at Winstowe and we hung more . . ." She shook her head, suddenly speechless, and took a moment to recover. "In other words, Majesty, it is hard to say for certain. It feels as if the last months have been one long observance of death."

The young woman's words struck Miriamele so deeply that she could only nod. She stood, holding back tears that she preferred to save until she could find some privacy. "Remember, all of you," she said, "secrecy is our first concern. If Pasevalles learns I am alive, he may flee."

"But is that not what you want, Majesty?" asked young Dregan.

"No," she said, as calmly as she could. "I want him in chains. I want to look in his eyes. I want the treacherous dog to know whom he has struck at and missed before he dies."

32

The Invisible River

Why did I die—or think I had died—only to come back to this? Simon wondered. *Why did I meet Jiriki's mother Likimeya on the Road of Dreams when I couldn't even dream for months?* The life he had once thought he understood now seemed as confusing as the Hayholt itself, something built on the ruins of the past, full of dark places that should have been exposed and cleansed. Instead, the secrets had only been locked away, but could not be forgotten. *Who am I? Was everything I thought I had done or learned, the things Miri and I built—were they all wrong? Why am I still alive, O Lord my God? To be punished?*

He had been trying to remember one of Miri's more common expressions, eyebrow cocked and smile crooked—a sign that she found something Simon said foolish or beside the point. But he could no longer summon it from his memory, not exactly, and that was maddening. Every time he concentrated on one aspect, her pursed smile that held both love and frustration, or her doubting gaze that seemed to see him in a way no one else could, the rest of her dear face faded into vagueness.

Why can't I dream of her? Usires Aedon, my Ransomer, why have you let this happen? All I have left to hold onto is the torn sack of my memory, poked full of holes by all the years that have passed. But dreams of her are denied to me. Why?

God must have a reason for this punishment, he told himself. If not, then everything he had been taught was lies. Did that mean he had been condemned because of his many mistakes?

You gave me everything, Lord. You put me on Your throne, to watch over the people as king in Your stead. I know I should have done better. For all my raging at selfish nobles, how was I any better? Already Simon had begun to think of himself as something finished, something that had been given a chance to do wonderful things, but then lost it to clumsiness and inattention. *We had the world. Now it is all broken.*

Like the most heedless of barons, he had ignored the most important things going on around him. Now, when it was too late, he could see so many signs he had been blind to when it mattered—the odd changes in the shipping laws, the bad advice Pasevalles had given about Nabban and the Thrithings, the gold that Archbishop Gervis should have noticed missing had he not been so busy with church duties and his own ambitions.

People fail. It is up to those above them to watch, to understand, to correct. But instead of watching, I left it all up to Miri and Tiamak and Eolair. A dark cloud was gathering in his thoughts. *And Pasevalles.*

Simon had not seen the turncoat Lord Chancellor for several days. Nor, for all Pasevalles's talk of the two Thrithings brutes being his jailers, had Simon seen much of them, either. The smaller one with the split lip occasionally brought him a bowl of cold pottage or an end of bread, and set them just beyond the reach of his chains, forcing Simon to lie down on the floor as far from the back wall as he could reach, then pull the meager offerings toward him with his foot. They were not going to give him a chance to overpower one of his captors, that was plain, and days of repeated testing had shown him that his chains, though old and flecked with rust, were far too sturdy for him to break. And the keys to his cell hung on the wall at the far end of the passage, hopelessly beyond his reach.

And when Pasevalles said he killed Josua—that couldn't be true, could it? No, I won't believe it. The devil wants me to suffer, and he has made up this story to pierce my heart, to make me even lower than I am.

But none of it mattered beside the horror of this helpless captivity, of his dreamless nights and his weary, dimming memories.

If I lose my Miriamele, I have lost everything. If I lose the memories of loving her, then nothing will be left of me but empty flesh, like a headless carcass on a butcher's hook.

Lillia was living in a world of utter darkness now, like a mole, and she feared that soon she would be eating like a mole as well, keeping herself alive with worms and crickets.

At least she had found a place where the thing hunting her from above could not reach her—or so she hoped. After discovering a stairway and climbing down it on hands and knees, heart beating fast as a bee's wings at the thought that the steps might suddenly end in a plunge down into unknown depths, she had found shelter beneath the bottom turn of the steps, and now she huddled there, hour after dragging hour, afraid to come out.

The rope that had dropped down on her had terrified her, but she was beginning to think huddling in utter darkness was just as bad. She was horribly hungry—she couldn't stop thinking about food. Memories of bread dripping with butter tormented her. She thought helplessly about tangy hunks of cheese, and crackling skin from a roasted goose, and especially her favorite pudding, a potage of raisins and apples topped with a sprinkling of aromatic galingale.

It must be nearly Aedonmansa up there. Just the idea brought her to tears again. *They will be making raisin potage right now for the holy day feasts, and baking fairy bread, and roasting whole beeves. Even the kitchen boys will get some. Everyone but me.*

Lillia could not stop thinking about food. She had found a place near her hiding spot where a little water leaked down from a cistern, and by drinking from the puddle at the base of the stone had avoided dying of thirst, but days had gone by since she had eaten the food off the tray she had found. Had it been meant only as a trap? Were there other trays, other traps?

I have to eat, she thought. *My belly hurts so much.* But how? And what? Dreadful as her hunger was, she was not ready to start on worms and beetles. Not yet. Not quite.

I can go look for another tray. I can look for another one and be quiet as can be. I'll listen for that person that tried to catch me, that . . . thing, so I'll know if it's a trap.

But what if I don't hear it? I didn't hear it before, and it almost caught me.

In Lillia's thoughts the thing she had glimpsed above her was a little like a ghost, a little like a spider, and a little like a demon she had seen in one of her books, a scrawny, grinning creature the color of blood trying—but failing—to tempt Saint Heanwig into renouncing God.

What if the red thing offered me an Aedonmansa supper for my soul? She was a little disturbed to find herself considering the bargain as she crept slowly up the long, spiraling stairway, feeling her way through the darkness. I *wouldn't do it,* she decided at last. *Because if I gave my soul away, I wouldn't get to see Mother and Grandmother Miriamele again after I die. I'd have to go to Hell.*

But even thinking about an imaginary demon's imaginary but delicious temptations was enough to make her stomach rumble, and suddenly the noise seemed fearfully loud. Lillia lay down as flat as she could against the steep steps, holding her breath. Had the red thing heard her?

As she clung to the stone, she did hear something. At first it was only a soft murmur, like a freshening wind, but then she heard voices in it, and the cadence of words too, though she could not understand them.

It must be people talking in the castle up above, she thought. A moment later, a happier idea followed the first: *Someone might be looking for me! Grandfather might have sent soldiers to find me down here under the castle!*

She almost shouted her presence, in defiance of lurking spider-ghosts, but then she realized that something about the voices was wrong: they sounded as if they were crying out, but not her name or anything she could recognize, and they sounded very frightened. She also realized with growing unease that the voices did not echo, though everything else down here, even the slightest scuff of her foot or a muffled sneeze caused by dust, reverberated like a shout.

Suddenly, a chill breeze wafted down the stairwell, flowing over her so that her skin instantly pimpled with the cold and she shivered.

Ruakha, Ruakha Asu'a! The shrieking voices suddenly seemed painfully loud and close, as if they spoke inside Lillia's own head. *T'si e-isi'ha as-irigú!*

Something horribly cold passed through her—not over her, not past her, but *through* her, so that she could almost feel her insides turn to ice. A moment later it was gone, but then another freezing emptiness passed through her, and another. The last one left a cry rattling in her skull, the first words she had understood.

The witchwood is in flames! The garden is burning!

Then the crashing waves of cold ended. A last whisper slithered through her like a serpent made of freezing fog.

Jinguzu! Aya'ai! O Jingizu!

The pain and terror of the voices frightened her so badly that Lillia could only cling to the hard stone steps and weep.

Her fit of shivering ended at last. Any questions she had ever had about spirits of the dead had been answered in the most frightening way possible. *Ghosts*, she thought. *Our castle is full of ghosts. They're truly here.*

She clambered back onto her hands and knees. She was still shivering, but her hunger had returned—a harsh, painful gouging in her stomach as though she had eaten something sharp that was not food.

The ghosts can't hurt me, she told herself, though she was far from certain that was true. *They went right through me.*

She began to climb upward again, through blind darkness. When she reached the top of the stairs, she clambered out onto wide, broken stones and began crawling, but to her dismay, the turnings were no longer where she remembered. What she thought would be an opening was now a flat stretch of wall; meanwhile, another spot where she was sure there had been a wall earlier now opened out onto something else, a gap full of moving air.

How can walls move? she wondered. *Is the castle really alive?*

Lillia struggled against the urge to flee back to the place under the stairs, but despite her terror, the pain of her empty stomach was only growing worse. *It must be another trap,* she decided. *But if it's a trap, there must be something to lead me into it—something worth having. Food—and that's what I came to find.*

She crawled along the new passage, belly against the ground like a lizard, stopping frequently to feel for what was ahead. Her world had become only what she could touch, and by touching recognize. It might only have been hours since her candle had consumed itself, but for all she could tell, it might have been days or even weeks.

No, silly, she told herself, trying to stay brave. *I'd be dead from hunger if I hadn't eaten for weeks.*

She crawled for a long time before reaching the top of another flight of stairs. She descended cautiously, sliding on her rump and testing what was below her with her feet, until she found herself at last in what sounded, by its distant echoes, like a large open space. She listened in silence for long moments, but heard neither ghost voices nor anything else, so she crawled forward into the new place.

Lillia had grown used to the dusty stone and the areas of damp earth that passed under her hands and knees as she crawled through the darkness. She had even taught herself to stay silent when she flicked away the invisible things that sometimes crawled on her, but what she'd just felt made her stop in surprise. Every other passage and place she had entered had been empty except for grit and an occasional, startling growth of roots or mushrooms, but the floor of this chamber seemed to be littered with small objects.

She crept cautiously forward, picking up some of them and turning them over in her fingers, trying to make out what they might be. One seemed to be a simple bracelet, the copper kind her nurses wore to ease their aching joints. Another felt like the wishbone of a capon or other small bird. But most of the things in her path seemed to be only broken shards of bigger objects—rusted iron nails, the remains of shattered pots, and even bits of window glass that might have come from the chapel. Then, when she had crawled some way across the open space, she encountered a large chunk of stone standing upright. Her fingers were so raw to sensation that when she reached out to touch it, she could feel every smoothed bump of the stonework. It seemed to be the broken stump of a pillar, very broad but only about half her own height. As she moved closer to investigate, her knee came down on what felt—and snapped—like a pile of dry, poking branches on the floor, but branches didn't interest her. She felt her way across the broken upper surface of the pillar until her fingertips encountered something—another tray.

Lillia's heart, already racing, now threatened to pound its way out of her chest. The tray seemed empty as her fingers explored it, and she was cast down into despair to think she had crawled all this distance through terrible darkness just to be cheated. Then her fingertip brushed something irregular and hard. She clutched it and brought it close to her face. It had a faint scent of grain.

Bread. It was a lump of bread—old and hard, but still food—and Lillia nearly cried aloud with joy. She searched the rest of the tray and found something else at the far edge, a round, hard object the size of a fat cherry, but smoother and heavier than anything that grew on a tree. She lifted this to her nose and sniffed it too, then brushed it off on her tattered dress and touched it with her tongue, but it was stony and cool and tasted like nothing. An ornament, she decided—something meant to be beautiful, but of no earthly use to her at all. She was about to drop it and take a bite of the rocklike hunk of bread instead when she heard a quiet noise from somewhere nearby. She froze like a startled hare—for a moment she almost felt she had *become* a hare, every whisker twitching, ears grown half as big as her body as she strained to listen.

There. Another quiet *skritch*. Something was moving, and it was close. It might be a rat, or a snake slithering between stones. It might be the Red Demon itself. Lillia did not want to move for fear of making the sticks rustle or snap beneath her, but she could not make herself wait until whatever it was touched her. She put her hands out to balance herself against the stone, meaning to spring upright as soon as she could get her feet under her. She clutched the precious heel of bread in one hand and squeezed the round, hard thing in the other as she strained to listen, but now the chamber was silent.

An instant later she heard a sudden flurry of sounds from somewhere far too close. To her astonishment and fright, her hand began to glow red until she could see her bones through the skin, then a bright white light blazed out in all directions, leaking from between her fingers as though she clutched a living star.

The terrible shape that was bending over her lurched back with a wailing cry, ragged red robes flapping, hands flung up as though trying to shut out the light. Its fingers ended in curving claws. Lillia screamed and kept screaming, but instead of attacking her, the ragged thing turned and lurched off toward a doorway on the far side of the chamber, staggering and snuffling as though it had been burned. Lillia's scream ended in a ragged gasp, and she watched in terror as the thing vanished through a rotted curtain of hanging cloth. As she tried to clamber to her feet to flee the chamber, still clutching the flaring orb of light, she found her dress was tangled in the crackling branches beneath her. She looked down and saw that she was not kneeling on dried branches, but on a pile of bones. When she saw the skull, she screamed again and dropped the shining sphere. The blazing light that had bloomed so suddenly in Lillia's hand now flickered and died, leaving the girl in darkness once more.

"I grew up in Chasu Metessa, a modest barony in the north of Nabban. You would not know it, of course, Simon—you have never been there. It was not important to you." His voice sharpened. "Or, rather, you did not know how important to you it would be. Because as it turned out, that place was home to one who would bring down your entire kingdom. My uncle Seriddan ruled Metessa. My father Brindalles was his younger brother, a mild, weak man—"

"I have heard of Brindalles," Simon said. "And he was neither mild nor weak. He sacrificed his life for—"

"Hold your tongue, or I will summon Hulgar to beat you into silence." Pasevalles said it so flatly that Simon could not doubt him. "Not a word until I say you can speak. You are no longer king, Simon. In this place, you are not even a man. Remember that."

Pasevalles waited to make sure of silence, then continued.

"My father gave me one good thing, and that was a reverence for reading and for history. He gave me something else, too—the mystery in my blood which set me apart from others. I came to understand at a young age that I was not like anyone else. Even as a child, I could see the lies that my parents and my uncle told themselves, the lies that flowed through every day and every deed in that castle like an invisible river—pretenses, half-truths, all the flummery that men employ to avoid saying what they truly mean, what they truly think. But even with a child's eyes, I could discern the animal selves they tried to hide, their lust, rage, and greed. Foolish people like you think that mortal men are half angel, only a short distance from God. They are not. They are animals that have learned to stand on their hind legs and to hide their true needs behind *words*. Men are simply beasts that can lie.

"I discovered that life was no different among men than it was among my uncle's cattle. The biggest bulls took what they wanted while the smaller ones lived out their miserable span waiting for a change that would never come. I vowed that I would not be one of those smaller bulls.

"There is one thing, though, that separates us from cattle. We men can create a world of words that seems as real as anything we can touch and taste. I learned that it is not always the biggest and strongest who takes the prizes. Sometimes—often—it is those who can think, who can plan, and who know how to tell the stories that others want to hear.

"You know the tragedy of my family. Your throne sits atop that tragedy like the Hallowmount—the great rock of Khand where their ancient kings were crowned. My father and uncle both died here at the Hayholt, pretending to be the hero Camaris and your esteemed Prince Josua, giving their lives to distract the Norns while your friends made their way into the castle from below. But their 'noble sacrifice,' as I have too often heard it called, was nothing noble at all. It was a simple trade—your success for my loss. No, do not say a word—do not dare! I have heard the praise you and others gave them. I have seen that cursedly pious stone in the garden that commemorates their deaths. If you had even once admitted it, if you had said, 'It was a terrible bargain, but for me to reach the throne they had to lose their lives,' I would almost have respected you. But like all the rest, you painted over your own sins with words that hid the ugly truth. *'Sacrifice.' 'Nobility.' 'Bravery.'* No, the truth is that my father and his brother were traded like stones on a game board for what you and your allies all wanted—a throne for you, their golden lad, to share with the mad king's daughter."

Simon could only clench his teeth. To hear this murderer twist the truth of how he had been forced onto the throne into a tale of heartless ambition—it was all he could do to swallow his rage and stay quiet.

"I was only a young boy when Prince Josua and your other dear friend Isgrimnur came to Chasu Metessa and took my father and uncle away to their war with the Storm King. I still had a few of my childish illusions then. I thought that knights, at least, tried always to do what was right and to tell the truth, though I knew they were only men and thus fallen and fallible. Isgrimnur, that fat old fraud, even came close to convincing me that he and Camaris were different from the others—that in those two, at least, some true spirit of knighthood still lived. In fact, it was I who brought the battle-helm of Camaris back to him! He said that *I* honored *him* . . ." For a moment Pasevalles voice trailed off, but when he spoke again, the chill had returned to his voice. "Yes, of course I ached to go with them, to live in a world of men who lived by their honor and their strong arms! But it was not to be. Prince Josua took my father and my uncle, and they all went away to war, leaving me alone with my grieving, hapless mother and a castle full of sycophants. And then they both died in Erkynland."

For a while then Pasevalles was silent, and even paced a bit before the cell door, as if trying to put his thoughts in order.

Is there a spark of decency still in him? Simon wondered. *Does the death of his father still hurt him so much?*

"I will not bother with the tale of the years that passed between then and the time I came to Erchester and the Hayholt," said Pasevalles abruptly. "I was treated badly by relatives and my uncle's friends. I was robbed of my patrimony and left to fend for myself. And that I did. I had learned that so-called knights and nobles were no different than anyone else, hiding their bestial natures so shallowly that only fools could not see the truth. But I could no longer stand to be surrounded by fools, so I left and made my way north. I chose the Hayholt as my destination, wishing to see not only the place where my father and uncle had died, but to see *you*, the peasant lad whom Isgrimnur and Eolair and the rest had set on the High Throne, to rule over all nations. I could not help wondering what they had seen in you to lift you up so high."

Simon was astonished by the man's cold hatred. How had he never seen it?

"When I finally reached the Nearulagh Gate after a long, difficult journey," Pasevalles continued, "I discovered that the castle had been closed up for the night. Several others who had also arrived too late were gathered at an inn on the edge of Erchester, and among them was a traveler who looked strangely familiar to me. He kept to himself, talking only a little with the others, but I knew that I recognized him. It was only when the middle-night was upon us and most of the other travelers had bedded down on the floor near the inn's fireplace—or, if they had no coins, had slunk off to try to find a place to sleep in the stables—that I finally dared to approach him.

"He was, as I had guessed, Prince Josua. How like him that was, to sit with the others as if he was nobody, waiting for the gates to open at dawn. He could have demanded the Erkynguards let him in—after all, he was the queen's uncle and the king's mentor!—but instead he had to play the part of the perfect knight, the kindly noble who despite his high rank would not put himself above the common herd." Pasevalles paused; a grim amusement crept into his voice. "And that self-satisfaction was his downfall.

"I revealed myself to him, and he remembered—not me, of course, though he pretended to, but my uncle and father and the castle where I was born. 'Your father's sacrifice still weighs heavily upon me after all these years,' he said, with a humility so false I could have struck him then and there. 'Lord Brindalles took my place,' he said. 'It is a debt I can never repay, but perhaps I can offer help to you and thereby ease a little of the sting of your loss.' Oh, yes, your beloved Josua was full of poetic words and grand promises. He said he would introduce me to you and your wife, that the two of you would raise me up in my father's memory, give me honor and position. And of course, every word from his mouth was a lie."

Simon had been listening in numb disbelief to Pasevalles' tale. He could not reconcile these mad, hateful words, a dark tangle of ideas Simon himself could not entirely understand, with the bland, helpful man who had been his Lord Chancellor, a steady shoulder for him to lean upon, a calm voice in the middle of many fierce disagreements. It was as though someone had pried off the top of Pasevalles's skull to reveal a squirming nest of snakes.

"Josua never told a lie in his life!" Simon was almost breathless in his fury. "If he said he would help you, he meant it. He would have done everything he promised and more. Anything else was only in your own sickened, evil thoughts."

Pasevalles only stared at him through the bars for a span of several heartbeats, his face like stone. Then he called, "Hulgar, bring the keys."

The huge clansman appeared, bearing a ring with two keys on it, one large, one small. Pasevalles said something in the grassland tongue, then a key turned in the lock and the cell door swung open. The torchlight dimmed, blocked for a moment by Hulgar's massive form. Simon did not even have a chance to get to his feet: the clansman grabbed him and heaved him upright as though he were a child, then swung a knee into his stomach. Simon dropped to his knees, gagging and gasping for breath. The Thrithings-man began to hit him on the face and head with his huge hands, not even bothering to ball his fingers into a fist, blow after open-handed blow like the pounding of a great mallet. When he had finished, he lifted Simon up and stared at him, then a broken-toothed grin spread over his face and he dropped the onetime king back onto the floor of his cell. Simon heard the key turn in the lock once more. He could barely think. His mouth was full of blood, and it drooled onto the straw-matted stone.

"You are lucky that was brief," said Pasevalles. "I told Hulgar I wanted you able to listen to the rest of my tale. After all, this is the answer to the questions you and little Tiamak and the others have been asking for twenty years. Because as I sat listening to the mockery of Josua's insincere apologies, I decided that he had to die."

Simon gurgled and spat more blood onto the floor. *God, take me now,* he thought. *If my life must end in this place, make it today. I do not want to hear any more.* But he could not summon the courage to speak again. His body and head felt broken, as if his bones were in pieces, sliding beneath his skin.

"I told Josua I had something I wished to show him, something he would not believe," Pasevalles continued in the matter-of-fact tone Simon had heard so many times without ever guessing what might lie beneath it. "He asked if the place was far, and I told him no, it was close by, as close as the edge of the Kynswood. By moonlight I led him into the edges of the forest until I found what I was looking for, then told him, 'Look there! Do you see?' Trusting fool that he was, believing in others' falsehoods as much as his own, he turned his back on me to look where I was pointing. I lifted the heavy stone I had found and I bashed in his head. Yes. Yes, at that moment my path had become clear before me. Yes, I hit him again and again, until his skull was broken and he lay dead at my feet. I dragged his body deeper into the forest until I reached a deep gully, then rolled his body into it. Yes. He is likely there still." Pasevalles's breathing had become heavier and his voice more excited, as if he were seeing it all again. "Yes! Just think, Simon. All these years you have been looking for Prince Josua, sending people across the world to find even a hint of his whereabouts, and all that time his moldering bones lay at your own doorstep."

Simon was weeping, salty tears making the gashes on his face burn like fire. "You lie!" he said. "You are a liar!"

"Oh, I am—but not about this." Pasevalles waved a careless hand. "I am the only man in this castle—perhaps in all the world—who understands what truth really is, and I am the only one who is not afraid to look at it with open eyes. When you call me liar, you only prove what a rarity I am."

Simon could only push his head against the stone flags, sobbing. "Monster!"

"We are all monsters," Pasevalles said. "Only a man like me admits it. Pretending is for children."

And with that he turned and walked away. The heavy footfalls of the giant clansman followed him down the passage. Simon heard the outer door open again, then close behind them.

33

A Great Madness

"I thought the Grass Thunderer had come for me."

For a distracted moment Fremur could not understand her. She was still so pale! "You mean the Stallion," he said at last. "Your clan's spirit."

"Yes. I felt sure I would die." Hyara reached up to touch the place the knife had gone in. "I thought I had been struck to the heart."

He took her hand in his. "Your skin is cold," he said. "You," he told the old woman tending her, "put more wood on the brazier."

"I can scarcely remember it." Hyara did not seem to have entirely returned to the world, though weeks had passed; she still spoke like someone relating a dream. "There was shouting, and my sister, too, and that man Eolair—"

"The man who tried to kill you," said Fremur. *As Kulva was killed by our pig of a brother on her wedding day.* That was an anger he had to keep pushing down. It came back time and again, as though despite all that had happened since, his sister's spirit still could not rest. "If that coward was here now, I would show him what I think of one who would attack a woman."

Hyara patted his hand. "Did he truly try to hurt me? That seems strange. I would not have thought it of him. But it is lost to me. I can remember feeling the knife in my chest—it was like ice! But all else . . ." She fluttered her hand as if fanning away smoke. "Lost. Gone." Her wan face brightened. "But I remember when I first woke. There you were!" She reached for his hand again. "No one has ever cared so for me. No man, anyway."

"No bad things will ever happen to you again. He bent to stroke her dark hair and kiss her brow. "I will make sure of that." He saw she was looking at him strangely. "What is it?" He felt her forehead, wondering if he had missed something. "Is it the fever again?"

"No, no." She smiled, but for a moment he felt sure he had seen worry, even fear. "I was only thinking how handsome your chin is, Fremur. It will be a shame to cover it up with your man's beard. After we marry, I mean."

Hearing her speak of their marriage swept away all other concerns. "If you wish me to remain beardless, I will," he said bravely. "For you, I will suffer the taunts of the others."

"Oh, no!" She reached up to touch his cheek. "No, you are a thane now,

Fremur, thane of the Crane Clan. You have earned your dignity—you *must* have a beard. But I confess I will miss seeing your chin." She gave him a look that turned her smiling, weary expression into that of a mischievous child. "Perhaps from time to time, though, you might scrape it off. Just for a day, so I can admire your fine chin in secret."

He laughed. "And then spend many moons growing it back again. How will I explain that to the other thanes?"

"You will think of something. You are clever." Her look turned solemn. "Oh, no, dear Fremur, I only jest! You must grow a long and beautiful beard—it will hang down on your belly, which I will fatten with good meals. And I will never ask you to cut it off, my handsome young thane—never!"

The grasslanders' war-camp stretched far along the eastern bank of the Laestfinger. It was Bison Clan land, and its thane and elders were only too happy to share it with their triumphant leader. Unver Shan, in turn, seemed in no hurry to leave the borderland between Erkynland and the High Thrithings, though hundreds of his warriors were now departing.

As he left the wagon where Hyara was being tended, Fremur watched other wagons roll out. Unver had released many of the soldiers to return to the grasslands, to their families and clans, retaining only a comparatively small force of men beside the river. With winter coming on, the Shan could not keep too many warriors away from their clans without causing hardship. But even that did not explain why Unver himself was still camped by the river's edge as his warriors departed, days after the battle had ended.

Fremur headed toward Unver's wagon, which the Shan had set up on the outskirts of the camp, with a wide swath of brown grass and mud between himself and the rest of the grasslanders. The Shan liked quiet.

The two Crane men guarding the wagon nodded respectfully at their thane as Fremur mounted the steps. As Unver's star had risen, so had his own: at the end of the thane moot, Fremur's clan had confirmed him as thane, with full powers. As he knocked on the door, he could not resist a moment of satisfaction. Thane of Clan Kragni. Who would have dreamed it?

Unver's low voice bade him enter. Inside, he found the Shan, as he had expected, but two others he had not, Odobreg, thane of the Badgers, and Unver's mother, Vorzheva.

"Are all the clans to be present, then?" she demanded. "You said you wished to speak to me, Deornoth—or I suppose I must call you Unver, if you insist on it. Why are these others here?"

"Because I want them here, Vorzheva." The Shan was leaning against the back wall of the wagon, tattooed arms folded across his chest. His mother sat on a bench. Odobreg squatted on the floor, looking distinctly uncomfortable.

"Why do you always call me by my name?" Vorzheva asked. "Why do you not treat me the way a mother should be treated?"

"Because you are not my mother."

Fremur's eyes widened. He looked to Odobreg, but that large, brave man was staring intently at the wooden floor of the wagon as if trying to think of some way to burrow through it and escape.

"How dare you—!" Vorzheva cried, but Unver raised a hand to silence her.

"My mother for most of my life was a woman you do not even know—Ozdrut of the Crane Clan, wife of an unpleasant fool named Zhakar. She raised me after your cursed father sent me away, and even gave me a name fit for a clansman. That is the woman I call "Mother.'"

Vorzheva's face went pale. "You dishonor me."

"Dishonor you?" Unver pushed himself away from the wall so he could move closer to her. "Let us talk of dishonor. Who hurt your sister Hyara?"

"What are you talking about?" She looked to Fremur and Odobreg as if for help but saw no sympathy or support on either face. "You know what happened—it was as I told you! The high king's lackey Eolair tried to kidnap me out of your own camp! He was the one who stabbed Hyara! Is that not why you went to war with the Erkynlanders?"

Unver shook his head. "I went to war because we could not be soft. I went to war because a prisoner I had already paid for was taken from me without ransom. I went to war because the Erkynlanders bargained in bad faith." He crouched beside her, his face so close to hers that his mother looked away. "I did not attack Erkynland because of you or Hyara. In truth, I know what happened, Vorzheva. I know it was the knife that you were using that wounded your sister."

"Lies!" Vorzheva made to get up, but Unver laid a heavy hand on her shoulder and kept her from rising. "How can you say that?"

Unver drew something out of his tunic. "Because I have the knife. It is one of ours." He held it out for her to see—a simple thing with a bone handle and a short, sharp blade. "Look, there is a little blood still on its hilt."

She would not look at it. "That means nothing. So Eolair the coward snatched up one of our knives to stab me with!"

Unver shook his head again. "And as the menfolk came thundering back at your call, he took the time to wipe it clean? Because there is no blood on the blade."

Vorzheva finally looked at the knife. For a moment Fremur could almost see her trying to think of something else to say, then he saw her shoulders sag. "So, then," she said to Unver. "I admit it. In trying to defend myself, I struck my own sister. That is something I will live with forever. Will you cut off my head, too, as you did Volfrag's?" Fremur could not help being impressed by the steadiness of her voice, the calmness of her face. "Will that make you happy, to finally be rid of me?"

"Don't be a fool," said Unver. He walked back and leaned against the wall once more. "Why did you cut off your hair?"

"Your grandfather Fikolmij cut my hair off whenever I said something he did not like. 'That is no woman's tongue,' he would say, 'but the creaking of a crow. So you shall look like one.' And when the old devil was no longer thane, my brother-in-law, Hyara's husband Gurdig, did the same to me whenever I was not obedient enough."

"But I killed Gurdig," said Unver. "Then you cut off your hair again, during the last moon, long after I became the new thane of the Stallions." His voice was quiet and measured now, as though he were talking to a frightened child. "Why did you do that?"

"Because I was tired of being ruled by men! And you are only one more, Deornoth or Unver, whatever you choose to call yourself—one more man who wants to order me about. Your grandfather and Gurdig, even your father Josua—every one of them sought to rule me, to use me, to treat me like an old cooking pot. I did not want to wait until you too decided I was too difficult and cut my hair off so I could be mocked as unwomanly. I was sick of you all."

Odobreg, as if deciding he had no place in this argument, rose from where he had crouched on the floor and retreated to the front door of the wagon, but after a stern glance from Unver he went no farther.

"I did not bring you here to humiliate you, Vorzheva," said Unver.

"Strange, since that is exactly what you have done." Her eyes were red and brimming, but Fremur thought she looked more like a beast preparing to bite its captor than anything truly humbled. "I know you will laugh about me after I am gone. 'How like a woman! How like a thane's daughter, to think she is better than everyone else!'"

"None of that has happened or will happen," Unver said. "The shame you feel is your own. You know you did wrong and then lied. What if I had hunted down this Eolair and killed him for the sake of your sister's wound? What then?"

"It would be no more than the king's lackeys deserve," she said fiercely.

"I met High King Simon," Unver said. "Before he died, he said that he had searched everywhere for my father, Josua. That he loved him."

"They all lie," Vorzheva said. "They did nothing to help me—or you and your sister. When Josua left, not a one of them did anything."

"Perhaps they did not know he was gone," said Unver with surprising gentleness. "Perhaps they did not know what had happened, Vorzheva. Did you ever send for help to the king or his wife—to anyone who knew Josua?"

She sniffed. "Why would they help me? They were the ones who thought I was an embarrassment—a clanswoman married to a king's son!"

Unver took a deep breath. "Here we come to the true problem, my lady. I cannot trust you. That is painful, because you gave birth to me. But everything you say is weighted with your anger and poisonous hatred of my father's friends, and I can believe nothing you tell me."

For a moment it seemed that Vorzheva would lash out, that she would say something terrible, but instead, she suddenly began to weep. She covered her eyes with her shawl, then got up and stumbled blindly toward the door.

"Let her out, Odobreg," said Unver. "Let her go."

After Vorzheva had made her way down the steps, the wagon was silent for a time. At last, Fremur stirred and said, "Should we go too?"

"Sit down," said Unver. "You too, Odobreg. I brought you two here because you are my chief thanes and you need to know what I know, that you may understand what I do. But I warn you, whether you understand my design or not, you will not like it."

Fremur exchanged a look with Odobreg. "Tell us, then, Unver Shan. What are you thinking?"

"Many things. The first is about the letter meant for King Simon but given to me instead. You heard Volfrag's confession. He took money from this Pasevalles to poison Rudur. It is likely that he encouraged Rudur to punish me in the first place, so that my name and my deeds would be talked about all through the thane moot."

"But you discovered Volfrag's treachery," Odobreg said, frowning. "The traitor is dead now. Do you fear there are more among our folk?"

"Dozens, I do not doubt. But few of them likely even realize it."

This felt to Fremur like a slap in the face, surprising and painful. "Do you suspect *us*, Unver?"

Astonishingly, Unver smiled, the scars on his cheeks rippling like short snakes. "If I did, you would not be here, free and bearing weapons, while I have none." He picked up the knife that had injured Hyara. "Except this, which could not even kill a woman, and is meant for little more dangerous than cutting turnips." He tossed it to one side; it clicked and slid across the wagon floor. "No, I trust you two with my life—and something more important than my life. I trust you with the lives of our people."

"Thank you, Great Shan," said Odobreg. "Your trust will not be in vain."

"I am pleased to hear you say that," Unver told him. "Because soon *you* must become the Shan of the grasslands."

"What? Me? Madness!" protested Odobreg. Fremur said nothing, but it was all he could do to hide his amazement—and a little envy. "What do you mean?"

"What I said. But I do not mean you will overthrow me. I need you to rule the clans in my stead—but only for a time. Do not fear. I will speak to all the thanes, and they will swear to follow you as if you were me."

Odobreg's eyes were still wide with alarm. "But why?"

"Because something much greater is at stake here, though I cannot see the whole shape of it yet. And our people could benefit—or regret a lost chance if we do not take advantage. If the spirits desert us, we could even be destroyed." He lifted a drinking skin and had a long swallow, then passed it to Fremur, who was grateful but still confused about what Unver planned and why the Shan would elevate Odobreg over him, when Fremur had been his ally before anyone else.

"I still do not understand," Odobreg said.

"I have been thinking long and hard, you see." Unver pulled over the bench on which his mother had been sitting and lowered himself onto it, long legs bent like a grasshopper poised on a blade of grass. "The stone-dweller noble Pasevalles sent gold to Rudur Redbeard, but it seems that the thane of thanes disappointed him. And he also gave gold to Volfrag, who poisoned Rudur. It *seems* simple enough—this Pasevalles decided to discard a thane who would not fight against the stone-dwellers for one who would."

Fremur nodded, but already he was finding it hard to keep track of the Shan's reasoning. "But why should it not be simple, Unver? This Pasevalles is not the stone-dweller king, just a rich lord with ambitions, who reached out to find allies in the grasslands. Many powerful city-men have done that before. That is why so many of our folk end up as sell-swords in the stone-dwellers' wars."

Unver nodded. "True. But Volfrag did not keep all that gold for himself. I have heard that the dead king's wife was killed by grassland mercenaries only last moon—by Thrithings sell-swords. I suspect Volfrag bought that murder with more of Pasevalles's gold."

Odobreg shrugged. "You cannot take on yourself the blame for what sell-swords do. They are no longer clansmen—they were cast out."

"I know," said Unver, "and I do not care about blame. But those sell-swords were not merely protecting one nobleman from the ambitions of another. Killing the queen was a strike at the heart of Erkynland and all the High Ward."

Odobreg shook his head like a buffalo plagued by biting flies. "I know little about the fights between stone-dwellers, Unver Shan, and I only know of the High Ward because you have taught me. Why should this matter to us?"

Unver lifted the drinking skin and took another long swallow of *yerut*. "Because everywhere I turn, I see the hand of this Pasevalles. He is clearly a man who thinks and plans, and who has been at work a long time. It does not pay to underestimate such a one. And there are other dangers to our folk that we have not even discussed, like the White Foxes that have marched into the north, spreading death."

"Spreading death to the city-men who held the fortress called Naglimund," said Fremur. "That is no concern of ours."

"Is it not? What if the witch-queen decides she wants more? It is not only stone-dweller lands that once belonged to the whiteskins—our grasslands were once theirs, too. If these White Foxes destroy the Erkynlanders, what is to keep them out of the Thrithings?"

"Many thousand clansmen, that is what!" said Fremur. "We would fight them to our last man!"

Unver looked grim. "I see you have not been listening to the tales of those who escaped Naglimund—tales of monsters and magic far beyond anything we have ever had to fight. A single giant can kill a score of mounted men as quickly as I can eat an apple, and the Queen of the North has many, many giants in her army, along with thousands upon thousands of silent, whey-faced killers."

"You make me feel hopeless, Great Shan," said Odobreg. "I had hoped our troubles were over when we defeated the Erkynlanders. Can we do nothing except wait for destruction?"

"The king and queen of the stone-dwellers are both dead," said Unver. "From all I can learn, their heir is still missing—he may be dead, too. This Lord Pasevalles seems to be the only one among them capable of wielding power. He has clearly planned long and carefully." He held out the *yerut*. "It might be worthwhile to make a pact with him."

Odobreg took the drinking skin from Fremur but stared at it as though he had forgotten how to use it. "If that is your plan, we will all bow to your wisdom, Shan. But how can you trust a noble who would kill the wife of his king?" Now he upended the bag and drank the last of it.

Unver laughed. "Making a pact is not the same as trusting someone. I do not trust this Pasevalles in the least, but it is his very cleverness that makes him interesting. I see dangerous, desperate times ahead. The northern fairies are playing some subtle game of their own whose end is still unrevealed. If that means we must ally ourselves with a stone-dweller usurper to survive, at least we should choose a clever one." He reached out and squeezed the older man's arm. "And now we come to the heart of things, so listen carefully. I am going to make you the Shan, Thane Odobreg—for a little while, anyway. You must take the clanfolk who are still here and return to the camp at Blood Lake."

Odobreg looked helplessly at Fremur, then back to Unver. "But what of you, great Shan? Why must I take your place? Where will you be?"

"In Erkynland, seeking allies."

Fremur was even more surprised now. "You have just won a mighty victory that will be hailed by our people forever, Unver. This seems like a great madness."

"You may think it madness now," said the Shan with a hard grin, "but after you hear what I plan, you will think it even worse."

"It is a terrible thing to see, my beloved. But why does it fascinate you so?"

Binabik looked up from the tangle of footprints. Before them stood the blackened remains of a barn, stark against the snow. "It is terrible, yes, but it is not what happened here that puzzles me so much as why."

"Why? The Norn army is foraging as they march, leaving only destruction behind." Sisqi picked up a scorched bit of pottery, then tossed it aside. "Share your thoughts with me, husband. Should you not call back Vaqana so we can move on?"

"I suppose," said Binabik. "It seems strange, though. I have never heard of an army, either immortal or mortal, traveling in such an orderly way—or so cautiously."

"Cautiously? You astound me, husband. The Norns have burned buildings all along their path, stolen everything they could find, and killed the few people they encountered. If that is caution, I'm sure those living here would think otherwise."

Binabik was still frowning. "It is an army of thousands, but they are pillaging only what lies in front of them, which would never be enough to feed them all. They must have brought a vast amount of food with them to have left such a narrow track of destruction."

"And that troubles you?"

"It does. Why would they carry so many supplies with them? It is still early winter, and they must have known the barns in these lands would be full and the livestock fattened."

"Perhaps they wanted to move quickly and not need to stop. You said they travel swiftly."

"But only by night." He smiled sadly. "If they want speed, why not travel in the daylight as well? The Norn soldiers are very hardy—a little sunshine does not stop them. And if they want so badly to surprise their enemies to the south, why did they wait so long after conquering Naglimund before setting out? I cannot understand it."

"I know you, beloved," she said. "You will make sense of it in time. I am going to find Ooki now. I have called him three times, but he is a stubborn ram when he does not want to hear."

"If you see Vaqana, call her too." Binabik was back on his knees, staring at the tracks of Norn boots. He was still staring at the muddy gouges in the snow when he heard something thump into the ground nearby. He looked up to discover that an ash spear, still quivering, had landed only a few steps away. Even more alarming, a half-dozen figures were charging toward him across the uneven ground.

He leaped to his feet and raised his arms high as another spear sailed past him. The newcomers were not Norns, but men, and at least two of them were young boys. All wore the tunics of local farmers. Binabik waved his arms. "Stop" he cried in the Westerling tongue. "Not enemies! We are being men like you!"

The men slowed but still came on. A few clutched spears, but the little army seemed to have been assembled quickly: one of the men had a wooden hayfork as his weapon, another a club that was only a heavy branch. Binabik waited as they approached. The strangers stayed close together, plainly fearful and the more dangerous because of it.

"That is no God-fearing creature!" one of the men said.

"A goblin," another said, wide-eyed, and lowered his spear as though Binabik might attack at any moment.

Without his wolf-mount, he knew he could not outrun these long-legged men. "We are being as much mortal as are you," he told them in Westerling. "Trolls from Yiqanuc, we are—friends of the king and queen, this is my swearing to you."

The men and boys who surrounded him were clearly farm-folk, but not the prosperous sort. They were gaunt and staring-eyed, and most were smeared with ash, as though they had been digging through burned ruins.

"What do you say, Stedman?" one of them asked the leader, but never took his eyes from Binabik.

The one called Stedman, a rangy, weathered fellow whose age was hard to guess, said, "They speak our tongue. But that means little, I think."

"Surely you have heard before about us?" Binabik said. "We are trolls of Yiqanuc, in the far north. I am Binabik of Mintahoq—a friend of King Simon's. We are trying to reach the Hayholt."

Stedman stared at him. "I took you for a goblin, or one of the fairies that burned our tithing barn. But I have heard of your kind." He frowned. "My sister's husband is a Rimmersman, and your folk have a bad name among the north-men."

Binabik nodded. "There are between our peoples many old grievances, but these days I am thinking trolls and men get on better in the north. My Rimmersgard friend Sludig and I pursued many adventures together, fighting for your Erkynland in the war of the Storm King."

Stedman eyed him up and down. "I know of that war, though I did not fight, being too young. And I believe you are not Norns nor goblins."

"It is so indeed." Binabik had seen a flash of white at the edge of his vision. "Hold yourselves still, please. I can promise you that my friend Vaqana would judge any spearing of me with great unhappiness." He raised his voice. "*Vaqana, ninit aia!*"

The white wolf appeared from behind the barn, trotting toward them. One of the boys let out a squeak of surprise and all the men took at least a few steps backward.

"Spears down, I ask of you," said Binabik. "The animal is my friend. Also, I am riding her." Vaqana slowed a little as she neared the strangers, but Binabik gave a swift whistle and she came to him. The farmers stared in amazement as the immense creature licked Binabik's face. "And my wife somewhere is here as well, searching for her own mount," he said. "Let me call her." He shouted, *"Sisqi! Come now! There are men here!"*

"What does your wife ride, a bear?" The look on Stedman's face showed his question was at least half serious.

"No, she is riding a mountain ram, like most of our folk," Binabik told him. "I am the only wolf-rider." He looked up to see Sisqi coming across the field, her head bobbing up and down as she made her way over the empty, ruined furrows with Ooki pacing behind her.

Stedman shook his head in wonderment. "And I thought we had seen the strangest things we would ever see."

"We troll-folk are small, but we are also being just men and women like you," Binabik told him. "We serve King Simon and Queen Miriamele—they are friends to us, and we are going to them now. We hoped to reach them before the Norn army, but I fear we cannot catch them up, so fast they are marching."

Stedman looked at him again. "Did you not hear? Good Queen Miriamele was killed. Murdered by Nabban-men or some such. Our liege lord rode to her funeral at the Hayholt not a fortnight past."

"What? Is this true? But it cannot be!" Binabik looked in desperation at the men's faces, but they all wore the same unhappy expression as Stedman. "Daughter of the Mountains, this . . . this . . ." Tears sprang to his eyes.

"What is wrong, my love?" Sisqi asked in the Qanuc tongue.

"I swear on the Book and our Lord it is true," the farmer said. "The baron's manor is draped in black. They have said masses for her soul in our village church."

Binabik told Sisqi what the farmer had said. Her round face grew pale. "Surely it cannot be true," she cried, but Binabik only shook his head, then brought his fist to his chest.

"But it seems to be. All . . . all the more reason we must be continuing with hurried speed." He was clearly finding it hard to catch his breath, let alone to talk. "Oh, my poor friend Simon! He will be full of despair. Curse the snake that was biting me! We might have been with him now."

Stedman kneeled and put his gnarled, callused hand on the troll's shoulder. "I see that your sorrow is real. I am sorry to give you this evil news. If you wish to rest before you ride on, the village is just over that rise. The Norns did not bother to burn it. We have no food to offer, I fear, but we may have a few jars of ale left, hidden away. We can drink to the queen's memory."

Binabik sat for a while, eyes shut and hands clasped together, as if in prayer. At last he looked up again. "We cannot stay, but we thank you for your kind words. I am sorry you are having no food." He reached into his leather pouch and pulled out a small sack. "These were given to us by King Simon, for helping us upon the road should we need such help. Perhaps they will help you buy food for your families to make up for what the Norns took."

Stedman took the sack and spilled it out into this hand. "There are more than a dozen silver pieces and two new gold crowns here!" he said in awe. The other men and boys leaned over his shoulder to look, as open-eyed as if they witnessed one of the Aedon's holy miracles. Stedman looked up at Binabik. "You do not mean us to have it all, surely?"

Binabik waved his hand. The troll looked as though he had dried in the sun, become as small and hollow as a gourd. "It has no use for us. We must be riding as fast as we can to King Simon's side. We will find food in our travel, as we are always doing."

As Binabik and Sisqi climbed onto their mounts, the older of the two farm boys stepped forward and held out a wooden Tree on a leather thong, a simple object he might have carved himself. He was not quite brave enough to meet Binabik's eye. "God'll watch over you if you wear 'un," he said in a quiet, shy voice.

"Thanks to you." Binabik took it from him and hung it carefully around his neck.

The other men were passing the coins around, wide-eyed and whispering, but Stedman turned back to Binabik and extended his hand, which enveloped the troll's completely. "Go with Heaven's grace," he said.

"And you," Binabik replied in a halting voice, then he and Sisqi rode on their way once more, bounding wolf and sturdy ram climbing the slope past the charred stones that were all that remained of the tithing barn.

"I have to leave you now," Porto told Levias. "I have been summoned to see Lord Pasevalles."

"To be honored, no doubt," said his friend. "You have earned it."

Porto could not feel quite so cheerful. Sergeant Levias had been in pain again and had spent most of the last sennight back in bed in the barracks. In that time, the mood of those in the castle had gone from shocked and mournful to terrified. The king was dead but still had not been given a funeral—his body was still with the funeral priests—and rumors had begun to spread that an army of Norns, in numbers that varied according to the teller, was marching down from the north to destroy the Hayholt in revenge for the last war. And though Lord Tiamak and his Nabbanai wife had never been the most beloved of the king's and queen's counselors, the shock of having them revealed as thieves and traitors had still shaken almost everyone in the castle.

"Whatever Pasevalles wishes of me, I will be back. You must do what the surgeon says and stay in your bed until then."

Levias seemed unperturbed. "God is watching over me. I had a most rare and unusual dream last night. I heard the voice of Elysia herself, mother of our holy Aedon, telling me to come north. That means she wants me to fight against the White Foxes, so I know the Mother of God will make me well enough to lift a sword in the Lord's name when the time comes."

"Perhaps. But remember also what the Book says," Porto cautioned him. *"The man who does not tend his flock, thinking that my Father will do his work, will find himself one day without any sheep."* Stay in bed as you've been told, *then* the Blessed Mother will likely heal you." He lifted himself off the stool he had pulled to the bedside.

"I never get over how tall you are," said Levias fondly. "You stand up like everyone else, but where they stop, you keep going!"

Porto hesitated, then turned back. "You say you heard the voice of Elysia in a dream."

Levias nodded. "I did. It could have been no one else. She called me "child of our people" and bade me come to her call."

Porto was a little jealous. "What did her voice sound like?"

"Lovely and strong and clear. Like music. And I swear that I heard angels singing as she spoke."

"You have been blessed indeed, to be given a dream like that."

"Wait," said Levias. "Before you go, dear old Porto, let us pray for the wounded Duke Osric, and also for Captain Zakiel, our good constable, and our fellow soldiers still at Winstowe." The Erkynlandish soldiers had still not returned to the Hayholt, despite the end of the siege in the Fingerdale—a subject of much discussion in the barracks.

Porto nodded. He came back to his friend's bedside and slowly lowered himself to one knee. "Next time," he said, grimacing as his joints made crackling noises, "ring the bell for prayer before I have stood all the way up."

Levias grinned. "Shush, blasphemer."

The sergeant had lost weight in the weeks since he was wounded, and the skin on his face hung a little loosely. Porto could not help feeling a surge of love for him, his fellow soldier and fellow Aedonite. They had survived much together. *I hope we both get a chance to rest now,* he thought, *and that this talk of the White Foxes' attacking us is just rumor.*

They prayed together for a long time, but the sergeant fell silent before he seemed to be finished—he had left three or four of their Erkynguard company unmentioned. Porto looked up in slight alarm and discovered his friend had fallen asleep.

Even with a fire burning in the great hearth, the barrack hall was never very warm. Porto pulled the blanket up to the sergeant's chin before he left, as if Levias were a large, bearded child.

Lord Pasevalles sat behind a table in the King's Retiring Room, apparently lost in thought, though the room was far from quiet. Several counting-priests from the Chancelry were clustered at both ends of the table, whispering and gesticulating to each other over stacks of parchments and account books. Lord Captain Zakiel stood at attention, darkly circled beneath his eyes, clearly waiting for Pasevalles to speak to him. Porto, the last and the least important, had stopped just inside the doorway, wondering whether he had misunderstood the time of his summons.

At last, fair-haired Pasevalles looked up and seemed to see Zakiel for the first time. A weary smile crossed his face. "Good of you to come, Lord Constable." Now he saw Porto and gestured for him to come forward as well. "I have much to say to both of you. Brother Wibert, will you bring something for these brave fellows to sit upon? Then you and the rest of the brothers may return to the Chancelry. We will meet later to finish this work."

Two priests brought a bench, then the robed monks filed out, carrying swaying towers of books and sliding bundles of scrolls in their arms like a hastily convened merchant caravan.

"I have news to share with you," Pasevalles said when the door had shut behind them. "But it must not go beyond this room."

Porto was surprised. What possible news would bring both him and Zakiel together? And why the two of them and no one else?

"You saw my helper, Brother Wibert," Pasevalles said. "This morning, he found this message. It had been pushed under the door of the Chancelry. He snatched it up before any of the other priests could see it, then brought it straight to me." He lifted a piece of parchment—very white, very clean—and spread it on the table. "No, do not get up. Here, I will read it.

"'*By order of Her Majesty, Utuk'ku seyt-Hamakha, Queen of the Hikeda'ya People and Mistress of Nakkiga*,' he began. Porto took a startled breath.

"'*Her Majesty directs that the King of Erkynland or his chosen emissary will meet with emissaries of the Mother of the People at the place where the River Nartha joins the River Greenwade, to discuss Terms of Surrender of the castle known as the Hayholt. If Her Majesty receives no reply to this command, the castle will be destroyed and its people made slaves. If the king's emissaries make promises and those promises are not kept, the castle will be destroyed and its people will be made slaves.*'"

Pasevalles looked up, grim-faced, as he finished. "That is the whole of it. Gentlemen, we have a grave puzzle before us."

"I say we spit on their extortion." Zakiel looked as though he had tasted something foul. "They mean to attack. They are only trying to save themselves the grief of besieging the castle, which they know will be no easy task."

"I beg your pardon, Lord Pasevalles," said Porto. "But why am I here? Surely you have better minds than mine to offer wise counsel."

Pasevalles summoned a weary smile. "You misunderstand, I fear—both of you. I *must* ride as emissary to the Norns—we have no other choice. His Grace, Osric, is still recovering. The king is dead and has not even been buried. His heir Morgan is missing, and the traitor Tiamak of the Wran seems to have stolen away with Lillia, the granddaughter of the late king and queen. After so many days, who knows if she is even still alive? No, I fear the weight of this falls on me, as acting regent."

"But why, my lord?" asked Zakiel. "Why honor them with any response at all? Let us finish the hoardings and bring in the last of the local musters. The Hayholt has outlasted several sieges, and we are surrounded by allies."

"Our field of allies has been picked clean by the fighting at Winstowe and the Fingerdale," said Pasevalles. "We may find a few more men in the outer provinces, but the muster-companies are still out. Anything we can do to delay the siege will help us. Even if it means risking treachery from the Norns under the cover of a parley, I see no other choice."

"But surely it cannot be you," said Zakiel. "Who will lead us if anything happens, Lord Chancellor? You have been our only touchstone in a terrible year. The people know you and trust you. What if we lose you to some dreadful trick of the Norn Queen?"

"I am only a man," said Pasevalles gravely. "But God arranges all." He made the sign of the Holy Tree and Zakiel and Porto followed suit. "We must trust in the goodness of our God, Lord Captain. Remember, Duke Osric has all his wits, even if he is still too unwell to leave his bed. The duke is a strong man and he is healing fast. It will not be long before he can rise and take command of the kingdom, as our noble King Simon and our dear, lost Queen Miriamele would have wished it. No, what we truly need most, gentlemen, is time. And answering this summons may purchase us a little."

Zakiel began to ask questions about finishing the siege preparations, but Porto only sat, puzzled and disheartened. The battle against the fairy-folk was coming, that seemed indisputable now, but Porto did not have quite as much faith in God as his friend Levias did.

"Your pardon, my lord," he asked. "I will gladly lay my life down to defend the castle, but I still do not understand. Why did you single me out to hear this grave news?"

Pasevalles leaned closer. "You are a veteran of many battles, Sir Porto. This time, however, you must serve a deeper purpose than just to swing your sword and deal blows. Duke Osric is recovering, and he is the regent. If the Hayholt is besieged, Osric will need to communicate with Lord Captain Zakiel—*but* . . ." Pasevalles spread his fingers to suggest a matter of some delicacy, ". . . it is possible that some of his orders may clash with Zakiel's plans. Therefore, Porto, you must be a conduit between them, knowing when to pass along Osric's commands directly or when to . . . delay them. Osric is angry and mournful, you see. He has suffered great losses and is recovering from a terrible wound. You must help him to lead, but also understand that sometimes he may not make the best choices."

Porto was uneasy. "You wish me to pick and choose which of his orders to pass along to Zakiel?"

Pasevalles shook his head. "No, not precisely. All the duke's orders must be passed along, of course—he is our regent!—but sometimes you might help him come to a different conclusion, one more in line with what the lord captain here is doing. Other times, you might need to make certain a messenger from Osric does not reach Zakiel until something long and carefully planned has been completed." He looked closely at the older knight. "Do you grasp my meaning?"

"We will have to work together closely, Sir Porto," said Zakiel.

Porto was not entirely comfortable with what he was being asked to do, but things were coming to the point where he needed to say yes or no. He was leery of the role Pasevalles wanted him to fill, but he also knew it was a high honor. If they survived the siege, it might mean he would never have to fear for his future again and could live out the rest of his life in something like comfort.

Send me a sign, Usires, my Ransomer, he prayed. *Just send me a sign so that I might know Your will.*

Someone knocked three times on the retiring room door.

"And that is Wibert," said Pasevalles. "I have arrangements to make, and you two are not the only ones who must be instructed in your new roles. Do I have your agreement, both of you, to do what must be done to protect the Hayholt in my absence?"

'Three times I came to you,'—the words of Usires himself, straight from the Book of

Aedon, Porto realized. *'Three times I came to you, yet you pretended not to hear me. What use your caution now, when all the world stands at risk?' Thank you, Ransomer,* he thought, *for sending me this sign of Your intent. You are most great.*

"I will heed your words, Lord Pasevalles," said Zakiel. "And may God grant us victory."

"I too will do what you ask, my lord," Porto agreed. "And may Usires the Aedon guide our steps in this terrible time."

"Amen to that, my friends," said Pasevalles. "Amen."

34

The High Citadel

By the end of her first day riding the great stag, Tanahaya had learned that while Quarrel might be faster than a horse for short sprints and could leap over obstacles that would balk even the most nimble of chargers, he did not have a horse's endurance. A swift gallop exhausted him in a fairly short time, so Tanahaya dismounted nearly every hour and led him until he had regained his strength. But she was feeling the press of time and of mysteries unsolved.

As she rode through the lowlands of the Coolblood Valley, keeping the splash and rush of the river T'si Suhyasei always within earshot, those unanswered questions only came to trouble her more. She desperately wanted to speak with Jiriki but she had no Witness. She also needed a proper archive to search for answers, now that Da'ai Chikiza's was beyond her reach.

Each day Tanahaya rode Quarrel until the great stag began to gasp with weariness, then walked beside him until he was fit again. Each afternoon she waited for several frustrating hours while the deer slept, although they still traveled faster than she would have on foot. Her main consolation as she made her way north toward the high peaks where Anvi'janya hid was that she encountered very few signs of the Hikeda'ya, though they had been thick as maggots around ruined Da'ai Chikiza.

But why are they even here? she wondered. *Why has the witch-queen of Nakkiga filled this ancient forest with Sacrifice troops if the mortal castle is her true objective?* A sudden and frightening thought struck her. *Does she mean to attack Anvi'janya?* The high citadel was the last of the Zida'ya cities still occupied as in the old days, protected by steep mountains and narrow trails. *But why would she bother? There are only a thousand or two of our people still living there. Does Utuk'ku plan some strike against the Year-Dancing ceremonies?*

She stopped to let Quarrel drink, and as she waited she thought yet again about Himano's parchment and its tale of the witchwood seeds buried beneath the present-day Hayholt. Even now, she knew, a Hikeda'ya army must be marching toward the mortal castle to take those seeds—but that did not explain the large Sacrifice presence here in Oldheart Forest.

A new thought came to her. Could the mysterious, forbidden valley of Tanakirú, beyond the hills to the east, have something to do with Utuk'ku's oblique strategy? Might a cache of witchwood seeds—or even an entire grove of witchwood trees—be hidden there?

Ever since the Zida'ya and Hikeda'ya clans had escaped the ruin of the Garden, they had carefully cultivated the sacred witchwood trees they brought with them, each tree watched over and protected as carefully as a child. But it had never been easy for witchwood to thrive in these new lands—the groves in most of the Nine Cities had died out long ago. Then the trees that had been rescued from old Asu'a when it fell and replanted in Jao é-Tinukai'i had withered and died not long after First Grandmother Amerasu's murder. The groves of Nakkiga had begun to fail after Utuk'ku lost the Storm King's War—even those last trees were now dead. So if there had been a witchwood grove in Tanakirú all this time, even one guarded by some monstrous ogre, why would her own people have gone without it so long?

Was this war truly about witchwood? Or something else? *My thought is so full of questions, but I cannot unpick any of them until I reach Anvi'janya.*

She swung up onto Quarrel's back once more and tapped the stag's barrel of a chest with her heels.

"Away, now," she whispered in his ear, and sang a little of the taming song. Quarrel's ears flicked as if in annoyance, but she had woven her song carefully and well: a moment later, he leaped ahead, his hooves throwing up spurts of damp earth.

"I cannot do it," Jarnulf groaned. "I cannot face the Lord of Song again."

"But you are strong, little man," said the giant Goh Gam Gar, "if you kept secrets from the wizard. Stolen Face is very old and very powerful."

"I held onto those secrets only because of a trick," he said. "And Akhenabi will not be fooled the same way twice."

The giant let out a rumble of interest. "You tricked him?"

Jarnulf could hardly move. It was not merely the pain of his scorched and ruined finger, though that was excruciating. Akhenabi's offhanded exploration of his thoughts had wracked his entire body, so that he felt as if he had been beaten by several men. His head throbbed as if his skull was cracked, and the agony of his burned flesh was even worse. "It is dragon's blood from the mountain," he told the giant. "I still have a bit of it in this jar. I put my finger in it when he was questioning me." He held up his hand, showing Goh Gam Gar the charred, shapeless lump of skin, which was all that remained beyond the first knuckle. "But I do not think he will be fooled that way a second time."

"And what secrets do you have that are worth so much suffering, man?"

Jarnulf hesitated. The giant had shown in the past that he did not care much for his Hikeda'ya masters, but how could he trust such a monster? "I could ask you the same," he said at last. "You are by far the largest giant I have ever seen, and the strongest. Why are you not marching south toward the Hayholt with the rest of the queen's army?"

"Perhaps because I tried to kill some *Higdaja*." Goh Gam Gar's voice rumbled again, and this time Jarnulf recognized it as a laugh. "After the queen sang up the dead Zida'ya, Hakatri, I was sick and angry. When the soldiers came to lead me away, I knocked one down and picked up another and squeezed him until his bones cracked and his eyes flew out. Then that little turd Saomeji came running with the pain-stone and I was thrown down, my limbs on fire. He said, 'Chain him up. The Lord of Song will decide what to do with him.' So here I wait."

Jarnulf felt torn. If he told the truth, the giant might offer him up to the Norns to save his own life. But the monster had proved himself more honorable than any of the Hikeda'ya with whom they had traveled. *Except for the female, Nezeru*, Jarnulf reminded himself. *She had a sense of honor, too. I hope she is far away from this madness, this war.* And as he thought it, he realized for the first time that he had been lying to himself all along. His reasons for taking Nezeru away from her Talon had been confused because she had offered him her body. That offer had disturbed him, but despite that, he had still felt sorry for her.

So I saved her, he realized. *Saved her from the war and her life of slavery under her monarch, the hell-witch Utuk'ku. As I would have saved my mother or my sister too, if I could have.*

"You are quiet a long time, man," said the giant.

"I have many things to consider. But one thought is about you, and it is this—I think you hate your Hikeda'ya masters."

The rumble again, slowly growing until it made Jarnulf's bones quiver. This time, Goh Gam Gar was not laughing. The giant pounded his huge fist on the floor of the storage room until the earthen floor jumped, making Jarnulf groan again in agony. "Masters!" he snarled. "Jailers! They took my people and made us slaves. They breed us like hounds to kill their enemies, but even hounds get more kindness. I saw my entire family die at the place you call Hayholt, fighting for the masked queen, because if they do not fight, they are killed by the queen's soldiers." For a moment the giant was silent except for the loud rumble of his breath. "Hate them? Without this collar on my neck—" he slapped at the great witchwood yoke, "—I will tear them apart, one by one, until all hairless whitefaces are dead."

Thank you, Lord, for this blessing, Jarnulf thought. *You have shown me that I am not alone, that my holy mission still stretches before me.*

"Then listen," he told the giant. "Listen and I will tell you of all I have done. And if you hate the Hikeda'ya, you will bathe in bliss when you hear my story."

"Move close and be quiet," said the giant, patting the floor with a vast, meaty hand. "A window is over us, and the smell of *Higdaja* in this place is too strong for me to know when one is near enough to hear our talk."

Jarnulf was fearful of venturing within reach of something that could tear him in half as easily as he might pull the wing from a cooked pigeon, but he also dimly remembered the giant lifting him up to drink as water was poured down from above, and he suddenly wondered at that. "Who brought us water?"

"I do not know, though I have had their scent before. Some mortal women. They live in the place beside us, but do not seem to be prisoners."

"Blessings on them, then." *Another sign,* Jarnulf thought. *Like Saint Pelippa bringing water to the dying Aedon—risking her own freedom to let our dying Ransomer drink.*

He had decided. *I am trusting in Your sign as proof of Your protection, my Lord God.* He slid closer to the great, man-shaped beast, near enough to speak without raising his voice above a whisper. The giant's stink was eye-watering, but he reminded himself that God's hand was in every creature—the Book said so, and the Book was Heaven's manifested will.

I open my heart unto You, my Ransomer.

"Listen, then," he began. "I was raised in the slave barns of White Snail Castle, and Jarnulf was not the name I was born with."

When Jarnulf had finished his tale, the giant did not speak, but only chortled, low and quiet, like a thunderous snore.

"So when you helped them, it was just to reach the queen." Goh Gam Gar laughed again, making Jarnulf's ribs vibrate like a tolling bell.

"Not so loud. You said they might be listening."

"I cannot stop. That Makho, with all his hate for you—and he was right!"

"I told you this so you will understand why I need to escape before Akhenabi sends for me again. He will be prepared for my trick this time. He will learn every secret I have."

"What do you care?" The giant rubbed at his eyes with the back of a huge hand. "You are dead either way. Do you fear the pain of the Singers' tortures? That too will pass." The creature frowned suddenly, his leathery brow wrinkling. "Or is there something else?" He took a pose of deep pondering, hand on chin, that was so comical Jarnulf realized he was being mocked. "Is it the little *Higdaja* girl? If you tell the Lord of Song your secrets, she will no longer be a deserter to be executed, but a traitor for not reporting you to the chief of her Talon." He nodded his huge head. "That must be it. She has taken away your heart."

"No!" Jarnulf realized he had spoken too loudly, too emphatically, but the giant's words had touched on something almost as painful as his mutilated finger. How could he expect a monster to understand the complexity of that strange situation? "No, I do not care for her that way. But she is not beyond salvation."

"Salvation?" Goh Gam Gar rumbled again. "Old Gam has not heard that word before, but he can guess what it means. You think to win her for your God."

"Perhaps. But my God also commands me to spare the innocent. It is in His book."

"Do you think your God is going to save all people the *Higdaja* queen means to kill?"

Jarnulf took a deep breath and let it out. "My God does what He thinks best. It is not up to me to seek to know His ways."

"A clever way not to blame your God for all the blood spilled in the world."

Jarnulf's entire body ached and his burned finger felt as though it had been skinned of its flesh and sinew, leaving only tormented nerves. He did not want to spend what little time remained before Akhenabi called for him arguing morality with a heathen giant. "I must get out of this place," he said. "If you do not care for me—and why should you?—you might at least wish me to succeed in my task, since I will be striking at the enemy we share." He glanced up at the storeroom window, the blackness beyond dotted with faint starlight. "Will you help me?"

"How? Do you forget you owe me for two favors, mortal man? Two times I hid you from Makho's anger."

"No, I have not forgotten. And I swear I will make good on all my debts. But perhaps if you could tear those bars from the window, I could get through." He squinted. "The opening looks as if it might be big enough . . ."

"Ha!" A wave of carrion stench followed on the giant's exclamation. "And leave me here with this yoke on my neck, to suffer much pain when Akhenabi's Singers find you are gone? That will not happen, man. There would be nothing left of me for you to repay."

Who knew when the Lord of Song would send for him again? Desperation threatened to overwhelm Jarnulf. He had one trick to keep himself alive, and he had used it already. But thinking of the jar of dragon's blood gave him an idea. "What if I used the burning blood to break the yoke you wear? Then you could escape with me." The thought of following an angry giant out of Naglimund gave him sudden hope. At the very least, he would be almost unnoticed in the midst of the death and destruction Goh Gam Gar would loose among the Norns.

The giant let out a splutter of scorn. "My collar is witchwood, made by the Singers. Not even dragon's blood will destroy it before they learn of it and stop us. No, that will not work."

"Then it will be the Cold, Slow Halls for me."

"Your dragon's blood might harm the bars on the window. They are only iron."

Jarnulf was angry at himself for not having thought of it already. "By the Sacred Blood of Usires, yes! But how will I reach the window?"

"Climb onto me. I will pretend to be asleep if anyone comes. I will say you used *kei-vishaa* powder on me to take away my wits." He reached out a hand and enfolded Jarnulf's face so that his fingertips touched each other at the back of Jarnulf's skull. "But do not drip any of that burning stuff on me or I will roar. And I might crush your head as well."

"I stand warned." Jarnulf looked around. After what had happened to his finger, he knew he could not use his hands to smear the pasty black blood onto the bars. He searched the floor around him and found a handful of stiff, pale bristles lying in the filthy straw. "I will use these."

"My own hair?" The giant chuckled, but gently this time, a noise like a large stone being dragged across the ground. "You may burn them if you wish, but the ones still growing in my hide must be left alone."

Jarnulf still had the jar clutched in one hand. He lifted his legs through his shackle chain until his arms were in front of him, then picked up the giant's wiry hairs, each one almost as thick and stiff as the shaft of a hawk's feather. When he had gathered enough, he tied them together in a makeshift brush. He wanted to remove his chain close to the shackle, so he dipped the thick hairs into the pot, then—as they began to smolder and curl—painted the black ooze around the last link of the chain. It did not immediately part, but after a few moments he could see that the blackened metal looked pitted and weak, so he stepped on the chain and yanked with his arm. The link snapped and fell away. Jarnulf offered a silent prayer of thanks.

He scooped up a little more of the black blood before the giant's shed hairs shriveled away, then daubed the link below the shackle on his other hand. Soon he was entirely free of the chain and was able to lift his arms and even stick his wounded finger in his mouth, tasting his own charred flesh.

He gathered another handful of the giant's hairs and made a new brush. The first had withered away, smoking like a rushlight. "Now for the bars."

"Do not get any of that foul muck on me," the giant warned as Jarnulf began to climb him. "I will tear off your leg if you do, little man." A huge, clawed hand closed around Jarnulf's knee, but only to help him up onto a vast shoulder. "Now I pretend to sleep, in case anyone sees you climbing out." The giant let his head loll and began to utter quite convincing snores, so that Jarnulf felt as if he climbed a fire-mountain just coming to life.

He peered through the bars, but the narrow alley between the storeroom and the wall was empty of anything except rain-splashes and rubbish. He carefully dipped and smeared the blood until he had coated the base and the top of one of the bars. The iron was much thicker than the link on his shackles, so he waited, painfully conscious that his next meeting with Akhenabi loomed closer with every moment. At last the thin trails of smoke died away, so he gave the bar a careful tug. It did not come loose, but he thought he could feel it give a little. He grabbed one of the other bars and dug his feet into the giant's shoulder just at the base of his massive neck, then pulled as hard as he could.

"I do not like this," rumbled Goh Gam Gar as Jarnulf adjusted his footing to get a better purchase. "Which leg should I tear off?"

"Neither." Then, with a crunch and a scrape, the bar finally broke loose.

Jarnulf hastily dipped and dabbed at the remaining bars with his heart beating very fast, hating each vulnerable moment. *My freedom is in Your hands, Lord,* he thought. *Help me now, I pray.*

Again, he set his feet, and this time the giant reached up his great paw to steady him. When the last bar came out, Jarnulf dropped it into the straw beside the others.

"I am going to climb out now," he said. "Are you sure you do not want to risk it with me?"

"If you think a little burnt finger hurts you," the giant said, "you cannot even imagine what the queen's collar feels like. And I do not think I will fit through that hole. No, you go. But do not forget what you owe me."

"Never." He clambered up onto the stone sill, then pushed his head and upper body through the now empty window frame. The alleyway was still deserted, rain hurtling down like spears from Heaven. Gratitude washed through him. "I thank you, Sir Giant," he whispered, "and I will remember."

Goh Gam Gar did not reply. Jarnulf folded his legs up beneath him, then turned around until he could grasp the sill with all his fingers except the wounded one. As he let himself down, he could hear the giant's mock snores begin again.

My hand is in every creature, sayeth the Lord, and I can make anything an instrument of salvation.

He jumped down, his bare feet splashing in the muddy water beneath the window. He nearly fell over, but flung out his arms, now free of every restraint except the metal cuffs around his wrists, and regained his balance.

Thank you, O my great God. You have shown me that a good heart can wear many guises, just as evil can wear fair appearance. I will not forget that lesson.

Tanahaya could feel the stag laboring as she guided him up the steep hill track. She had been riding the great red creature for many days, but she knew she could not hope to do so much longer.

I have pushed you too far and too fast, forest lord, she thought. *Much more of this and that brave heart of yours will burst.*

She slid down from Quarrel's back then and began leading him up the slope. He followed her now like an obedient dog, which made her heart even sadder. *He did not ask for this. He had no choice. Am I only a lesser shadow of Utuk'ku herself, who ignores all costs, sacrificing even innocents to achieve her aims?*

When they reached the crest, a low promontory that sat among higher hills, she looked down, marveling at how far she could see. Every tree seemed a perfect work in miniature, leagues of countryside displayed below her like the work of the world's most gifted maker of tapestries.

The Garden is not just in our memories, Tanahaya thought. *It is here, if we only look for it.*

But she had clambered up the hill in the hope of getting some idea of how far away Anvi'janya might be, and even from this elevated spot, she could see no trace of the legendary citadel.

I should have known that a city which has stayed safe for so long by its invisibility would not reveal itself to me just because I climbed to a high place.

She saw movement below her and dropped into a crouch. To her dismay, she saw that a company of Hikeda'ya Sacrifices had entered the valley, marching along the winding road in their swift, seemingly disordered way. Tanahaya made a hurried count and decided that several hundred warriors must be hurrying across the valley in stark daylight. It made her shiver. *So many!* she thought. *Where are they bound? They are leaving Da'ai Chikiza and heading east—could they be marching toward Tanakirú?* The size and boldness of the Hikeda'ya force startled her. *Nothing is hidden anymore. Whatever Utuk'ku wants, she is reaching out for it now and does not care who knows.*

Tanahaya watched for no little time as the Sacrifices passed through the valley and out of her sight, then she continued her survey of the surrounding hills, craggy limestone masses in odd shapes. Within moments she spotted more movement, this time north of her vantage point.

A small group of riders were making their way around the base of one of the higher crags. Tanahaya could not be certain from so far, but she thought this group numbered less than a dozen, and as she watched them, her heart grew lighter within her breast: if those were not her own Zida'ya people, she told herself, then she could no longer trust her eyes. No Hikeda'ya soldiers would dress in the earthy colors these riders wore—the Order of Sacrifice went always in black, or white-clad in snow. More importantly, though, they seemed to be headed toward the cluster of mountains where she thought Anvi'janya must lie. If they were her own folk, she could join them. She had heard that the way up to the citadel was confusing and dangerous, and she had worried about finding the hidden track that led up to the city.

"I am sorry, my friend," she said to Quarrel, gently rubbing the spot between the roots of his antlers. "One last race, then I promise that I will release you to your forest." She leaned close and sang, reminding him of his taming, and he stood patiently as she climbed back on. "Be grateful I wear no armor," she said, "and that I am small and slender."

The stag turned his head and gave her a sidelong glance. If it was a look of gratitude, he hid it well.

"Haste, good Quarrel," she said, using her knees to turn him gently toward the track they had just climbed. "Your reward will come when we have caught them up."

It took all that day and part of the next, with only a few short stops to let the stag rest, before Tanahaya reached the place where she hoped to cross the travelers' path. The stag was stumbling a bit now, bone-weary, and she was growing more and more concerned for him.

"A bit farther, only," she whispered in his ear. His head was down like a weary ox dragging a plow, and she feared she would have to release him before she could catch up with the riders she had seen. And if those travelers were themselves hurrying, they might already be gone. She had considered moving to higher ground to try to find them again—guessing at their path was much more difficult at ground level, where one stony outcrop looked much like the next—but the sky had gone witchwood-gray, and she could see a storm coming down from the north which would likely blanket the peaks in snow.

"I will not force you to climb into that," she told Quarrel. "You deserve a better reward for your labors."

The stag snorted, his chin wet with foam, his tongue dangling. She slid off to let him rest and browse on a patch of mountain sedge while she climbed onto a stone that jutted from the soil like a half-buried spearhead. Once atop it, she could see that the storm was coming faster than she had thought, and she was about to jump down and lead Quarrel to shelter when she caught a glimpse of the riders she was chasing. They were less than half a league ahead of her now, following the course of a stream at the bottom of a steep gorge, and the sight of them lifted her heart again.

"One last run, brave Quarrel," she said, swinging herself onto the stag's back. He made a groaning noise, but even without the prompting of the Song, he let her guide him downward toward a place where her path would join the river valley. "Now, fly," she said. "Your freedom is only an hour away."

Whether he understood her or not, the stag leaped down the slope as Tanahaya clung to his broad chest. Several times she had to grab at his antlers to keep her balance, but she feared breaking them off and let go again as quickly as she could. The sound of running water rose to her ears, and soon after that they reached the mouth of the gorge. Its walls rose high on either side, massive rock faces that looked as though they had been sliced with a dull blade and then pried apart. A few pines and spruces clung to the lower reaches, but otherwise the gorge was all gray stone.

She held on tight and urged Quarrel into his version of a gallop. At last, as he began to slow with weariness, she saw the travelers at the far end of the gorge.

"Now give me your best!" she cried. Quarrel did not disappoint, though she could feel his chest heaving as he raced along the gravel and broken stone that had collected beside the stream. As she drew closer, she became more and more certain that these riders were her own kind. The last of them heard Quarrel's hoofbeats and turned to look back.

"Stay!" she cried. "Stay for me, kinsfolk! Stay for me!"

The endmost rider had apparently called to the others: they all turned in a narrow place where the stream ran between the close-leaning hills. One of the riders jogged back toward her with his bow ready, an arrow already on the string. Tanahaya slowed Quarrel and sat up straight, hands lifted to show she held no weapon.

"Who are you?" the stranger shouted. "These are the wrong lands in which to go nameless. Speak!"

"I am Tanahaya of Shisae'ron," she called back. "A friend of Year-Dancing House. I seek Anvi'janya!"

He pulled up and watched her approach, bow still in his hands, but held more loosely now. As she neared him, she threw back her hood and he did the same. His hair at first looked gray, but on closer view revealed itself to be flecked with both black and white.

She slid down from Quarrel's back. The animal stayed where she left him, his sides heaving, for once not even interested in finding food. The Zida'ya stranger watched her carefully as she walked toward him, but his eyes kept straying to the big red stag.

"A strange mount you have chosen," he said.

"The Garden gives what the Garden gives."

He lowered his bow. "You call yourself Tanahaya? That is strange—I have heard that name many times in these last days."

Before she could ask him what he meant, she heard the drumming of hooves and looked up to see another rider galloping back toward them, cloak billowing. *"Spark!"* the newcomer cried. "Spark, is that truly you?"

"Rabbit?" It was almost too good for Tanahaya to believe it possible. "Aditu, my beloved friend!" She ran toward the approaching rider. "What are you doing here?"

Aditu reined up her horse, then dismounted, though not without some effort. Her belly had grown even bigger since the last time they had been together, a beautiful roundness like a full moon. She even had to turn sideways to embrace her friend. "My own dear Spark," she said, "I have worried for you since you spoke to Jiriki. Where is the mortal princeling, Morgan?"

"I do not know—I fear he may have been lost. A large company of Hikeda'ya attacked Da'ai Chikiza as I was using the Witness to speak to your brother. We were overwhelmed but Vinyedu of the Pure and I managed to bring down the Place of Sky-Watching's roof, trying to even the odds. Vinyedu perished, and I was separated from Morgan. I could not find him in the rubble."

Aditu shook her head. "Terrible. Jiriki said nothing of any Hikeda'ya attack."

"He did not know. Some fell spirit reached out from Nakkiga and ended our talk."

"This is grave news about young Morgan." Aditu pulled Tanahaya to her again. "But I rejoice to see you alive."

"Where is Jiriki? I must speak to him."

"He is gathering fighters to ride to old Asu'a because of your discovery of Himano's scroll. I do not know where he is."

Tanahaya's heart, so buoyant at seeing Aditu again, now grew heavy. "Ah. I feared this. Who do you travel with? Do any of your companions have a Witness so I can reach out to your brother?"

Another rider approached. "I have a Witness, but it will do you no good," she said. Her hair was silver-white, her face handsome and strong.

"I know you, my lady," said Tanahaya. "You are Ayaminu, mistress of High

Anvi'janya. But this is another mystery—at least to me. Why are you and Aditu here, in the middle of the mountains?"

"The Great Year is ending," Aditu explained, "but my mother still sleeps in the Yásira of H'ran go-Jao. The witchwood is all gone, of course, but the Year-Dancing Ceremony was always more than just the witchwood." She made an ancient hand-sign—*The Garden Abides*. "I am not yet our people's Sa'onsera, but I cannot turn my back on our most important ritual. Lady Ayaminu and her grandson came to meet me."

Ayaminu turned to the rider with black and white hair. "Liko, hasten ahead and tell the others that all is well. We will catch them soon."

He nodded and rode away up the track.

"Lady Ayaminu, you said your Witness would do me no good," Tanahaya said. "I mean no disrespect, *S'huesa*, but I must ask why that is so. I have a most important message to give to Jiriki."

"Your conversation with him, though it was days and days ago, was the last time we could use the Witnesses," Ayaminu told her. "At the same time as the Hikeda'ya must have attacked Da'ai Chikiza, some great force rendered the Witnesses silent—both Jiriki's and my own."

"Utuk'ku," said Tanahaya in dismay. "This must be her work."

"It seems likely," Ayaminu agreed. "It seems we have much to discuss, but as you can see, a storm is coming and we have one last climb still to make. I do not wish to be caught in the open when the weather changes."

"One last thing, then," said Tanahaya. "I made a promise, and I intend to keep it. Do you have a horse to spare?"

"Sadly, we have several," Ayaminu told her. "Three of our companions died at the hands of Sacrifice troops. You may ride poor Yiyuna's mare, Feather. She knows the mountain trails well."

"Then the time has come for me to release my courageous mount. He has labored bravely on my behalf—although not by his own choice." She turned and took the stag's face between her hands. His shoulder was by her head, and his antlers stretched higher and farther than she could reach, but as she leaned close, he stood motionless but for a slight trembling in his legs. "You have served me nobly, friend Quarrel," she told him. "I set you free now to find your own way. But if I am in great need, I may call for you again one day, and I pray you will come if you hear my song. My thanks to you, excellent creature."

Quarrel raised his head then and looked at her for no little time before suddenly prancing backward and thrashing the air with his antlers. A moment later he turned and bounded away back down the river valley until he was lost to sight.

"I see we all have stories to share," said Aditu. "Come, dear one, ride with me until we catch the others. Ayaminu says we will reach Anvi'janya's gates well before tomorrow's sunset."

Tanahaya looked at her friend's swollen belly and smiled. "In the midst of all this fear and bloodshed, I have at least one piece of good news, my better-than-sister." She leaned close so she could speak in a whisper. "I carry a child."

Aditu's eyes widened. "Glory!" she said. "Oh, Spark, this is such happy news. It almost makes me feel hopeful. Have you told Jiriki?"

She shook her head. "No. But sadly, it is not the thing I most need to tell him."

Her friend's smile faltered. "Oh. Oh, Spark, I do not like the sound of that."

"Nor will you when I tell you what it is. But do not despair—it might only be my own over-loud worries. Still, I will be glad to reach Anvi'janya and its libraries."

Aditu managed another smile, though it was smaller than the first. "My dear Tanahaya. Nothing is entirely real to you until you have read it in some chronicle."

Tanahaya shrugged. "That is what I am, dear Rabbit, and I have always believed it is what the Garden wants of me. I am a scholar. My only monarch is truth."

"It is a pity you chose such a demanding master." Aditu embraced her once again. "You may pursue truth for a long lifetime and still never get to meet it."

Feather proved to be as steady as Ayaminu had said. Now that she could ride without concern that she might be injuring or overstraining her mount, Tanahaya could finally give real attention to the landscape around her as they climbed higher into the hills. Here the earth's rocky bones stuck up in gray masses that wind and rain had carved into strange shapes, fluted spires and great slope-shouldered mounds like hooded figures. As Tanahaya and Aditu talked in undertones, sharing all that they had experienced since they had parted in H'ran Go-jao, Ayaminu named the peaks that loomed on either side of their winding track.

"Pe Ni'yo," she said, gesturing toward the nearest, "—Watcher of the Way. There, the Twin Hunters. And that one is Jumi'iru—Moon Cradle. Behind her, Gundao, The Marshal."

"I have never seen such strange mountains," said Tanahaya. "Not a single one has the same shape as another."

"Soft stone," Ayaminu explained. "These ranges are full of caves, too, because the water wears them away."

"In the terrible flood ten Great Years ago," Liko said. "Whole cliffsides fell away and broke up. The water carried stones as big as houses down the valley."

"I was not alive then," Tanahaya said, "but I have heard much of the flood, and I was lately in Da'ai Chikiza, which I know was drowned for some time. Did Anvi'janya take any harm from the water?"

Ayaminu turned back and favored her with a smile. "That is right. I forgot you were one of our younger folk, like Aditu. No, Anvi'janya was not harmed by the flooding. You will see why soon enough."

Aditu was so front-heavy now that Tanahaya could not help fearing she might overbalance as they followed the twisting track, but she reminded herself that in all the time she had known Jiriki's sister, she had never seen her do anything gracelessly. "You would probably fall as gently as a leaf," she said, not realizing she had spoken aloud.

"What is that, dear one?" Aditu asked.

"Nothing. I am so pleased to see you again that the thoughts in my head are bubbling like a hot spring."

"My heart has the same feeling," said Aditu, laughing, but a moment later she grew more sober. "When I heard that you were in Da'ai Chikiza, and then learned that Utuk'ku's soldiers were in the forest nearby, I feared for you, though I did not know the Sacrifices had entered the city."

"I was lucky to escape." A clutch of sadness made her take a deep breath. "I can only hope that the mortal youth made his way out, somehow. But I fear it is not likely."

"Do not give up hope. Young Morgan is a grandson of Simon—and Miriamele too, of course. Did you know I found Simon once when he was only his grandson's age, lost on the forest's edge in midwinter. I led him back to Jao é-Tinukai'i through the Summer Gate."

"Yes, I know that story well," said Tanahaya, smiling.

"Then know this. I spent much time around Simon in that year, and though he was little more than a child, even by his own people's reckoning, he had a strong *suya'do.*" The word was an old one, a Garden word for "thread" that meant something like "fate" or "destiny," but even Tanahaya, despite all her years of study, could not have easily translated it into the mortal tongue. "Happenstance will not take young Morgan's life. Only a destiny greater and more potent than his own could do that. At least, that is what I feel. We are all part of a tapestry, under the hands of some unknown weaver who creates a pattern too vast and intricate for us to see."

They rode on in silence for a while, until Aditu said, "Tell me of the life you carry inside you. When did you know?"

Tanahaya made a finger-sign—*frailty.* "In truth, I still do not know for certain, though I *feel* certain. It came upon me over a time. Dreams told me, but I did not recognize them at first. Only when I dreamed of my poor, lost mother did I wake to realize what was inside me." She hesitated. "This will sound strange, but I thought that in the dream my mother spoke with your mother, Likimeya's, voice."

Aditu looked troubled. "I have only heard her voice once since she slipped into the deathlike trance of the *keta-yi'indra.* Strangely, I did not even hear her words as well as the mortal boy Morgan did."

Tanahaya found that startling. "Truly? What did she say?"

"Morgan told us she said, *All the voices lie except the one that whispers. And that one will steal away the world.* I did not hear so much—her voice only murmured in my thought briefly, as faint as the sea in an empty shell. Still, I heard enough to know he spoke truly, which does not explain why she spoke to him and not to her own children."

"I cannot make sense of it either," said Tanahaya. "But I have other questions, other grave fears, that might be answered by Anvi'janya's archives. Perhaps there we can also find an answer to what Morgan heard."

The company rode through the night, resting the horses when it seemed necessary. Dawn found them at the base of a mountain whose rounded top loomed high above them. "Now we climb," said Ayaminu.

Tanahaya was puzzled. "Forgive me, my lady, but this mountain does not look like what I have been told of *Soori K'yan*—the Sun's Eye."

Ayaminu smiled. "That is because it is not the Sun's Eye. This is *Funida*—the Step. Be patient and you will soon understand."

Tanahaya had been told to be patient so many times by her old mentor that she almost felt comforted. "I hear," she said. "And when I hear, I learn."

"And I hear Master Himano in your words," said Ayaminu, smiling. "I was very sorry to hear of his death. You had a good teacher."

"I miss him every day."

As they made their way up the Step, the air grew colder and snowflakes swirled around their heads, though most of them melted before they reached the ground. Tanahaya had never been to Anvi'janya, though she had heard much about it, and she was puzzled why they should be climbing a different mountain than the one she had been taught was the seat of the ancient city. Then, as they followed the track around *Funida's* base, she saw what had been hidden from her eye behind it—a mountain standing nearby that was almost twice as high as the Step, its peak like the tip of a sword blade. "Is that not the Sun's Eye over there?" she asked in confusion. "What do I not understand? Are the stories wrong?"

Aditu gave her a merry look. "It is good you are seeing something of the world, Spark," she said mockingly. "I pity anyone who has only traveled in books."

"I have traveled to the old site of Asu'a and back," Tanahaya retorted. "Though in truth I only remember the first trip, not the return. And I have just made my way through what felt like much of the Oldheart and into and out of Da'ai Chikiza before I caught up with you. That feels like traveling to me."

"Do not pout," said Aditu. "Though it improves your usually too-serious face. I wonder that my brother thinks so highly of you, when you go about looking like a thundercloud."

"You are a wretch. And you are teasing me, Rabbit."

"And you are correct."

They climbed for no little time up a track so steeply perilous that at times they had to dismount and lead even the sure-footed Zida'ya horses. By the time they had traveled halfway around the Step, the stark bulk of the Sun's Eye filled

Tanahaya's vision. Though it looked to be only a few furlongs away from where they rode, the distance down to the valley floor that lay between the two peaks would have been enough to make a weaker head dizzy. But that was not what caught Tanahaya's eye as she pulled up in astonishment. "By the Garden Eternal, tell me I am not dreaming!"

"No," said Ayaminu, "you are not. Before you stands High Anvi'janya, home of my family and clan since my ancestors came from the Garden."

A vast cavern in the side of the steep-sided Sun's Eye had now been revealed. Tanahaya could see what could only be city walls standing tall inside the great opening, gleaming in the afternoon sun.

"Is that Anvi'janya? But we are on the wrong mountain!" Tanahaya said in confusion.

"Not for long," Ayaminu assured her. "Come. We have a little farther to ride."

They continued along the track, around the rounded bulk of the Step, and then something that had been almost invisible against the background of ragged limestone peaks finally revealed itself to her.

"Is that . . . a bridge?" she asked, staring. "Is that the Silken Span?"

"Yes, it is, Spark!" said Aditu. "You will see it from very close, very soon."

Tanahaya had known that Anvi'janya had a famous rope bridge, but she had never guessed that it stretched between two mountains, with nothing beneath its gently sagging length but empty air and the valley floor far, far below. So fixed was her gaze on the bridge as they approached it that she hardly looked up at the city itself, though she could see the towers were beautiful and shapely. The city shone within the overhanging cavern like a pearl in an oyster or a marble statue in an alcove.

She lost sight of the crossing for a little while as they made their way around a place where the mountain bulged outward like Aditu's belly, but soon they reached the near end of the bridge. In all her reading, Tanahaya had never imagined the famous Silken Span to be so small, so fragile. Its ropes seemed little more than threads, as if it might shred and blow away in the next strong wind. As they reached the twin posts that marked its entrance, she could see the bridge sway in the wind, its guide ropes powdered with new snow.

"I never thought it would be so . . . slight," she said.

"If it will hold me and this almost-born child inside me," Aditu told her, "I think you need not fear your slenderness will be too much for it."

"Just the same, you go first," said Tanahaya. She tried to make a joke of it, but it came out wrong, a little anxious.

"We are all going over it, Spark—a dozen horses and riders." Aditu's eyes sparkled with mischief. "But you may wait until we've all crossed if you want, just to make certain."

"No. It's not that. And if I truly thought there was danger, I wouldn't let you go—not first, not ever."

Ayaminu had already ridden out onto the planks of the bridge. It was wider than Tanahaya had guessed at first—a good-sized wagon would make it across with a little room left on either side. "Come, you two," said the mistress of Anvi'janya. "You can finish your gossiping when we have reached the city." Ayaminu rode out onto the span with Liko behind her, followed by the rest of the company. Aditu urged her horse after them, and Tanahaya could do nothing but follow.

It is not that the bridge seems fragile, she thought. *It is that, suddenly,* everything *seems fragile.* The mood had swept down on her like one of the fierce winds from the mountain's heights.

She followed her friend across the swaying span. Far below, a river that looked as small as a thread wound through the gorge, but if its waters sang or splashed, Tanahaya was too high above it to hear.

35

Honor-Bound

Pasevalles rapped on the door of Simon's cell. "Wake up, king without a throne."

Simon kept his eyes shut. "I don't need to hear more of your lies."

"Lies? You mean truths that you would rather not learn. Are you trying to convince yourself that things are not as bad as they seem?" He laughed. "But they are. And they will soon grow worse—at least for you."

"You are a madman, Pasevalles—sick in your wits. It's too bad your father died after your birth instead of before you were conceived."

"Very good." He almost sounded cheerful. "You think to make me angry so that I will come into your cell and somehow give you a chance to get free. Do you imagine yourself overcoming the weight of your chains and your age and then holding me hostage? Then *you* are the madman. Come now, Your Late Majesty, how do you think all this came to be? I have been preparing carefully for years. Why would I throw all that aside now that my work is almost done?"

Yes, he has been careful, and because of that he has been silent a very long time, Simon thought. *That long silence might be my only hope. He wants his cleverness to be known.* "I underestimated you," he said aloud, letting some of his true frustration into his words.

"Underestimated? That word is hardly adequate. But do not blame yourself. The world is full of people like you. Most men want to believe things that make them feel comforted, and they will ignore any difficult truth to keep believing."

"Most men are not liars. Most men are not traitors."

"You think not? But in any case, most men are cowards. Only a few are like me, men who see that anything is possible if you throw away the rules that everyone else obeys. But none of them truly understand."

"Why did you kill Josua, as you claim? It would have been much easier to let him help you. He would have given you out of kindness everything you stole instead."

"Perhaps. But he was the one who came to my home and took my father and uncle away to offer them up as sacrifices so that you and your demanding bitch of a wife could rule."

Simon thrashed uselessly in his chains. "Murderer!" he cried, forgetting for a moment that he had meant to keep his captor talking. "You are not worthy to speak of my wife."

Pasevalles shook his head. "Do you see? You try to practice strategy on me, but you are not good at it. Why do you think Eolair and Isgrimnur and the rest chose you to be their Commoner King? For your bravery? For your good heart?" He laughed again. "The stories that people tell themselves! No, they wanted Miriamele as queen, but her father had put the world in peril and almost destroyed Erkynland. They needed someone to sit beside her, a young hero whose presence would soothe the other nobles—a green fool who could be guided and directed by the rich barons but not have the wit to realize it."

"Begone. I will no longer listen to you."

"Ha. You will be listening to my voice for the rest of your short life, if only in your memory as you think of all the foolish things you have done and all the ways I have humiliated you and ruined you." Pasevalles' voice rose, as if he defended himself. "First, I killed your precious Prince Josua. Later, I helped your foolish son to doom himself. Then I killed Idela, your son's widow, with my own hands—I threw her down the steps of your own residence. And your wife, Miriamele? Dead at the hands of men I hired, burned like an Aedonite martyr! In fact, I brought down all Nabban from my chambers here in the Hayholt—and with your own gold, Simon! So even in your last moment you will be thinking of me, cursing me, hating me. It does not matter whether you listen or not—I have destroyed everything you cared about."

Simon pulled desperately at his chains after Pasevalles had gone, as if anger alone might give him the strength to break iron shackles. He struggled until his wrists and hands were slick with blood, then he fell to the floor of his cell once more, sobbing in helpless fury.

He awoke from another dreamless, deathlike sleep. This time the moment of innocence was so short that he had not even opened his eyes before the horror crashed in upon him.

Miri, he thought, then: *Please, God, if You are merciful, let me die. Let me be with her.*

But his heart continued to beat, breath to fill his lungs. He would live until Pasevalles no longer received pleasure from tormenting him.

Simon sat up, feeling like Saint Granis crushed under stones—but holy Granis had kept his courage to the end, crying out, "I come to you at last, O Lord!" even as more stones were piled on his broken body. Simon knew that he would not be so brave. He could not survive many more stones before his heart burst.

Josua, Miri, even poor Idela—that fiend murdered them all. And what did he mean about John Josua? He said he watched him doom himself.

These ghastly thoughts were interrupted by a flicker of movement at the door of the cell. Simon looked up and saw a shadowy figure on the other side of the barred window. It did not seem large enough to be the great beast Hulgar, or even the other clansman, Zhadu. The figure stood motionless outside the door, watching him.

"If that is you, Pasevalles, looking to see if I am dead yet, you will be disappointed to know I am not."

The shape did not move.

"So then, have you devised some new game? Enjoy it. I will not be playing." He pushed himself back against the wall, chains clanking and dragging.

The voice, when it came, was unfamiliar and spoke strangely. "You are the one called Seoman? King of this land?"

It must be another Thrithings-man, Simon decided. *Perhaps Pasevalles is selling glimpses of me to his minions for a silver-piece a peek.* "Go away, grasslander. You will get no pleasure from me. And tell your master I spit on him."

The one looking through the door moved a bit, but the flickering torchlight did not reveal any features Simon could recognize. "I ask again. Are you the one called Seoman? I have been sent to give news to him."

Something about the odd liquidity of the stranger's Westerling gave Simon pause. He sat up straighter. "Who are you?"

"Must I ask again? Are you the one called—"

"Seoman. Yes, that was the name I was given at birth. Who are you and what do you want?" What strange new misery had Pasevalles invented to torment him?

Now the newcomer turned to look back up the corridor, and in that instant the light caught his features. Simon did not know him, but he did know the stranger's kind. "Good God, you are a Sitha!"

"I am Zida'ya, yes. And if you are Seoman, I have a message for you from my *Hikka Staja*."

He had not heard the words for so long that it took him a moment to remember what they meant. "Your . . . arrow-bearer?"

"Yes. I owe this to him, so I am here. He sent me with a message for you."

"What? Who sent you? Who are you?"

His reply seemed almost grudging. "I was sent by Jiriki of the Sa'onserei clan to find King Seoman. My mother named me Yeja'aro."

Lillia was crawling in darkness. The small, round thing in her hand, the little magical lamp she had found, tried to help her by beginning to glow, but that was the last thing she wanted. She popped it in her mouth to try to make it stop, or at least hide it. It still glowed a little—she could see its gleam on the floor when she opened her mouth a tiny bit, so she closed her lips tight.

Her stomach was hurting, but she hadn't found anything to eat since the heel of bread, and all the passages seemed different since the last time she had left her hiding place, as if the underworld of the castle was changing around her. Was the red thing somehow making that happen? She could not stop thinking about the terrifying thing that kept trying to catch her.

Is it like one of those devils from my book about the saints?

She kept remembering a particular picture of a demon. It had worn a ragged red cloak, but its body and head had also been red. *Is that what's trying to catch me? Or is it a ghost?* Lillia had been trying to understand for a long time where all the dead people like her mother and grandmother went after they died. For a while, she had thought they might be hiding in the secret room Pasevalles visited. She had even wondered if that was what death was like, if it meant you just couldn't be with the people who loved you anymore, could only hear them and watch them through cracks in the wall. But now that she was lost beneath the castle, she was beginning to wonder whether all the dead people might not be hiding down here instead. She hadn't found her mother or grandmother, but she had heard strange voices whispering—sad voices, frightened voices—and a dreadful chill had passed right through her, as if someone had opened a window in her chest and let in a biting winter wind.

But all Lillia's wondering about dead people meant very little compared to the two things she had to think about all the time: she was so hungry she thought she might die soon, and she was being chased by a horrid phantom in a ragged red robe.

Or maybe it's not a robe at all, she thought suddenly. *Maybe that's the red thing's skin.* But that was too horrible a thought to linger on.

Her stomach growled again. Several times in the days since she had been trapped behind the door, she had come across trays with food on them, but she always left them alone, knowing that they were likely set there by the demon just to catch her. But to know that food was out there while she was starving was becoming more than she could bear.

I have to find something to eat. Even if I have to take it out of one of the red thing's traps.

It was painful to crawl for an hour over rough stone, and terrifying to make her way through utter darkness, never knowing when she might fall into a pit or tumble down a flight of stairs. It would have been different if she dared to use the little ball of light more, but she was terrified that she might give herself away to the thing that was hunting her. Instead, she kept the glassy sphere where she could always reach it quickly, sometimes in her mouth, sometimes in the bosom of her gown, but only used it for brief moments, clutched in her fist to keep most of the light shielded.

She did not want to think about what all the dirt and crawling had done to her dress. It was one of her favorites, with miniver on the cuffs, but now it had several holes and a tattered hem. Her poor, dead mother would have been horrified.

The passageway she was crawling through had seemed familiar, but it surprised her by turning at the end. Lillia could suddenly feel cooler air in front of her and decided she had to risk using the shining ball. She took it out of her mouth and gave it the smallest squeeze, then watched as it began to brighten in her fist until she could see the redness of her own flesh between the bones. The dim glow showed her that the passage was covered above by a cracked stone ceiling that ended when it met a broken archway. Beyond the arch the stone floor became dark earth, while the space above the passage was all shadow.

Lillia put the crystal globe back in her mouth and crept toward the arch. She paused just beyond it, where the ceiling ended, then stopped to listen as carefully as she could. When she did, she heard unusual sounds—not the whispery scrape she associated with the red thing but muffled steps, slow and cautious, directly in front of her. She spat the little globe back out, then wrapped her hand in her skirts and pushed back against the stone wall, ready to retreat. The noises grew louder. Lillia thought she could hear someone whispering, and her heart began to beat very fast.

A strong light was growing at the far end of the passage, bright enough to make her blink, even as the footsteps grew louder. For an instant, joy flooded her—*Someone is looking for me!*—but was replaced a moment later by a thought as frightening as the first had been exciting. *But it could be the red thing. Or something even worse.*

Two shapes came shuffling around the corner into the passageway, the first one carrying a torch, its light almost painfully bright to Lillia's eyes. Both figures seemed outsized and grotesque, and the leading shape walked strangely, dragging one leg. Even more disturbing, it was wrapped head to foot in thick cloth that covered all its head but for the eyes—even its hands looked lumpy and inhuman. The second figure was dressed the same way. Lillia lifted the globe and held it in front of her, heart pounding, uncertain whether to shine her light on the invaders or immediately scurry back down the passage.

The light flickered in her hand and the figure with the torch seemed to see her, for it stopped and lifted the torch.

"*Who is that?*" it demanded, voice muffled and strange.

Lillia shrieked despite herself, and the sphere in her hand suddenly burst into brilliant, glaring light, so bright that even the thing holding the torch cried out and took a staggering step backward. At the same moment, a heavy wall of wood dropped in front of her, blocking the passage between her and the two shrouded creatures. She turned and scrabbled away on her hands and knees, only to have another wooden barrier plunge down in front of her with a loud thump, trapping her between the two obstructions.

Lillia did not have even a moment to think before something dropped over her head from above and tightened around her neck and shoulders. She managed to get the fingers of one hand beneath the cord just before it closed on her throat. Something began trying to pull her upward, then her feet were off the ground and she was dangling, kicking helplessly.

Simon felt his first moment of relief in a long time. "Is this true?" he asked. "You come from Jiriki?"

"I told that," said the strange Sitha. "Do you not listen?"

"Oh, praise to the Highest! Thank Usires and His Father and His divine mother." Simon even moved toward the door, as though he were not shackled head and foot, but his chains brought him up well short. "Quick, there are keys hanging on a nail down the corridor. Bring them to me, please."

"I bring you a message from Jiriki i-Sa'onserei," the other said again, as though he were the one who was having trouble hearing. "I have come far and risked much to do so, mortal. Stop making noise and listen to me."

Simon stood, panting with excitement. "Yes, fine! But bring me the keys! I might have known it would be Jiriki. Thank God!"

"I do not know what you mean about keys. I am here to give you a message from Jiriki i-Sa'onserei, my *Hikka Staja*. His message is this—not long ago, during the Sky-Singer's Moon, Tanahaya of Shisae'ron found your grandson, Moor-Gan."

"Do you mean Morgan? Is he safe? Please, tell me he is safe."

The Sitha spoke flatly. "When Tanahaya spoke to Jiriki, your grandson was safe. He was traveling with her, though she is a scholar, and I doubt she is much use protecting him." He ruminated on this for a while. "It is too bad he did not find one of our people better trained in fighting. Like me."

Simon felt as though his heart had been half-turned to stone, but now had been cured by some magical spell and was becoming flesh and blood once more. "Ah, God is good," he said, ignoring Yeja'aro's afterthought. "Where is my grandson now?"

"Who can say?" The Sitha seemed impatient, as though Simon was failing to understand something important. "Your Moor-Gan was in Da'ai Chikiza with the scholar Tanahaya."

"Da'ai Chikiza?" The name filled Simon with sudden concern. He remembered the ruined city all too well. He and Binabik and Miri had been ambushed there when they had fled the Hayholt all those years ago; Binabik had been shot with an arrow and had almost died of his wounds. Later they had been menaced by a shaggy giant, and only the arrival of Josua's hunters had saved them from a grisly death. "But why is Morgan there? Why go to that old, dead place?"

Yeja'aro shook his head. Simon could barely see him—the torch was almost directly behind the Sitha—but he thought he saw something like disgust in the immortal's posture. "I know nothing of this. I had a duty to Jiriki. Now I have fulfilled part of it—if you are indeed Seoman the king." He backed away from the barred window in the door. " I must go next to complete my last errand for Likimeya's son, then my honor will be my own once more."

"Wait!" Simon all but shouted it. "You are not going, are you? Are you mad? I am Jiriki's friend. He would not want you to leave me here as a prisoner. A traitor has killed my wife and stolen my throne. All you need to do is give me the keys hanging at the other end of the corridor and I will be able to make things right again." But something was wrong about the entire exchange, something Simon could not understand. "Speak to me!"

The Sitha remained silent a long while, as if pondering Simon's words, but when he spoke, all he said was, "That is not my task. I did what Jiriki commanded me to do. By my White Arrow, which he holds, I was bound to do only that. 'Take this message to Seoman, King of Erkynland,' he told me, 'who lives in the castle where Asu'a once stood.' Jiriki said nothing to me about helping you or freeing you."

Simon could not believe his ears. "Are you saying you will walk away now and leave me chained here, just because Jiriki did not tell you to help me? The traitor Pasevalles will murder me and it will be your fault. Jiriki will be in a rage."

"I do not see how any of this could be my fault." Yeja'aro almost sounded insulted. "I did not put chains on you. I have not harmed you. I came and did as I was told. Now I must ride west to complete my last task for Year-Dancing House, then my honor will be regained."

"Honor! The Devil with your honor! Jiriki would want you to help me."

"It is not for me *or* you to decide what Jiriki would want." The Sitha might have been a magistrate, quickly handing down some gruesome sentence because he was in a hurry to get to his country estate. "I know what he told me. I have accomplished that. Beyond that, the Garden waits." He turned then and vanished from the opening in the door.

"No!" Simon shouted, not caring anymore that Pasevalles or one of his grasslander henchmen might hear him. "Don't leave. It would take you only a moment. Jiriki will never forgive you if you go without helping me! Don't you understand—they're going to kill me!"

His cry was followed by a long silence. Despair and disbelief crept over him. How could salvation be so close, yet turn its back on him this way? "Please!" he shouted. "If not for my sake, then for Jiriki's. And Aditu, his sister—she is my friend, too."

The continuing silence felt like a body blow. Simon sagged back against the wall, then slowly slid to the hay-matted floor. Something small squeaked and fled from beneath him, but he barely noticed it.

How could this be? To be so close—

A shadow appeared once more at the barred window. "I have considered what you say," the Sitha said. "You mortals think our people are monsters, things without soul. This I know. But we are not." He pushed his hand between the bars. "Take this. One way or another, it may save you." He flicked his wrist and something flew through the air, skidded on the floor, then landed a couple of steps from Simon's feet. "Now I return to my sworn task." He vanished from the window.

Desperate, elated, but confused—why had the keys made so little noise?—Simon dragged his chains to the place where the object had vanished into the damp straw, but it had landed a good half a pace beyond his reach. He stretched out on his side and extended one leg, probing as more small, live things scattered away through the muck, until at last his big toe touched something hard. He stretched a short, painful bit farther and got his foot behind it, then pulled it toward his hand.

It was a knife, he realized as his fingers closed around it. Baffled, he lifted it up to the thin light from the door. The handle was wrapped in shiny cord, but otherwise it was made from a single piece of witchwood a hand-span and a half long, incised with symbols.

Simon stared at it for a long time. He did not weep, though he felt as if he wanted to. To be so close to rescue, only to be left this way!

"One way or another, it may save you," the Sitha had said. *So at least I can take my own life. That's what he meant.*

It was better than nothing, he had to admit. But not very much.

36

A Distant Relative

"It truly is you." The gray-haired man with the eyepatch dropped to his knees before her. "May God strike me blind!"

"Do not risk the one eye you have left with such a careless oath," Miriamele cautioned him, but she was smiling. Baron Norvel had always been prone to elaborate curses and invocations.

He rose, though not without a moment's struggle. "This is a miracle worthy of Blessed Tankred himself! I was desperate sad when I heard you were lost, Majesty. Now that I see it was a terrible lie, my heart is full again." As if to prove what he said, a tear ran down one cheek.

"The story of my death was false, but it came from a cruel truth. Duchess Canthia of Nabban died in that carriage—not me. But I will give you the whole of the tale when we sit down to eat, Baron. For now, tell me, please, have we found ships?"

"Aye, right enough, Your Majesty. First things first, as I always say, though it is hard to stop looking at you. What a wonder! You have not aged since I saw you last, ten years gone, at . . . at the funeral."

"Not quite ten years, and I have most certainly aged, but I take the kindness as it was meant. I was very grateful to have you with me that day, my lord." In truth, though, when she recalled the day of John Josua's funeral, she could only ever remember Simon's shocked and helpless face. In her memory, the days and weeks and even months afterward were still blanketed in shadow, as though the sun had entirely ceased to shine during that time and she and Simon had stumbled in darkness.

"Aye, well, it seems I must again share my sorrow with you," said Norvel. "I have only just heard about the king and I am gutted by the news."

Miriamele thought she had armored herself, but every time someone mentioned Simon it felt like she was being kicked in the belly. She let out a long, shaky breath. "Thank you for your sympathy, my lord. It is . . . hard."

"Now tell me what is what, then. By the freckled paps of Saint Rhiappa, I hear that Lord Pasevalles has proved a traitor! Who would have thought? He seemed such an orderly man."

"Who told you about Pasevalles?" She turned to Dorret, the sick Earl's daughter. "I said that none of this was to be shared, not by message or gossip."

"Not a word of it came from me, Majesty," Dorret replied.

"Nay, nay, I heard it from the young viscount, Lord Dregan, after I arrived," said Norvel. "All Lady Dorret wrote was that I was needed most urgently at Prince's Hall, and by God's Bloody Wounds and Beating Heart, that was all I needed to know! I came right sharpish, and here I am."

"I am grateful. Lady Dorret, *please* remind your brother the need for secrecy is real. Now, Baron, what about ships?"

"We have impressed three merchant cogs in the harbor, Majesty. We think we can put as many as two hundred men on each, since it is a short journey up the river to Erchester and the Hayholt and they will not have to be so crowded for long."

"But do we even have six hundred men?" she asked.

"In truth, my count comes closer to five hundred than six," Norvel admitted. "If we could wait a little longer—"

"I wish I could," said Miriamele. "But the usurper has my granddaughter and perhaps my grandson as well. I do not want to give him an extra moment. That is why we are taking ship and going up the Gleniwent instead of marching. I want to come down on Pasevalles like a thunderbolt."

"By Saint Algor's shriveled hand, I like the thrust of your thought, Majesty!" Norvel crowed, his ruddy face glowing with excitement. He was well past his prime, but he was one of the few southern nobles she knew well and trusted; planning to retake the kingdom with someone she could trust seemed more important to her than it ever had before. "But we are a fair small thunderbolt, it must be said."

"Does this traitor Pasevalles truly command the Hayholt?" asked Lady Dorret. "Most rumors say that Duke Osric holds it until the heir, Prince Morgan, returns."

"If Osric truly has the throne," said Miriamele, "then all the better for us. The Osric I know would never try to take the crown from his own grandchildren. But remember, the same rumors say the duke was badly wounded at Winstowe, so we cannot be certain of anything. The usurper has planned this for a long time. Until I sit on the throne myself, or our heirs do, not a single word out of the Hayholt can be trusted." In her heart, though, she prayed that at least one piece of the story was true—that Pasevalles did not yet have Morgan in his power.

"When do we move against him?" young Dregan asked. Dorret's brother had appeared in the doorway in his martial finery, looking as though he planned to lead the assault on the Hayholt himself. Miriamele shuddered at the thought.

"Let us go down to eat," she suggested. "Baron Norvel has ridden far and is no doubt hungry. We will discuss our plans afterward."

★ ★ ★

Even with the gathering limited to Durward's family and close retainers—but not the earl himself who, as always, took his meals alone in his bedchamber—Miriamele wanted to minimize the chance for loose tongues to give anything away. She led the conversation, inquiring about various Meremund nobles, and the others dutifully followed her lead. Baron Norvel, overjoyed at the queen's return, drank too much and fell asleep, chin on chest, even before the pastry was brought in.

Miri looked askance at the monstrous honey-cake, which could have easily fed a small parish. "What have you told your household?" she asked Lady Dorret.

The earl's daughter leaned close. "That one of my father's distant relatives escaped from the chaos of Nabban and is staying with us for a short while. Only my own servants will wait on you, and do not fear—they will keep the secret. I chose them for their discretion and loyalty."

"I do not doubt you did." Miri had already decided that Dorret was the most sensible person in Prince's Hall. "I am going to my chambers. Will you see that Norvel is helped to bed?"

"Of course," said Dorret. "He is like a dear uncle to me. When I was a child, he used to bring me toys he had carved himself."

Miri laughed. "The same for me! Although I could never tell exactly what animals they were supposed to be."

Dorret shook her head. "He was never a very good carver, but he has an excellent heart."

"Just so. When you have seen off the rest of the company, will you come to my chambers so we may speak privately, just the two of us?" She looked at Jesa, who had sat quietly and even apprehensively through the meal, holding baby Serasina as if someone might try to snatch the child away. "The three of us, rather. Jesa needs to be part of this as well."

Dorret raised one eyebrow, but then immediately smoothed the curiosity from her face. "Of course, Majesty. I will knock thrice, like this." And she squeezed Miriamele's hand once, then twice more in rapid succession.

"Good." Miri stretched, feigned a yawn, then stood. "I thank you all," she said to those at the table, "but the time has come for rest. It has been a wearying day."

"Let us toast the queen!" said young Dregen.

"No, please, it is not necessary," Miri told him, but there was no stopping him as he climbed to his feet and lifted his cup.

"*The queen!* Thanks be to God for giving her back to us!" Dregen cried, and the others present echoed him. *"The queen!"*

Now every servant within earshot will have heard that, Miri thought. *And I should have seen it coming. I truly am tired, but that's when the worst mistakes are made.*

Even though he had not lived in the St. Sutrin's Cathedral dormitories for many years, the habits Brother Etan had learned as an acolyte still ruled him. Though he was imprisoned in one of the Hayholt residence's less luxurious bedchambers on the orders of Lord Pasevalles, he still rose before sunrise each day to say his prayers.

Most of the prayers he had memorized from the *Librin Horas* were pleas for peace and Heaven's grace, but after several days of confinement and meager meals, the monk's thoughts were tending toward vengeance, and he chose the more militant prayers from the *Sacranai* for his meditation instead.

Yea, and we were held down in those days by jealous hands,

By ungodly hearts

And could not find our voices to pray

And yet You gave us back our tongues to speak, our hearts to sing Your praises, when Your Song had been stolen from out of our mouths.

Just as it was You, O Lord, Who once cast down the walls of Khand and made of that evil place a wasteland,

And as it was You, O Lord, who sent Your Son to speak unto us the truth of Your Love and ransom our souls.

Now a shadow stands upon our hearts again, and our song is silenced, for an evil man has tried to spite your name by murdering the hope of the world . . .

He broke off, distracted by the clatter of horses' hooves on the cobblestones outside his prison-chamber. Etan drew a chair to the window and stood on it, peering down to the courtyard far below. A group of mounted men were gathered there, and though they wore the livery of Pasevalles' barony in Hewenshire, Etan did not think they looked much like the Hewenshiremen he had met—several had tattooed arms that made them look more like grasslanders than men of Erkynland. It was true that a few Erkynlandish nobles hired Thrithings mercenaries for their personal guard, but it seemed odd that Pasevalles would do so when the lands he had been gifted by the king and queen lay so far west of the wild grasslands.

Whatever the Lord Chancellor may say, I cannot believe that Tiamak and Lady Thelía have turned traitor—it goes against all that I know of them. Tiamak loved King Simon like a brother. I can only pray that Pasevalles discovers the truth soon. And on that day, I too will be free once more.

He had turned from the window and its cold breeze, determined to finish his prayers, when he heard a noise—*paff*!—from just outside the window. He went back and saw a mass of pale fluff lying on the stones below, surrounded by a strew of small white dots. Had someone thrown a snowball at his window and missed? He looked up, but though the roofs all had a dusting of white along their peaks, there did not seem to be enough for anyone to be making missiles of it. And who would have thrown it? The riders who had assembled below were already on their way across the inner bailey toward the gate, the iron-shod hooves of their horses clock-clocking on the stones. As he wondered idly where these dozen or so armored men might be going, and if Lord Pasevalles was with them, something flew in through the window and past his face, making him start in surprise.

The bird, for that was what it was, flew madly from wall to wall, but did not seem to be merely looking for a way out. Instead, it dashed itself over and over against the walls, sometimes tumbling to the floor, only to leap up again and continue its reckless flight around the room.

Brother Etan watched, faintly sickened. *It seems more intent on bashing out its brains than escaping, poor thing.*

The bird struck the wall one last time and fell. This time it did not rise again.

Etan picked it up. The pigeon's neck was broken, the warmth already leaving its battered little body. He set it on the pitted oak table, which, along with the narrow bed and one stool, constituted all of his furniture, then he returned to the window to see if he could puzzle out what had caused the bird to behave so strangely. Two or three more motionless snowball-shapes had joined the first, and he realized that they were all of them dead birds. Even as he watched, another darting shape appeared from the north beyond Erchester, a peregrine falcon, and flew unevenly until it hurtled against the high roof of the building across the courtyard from his window and plummeted down to the courtyard stones.

Stunned, Etan looked out in the direction from which the last bird had come. A band of smeared gray covered the northern horizon, as though a great fire burned there, obscuring the boundary between Earth and Heaven with smoke. But it lay too close to the ground to be smoke, as though a liquid thunderstorm had been poured from a jar like an offering of wine to some pagan god.

Etan's heart went cold and the hairs on his neck and arms stood up. *What is that coming toward us,* he wondered. *Surely that darkness is nothing earthly. Surely it is something to be feared.*

He went and pounded on the locked door of his room, but nobody answered. "Hoy!" he shouted. "Can anybody else see what I can see? Hoy! Something is coming from the north!" But nobody answered him.

Powerless to do anything else, he returned to the threadbare rug beside his bed and began once more to pray.

The queen's outer chamber was lit with so many candles that Jesa thought everyone else in Prince's Hall must be sitting in darkness. She looked down at Serasina, wondering whether the room might be too bright. The baby had fallen asleep right after being fed and could have been put in a cot, but Jesa was feeling anxious and wanted the child near. Beside them, Miriamele wore a look that Jesa recognized: the queen's mind was on larger, more important things even as she made small talk with Lady Dorret and young Lord Dregan.

"So," Miriamele said. "Now that we are alone, we can speak of important matters. Lord Norvel said that he had located enough ships to take a fighting force to Erchester. But where will we find the fighters themselves?"

Dorret looked worried, but Dregen spoke up immediately. "We will find them, Your Majesty, never fear."

Miriamele turned to Dorret. The queen said nothing, but it was clear to Jesa she wanted the young woman's opinion.

"I expect my brother is right, Majesty," Dorret said. "But it may take some time to find them. We sent our best fighters to Winstowe."

"I am not as concerned about numbers as I am about delay," said Miriamele. "We would need far more men than we can gather to besiege the Hayholt in any case—it is a strong fortress. All we need is enough shields and spears around us to prevent treachery before we can make ourselves known to the people. I cannot imagine that Pasevalles will be able to keep the throne when our subjects find out I am still alive."

"Norvel said the ships could hold six hundred soldiers," Dregen said.

"But he doubted he could find more than five hundred," replied Miriamele. "So, with a few score more to be found, and the ships being refitted, when can we head north?" Miriamele asked.

Dorret looked to her brother, but he clearly did not have a figure to offer. "Perhaps a sennight, Majesty," she suggested.

Miriamele nodded. "Good. We dare not wait much longer than that. When we have fitted out the ships, we will sail as far as Storm Cove, a league south of the Erchester docks. From there, we will be able to discover what is happening at the Hayholt—perhaps even send a few men in disguise to find out who is in the castle beside Pasevalles. If we could get a message to Osric telling him I live, it might mean we do not have to fight at all. Pasevalles could be arrested quietly and easily."

"If Duke Osric is not a traitor, too," said Dregen.

Jesa thought the queen was going to say something sharp to him, but by the time she spoke her voice was calm. "Osric has always been loyal to our family. I trust him with my life. And do not forget, he has been badly wounded and probably knows little of what has actually happened."

Young Dregen quickly said, "Of course, Your Majesty. I meant no slander against the duke. But you trusted this Pasevalles, too."

The queen nodded. "That is true. And I am doing my best to learn from that lesson. You are correct, my lord—we can take nothing for granted these days. Nothing."

Dregen looked relieved.

"But what of the talk of the fairies—the White Foxes?" asked Dorret. "Is it true they are in Erkynland now?"

Listening, Jesa felt her skin prickle. So many dangers, but waiting behind them all, these creatures out of fearful legend—!

"That is one reason I wish to act quickly," Miriamele admitted. "All we know for certain is that the Norns attacked Naglimund and captured it. They seem to have a strange connection to the place, so I can only hope that alone was what they wanted—although I doubt it. But we can hope that at least they will stay there until we have dealt with the usurper Pasevalles. As it is, we can barely gather enough soldiers to play a game of town ball—we dare not split our forces."

"And who will lead our army?" Dregen asked. "After all, Lord Norvel could not even stay awake—"

"The baron was celebrating my unexpected return," Miriamele pointed out, quietly but firmly. "He is a good man. When I was a girl, I thought him the most amusing man in Meremund. I did not understand his true depths, his true worth." The queen folded her hands in her lap. "Now we come to other matters—things that can be put off no longer."

Despite herself, Jesa pulled sleeping Serasina a little closer. How could she dare to argue with the queen? But she did not want to be left behind in a strange place.

"I have thought long and hard," Miriamele began. "Lord Dregen, I know you wish to go to war. But I cannot let you."

"But Majesty—!"

She held up her hand. "Your bravery honors you and your family. But after only Erchester and the Hayholt, Meremund is the heart of our kingdom. Your father is ill—no, let us be truthful here. The earl is dying."

"There is hope," said Lady Dorret, but Jesa thought the young woman only partly believed it herself.

"Perhaps. But what if the fight to take back the throne becomes a wider war? We do not know what mischief Pasevalles has done over the years as he hid like a viper in our midst. We do not know how many of those we thought loyal he might have bribed or threatened into supporting him. I cannot leave Meremund with only your ailing father to rule it."

Dregen's face was flushed. "Dorret will still be here. She already makes most of the decisions."

His sister shook her head. "All rulers need advisers, Dregen. But yours is the final say while Father is ill."

"A wise leader listens to wise counselors," the queen told him. "I do not doubt Lady Dorret wants what is best for you and the earldom. But in any case, my mind is made up. I need you both here so that I need not fear for Meremund. And if the fight with Pasevalles goes badly at first, I will need a place of safety waiting. Prince's Hall and the city held out even against King Tethtain. It has a long history of scorning usurpers."

Young Dregen looked as though he might argue more, but his sister caught his eye. After a moment, he bowed his head. "As you say, Your Majesty."

"Then that is well," Miriamele said. "I bid you both goodnight, and again I thank you for your fidelity, Lord Dregen and Lady Dorret. Meremund is in good hands." She rose to accept their farewells, then turned to Jesa. "Come with me, my lady. I would talk to you before you put the baby to bed."

Jesa felt her heart grow heavy in her breast.

When they reached the bedchamber, the queen sat down on the edge of the bed and let out a deep sigh. "Please, help me take off these monstrous, heavy clothes."

Jesa could not bear to wait any longer. "Of course, Majesty. But first I must say some things. I ask for your pardon, but I do not want to stay in this place." The words came tumbling out. "I know you mean to leave little Serasina here, and I see the wisdom in this. But . . . oh! Queen Miriamele, I have had so much worry!"

The queen gave her an odd look. "Tell me what is troubling you, Jesa."

"You know—you must know. You want to leave the child here, where she is safe. But you know I cannot bear to leave her. So you think you must leave me here too, to watch over her." She stopped to take a breath, her heart racing. "I do not speak the Westerling tongue so well. Forgive me. But I have had dreams, many dreams, and always in them I take Serasina and run away. Run back to the Wran. I know it is wicked, a crime against the trust you and her mother both gave to me, but these are my dreams and they come every night! I am full of sorrow. I do not want to leave her, but I do not want to leave you either, because you have been good to me. And I do not want to stay in this strange place. It . . ." She took a deep breath, trying to calm her pounding heart. "It is very hard to say this. Serasina means very much to me—but so do you, Queen Miriamele. I know you mean to leave us behind. I would not run away with the baby, not after all the kindness you have given me, but I do not know what else to do."

Jesa stood before the queen, chest heaving. She felt a pain inside her, as though something important had come loose, and she was frightened to have said so much, to have told the queen about her traitorous dreams.

"Oh, my dear," said Miriamele at last. "I wondered why you have been so quiet. Did you really think I would leave you behind? You saved my life. You saved little Serasina's life. Of course you must go with me."

"But I cannot leave—"

"You cannot leave the baby—you will not. I know that. By the Sacred Mother Elysia, how could I not know that? No, you will both come with me." She raised her hand, even as Jesa swayed in ecstatic disbelief, her knees suddenly weak. "But you will not come to the Hayholt with me, not at first, because only the good God knows what we will find there. No, when we dock in Storm Cove, you and the little one will stay in the village there, guarded and safe, until I call for you. Do you understand? And do you agree?"

"Yes, Majesty." Jesa could breathe now. At last, she could breathe.

"Good. Then please put the baby down and help me out of this foul dress. I don't know who wore it last, but she must have been as slender as a needle—it is squeezing the life out of me."

Duke Osric was wrapped in bandages from just below his neck to the bottom of his ribcage. Only an hour before, the bandages had been white as the snow falling outside, but a flower of blood had bloomed through the linen for each time he had tried to rise and failed—three blossoms in all.

"God curse this nonsense!" He fell back again. "What did that traitor-woman do to me?"

Porto winced. "Please, Your Grace, stop trying to get out of bed. Whatever else they may be saying about her and her husband, I think Lady Thelía tended you well."

"I will go mad. It is like being wound up in a shroud and laid in my coffin while I still live. I cannot even lift my arms!" As if to prove it, the duke tried once more to reach above his head to where a holy Tree hung on the wall. The effort was useless—his shoulders had been bound as well. Porto guessed it had been an attempt to keep him from opening the wound, but that precaution too was being overmatched by Osric's stubbornness and fury. "I cannot lie here like a butchered beeve. The king is dead—the poor queen is dead too! My grandson and granddaughter have both been taken from me, and treachery is all around. I cannot lie here helpless!" A few flecks of spittle landed on his beard and trembled there like sea foam blown onto the deck of a ship. "And what are you doing, you sad-eyed old Nabbanai tent pole?" he demanded of Porto. "You do nothing but tell me, 'Lie down, milord, lie down' like a be-damned nursemaid."

"Because the more you try to get up, the more you make yourself bleed," Porto replied as calmly as he could, but he did not manage to keep his tone entirely free of irritation. He had not been looking forward to this posting, but it was proving even less rewarding than he had guessed. "And you have scared off all the maids who should be tending you. Now lie down and stop heaving about like a speared whalefish, Your Grace, before you make yourself bleed to death."

Something in Porto's voice finally caught the duke's attention. He stared at the knight for a moment, and his face fell a little. "I am making an ass of myself. That is what you think, don't you?"

"I would not have put it that way, Your Grace, but these fits of temper are not helping your recovery. And I may be tall as a tent pole, but I am not from Nabban. I am Perdruinese."

"God save us," said Osric. "Don't take offense, man. I am hurting, and I am tired of being a prisoner of maids and healers. And all the thunder gets into my ears and makes my skin crawl. I wish that cursed storm would hurry up and do whatever it's going to do."

Porto could not argue with him on that count. Since he had risen with first light that morning, the approaching storm could be felt everywhere and every moment. The air was tight and surprisingly warm for Novander, and the low murmur of distant thunder seemed continuous, like some huge beast growling and pacing just outside. "I understand, Your Grace. We are all made uneasy. But storms come and go. The threats we face are real, and—I beg your pardon, my lord Duke—we need you hale and whole. So please, I beg you, lie still and try to rest."

"If I must. But fetch Zakiel to me. I can at least learn something of the state of our defenses."

Porto stifled a sigh. The state of the defenses was not good, as Osric and, in fact, almost everyone in the Hayholt already knew. Few of the projects that Lord Chancellor Pasevalles had sworn to finish had been completed before his departure from the castle.

Porto took his leave of the duke, then spent an infuriating stretch of time trying to find one of the maids to watch over him. He was successful at last, although the poor thing looked like she might bolt the first time Osric started shouting.

"You don't have to answer him," Porto told her. "If you're frightened, just stay out of his reach and let him bellow. I'll be back soon enough."

The young maid shook her head, eyes wide. "But the things he says, my lord—!" She shuddered.

"Duke Osric is a proud man," said Porto. "He wants to do his duty to the castle and the throne. Be a little understanding." He patted her arm, then turned to go. "Sing him a song or two," he called over his shoulder.

"But I do not sing well," the maid said.

"Neither do I. But in any case, he will find you more pleasant to look at than me, so sing. And try not to let him frighten you. He will do you no harm."

Porto found Lord Captain Zakiel on the top of Holy Tree Tower, looking out across the middle and outer baileys at a sea of people crowding their way through the Nearulagh Gate.

"All the folk of Erchester are trying to get in," said Zakiel. "Damn these rumors and whispers. How are we going to feed them all?"

"Look to the north, my lord." Porto was still struggling for breath after climbing so many stairs. "Do you think it is only rumors that have frightened them?"

"It is only a storm," said Zakiel, his face even more grim than usual. "Surely they can face it just as well in Erchester. What better defense will castle walls provide against bad weather than city walls? No, they are behaving foolishly, and we cannot take them all in. It endangers the safety of the castle itself. I will send more men to the gate to keep them out."

"But isn't that the point of a castle?" Porto asked. "To provide shelter for the people in times of war?"

"Not when there are more people than we can feed." Zakiel looked around, then finally saw some of his Erkynguards sheltering in the lee of the tower's capital. He called one over and the man put his head down and hurried across to him as if facing a deadly flight of arrows. The sound of the wind was so loud that Zakiel had to lean close to the soldier's ear and shout his orders.

Porto's gaze drifted to the Kynswood, the dark mass of trees, barely visible under a blanket of streaming mist, and then toward the downs beyond Erchester, which lay under an even deeper pall of gray nothingness. It was a strange storm, there was no question of that. It had arisen the night before, but was still huddled on the downs north of the castle, invisible except as a deeper darkness painted across the bottom of the sky. Porto thought it should have reached them by now, even passed over the Hayholt and spent itself to the south. Instead, its winds had been hurling flurries of snow and darts of hard sleet against the castle walls all day, but the storm itself had stayed in one place, crouching like a beast while its thunders rolled on and on across the sky, as if the smithies of Heaven were working all the hours God gave. Now, with twilight coming on quickly and the sun utterly hidden, Porto felt a moment of strong, superstitious unease. It seemed very strange that the wind blew so powerfully but the bank of dark cloud still hovered in the distance, like something that resisted the winds instead of traveling with them. *Surely that is unnatural*, he thought, but then was distracted as Zakiel dismissed the soldier and gestured for Porto to come nearer.

"I do not like this," the captain said. "It feels like more than bad weather. And the thunder—the thunder! It never stops. I can scarcely think." He stared out at the horizon, squinting against the wet, cold wind. "And now we will have riots in front of the gate. Damn those fools, why don't they—" He fell silent and stayed that way.

"Lord Captain?"

Zakiel's face seemed to have lost its hard edges, as though the shrieking winds had scoured them away. And he had gone pale, pale as ice, pale as bone. "I do not think that is thunder at all," he said.

Porto did not think he had heard him correctly. "What do you say?"

Zakiel leaned toward him and put a hand on Porto's shoulder. It was an odd gesture from the taciturn, nerveless captain, and it became odder still when Porto realized that Zakiel's hand was trembling.

"I sent my wife away," he said into Porto's ear. "I could not bear to see her mewed up like a beast, and I thought there was a chance the castle would be besieged." He spoke like someone in a dream, his words slow and hard to hear over the storm. "I sent her away."

"That was a good idea," said Porto, raising his voice. "I hope you are not regretting it." It was hard to believe that Captain Zakiel could be a-quiver with sentimentality, but Porto could find no other explanation. "If I still had my wife and child, I would send them somewhere safe as well."

Zakiel shook his head. "But now I fear I will never see them again."

"What do you mean by that? Captain, are you ill?" Zakiel's face had gone white as a split root. Porto thought the man might be having a deadly fit, like the one that had taken poor King Simon. "Captain, speak to me! What is wrong?"

"The thunder," the captain said in a strange, doomful voice. "I can hear it better now. Can you not hear it, Porto?"

"Of course," he shouted over the wind. "It has been deafening me all day!"

"No, can you not hear the steady beat? Can you not hear it—*bom-ba-bom-ba-bom-ba-bom*?"

For a moment Porto was certain that whatever had struck Zakiel had crippled the captain's wits as well. But as he reached down to take the captain's elbow and lead him toward the stairs, he suddenly noticed what Zakiel had already heard—a rhythm in the inescapable rumbling, buried deep, but steady as a heartbeat. The wind shrieked and then grew quieter, and in that long moment of comparative silence, Porto could at last hear it clearly.

Bom. Ba-bom. Ba-bom. Ba-bom. Ba-bom.

"What is that?" To his own ears, his voice sounded like a fretful child's. "I have never heard anything like it."

"Yes, you have," Zakiel said. The color seemed to have leached from his features, so that for a moment Porto could almost believe it was the captain's ghost that stood beside him, not a living man. "You must have—you went north with Duke Isgrimnur, did you not?"

"Drums." Porto's innards were like ice. "May the Ransomer save us, I do hear them now. Those are Norn war-drums."

Lord Captain Zakiel suddenly bolted toward the stairs. For an instant Porto thought the constable had abandoned him in terror, but then he heard the faint sounds of Zakiel's voice as he hurried down the steps, calling out for the Erkynguard.

"The White Foxes are coming! *To arms! The Norns are here!"*

The captain's retreating voice was swallowed up by the shriek of wind and the now-unmistakable, growing clamor of drums—hundreds of them, beating, beating, beating in the impenetrable darkness of the storm.

37

The Boiler

Something seemed to have changed between the two of them. When Morgan woke, gray morning light filled the sliver of space where they had sheltered beneath the jutting stone, and Nezeru was still wrapped in his arms. He was surprised to see she was already awake; for a moment, they only stared at each other.

"I feel we should get up," she said at last, "though in truth I do not know what we should do." She peered past his arm at the deep mist that surrounded their hiding place. "Is it always as thick as this?"

"I was only in the valley for an hour or two the first time," he said, relishing the feel of her body against his, reluctant for their intertwining to end. "But I never saw anything else."

"We must make a plan." But she still did not pull away. Nezeru almost seemed to want to be talked out of leaving their meager shelter, which did not seem too surprising after their near-fatal encounter with the ogre.

Morgan pressed his face against her neck. Her hair smelled of pine sap. "What plan can we make?" he asked. "You wanted to come here. I told you what it was like."

She stiffened, and for a moment he thought she would say something angry or push him away, but she did neither. "I have already said that I misjudged your tale, Morgan. I was wrong. It does me no harm to admit that. The Order of Sacrifice did not teach me to hold on to my ideas after they have been proved wrong. And, in truth, I do not know what to do, either." She was silent for a long time. Morgan listened to her breathe and wondered at finding himself in a world where he embraced a white-faced fairy as they hid from a monster big as church tower.

"Are you truly a prince?" she asked.

He laughed a little. "Yes. That was also true." He took a breath, aware that he was stepping off familiar ground, however dangerous, and into a new country where he had never been. "My father was the son of High King Simon and High Queen Miriamele of Erkynland. Yes, I truly am a prince."

"And I have led you to this terrible valley," she said. "We must trust each other, it seems, and completely. Tell me the whole of your story, and I will tell you mine."

Their tales took no little time to relate, and though the mists lay so thick in the vale that it was hard to know for certain, by the time he had told Nezeru about all his travels and she had done the same, the invisible sun seemed to have risen high in the sky. Both had been surprised by parts of the other's revelations—he perhaps more than she, since he had told her his greatest secret already.

They had not made love again—or "coupled," as Nezeru would have it—but some barrier between them had clearly fallen with her escape from the shadowy ogre. For Morgan, only the smallest sliver of his earlier caution remained. That quiet voice could not be silenced completely—this woman, this *girl*, was still one of the White Foxes, ancient enemies of his people, and could conceivably be tricking him, somehow—but Morgan could no longer make himself believe that.

"Where did your mother come from?" he asked. "Was she born a slave?"

Nezeru shook her head. "I did not pay as much heed as I should have to what she told me of her early life." Her face was solemn, sad. "She was a mortal. I was ashamed of that, so I clung to my father's high station. *I am the daughter of a magister,* I told myself, never *I am the daughter of a mortal slave.* I believe she came from Rimmersgard, where she lived in a community of women, but she once said something of your Erkynland as well." She made the wriggling, serpentine gesture he now recognized as a helpless shrug, an admission of mistakes made. "I should have learned more."

They were lying side by side, wedged so deeply into the small, slanted space that if Morgan sat straight he would crack his head against the shelf of stone. He could hear water gurgling somewhere beyond their shelter but could not tell if it was a nearby stream or the Narrowdark River down on the valley floor. "I think we must all wish we had listened better and understood more." He frowned. "That thought has certainly nagged at me many times since I escaped into the forest."

"Do you miss your father?"

"Of course—or at least what he used to be. In his last months he was very angry and grim. My mother was carrying my sister in her belly, and I heard him murmur, "I pray she is born dead."

Nezeru remained silent for no little time. Morgan was lost in memory, so he was a little startled when she said, "My people understand regret better than we understand ourselves."

"What do you mean?"

She turned on her side and placed her hand on his chest. Just the touch set him tingling, but this intimacy seemed to betoken more than lust, something much larger and more mysterious. "I think," she finally said, "that I am waking up."

Her features were so delicate and so strange, her eyebrows pale enough to be almost invisible, her eyes so dark that they seemed a door into unknowable depths. And yet she was only his age! "I still don't understand," he said. "Waking up?"

She ran her fingers over the curved plates of his Norn armor. "In Nakkiga, the queen is our sun and moon. Everything is given by her, and everything is done for her. She is the Mother of All. We owe her everything." Her voice had fallen into a rhythm that sounded like a recitation. Nezeru may have noticed it too; when she spoke again, it was in a more ordinary way. "At every step, from childhood to death, we are told to ask one question—*What would best serve the queen*? And if laying down your life is the answer to that question, then you lay down your life. We Sacrifices are the greatest example, of course. It is in our name.

"But it is not only the nobles and the members of the higher orders who owe the queen their lives," she went on. "Every child of the mountain belongs to her from birth—that is why we call her the Mother of All. And the price to be one of the queen's children is very high. Any infant born with a taint of any kind, any flaw, is taken away before the mother even sees it. The philosopher Yedade, the one who created the Box by which children are judged and selected for one order or another, taught the healers what to look for—the signs of an 'unhelpful child,' as they are called. And when the Healer's Order declares a newborn 'unhelpful,' that one is removed. We are not a sentimental people. We all know that means they are killed. And that too seemed to me merely a way to keep the race strong, to best serve the queen. If I had looked less like a Hikeda'ya and more like my mother, I likely would not have been allowed to live, either."

She was talking faster now, as if she traveled through a place she wanted to leave as quickly as possible. "During my childhood in the order, such things seemed beyond questioning. Keep the race strong. Remove the flawed, the crippled, and the witless. Only then could Nakkiga and the queen take back the world that was stolen from us.

"But since I have been out of Nakkiga—I could never have dreamed there was so much world outside the mountain!—I have begun to see things I never knew existed, and to have new thoughts. Disturbing thoughts." Her hand slid down from his chest to find Morgan's own hand, which she clasped in her chill fingers. "Some of that is because of the mortal I told you of—Jarnulf, curse his name! Before he stole me from my Talon and made me an outcast, he always asked me questions, forced me to defend what I believed. But some of his questions I could never answer."

"What kind of questions?"

She sighed. It sounded no different to Morgan than the sound any regretful mortal would make. "The most hurtful—and the most potent—were about my own place in our undertaking. Why had I, among so many Sacrifices, been chosen as a Queen's Talon, and for such an important mission? I had scarcely finished my training in the order when the command came. I was skilled, yes, but I had no experience in the world outside our mountain, and yet I was sent with a hand-picked company to distant places no other Hikeda'ya had ever seen. We found the bones of legendary Hakatri, and captured a dragon alive on the peak of a snowy mountain! The things Jarnulf asked angered me, but in the dark of night, when I lay trying to sleep, they came back to me again and again. Why me, indeed? There were dozens of Sacrifices more experienced, dozens with lists of accomplishments that dwarfed mine."

He felt an urge to defend her. "You are more than skilled. I saw you fight. You are terrifying."

"Thank you, Prince Morgan." She almost smiled. "Do you see? I have learned to believe you. But if you think I am a fearsome fighter, you should have seen Makho, our Hand chieftain, before he was crippled and burned by a dragon's blood. He was one of the younger leaders, but everyone in our order knew of his deadly skill. No, after the mortal questioned me about it, I could not find anything to explain it. My father is a high noble, but of the Builder's Order, which to the warriors of the Order of Sacrifice is no better than being a Harvester or of some other mean order. Even my father's magistracy would not have earned me a place in a Queen's Talon, let alone in one with such important tasks. So Jarnulf was right, I came to realize—I did not belong on such an important mission. I just had not wanted to think about it before he forced me to confront it."

"But you did everything the queen wanted," Morgan pointed out. "You succeeded in your tasks."

"Yes, we succeeded. But I still do not understand why I was chosen, and I do not think I ever will."

Moved by a sudden sympathy, Morgan squeezed her hand. She looked at their two hands for a moment, puzzlement obvious on her face. *Do they not take each other's hands in Nakkiga?* he wondered. Then she folded her fingers around his.

"I prattle like a child," she said. "We cannot stay here. We have no food, and it is plain the valley floor is not safe. Let us find a place to cross the river, then we can climb up the slope on the far side and look for better shelter."

Morgan had not fully remembered the strangeness of this place Tanahaya had named Misty Vale and Nezeru called *Tanakirú*, but as they made their way downhill toward the invisible line of the river, he was quickly reminded. The plants along the slow-moving Narrowdark seemed to have been leached of color. Much of what should have been green even at this time of year was gray or black instead. Even the few flowers he saw were pale, ghostly things that sagged like wet linen.

"Some of these trees and plants remind me of stories I have heard," said Nezeru. "Of things that grew in the Lost Garden and the mountains around it. But that cannot be. Still, it is an odd, uncomfortable place."

Morgan guessed they must be several leagues north of the spot where he had first approached the valley with ReeRee and her tree-dwelling troop. The steep slate cliffs that had kept him on the ground while the more nimble Chikri had left him behind were supplanted here by high, uneven limestone walls, like crumbling, abandoned fortresses standing shoulder to shoulder. The mists were so thick along the hill slope that it was hard to see these cliffs even from only a few dozen paces away, but Morgan still felt as if eyes might be watching them from both sides of the gorge, and he began to worry about Norn patrols as much as about the ogre.

Once Nezeru stopped abruptly. Motioning him to be silent, she pointed back up the slope. Morgan stared into the gray swirl until a stag appeared from the fog and stood looking down at them. It was altogether ordinary except that it only had a single antler sprouting from the center of its forehead and trailing over its back like a leafless bush. Just seeing it made Morgan's stomach clutch.

"How strange," Nezeru said when it had vanished into the mists once more.

"Wait until you see the salamanders."

The descent was steep, and in many places dangerous, but at last they reached the riverbank. The Narrowdark flowed smooth as a stream of quicksilver. It was wide here, too, an arrowshot across, and surrounded on both banks by the sickly cattails he had seen his first time in the valley.

"You're not planning to use that same river-crossing trick as before, are you?" he asked, staring at the sluggish, opaque water. "Because I'm not going to swing on a rope over that. It looks like poison."

She shook her head. "It is too wide for that. We must find a place where we can cross it some other way—preferably without getting wet, because I do not like the look of it either."

The sun had dropped behind the valley's western wall and the light was fading. They avoided the muddy bank and made their way across drier land higher up the slope, following the Narrowdark's snaking course northward up the gorge.

They were lucky: less than half a league onward they found a great ash tree that had fallen across a narrow spot in the river to form a natural bridge. It had toppled recently enough that its roots were still thickly covered in dark, loamy soil; black winter buds that looked like the hooves of tiny deer sprouted from its branches. Nezeru immediately sprang onto the trunk and began walking across. Morgan almost called out to her to wait for him, but his pride silenced him.

She is my same age. I have been living in trees for months. If I cannot manage to walk a tree trunk as broad as my waist, I belong in the river.

But the diamond-patterned bark of the ash was more slippery than he had expected, and when he reached the middle a pall of stinking mist swirled up from the river and all but blinded him. He could barely see his own feet, and the uneven weight of the sword on his back and his bag tied to his belt suddenly made everything feel precarious. As he stopped, waiting for the worst of the murk to billow past, he made the mistake of looking down. A large, shiny something breached the dark, sluggish water below him, wide as a harbor dolphin but shaped like an eel, long and smooth. A moment later it slipped under again. His legs suddenly wobbly, Morgan crouched and held onto the damp, slick bark of the trunk as he fought a moment of dizziness.

"Morgan?" It was not a shout but a quiet call. He rose to his feet and began inching forward, spreading his arms for balance. The Narrowdark beneath him looked more like one of Erchester's sewers than a forest river, with an oily sheen and writhing streaks of black and gray like the flourishes in an illuminated manuscript. "Morgan," Nezeru called again, "where are you?"

"I'm still here," he called back, but softly. The valley had a watchful air, and he felt sure there were things watching them from every side. When he finally reached the far side and jumped down from the cluster of branches onto the muddy ground, his heart was beating fast and his legs were shaky. He was ashamed of himself, until he saw that Nezeru did not seem to be her usual brisk self either.

"I do not like this place," she said.

"I told you it was bad! But you wanted to come here. You didn't listen."

"I have admitted my mistake," she told him sternly. "Instead of throwing words at each other, Morgan, let us make our way up from the valley floor. Remember, we are aiming for the heights, hoping the *Uro'eni* cannot climb them easily."

"But why should we even stay in this valley? There must be a curse on this place. You've seen it. Everything is wrong here. The plants, the water—everything."

"It is true that I have never seen anything like it," she confessed. "Not even in the depths of Nakkiga or on the dragon-mountain. As to staying in this valley, let us save that discussion until we are somewhere safe."

He could not argue with that, though he wished he could. He had half-hoped she would decide to lead them back out of Misty Vale to some more wholesome spot, but he had already learned that Nezeru could be stubborn. "Well, then," he said. "Lead on and I will follow."

The eastern wall of the gorge rose steeply and the climbing was difficult; it was all Morgan could do to keep up with his companion. Bits of loose stone kept sliding down from above, sometimes by the barrow-load, and he had to spend as much time watching the heights as looking down to pick his way between outcroppings.

They had climbed perhaps a quarter of the way up the rocky slope, and the sky was quickly growing dark when Nezeru stopped, waiting for him to catch up. When he reached her, he bent over to catch his breath, but she hardly looked at him.

"I am trying . . ." he began, but she lifted her hand.

"Quiet. I think I can hear . . . and smell . . . a company of Sacrifices below us."

Morgan froze like a startled hare. "What should we do?" he said. "Will they hear us?"

"Unlikely, from this distance," she whispered. "The wind is in my face. And they will not catch our scent either, unless the wind changes." She turned to look up the slope. "Do you see that jut of stone above us?"

He looked up. A great, folded lump of rock the color of a dove's breast stood out from the dead grass, loose rocks, and dark soil of the slope. Morgan nodded.

"Good. Make for it. It will be a better place to see if I am right."

And what if you are? he wanted to ask. *How are we going to fight against a whole troop of Norn soldiers?* Instead, he bent low and scrambled up the slope, using his hands almost as much as his feet.

Nezeru reached the stone first and stretched out on top of it, hidden from the valley floor beneath. Morgan climbed wearily up to lie beside her. The sky was mostly dark now, twilight spreading rapidly, and he could see little below them except the pale mists that had thickened above the river. "Where are they?" he whispered.

"It is hard to say—Sacrifices move very quietly, of course, as they have been trained to do. But I would say they are there, on the river's far side." She pointed. "Now be silent for a while so I can listen."

Morgan did his best not to move or breathe too loudly.

"They have found the tree we crossed on," she told him after a long silence. "They are going to use it to get over the river."

Morgan felt a tightening in his chest. "Are they following us?"

"I do not think so. But I can only hear a few words here and there. Now be silent!"

But even as she finished speaking, a great, booming sound reverberated down the gorge. *Thoom!*

"It's the ogre!" said Morgan, much louder than he had meant to. "We have to find a better place to hide."

Nezeru shook her head. Another crashing footfall made the hillside shake and sent chunks of stone bounding down the slope to disappear into the mist. *Thoom!*—another bone-rattling impact, closer and louder.

"Where is it?" Morgan's heart was beating hard. "I can hear it, but I can't see it!"

"It is coming down the river course," said Nezeru. "I hear the Sacrifices shouting." Her eyes widened. "By the Garden, they are screaming!"

Then Morgan could see the ogre, or at least its huge shadow looming in the mist, as if a massive merchant ship had somehow found its way into a mountain stream. The thunderous footfalls stopped, and now even Morgan could hear the shrill cries—the Sacrifices did not sound like thinking beings but terrified animals. Trees crashed and splintered, then the shrieks stopped. After that, the great shadowy mass began to move down the river once more and soon vanished utterly, though its footfalls kept the ground trembling for some time. The valley fell back into silence.

Morgan was sweaty and trembling. He wanted nothing more than to get out of this cursed place as quickly as possible. Thus, he was more than a little disturbed when Nezeru said, "We must go down and see what happened."

"Are you mad? Why?"

"Because it may tell us something about this creature. If it was walking along the riverbed, it may have left its track in the mud."

"Not in the dark. No. What if it comes back while we're down there?"

"Very well," she said, though he could tell she was frustrated by his caution. "We will wait until first light."

She prodded him awake in the rocky shelter they had chosen, another overhang high on the slope above the river. Morgan had slept badly, and the only dreams he remembered were of hiding and being pursued. "Come with me," she told him. "The sun is up. I want to see what traces the ogre has left behind."

"Why bother? We can't fight it. It's as big as a steeple!"

"Then you may stay here," she said. "I will go look for myself."

Every sane impulse told him to do just that, to let this Norn madwoman go down to the river alone if she wanted. Still, before Nezeru had descended far enough to vanish into the murk, he was sliding and scrambling down after her, cursing her for being a fool and cursing himself for being a bigger one.

It took no little time to make their way down to the valley floor. Morgan covered the last part of the descent half-sliding on gravel and fell painfully onto his rump several times. For once he was grateful for the cloaking fogs.

Nezeru was only a few steps from the marshy riverbank when he caught up. "Come see," she said, and flared her fingers in a gesture he had not seen before.

"What does that mean?" he asked. "When you spread your hands like that?"

For a moment she did not seem to understand his question. Then she slowly straightened her fingers again. "Do you mean like this? It is just a sign. It means, 'I am surprised.'"

He wanted to see it again, just for the captivating way her fingers moved, like a newly woken cat unsheathing its claws as it stretched, but instead he stepped closer. "What are you surprised about?"

"These tracks from the *Uro'eni*. They are not like anything I have seen before."

Morgan stared down at the massive depression in the soggy riverbank. Reeds and even small trees were crushed into the muck at its bottom. "That's a track? It just looks like a hole."

"That is only one of them. There are more, and they circle down and then lead back up the valley."

"We know that thing is huge. What is surprising?"

She gave him a cool look. He knew he had annoyed her somehow. "Does that look like the track of any foot you have ever seen? Does it look like a deer's slot, a horse's hoof, or a soldier's boot?"

"How could it? It's as big as a house!"

"But even a giant as high as Nakkiga's mighty Tearfall must have a foot. But whatever stepped here left a print so strange that it must have been wearing something on its feet, something odd and irregular. See the edges? The places where parts of it stick out to one side or the other?"

Morgan felt a chill. "The Boiler."

"What is that?"

"When I was a child, I heard stories about a giant so big he could take the roof off a church, pick people out of it, and then throw them in his cooking pot. He was called the Boiler. He wore iron cauldrons on his feet because no shoes were big enough."

She gave him a bemused look, then straightened. "Whatever this creature might be, at least we know it has gone back up the valley. We will follow in that direction."

Morgan was stunned. "What do you mean, follow? That's exactly where we shouldn't go!"

"As long as the footprints lead away, we are safe. Would you rather wonder whether it might be behind you?"

He shook his head furiously. "That makes no sense at all. We should stay as far away from it as possible."

"If we are to hide in this valley from the armies of the Hikeda'ya and the Zida'ya, we must know always where the ogre is."

"I don't want to hide in this valley. That's *your* idea."

"I said that you do not need to stay with me."

"You know I wouldn't have a chance getting back across the valley and the forest on my own. But if you want to be rid of me, Nezeru, just tell me so."

She watched him calmly for a moment, then made another unfamiliar gesture, this one with her two hands sliding across each other and then apart. "You are hungry, perhaps. Mortals cannot go long without food."

His anger softened to mere exasperation. She was right at least about one thing—he *was* hungry. They had found nothing he dared to eat in the valley so far. "Yes," he said. "Let's look for food. If you're going to drag me off to get killed, it might as well be on a full stomach. But first, what did that mean? The thing you did with your hands just now."

She gave him a look of puzzlement that required no translation. "You are full of questions today. Do you mean this?" She repeated the sliding gesture. "It means *Passing in the Corridor*—something we say when we have an argument that cannot be settled, at least not in the moment."

"Why do you talk with your hands so much?" he asked. "You said you grew up inside a mountain. What use are hand-signs in the dark?"

Unexpectedly, she laughed. For a moment she could have been any other girl his age, amused by the stupidity of the male animal in general and this representative of the sex in particular. "Do you think the Hikeda'ya live in utter darkness, like cave fish?" she asked. "It is true that sometimes we must communicate in true darkness. Then our gestures are not meant to be seen but to be felt, and we make them against the hands of those we are speaking with." She demonstrated by letting the fingers of one hand dance over the other.

He could not help staring at her. There were moments, and this was one, in which despite all the dangers that threatened them, he found Nezeru and her ivory-pale face so captivating he did not want to think about anything else. *She's like a song,* he thought. *A living, breathing song.*

"Why do you look at me like that, Morgan?"

"Do you have a hand-sign to say, *'You are very beautiful'*?"

For the first time in several days, he seemed to have caught her completely off-guard. "Why would you want to know that?"

"Just curious."

She looked back at him, lips pursed. "My people are not much given to flirtation and flattery of that sort—not outside the bedchamber. But we do use this sign sometimes, which has several meanings. One of them is close to what you ask." She raised one finger to the outer corner of her eye. "It means, simply, 'I see you.'"

"Thank you." He lifted his finger to his eye. "So lead on, then. But remember—food first, *then* painful death."

She gave him another look, this one harder to decipher. "You are a strange young mortal, Morgan. Come, let us waste no more time. We need to get back up out of the valley and into the heights."

The longer she traveled with the mortal boy (or young mortal man, Nezeru reminded herself, at least by the terms of his own short-lived people) the less she felt she understood him.

When they had first met, she had considered him to be like any other of his kind, unworthy of even the most ordinary respect. His people had infested the Hikeda'ya's ancient lands like verminous insects—pink, useless creatures who bred and bred until they erupted into great swarms, sullying everything around them, devouring all they could find.

But their time together had changed things, although she was still not entirely certain how it happened. He was not much of a fighter, she knew—he would not last for even the briefest time in the proving-ground of the Reach, as Nezeru herself had done time and again, sometimes standing over the dead and disfigured bodies of Sacrifice order-mates who had fallen, fighting on desperately until the horns blared to end the exercise. But despite his lack of battle-skills, Morgan had proved himself no coward by coming to her aid several times. Did it take more courage or less to leap into a fight when you were not a hardened fighter?

Then they had spent all those hours trapped in the yew tree at the Gate of the Star, and her own body had betrayed her. She regretted a little that she had given in to the hunger of her flesh. What apparently had been lovemaking to him had been only the scratching of an itch to her. But now he seemed smitten by her, and Nezeru didn't like that. It added an air of responsibility to everything that was happening. He was right, in a way—she hadn't given him much choice about coming with her.

But I did not bring him to the forest in the first place, she told herself. *I did not pluck him out of this Vale of Mists as the Zida'ya creature Tanahaya did, then promise to take him home. None of that is my fault!*

Still, she was troubled. And because of her relentless self-honesty, instilled not just by the training of her order, but by things she had learned from her father and mortal mother, she had to admit that the affection was not entirely one-sided.

I think he must be handsome for one of his kind. His features are regular, and his hair, though always disarrayed, is a fine shade of brown like an otter's pelt. Her own people, even halfbreeds like herself, were all born with the same colorless locks, though some of the most self-confident or fashionable chose to dye theirs black with lead and slaked lime. Any other shades were frowned upon, seen as trying to lift oneself above one's place or to flaunt the endless public mourning her people had adopted after the queen's beloved son had died.

Sometimes he is endearing, like a pet, she thought. *Sometimes he is frustrating, like a child. But he means well, and in his way, he is honorable.* Worst of all, as far as resolving her confusion, there were times when she even found him oddly attractive. His face was rounder than she was used to, and his eyes, though an interesting shade of green, seemed small, but those ocean-colored eyes revealed many things, particularly when he was concerned for her, or amused by her. Nezeru had come to realize that when Morgan smiled or even laughed at her, he was not showing contempt, as one of her fellow Sacrifices would have been doing, but honest amusement. And she had been amused by him as well, by his peculiar ways, his self-mockery, and, strangest of all, his kindness toward her.

I should despise him, she thought. *His people are my people's eternal enemies. The mortal Jarnulf interested me, and I acted on it, only to be rebuffed. But this mortal makes me feel differently. Still, that can only be weakness in a time and place where I cannot afford it.*

In the days that followed they made their cautious way up the valley toward the headwaters of the Narrowdark. It was more difficult to travel through the high, rocky hills on the eastern side—the slopes there were made even more treacherous by snowfalls and icy stones—but Nezeru did not want to be surprised by Sacrifice troops coming from out of the west.

On the sixth day of their journey they stumbled on a battle between Hikeda'ya and Zida'ya in a high, narrow gorge that joined the Coolblood Valley to Tanakirú. Nezeru heard it long before she could see anything, and when they could finally make out the distant struggle far below, she led them upslope to an even higher spot.

"I can see a Zida'ya fort at the top of the gorge," she told him. "But there look to be far more Sacrifices than there are defenders."

"Let's leave them to it," Morgan said. "The only thing we could do would be to get killed, and you don't even know which side wants to kill you more."

"I suppose you are right. Let us move on—but stay low. Even from so far away, some of them might see us." She was still puzzled as to what had been going on at Naglimund and Da'ai Chikiza, and why that fight was spilling over into what should have been an empty landscape of high hills and bleak, unpopulated valleys. She also could not help wondering why, if her Hikeda'ya colleagues were so interested in the Vale of Mists, they were going about it so obliquely.

Why don't they just send an entire Sacrifice legion into the valley, ogre or no ogre? That was what Sacrifices were for, after all, what they had been trained to do—give their lives for the good of Nakkiga and the queen. Surely a large enough force of trained fighters, armed with arrows and fire, could deal with even the most monstrous of giants. Why did High Marshal Muyare or whoever commanded the queen's army here not simply enter the valley in force? And that thought brought another: Why were the Hikeda'ya's enemies defending the place so desperately? Why would the diminished clans of the Zida'ya build a large fort and expend so many lives to defend an empty wilderness? Surely most of their villages—their "little boats" as they called them—lay far away to the east and south. What could be important enough here to spend many precious lives defending it?

The more she puzzled, the more Nezeru wanted answers.

My Talon was sent to catch a dragon, she thought suddenly, *though we never found out why. Could it be that our queen means to capture the great ogre as well?* Nezeru was both amazed and terrified by this unexpected idea. What a horrifying weapon of war such a monstrous creature would be! And it might explain the zeal with which the Zida'ya were laying down their lives to keep the Hikeda'ya army out of the north end of Tanakirú, where the ogre seemed to shelter.

As darkness fell and they left the battle in the gorge behind, the pair took refuge in a cavern in the rocky hillside. Like most of the holes they had found in these mountains, it looked to have been cut by water over a long, long time; indeed, a small stream with no visible source in the hills above trickled out of the cavern's entrance and flowed away down the gully it had cut into the slope.

Nezeru, well-trained in foraging, had found beech nuts growing in a place where the stream widened into a pool, and even some mushrooms, mostly waxcaps and pheasant's tails. Unlike the much larger Narrowdark, this water smelled clean, so she filled her drinking sack with it. Since the valley was so full of shielding fog, she built a small fire, walling it with stones to make sure it would not give them away to anyone below, then toasted the nuts and mushrooms and added them to hot water to make a thin broth. Nezeru would never have admitted it out loud—too many years of Sacrifice training—but she was hungry too, and the pleasure with which Morgan sucked down the soup was gratifying.

"By all the saints," he said breathlessly after he had finished his second helping, consumed straight out of the field cup they shared despite burned fingers and tongue, "that was good. My head doesn't hurt now."

"Then it is a good time to sleep," she said. "We have a long way to go tomorrow, I think."

"You say that like you have a destination in mind."

"You saw the Zida'ya fort we passed, and the fighting in the gorge. I do not want to go there—either side would shoot me full of arrows as soon as they saw me—but I do want to sneak back and discover what is happening there. The more we know about the movements of both sides, the less chance we will be captured."

"You want to watch from far away, yes? Very far away?" He nodded his head. "Then I have no objection. But I still don't know where you think we're going."

"Nor do I. But I will tell you when I have decided."

She was amused that a full stomach seemed to make him far less argumentative, and when he rolled himself in his cloak and lay down to sleep, she felt a kind of contentment. She was still alive. She was keeping the mortal youth alive, too. After all they had been through, both of those things felt like rare and impressive feats.

While she watched Morgan fall asleep, snorting and fidgeting until he finally grew silent, Nezeru had a feeling she did not remember having before, at least not since she had left her family's clan compound for the order-house of the Sacrifices. It was nothing so simple—or so unlikely—as feeling truly bound to another person, but there was unquestionably a link between them. She felt *comfortable* in the mortal boy's company. She felt as if for once she was not simply a lone thing in a dangerous world. The world was still dangerous, but the danger being shared, even with this strange creature from an enemy race, made it seem a little less daunting.

It is wrong to rely on anyone but another Sacrifice, her old training warned her. *Dangerous, and a betrayal of the Mother of All.*

Perhaps. But this is another world, she told herself. *Everything is different now.*

Waking in the darkness, Nezeru realized she had curled herself around sleeping Morgan from the back, and she felt another infrequent sensation—she wanted to couple.

It did not take much to rouse him, and though he did not seem quite awake, he understood very quickly. As they peeled away their garments, Nezeru leaned to kiss his mouth, surprising herself with how quickly she had taken to this strange mortal practice. But Morgan was not content simply to kiss her mouth, and soon had begun practicing the same art on her neck, breasts, and belly.

This is not just coupling, she realized. *This must be what I have heard of—lovemaking.* It was a revelation to her. Since she had first begun to couple with others, mostly fellow Sacrifices in stolen moments at the order-house, the activity had meant different things—an exciting transgression against the overwhelming rules of the order, or sometimes just a bodily itch that demanded to be scratched. But she had never thought of it as a way to show affection, to give and receive pleasure. And whether Morgan was a rarity among his own kind or not, he clearly knew that part of it.

Is this why the high nobles, the Hamakha and such, sometimes have many concubines or coupling partners? Does each one bring a different kind of excitement to the game? For that was what it seemed to her at the moment, not a duty, not merely a way to relieve a need, but a kind of game of shared partnership, of innovation and surprise.

In that way, lovemaking is a bit like shaynat, she thought. *Perhaps mortals never bothered to learn that game because they have this instead.*

Nezeru knew she was inexperienced, at least in these more subtle aspects of what she now thought of as "the mortal sport," but she had studied strategy and she was strong, lithe, and flexible. As she tried different things, and was rewarded with happy murmurs, sighs, and—perhaps inevitably—an occasional quiet yelp of pain, she began to lose herself.

This is an entire world, she realized. *It is a world that exists only for a time, and only for those who are in it together.*

At last, panting in the dark, the fire long since burned down to ashes, they fell apart. Morgan almost immediately slid back into sleep, but Nezeru lay next to him savoring his warmth and thinking, remembering, and even wondering at where her travels had brought her.

My life is not over. The sudden thought surprised her. *If I live, there are still things for me to learn and to experience, things that the Order of Sacrifice would never have brought me. I had not realized that until now.*

38

The King Below

His dreams had been taken from him. He did not know how or why. But his memories, his wretched, punishing memories, remained. As Simon huddled against the wall of his cell, the worst moments of his life came trooping past him like visiting phantoms.

"Our son cannot be dead!" his wife had cried. *"God could not be so cruel!"*

But God could, and God had. John Josua would always be the little child Simon had carried on his back through the Hedge Garden, and also the serious, bearded young man who had been so astonished to hold his own first child that he had wept at Morgan's birth. He would always be every age his loving parents remembered, but he would never be old.

John Josua had not died in his wife's arms, but his mother's. Miri had been inconsolable for months, almost a phantom, and Simon had felt as if his own pain, great as it was, was a weight he could not share for fear it would crush her.

And that night on a hilltop at the edge of the High Thrithings, waiting for the sun to rise and the fighting to begin again. Gunkar Blood-Eye and his Boar Clan fighters, who waited in the darkness below, had meant to drive the king and his forces back out of the Thrithings—perhaps for good. Isgrimnur, good old Isgrimnur, had said to him, "This is the worst part of ruling other men, Simon. When you must send them to die, though you would rather those hundreds or even thousands of deaths could be your own, over and over, instead of making widows and orphans of the women and children who have trusted their men to you."

"Is it worth it?" Simon had asked. "Can you kill some men to make others happy? Is that the bargain that God wishes on us?"

Isgrimnur, bless him, had known exactly what he meant. "No, of course not. But sometimes you have to cause the death of some men—including your own—to keep even more of them safe."

Later Simon had stood in the wreckage of the thane's charge, with bodies lying everywhere, some still alive but breathing their final breaths, and he had been violently sick.

"I can never eat before a battle," Isgrimnur had told him, patting him on the back as Simon tried to wipe his beard with the sleeve of his mail shirt.

But his memories did not come in an orderly fashion, like fighting men lined up for a last inspection before the charge. As Simon lay in misery and shame, in a cell so full of rats and other vermin that he had long since stopped paying attention to them, all the worst moments of his life now came back to him, as though they crowded in to see his ending—his final humiliation.

How could Jiriki's messenger leave that way? How could he see me in chains and do nothing to help me? Do the Sithi hate us so much? Simon had hoped to make things better between their two races, but that had been another failure, another task he had set for himself but never finished. *Perhaps they prefer it this way,* he thought. *Not Jiriki—not Aditu. But the rest might be happier with mortals they can despise, who are their clear enemies, not confusing, half-allies like I was. Because what did I ever manage to do for them? A few proclamations that my subjects should not spite the Sithi, that they had been our allies against the Storm King. But those proclamations did not keep mortals from hating and fearing Jiriki's people, and they certainly did not bring the Sithi closer to us.*

Thoughts of the Storm King inevitably also brought back those last terrible days before Green Angel Tower fell—of his days as a prisoner on the wheel.

Inch. That horror. He saw the man again in his mind's eye, huge as a half-giant, lumbering, with a face as round and empty of expression as a wheel of cheese. *He hated me. I could not understand it. How could he hate me without ever knowing me? Did he truly think he might become Doctor Morgenes's assistant instead of me? A shambling brute of a creature like that?*

As a child, with old Prester John on the High Throne—seemingly since the world had begun—Simon had assumed God would only give power to worthy men, to those who deserved it. But Miri's mad father had showed that it was not so simple, and the treachery of Pasevalles had sealed the proof that dominion could also be given to the unworthy.

The power to rule others brought out what was hidden inside someone, Simon saw now—or sometimes not even hidden. When the red priest Pryrates had controlled the Hayholt and mad King Elias, Pryrates had given the sullen beast Inch what he always wanted—power. Power over the life and death of all the men who had to labor in the forge and tend the furnaces. *And then Pryrates gave me to Inch, too, and he hung me on the wheel.*

Memories of those hopeless days fastened on him like sucking leeches—the hopelessness, the agony. The lost, helpless hours had been worse than death in some ways, so dreadful that Simon had prayed for his life to end. But an unexpected ally had found him, and he had escaped.

And now, when I am most alone, what do I get? An immortal who gives me a message and then walks away—who thinks he is doing me a favor by leaving me a knife so I can kill myself.

How few are there, he wondered, *whether men or immortals, that can be trusted with power over others? Not many. Not many at all.*

He lifted the Sitha's dire gift into the torchlight. In its way it was a beautiful thing. Simon had no idea how the Sithi and Norns worked witchwood—was it grown? Forged? Carved? All he could tell was that a careful and supremely talented hand had shaped it. The blade had been scraped into ripples along its edge that caught the light like the scales of a tiny fish, and the narrow point was clearly meant for more than just cutting rope or meat. It was a fighting knife.

A distant memory drifted up, of Jiriki or someone telling him, *"The witchwood must be cured and shaped at the same time. Once the making is complete, it cannot be changed again."* And that must be why, despite all the bits of witchwood in the world that still survived in knives and swords and armor, the loss of the witchwood trees must be so terrible for the Sithi: they would make nothing new. In a way, he realized, the annoying messenger who had tossed this to him so casually was making a great sacrifice.

But I didn't want a sacrifice. I didn't want a knife. I wanted the keys to these damnable shackles.

He tested the knife's point with his thumb and immediately wished he hadn't. He put his thumb in his mouth, sucked away the blood, then spat. It was certainly sharp.

Simon set the point in the keyhole of his wrist shackle and began to try to move the mechanism. Once he thought he felt something inside the lock slide a little, but then it slipped back; he cursed loudly, then forced himself to be quiet, listening to see if anyone was coming before he went back to work. He kept prying at the shackle, shaking sweat from his forehead because his hands were occupied, teasing and poking with the sharp end of the Sithi knife, but at last he had to give up.

Useless. Useless, useless. Like me.

He began probing at the other shackle, hoping it might be easier to open. It was not. At last, he gave up on that one too, and felt a wave of despair wash through him.

No, he told himself. *I cannot give up. Lillia and Morgan are still out there somewhere, and Pasevalles will kill them to steal their birthright.* But he had been fighting the shackles and heavy chains for days, and he was weary beyond belief. Perhaps the Sitha had been right. At least if he took his own life, he would deny that monstrous traitor the pleasure of killing him.

It was not as though he feared his ending: he had already died once at the hands of Unver, the chieftain of the grasslanders, or at least it had seemed so. Would it be so much worse simply to slide this witchwood knife between his ribs and into his own heart? Doctor Morgenes had once told him that in ancient times it had been considered a noble way to die, a rebuke to your persecutors, a message to your allies that you had commanded your own life to the very end. But as he pondered whether he could flaunt the Lord God's own words from the Book of the Aedon—*"He who takes his own life spites Me, because he who believes in Me can never be without hope"*—Simon straightened his legs and his chains rattled. He stared at the irons that had worn his shins and ankles raw, then drew his legs up beneath him and sat like a tailor so he could reach the shackle on his right ankle. He let his fingers roam over it because he could not see it clearly, and thought it felt a little older and a little more corroded than the irons around his wrists. He slipped the narrow tip of the witchwood blade into the shackle, then began to twist it until he felt an answering pressure from inside the lock. He softened his grip: he did not want to break off the point inside the shackle. That could not only ruin the knife for further use, but also wedge the lock shut.

He kept working the tip of the knife until he felt more resistance, then did his best to pry whatever was impeding the knife out of the way. The knife slipped forward a little farther into the lock, and for a moment he was full of despair, certain that he had snapped off the tip. But instead, he felt enough weight against it that he decided he had really moved something inside the lock.

After that tiny portion of success his thoughts grew so fixed that he almost felt as though he were inside the shackle, a dark cave full of levers that must each be tested and tried. He worked with all the patience he could summon, and time crawled past as his fingers cramped and his sweat dripped. Then, almost without warning, the metal shuddered and the lock popped open.

Simon could not believe his good fortune. He took the shackle in trembling hands and twisted it until the two halves parted. His right leg was free!

His excitement cooled when he discovered, after another hour or more of taxing labor, that the other leg iron was not going to be as accommodating. He did his best to repeat the process that had freed his right leg but could not duplicate his success. At last, with his hands too slippery with perspiration and the blood from small cuts to grip the knife anymore, he stopped. He leaned back against the wall of his cell, then slid down to the filthy floor, his strength gone, his moment of excitement and relief gone as well.

I have reached the end of my powers, Lord, he prayed. *I cannot do this without Your help.*

But nothing answered him except the scurrying of tiny feet beneath the straw. God, it appeared, was in no hurry to intervene.

The cord had pulled tight around Lillia's neck, crushing the tips of her fingers as her captor began to drag her upward. Her feet were only just touching the ground. A dark shape crouched like a spider at the top of the wall above her, and her thoughts were shrieking *No, no, no, no!*

She reached up her other hand to clutch at the strangling cord. Her fingers hurt like they were being burned, and she was already dizzy from lack of air. She wriggled desperately, but her feet slipped and for a heart-stopping instant she spun at the end of the choking cord with only the tip of one toe on the ground. Her shining sphere was gone, dropped in the first instant of her desperate struggle. The only light was a dim glow somewhere far, far above her, and she had no weapon except the strength of terror and her fury at the thing that was trying to kill her. A red fog was beginning to blot out everything when her captor's grip on the cord slipped.

Lillia found herself stumbling backward, both feet suddenly on the ground once more. In blind panic, she grabbed at the noose, but before she could get it off her neck, her legs buckled and she collapsed. This sudden downward pull on the cord caught her attacker by surprise. The shape that crouched above her was dragged to the edge of the wall as the rope tightened between them again. Then, with a hiss of rage, it tumbled over the edge and landed almost on top of her.

Lillia screamed and struck at the stinking, clutching shadow, which seemed to be made of rags and claws. She kicked and kicked, crying aloud, but the flapping shape fought back. It tried to pull the strangling cord tight again, but Lillia still had her fingers under it, and managed to drag her head out of the noose before it tightened on her throat. Her attacker wrapped its horrible hands around her neck as Lillia struck at the hissing, near-invisible thing. She felt ragged nails digging at her cheek and chin, then something foul was pressed against her mouth, something that smelled both flower-sweet and rotten. Lillia thrashed, shaking her head violently from side to side until she felt the cloth slide away and was able to suck in a little air. Bony, clawed fingers were still trying to push the sickly-sweet rag back into place, and Lillia bit down on those fingers as hard as she could.

The cry that followed was like nothing she had ever heard, a wordless, high-pitched screech like a bird of prey. Her attacker dropped to the stony floor, wailing wordlessly, and Lillia clambered onto the red thing's bowed back. A moment earlier she had been terrified by the thing's mere touch, but now she had only one thought—escape. The ragged shape shrieked again and reached up to claw at her, but Lillia's weight held it down for just long enough for her to jump to the wall and catch its top. With a strength she had not known she had, she managed to pull herself up high enough to get her elbows onto the top of the board. Then, her heart beating fast, her head full of swirling, confused thoughts, she swung one leg up onto the top and then pulled herself the rest of the way onto the barrier. When she dropped down on the other side, she realized she was in a stairwell: the red demon had been fishing for her from the steps.

The murderous thing was trying to climb out of the makeshift pit below her, scrabbling at the wall. Lillia clambered up the stairs on all fours as fast as she could, our of near-darkness into more near-darkness.

Up, she thought. *Have to get up. Have to find some light.*

She struck her knee against a step and let out a gasp of pain. She thought she heard the red thing's claws rasping along the wooden wall of the trap as it dragged itself out. Weeping, terrified, Lillia climbed.

Exhausted by the effort of prying open just one of his shackles, Simon slept until heavy steps coming down the passage toward his cell startled him into wakefulness. A massive shadow blocked the torchlight outside. The lock clicked, the bolt slid, and the door swung out into the corridor, revealing a broad-shouldered figure.

It's Inch! Simon thought. *He's come back for me!* He closed his hand around the hilt of the witchwood knife, then remembered where he was, and when. *No, Inch is dead. It's one of Pasevalles' barbarians.*

He kept his eyes closed as the clansman entered. He heard a dish being set down, but though he was achingly hungry, he did not move.

"Your last meal, stone-dweller."

Simon recognized the voice: it was split-lipped Zhadu. *Last meal?* he wondered, heart speeding. *Are they going to kill me now? Then why feed me?* He could feel the lure of the open door like a cool breeze in roasting summer—it was so close! But he knew all too well that his remaining shackles would keep him well short of that falsely beckoning freedom.

"Are you dead, stone-dweller?" Zhadu came closer, boots scraping through the muck. Simon was weak, near-starving, and the Thrithings-man was burly and well-fed, but the grasslander still showed caution. He kicked Simon's leg, tentatively at first, then again, harder.

Simon did his best to ignore the pain, forcing himself to stay limp. He was on his back, eyes closed, expecting at any moment to feel a heavy boot smash down on his face or his groin. Zhadu was talking to himself in the Thrithings tongue, but Simon recognized a few words—"*kven*" and "*vit vukaz.*"

Queen of the White Foxes. But what did he mean by it? The grasslander kept kicking him, trying to rouse him. *Does that mean the Norns are here?* Simon hadn't seen Pasevalles in two days. Had his treacherous chancellor fled the castle ahead of an attack by the immortals?

Simon could feel straw rustling against his legs as the Thrithings-man, apparently believing Simon must be nearly dead, leaned over him, one foot on either side of his body. "Wake up, king," Zhadu growled. "Soon someone comes for you. The chief makes a bargain." The clansman's thick fingers curled in Simon's hair and began to drag him upright. It felt as though his scalp was being ripped loose.

A thought flashed into his head like a spark flung out by the burning pain: *I've got one leg free.* He kicked upward as hard as he could between Zhadu's legs, slamming his shinbone against the clansman's crotch. Zhadu let out a gurgling cry of shock and fell to his knees, half atop of Simon, who thought his ribs might break from the weight. He squirmed, trying to pull his shackled arm out from underneath the writhing mass, but before he could free the hand that held the witchwood knife, the clansman gasped in a great scrape of air and his huge hands wrapped around Simon's throat. Simon thrashed in his chains trying to escape that grip, but Zhadu was squeezing his windpipe closed, and within a few seconds the heavy grasslander had straddled the king's heaving chest. But now Simon's hand was finally free.

He knew he might have but one try. He did not believe he could reach his enemy's throat with those thick arms in the way so he drove the blade into Zhadu's back just below the ribcage. The witchwood knife slid through the sweaty leather jerkin as if it were suet, deep into the clansman's flesh and muscle. Simon tried to twist it then, but Zhadu was heaving atop him like a gaffed fish and the hilt was yanked from his hand. His enemy's fingers were still crushing his throat. Zhadu had lost some strength, but so had Simon.

The dark cell was becoming darker, as if the lone torch outside was guttering, and he was becoming more desperate with each heartbeat. *I don't have a knife now,* he told himself, *but I still have slack in my chains.* Zhadu had made the very mistake that Pasevalles had scoffed at: he had come too close.

With what felt like his last strength, Simon threw the loop of chain from his right-arm shackle around the bigger man's neck, then yanked it as tight as he could. As Zhadu fought to get free, Simon was able to loop the other chain over his head as well, then began to pull with both hands, blocking his enemy's clawing fingers with his forearms and elbows. He drove his free leg into Zhadu's belly over and over, hoping to make the man's wound bleed faster.

Simon had no idea how long they struggled. It felt like hours. The blackness that had almost overwhelmed him retreated a little, but flares of light still danced before his eyes, and his head felt as though it were on fire, but Simon pushed the pain aside. Something was in him now, a grim, murderous glee, as if it were Pasevalles himself whom he was throttling.

It happened in a moment. The grasslander's resistance had weakened only a little even after he had been stabbed, but now, with no more warning than slackening pressure, his hands on Simon's neck seemed to turn utterly boneless, then slipped off. Simon felt the man's weight change from something with a shape into something like a massive sack of flour, but he did not dare let go yet.

After he had taken a dozen huffing breaths, filling his lungs with glorious air, Simon finally let the chains go slack. He tried to wriggle free, but could not shift the fleshy, foul-smelling bulk that lay over him like a collapsed wall. He settled for moving his face out from under Zhadu's meaty arm.

"Didn't expect . . . to get kicked . . . in the ballocks, did you?" Simon wheezed. He could just see the bulge-eyed face at the edge of his vision, and he laughed, a dry, cracked sound like a stick breaking. "Hah! Maybe you . . . didn't remember . . . that I am the Commoner King."

After a long, painful struggle, Simon at last managed to get his chains unwound from his attacker's neck so he could search the hulking, inert body for the keys to his shackles, but they were nowhere to be found. He turned his head to the side, far too exhausted and too battered to push off Zhadu's sprawling weight, and saw that the ring of keys still dangled from the lock on the cell door, far, far beyond his reach.

All for nothing! Despair swept back over him. Half-crushed beneath his dead enemy, he struggled to get air into his lungs, but it was difficult because his ribs hurt so badly that he could barely expand them. The dead man was too heavy, and Simon was too weak to push him off.

This ugly bastard tried to kill a king, he thought in growing desperation as he struggled against the limp weight of Zhadu's corpse. *And he still might succeed.*

They retreated through the darkness, back down the corridor they had been following through the Hayholt's deep, hidden places. Clumsy in their thick garments, they had almost become stuck when they both tried to squeeze around a narrow corner at the same time, and now they stood, faces close, whispering as they struggled to catch their breath.

"What did you see?" Thelía asked.

Tiamak said, "Very little. A flash of light, a scurry of movement, then that heavy board came down."

"Do you think it is Pasevalles who is trying to catch us? And how can a wall drop from nowhere?"

"Whatever has stalked us through this underground maze is not Pasevalles or any soldier," Tiamak declared. "I have glimpsed our pursuer, remember, and he is small and thin and ragged." He slumped back against the wall of the passage. "As to the barrier that came down, that is easier to say. Remember, these depths beneath the castle were once the domain of the red priest Pryrates. Hjeldin's Tower and the depths below it were given over to him. The gods alone know what evil he was up to down here—what strange things he might have done. He had the freedom here to shape a world that matched his own corrupted mind."

"It is horrible—all of this is horrible," Thelía said. "We must go bundled up like trolls to avoid poison, and something is hunting for us, some hell-demon that Pryrates summoned, I do not doubt." His wife, usually so calm and good-natured, was beginning to fray at the edges, and Tiamak did not blame her. They had spent days living with the dreadful knowledge that they were not alone in the Hayholt's depths, that something was hunting them from the tops of ruined walls and along the ceilings of collapsing passageways, something preternaturally nimble that could vanish from one spot and appear again in another, far away, just moments later.

"There must be reason behind all of this," he assured her, though he did not feel as much confidence as he tried to show. "Someone is living down here in this maze of foundations and ruins, someone who wishes to keep out or kill any who tread on his territory."

"You make it sound like a living, mortal man!"

"Until I know otherwise, that is what I must guess our shadow is," he said. "Certainly, it is something intelligent—careful there!" He sprang forward, almost dropping the torch, and pulled Thelía away from the wall. "Look, there is another," he said, holding the torch close. A iron barb not much bigger than a sewing needle stood out from between two stones, its point daubed in black. Tiamak sniffed it. "The same poison that was on the other wall-spikes—and also on the arrows that wounded the Sitha envoy, I wager. The dragon-blood poison that *you* discovered, my clever wife."

She looked at the blackened point with disgust and fear. "Elysia's mercy on us, they are everywhere!"

"And that is why we go about in this padding of spare coats and cloaks, like roasted pigeons wrapped in bacon. Whoever or whatever lives down here is jealous of its territory—but I do not need to tell you that. We have both seen stones propped on a ledge over passages, ready to fall, and pits dug in the middle of corridors so that someone walking in the dark would fall in. And of course, these devilish needles—dozens of them!—meant to scratch and poison the unwary."

"We should not linger here," Thelía said in a strained voice. "That red thing might be following us even now."

They descended carefully to the sheltered place where they had been making camp, a spot that Tiamak remembered from the last hours of the Storm King's War, when he and Prince Josua, guided by several of the Sithi, had made their way up from caves near the Kynslagh shore, through these very ruins, and into the castle itself. He had not been able to find the route leading back to the caves—many old stone walls had collapsed since that long-ago day, perhaps during the building of Holy Tree Tower—but he had found again the wide and deep stone basin that the Sithi had named the Pool of Three Depths. Nothing was left in it now but a layer of damp mud, though it still seemed one of the few places the red creature preferred to avoid.

When they had returned to the echoing, high-ceilinged emptiness of the pool chamber, Tiamak lit a small oil-lantern and extinguished his torch in a crevice in the floor. It was one of only two torches they had left, and it would only last for another journey or two up from the Pool, so Tiamak was determined to save it as long as possible. The inconstant labyrinth beneath the castle had proved too dangerous for the weak glow of a rushlight or even their oil lamp.

His wife leaned against him, but already her head was nodding. He took a sheaf of parchments out of his pack and leaned close to the lantern to begin reading John Josua's words again. He had only read part of it—time for study had been scarce since they had fled from Pasevalles and hid themselves beneath the castle—but the more Tiamak read, the more disturbed he became and the more certain that whatever was hunting them through the dark places under the Hayholt had also been responsible for John Josua's fever-ravaged death. But he still had no idea what their enemy was, or how it had come to hide down here.

His chest tight with worry, he sighed deeply as he opened John Josua's book, and felt his wife stir against him in her exhausted sleep.

I believed one day I would answer all the Hayholt's questions, he thought—*uncover all its secrets. What an arrogant fool I was! This castle is* made *of secrets.*

Lillia was lost in the dark. She had lost her glowing ball. She had lost the place where she had been safe. Now she had no idea where she was, but she knew the red thing must be chasing her so she could not stop.

But what is it? She could not help remembering what it had felt like beneath her hands as they struggled, the dry, scaly skin and its thin fingers, knobby, strong, and clawed like one of the ospreys that hunted over the Hayholt's moat. She had managed to kick and struggle her way free, but she did not think she would be so lucky another time.

These depths beneath the castle foundations were chaotic with fallen stones, the half-buried remnants of older structures, but as she scrambled up one staircase, then another, things had begun to seem a little more orderly. She was walking on paving stones, and when she stopped to touch the walls they seemed unbroken. The echoes of her movement also came back to her quickly and cleanly, which meant she must be inside something with a roof. She did not know if that was good or bad—she would not have to fear one of the red thing's nooses, but she might find herself trapped in a dead end, as she almost had just a short time ago. Still, what she wanted more than anything was to be safe from her pursuer. She had managed to pilfer just enough food from the red thing's traps in past days that even the constant ache in her stomach was less important than finding a hiding place.

Lillia had never thought about the dread that a fox or a deer must feel with a host of shouting men on horses chasing after it, but now she knew. She also knew she would never like hunting again. Something was after her, for no reason she could understand. Her heart was beating as fast as that of any quarry, and she kept thinking she heard footsteps behind her, but worst of all, as each hour passed it became more and more clear to Lillia that nobody at all was searching for her except the red thing.

Where are the soldiers? Why isn't my grandfather or Uncle Timo down here, trying to find me? She could not imagine an answer, unless she had been forgotten.

The staircase she was climbing ended in a pile of rocks and broken timbers. Lillia sat and wept, but even as tears streamed down her cheeks, she was angry at herself for doing so. She forced herself to get up and feel the obstacles in front of her, and to her great relief, discovered an opening in the rubble. If whatever space lay beyond it was small enough, she decided, it might even be a place where the red thing couldn't follow her. Or would she get part way inside and be stuck until the red demon found her? She wondered if God might be tired of helping her.

She wiggled between the two leaning stones that made the gap, then crawled forward, using her hands to find her way, as if her fingers were the twisty horns of a snail. In some places, the upward path actually became easier—too easy to be safe if the red thing was close behind.

What if it's only bones? she suddenly wondered. *Bones in red rags. Could it squeeze through behind me? Or if it's a ghost, it maybe could just—*

No, Lillia. Stop scaring yourself. Don't be a blower like Aedonita's little sister. It's not a ghost or it wouldn't have food.

Yes, the small but not easily silenced part of her suggested, *but it could still be bones. Just bones, like in that picture of Weighing Out Day where the dead come back alive.*

She was truly angry with herself now, angry at being small and young, angry at being left alone, angry at the dark and the horrible thing that kept trying to catch her. Her anger did not push her fear away, but it gave her something to hold.

Keep going, she told herself. *A princess does not give up, never.*

She wiggled upward through another series of small spaces, then was momentarily stuck in a very narrow place between two chunks of stone. She grew so terrified that she almost began to shout, even though the only ears that would hear her belonged to the noose-demon, but after a while she managed to wriggle her arm through the top of the narrow crevice. Now that she could tilt her shoulders to squeeze through the gap, she finally slithered free of the obstruction.

As she rested, letting her heart slow down, Lillia thought she heard something breathing nearby. She froze, heart rabbiting again. It sounded something like snoring—like the noise Grandmother Nelda always made in her chair after the afternoon meal, a hoarse, breathy in-and-out. (Nelda always got angry when Lillia told her she had been sleeping, as if sleeping was something shameful.) But as she tilted her head to hear better, she discovered something startling: the noise was coming from above her.

Was it the red thing, crawling down toward her through the rubble? She stayed still as a frightened deer, holding her breath and listening, and although whatever it was continued to rasp away like a sawyer stripping the branches from a trunk, it did not seem to be getting closer.

Lillia sat motionless for so long that her feet, tucked beneath her at an odd angle, began to tingle. She did not want to go back, so at last she began to climb toward the noise, through the jumble of fallen rock and wooden beams, moving as quietly as she could. Once a sudden small avalanche of fist-sized stones tumbled painfully down on her, covering the lower part of her up to her knees. For a few heartbeats she was panicked again, certain that the whole mass would now slide down and bury her, but the fall of stones ended as quickly as it had begun; after pulling her legs loose, she continued her climb.

As Lillia wriggled upward she wondered whether this was what it felt like to be a worm swimming through the dark earth, ever upward, desperate for the sun.

But then they stick their head up and a bird grabs their neck and pulls them out and eats them.

That was too much like what had almost happened to her. Lillia did her best to stop thinking about worms.

It was no longer just rocks and wooden beams that blocked her way, but showers of damp dirt as well. Some of it got in her mouth and she spat it out, tasting mud. She wanted to cry again, but she had climbed too far upward to give up now: if the red thing was still following her, it must be close behind now. She had to keep going. She had to.

As she wiped another stinging shower of dirt from her eyes, Lillia saw something that made her wonder. Light was leaking down between the stones and wood—just a faint glow, but enough that she could make out a little of what was in front of her. The first glimpse made her heart sink—the rubble seemed to stretch above her forever—but she decided that if there was light shining through, it must come from somewhere.

More climbing, more wriggling, more getting stuck, but she kept going, even though weariness pulled on her like heavy chains.

Just a nap, she begged herself. *Just a little sleep to get stronger, then I'll finish.*

Don't, Lillia, the princess-voice told her, haughty and commanding. *Stop making up reasons to stop. Just climb. If you don't climb, you'll stay in the dark forever.*

Sniffing back tears, she wiggled through another tight spot, and this time when her head came through and her shoulders after, she could see.

She couldn't see well, not with so little light, but enough to tell that some kind of open space was beyond the next set of fallen stones. She aimed herself forward, thinking helplessly about what her dead mother and dead Grandmother Miriamele would think if they saw her now, filthy, dress torn, fingernails broken, and face covered with dirt. Were they still watching over her, as everyone kept saying? Or had she left them behind in the black underneath?

She finally wriggled her body upward out of the last tight spot and found she was in a sort of square hole in the floor of a shadowy passage, with a dirty, plastered ceiling above it and cobwebs everywhere, like bed hangings. Her exultation at reaching freedom dropped suddenly into fear once more. *Still under the ground, under the castle.* She rubbed at her cheek but could not tell the difference between tears and mud.

Still, she could finally stand upright. Her legs felt weak, like a newborn calf's, like a colt just tumbled out of its mother's belly, and it took her a moment to find her balance.

She could see light in front of her. It came from the other end of the passage, where it bent to one side, so she climbed out of the hole in the floor and went slowly toward it. The sawing noise had stopped. The only sound was her own scuffing footsteps.

Beyond the turn of the corner she discovered a stairway, a spiral leading up out of the dim passage into something brighter beyond. She mounted from one tall step to another. Sometimes her exhausted legs failed her, and she had to climb to the next step on hands and knees, but she kept going.

At the top, she crouched and looked around. She was in yet another empty passage, a long one, but a torch burned in a sconce high on the wall, and for the first time Lillia felt a breath of real hope. On her left the corridor ended in a wooden door, so she staggered to it and tried to open it, but it seemed to be barred on the other side and did not yield even a fraction of an inch. She turned to the torch, but it was bracketed high on the wall: even on tiptoes she could not reach it.

Another storm of sobbing threatened to overtake her, but Lillia fought it down and crept farther along the corridor. Several doors with barred windows stood along one side of the passage, but they were all shut. Lillia stretched up and peered cautiously into each in turn but could make out nothing but shadows. Then, as she neared the end of the corridor, she saw that the last door was not closed, though it was not open very wide, either. And Lillia now heard the breathing noises again, slow and harsh.

It was almost enough to make her turn around, but she knew the only way out of these corridors was to climb all the way back down through the stones and other rubble, and nothing could make her go through that again. She crept as quietly as she could toward the open door, holding her breath, then carefully pushed it open enough to look inside. The snoring sound was very loud now, coming from the center of the dark space. But as she leaned in for a better look, she saw something that terrified her: a great dark mound lay against the back wall of the little room, and it had at least three arms.

Lillia couldn't help herself. She let out a shriek of terror. One of the arms moved, and she darted out into the passage again.

"Who is that?" a voice cried, deep and ragged. "Who is there? Is this another trick of yours, Pasevalles?"

Lillia stopped running. Something about the voice was familiar, though it sounded pinched and pained, as if whoever it was couldn't get any breath. *But he said Pasevalles!* If it was someone who knew Pasevalles, maybe the Lord Chamberlain was somewhere close! Perhaps if she called his name loud enough, he would come and find her.

"Is someone there?" the hoarse voice asked again.

Something about it, though it was angry and sick-sounding, touched something in the child. It sounded like . . . *"Grandfather?"* she asked. "Grandfather, is that you?"

"If you have brought my granddaughter down to threaten her, you bastard rogue, I will have your heart," the voice said, even angrier.

"Grandfather!" she cried, joy rushing through her. "Grandfather, it's just me! It's just me!"

"Lillia? I don't believe it, I can't . . . Come to me, child, if it's truly you. Oh, Blessed Mother Elysia, I cannot believe it. This is a trick, it must be!"

"Where are you?" she called, poking her head into the damp, stinking cell once more. "Grandfather?"

"Sweet Usires on the Tree," he said, voice breaking. "Oh, praise God in the highest! Lillia, if that is you and I am not mad, take the keys out of the door. The keys! Get them and bring the ring to me!"

She finally noticed the ring hanging from the lock on the door. She wiggled the key in the latch until it came loose, then moved forward slowly and carefully—she was still uncertain, and a little fearful it might be something that was only pretending to be her grandfather—until she stood by the strange shape with too many arms. One of the hands opened and closed, then opened again and lay flat. "Put the keys in my hand, dear," her grandfather's voice said.

The hand was entirely red, and again Lillia fought a moment of terror, fearful that she was being tricked. How could her grandfather be that way? How could he be red and have more than two arms?

"If you're really my grandfather, tell me what you like to call me," she demanded in a trembling voice.

"Call you! Child, I will call you 'trouble' if you don't give me those keys." But even full of anger and frustration, the voice still sounded just like her grandfather's. "I call you lots of things, little one—dearest, honey, little lion cub."

"Then what's my horse's name?"

"God's Bloody Tree, child!" Now it sounded more than ever like her grandfather Simon. "It's not a horse, it's a pony, and its name is Moth."

Thrilled beyond all measure, she dropped the keys into the waiting hand.

"Now turn away, dear," her grandfather said. "There's a man on top of me—a very large man—and I have to push him off me. I don't want you to see him. It's not a pretty sight. Go on, turn your back like a good girl."

She had a hundred, hundred questions for him but at that moment could not think of even one. She turned her back, and heard her grandfather breathing loudly, gasping even, then a dull thump as something large rolled onto the floor. "Look away!" Grandfather warned her again, then she heard keys clicking against metal, and a moment later a hand came down on her shoulder.

"Out the door," he said. "Let us go—hurry! By all the saints and angels, child, what are you doing down here?"

Lillia burst into tears again. "I was lost!"

"But you found me! Stay with me now, little cub—I'll keep you safe." He prodded her toward the door. A moment later they were back in the corridor where the light was brighter. Lillia looked up at him and screamed.

"What is it?" her grandfather asked. "Are you hurt?"

"You're all red!" she said, pulling away. "Like the bad thing."

He shook his head. The king was indeed red and wet all over—his face, his beard, his hands, his shirt. "It's only blood," he said. "And most of it isn't mine, thank our Ransomer."

"I thought everything down here might turn red after—after it dies. Like that devil. Are you dead too?" She didn't want to believe it, but she still couldn't quite be certain that she was safe again with her beloved grandfather. "You won't hurt me?"

"Bless you child, no. I'm not dead and I would never, ever hurt you." He suddenly dropped to his knees and embraced her. As she felt his strong arms and smelled the living, real smell of her very own Grandfather King Simon, the tears came even harder.

"It's you! It really is!"

"And you have saved me, my wonderful, clever granddaughter. And maybe saved the kingdom as well." He hugged her hard, burying his face in her hair. She didn't even care that he was getting it all sticky with blood. "I will take you to someplace safe, I promise," he said. "After that—well, your grandfather is going to have an ugly fight on his hands. But this time, the fight won't all go one way."

39

The Queen's Device

The Silken Span swayed in the wind, creaking with each step their horses took. Tanahaya did not fear high places, but it was still strange to look down into the occasional gap between boards and see the narrow valley so very, very far beneath them.

"The bridge will not fail," Aditu reassured her.

"I am not such a craven," said Tanahaya, smiling. "But I admit it is an arresting sight from here. Look, the river is just a blue thread."

"The water is much higher in the spring," said Ayaminu. "It climbs far up the wall of the gorge."

Tanahaya turned her attention back to the city itself, still a furlong away at the end of the slender, swaying bridge. Although it showed many touches of vivid color—golden and red banners, roof tiles of green and pale blue slate—most of the city's facing, including the outer wall and the towers that loomed on either side of the gate, was cased in ice-white limestone. The towers tapered upward, ending in clusters of needle-thin spires three times the height of the gatehouse.

"Your city is very beautiful, my lady," said Tanahaya.

"This is only the mask it shows the world," Ayaminu replied, "—or what small portion of the world ever ventures into these high, cold lands. You will soon see the face it keeps for its inhabitants and friends. Then tell me what you think."

"The towers are called the Eyes of Anvi'janya," Ayaminu's grandson, Liko, called back to her. "From their tops, sharp-sighted sentries can see for fifty leagues north, east, and west."

"Fifty leagues, yes," Ayaminu said. "But only to discern something large—a signal fire or a coming storm. Do not make it sound as if we can count the fleas on a bear's back from such a distance."

Ayaminu, Tanahaya thought, was in no hurry to boast, though High Anvi'janya was worth boasting about, if only because it was the last stone settlement of the Zida'ya still thriving. But Tanahaya knew that the mistress of this isolated place was famously quiet about herself, and apparently about her city as well.

"I have read that this place was built not long after the Nine Cities began," Tanahaya said as the length of remaining bridge shrank and the walls loomed higher and higher.

Lady Ayaminu made the sign for *days long past.* "My ancestor, Tululiko the Herald, found this place less than ten Great Years after our people arrived from the dying Garden. Jenjiyana and her husband Initri had sent him to search for others of our people, since the Eight Ships had all landed in different places. On his way from Tumet'ai to Mezutu'a, Tululiko saw this spot, a great cavern in a tall peak, and decided that he would claim it for his clan, the Anvi. Then, after almost another Great Year had passed, and he had completed his mission for the Sa'onsera and the Protector by finding the landing places of several of the other Great Ships, Tululiko asked Tumet'ai's permission to begin a new settlement here. He and others of our people built this place—though not without help from the Vao, who were skilled in crafting in stone and metal and shaping the materials of the earth to their own ends, both in our lost Garden and here."

Tanahaya was intrigued. "You call them Vao, not Tinukeda'ya?"

"I call them what they call themselves." Ayaminu gave her a sharp but not unfriendly look. "You seem preoccupied, young scholar. Have I told you only things you already knew?"

"No, Mistress." She made a sign of emphasis. "Not at all. But I confess I am wondering why your people chose to live here instead of where one of the great ships would provide the necessities to build a city."

"Necessities? Here we are surrounded by stone and wood and water—everything needed to build. But I deem that was not the only meaning of your question. Among the Anvi, it has long been told that Tululiko was weary of the contending of the two great Keida'ya clans, the Sa'onserei and Hamakha—that he wanted to make a home for himself and his followers without having to choose a side in a conflict he thought was dangerous to both parties." She fell silent for a while, thinking. "My father Kuroyi was much the same. Always he fought to be independent of the great clans, and to keep our city that same way. Alas, in the end, Utuk'ku—may her name and deeds wither into dust!—took that choice from us when she murdered First Grandmother Amerasu. And then she killed my father, too."

"I never met him," Tanahaya said as they rode off the bridge and onto the tongue of stone that led to the massive gate. "But I know he was one of the greatest of our kind."

"If you truly wish to know more about Anvi'janya and our clan," Ayaminu said, "I will be happy to tell you all I know—when our larger troubles permit it."

"That would be a gift indeed." Tanahaya looked at the stone eagle, whose unfurled wings formed the lintel of the gateway, and could not help but be impressed. She had never seen an ancient city of her people that was not in ruins. "But first, *S'huesa,* I must beg your leave to visit your archives. I have a great fear and will not be able to rest until it has either been proved or disproved."

"I hope the fear proves groundless, but I will summon Dineke, Master of the Repository. He will help you find what you seek."

Aditu said, "And I hope the same. I also hope you will not disappear into your dusty books for days and days, dear Spark. I long to sit with you at ease and share all our news."

"Hah!" Ayaminu shook her head. "You will have small time to ease yourself in the coming days, *Mu-Sa'onserá*," she told Aditu. "Have you forgotten why you are here?"

"Of course not. But it is still many sunsets until Year-Dancing. If I cannot find a few moments to talk to my dear friend in that time, I shall have to give the hospitality of Anvi'janya a poor report."

"Oh, would you?" Ayaminu frowned, but Tanahaya had begun to realize that this was the mistress of Anvi'janya's way, to seem short-tempered when in truth she was not. "I always suspected that you children of the Second Exile, running wild in the forest since birth, would lack for proper manners when you grew. Now my worst fears have been proved real."

"You were right to worry, Mistress," Aditu said, smiling at Tanahaya. "We have given over the old ways completely and are like animals. Just ask the Pure."

Her friend meant it as a jest, but Tanahaya suddenly remembered that there might not be any of the Pure left alive, and Aditu saw it on her face. "At least let us eat and drink together, Spark," she said quickly, "before you go off to hunt among the old tales. I beg you give me that much, at least."

"Of course, Rabbit," Tanahaya answered, but already she felt a pull, the worrisome weight of sliding time.

Anvi'janya was small compared to any of the Nine Cities—at least four or five settlements the same size would have fit within the toppled boundary stones of Da'ai Chikiza, to name only one—but it had been crafted with great care and an eye for the beauty of simplicity. It did not lack for decoration, but compared to the teeming scenes of nature rendered in stone that ornamented the other ancient settlements of her people, the city in the mountain cavern was simple, almost spare.

"I must ride ahead," Ayaminu announced. "I have been gone since the middle of the Tortoise Moon, and there are many things waiting for me. But you two have no need to hurry—Liko will accompany you."

"I do have some need for haste, remember," said Tanahaya.

"All will be ready when you reach the Clanhold." Ayaminu led her riders away down the wide main road toward the far end of the city, but Tanahaya and Aditu followed her grandson, who chose a more roundabout route. Soon they were passing a great curving wall of stone more than half as high as the cavern roof. Thin streams of water ran twinkling down its face and splashed into a wide canal at the base.

"Are those the famous waterfalls?" Tanahaya asked. "I mean no slight, Liko, but they seem more like trickles."

He laughed. "You arrived in the time of the year when the mountain crevices thicken with ice, Tanahaya. Come back in springtime and you will see them thundering down in great swoops of water and foam!"

"I meant it partially in jest. Your city is beautiful."

"It is, or so I have always thought." He pointed to a cylindrical building with a domed roof at the farthest end of the city. "There is the Clanhold where you will stay."

"What is the thing that stretches out in front of it? That canopy or roof held up by pillars?"

"Ah, that you must see from beneath to appreciate it, though this is the wrong time of day, just as it is the wrong time of year for the cataracts. Again, scholar, you must plan your visit better next time."

She smiled. She had assumed his name, "Starling," had been given because of the piebald coloring of his hair, but he had more than a little of the bird's cheekiness as well. "I confess I did not give as much thought as I could have to seeing all these celebrated sights in their proper seasons."

"And I hear you are interested mostly by the Repository, in any case," he said. "That to me is sad, because ours is likely no different than any other you have seen—dark, sunk deep in stone, and with few windows, so as not to distract scholarly types like yourself. But Anvi'janya has other sights far more grand and unusual."

"Those will have to wait," she told him. "But I am sure they are worth seeing."

Aditu rode up close beside her. "I think Ayaminu's grandson has taken a fancy to you," she whispered. "Should my brother be concerned?"

"Rabbit! You are very wicked." She made an exaggerated version of the gesture that meant *shame upon our house*, giving Aditu a stern look. "How could you say such a thing? In any case, I think it is you he fancies. He must like his females fat."

"Oh!" Aditu laughed. "Well, he would not be a fool if he did. I think my great belly is very fetching."

"It is," said Tanahaya, relenting. Indeed, she thought that her friend had never looked more hale and full of life. *I suppose that is because she truly is*, Tanahaya thought, amused. *Full of life.*

As they rode along the wide, curving street, Anvi'janya's inhabitants called and waved. Liko was clearly well-liked, and though nobody recognized Tanahaya—she would have been surprised if anyone had—many seemed to know Aditu and greeted her as well, some crying, "Year-Dancing is here!" as if Aditu were the living embodiment of the ceremony. "The People will not fail!" cried others, and Tanahaya wondered whether they were referring to the coming days of ritual or the roundness of her friend's belly.

One child will not save us, she thought, and put her hand on her own, still-flat stomach. *Nor will two.*

Tanahaya's first impression of the cavern city as a pearl in an oyster only became stronger as they followed the secondary road through the crowded city toward the curving, many-windowed wall of the Clanhold. Most of the buildings they passed were made of polished white stone. Many of the taller structures were connected to others by walkways or sheathed in exquisite staircases that climbed the outside of the graceful towers like tangles of snow-white ivy.

They certainly like high bridges and perches, she decided, eyeing the arc of one such span far above her head. *It is like the descriptions I have heard of Hikehikayo, but brighter and more spaciously arranged.* In its great days, the city of Hikehikayo had often been called "the Shadow-Forest" because its buildings huddled so close together, like barnacles growing on a pier, and were mostly made from light-swallowing black basalt. But Anvi'janya's structures, both grand and humble, were covered in identical pale stone and decorated with simple, curving shapes as delicate as the gills and rings of a snowdrop mushroom, so that the city seemed almost a single living thing.

"Now we are beneath the Pavilion," Liko announced as they rode out between a row of tall, graceful houses into an open area roofed in sparkling colors. Tanahaya looked up and saw that panes of colored crystal, blue, yellow, and green, had been set into a meshwork of stone that arched high above the paving. The individual crystals had an hourglass shape, so that they looked much like spread-winged butterflies, although she thought they were oddly dark and muddy.

"Only once a day do our butterflies take the light," said Liko. "At noon, when the sun's rays knife down from a crevice high in the mountain. We Anvi call this place the False Yásira—meant with no disrespect, Lady Aditu, I promise you. It was Tuliliko's jest, a way of saying that though we would never be Tumet'ai or Asu'a, where the clans and the sacred butterflies gathered, we still considered ourselves sovereign in our own country."

"I look forward to seeing it when the light is upon it," Tanahaya told him.

They came at last to the Clanhold and its great doors carved with images of mountains. The guards there took their horses away to the stables, and they entered the great antechamber, a hall that covered much of the bottom floor of the residence. An irregular stone table, wide enough to seat many, dominated the room. The table looked to have been shaped directly from the naked rock, and its base seemed part of the floor, as if it had sprouted there like a mushroom.

A Sitha Tanahaya did not know approached Liko and whispered in his ear. The Starling's face, cheerful only moments before, took on a serious cast. "Apparently a messenger has arrived from Tanakirú," he said.

"Have they news from my brother?" asked Aditu. "Are his whereabouts known?"

The look on Liko's face gave Tanahaya a shudder of worry. "Better you should come and learn for yourself, Lady Aditu," he told her. "I only know my grandmother sends for us." He turned to Tanahaya. "I apologize. We must wait before we bring you to Dineke the Scholar—*S'huesa* Ayaminu asked for both you and Aditu."

Ayaminu's chambers on an upper floor of the Clanhold were as plain as any scholar's, though they lacked the clutter of books and scrolls that would litter most places of study. Instead, a few branches of white mountain bell stood in a fluted vase atop a table, where Ayaminu sat waiting. Her guest, Tanahaya was not particularly pleased to see, was Dunao the Gray Rider, one of Khendraja'aro's chief allies, and she was disturbed by his appearance. Dunao had the look of someone who had ridden far and fast. Worse, his garments were stained with dried brown splashes that looked like blood, and his thin face was weary and full of gloom.

"Lady Aditu," he said. He did not rise but made a sign of courtesy. His eyes shifted to Tanahaya. "And the scholar, too. I had the idea that you had gone to the mortal castle that roosts on the bones of Asu'a. You certainly proclaimed that choice loudly enough."

"What brings Tanahaya here is not under discussion," said Aditu sternly. "Why are *you* here, Lord Dunao?"

His face grew even more grave, and Tanahaya could see his deep weariness and pain even more clearly. She did her best to push her resentment aside. "I am afraid I bring no good news," he said. "The Hornet's Nest fortress above Wormscale Gorge has fallen to the Hikeda'ya. Now almost all the Narrowdark Valley is theirs." He turned to Aditu. "I regret to tell you also that your uncle, Protector Khendraja'aro, is dead."

"Dead!" Color drained from Aditu's golden skin. "By the Garden, that is ill news indeed. And the Hornet's Nest has fallen to our enemies?" She passed both hands over her face as if to wipe away the dreadful tidings. "How did this happen?"

"I have heard no more than this myself," Ayaminu said, "because we waited for you two to arrive. Please, Lord Dunao, give us your tale now. I have sent for refreshment for you."

"Neither food nor drink will fill the hole in me," he said. "But I thank you. Lady Aditu, in light of your condition, please be seated."

"I am well as I stand," said Aditu, not without a hint of brittleness, but after a moment she chose one of the seats around the table and lowered herself into it. She sighed. "I ask your pardon, Dunao. My last words with my uncle were also harsh ones. I wish I could amend that, but an arrow cannot fly backward to the string. May he find the light that shines above the bow." She took a shaky breath. "Tell us what happened, please."

"As you know, we have held Wormscale Gorge for years against the Hikeda'ya, and fought on through each blood-red moon of this year, as Utuk'ku and her generals sent more and more of their Sacrifices against us. Before Utuk'ku finally showed her true intent in Jao e-Tinukai'i, turning the long Mirror War into open conflict, the Hornet's Nest had never been overcome, so even though we were much outnumbered, we felt confident we could keep the Hikeda'ya out of the Narrowdark and far from Tanakirú."

Tanahaya remembered the strange fogs and the sluggish waters of the valley where she had rescued the mortal prince, Morgan. "But why would the Hikeda'ya want to take that strange, empty place? And why are we losing our people's lives to defend it?"

A brief look passed between Aditu and Ayaminu, but Dunao continued as though she had not spoken. One of his braids, Tanahaya saw, had come loose; his hair hung down on one side like a curtain pulled over half a window.

"Lady Aditu, your brother Jiriki came to Protector Khendraja'aro in the Hornet's Nest a short time ago and asked for fighters to defend the mortal kingdom's castle, the one built on the bones of Asu'a, because of news he had been given that it was threatened somehow. After much argument, Khendraja'aro gave him permission to take such warriors as were willing to follow him. Something less than ten score of our people chose to go with your brother."

Tanahaya could not help asking, "Was Jiriki well when you saw him last?"

"Well enough to take away a goodly number of our fighters," Dunao said with a look like sour milk. "Well enough to hurry off to defend mortals while we fought for our lives between the two valleys." He fell silent for a long moment before speaking again. "Then, only a few sunsets ago, as we sat at our meal in the hall of the Hornet's Nest, a figure appeared as if from nowhere, climbing in the wide window that overlooked the pass. Do not ask how we could let this happen," he said, though no one had spoken. "Every finger-span of the track up from the valley below was guarded. The intruder must have made his way up the sheer stone cliff from the bottom of the pass, climbing like a lizard—silently too, since no one heard or saw him until he appeared in the hall."

"What kind of creature could accomplish such a thing?" Aditu asked.

"So you might ask." Dunao bunched his hands into fists. "I still do not know what he was, except that he had been Hikeda'ya—once."

"What does that mean?" said Ayaminu.

"It means that he was no longer anything natural. I saw him, Mistress—I was there. He wore the armor of a Hikeda'ya chieftain, but his face was as gray and leathery as the hide of a tortoise. He had but one eye, burning bright as a flame. I swear by the ship that brought my ancestors here, he was a walking corpse. I have never seen anything like it."

"I have," said Ayaminu in a grim voice. "Outside Nakkiga, when the mortals tried to take the mountain city in the days after the Storm King was defeated. The Hikeda'ya Order of Song used their foul knowledge to raise the dead there, too. This creature must be Akhenabi's work."

Aditu reacted with dismay. "Akhenabi? Utuk'ku's chief conjuror? That cruel, slithering beast?"

"Of course," said Ayaminu. "When Duke Isgrimnur and his soldiers besieged Nakkiga, Akhenabi raised many dead mortal soldiers from their shallow graves—made them walk and even slay their living comrades. This thing that attacked the fortress is of the Lord of Song's making, I promise."

"Whatever it was," said Dunao, "none could stand against it. I tried, many others tried, but its strength was like that of a giant, and its sword swift as a striking serpent. The closest of our fighters were surprised and killed by him just in the first instants, and when the rest of us hurried toward him, he picked up the stone table, which must have weighed as much as ten of us, and threw it, scattering us like leaves in a gale. Ganida of the Limberlight was crushed beside me, and several more were crippled. My arm was broken." For the first time, Dunao threw back his cloak to reveal his hand. The fingers were puffed like overripe seed pods, the skin purple and black where it showed between his linen bandages. The rest of his arm was hidden by his bloody, tattered sleeve. "But when the creature would have finished me, your uncle Khendraja'aro leaped between us. He put up a strong fight, but the thing that attacked us was truly terrible. In a short while Khendraja'aro was beaten down to the floor. Then, while he struggled to rise, the creature cut off his head."

"By the Grove," said Aditu, her voice more fearful than Tanahaya had ever heard. "My mother's brother. This is foul. This is foul!"

"You have not heard all the foulness yet," said Dunao. "Though the dead thing scaled the crags leading to the Hornet's Nest by itself, Hikeda'ya troops followed not long after. When the sentries nearest the fort heard the cries from the hall, many of them left their posts to help and, in their wake, the attackers swarmed up the hill's trackway like termites. Those of us still alive in the hall could hear the fighting getting nearer and knew that the Sacrifices would soon reach the fortress. Meanwhile, the thing—the dead thing—was hacking to pieces all who came against it. I could no longer hold a sword in my hand, so I gathered all the Zida'ya I could save and we fled the hall." He looked at Ayaminu, then at Aditu, and it was hard to tell whether his fury or shame were greater. "Yes. We fled. I fled."

"Nobody has spoken against you, Lord Dunao," said Ayaminu.

"I feel what you do not say," he countered. "But it matters little what you think—or what I think, for that matter. Our warriors were caught between the upward-rushing Hikeda'ya and the deadly gray thing in the hall. I led as many as I could down a second, secret track the Hikeda'ya did not know. When we reached relative safety, I dispatched most of the survivors up the valley, to . . ." He paused then and looked at Tanahaya and Liko, as if suddenly uncertain of what to say.

"You sent them to the headwaters of Tanakirú," said Ayaminu.

"Yes. If they can harry General Ensume and his Spider Legion from behind, then it may help Chekai'so, Yizashi, and the others to hold out longer."

"*What* others?" Liko asked. "And what are these headwaters? *S'huesa*?"

"Soon you will know everything," Ayaminu told her grandson. "But first we have more immediate things to discuss. You sent the fort's other survivors up the valley, Lord Dunao, but you came here to Anvi'janya. Why?"

"Why? Because this is the closest settlement of any size. Because we have lost our commander, Khendraja'aro, and our fortress in the pass as well. Nothing remains but a shrinking army of our people defending . . ." Again he paused.

"It is likely we now hold only the very northernmost part of the vale. If there is a more dangerous spot on this teeming world, I cannot imagine it. We need every one of the Zida'ya at our side now or we will perish and Utuk'ku and the thrice-cursed Hamakha will have the victory." Dunao's face looked as if his many Great Years of life had all caught up to him at once. "We will none of us survive that, I think."

"Even in my ignorance, I can see this is terrible news," Tanahaya said. "Aditu, my dear one, I pray that your uncle will find the Garden we all seek. You know he and I did not agree—we saw the world through very different eyes—but I never wished him harm. My sorrow is with your house."

Aditu nodded but did not meet her friend's eye.

Like me, she is fearful for Jiriki, she recognized. *But something else is troubling her as well—something I do not understand.* "*S'huesa* Ayaminu," Tanahaya said then, "I know there are things to be decided here, but I know just as well that they are not mine to decide. I still have an urgent need to visit your archives. Please believe me when I say my search may be just as important as Lord Dunao's ill news."

Ayaminu nodded. "Liko, take her to the Repository."

Tanahaya made a hand sign of apology. "I have one last question, I fear. Are all the Witnesses still silenced?"

"Why do you think I nearly killed my best horse coming here, scholar?" said Dunao.

"So we cannot speak with Jiriki, even in great need." It seemed unreal, as if Tanahaya had wandered in her sleep onto some dark and frightful stretch of the Dream Road. "Still, I must learn what I can." She rose, made a brief gesture of leavetaking, and followed Liko out of the chamber.

As she went out, she heard Ayaminu tell Dunao, "I do not know what this city has left to give. Even if we send word out to the nearest settlements, I fear we will find only a few score more fighters who can ride back to the vale with you. We must keep some few behind to defend Anvi'janya."

"If Utuk'ku wins the vale, how will you defend this place?" Dunao demanded. "Nothing will stop her. Nothing."

The door closed behind Tanahaya.

"Follow me," said Liko. His earlier light-heartedness was now quite gone.

Archive Master Dineke was small and slight, with an air of serenity that did not entirely obscure a trace of irritation at having been called away from a task of his own. "Liko says that Mistress Ayaminu directs me to give you every courtesy in using the Repository. Tell me what you require."

"Thank you, Archive Master." Tanahaya's fear had been growing since she had heard Dunao's news; she needed to discover as quickly as possible whether it was justified. "Please show me where you keep the archive of writings from Nakkiga."

"From Nakkiga?" Dineke's eyes narrowed. "What do you mean, 'from Nakkiga,' young scholar? We have countless tomes in which that place is mentioned, and almost that many in which Queen Utuk'ku and her rogue clans are discussed at length."

"No, I need writings from Nakkiga itself. Official documents from the Hikeda'ya, especially anything from just after the Parting."

Dineke looked doubtful. "We have precious few of those, as you may imagine. When the so-called queen separated her people from ours, she also stopped trade and discourse between us. But I will take you to what small amount we have." He led her into the broad archive hall, an eight-sided building with a high ceiling, like an immense beehive lined with square alcoves that stretched high up the walls. Dizzyingly tall ladders stood against the shelves on all sides, several of them occupied by librarian-scholars. Below them, a half dozen more archivists stood at the various stone tables. It was not unlike the library in Da'ai Chikiza, but much more clean and ordered.

No surprise there, she thought. *Anvi'janya has never been deserted. Nothing much has changed here since before the Parting.* She was struck with a sudden pang at the realization at how much of their people's story had already been lost with Tumet'ai, Asu'a, and all the other fallen cities.

Dineke led her to a ladder and pointed to a dark alcove halfway up the wall. From where Tanahaya stood it looked empty, and she said so.

"There are documents there, never fear," said the Archive Master. "But they are few, as I warned you. You will see them when you have climbed high enough."

As she mounted a ladder, Liko the Starling called up to her, "Now that you are in Master Dineke's good hands, I must leave you. My grandmother will likely need me for other errands."

"Go with the Garden's blessing." She climbed past alcove after alcove stuffed with dusty scrolls, some bound with twine, others with the *srinyedu* cord that marked them as important documents. As she reached the one Dineke had pointed out, she saw that he had been right: at least two dozen scrolls and several loose sheets of vellum covered the bottom of the square space, all curling with age.

Tanahaya opened the first and began puzzling her way through the Hikeda'yasao text, Dineke now quite forgotten beneath her at the bottom of the ladder. The Master Archivist, long inured to the obliviousness of scholars pursuing answers, shook his head and went back to his study.

Jiriki and his company rode for days across the southern reaches of the great forest and at last out onto the grasslands, stopping only long enough to water their horses. The impossibly swift, near-silent company swept through the fallow fields and past the hamlets of mortal men like something out of legend.

By day they seemed little more than a blur of horses and bright armor; by night they were a streaming silvery dream that would, in more ordinary times, have been talked about for years afterward by those who had caught sight of them.

The nearly full moon was a pale, weary blue, and its light washed the surrounding meadowlands in shades of pewter and ivory as Jiriki, Ki'ushapo, and the two volunteers from Peja'ura, Shen'de the Bowman and his great-granddaughter Rukayu Crow's Claw, led the troop up the steep hill toward a ring of trees. Despite the size of the host, their horses' hooves were almost silent—a mortal a hundred paces away would not have heard them riding at all.

"Why do we come here, kinsman?" asked Ki'ushapo. "This place had an ill name even before you and I were born—before the northern mortals came and threw down Asu'a."

"It did indeed," said Jiriki. "*Ukamu-e-noka,* the shadow hill. The mortals call it Thisterborg, and it has seen more than its share of ugly doings. It was here that the mortal king Elias made his bargain with Ineluki Storm-King."

Ki'ushapo gave him a look of dismay. "Then why do we climb it? Have we not enough dreadful omens already to last ten lifetimes?"

"Because this is the highest spot for at least a league in all directions," Jiriki said. "I wish to see what I can of the Hayholt."

Old Shen'de made a face. "Hayholt. Even the name is ugly in the mouth. I may not hate the mortals as many of our fellows do, but I can never forgive them what they did to our beautiful Asu'a."

"That was long ago—almost a score of mortal generations, though barely one of ours," said Jiriki. "And the north-men that destroyed Asu'a were not the same as those who live there now. Not all mortals are alike, any more than all Garden-folk are the same. In any case, the worst deeds of all were done there by Ineluki—my own ancestor."

"I concede your point," said Shen'de. "But it still does not make me love them."

"What do you see, Jiriki of the Year-Dancing?" asked Rukayu, the bowman's granddaughter. "You have always had the clearest sight of any of us."

Jiriki shook his head. "I see only the false storm that the queen's Singers have called down to hide themselves. It cloaks the mortal city of Erchester like muddy water, obscuring all beneath it." He leaned forward. "No, I do see something—mortals."

"What do you mean?" Ki'ushapo asked. "Coming toward us?"

The rest of the company, several hundred mounted male and female Sithi, had now reached the top of the hill and waited, still as statues. A few of them had hung bright house-pennants on their lances, but in all other ways it was a quiet, grim company. "Do not mistake me," said Jiriki. "When I said mortals, I did not mean an attacking force. See, look for yourselves. The downs to the south of us are full of them. They are fleeing their city."

"I see them!" Rukayu said. "Scores and scores of them scattering in all directions! What do they flee? The Hikeda'ya?"

"What else?" Jiriki settled back into his saddle. "That mortal city has suffered beneath the icy hand of Nakkiga before. Even short-lived mortals must remember it all too well."

"It is sad, but we can do nothing to help them," said Ki'ushapo, as though he feared Jiriki might try to rescue every straggler, every stumbling mortal.

"No," said Jiriki. "We cannot. And we dare not linger here any longer."

"Look there!" cried Rukayu. "I see a great flame leaping toward the sky!"

"It is the castle," Jiriki said, and his voice was strained. "They have already reached it. Ride now!" he cried, turning to the waiting Zida'ya. "Ride! The Hikeda'ya await!"

"But they are thousands," said Ki'ushapo. "And we are only a few score. What can we do?"

"What can true hearts ever do?" Jiriki asked. "Whatever good they can manage before the end of things. Now we must ride!"

A stir went through the gathered ranks, and a few of the Zida'ya horses reared and flaunted their hooves at the air, as if already come to battle. Then, as Jiriki spurred Ayaminu's Cloudfoot down the hill toward the storm-darkened city and the castle, the rest of his company leaped out behind him, as if one thought guided them.

Lances shimmering in the light of the moon and the cold stars, the Zida'ya raced down the hill toward what had once been their people's home, toward the deadly battle they knew they would find there. A few voices even rose in war-song, but soon fell silent again, swallowed in the muffled thunder of hooves.

After several hours of working her way through ancient Hikeda'ya writings, Tanahaya believed she had finally found what she was searching for. Her sinking heart certainly seemed to agree, but she wanted confirmation from an experienced eye.

She clambered down the ladder and headed for Dineke's study. "Archive Master!" she called. "Are you there? I need to ask your help."

He came out, rubbing his long chin, looking for a moment as though he did not remember who she was. "What is it? Ah, you—it is you. What can I do? I am in the middle of a most perplexing—"

She did not wait for him to finish. "Look at this. Tell me what you see."

He took the scroll from her reluctantly—it was dirty, smirched with lampblack. "Much of it has been obscured," he said. "It seems to be from the time of High Celebrant Sumizhe."

"It is. Just tell me what this is, here."

"It is Utuk'ku's own mark, of course, may her cursed name vanish from our people's story." He frowned. "Why such an alarm, Tanahaya of Shisae'ron?

Nothing comes out of Utuk'ku's royal palace, the *Omeiyo Hamakh,* without the queen's hand upon it. See, that is her initial, and there is her device." He pointed at the seal beside the stylized U-rune.

"Exactly—her device. The queen's device!"

Dineke gave her a puzzled look. "As I said, you will not find any important palace letters from that time—or this, I would guess—that do not have the queen's signet upon them."

"But where is the scribe's device? Where is the seal of the scribe who actually wrote it?"

Dineke squinted, bringing his straw-colored eyes close to the parchment. "I do not see it. In truth, I do not believe that scribes signed their own names in those days. Back then, clerics were held in little regard by Utuk'ku's folk—"

Again she interrupted him. "Thank you. You have answered the first part of my need. Now, tell me what you see here." She held up another parchment, this one almost pristine except for the wrinkles where it had been folded too tightly, perhaps while being carried.

"This is something more mundane and much more recent," Dineke said, running his eyes across it. "Another court document, some matter of military accounting from the Sacrifice order-house. There is the mark of Nakkiga's old High Marshal, Ekisuno, who died in the Storm King's War, and beneath it are the seals of various other Sacrifice officers."

"Yes, but at the very bottom?"

"The chronicler's seal. I have seen it before but cannot bring it to mind."

"Here it is again." She held up another document. "Who might know whose seal this is?"

"Why so much concern over a chronicler's marks?"

"Because I have seen it before, and that is of terrible importance. But, please, I must know to whom this belongs."

He waved his hand in frustration. "Young scholar, you are making a great deal of trouble for me . . ."

"Please! I need to know this one thing, then I promise I will leave you alone." Her heart was beating swiftly now, and a creeping cold stole through her.

Dineke considered for a moment. "Mayara is one of our oldest archivists, and she once made a study of Nakkiga's methods for making and storing documents."

"Take me to her. Please."

Although Tanahaya's thoughts were in such a storm that she could barely find her way back through the confusing, unfamiliar corridors, after a false start or two she discovered the antechamber of the lower hall and from there was able to make her way to Ayaminu's residence.

She discovered the mistress of Anvi'janya deep in talk with Dunao the Rider. The tabletop was covered in maps and lists. Neither looked up when she came in.

"Lady Ayaminu," she said. "Lord Dunao. I beg your pardons, but I must speak to you both. I do not think it can wait."

Dunao frowned, but Ayaminu's look was more tempered, bemused rather than annoyed. "I hope you have brought good news, young scholar," she said. "We are in sore need of some."

Tanahaya's heart felt bruised. "I fear my news may be only a little less grim than Lord Dunao's. But first let me tell my own story, since Lord Dunao has not heard it." She quickly explained the discovery of the parchment on her beloved teacher Himano's body, how she and Lady Vinyedu of the Pure had translated it, and how Tanahaya had relayed what the document said to Jiriki just before Vinyedu's Witness was silenced. "And I still have Himano's parchment."

Tanahaya unfurled it on Ayaminu's table. "Look," she said, "it speaks of the Witchwood Crown, a mystery that has puzzled us since we first heard the whispers that Utuk'ku was seeking it. It tells that the Witchwood Crown taken from Hamakho the Great in the Garden contained living seeds of the witchwood trees, and that the crown had been buried in what are now the ruins of old Asu'a, deep beneath the mortals' Hayholt castle."

Dunao leaned in, not to look at the parchment, but to stare angrily at Tanahaya. "Are you saying it was this single written record that caused Jiriki to deprive us of needed fighters in the Narrowdark Valley?"

"Please," said Ayaminu. "Let her finish speaking."

Tanahaya took a deep breath before continuing. "While I was with Vinyedu and her Pure, Utuk'ku's Sacrifices swept down on Da'ai Chikiza in great numbers, killing Vinyedu and her Jonzao Clan. I barely escaped with my life. Soon after that, the queen of Nakkiga led her vast army south. It seemed clear that she aimed to take the mortal castle and recover the only remaining witchwood seeds in this land."

"I have heard much of this already from Jiriki, when he came to the Hornet's Nest." Dunao seemed a little less resistant now, but still angry. "So it *was* you who set Jiriki on his mission."

"Enough, Rider." The mistress of Anvi'janya wore a grim look. "Just tell us what you have learned, Tanahaya."

"Vinyedu said this document about burying the Witchwood Crown under Asu'a had been written many Great Years ago. Something about that, though, seemed strange to me, and now I have found out why. Do you see the chronicler's mark below the queen's device?"

"We see it," said Ayaminu.

"Then look now to these other parchments from Nakkiga, created in the same era." Tanahaya held up a handful of scrolls she had brought from the Repository. "Do you see? Even these, some created later than the one I took from Himano's body, have no chronicler's mark. That custom did not begin in Nakkiga until many, many Great Years later. And yet the parchment that tells of the Witchwood Crown being buried underneath the mortal castle has just such a seal at the bottom!"

"That does not prove anything except that Himano's document may have been unusual," Ayaminu pointed out.

"I wish I could agree. But see this sign here at the bottom of Himano's parchment." Tanahaya pointed. "It is the mark of the scribe who wrote it. After searching, I found others like it in the archive—it is the mark of a Lady Miga seyt-Jinnata."

Ayaminu took a surprised breath. "I know her."

"I do not," said Dunao, glaring like a bird of prey. "Why is this meaningful?"

"Because," Ayaminu replied, "Lady Miga was not born until twenty Great Years or more after this document about the Witchwood Crown was supposedly written."

Now that Ayaminu had confirmed it, Tanahaya felt the full weight of her own foolishness. *Jiriki*, she thought, *my beloved, I have sent you into a trap.*

"So you are telling us that this document she found with Himano was false," said Dunao. "That we gave up those warriors to Jiriki for no good reason."

Ayaminu turned to Tanahaya, face grim. "Could there be any less disheartening conclusion?"

"I cannot think of one," she said. "Worse than that, I fear this trick was meant to make us do exactly what we have done." She lowered her head in shame and despair. "What *I* have done."

"Lady Miga is one of the Hikeda'ya who do not love what the queen has done to her people," said Ayaminu. "She must have risked her life to warn us, hoping that we would see her sign on this supposedly ancient document—a false document, forged at the queen's own order, I would guess."

"And Jiriki is rushing to the Hayholt because I told him of it." Tanahaya wanted nothing more in that moment than to be alone. "Which, it seems, is exactly what the Hikeda'ya queen and her counselors wanted to happen."

"But why?" Dunao asked. "Even if all this supposition is true, why should Utuk'ku go to such lengths?"

"To weaken our defenses in Tanakirú—the Vale of Mists," said Ayaminu slowly. "And to draw our attention away from what is happening there, where the fate of our people may hang in the balance. And the mistress of Nakkiga has succeeded in her aim—in fact, by doing so, she may have already won the war." She turned to Tanahaya. "Ask my grandson Liko to bring Aditu here. I know what it is that Utuk'ku truly desires, and so does Lord Dunao. I have a tale I must reveal to you now—a terrible secret."

Hakatri

Third Interlude

He awakened into horror, his home in flames.

The walls had been thrown down, the marble facing shattered like thin ice, the very stones uprooted and tumbled. Squat, animalistic figures raced through the evening gloom—bearded, bloody-handed men who howled like wolves as they chased down the palace's last survivors.

Mortals. Mortals were destroying Asu'a! Where were his people? Was this a dream of what was to come? He felt helpless rage boiling through him. He had no fists to clench, no hands to wield a sword. He yearned to grip Thunderbolt's hilt, but he might as well have been a cloud floating uselessly over the death of the city.

This is what they did. The voice had returned, the strange voice that seemed to speak with more than one tongue. *This is what the mortals, the Sunset Children, did to great Asu'a.*

He could not believe it. This was some nightmare, some unlikely possibility, like the fractured visions he had once seen in the deserted ruins of Sesuad'ra, the sacred hill called the Leavetaking Stone.

No. The voice was stern, even harsh. *No, it happened. After you left your people behind. The mortals came and destroyed everything.*

He finally found a voice of his own. *How could this happen?*

A mixture of fury and weakness. A fatal reluctance. Your brother tried to stop it, but in the end, it took his life.

Ineluki? The name came back and with it, the phantom of his brother's face, his fair, laughing features. *My brother is dead?*

Long since. But he fought the mortal destroyers so fiercely that his name became a curse among them. And as the nameless voice spoke, he felt a presence too, for the first time, felt it reach out and enfold him in the warmth of its power. *But our race survived. We fought back, led by the proud Hikeda'ya and the unkillable strength of your brother's spirit. We came within a hair's-breadth of spinning time backward on its axis, of undoing the unimaginable. But again we failed, and this time your noble brother's spirit was banished, cast out into the cold void forever, for the sin of loving his people.*

No! The slaughter still raged around him, but he could not touch it, could not stop it. He saw his kin fall beneath the crude weapons of the mortals, saw the tiles of the Tan'ja Stairs run scarlet with their blood. *Stop it!* he cried. *Stop this!*

It is too late, the voice told him. *It was finished long ago. And it was not the last of their attacks on the survivors.* A thunderous wave of vision crashed upon him, a fractured mirror of destruction and death, immortals mowed down like dandelions, crystalline beauties smashed to pieces, the great towers crumbling into dust and rubble. Dark eyes and golden eyes stared out at him in helpless despair as the mortals beat his people down, skewered them, set them on fire. And then the voice again, tolling like a doomful bell. *Because you left.*

But the burning inside me! And even as he said it, he felt it once more, his bones kindling with agonizing whitefire, his blood boiling from the cursed black blood. *I could find no peace! No aid!*

You fled your people, the many-tongued voice declared, harsh as a crow's screech. *You left them, and then they were all but destroyed.*

But what could I have done? I could not even be a father or husband to my family! Every waking moment was agony.

And now every waking moment is agony for your people. Your parents were betrayed. Your brother was not strong enough by himself to stem the tide, to turn back the flood of mortals, to save your home and your kin from annihilation. They slew your wife at the foot of the great staircase—yes, they killed the Lady of the Silver Braids in her own house. Do you see her, lying in her blood as life ebbs? She is wondering how it all came to this—wondering with her last thoughts where in the world her husband is while his family dies.

Before him was the greatest horror of all, but for a terrible moment he could not even remember her name. Then it came to him.

Briseyu. Oh, by our sacred grove, I loved her. I loved her!

Not enough to stay. And your people? Did you not love them? The scornful words surrounded him and forced their way into the sore spaces between his thoughts. *And your daughter Likimeya, who had to flee alone into the forest like a hunted animal?*

Did she live? Tell me that she lived!

For a little while. But now she is with us—one of the lost, the abandoned. Listen to the wind of our thoughts and you will hear her. Listen, Protector Who Was Not. You are the only hope she has left.

And in that acute, agonizing instant, he *could* hear his daughter in the knot of voices, though she spoke the same words as the rest, blamed him with the same angry mind and heart. The voices filled all his thoughts now even when they did not speak with words, the continuous roar of a windstorm made from shame and fury. *How can this be?* It was a scream, though he had no lips or tongue. *How can this be?*

We have told you. The mortals destroyed Asu'a. They killed your brother and your wife, and they drove your mother and daughter into exile. Then a mortal slew your mother Amerasu, and later a band of mortals ambushed your daughter Likimeya, so that she barely clings to her life and to the world. All because you were not there when you were needed. Our people are all but ended. The mortals and the traitors who sided with them now are trying to destroy the rest, to make a world in which only mortals remain, breeding like vermin, infesting every inch of this world.

And can we do nothing to stop it? He had thought he could not feel any pain to rival the burning blood, but now his heart faltered before a horror he could never have imagined. *Nothing?*

You are Hakatri. You are the true Protector, though you fled your responsibilities. But a moment is coming, an instant of balance where everything might change. Would you repair the harm you have done?

Yes! Yes! He could not imagine knowing what he had learned, seeing what he had been shown, and still doing nothing. *I have sinned against my people. I have let my pain make me weak!* He was Hakatri i-Sa'onserei, scion of his clan. He had been reminded, and now he remembered. His fierce love for all that he had inherited smoldered inside him, perhaps even hotter than the dragon's blood. *Tell me what I can do to save our people!*

Prepare yourself, the voices told him, speaking as one. Again the flames rose before him, and again he was assaulted by the shrieking of innocents, the red wash of lives cut to pieces in an instant. *Store up your anger. Seize your fury and prepare to wield it like a weapon. Only that way can our people be saved.*

I will do it. I will make it all right again. And for a moment the pain of his terrible injuries subsided, the pain that had so long been a part of his very being, not merely a malady of his long-lost body. An icy determination rushed in to fill the empty place. *I will undo what the mortals have done. Because I am Hakatri of the Year-Dancing, Asu'a's heir and its avenger. I am our people's last Protector.*

Yes, the knotted voices told him. *Yes. Now you understand.*

40

Fire in the Keep

"I swear by the Holy Wounds of the Aedon, there are thousands upon thousands of them," whispered Zakiel in sickly astonishment. "How could this be? We are undone."

The captain and Sir Porto stood atop the Nearulagh Gate's western gatehouse. The slope at the base of the Hayholt's great outwall was swarming with dark shapes. More Norn soldiers than Porto had dreamed existed were assembled in front of the castle, and though only one in every score of them held a torch, the light of the flames still turned the night into yellow daylight. Every time one of the invaders looked up and Porto saw a pale, corpse-face, he shuddered like a man with a fever. Nightmarish memories of the fighting on Nakkiga's deadly slopes threatened to sweep him away into madness.

"How can there be so many?" he asked in a strangled voice. "How? When Duke Isgrimnur led us against the Norn fortresses, only a handful of White Foxes were still alive." But this horde filled the wide hillside and stood in dark, armored ranks all the way back to the town wall of Erchester.

"May Hell take them all!" said Zakiel. "They must have some dark magic of the Adversary." A few arrows came whistling up from the Norns' front ranks; the lord captain hurriedly moved back from the parapet. The guards inside the gatehouse drew and loosed, but their arrows seemed to fall among the Norns without effect. "I realize now I do not know anything, Sir Porto," he said. "The world is a vile pit, and we are abandoned by Man and God alike."

"Hold fast to your courage, Captain. God would not abandon us!" But Porto's own newfound faith was badly shaken. "He tests us!"

"This is no mere test. This is the end of the world." Zakiel was almost as pale as the Norn soldiers milling below.

Porto could think of nothing to prove the Lord Captain wrong. As they stared down at the enemy, a procession came marching out of the center of the besieging army, a strange, hard-shelled line with many legs.

"The Norns are holding shields above their heads," said Zakiel. "Look how big those are—it takes five of them just to hold up one shield! They must be bringing up their miners. The whiteskins mean to topple the gate from beneath." He raised his voice to a shout. "Loose at those carrying the shields! Aim at their legs!"

More arrows sped from both gatehouses, but even those that flew truly only smacked against the huge, curved shields and bounced away. Porto risked moving up to the edge of the parapet once more, head low as black arrows buzzed past him. "See that one at the front!" he called to Zakiel as the first shield to reach the gate stopped in front of the great, carved facade. "A Norn who carries some kind of crystal hammer."

"No hammer will break this gate," Zakiel declared, recovering a little of his confidence. "Nor will they dig under. The foundations of these towers are set all the way down into the walls of the old fairy castle."

But even as he spoke, the Norn warrior with the strange hammer summoned the other shield-bearers forward, until it looked as though the base of the gate house was surrounded by monstrous beetles.

Beetles, Porto thought in despair. *Earthchafers, that's where those shields come from. They are made from the plated shells of those terrible, rock-chewing beasts that brought down the walls of Naglimund.*

The entire guard tower quivered like a plucked string, but with no sound other than the scraping of sliding masonry. Porto grabbed at the battlement to keep from falling and looked down. Another hammer-wielding Norn had struck the base of the tower, and now swung back the long pole of gray wood with its faceted crystal head to strike again. Elsewhere along the wall, archers and soldiers manning great pots of flaming oil were fighting back, but, nightmarishly, their efforts seemed to accomplish almost nothing, as though the Norns were impervious to harm. A few of the besieging Sacrifices fell to the defenders' darts, or caught fire and ran, burning, but most of the enemy host stood untouched and seemingly unconcerned even as catapult-stones and arrows fell among then.

How can this be? The world has run mad—! Porto swayed and almost stumbled as the tower shook beneath him, then lost his balance and fell to his hands and knees.

"Loose your arrows!" screamed Captain Zakiel at the archers on the rampart beside them, sounding more panicked than Porto had ever heard him. "God's Blood, men, now—before they bring the whole gate down!"

But even as more arrows flew from the eastern gatehouse, the tower beneath Zakiel and Porto continued to shudder. Porto could feel every hammer blow, though he still could not hear them—the impact seemed to travel up through the masonry and shake his bones to jelly.

"This tower is going to come down and take us with it!" Porto shouted to Zakiel. "We must get the men out."

Zakiel stared at him, face almost empty of expression, as if he had lost the ability to understand his own spoken tongue. Then the tower swayed again. A piece of the parapet tipped a little, then slowly fell outward, taking with it a large section of the tower's upper wall. Zakiel was finally startled into movement. "Down!" he cried to the other soldiers. "Down! Make haste!"

The thunderous blows had stopped. Porto prayed that the chunk of falling parapet had killed the hammer-wielders, although he knew there was scant chance it had stopped them all. The tower swayed alarmingly around him as he hurried down the stairs. He heard a dreadful sound as the straining stone gave way and the stairwell behind him suddenly wrenched to one side and began to fall to pieces. Porto vaulted down the steps two at a time as bits of stone rubble bounced past him. He could see no sign of Zakiel following, but he dared not wait or go back for him.

Porto staggered down to ground level and joined a dozen other soldiers, some of them bleeding from their heads and other wounds, stumbling together onto the mud of the outer bailey. Above the shouts of the men in the eastern gatehouse and the screams of those still caught in the collapsing western side, he could hear the Norns chanting on the hill outside the walls, a dark, triumphant song, a celebration of blood spilled and blood yet to be shed.

As they staggered across the bailey toward the inner gate, Porto heard a groaning sound so loud that it seemed the death rattle of God Himself. He looked back and saw the tower they had just quit fall in on itself in a vast, booming rattle of stone and timber. A host of dark shapes, many bearing torches, came scrambling over the collapsed structure; a moment later, the massive Nearulagh Gate swung off its hinges on the west side and sagged inward as more dark shapes pushed through the gap. Several of the soldiers with him lifted their bows, but Porto shouted, "Save your shafts! There are too many of them to fight here!" But even as he tried to lead the surviving Erkynguards through the gate into the middle bailey, he wondered, *What good will any wall or gate do? They will just break them all down with those cursed hammers!*

Still, and especially if Zakiel had been killed in the collapsed tower, Porto could not leave these other Erkynguards, many of whom he knew, to die alone.

Black Norn arrows spattered against the iron-bound doors of the second gate, but the guards there had not deserted; as Porto's ragged company fled toward them, they opened the postern to let them through. He fell back to help the last men, who were carrying a wounded guard.

As they finally squeezed through the postern, Porto looked back and saw that many of the scores of Norns swarming into the outer bailey were carrying earthenware jugs on their shoulders. One of the invaders turned and threw his jar against the base of the crippled eastern gatehouse where it broke against the stone. Another white-faced Norn soldier threw a torch into the thick black liquid now oozing down the wall, and flames leaped up like dancing, capering demons. Within moments the fire had caught in the timbers of the gatehouse roof and set it blazing like a monstrous bonfire, flames leaping high into the sky. Erkynlandish soldiers tumbled from the upper windows, many of them burning.

Dear Merciful God save us, we are in Hell, was all Porto could think. Roaring flames were springing up along many of the buildings in the outer bailey. The viscous liquid in the jars was as black as pitch but seemed to burn much faster and hotter: already Porto could hear stones cracking in the heat.

Aedon preserve me, poor Levias is asleep in the guard barracks! Shadow-shapes were all around him, an army of white-faced ghosts, and even buildings in the middle ring of the castle had begun to burn. The air stank of smoke and of acrid, burning tar, as well as a stranger odor like smelted iron.

He almost ran into a dark figure, and only realized when it turned toward him that it was one of the White Foxes, eyes like black holes in a bloodless face. The Norn had just thrown a jar against the wall of the inner bailey and was about to set the black stuff alight, but Porto had his sword up. He swung at the surprised Norn and took off the hand that held the torch. The blow made his enemy stumble backward into the black puddle at the base of the wall just as the fallen torch—still clutched in the Norn's severed, bone-white hand—set the liquid ablaze. Astonishingly, the Norn did not let out a sound as flames ran up his legs and belly, but instead tried to draw his sword with his remaining hand. Porto did not want to fight someone who was already on fire, so he hacked at the creature's head until his foe staggered back into the blaze. Porto turned and ran. Smoke was everywhere, making it harder to breathe by the moment.

The gateway to the inner bailey was deserted. As Porto limped through it, a bolt flew past his head, nicking his ear. He did not stop. The middle bailey was now filling with the same dark-eyed, white-skinned demons that had overrun the outer part of the great keep.

Levias and I can pray together at the end, was all he could think. *If I can only reach him!*

Etan watched in terror from the small window of his room on the uppermost floor of the castle's royal residence. Torch-bearing Norns were flooding in through the Nearulagh Gate. The whole of the castle's outer ring was ablaze, flames writhing up toward the clouded sky, as parts of the middle bailey burned as well.

I'm trapped. The terrible thought kept interrupting his attempts to pray. *Trapped. I'm going to burn to death here like one of the ancient Aedonite martyrs.*

But Etan was not content to sit and wait for it. He ran to the door of the chamber in which he was imprisoned and examined the hinges, but they were elaborate works of cast iron, the straps bolted firmly to the wooden door, and he had nothing with which to pry them loose.

So meet your end with proper Aedonite grace, he told himself. *Try to be as brave as your Ransomer.*

But some animal part of him could not simply wait for death. Smoke was rasping in his nostrils and lungs as he searched in growing terror for something he could use to smash the door open. His makeshift prison was a seldom used bedchamber meant for the companions of visiting dignitaries. It contained a number of everyday items, a tray with a ewer of water and a heavy bowl for washing set on an upright chest, another chest full of linens, and a canopied bed, but nothing he could use to pry off the hinges or break the heavy latch.

He could see the light of the fires flickering in the building closest to his window, and he knew that unless some miracle occurred, the Norns would burn the residence down around him. In a sweating panic, he kicked against the post of the canopied bed until it broke away, then he ran to the door with it. He rammed the heavy bedpost against the door, again and again. At first he tried to smash the hinges; when that did not succeed, he tried to break off the latch on the inside. Hard as he struck it, though, he could not achieve anything except to bend the handle, and the bedpost was beginning to splinter and come apart. The smoke was thickening, burning his eyes and nostrils and throat. Etan hammered the post as hard as he could against the door, and as he did so he shouted out his rage and fear. At last he stopped, panting and desperately short of breath, his eyes so watery that he could barely see, and as he slumped there with his hands on his knees, the handle of the latch suddenly turned and the door swung inward.

Smoke filled the air outside, and for a long, confusing moment Etan could not make out the person standing there well enough to know if it was a mortal or one of the White Foxes. As he raised the splintered bedpost to defend himself, trying to blink clear sight back into his eyes, the shape in the doorway threw hands up in alarm. "Do not strike at me!" the figure cried. "I am only Brannan, Aengas's man!"

For a couple of heartbeats Etan could not make sense of the man's words at all, then remembered Tiamak's friend, Lord Aengas, the factor for the sea merchants. This was his cook.

"Praise God, you've saved me," he said, caught between laughing and crying. "Let us get out of this place—if the residence is not on fire yet, it will be in a moment."

"It is!" said Brannan. Now that they were moving down the corridor side by side, Etan could plainly see the terror on the young man's face. "Please—I need help! My lord Aengas is too large—his chair is . . ." He waved his hands in desperation. "He will die if we can't get him out. I have been trying to find someone to help, but they all are running like mad things."

"Not so mad to run from fire," said Etan. "And I have seen your master's chair. It would take more than one or two men to get that massive engine out of the residence. Half a dozen soldiers might manage it—we cannot. We will have to try to carry out just the man. But Aengas is a large fellow."

"I know! And he cannot walk or even sit up without help."

Etan shook his head and ran toward the stairwell at the end of the passage where the air was cleaner. Most of the windows on either side were shuttered, but shrieks of panic, shouts of confusion, and the sharp smell of burning still drifted in.

Lead me, O Lord, he prayed. *Help me to do Your will.*

And as he reached the stairs and began to descend, Etan suddenly felt a greater clarity, as if his prayer had not been in vain. *It is likely we will all die,* he realized. *I might find myself standing before my Redeemer before the hour is out. What deeds can I do in that time that I would dare to look into His eye and confess? That is all that matters now.* "We must find more men to help us," he told the young secretary.

"But where could we take him, anyway?" Brannan cried. "Those cursed whiteskins are all over the keep."

"We will decide after we reach him," Etan said. "No, hold, hold, I have thought of something—the seagate! The gate down to the old docks in the west wall. If the Norns haven't already found it, and we can open it, we might still be able to get down to the Kynslagh."

"And then what?" Brannan sounded close to utter despair. "Be caught between the White Foxes and the water?"

"One thing at a time. Let us solve the first problem before the second, and the second before the third—"

"I don't even know what you're talking about." Brannan pressed his hands to his head. "I don't understand!"

"Then close your mouth and follow me."

They reached the bottom of the stairs quickly, coughing and blinking in the growing drifts of smoke. The mad light of the flames danced in the windows of the ground floor, and when Etan took a quick look outside, he saw three Erkynguards fighting with a pair of dark-clad Norns.

"Go try to get your master out of his chair," he said. "I'm going to find more help." He did not watch to see if Brannan followed his instructions. Somebody had shot a fiery dart or thrown a torch onto the roof above him, and already Etan could see fire licking along the beams at the edge of the building's roof, wriggling between the slate shingles like demonic tongues. If the residence started burning from both bottom *and* top, Etan knew, the fire would engulf the structure in mere moments. They needed to get Aengas out as quickly as possible.

A pike caught one of the Norn soldiers from behind, dropping him to his knees—three more Erkynguards had appeared to join the struggle. The first two guardsmen stabbed him as he struggled to get back onto his feet. With five of them now encircling the remaining Norn, one of them was able to stab the enemy in the side, then another finished him with a two-handed sword blow to the neck. The jar of black ooze the Norn warrior was carrying fell from his twitching fingers and burst on the cobbles.

As the other Erkynguards tried to make sense of what was happening, the one nearest the front of the residence picked up a fallen torch and bent to look at the dead Norn even as the spilled black liquid slowly formed a puddle around his feet. Etan leaped out of the door and ran forward to yank the soldier away, ignoring the man's surprised curses.

"If you drop a spark in that, you will burn to death before anyone can help you," Etan shouted in the guard's ear, struggling to be heard above the din of castle folk screaming for help in several nearby spots. "You men are needed in the residence," he called to the others. "Follow me."

The soldiers were bewildered but seemed willing to be led by anyone less confused than themselves. Etan hurried them back into the residence and up to the chambers Aengas occupied. They found him half out of his chair, his cook Brannan desperately pulling on his ankles as the crippled Aengas struggled to stay in his seat.

"Help! He's gone mad!" Aengas cried, his face wan with fear and streaming with sweat.

"No, he hasn't," Etan said. "He's trying to save you. Come, men, slide him out of there. We must carry him to safety. Do any of you know where the old seagate door is? You? Good. Carry Lord Aengas down to it—he cannot walk or much move his arms, so you all must lift him down the stairs and take him to the docks."

The guardsmen looked at Etan as though he'd lost his mind. "He weighs more than all of us put together!"

"Then get more helpers. This man is important to us all."

They finally managed to heave Aengas out of his chair and out of his rooms, carting him awkwardly into the entry hall of the residence. Etan, following close behind them, now spotted a familiar figure staggering like a drunkard past the residence's main door. He slipped away from the men struggling with Aengas and hurried down the smoky stairs.

"Hoy!" he cried, running after the stumbling figure. "Lord Captain! Lord Captain Zakiel, is that you?"

The figure stopped and slowly turned. Etan saw the ashen mask and had a moment of terror—it was not Zakiel, but some Norn wearing the captain's armor! But he realized a few heartbeats later that the captain was covered in stone dust, with bloody cuts all over his face and hands and a dark splash of blood in the hair beside his temple. He had fallen, or something had fallen on him.

"Zakiel, your men need you. Are you badly wounded, man? What happened to you?"

The captain's eyes were mild and calm, in startling contrast to the rest of his appearance. "Where are the children?" he asked. "I am looking for them, but they are hiding from me. Very naughty of them. Naughty."

Sweet Ransomer save us all, thought Etan, *his wits are addled.* "If you want to help the children, come with me, Captain. I will take you."

Zakiel gave him a slightly puzzled look but then followed Etan back toward the residence as the guards trudged out, cursing and sweating as they struggled with Lord Aengas's limp weight while Brannan tried to direct them.

"It's the captain!" one of them said when he saw Zakiel.

"It is," agreed Etan, "but I think his brains have taken a knock. All of you, follow me down to the seagate. The stairs are steep, so step carefully."

A figure wreathed in flames came screaming out of the smoky darkness and ran past them without stopping.

"The children have been kept up too late," Zakiel said sadly. "And playing such rough games."

"Haste!" cried Jiriki, standing in his stirrups. "I see a great blaze. The Norns are burning the castle!"

As they burst out of the trees and into the outer reaches of the graveyard the rest of the Zida'ya saw it too, a glare so bright that it reflected from the low thunderclouds, as if the sky itself had caught fire. "By the Garden, there are thousands of Sacrifices there!" shouted Ki'ushapo. "See all the banners! How could there be so many Hikeda'ya?"

"Who can say? But we will never make even a dent in such a vast force," Jiriki shouted back, then angled his racing horse toward the castle's massive broken gate. "Strike the vanguard instead!" he called back to the others. "If we can behead the Hamakha serpent, we may be able to make a stand inside, where the walls will help us against their numbers!"

The Zida'ya swept across the cemetery, their mounts leaping high over fallen stones, then followed Jiriki along the Erchester town wall toward the blazing castle. "Remember!" Jiriki shouted again, "under this mortal burying ground lie our own people, deep in the earth! This was our land first, not Utuk'ku's! Strike at the head of the serpent!"

A heartbeat later a blinding glare filled the sky. Jiriki could almost believe the clouds had caught fire, but it was only lightning leaping through the storm. In the flash, he saw a slender white figure standing atop the largest wagons, garments rippling in the rising wind as it raised its arms to the sky.

"See! That is Utuk'ku herself!" he called to Ki'ushapo. "What is she doing here?"

"She no longer fears anything!" his friend shouted back. "She thinks she has won!"

"Let us make her think again!"

As they rushed uphill toward the castle outwall and onto the leading edge of the Hikeda'ya invaders, startled white faces turned toward them and dark eyes widened in startlement. *"The Zida'ya have come, the cursed traitors!"* a Sacrifice officer cried, and others echoed her. *"Traitors! Kill the traitors! Long live the Mother of All!"*

Jiriki's horse leaped in among the Hikeda'ya fighters crowding the ruined gate, striking with the force of a catapult stone; nearly a dozen Sacrifices were knocked aside or trampled in the first moment. Jiriki's spear snapped out once, twice, thrice, each time leaving a black-armored warrior writhing on the ground, but the fourth, though mortally wounded, managed to drag the shaft from Jiriki's grasp as he fell. Spear gone, his horse rearing and flailing its hooves among the reeling Sacrifice soldiers, Jiriki drew his witchwood sword Indreju and began to cut his way through the attackers, aiming for the castle's main gate.

"Follow me," he cried. *"For the honor of Hakat—"* An arrow struck him in the side. Jiriki almost fell from his saddle, but though the dart had pierced him between two plates of his witchwood armor, it had not gone deep. He plucked it out, tossed it aside, then rode tireless Cloudfoot into the thickest part of the Hikeda'ya vanguard.

Within moments the Sacrifice warriors surrounded him, and Jiriki could no longer see the rest of his company. Gauntleted hands reached up to catch at his bridle. Jabbing pikes scored his armor and scraped his legs. Jiriki could no longer waste his breath on shouted exhortations but stood as tall in the stirrups as he could, dealing death with first one hand, then the other, as his horse trampled through the milling Hikeda'ya. Jiriki did not know how long his mount's armor would protect her, but whatever wounds she had taken did not slow Cloudfoot at all: she struck out with her hooves, smashing heads and denting chest-plates, throwing crippled enemies to either side of her like the bow of a fast ship.

But Jiriki knew that the element of surprise was gone and his company was far too small to change anything. The great majority of the Hikeda'ya army had not even bothered to move forward, but simply stood in its endless ranks about the castle walls and the western edge of Erchester, as though the sudden appearance of the Zida'ya riders was of no import at all.

Jiriki found the breath to cry out once more. "If this is the last moment we live, let it be a great moment! Follow me, defenders of the Garden!" A moment later Cloudfoot shouldered her way through a last mob of Hikeda'ya fighters, and suddenly Jiriki burst past the tumbled gate towers and into the castle's outer ring, where he was quickly surrounded by torches and fierce white faces. "Ki'ushapo! Shen'de!" he cried. "To me! The last hour is come! Let us bloody Amerasu's murderers so that they will never forget us!"

A dozen Sacrifice foot soldiers now closed around him, jabbing with pikes and swords. The wind was rising. The world seemed painted in flame and flaring light. An arrow pierced Cloudfoot's shoulder through the armor and into flesh; as the horse stumbled, Jiriki's enemies grabbed his legs and tried to pull him from his saddle. Indreju rose and fell over and over, like a smith's hammer, but other hands caught at his arm and pulled it down until the gray blade could strike no more. Then Jiriki was torn out of his saddle and dragged to the muddy ground.

Lillia was too exhausted even to walk, so Simon carried her through the long-unused corridors and up several stairwells. He knew all too well where he was. *I was here the day that Doctor Morgenes died.* He forced his weary legs to climb another flight, this one half-blocked with broken furniture. *The day I found*

Prince Josua in the same cell that Pasevalles put me in. But how could he have known about that? What manner of monster has been so close to us for so long?

His granddaughter murmured something against his chest, and though Simon could not make out a word of it, he tightened his grip on her. Strange noises drifted down into the deep, stony quiet of the dungeons, and the more Simon listened, the more it sounded like people shouting, even screaming, far above them.

"I do not know what goes on up there, little cub," he told Lillia, his mouth against her ear. She squirmed away from his tickling beard—it had grown much longer since he had fallen on the Winstowe battlefield. "And if I put you down, then you *must* stay where I leave you. Do you understand, child?"

She whispered what he thought was an agreement into his chest.

He could feel a growing heat now and stood uncertainly before the door that he knew led into a storeroom beneath the old dining halls. He kicked at the latch and shoved the door open with his foot.

Fire. The Inner Bailey was in flames! Simon looked around the room and saw a dark figure flit past, moving so swiftly he could almost believe it was a shadow. As it sped through the open door leading to the outer hall, he caught a momentary glimpse of black armor and a whey-colored face.

"Norns," he said, but only quietly—he did not want to terrify his granddaughter. *God's Bloody Tree,* he thought, *my worst nightmare. The Norns have attacked the Hayholt.* Rage boiled inside him. *This must be your work, too, Pasevalles—or at least had your help. What did the Norn Queen promise you, traitor?*

He had to get Lillia to safety. The tapestries in the hallway were ablaze but he could still get across the room. For a moment he wondered if he could stop the fire before it spread, but the wall of flames outside the windows told him it was too late for anything except escape. He clutched Lillia tightly against his body and ran on weary, staggering legs toward the great double doors. Once, he almost dropped his granddaughter when he tripped on something—a body, though whether one of the castle's defenders or attackers he could not tell through the thick smoke. He hurried on before Lillia saw the sprawled corpse.

If the burning hall had been a horrible surprise, what lay outside the building was a waking nightmare. Even the castle's stony outer walls were on fire, although how that could be true, Simon could not even guess. Flames billowed everywhere, throwing bizarre shadows, but he could also see corpse-faced Norn warriors retreating toward the front of the castle with a few doughty Erkynguards—far too few—chasing after them.

As he stood at the top of the rise on which the residence stood, Simon could see across most of the keep. The Throne Hall was not yet in flames, although tongues of fire licked hungrily at its outer walls. But beyond them he saw something that threatened to freeze his blood. On the slope beyond the castle, stretching as far as he could see beyond the ruins of the Nearulagh Gate, waited an impossibly vast horde of White Foxes, many with torches—thousands of dead, white faces watching the Hayholt burn.

Why does the rest of their army wait instead of attacking? he wondered even as he stumbled out. *Does Utuk'ku fear to lose soldiers in a fight she has already won?*

It was clear that there were no safe places left inside the inner bailey, and the burning residence and dozens of Norn shadows blocked his way toward the seagate. Simon headed for the shadows of the inner wall instead and followed it toward the middle bailey gate, Lillia all but insensible in his arms. The wind was blowing so hard now, in great sweeping gusts, that several times he almost fell.

The walls were burning in the middle bailey, too. Great swathes of the stonework had fallen and lay in smoking heaps; Simon could only hurry on through the baking heat, head bent over his granddaughter to protect her from flying sparks. He half-limped, half-ran through the gate, expecting at any moment to be pierced with arrows, but the figures he saw seemed to be busy fighting each other. In the flickering, firelit darkness he could not tell the difference between enemy and ally.

The walls of the outer bailey were sheets of towering flame, as though the very stones were burning. Increasingly desperate, Simon headed toward the smashed and blackened remains of the Nearulagh Gate. Even in his terror, he could only marvel at the destruction. What terrible magicks had caused this? And why were Utuk'ku's thousands of soldiers still waiting outside the gates, as though events in the blazing, dying castle had not yet grown interesting enough to demand their presence?

In that instant, he saw a great company of riders appear out of the darkness and crash into the thickest knot of Sacrifice invaders at the Nearulagh Gate. Stunned and confused, Simon halted, trying to understand why the Norn Queen was sending cavalry to attack her own warriors, then he saw a horse rear up in the middle of the skirmish, forelegs shoving at the air. To his amazement, he thought he recognized the rider's witchwood armor.

"Jiriki?" he shouted, but his voice died beneath the screams of mortals and immortals battling just inside the shattered gate. *"Jiriki!"* A moment later the Sitha vanished, pulled down by Norn soldiers.

Simon was about to plunge bare-handed into the struggle when he remembered he was carrying Lillia. He looked about frantically until he saw a dark spot far away from the flames. He set her there, then pried her arms from his neck when she would not let go. "Grandfather, don't leave!" she cried. "I'm afraid!"

"Just stay here and don't move, little one. I'll come back for you, I promise."

As he set her down, a half-dozen Erkynguards appeared from behind a building and stumbled toward him. They looked as though they were heading away from the fight at the gate, so Simon lurched out in front of them.

"Stop, you men of Erkynland!" he shouted. "It is not too late! Follow me!"

The soldiers stared at him in astonishment, and Simon wondered how bad he must look to cause such dismay.

"If you try to flee the castle, ten thousand White Foxes are waiting!" he cried. Something lying on the ground nearby caught his attention and he snatched it up. It was a Norn sword of dark witchwood, curved down toward the cutting edge like some strange butcher's tool. He lifted it over his head. "What are you waiting for?" he cried. "For the Hayholt! Follow your king!"

He turned and hurried toward the spot where Jiriki's horse still stood over its master, kicking at the Norn warriors who were trying to reach its fallen rider. Simon ran straight at the nearest Sacrifice and swung the blade down, driving the curved point through the top of the Norn's helmet; his enemy died without a sound. Then the Erkynguards Simon had rallied caught up and threw themselves into the thicket of swords and spears. The Norns who had pulled Jiriki down turned to defend themselves. One of them was crawling over bodies to meet Simon when something struck the Norn from behind and he fell back, the blood gouting from his mouth almost black against his parchment-colored skin. The dying Norn was shoved to one side, then Jiriki climbed out from beneath him, got to his feet, and began plying his gray witchwood blade. Within moments, the now outnumbered Norns scattered, fleeing deeper into the burning Hayholt with the mortal soldiers in pursuit.

Jiriki let his sword drop to one side and reached out to calm his snorting horse. "Seoman, my friend," he said. "I should have known that you would come to my aid if you still lived."

Eyes filling with tears, Simon hurried across the muddy, blood-slicked ground and pulled Jiriki into his arms. "God save me, it really is you!" He felt something wet and slippery beneath his hand. "You are wounded!"

"It is nothing—an arrow that barely pierced the skin. I plucked it out and tossed it away."

Simon was so exhausted he could barely stand upright. "I did not think I would ever see you again," he said, "but here you are at the end."

"I could not leave my mortal friends to face the queen's army alone." Jiriki wiped Indreju's blade clean against the leg of his breeks. "But I fear you speak truly about the end—my few warriors will not save us against such a huge and fearsome host."

Simon looked out between the tumbled, smoking ruins of the gatehouses. "We have no chance against such a vast army. Is there any way to block the gate—?" His eye was caught by a fierce, spreading glow that outshone even the fires. A figure stood atop a huge wagon near the front of the waiting Norn soldiers. "By Heaven, is that the witch queen herself?" The shape seemed human, but it was tattered as though clothed in ancient rags, and shone with a light so deep and so disturbingly red that it out-smoldered even the burning walls and made the clouds overhead gleam as red as sunrise. Looking at it, Simon felt something clutch painfully at his heart, so that he almost fell to his knees.

"No," said the Sitha, steadying him with a hand under his arm. "I saw Utuk'ku atop her wagon, dressed in white."

"Then who is that? *What* is that?"

Jiriki's face was grim. "It looks like one of the Red Hand."

"The Red Hand!" Simon could make no sense of that. "But they're all dead! They died in the Storm King's War!"

"They died long before that, when Asu'a fell." Jiriki stared at the glow surrounding the wagon, a glow that billowed and wavered as though the rising wind plucked at it. "But it seems that somehow Utuk'ku has raised one of them." He shook his head. "If it truly is one of those cursed things, it is an enemy beyond my power—perhaps beyond any power on this earth."

Simon had never seen Jiriki look so defeated. Terrified, he abruptly remembered his granddaughter, left to wait in a shadowy corner of the wall, but before he could run to retrieve her, the burning figure atop the wagon lifted its ragged arms high in the air. A blinding flare of scarlet light played across the whole of the battlefield, from one side of the Hayholt's outer wall to another, as if the morning sun had suddenly burst into view on the smoky horizon. A moment later, with a crack louder than any thunderbolt, the bright red glare and the windblown figure both vanished. The night swept back in, and, as if it had been held back until this moment, rain began to pour down in brutal shards, hissing into the mud around their feet.

The slope beneath the burning gates was suddenly and utterly empty. The entire Norn army had disappeared.

Simon stared out in utter amazement, unable to believe what he saw. "What happened? *What just happened?*"

"I do not know!" Jiriki seemed just as dumbfounded as Simon. "But see, the bodies of those who were slain are still here. Dozens still lie all around."

"But where is all the rest of their army? And the Red Hand? What happened? All those thousands can't have just . . . *vanished*!" Simon wondered if he had been struck in the head without knowing it. Nothing else could explain what he had just seen. The vast host of Norn soldiers that had surrounded the castle mound only moments ago had simply ceased to be, as if some great hand had swept them up and flung them far away. The fires still lit everything, sparking and dancing beneath the heavy rain: Simon could see the empty slope beyond the gate and the nearest part of Erchester's city wall, but the whole of the hillside between them was naked of anything but a few sprawled corpses. All that remained of the massive army was one great black wagon standing on a low rise. Whatever beasts had pulled it had broken their traces and fled.

Jiriki took a few steps forward and nudged one of the Norn corpses with his foot. "The Hikeda'ya are gone but their dead remain!" He looked at the body beside it and said, "No, not only the dead. Here is a Hikeda'ya who still lives, though sorely wounded." Jiriki sank to his knees beside the supine figure; when he looked up, he seemed even more astonished. "By the Grove, this is Muyare himself, the High Marshal of all Utuk'ku's troops!"

The slumped figure Simon had thought was just another dead Norn, one of the pack that had tried to kill Jiriki, opened his eyes, his hands clutched over his midriff. The mouth gaped in the Norn's white face as he groaned in pain.

"Muyare, what are you doing here?" Jiriki said. "Why would you lead the attack yourself? And where is the rest of your great army? They have gone, blown away like smoke."

Muyare half opened his eyes. "I leave you with my curse, you and the mortals. The Garden will welcome me soon." Surrounded by flames and the sprawled bodies of dead comrades, and clearly in terrible pain, he spoke the mortal Westerling tongue with surprising skill. A moment later, the Norn's eyes widened. "Jiriki of the Year-Dancing, is that you? You were fools to fight against us. You cannot defeat the queen."

"We *have* defeated her," said Simon hotly. "Your mighty army has run away. Do you call that nothing?"

Muyare's half-lidded gaze slowly moved to Simon and his bloody mouth curled in a pained smile. "It is *exactly* nothing, mortal. There never was an army—only the few hundreds I commanded. The rest of them were a song of deception that the dead thing Ommu sang—the greatest enchantment ever woven!" He coughed, and blood dribbled onto his chin.

"What game is this?" Jiriki demanded.

"It is Queen Utuk'ku's game, of course," Muyare said, fighting now for breath. "She . . . made it. The pieces . . . are hers. You and the mortals cannot win."

"You had honor once, Muyare," said Jiriki. "You fought the giants and the Northmen at our side, like a true son of the Garden. How could you serve that mad creature?"

Another deep shudder creased Muyare's face, and for a moment he did not speak. Then he took a rattling breath and said, "The queen holds . . . my family's safety. She . . . sacrificed one of my grandchildren to summon Ommu the Whisperer back from beyond death, just to . . . to punish me . . . for telling my wife of the Witchwood Crown." He struggled to take in air. "I had no choice."

"There is always a choice," said Jiriki, but his face seemed almost pitying. "And all for nothing. You came for the Witchwood Crown, but I do not think you or your queen have found it."

"We never . . . sought it . . . here . . ." Muyare coughed weakly again, and this time a gout of blood spattered the front of his breastplate. He took one last rattling breath, then sagged and was still.

"Utuk'ku corrupts everything she touches," said Jiriki, staring down at Muyare's corpse.

"What did he mean about the Witchwood Crown?" Simon asked. "I don't understand—"

"Seoman, look there!" Jiriki pointed out through the broken gate. On the nearly empty hillside below them a gleam had kindled once more near the black wagon. The point of red light rose from the ground, then floated slowly and unevenly toward them, bobbing up the slope like a determined firefly. Simon lifted his salvaged Norn sword as the scarlet ember reached the cleared space in front of the ruined gate and was revealed as a shadowy figure with two legs and two arms, glowing in spots but weirdly indistinct at its edges. Burning remnants of winding cloth floated around it, the sparks drifting up and away as the figure trudged toward them.

" 'Ware!" shouted Jiriki. Arrows flew outward from somewhere nearby—Simon did not know whether they came from his own soldiers or Jiriki's folk—and struck the staggering figure, knocking it back a step. Though Simon could see at least three shafts now jutting from the charred, bandaged midsection, the ember-red around the wounds shrank and vanished as the thing continued stumbling uphill toward the gate, the eyes in its shadowed face burning like coals.

Another arrow struck the figure full in the chest. Another tongue of fire leaped up around the shaft. The thing continued toward them.

I am failing, a voice said.

Simon heard it plainly, though not with his ears: the words flew straight into his head, cold as death itself, but whatever power the smoldering thing might have once had seemed all but gone. *I have no choice*, it moaned. *No choice . . .* An instant later the figure burst into sparks and leaping flames too strangely red to be ordinary fire, then collapsed in front of the gate. Its embers glowed, then died.

Jiriki went forward and stood over it. "Nothing is left but ash," he called. "I do not understand what has happened here."

Simon heard footsteps behind him and whirled to look for an enemy, but saw only Lillia walking unsteadily toward him, her pale face twitching. "Dear God, are you hurt, child?" he cried.

"Grandfather," she said in a small, terrified voice. "Grandfather, something got inside of me! It hurts! Grandfather, it hurts!"

"Jiriki!" Simon shouted in desperate fear. "Jiriki, come quickly!"

As he ran toward her, Lillia stumbled a few more steps, then fell into her grandfather's arms. Her skin was ice-cold. As Jiriki hurried toward them, the girl's eyes rolled up until only fingernail-slivers of white remained. "No, no!" cried Simon. "Jiriki, please, help her!"

When Lillia spoke again, the childish pitch was still hers, but the words were not: no mortal child could have sounded so grim, so bitter. *"You have been tricked. The Queen of Nakkiga has fooled everyone—and now the last part of her game begins."*

Afterword

I am distressed by life
Because it is always too short.
I am angry with death
Which always comes too late.
Why can we never find
The peaceful home,
The valley with its needful, singing stream,
The land of clear golden light,
Where each is given what is needed —
And only that —
As was promised long ago?
Now it is time to ride home
To the place I was born
And begin again.

—BENAYHA OF KEMENTARI

In Viyeki's dream, the peak called Kushiba stood before him like a finger raised in stark warning. No, he dimly recognized, it was not Kushiba, but a mountainous and solitary pillar of stone, alone in a wide, empty meadowland, its high summit thatched with long grasses, stunted trees, and a clutter of ancient ruins.

What is this place? he wondered, staring helplessly at the great stone hill.

You must go through it, a voice told him. He thought it might be his old master, Yaarike, but could not be certain. *You must cut through to the center. To the heart of what was lost.*

He was confused. *But the queen's troops,* he protested. *They have to get past it, or I will be punished. It is so tall, so narrow—surely they should go around it instead.*

You cannot avoid it, the voice told him. *You must go through it. Otherwise, you will never know . . .* The voice had begun to fade.

Know what?

What lies beneath, said the fading voice that might be Yaarike's—or perhaps it said, *The lies beneath.*

A moment later Viyeki awoke to noises outside his tent, sounds of a strained, whispered argument and something else—a swelling murmur like the arrival of a rainstorm.

"What can you want?" He recognized the voice as that of Dayago, the chief of his household guard. *"He has only just begun his rest."*

"He would want me to wake him." That one belonged to his secretary, Nonao, and there was a desperate edge to his words.

Viyeki sat up. The two of them were still talking in hushed tones just on the other side of the tent flap, but now he could hear other voices, many of them, quiet yet full of urgency. He rose and pushed his way out into the night.

"What is happening here?" he demanded.

His guard captain and secretary looked up, faces close together like lovers surprised, startled by his sudden appearance. "He insisted—" Dayago began.

"High Magister," Nonao interrupted, "I knew you would want to hear. It is the . . . the Zida'ya. He is out."

"The Zida'ya? Do you mean Hakatri?" Viyeki was far from fully awake. "*Out*? What does that mean?"

"He has left his wagon. He cannot be found anywhere in the camp."

It was like an unexpected plunge into icy water—a moment of numbness, then something much worse. "By the Lost Garden, who is responsible for this?" Upsetting as the news was, he could not suppress a moment's secret glee. *Smug General Kikiti, with his boasting and preening—this will fall straightly on him.* But an instant later Viyeki saw Prince-Templar Pratiki in the center of the camp, grimly delivering orders to various underlings, and realized that losing something Queen Utuk'ku had gone to so much effort to gain might send every single noble and officer on Kushiba to the Cold, Slow Halls. "I will be out again in a moment," he told his underlings. "Round up the rest of our guards and alert the overseers. We must help in the search."

Back in his tent, he pulled a heavy hooded coat over his robes and belted it tightly with a sash, then pulled on his heavy goatskin boots. Even for Viyeki, raised in the mountainous north, this late autumn midnight in the heights was unpleasantly cold.

More suitably dressed now, he hurried to Pratiki, who was in conversation with one of Kikiti's Sacrifice lieutenants. When he saw Viyeki, however, he gave a nod. As he waited for the prince-templar to finish, Viyeki watched Sacrifice soldiers, many carrying *ni'iyo* spheres or torches, darting here and there about the camp to no visible purpose, like fish feeding on prey too small to see. By the strong light of the moon, only a single day past full, he could see Hakatri's wagon at one edge of the Sacrifice camp, its door open and swinging slowly in the mountain wind.

When the general's emissary had departed, Pratiki turned to him. "Collect some of your workers, Magister. I think we must search the caverns."

"Of course, Serenity." But before he could move, a small figure came toward them, dark robes flapping in the icy wind. Viyeki saw a flash of pale features crisscrossed with black runes—Sogeyu, the leading Singer in the camp.

"Serene Highness, I beg an audience," she said, ignoring Viyeki as though he were only another of the prince-templar's clerics. "General Kikiti is certain that Hakatri is hiding in the caverns, or even tried to escape down the mountain."

"Stay, please, Magister," Pratiki told Viyeki, then turned back to Sogeyu. "I take it you think otherwise, Singer. Where has our guest gone, then?"

"Up." Beneath the distracting symbols, her face was solemn. "Higher up the mountain. We of the order sense him only imperfectly, though, and Kikiti will not listen. You must trust us, Serenity, or everything could be lost."

Her words shocked Viyeki. Could all of Queen Utuk'ku's plans be so delicately, even precariously, balanced? "But why would he go up?" he asked. "Is there something he seeks on the mountain above us?"

Sogeyu shook her head. "No, Magister. But he does not know that. He feels it. He hears its music—" She abruptly fell silent.

"Feels what?" Viyeki asked, but the Singer only looked at Pratiki. "What does he feel? What music does she speak of, Serenity?"

Pratiki shook his head. "There is no time for talk now, High Magister. Singer Sogeyu, if you know these things, why are you not already pursuing him?"

"Hakatri is beyond our power to restrain, Serenity—at least without causing him harm, or perhaps defeating our queen's hopes entirely. It is possible that if we find him, we can calm him, but the mountain is a dangerous place. We must have help." She made a gesture Viyeki did not recognize. "I will speak honestly, Highness. I also do not trust Kikiti's Sacrifices to be sufficiently cautious with him if they find him."

"Cautious?" Viyeki asked. "You say you cannot restrain him, this . . . thing that has died and come back, this power. Even if you find him, how will you bring him back?"

Sogeyu threw him a cold stare, then turned back to the prince-templar. "The general has already dismissed us, Highness. Must I argue with the magister of the Builders as well while our time slips away?"

"If your Singers cannot restrain or compel Hakatri," Pratiki said, "and you do not trust the Sacrifices, that leaves us only Viyeki's Builders to do what you ask. He has the right to ask questions."

For a brief instant, Sogeyu's imperturbable expression slipped, and Viyeki saw how disturbingly fearful she was. "I know that you have had quarrels with our order, Serenity," she said. "Please believe me—this is an hour we must trust each other."

Sogeyu and Pratiki both stood silent for a long moment, staring fixedly at each other as if they spoke, even argued, without any words Viyeki could hear. The sudden madness of the night had all but overwhelmed him. He felt as helpless as in his far-distant childhood, when his parents would talk heatedly about things he did not understand.

"Very well." Pratiki spoke quietly. "We will follow you, Singer. High Magister, we need a small company of your most trustworthy workers."

Viyeki summoned Nonao and Dayago, who had been waiting at a courteous distance. He did not want Kikiti interfering with what they were doing, but he knew that his own secretary Nonao had many friends among the Sacrifices, so he commanded Nonao to take a party of tunnelers to search the cavern. "But be cautious," he told him. "We have barely begun making them safe. And if you find Hakatri, do not approach him. Keep him in view and send for help." When his secretary had gone, he turned to the guard-chief Dayago. "We will need at least a handsworth of our house guard to go up the mountain with us. Choose the most trustworthy—those who are bravest, and who will keep silence no matter what happens."

"I have them already waiting, High Magister," said Dayago. "Five of my most reliable."

"Will that be enough, Sogeyu?" Pratiki asked.

Her face had become impassive once more. "Yes. I think we will be better with a small company, for greater speed. I will bring only two of my most trusted Singers. If we do find Hakatri, we must rely on persuasion, not force."

Prince-Templar Pratiki still wore the stern but calm expression appropriate for a noble in a dire situation, but Viyeki knew him well enough now to sense the noble's deep unease. *If Utuk'ku's own relative is frightened,* he wondered, *what hope for the rest of us?*

The moon had begun to slide down into the west, and new snow was falling, whipped by the wind into elaborate swirls that danced like gleeful spirits. Their small company had been climbing for some time, following mountain tracks that even keen-eyed Viyeki could barely make out, led by Sogeyu and her two Singer companions. For the last part of the hard-fought ascent the whole company had been slowing, and now they came to a halt.

"I regret to say that we have lost his essence, Serenity," Sogeyu told Pratiki.

Garden preserve us, Viyeki thought, *the benighted creature who Utuk'ku brought back from death may have stumbled and fallen from some high place. Is it possible to die twice?* The idea that Hakatri might be gone brought a bizarre mixture of relief and dread. The thing in the Navigator's armor had disturbed him since it first thrashed into a semblance of life back in the mortal fortress, but he could only guess at the peril they were in if the queen's prize was truly lost.

"Have we chased a phantom all this time?" the prince-templar demanded. "Or has he met with some accident?"

"I cannot say." Sogeyu exchanged glances with the other two Singers, one tall, one short, both fixedly silent. "We have experienced such a thing before, even when he is close by. Sometimes he . . . turns within. Then we cannot feel him at all."

Pratiki looked down. "The snow has covered any tracks he might have left, and now you say you cannot feel him, either. The Mother of All will call this a disaster, and she will be right. I promise, she will not be kind to any of us." He looked up through the flurrying white to the dangerous mountainside above them. "Soon we must go roped together if we are to continue at all. Did your Builders bring rope, Magister?"

Viyeki had not spoken in some time. His lips were dry and chapped, and it took him a moment to form the words. "Of course, Serenity. But in truth we would need more precautions than that to climb much higher. There are many loose stones and protruding boulders above us, and the new snow now falling will also make the footing treacherous."

"You heard the magister," Pratiki said. "So tell me, Singer, what do you propose? Important as this is, I am not eager to risk a fall to my death."

"If we do not recapture Hakatri, Prince-Templar," she said, her face almost invisible in her snow-spattered hood, "then falling to our deaths might be the best we can hope for."

Viyeki had turned his eyes to the mountainside above them, hoping to spot some other route upward, and as he did, he noticed something dark lying atop the snow a few paces above where they stood. He lifted his *ni'yo*; when the light fell on the object, he saw that it glinted. He scrambled up the track toward it, boots sinking deep with each step, all too conscious that a misstep could send him sliding to his death. When he reached the object, he stared at it for long moments, trying to make sense.

"What are you doing, Magister?" Pratiki called.

"I have found something, I think." He picked it up, then carefully waded back to the others and held it out for them to see—a violet-colored, translucent cube as wide as his thumb, stuck to a larger piece of limestone like a barnacle. "It is a crystal of flowstone that has fallen from a vein in the mountainside."

"Our lives—and more than our lives—are in peril," said Sogeyu, contempt plain in her every word. "And the magister of the Builders collects interesting pebbles."

Viyeki took a deep breath before speaking: it was the wrong time for angry replies. "You are not looking carefully, Singer. This was lying in the open on a bank of snow. More snow has been falling, and yet there is scarcely any on it. It must have tumbled down from above only a short while ago."

Prince-Templar Pratiki stared at the purple shard. "Are you saying it was knocked loose?"

"It seems likely. And we have seen no mountain-sheep or anything else alive here. Perhaps it was dislodged by Hakatri as he climbed."

Pratiki shook his head, but said, "Then we continue upward as long as we can. Magister Viyeki, you found this prize, so you may lead."

This is not what I was trained to do, he thought, but of course did not utter the words aloud. The sifting whiteness had covered any distinct tracks, but he thought he could see faint impressions that might have been footprints only a short time earlier, so he followed them carefully as they meandered across the face of the mountain. They had climbed far onto the southeast side of Kushiba by now, the lights of their camp long since lost from sight. The wind here seemed a living thing, alternatively tugging and shoving Viyeki like a prankish child, though such pranks could easily prove fatal in such a high, precarious place. One look down where the steep, rocky slope fell away into darkness was enough to keep Viyeki's eyes fixed in front of him.

The latest snow flurry had finally ended, and he could see a little of what was around them for the first time. Where they climbed now, Kushiba's western flank dropped down into what must be Tanakirú, but the steep-sided gorge was so full of mist that it might have been a pot boiling over: he could make out nothing of the valley beneath.

As he held onto a limestone outcrop to catch his breath and wait for the others, Viyeki thought he glimpsed movement on a spur of stone not far above them. His heart stuttered and then sped. He raised his hand to bring those behind him to a halt.

"What is it, Lordship?" asked Dayago, who was closest.

"Quiet," he whispered. "Go back down and tell His Serene Highness that I think I see something moving above us."

Within moments, Pratiki, Sogeyu, and the other two Singers had clambered up to stand beside him.

"There." Viyeki pointed. "At the edge of that outcrop, overlooking the Valley of Mists. Do you not see it?"

For a moment they all stared at the shape in silence. Then the figure on the precipice lifted its arms high, and it became clear they had found what they were seeking.

"By Hamakho's Sword," breathed Pratiki, "does the mad creature mean to jump?"

Sogeyu and her two followers abruptly shouldered past him. Viyeki heard an odd, whining sound, and when the wind eased a little a moment later it became clear the Singers were chanting, a song whose words Viyeki could not make out, but doubted he would recognize in any case. It was hard to separate their song from the cry of the wind, but he thought he could feel it, its strands intertwining, crossing then parting—a song of binding, as carefully made as a spider's web, meant to lull, catch, and hold.

As he and the prince-templar stood motionless, the three Singers moved toward the figure, which still stood with outstretched arms, staring down into the wind-whipped mists. Viyeki held his breath as they neared the solitary shape, but Sogeyu and her minions stopped short. Their voices rose, and though their melodies seemed discordant, they nevertheless began to come together like stones perfectly cut and joined. Their song seemed to fit the hour and the place as if it came from the mountain itself, a chant that felt like slow time and inevitable change and the ultimate end of all things—an end not to be feared but welcomed.

They sang for so long that the cold had Viyeki shivering badly, but the weird figure only sat unmoving, still with its back to them, still but a single twitch from falling away into the empty air. At last the song resolved in a gradual mounting of individual, incomprehensible words, each one uttered into a moment of stillness, like a drop of blood splashing on an ancient sacrificial altar.

Then it ended. In the silence that followed, the thing on the outcrop turned slowly to look back at them. Twin lights smoldered in the eyes of the helmet. After what seemed an achingly long time, the creature in the gleaming, moonlit armor pivoted awkwardly, then came shambling back across the outcropping toward them, its walk so unsteady that Viyeki felt a painful clutch in his stomach, terrified that Hakatri might misstep and fall.

When the thing they had been pursuing so long reached safer ground, it stopped, swaying a little, and the Singers moved in around it. They were singing again, but so quietly now Viyeki could barely hear them, a murmurous hum like contented bees. Their hands hovered over the crystal-armored shape, never touching but always in motion, as they coerced it with pale, fluttering fingers back toward the rest of the small company. Hakatri went with them like a sleepwalker.

Pratiki let out an audible sigh of relief. "You did well, High Magister," he said, but the raggedness of his voice made it plain how close to disaster they had come. "But walk carefully, I beg you. It is still a long, dangerous way back down to our camp."

Viyeki only nodded, saving his breath. He signaled to Dayago and the rest of the guards, who turned and began to descend. Viyeki and the prince-templar went just behind them, following their own tracks down the slope.

He looked back to where the Singers were guiding the strange thing in crystal armor back down to safety. The round eyes and circular mouth of the revenant's helmet seemed frozen in a look of perpetual surprise or confusion, and its scuffing, clumsy steps made the terrifying Hakatri seem like nothing so much as a lost and weary child. But inside the depths of the strange helmet, behind holes like the eye sockets of some brute beast's skull, the twin fires still smoldered.

Appendix

PEOPLE

ERKYNLANDERS

Agga—a riverside dweller in southern Erkynland
Aglaf, Count—the ruler of Winstowe
Algor, Saint—an Erkynlandish holy figure famous for a shriveled hand
Ardith of Cellodshire—an historical noblewoman who rode onto a battlefield to save her son
Avel—King Simon's body servant
Boez, Bishop—recently elevated Chief Almoner of the Hayholt
Culby, Father—a monk helping Jesa during her flight from Nabban
Dorret, Lady—Earl Durward's daughter
Dregan—Earl Durward's young son and heir
Durward, Earl—ruler of Meremund
Elias, King—the former High King of Osten Ard; Queen Miriamele's father, killed in the Storm King's War
Erol—King Simon's squire
Etan, Brother—an Aedonite monk; a confidant of Tiamak entrusted with a secret mission
Finias, Sir—King Simon's standard bearer
Gervis, Escritor—the highest religious authority in Erkynland; Lord Treasurer of the Hayholt
Gytha, Lady—a Hayholt noblewoman
Heanwig, Saint—an early Erkynlandish saint
Idela, Princess—the widow of Prince John Josua, killed by Pasevalles
Izaak—a childhood friend of King Simon
Jeremias, Lord—the Lord Chamberlain of the Hayholt; King Simon's boyhood friend
John Josua, Prince—son of King Simon and Queen Miriamele; father of Prince Morgan and Princess Lillia, died of a fever several years earlier
John Presbyter, King—former High King; Queen Miriamele's grandfather, aka "Prester John"
Josua, Prince—Queen Miriamele's uncle, who disappeared twenty years ago
Judid—a slave in Nakkiga
Jurgen of Sturmstad, Sir—Queen Miriamele's protector, killed defending his queen
Levias, Sergeant—an officer of the Erkynguard; wounded battle companion of Porto

Lillia, Princess—granddaughter of King Simon and Queen Miriamele, lost beneath the castle
Loes—one of Princess Lillia's nurses
Marchlings—residents of northern Erkynland, near the Frostmarch
Miriamele, Queen—High Queen of Osten Ard; currently presumed dead, but lost in Nabban
Morgan, Prince—heir to the High Throne; grandson of King Simon and Queen Miriamele, lost in Aldheorte Forest
Morgenes, Doctor—a Scrollbearer; young Simon's friend and mentor, killed before the Storm King's War
Nelda, Duchess—wife of Duke Osric; Princess Idela's mother
Norvel, Baron—a nobleman of Meremund
Obed—"Rightmark Obed": a guard captain of the Erkynguard
Orvyn—Archbishop of Meremund
Osric, Duke—Lord Constable, Duke of Falshire and Wentmouth; Prince Morgan's grandfather
Pieres, Count—a Sistanshire noble, ally of King Simon
Rachel—the Mistress of Chambermaids during King Simon's youth
Rowson, Earl—a nobleman of Glenwick
Shem Horsegroom—a Hayholt stablehand during King Simon's youth
Sherwyn, Lord—an Erkynlandish noble from the Westfold
Simon, King—the High King of Osten Ard and husband of Queen Miriamele; also known by his birth name, "Seoman," sometimes called "Snowlock"
Snell, Baron—the lord of Brockfordshire
Stedman—an Erkynlandish farmer
Swidelm, Father—a priest in Meremund
Strangyeard, Father—a deceased Scrollbearer and former royal chaplain of the Hayholt
Timmas—a priest in Meremund, Earl Durward's chaplain
Tzoja—Lord Viyeki's mistress; mother of Sacrifice Nezeru and daughter of Prince Josua and Lady Vorzheva. Unver's twin sister, named "Derra" by her parents
Wibert, Father—a counting-priest at the Hayholt, Pasevalles' assistant
Wilona, Lady—the Baroness of Haestall
Zakiel of Garwynswold, Sir—the Captain of the Erkynguard; Sir Kenrick's commander; later Lord Constable

HERNYSTIRI

Sir Aelin—a knight, grandson of Count Eolair's sister
Aengas ec-Carpilbin of Ban Farrig—a merchant and scholar of ancient books
Aeth, Tarn—an older clan leader

Airgad Oakheart—a legendary warrior
Bagba—a cattle god
Brannan—a former monk and Aengas' cook
Brygit—goddess of the sun, daughter of Brynioch
Brynioch of the Skies—sky god, called "Skyfather"
Cuamh Earthdog—earth god
Curudan, Baron—the Commander of the Silver Stags
Deanagha—a minor goddess, called "of the brown hair"
Dunn—a death god
Elatha—Count Eolair's sister, Aelin's grandmother
Eolair, Count—the Count of Nad Mullach and Hand of the Throne, sent to Hernystir by King Simon
Evan—an Aedonite soldier; one of Sir Aelin's companions
Fintan—an Aedonite soldier and member of the Silver Stags
Garrad of Duncroich, Tarn—a noble following King Hugh
Glinn—a member of the Silver Stags
Gurryn, Sir—a member of the Silver Stags
Gwynna—Eolair's grand-niece
Gwythinn, Prince—King Hugh's father, killed during the Storm King's War
Hern, King—the legendary founder of Hernystir
Hugh ubh-Gwythinn, King—the ruler of Hernystir
Inahwen—Dowager Queen of Hernystir; last wife of Hugh's grandfather King Lluth
Isleen—Earl Murdo's daughter
Jarreth—one of Aelin's men, killed during the fall of Naglimund
Larkin, Count—one of Sir Aelin's companions and an ally of Count Eolair
Lluth, King—former ruler of Hernystir; father of Maegwin and Gwythinn; killed at the Battle of the Inniscrich in 1165
Maccus Blackbeard—a soldier; one of Sir Aelin's companions
Mircha—goddess of rain; Brynioch's younger daughter
Murdo, Earl—a powerful noble; ally of Count Eolair and Sir Aelin
Murhagh One-Arm—a war god
Nial, Count—nobleman of Nad Glehs; Countess Rhona's husband
Rhona, Countess—noblewoman of Nad Glehs; friend to Queen Miriamele; guardian of Princess Lillia
Rhynn of the Cauldron—a battle god
Samreas, Sir—Baron Curudan's lieutenant; member of the Silver Stags
Sinnach, Prince—a historic prince of Hernystir, also known as "The Red Fox"
Silver Stags—a Hernystiri elite troop, loyal only to King Hugh
Talamh of the Land—ancient Hernystiri goddess associated with the Morrigu
Tethtain, King—fifth king of the Hayholt; called the "Holly King" and "Tethtain the Usurper"
Tylleth, Lady—fiancé of King Hugh

NABBANAI

Astrian, Sir—a member of the Erkynguard and former drinking companion of Prince Morgan, now part of Duke Osric's host

Blasis—the son of Duchess Canthia and Duke Saluceris; killed while fleeing Nabban

Brindalles—Pasevalles' father, killed during the Storm King's War

Camaris-sá-Vinitta, Sir—King John's greatest knight, also known as "Camaris Benidrivis"; disappeared at the end of the Storm King's War

Canthia, Duchess—the wife of Duke Saluceris; mother of Blasis and Serasina. Killed while fleeing Nabban

Crexis the Goat—historic Imperator who executed Usires Aedon

Dominiate—the ruling council of Nabban, consisting primarily of the fifty noble families

Drusis, Earl—Earl of Trevinta and Eadne; Duke Saluceris' late brother and rival

Envalles, Marquis—counselor to and uncle of Duke Saluceris, traitor to the High Throne

Elysia—the mother of Usires Aedon; called "Mother of God"

Goody Carpenter—Father Culby's housekeeper

Honora, Saint—an Aedonite martyr

Matreu, Viscount—nobleman; son of the ruler of Spenit Island

Oliveris, Sir—knight; former drinking companion of Prince Morgan, now member of Duke Osric's host

Pasevalles, Lord—Lord Chancellor to the High Throne, acting Hand of the Throne

Pelippa, St.—Aedonite saint, called "Pelippa of the Island"

Pryrates—priest, alchemist, and wizard; believed killed during the fall of Green Angel Tower

Sallin Ingadaris—current ruler of Nabban; cousin of Turia

Saluceris, Duke—previous ruler of Nabban

Serasina—infant daughter of Duchess Canthia and Duke Saluceris

Seriddan, Baron—lord of Metessa, Pasevalles' uncle, killed during Storm King's War

Tercis—character from an old tale; an imperator's son who supposedly got lost in Aldheorte Forest

Thelía, Lady—a herbalist and healer; Lord Tiamak's wife

Turia Ingadaris, Lady—wife of late Drusis, cousin to Sallin Ingadaris; supposedly pregnant with the heir to Nabban

Usires Aedon—Aedonite Son of God; also called "the Ransomer" and "the Redeemer"

Varellan, Duke—the unlamented former Duke of Nabban; Saluceris' father

NORNS (HIKEDA'YA)

Akhenabi, Lord—High Magister of the Order of Song, also called "Lord of Song"
Anchoress–name for Queen Utuk'ku's female body-slaves
Drukhi—historic figure; son of Queen Utuk'ku and Ekimeniso; killed by mortals centuries ago
Enduya, Clan—Viyeki's clan, a middling noble family
Ensume—Sacrifice general of the Spider legions
Gayu—Builder overseer of Viyeki's "stonecrackers"
Hamakha, Clan—the clan of Queen Utuk'ku
Hamakho Wormslayer—an historic figure; clan founder and famous warrior of the Garden
Hezidri—Sacrifice commander, Kikiti's lieutenant
Hidden, the—group of malformed outcasts living in the depths beneath Nakkiga
Ijikho—one of Pratiki's clerics
Jijibo, Lord—a close descendant of Queen Utuk'ku, called "the Dreamer"
Jikkyo, Lord—a high noble of the Order of Song
Khimabu, Lady—Lord Viyeki's wife
Kikiti, General—General of the host accompanying Viyeki's builders to an unknown destination in Aldheorte Forest
Lord of Dreaming—the Hidden's nickname for Lord Jijibo
Makho—a Hand Chieftain, former companion of Nezeru, now transformed by Akhenabi
Muyare sey-Iyora, Marshall—High Magister of the Order of Sacrifice
Nezeru Seyt-Enduya—daughter of Lord Viyeki and his mistress Tzoja, who travels with Morgan through Aldheorte Forest
Nonao—Lord Viyeki's secretary
Northeastern Host—previously secret Sacrifice army
Ommu the Whisperer—a Singer; former member of the Red Hand, resurrected by Queen Utuk'ku
Oroji—Builder foreman of Viyeki's "proppers and pillarers," called "Oroji One-Arm"
Pratiki—Prince-Templar; descendant of Queen Utuk'ku, now leading a host on a mysterious mission through Aldheorte Forest
Queen's Teeth—Queen Utuk'ku's personal guard; rumored to be tongueless
Saomeji—a Singer involved in the resurrection of Chieftain Makho
Sumizhe—a past High Celebrant of Nakkiga
Suno'ku—a famous general killed in the aftermath of the Storm King's War
Utuk'ku Seyt-Hamakha—the Norn Queen; Mistress of Nakkiga; oldest being in Osten Ard

Viyeki seyt-Enduya, Lord—the High Magister of the Order of Builders, father of Nezeru
White Foxes—a pejorative mortal name for Norns
Yaarike sey-Kijana, Lord—former High Magister of the Order of Builders, Viyeki's mentor, now deceased
Yedade—a Hikeda'ya philosopher
Zinuzo—a war poet, popular with the Order of Sacrifice

PERDRUINESE

Peronella—one of Yissola's ladies-in-waiting
Porto, Sir—hero of the Battles of Nakkiga; veteran soldier, friend of Prince Morgan
Yissola, Countess—ruler of Perdruin; daughter of Count Streáwe

QANUC

Binabik (Binbiniqegabenik)—Scrollbearer; Singing Man of the Qanuc and dear friend to King Simon
Kikkasut—the legendary king of birds
Little Snenneq—Qina's betrothed ("nukapik")
Merewa—one of Qina's rivals, called "Skinny Merewa"
Qina (Qinananamookta)—the daughter of Binabik and Sisqi
Ookekuq—a former Scrollbearer; Binibik's master, killed on the Road of Dreams in 1165
Sedda—the moon goddess, also known as "Moon-Mother"
Sisqi (Sisqinanamook)—a daughter of the Herder and Huntress (rulers of Mintahoq Mountain); Binabik's wife
Yutu—a jacket-maker's son; one of Little Snenneq's rivals, called "Ugly Yutu"

RIMMERSGARDERS

Gilhedur—a mortal slave of Nakkiga
Grimbrand of Elvritshalla, Duke—son of Isgrimnur and Gudrun, current ruler of Rimmersgard
Hjeldin, King—the second ruler of the Hayholt, called the "Mad King"
Isgrimnur of Elvritshalla, Duke—Duke Grimbrand's late father
Jarngrimnur—Jarnulf's deceased brother
Jarnulf Godtru—a man of unclear allegiance on a mission to kill Queen Utuk'ku
Roskva—the leader of the Astaline Sisters; Tzoja's surrogate mother, called "Valada"

Skalijar—a troop of pagan bandits in northern Rimmersgard
Sludig—a friend of King Simon and Binabik, currently a cattle breeder
Vordis—Tzoja's blind companion, born as a slave in Nakkiga

THRITHINGS-FOLK

Anbalt, Thane—the leader of the Adder Clan
Burtan—a shaman of the Crane Clan
Etvin, Thane—the leader of the Wood Duck Clan; born by Shallow Lake
Fikolmij—the former March-thane of the Stallion Clan and the High Thrithings; Vorzheva's father, killed by her
Fremur, Thane—the new leader of the Crane clan; Unver's first follower and closest friend
Gunkar Stonefist—the thane of the Boar Clan during the Second Thrithings War
Gurdig—the former thane of the Stallion Clan; husband of Hyara; killed by Unver
Hulgar—Zhadu's larger and uglier brother
Hyara—Vorzheva's sister; Unver's aunt, beloved of Fremur
Odobreg, Thane—the leader of the Badger Clan
Ozdrut—Unver's stepmother, a woman of the Crane Clan
Rudur Redbeard, Thane—the former leader of Black Bear Clan; March-Thane of the Meadow Thrithings, who was poisoned
Tasdar of the Iron Arm—a tutelary spirit; a metal-working deity worshiped by all the grassland clans, also called Tasdar the Anvil Smasher
Unver—"Nobody," the Thane of the Stallion Clan and Shan of the Thrithings; Tzoja's twin brother, named "Deornoth" by his parents, Prince Josua and Lady Vorzheva
Volfrag—Rudur Redbeard's chief shaman
Vorzheva—Unver's mother
Zhadu Split Jaw—a clansman in Erchester, in league with Pasevalles
Zhakar—Unver's stepfather; of the Crane Clan

SITHI (ZIDA'YA)

Aditu no'e-Sa'onserei—the daughter of Likimeya; Jiriki's sister
Amerasu y-Senditu no'e-Sa'onserei—the mother of Ineluki and Hakatri; called "First Grandmother" and "Amerasu Ship-Born," killed during the Storm King's War
Ayaminu—the mistress of Anvi'janya, daughter of Kuroyi
Ba'atigasa—leader of Peja'ura's Redstart Clan
Chekais'o—called "Amber-Locks"; a member of Zida'ya clan

Dinike—master of Repository, the archive of Anvi'janya
Dunao the Gray Rider—a supporter of Khendraja'aro
Ember—Aditu's nickname for Yeja'aro
Ganida of the Limberlight—a fighter at the Hornet's Nest
Hakatri—resurrected son of Amerasu Ship-born, father of Likimeya
Heart-Seed Clan—Tanahaya's clan
Himano of the Flowering Hills—a scholar; Tanahaya's teacher; recently murdered
Ineluki—son of Amerasu Shipborn, called the "Storm King," dead at the end of the war named after him
Jakoya the Gatherer—near-mythical figure from the Lost Garden
Jenjiyana of the Nightingales—historic figure; mother of Nenais'u
Jiriki i-Sa'onserei—son of Likimeya; brother of Aditu
Jonzao—"the Pure," a faction with a strictly traditional lifestyle
Ki'ushapo—Jiriki's cousin and friend, his name means "Onionskin"
Kuroyi—former ruler of Anvi'janya, killed during the Storm King's War; Ayaminu's father
Khendraja'aro—Likimeya's half-brother; uncle of Jiriki and Aditu; self-styled "Protector" of House of Year-Dancing
Likimeya y-Briseyu no'e-Sa'onserei—the Sa'onsera; mother of Jiriki and Aditu
Liko the Starling—a Zida'ya of Anvi'janya; Ayaminu's grandson
Nenais'u—the wife of Drukhi and daughter of Jenjiyana, killed by mortals thousands of years ago
Niyanao of the Lake—a fighter killed by the Hikeda'ya general Ensume
Rabbit—Jiriki's nickname for Aditu
Rukayu—also known as Crow's Claw, a young archer from Peja'ura
Saon'sera the Preserver—historic figure; wife of Hamakho Wormslayer; founding-mother of House of Year-Dancing
Sa'onserei—Jiriki and Aditu's clan; also called House of Year-Dancing
Selusana Moonhouse—a woman killed in fighting at Wormscale Gorge
Shen'de the Bowman—one of the oldest remaining Landborn
Shima'onari—the father of Jiriki and Aditu; killed during the Storm King's War
Silver Fir Clan—a clan in the northern part of Aldheorte Forest
Siriaya—Tanahaya's mother
Spark—Jiriki and Aditu's nickname for Tanahaya
Tanahaya of Shisae'ron—a scholar of Shisae'ron
Tululiko the Herald—Ayaminu's ancestor
Vinyedu—a scholar, leader of the Pure; sister of Zinjadu
Willow-switch—Aditu's nickname for Jiriki
Yeja'aro of the Forbidden Hills—Khendraja'aro's nephew, father of Aditu's unborn child
Yiyuna—a follower of Ayaminu, killed in battle with Norns

Zinjadu—lore-mistress of Kementari; sister of Vinyedu; killed during the Storm King's War

TINUKEDA'YA

Chikri—seemingly self-aware dwellers in Aldheorte Forest, somewhat resembling squirrels
Delvers—a mortal name for the Tinukeda'ya who shape stone; also called "Dwarrows" and "Dvernings"
Jun Dar Kran—a giant fighting for the Hikeda'ya in Aldheorte Forest
Gan Doha—a Niskie; a relative of Gan Itai, who helped Miriamele thirty years ago
Gan Lagi—a Niskie; Gan Doha's oldest living relative
Geloë—a wise woman, called "Valada Geloë"; killed near Sesuad'ra during the Storm King's War
Giants—large, shaggy, manlike creatures also known as "Hunë"
Goh Gam Gar—a very old, very large giant
Hidden, the—a faction of Tinukeda'ya hiding in the deeps below Nakkiga
Hin-Goda—leader of a Niskie family
Kuyu-kun Sa'Vao—current Voice of the Dreaming Sea; the "memory" of the Vao
Niskies—a type of Tinukeda'ya who serve aboard ships to "sing the kilpa down"
Ruyan Sho—a son of Ruyan Vé, called "first Sa'Vao"
Ruyan Vé—fabled patriarch of the Tinukeda'ya; called "The Navigator"
Sea Watchers' Guild—another name for the Niskies
Tih-Rumi—a Tinukeda'ya who Qina and Little Snenneq meet in Aldheorte Forest
Vao—the Tinukeda'ya's name for themselves; also known as Changelings
Yem Suju—Hin-Goda's grandson
Yem Gili—Yem Suju's wife
Zin-Seyvu—the leader of a Tinukeda'ya group traveling through Aldheorte Forest

WRANNA-FOLK

Aponi—a figure out of folklore who married the sun
He Who Always Steps on Sand—a god
Dula—an alias used by Jesa
Green Honeybird—a mythical Wranna spirit; Jesa's namesake
Jesa—nurse to Duke Saluceris' and Duchess Canthia's infant daughter Serasina; named "Green Honeybird" by her elders

Keleg—Jesa's relative, called "Cousin Keleg"
Mukah—swamp spirits who lure travelers off their path
Night Eater—a mythical demon
Pok-Pok—the brother of Jesa's father, called "Uncle Pok-Pok"
She Who Waits to Take All Back—a death goddess
They Who Watch and Shape—gods
Tiamak, Lord—a Scrollbearer; scholar and close friend of King Simon and Queen Miriamele

OTHERS

Adversary, the—the Aedonite devil
Madi—a Hyrka who guided Brother Etan during his recent travels
Qo'sei—islanders, one of Osten Ard's earliest mortal peoples along with Qanuc and Wran-folk

CREATURES

Bluejay—Tanahaya's horse, killed by a giant
Bonog—horse named after Jesa's uncle
Cloudfoot—Anvi'janyan horse given to Jiriki
Ebur—ancient name for elephant
Falku—Snenneq's large ram
Feather—Yiyuna's horse, later ridden by Tanahaya
Ghants—shelled, crablike Wran-dwelling creatures
Hollyhock—Etan's rented farm horse
Kilpa—manlike marine creatures
Kallypook (Qanuc name: "Qallipuk")—"River Man"; a water monster
Minku—Nezeru's childhood pet ermine
Mite—a cat in the Hayholt
Ooki—Sisqi's ram
Orla—a goat
Orn—Sir Jurgen's horse
Salt—Jarnulf's horse
Scand—a donkey
Sekob—fabled giant Wran crocodile
Silvershod—Simon's war horse
Swiftwing—Isleen's horse
Tipalak—Qina's ram
Uro'eni—the Zida'ya name for "ogre"—a legendary creature larger than a giant
Vaqana—Binabik's wolf companion

Windrunner—a fabled Zida'ya horse
Witiko'ya—a ferocious wolf-like predator of the far north

PLACES

Abaingeat—an important trading town in Hernystir along the coast, near the Barraillean River
Aldheorte—also known as Oldheart; a huge forest to the north and east of Erkynland
Anvi'janya—a famous Zida'ya settlement in Aldheorte Forest
Asu'a—Zida'ya name of the Hayholt, their most important city before mortals conquered it
Baraillean—a river in Hernystir
Bernet—an Erkynlandish town
Blue Mud Lake—a body of water south of the mountains of Yiqanuc
Blue Top Hills—a mountain range in Hernystir
Brockfordshire—a barony in Erkynland
Carn Inbarh—a castle in Hernystir; home of Earl Murdo, Eolair's ally
Clanhold—the chief residence of Ayaminu's family in Anvi'janya
Clontub—al walled town in Erkynland
Cold, Slow Halls—a place of torture in Nakkiga
Coldwater—a river flowing from Nabban into southern Erkynland
Coolblood River—the translated name of *T'si Suhyasei*, a river in Aldheorte Forest that runs past Da'ai Chikiza, and gives its name to the Coolblood Valley
Cuihmne, the—a river in Hernystir
Curath Tor—a steep peak in Hernystir
Da'ai Chikiza—a ruined Zida'ya city in Aldheorte, called "Tree of the Singing Wind"; one of the nine Gardenborn cities
Den Haloi, Mount—according to the book of Aedon, where God created the world
Drochbor—a bridge-town in eastern Hernystir
Dubh Moinar—scene of a fabled battle won by Murhagh One-Arm, Hernystiri god of war
Dunath Tower—a guard tower along the Inniscrich near the border between Hernystir and Rimmersgard
Duncroich—a Hernystiri holding
Erchester—capital of Erkynland and seat of the High Throne
Erkynland—a kingdom in central Osten Ard
Eywick—a settlement in southern Erkynland
Fallaferig Hills—the hills that surround Nad Glehs
Fearanthar—Hernystiri meadowlands

Fellmere Castle—the first sanctuary of Duke Osric's retreating army; a keep on the Laestfinger River near the eastern Erkynlandish border
Fingerdale—the river valley around Winstowe Castle
Flintwall—a town between Hayholt and the Fingerdale
Flowering Hills—a region in Aldheorte Forest; home of Himano
Forbidden Hills—a Zida'ya stronghold in Aldheorte Forest, home of Khendraja'aro
Funida—"the Step," a mountain near Anvi'janya
Gadrinsett—a refugee settlement near Sesu'adra, founded during the Storm King's War
Garden, the—Venyha Do'sae, the fabled place from whose destruction the Keida'ya fled
Gate of the Star—an entrance to Da'ai Chikiza
Gleniwent—a river connecting the Hayholt to the sea
Goddinsborough—a market town in southern Erkynland
Go-jao'e—Little Boats; the name for small Zida'ya settlements in Aldheorte Forest
Granary Tower—a tower in the Hayholt that housed Prince John Josua's chambers and study
Greenwade—the Erkynlandish name for river known in Hernystir as the Barailleam
Gundao—"The Marshal," a mountain near Anvi'janya
Hallowmount—the great rock of Khand where their ancient kings were crowned
Hayholt, the—the seat of the High Throne of Osten Ard, located above Erchester
Hernysadharc—the capital of Hernystir
Hernystir—a kingdom in the west of Osten Ard
Hikehikayo—one of the nine Gardenborn cities, located in the far northwest; called Cloud Castle and long abandoned
Hjeldin's Tower—a sealed tower of ominous repute in the Hayholt
Hornet's Nest—Zida'ya fortress in Aldheorte
H'ran Go-jao—the most easterly of the Go-jao'e (Little Boats)
Jumi'iru—"Moon Cradle," a mountain near Anvi'janya
Kementari—one of the nine Gardenborn cities, now only ruins
Khand—a lost and fabled land; also known as "Khandia"
Knacker's Yard—a Nakkiga parade-ground for sacrifices in training
Kushiba—"the Beak," a mountain at the northern end of the Wealdhelm
Kwanitupul—trading port, the biggest city in the Wran
Laestfinger—a river at Erkynland's eastern border
Lismoor—a settlement in Hernystir
Little Thrithing—a district of Erchester
Main Row—a major thoroughfare in the city of Erchester
Market Square—a marketplace in Erchester

Marshal, the—a mountain peak in Aldheorte Forest
Melcolis—a port town in Nabban
Meremund—an Erkynlandish town on the rivers Greenwade and Gleniwent; birthplace of Queen Miriamele
Metessa—a Nabbanai barony where Pasevalles was raised
Mezutu'a—"the Silverhome"; an abandoned Zida'ya and Tinukeda'ya city beneath the Grianspog Mountains. One of the nine Gardenborn cities
Moon Cradle—a mountain peak in Aldheorte Forest
Nabban—a duchy in the southern part of Osten Ard; former seat of empire
Nad Mullach—Count Eolair's home in eastern Hernystir
Naglimund—a fortress in northern Erkynland; a place of battles during the Storm King's War, now a stronghold of the High Ward
Nakkiga—a Gardenborn city beneath Stormspike Mountain—"Mask of Tears"; home of the Hikeda'ya
Nartha—a river that runs north to south along the base of the Wealdhelm
Narrowdark, the—a river that runs through Misty Vale, also known as *Dekusao*
Nascadu—desert lands south of the Wran
Nearulagh Gate—the main entrance to the Hayholt
Ocean Indefinite and Eternal—body crossed by the Gardenborn on their way to Osten Ard
Onestry—a town in southern Nabban
Osten Ard—the mortal kingdom ruled by King Simon and Queen Miriamele (Rimmerspakk for "Eastern Land")
Palano—a city in southern Nabban famous for its swordsmiths
Peck, the—a tall rock in Meremund, location of Prince's Hall
Peja'ura—a Zida'ya settlement in Aldheorte, home to the Redstart Clan
Pe Ni'yo—a mountain peak in Aldheorte
Perdruin—an island in the Bay of Emettin; ruled by Countess Yissola
Place of Sky-Watching—a great chamber in Da'ai Chikiza
Prince's Hall—a central stronghold in Meremund
Red Campion Bridge—a span over the Coolblood River
Red Pig Lagoon—Jesa's home village in the Wran
Re Surieni—a river flowing through the valley of Shisae'ron
Rimmersgard—a duchy in the north of Osten Ard
Rhynn's Beacon—a mountain in Hernystir
Sistanshire—a county in Erkynland
Silken Span—a bridge leading to Anvi'janya, connecting two mountain peaks
Soori K'yan—"the Sun's Eye," the mountain home of Anvi'janya
Stone Root—a Hikeda'ya fortress in Aldheorte
St. Rumen's Way—main street in the center of Wentmouth
St. Sutrin's—a cathedral in Erchester
St. Tankred's—a cathedral in Meremund
Shisae'ron—a valley in the southwestern part of Aldheorte; birthplace of Tanahaya

Stile, the—an ancient pass over the hills between Da'ai Chikiza and Naglimund
Stormspike—the mountain also known as *Ur-Nakkiga* or *Sturmrspeik*, home to the Hikeda'ya
Tanakirú—a valley in Aldheorte Forest, also known as "Misty Vale" or "the Valley of Mists; specifically, the far northern end of the valley
Taig, the—a wooden castle, home to Hernystir's ruling family
Tebi Pit—a magical device used to change the dead or dying into undead warriors
Thrithings—a plain of grassland in the southeast of Osten Ard, divided into High Thrithings, Meadow Thrithings, and Lake Thrithings
Tower of the Holy Tree—newer tower in the Hayholt
Tower of the Reaching Hand—a tower in Da'ai Chikiza
T'si Suhyasei—a great river in Aldheorte; called Aelfwent in Erkynland
Twin Hunters—a mountain peak in Aldheorte Forest
Urmsheim—a fabled mountain in the far north
Watcher of the Way—a mountain peak in Aldheorte Forest
Wealdhelm—a range of hills in Erkynland, called Yi'ire Highlands by the Zida'ya
Wentmouth—a port town at the mouth of the Gleniwent River
White Snail Castle—a Hikeda'ya castle on the shoulder of Nakkiga Mountain
Winstowe Castle—a fortress in Fingerdale
Willow Hall—the place where Tanahya grew up
Wran, the—marshland in southern Osten Ard
Wormscale Gorge—location of the Zida'ya fortress Hornet's Nest in Aldheorte Forest
Ya Mologi—"fire mountain" located in the Wran
Yiqanuc—home of the Qanuc people; also known as the Trollfells

THINGS

Aedonites–followers of the faith of Usires Aedon and Mother Church
Analita-zé—Hikeda'ya fermented beverage
Battle of the Hollows—famous struggle between Qanuc trolls and Bukken (goblins)
Book of the Aedon—Aedonite holy book
Bloodwood—a wood used to make Norn armor, also called "ki'tzi"
Brookstem—an edible plant
Bullace—a shrub with plum-like fruit
Cold Root—Makho's witchwood sword, stolen and given to Nezeru by Jarnulf; once belonged to General Suno'ku
Dance of Sacrifice—a Hikeda'ya term for combat
Dawnstone—the Master Witness of Da'ai Chikiza, lost during a flood

Day of Weighing Out—the Aedonite day of final justice and end of the mortal world
Drukhi's Day—a Hikeda'ya holiday commemorating Queen Utuk'ku's dead son, celebrated during Stone-Listener's Moon
Ereb Irigú—the site of a famous battle between the Zida'ya and Rimmersmen centuries ago
Erkynguard—the elite soldiers of the Hayholt and Erkynland
Forrest myrrh—a seasoning herb
Foxberry mats—a bog-loving plant in Nakkiga
Fulaith—an ancient Hernystiri holiday celebrating the Morrigu
Gardenborn—all who came from the Garden, both Keida'ya and Tinukeda'ya (or "*Vao*")
Gate of the Fifth Ship—the water gate of old Asu'a
Great Year—a Gardenborn time span, roughly 60 human years
Hall of the Five Staircases—a place in Asu'a; site of Briseyu's death
Hall of the Great Circle—a hall in Asu'a
Hayefur, the—a beacon at the mouth of the Gleniwent River
Hikeda'yasao—the language of Nakkiga
Juya'ha—an art weaving stories from cord
Keida'ya—the Zida'ya and Hikeda'ya; the Witchwood children
Kei-mi—precious powdered witchwood sap
Kei-vishaa—a substance used by the Gardenborn to make enemies drowsy and weak
Kei soma—an elixir made from the essence of witchwood
Landborn—the Keida'ya born after the arrival in Osten Ard
Librin Horas—"Book of Hours," collection of Aedonite prayers
Lismoor—a Hernystiri manor, home of Isleen's aunt and uncle
Mansa sea Cuelossan—an Aedonite prayer for the dead
Mooncloud—a Master Witness, currently beneath the Hayholt
Mother Church—the Aedonite church, led from Nabban's Sancellan Aedonitis
Ni'yo—a glowing sphere
Parting, the—the separation event of the Zida'ya and Hikeda'ya
Pu'ju—bread made from the white barley grown in the cold valleys below Stormspike
Rightmark—a military deputy of an Erkynlandish captain
Queen's device—Utuk'ku's signature rune
Queen's Huntsman—an honorific given by Queen Utuk'ku to a skilled mortal hunter of escaped slaves
Sacranai—a set of prayers from the Book of Aedon
Sacrifice—a trained Hikeda'ya soldier
Shent—a strategic board game played by the immortals; called "Shaynat" by Norns
Softfoot—a common mushroom
Song of Challenge—a Zida'ya way to settle disagreements
S'rin-yedu—a special cord used in Juya'ha art

Talon—a squad of five elite, specially-trained Sacrifices
Thanemoot—a yearly gathering of all Thrithings clans at Blood Lake
Tree, the—"Holy Tree," or "Execution Tree"; a symbol of Usires Aedon's execution and the Aedonite faith
Tutor Sleeps, the—a Hikeda'ya hand-sign of approval and teasing mockery
Unbeing—an ancient threat which destroyed the Garden
War of Return, the—Hikeda'ya name for the Storm King's War
Westerling—a language originating from Waristen Island; now the common human tongue in Osten Ard
Witchwood—rare wood from trees brought from the Garden; hard as metal
Witchwood Crown, the—"kei-jáyha". Has several meanings: a circlet awarded to heroes; the supply of sacred witchwood trees; a move in Shent
Witness—a Zida'ya device to talk over long distances and enter the Road of Dreams, oftentimes a dragon scale, special stone, pool, or pyre
Yedade's Box—a Hikeda'ya device for testing children
Yerut—fermented mare's milk drunk by the Thrithings-folk

STARS AND CONSTELLATIONS

Attara's Belt—the largest constellation in the skies of Osten Ard
Bend of the River—one of the stars of *Venyha Do'sae*, the Lost Garden
Blade—a star of *Venyha Do'sae.*
Dancer—a star of *Venyha Do'sae.*
Horned Owl—Erkynlandish
Lamp—Erkynlandish
Lantern—Hikeda'ya
Pool—a star of *Venyha Do'sae.*
Staff—Erkynlandish
Swallower—a star of *Venyha Do'sae.*

HOLIDAYS (AMONG AEDONITE MORTALS)

Feyever 2—Candlemansa
Marris 25—Elysiamansa
Marris 31—Fool's Night
Avrel 1—All Fool's Day
Avrel 3—St. Vultinia's Day
Avrel 24—St. Dinan's Day
Avrel 30—Stoning Night
Maia 1—Belthainn Day
Yuven 23—Midsummer's Eve
Tiyagar 15—Saint Sutrin's Day

Anitul 1—Hlafmansa
Septander 29—Saint Granis' Day
Octander 30—Harrows Eve
Novander 1—Soul's Day
Decander 21—Saint Tunath's Day
Decander 24—Aedonmansa

DAYS OF THE WEEK

Sunday, Moonday, Tiasday, Udunsday, Drorsday, Frayday, Satrinsday

MONTHS OF THE YEAR

AEDONITE	SITHI	HIKEDA'YA	THRITHING
Jonever	Raven	Ice-Mother	Second Blue Moon
Feyever	Serpent	Serpent	Third Blue Moon
Marris	Hare	Wind-Child	First Green Moon
Avrel	Grieving Sister	Dove	Second Green Moon
Maia	Nightingale	Cloud-Song	Third Green Moon
Yuven	Lantern Bearer	Otter	First Yellow Moon
Tiyagar	Fox	Stone-Listener	Second Yellow Moon
Anitul	Lynx	Lynx	Third Yellow Moon
Septander	Crane	Sky-Singer	First Red Moon
Octander	Tortoise	Tortoise	Second Red Moon
Novander	Rooster	Fire-Knight	Third Red Moon
Decander	Moon-Herald	Wolf	First Blue Moon

KNUCKLEBONES

Qanuc auguring tools
Patterns include:
- Wingless Bird
- Fish-Spear
- The Shadowed Path
- Torch at the Cave-Mouth
- Balking Ram
- Clouds in the Pass

The Black Crevice
Unwrapped Dart
Circle of Stones
Mountains Dancing
Masterless Ram
Slippery Snow
Unexpected Visitor
Unnatural Birth
No Shadow

THE EIGHT SHIPS

Lantern Bearer, Singing Fire, Time of Gathering, Yakoya's Dream, Dance of Sacrifice, Gate Opener, Cloud of Bird, and Sacred Seed

HIKEDA'YA ORDERS

Order, Ordination, Ordinal
Order House—actual location of Order's school, offices
Orders mentioned: Sacrifices; Whisperers; Echoes; Singers; Builders; Tillers; Celebrants; Gatherers
Order hierarchies: Magister or High Magister (Highest official outside Royal Household—master of an Order)

THRITHINGS CLANS AND THEIR THRITHINGS

Adder—Lake
Antelope—Meadow
Bison—High
Black Bear—Meadow
Crane or "Kragni"—Lake
Dragonfly—Lake
Fitch—Lake
Fox—High
Grouse—High
Kestrel—Lake
Lynx—Lake
Polecat—Lake
Sparrow—High
Stallion or "Mehrdon"—High
White Spot Deer—Lake

Wood Duck—Lake
Other clans include:
Badger, Bustard, Otter, Pheasant, Roebuck, Snake, Sparrowhawk, Vulture, Whipsnake, and Wild Horse

WORDS AND PHRASES

HERNYSTIRI

Bennach—"Greetings!"
Fa'sos!—"Get down!"
Mu' harcha—"Sweetling"

NORN (HIKEDA'YASO)

Kaddara!—"Get her!"
Ki'tzi—Bloodwood
M'shi—water / watery / that which fits where it is put
S'huo-gan—mentor
Uro'eni—ogre
Uro'ye—giant
Ujin-do — trap

QANUC

Ninit!—"Come"
Ninit aia!—"Come (emphasized, as in "come *now!*")
Nuluk–rump
Nukapik—betrothed
Agaki—Qanuc name for Tinukeda'ya "Delvers"

SITHI (ZIDA'YASO)

Hikka—"Bearer"
Jingizu—"sorrow"
S'rin-yedu—special cord used in *Ju'yaha* art and to mark important documents
Staja—"arrow"

sa'juya—"weave word," the art of thought-shaping by singing; Sithi debate form
T'si e-isi'ha as-irigú!—"There is blood on the eastern gate!"

THRITHINGS SPEECH

Kven—"queen"
Varn—the Wran
Vit vukaz—"White Foxes"

OTHER

Nebbu—"Gold" (Khandian)
Panuk—"Chisel" (Wranna)